Fritz Reuter Leiber

SF Ultimate Collection: 20+ Time Travel & Dystopia Stories

OK Publishing 2021

Fritz Reuter Leiber

SF Ultimate Collection: 20+ Time Travel & Dystopia Stories

Published by

MUSAICUM
Books

- Advanced Digital Solutions & High-Quality book Formatting -

musaicumbooks@okpublishing.info

2021 OK Publishing

ISBN 978-80-272-7918-0

Contents

The Big Time

Chapter 1
Enter Three Hussars

When shall we three meet again
In thunder, lightning, or in rain?

When the hurlyburly's done.
When the battle's lost and won.

—Macbeth

My name is Greta Forzane. Twenty-nine and a party girl would describe me. I was born in Chicago, of Scandinavian parents, but now I operate chiefly outside space and time-not in Heaven or Hell, if there are such places, but not in the cosmos or universe you know either.

I am not as romantically entrancing as the immortal film star who also bears my first name, but I have a rough-and-ready charm of my own. I need it, for my job is to nurse back to health and kid back to sanity Soldiers badly roughed up in the biggest war going. This war is the Change War, a war of time travelers-in fact, our private name for being in this war is being on the Big Time. Our Soldiers fight by going back to change the past, or even ahead to change the future, in ways to help our side win the final victory a billion or more years from now. A long killing business, believe me.

You don't know about the Change War, but it's influencing your lives all the time and maybe you've had hints of it without realizing.

Have you ever worried about your memory, because it doesn't seem to be bringing you exactly the same picture of the past from one day to the next? Have you ever been afraid that your personality was changing because of forces beyond your knowledge or control? Have you ever felt sure that sudden death was about to jump you from nowhere? Have you ever been scared of Ghosts-not the story-book kind, but the billions of beings who were once so real and strong it's hard to believe they'll just sleep harmlessly forever? Have you ever wondered about those things you may call devils or Demons-spirits able to range through all time and space, through the hot hearts of stars and the cold skeleton of space between the galaxies? Have you ever thought that the whole universe might be a crazy, mixed-up dream? If you have, you've had hints of the Change War.

How I got recruited into the Change War, how it's conducted, what the two sides are, why you don't consciously know about it, what I really think about it-you'll learn in due course.

The place outside the cosmos where I and my pals do our nursing job I simply call the Place. A lot of my nursing consists of amusing and humanizing Soldiers fresh back from raids into time. In fact, my formal title is Entertainer and I've got my silly side, as you'll find out.

My pals are two other gals and three guys from quite an assortment of times and places. We're a pretty good team, and with Sid bossing, we run a pretty good Recuperation Station, though we have our family troubles. But most of our troubles come slamming into the Place with the beat-up Soldiers, who've generally just been going through hell and want to raise some of their own. As a matter of fact, it was three newly arrived Soldiers who started this thing I'm going to tell you about, this thing that showed me so much about myself and everything.

When it started, I had been on the Big Time for a thousand sleeps and two thousand night-mares, and working in the Place for five hundred-one thousand. This two-nightmares routine every time you lay down your dizzy little head is rough, but you pretend to get used to it because being on the Big Time is supposed to be worth it.

The Place is midway in size and atmosphere between a large nightclub where the Entertainers sleep in and a small Zeppelin hangar decorated for a party, though a Zeppelin is one thing we haven't had yet. You go out of the Place, but not often if you have any sense and if you are an Entertainer like me, into the cold light of a morning filled with anything from the earlier dinosaurs to the later spacemen, who look strangely similar except for size.

Solely on doctor's orders, I have been on cosmic leave six times since coming to work at the Place, meaning I have had six brief vacations, if you care to call them that, for believe me they are busman's holidays, considering what goes on in the Place all the time. The last one I spent in Renaissance Rome, where I got a crush on Cesare Borgia, but I got over it. Vacations are for the birds, anyway, because they have to be fitted by the Spiders into serious operations of the Change War, and you can imagine how restful that makes them.

"See those Soldiers changing the past? You stick along with them. Don't go too far up front, though, but don't wander off either. Relax and enjoy yourself."

Ha! Now the kind of recuperation Soldiers get when they come to the Place is a horse of a far brighter color, simply dazzling by comparison. Entertainment is our business and we give them a bang-up time and send them staggering happily back into action, though once in a great while something may happen to throw a wee shadow on the party.

I am dead in some ways, but don't let that bother you —I am lively enough in others. If you met me in the cosmos, you would be more apt to yak with me or try to pick me up than to ask a cop to do same or a father to douse me with holy water, unless you are one of those hard-boiled reformer types. But you are not likely to meet me in the cosmos, because (bar Basin Street and the Prater) 15th Century Italy and Augustan Rome-until they spoiled it-are my favorite (Ha!) vacation spots and, as I have said, I stick as close to the Place as I can. It is really the nicest Place in the whole Change World. (Crisis! I even *think* of it capitalized!)

Anyhoo, when this thing started, I was twiddling my thumbs on the couch nearest the piano and thinking it was too late to do my fingernails and whoever came in probably wouldn't notice them anyway.

The Place was jumpy like it always is on an approach and the gray velvet of the Void around us was curdled with the uneasy lights you see when you close your eyes in the dark.

Sid was tuning the Maintainers for the pick-up and the right shoulder of his gold-worked gray doublet was streaked where he'd been wiping his face on it with quick ducks of his head.

Beauregard was leaning as close as he could over Sid's other shoulder, one white-trousered knee neatly indenting the rose plush of the control divan, and he wasn't missing a single flicker of Sid's old fingers on the dials; Beau's co-pilot besides piano player. Beau's face had that dead blank look it must have had when every double eagle he owned and more he didn't were riding on the next card to be turned in the gambling saloon on one of those wedding-cake Mississippi steamboats.

Doc was soused as usual, sitting at the bar with his top hat pushed back and his knitted shawl pulled around him, his wide eyes seeing whatever horrors a life in Nazi-occupied Czarist Russia can add to being a drunk Demon in the Change World.

Maud, who is the Old Girl, and Lili-the New Girl, of course-were telling the big beads of their identical pearl necklaces.

You might say that all us Entertainers were a bit edgy; being Demons doesn't automatically make us brave.

Then the red telltale on the Major Maintainer went out and the Door began to darken in the Void facing Sid and Beau, and I felt Change Winds blowing hard and my heart missed a couple of beats, and the next thing three Soldiers had stepped out of the cosmos and into the Place, their first three steps hitting the floor hard as they changed times and weights.

They were dressed as officers of hussars, as we'd been advised, and-praise the Bonny Dew! —I saw that the first of them was Erich, my own dear little commandant, the pride of the von Hohenwalds and the Terror of the Snakes. Behind him was some hard-faced Roman or other, and beside Erich and shouldering into him as they stamped forward was a new boy, blond, with a face like a Greek god who's just been touring a Christian hell.

They were uniformed exactly alike in black-shakos, fur-edged pelisses, boots, and so forth-with white skull emblems on the shakos. The only difference between them was that Erich had a Caller on his wrist and the New Boy had a black-gauntleted glove on his left hand and was clenching the mate in it, his right hand being bare like both of Erich's and the Roman's.

"You've made it, lads, hearts of gold," Sid boomed at them, and Beau twitched a smile and murmured something courtly and Maud began to chant, "Shut the Door!" and the New Girl copied her and I joined in because the Change Winds do blow like crazy when the Door is open, even though it can't ever be shut tight enough to keep them from leaking through.

"Shut it before it blows wrinkles in our faces," Maud called in her gamin voice to break the ice, looking like a skinny teen-ager in the tight, knee-length frock she'd copied from the New Girl.

But the three Soldiers weren't paying attention. The Roman —I remembered his name was Mark-was blundering forward stiffly as if there were something wrong with his eyes, while Erich and the New Boy were yelling at each other about a kid and Einstein and a summer palace and a bloody glove and the Snakes having booby-trapped Saint Petersburg. Erich had that taut sadistic smile he gets when he wants to hit me.

The New Boy was in a tearing rage. "Why'd you pull us out so bloody fast? We fair chewed the Nevsky Prospekt to pieces galloping away."

"Didn't you feel their stun guns, *Dummkopf*, when they sprung the trap-too soon, *Gott sei Dank*?" Erich demanded.

"I did," the New Boy told him. "Not enough to numb a cat. Why didn't you show us action?"

"Shut up. I'm your leader. I'll show you action enough."

"You won't. You're a filthy Nazi coward."

"*Weibischer Engländer!*"

"Bloody Hun!"

"*Schlange!*"

The blond lad knew enough German to understand that last crack. He threw back his sable-edged pelisse to clear his sword arm and he swung away from Erich, which bumped him into Beau. At the first sign of the quarrel, Beau had raised himself from the divan as quickly and silently as a —no, I won't use that word-and slithered over to them.

"Sirs, you forget yourselves," he said sharply, off balance, supporting himself on the New Boy's upraised arm. "This is Sidney Lessingham's Place of Entertainment and Recuperation. There are ladies —"

With a contemptuous snarl, the New Boy shoved him off and snatched with his bare hand for his saber. Beau reeled against the divan, it caught him in the shins and he fell toward the Maintainers. Sid whisked them out of the way as if they were a couple of beach radios-simply nothing in the Place is nailed down-and had them back on the coffee table before Beau hit the floor. Meanwhile, Erich had his saber out and had parried the New Boy's first wild slash and lunged in return, and I heard the scream of steel and the rutch of his boot on the diamond-studded pavement.

Beau rolled over and came up pulling from the ruffles of his shirt bosom a derringer I knew was some other weapon in disguise —a stun gun or even an Atropos. Besides scaring me damp for Erich and everybody, that brought me up short: us Entertainers' nerves must be getting as naked as the Soldiers', probably starting when the Spiders canceled all cosmic leaves twenty sleeps back.

Sid shot Beau his look of command, rapped out, "I'll handle this, you whoreson firebrand," and turned to the Minor Maintainer. I noticed that the telltale on the Major was glowing a reassuring red again, and I found a moment to thank Mamma Devi that the Door was shut.

Maud was jumping up and down, cheering I don't know which-nor did she, I bet-and the New Girl was white and I saw that the sabers were working more businesslike. Erich's flicked, flicked, flicked again and came away from the blond lad's cheek spilling a couple of red drops. The blond lad lunged fiercely, Erich jumped back, and the next moment they were both floating helplessly in the air, twisting like they had cramps.

I realized quick enough that Sid had shut off gravity in the Door and Stores sectors of the Place, leaving the rest of us firm on our feet in the Refresher and Surgery sectors. The Place has sectional gravity to suit our Extraterrestrial buddies-those crazy ETs sometimes come whooping in for recuperation in very mixed batches.

From his central position, Sid called out, kindly enough but taking no nonsense, "All right, lads, you've had your fun. Now sheathe those swords."

For a second or so, the two black hussars drifted and contorted. Erich laughed harshly and neatly obeyed-the commandant is used to free fall. The blond lad stopped writhing, hesitated while he glared upside down at Erich and managed to get his saber into its scabbard, although he turned a slow somersault doing it. Then Sid switched on their gravity, slow enough so they wouldn't get sprained landing.

Erich laughed, lightly this time, and stepped out briskly toward us. He stopped to clap the New Boy firmly on the shoulder and look him in the face.

"So, now you get a good scar," he said.

The other didn't pull away, but he didn't look up and Erich came on. Sid was hurrying toward the New Boy, and as he passed Erich, he wagged a finger at him and gayly said, "You rogue." Next thing I was giving Erich my "Man, you're home" hug and he was kissing me and cracking my ribs and saying, *"Liebchen! Doppchen!"* —which was fine with me because I do love him and I'm a good lover and as much a Doubleganger as he is.

We had just pulled back from each other to get a breath-his blue eyes looked so sweet in his worn face-when there was a thud behind us. With the snapping of the tension, Doc had fallen off his bar stool and his top hat was over his eyes. As we turned to chuckle at him, Maud squeaked and we saw that the Roman had walked straight up against the Void and was marching along there steadily without gaining a foot, like it does happen, his black uniform melting into that inside-your-head gray.

Maud and Beau rushed over to fish him back, which can be tricky. The thin gambler was all courtly efficiency again. Sid supervised from a distance.

"What's wrong with him?" I asked Erich.

He shrugged. "Overdue for Change Shock. And he was nearest the stun guns. His horse almost threw him. *Mein Gott*, you should have seen Saint Petersburg, *Liebchen*: the Nevsky Prospekt, the canals flying by like reception carpets of blue sky, a cavalry troop in blue and gold that blundered across our escape, fine women in furs and ostrich plumes, a monk with a big tripod and his head under a hood-it gave me the horrors seeing all those Zombies flashing past and staring at me in that sick unawakened way they have, and knowing that some of them, say the photographer, might be Snakes."

Our side in the Change War is the Spiders, the other side is the Snakes, though all of us-Spiders and Snakes alike-are Doublegangers and Demons too, because we're cut out of our lifelines in the cosmos. Your lifeline is all of you from birth to death. We're Doublegangers because we can operate both in the cosmos and outside of it, and Demons because we act reasonably alive while doing so-which the Ghosts don't. Entertainers and Soldiers are all Demon-Doublegangers, whichever side they're on-though they say the Snake Places are simply ghastly. Zombies are dead people whose lifelines lie in the so-called past.

"What were you doing in Saint Petersburg before the ambush?" I asked Erich. "That is, if you can talk about it."

"Why not? We were kidnapping the infant Einstein back from the Snakes in 1883. Yes, the Snakes got him, *Liebchen*, only a few sleeps back, endangering the West's whole victory over Russia —"

" —which gave your dear little Hitler the world on a platter for fifty years and got me loved to death by your sterling troops in the Liberation of Chicago —"

" —but which leads to the ultimate victory of the Spiders and the West over the Snakes and Communism, *Liebchen*, remember that. Anyway, our counter-snatch didn't work. The Snakes had guards posted-most unusual and we weren't warned. The whole thing was a great mess. No wonder Bruce lost his head-not that it excuses him."

"The New Boy?" I asked. Sid hadn't got to him and he was still standing with hooded eyes where Erich had left him, a dark pillar of shame and rage.

"*Ja*, a lieutenant from World War One. An Englishman."

"I gathered that," I told Erich. "Is he really effeminate?"

"*Weibischer?*" He smiled. "I had to call him something when he said I was a coward. He'll make a fine Soldier-only needs a little more shaping."

"You men are so original when you spat." I lowered my voice. "But you shouldn't have gone on and called him a Snake, Erich mine."

"*Schlange?*" The smile got crooked. "Who knows-about any of us? As Saint Petersburg showed me, the Snakes' spies are getting cleverer than ours." The blue eyes didn't look sweet now. "Are you, *Liebchen*, really nothing more than a good loyal Spider?"

"Erich!"

"All right, I went too far-with Bruce and with you too. We're all hacked these days, riding with one leg over the breaking edge."

Maud and Beau were supporting the Roman to a couch, Maud taking most of his weight, with Sid still supervising and the New Boy still sulking by himself. The New Girl should have been with him, of course, but I couldn't see her anywhere and I decided she was probably having a nervous breakdown in the Refresher, the little jerk.

"The Roman looks pretty bad, Erich," I said.

"Ah, Mark's tough. Got virtue, as his people say. And our little starship girl will bring him back to life if anybody can and if..."

"...you call this living," I filled in dutifully.

He was right. Maud had fifty-odd years of psychomedical experience, 23rd Century at that. It should have been Doc's job, but that was fifty drunks back.

"Maud and Mark, that will be an interesting experiment," Erich said. "Reminiscent of Goering's with the frozen men and the naked gypsy girls."

"You are a filthy Nazi. She'll be using electrophoresis and deep suggestion, if I know anything."

"How will you be able to know anything, *Liebchen*, if she switches on the couch curtains, as I perceive she is preparing to do?"

"Filthy Nazi I said and meant."

"Precisely." He clicked his heels and bowed a millimeter. "Erich Friederich von Hohenwald, *Oberleutnant* in the army of the Third Reich. Fell at Narvik, where he was Recruited by the Spiders. Lifeline lengthened by a Big Change after his first death and at latest report Commandant of Toronto, where he maintains extensive baby farms to provide him with breakfast meat, if you believe the handbills of the *voyageurs* underground. At your service."

"Oh, Erich, it's all so lousy," I said, touching his hand, reminded that he was one of the unfortunates Resurrected from a point in their lifelines well before their deaths-in his case, because the date of his death had been shifted forward by a Big Change after his Resurrection. And as every Demon finds out, if he can't imagine it beforehand, it is pure hell to remember your future, and the shorter the time between your Resurrection and your death back in the cosmos, the better. Mine, bless Bab-ed-Din, was only an action-packed ten minutes on North Clark Street.

Erich put his other hand lightly over mine. "Fortunes of the Change War, *Liebchen*. At least I'm a Soldier and sometimes assigned to future operations-though why we should have this monomania about our future personalities back there, I don't know. Mine is a stupid *Oberst*, thin as paper-and frightfully indignant at the *voyageurs*! But it helps me a little if I see him in perspective and at least I get back to the cosmos pretty regularly, *Gott sei Dank*, so I'm better off than you Entertainers."

I didn't say aloud that a Changing cosmos is worse than none, but I found myself sending a prayer to the Bonny Dew for my father's repose, that the Change Winds would blow lightly across the lifeline of Anton A. Forzane, professor of physiology, born in Norway and buried in Chicago. Woodlawn Cemetery is a nice gray spot.

"That's all right, Erich," I said. "We Entertainers Got Mittens too."

He scowled around at me suspiciously, as if he were wondering whether I had all my buttons on.

"Mittens?" he said. "What do you mean? I'm not wearing any. Are you trying to say something about Bruce's gloves-which incidentally seem to annoy him for some reason. No, seriously, Greta, why do you Entertainers need mittens?"

"Because we get cold feet sometimes. At least I do. Got Mittens, as I say."

A sickly light dawned in his Prussian puss. He muttered, "Got mittens ... *Gott mit uns* ... God with us," and roared softly, "Greta, I don't know how I put up with you, the way you murder a great language for cheap laughs."

"You've got to take me as I am," I told him, "mittens and all, thank the Bonny Dew —" and hastily explained, "That's French —*le bon Dieu* —the good God-don't hit me. I'm not going to tell you any more of my secrets."

He laughed feebly, like he was dying.

"Cheer up," I said. "I won't be here forever, and there are worse places than the Place."

He nodded grudgingly, looking around. "You know what, Greta, if you'll promise not to make some dreadful joke out of it: on operations, I pretend I'll soon be going backstage to court the world-famous ballerina Greta Forzane."

He was right about the backstage part. The Place is a regular theater-in-the-round with the Void for an audience, the Void's gray hardly disturbed by the screens masking Surgery (Ugh!), Refresher and Stores. Between the last two are the bar and kitchen and Beau's piano. Between Surgery and the sector where the Door usually appears are the shelves and taborets of the Art Gallery. The control divan is stage center. Spaced around at a fair distance are six big low couches-one with its curtains now shooting up into the gray-and a few small tables. It is like a ballet set and the crazy costumes and characters that turn up don't ruin the illusion. By no means. Diaghilev would have hired most of them for the Ballet Russe on first sight, without even asking them whether they could keep time to music.

Chapter 2
A Right-Hand Glove

Last week in Babylon,
Last night in Rome,

—Hodgson

Beau had gone behind the bar and was talking quietly at Doc, but with his eyes elsewhere, looking very sallow and professional in his white, and I thought-Damballa! —I'm in the French Quarter. I couldn't see the New Girl. Sid was at last getting to the New Boy after the fuss about Mark. He threw me a sign and I started over with Erich in tow.

"Welcome, sweet lad. Sidney Lessingham's your host, and a fellow Englishman. Born in King's Lynn, 1564, schooled at Cambridge, but London was the life and death of me, though I outlasted Bessie, Jimmie, Charlie, and Ollie almost. And what a life! By turns a clerk, a spy, a bawd-the two trades are hand in glove —a poet of no account, a beggar, and a peddler of resurrection tracts. Beau Lassiter, our throats are tinder!"

At the word "poet," the New Boy looked up, but resentfully, as if he had been tricked into it.

"And to spare your throat for drinking, sweet gallant, I'll be so bold as to guess and answer one of your questions," Sid rattled on. "Yes, I knew Will Shakespeare-we were of an age-and he was such a modest, mind-your-business rogue that we all wondered whether he really did write those plays. Your pardon, 'faith, but that scratch might be looked to."

Then I saw that the New Girl hadn't lost her head, but gone to Surgery (Ugh!) for a first-aid tray. She reached a swab toward the New Boy's sticky cheek, saying rather shrilly, "If I might..."

Her timing was bad. Sid's last words and Erich's approach had darkened the look in the young Soldier's face and he angrily swept her arm aside without even glancing at her. Erich squeezed my arm. The tray clattered to the floor-and one of the drinks that Beau was bringing almost followed it. Ever since the New Girl's arrival, Beau had been figuring that she was his responsibility, though I don't think the two of them had reached an agreement yet. Beau was especially set on it because I was thick with Sid at the time and Maud with Doc, she loving tough cases.

"Easy now, lad, and you love me!" Sid thundered, again shooting Beau the "Hold it" look. "She's just a poor pagan trying to comfort you. Swallow your bile, you black villain, and perchance it will turn to poetry. Ah, did I touch you there? Confess, you are a poet."

There isn't much gets by Sid, though for a second I forgot my psychology and wondered if he knew what he was doing with his insights.

"Yes, I'm a poet, all right," the New Boy roared. "I'm Bruce Marchant, you bloody Zombies. I'm a poet in a world where even the lines of the King James and your precious Will whom you use for laughs aren't safe from Snakes' slime and the Spiders' dirty legs. Changing our history, stealing our certainties, claiming to be so blasted all-knowing and best intentioned and efficient, and what does it lead to? This bloody SI glove!"

He held up his black-gloved left hand which still held the mate and he shook it.

"What's wrong with the Spider Issue gauntlet, heart of gold?" Sid demanded. "And you love us, tell us." While Erich laughed, "Consider yourself lucky, *Kamerad*. Mark and I didn't draw any gloves at all."

"What's wrong with it?" Bruce yelled. "The bloody things are both lefts!" He slammed it down on the floor.

We all howled, we couldn't help it. He turned his back on us and stamped off, though I guessed he would keep out of the Void. Erich squeezed my arm and said between gasps, "*Mein Gott, Liebchen*, what have I always told you about Soldiers? The bigger the gripe, the smaller the cause! It is infallible!"

One of us didn't laugh. Ever since the New Girl heard the name Bruce Marchant, she'd had a look in her eyes like she'd been given the sacrament. I was glad she'd got interested in something, because she'd been pretty much of a snoot and a wet blanket up until now, although she'd come to the Place with the recommendation of having been a real whoopee girl in London and New York in the Twenties. She looked disapprovingly at us as she gathered up the tray and stuff, not forgetting the glove, which she placed on the center of the tray like a holy relic.

Beau cut over and tried to talk to her, but she ghosted past him and once again he couldn't do anything because of the tray in his hands. He came over and got rid of the drinks quick. I took a big gulp right away because I saw the New Girl stepping through the screen into Surgery and I hate to be reminded we have it and I'm glad Doc is too drunk to use it, some of the Arachnoid surgical techniques being very sickening as I know only too well from a personal experience that is number one on my list of things to be forgotten.

By that time, Bruce had come back to us, saying in a carefully hard voice, "Look here, it's not the dashed glove itself, as you very well know, you howling Demons."

"What is it then, noble heart?" Sid asked, his grizzled gold beard heightening the effect of innocent receptivity.

"It's the principle of the thing," Bruce said, looking around sharply, but none of us cracked a smile. "It's this mucking inefficiency and death of the cosmos-and don't tell me that isn't in the cards! —masquerading as benign omniscient authority. The Spiders-and we don't know who they are ultimately; it's just a name; we see only agents like ourselves-the Spiders pluck us from the quiet graves of our lifelines —"

"Is that bad, lad?" Sid murmured, innocently straight-faced.

" —and Resurrect us if they can and then tell us we must fight another time-traveling power called the Snakes-just a name, too-which is bent on perverting and enslaving the whole cosmos, past, present and future."

"And isn't it, lad?"

"Before we're properly awake, we're Recruited into the Big Time and hustled into tunnels and burrows outside our space-time, these miserable closets, gray sacks, puss pockets-no offense to this Place-that the Spiders have created, maybe by gigantic implosions, but no one knows for certain, and then we're sent off on all sorts of missions into the past and future to change history in ways that are supposed to thwart the Snakes."

"True, lad."

"And from then on, the pace is so flaming hot and heavy, the shocks come so fast, our emotions are wrenched in so many directions, our public and private metaphysics distorted so insanely, the deepest thread of reality we cling to tied in such bloody knots, that we never can get things straight."

"We've all felt that way, lad," Sid said soberly; Beau nodded his sleek death's head; "You should have seen me, *Kamerad*, my first fifty sleeps," Erich put in; while I added, "Us girls, too, Bruce."

"Oh, I know I'll get hardened to it, and don't think I can't. It's not that," Bruce said harshly. "And I wouldn't mind the personal confusion, the mess it's made of my spirit, I wouldn't even mind remaking history and destroying priceless, once-called imperishable beauties of the past, if I felt it were for the best. The Spiders assure us that, to thwart the Snakes, it is all-important that the West ultimately defeat the East. But what have they done to achieve this? I'll give you some beautiful examples. To stabilize power in the early Mediterranean world, they have built up Crete at the expense of Greece, making Athens a ghost city, Plato a trivial fabulist, and putting all Greek culture in a minor key."

"You got time for culture?" I heard myself say and I clapped my hand over my mouth in gentle reproof.

"But *you* remember the dialogues, lad," Sid observed. "And rail not at Crete — I have a sweet Keftian friend."

"For how long will I remember Plato's dialogues? And who after me?" Bruce challenged. "Here's another. The Spiders want Rome powerful and, to date, they've helped Rome so much that she collapses in a blaze of German and Parthian invasions a few years after the death of Julius Caesar."

This time it was Beau who butted in. Most everybody in the Place loves these bull sessions. "You omit to mention, sir, that Rome's newest downfall is directly due to the Unholy Triple Alliance the Snakes have fomented between the Eastern Classical World, Mohammedanized Christianity, and Marxist Communism, trying to pass the torch of power futurewards by way of Byzantium and the Eastern Church, without ever letting it pass into the hands of the Spider West. That, sir, is the Snakes' Three-Thousand-Year Plan which we are fighting against, striving to revive Rome's glories."

"Striving is the word for it," Bruce snapped. "Here's yet another example. To beat Russia, the Spiders kept England and America out of World War Two, thereby ensuring a German invasion of the New World and creating a Nazi empire stretching from the salt mines of Siberia to the plantations of Iowa, from Nizhni Novgorod to Kansas City!"

He stopped and my short hairs prickled. Behind me, someone was chanting in a weird spiritless voice, like footsteps in hard snow.

"*Salz, Salz, bringe Salz. Kein' Peitsch', gnädige Herren. Salz, Salz, Salz.*"

I turned and there was Doc waltzing toward us with little tiny steps, bent over so low that the ends of his shawl touched the floor, his head crooked up sideways and looking through us.

I knew then, but Erich translated softly. "'Salt, salt, I bring salt. No whip, merciful sirs.' He is speaking to my countrymen in their language." Doc had spent his last months in a Nazi-operated salt mine.

He saw us and got up, straightening his top hat very carefully. He frowned hard while my heart thumped half a dozen times. Then his face slackened, he shrugged his shoulders and muttered, "*Nichevo.*"

"And it does not matter, sir," Beau translated, but directing his remark at Bruce. "True, great civilizations have been dwarfed or broken by the Change War. But others, once crushed in the bud, have bloomed. In the 1870s, I traveled a Mississippi that had never known Grant's gunboats. I studied piano, languages, and the laws of chance under the greatest European masters at the University of Vicksburg."

"And you think your pipsqueak steamboat culture is compensation for —" Bruce began but, "Prithee none of that, lad," Sid interrupted smartly. "Nations are as equal as so many madmen or drunkards, and I'll drink dead drunk the man who disputes me. Hear reason: nations are not so puny as to shrivel and vanish at the first tampering with their past, no, nor with the tenth. Nations are monsters, boy, with guts of iron and nerves of brass. Waste not your pity on them."

"True indeed, sir," Beau pressed, cooler and keener for the attack on his Greater South. "Most of us enter the Change World with the false metaphysic that the slightest change in the past —a grain of dust misplaced-will transform the whole future. It is a long while before we accept with our minds as well as our intellects the law of the Conservation of Reality: that when the past is changed, the future changes barely enough to adjust, barely enough to admit the new data. The Change Winds meet maximum resistance always. Otherwise the first operation in Babylonia would have wiped out New Orleans, Sheffield, Stuttgart, and Maud Davies' birthplace on Ganymede!

"Note how the gap left by Rome's collapse was filled by the imperialistic and Christianized Germans. Only an expert Demon historian can tell the difference in most ages between the former Latin and the present Gothic Catholic Church. As you yourself, sir, said of Greece, it is as if an old melody were shifted into a slightly different key. In the wake of a Big Change, cultures and individuals are transposed, it's true, yet in the main they continue much as they were, except for the usual scattering of unfortunate but statistically meaningless accidents."

"All right, you bloody savants-maybe I pushed my point too far," Bruce growled. "But if you want variety, give a thought to the rotten methods we use in our wonderful Change War. Poisoning Churchill and Cleopatra. Kidnapping Einstein when he's a baby."

"The Snakes did it first," I reminded him.

"Yes, and we copied them. How resourceful does that make us?" he retorted, arguing like a woman. "If we need Einstein, why don't we Resurrect him, deal with him as a man?"

Beau said, serving his culture in slightly thicker slices, *"Pardonnez-moi*, but when you have enjoyed your status as Doubleganger a *soupcon* longer, you will understand that great men can rarely be Resurrected. Their beings are too crystallized, sir, their lifelines too tough."

"Pardon me, but I think that's rot. I believe that most great men refuse to make the bargain with the Snakes, or with us Spiders either. They scorn Resurrection at the price demanded."

"Brother, they ain't that great," I whispered, while Beau glided on with, "However that may be, you have accepted Resurrection, sir, and so incurred an obligation which you as a gentleman must honor."

"I accepted Resurrection all right," Bruce said, a glare coming into his eyes. "When they pulled me out of my line at Passchendaele in '17 ten minutes before I died, I grabbed at the offer of life like a drunkard grabs at a drink the morning after. But even then I thought I was also seizing a chance to undo historic wrongs, work for peace." His voice was getting wilder all the time. Just beyond our circle, I noticed the New Girl watching him worshipfully. "But what did I find the Spiders wanted me for? Only to fight more wars, over and over again, make them crueler and stinkinger, cut the swath of death a little wider with each Big Change, work our way a little closer to the death of the cosmos."

Sid touched my wrist and, as Bruce raved on, he whispered to me, "What kind of ball, think you, will please and so quench this fire-brained rogue? And you love me, discover it."

I whispered back without taking my eyes off Bruce either, "I know somebody who'll be happy to put on any kind of ball he wants, if he'll just notice her."

"The New Girl, sweetling? 'Tis well. This rogue speaks like an angry angel. It touches my heart and I like it not."

Bruce was saying hoarsely but loudly, "And so we're sent on operations in the past and from each of those operations the Change Winds blow futurewards, swiftly or slowly according to the opposition they breast, sometimes rippling into each other, and any one of those Winds may shift the date of our own death ahead of the date of our Resurrection, so that in an instant-even here, outside the cosmos-we may molder and rot or crumble to dust and vanish away. The wind with our name in it may leak through the Door."

Faces hardened at that, because it's bad form to mention Change Death, and Erich flared out with, *"Halt's Maul, Kamerad!* There's always another Resurrection."

But Bruce didn't keep his mouth shut. He said, "Is there? I know the Spiders promise it, but even if they do go back and cut another Doubleganger from my lifeline, is he me?" He slapped his chest with his bare hand. "I don't think so. And even if he is me, with unbroken conscious-ness, why's he been Resurrected again? Just to refight more wars and face more Change Death for the sake of an almighty power —" his voice was rising to a climax —"an almighty power so bloody ineffectual, it can't furnish one poor Soldier pulled out of the mud of Passchendaele, one miserable Change Commando, one Godforsaken Recuperee a proper issue of equipment!"

And he held out his bare right hand toward us, fingers spread a little, as if it were the most amazing object and most deserving of outraged sympathy in the whole world.

The New Girl's timing was perfect. She whisked through us, and before he could so much as wiggle the fingers, she whipped a black gauntleted glove on it and anyone could see that it fitted his hand perfectly.

This time our laughing beat the other. We collapsed and slopped our drinks and pounded each other on the back and then started all over.

"*Ach, der Handschuh, Liebchen!* Where'd she get it?" Erich gasped in my ear.

"Probably just turned the other one inside out-that turns a left into a right —I've done it myself," I wheezed, collapsing again at the idea.

"That would put the lining outside," he objected.

"Then I don't know," I said. "We got all sorts of junk in Stores."

"It doesn't matter, *Liebchen*," he assured me. "*Ach, der Handschuh!*"

All through it, Bruce just stood there admiring the glove, moving the fingers a little now and then, and the New Girl stood watching him as if he were eating a cake she'd baked.

When the hysteria quieted down, he looked up at her with a big smile. "What did you say your name was?"

"Lili," she said, and believe you me, she was Lili to me even in my thoughts from then on, for the way she'd handled that lunatic.

"Lilian Foster," she explained. "I'm English also. Mr. Marchant, I've read *A Young Man's Fancy* I don't know how many times."

"You have? It's wretched stuff. From the Dark Ages —I mean my Cambridge days. In the trenches, I was working up some poems that were rather better."

"I won't hear you say that. But I'd be terribly thrilled to hear the new ones. Oh, Mr. Marchant, it was so strange to hear you call it Passiondale."

"Why, if I may ask?"

"Because that's the way I pronounce it to myself. But I looked it up and it's more like Pas-ken-DA-luh."

"Bless you! All the Tommies called it Passiondale, just as they called Ypres Wipers."

"How interesting. You know, Mr. Marchant, I'll wager we were Recruited in the same op-eration, summer of 1917. I'd got to France as a Red Cross nurse, but they found out my age and were going to send me back."

"How old were you-are you? Same thing, I mean to say."

"Seventeen."

"Seventeen in '17," Bruce murmured, his blue eyes glassy.

It was real corny dialogue and I couldn't resent the humorous leer Erich gave me as we listened to them, as if to say, "Ain't it nice, *Liebchen*, Bruce has a silly little English schoolgirl to occupy him between operations?"

Just the same, as I watched Lili in her dark bangs and pearl necklace and tight little gray dress that reached barely to her knees, and Bruce hulking over her tenderly in his snazzy hussar's rig, I knew that I was seeing the start of something that hadn't been part of me since Dave died fighting Franco years before I got on the Big Time, the sort of thing that almost made me wish there could be children in the Change World. I wondered why I'd never thought of trying to work things so that Dave got Resurrected and I told myself: no, it's all changed, I've changed, better the Change Winds don't disturb Dave or I know about it.

"No, I didn't die in 1917—I was merely Recruited then," Lili was telling Bruce. "I lived all through the Twenties, as you can see from the way I dress. But let's not talk about that, shall we? Oh, Mr. Marchant, do you think you can possibly remember any of those poems you started in the trenches? I can't fancy them bettering your sonnet that concludes with, 'The bough swings in the wind, the night is deep; Look at the stars, poor little ape, and sleep.'"

That one almost made me whoop-what monkeys we are, I thought-though I'd be the first to admit that the best line to use on a poet is one of his own-in fact, as many as possible. I decided I could safely forget our little Britons and devote myself to Erich or whatever needed me.

Chapter 3
Nine for a Party

Hell is the place for me. For to Hell go the fine churchmen, and the fine knights, killed in the tourney or in some grand war, the brave soldiers and the gallant gentlemen. With them will I go. There go also the fair gracious ladies who have lovers two or three beside their lord. There go the gold and the silver, the sables and ermine. There go the harpers and the minstrels and the kings of the earth.

—Aucassin

I exchanged my drink for a new one from another tray Beau was bringing around. The gray of the Void was beginning to look real pleasant, like warm thick mist with millions of tiny diamonds floating in it. Doc was sitting grandly at the bar with a steaming tumbler of tea —a chaser, I guess, since he was just putting down a shot glass. Sid was talking to Erich and laughing at the same time and I said to myself it begins to feel like a party, but something's lacking.

It wasn't anything to do with the Major Maintainer; its telltale was glowing a steady red like a nice little home fire amid the tight cluster of dials that included all the controls except the lonely and frightening Introversion switch that was never touched. Then Maud's couch curtains winked out and there were she and the Roman sitting quietly side by side.

He looked down at his shiny boots and the rest of his black duds like he was just waking up and couldn't believe it all, and he said, *"Omnia mutantur, nos et mutamur in illis,"* and I raised my eyebrows at Beau, who was taking the tray back, and he did proud by old Vicksburg by translating: "All things change and we change with them."

Then Mark slowly looked around at us, and I can testify that a Roman smile is just as warm as any other nationality, and he finally said, "We are nine, the proper number for a party. The couches, too. It is good."

Maud chuckled proudly and Erich shouted, "Welcome back from the Void, *Kamerad*," and then, because he's German and thinks all parties have to be noisy and satirically pompous, he jumped on a couch and announced, *"Herren und Damen,"* permit me to introduce the noblest Roman of them all, Marcus Vipsaius Niger, legate to Nero Claudius (called Germanicus in a former time stream) and who in 763 A.U.C. (Correct, Mark? It means 10 A.D., you meatheads!) died bravely fighting the Parthians and the Snakes in the Battle of Alexandria. *Hoch, hoch, hoch!"*

We all swung our glasses and cheered with him and Sid yelled at Erich, "Keep your feet off the furniture, you unschooled rogue," and grinned and boomed at all three hussars, "Take your ease, Recuperees," and Maud and Mark got their drinks, the Roman paining Beau by refusing Falernian wine in favor of scotch and soda, and right away everyone was talking a mile a minute.

We had a lot to catch up on. There was the usual yak about the war —"The Snakes are laying mine fields in the Void," "I don't believe it, how can you mine nothing?" —and the shortages-bourbon, bobby pins, and the stabilitin that would have brought Mark out of it faster-and what had become of people —"Marcia? Oh, she's not around any more," (She'd been caught in a Change Gale and green and stinking in five seconds, but I wasn't going to say that) —and Mark had to be told about Bruce's glove, which convulsed us all over again, and the Roman remembered a legionary who had carried a gripe all the way to Octavius because he'd accidentally been issued the unbelievable luxury item sugar instead of the usual salt, and Erich asked Sid if he had any new Ghostgirls in stock and Sid sucked his beard like the old goat he is. "Dost thou ask me, lusty Allemand? Nay, there are several great beauties, amongst them an Austrian countess from Strauss's Vienna, and if it were not for sweeting here ...Mnnnn."

I poked a finger in Erich's chest between two of the bright buttons with their tiny death's heads. "You, my little von Hohenwald, are a menace to us real girls. You have too much of a thing about the unawakened, ghost kind."

He called me his little Demon and hugged me a bit too hard to prove it wasn't so, and then he suggested we show Bruce the Art Gallery. I thought this was a real brilliant idea, but when I tried to argue him out of it, he got stubborn. Bruce and Lili were willing to do anything anyone wanted them to, though not so willing to pay any attention while doing it. The saber cut was just a thin red line on his cheek; she'd washed away all the dried blood.

The Gallery gets you, though. It's a bunch of paintings and sculptures and especially odd knick-knacks, all made by Soldiers recuperating here, and a lot of them telling about the Change War from the stuff they're made of-brass cartridges, flaked flint, bits of ancient pottery glued into futuristic shapes, mashed-up Incan gold rebeaten by a Martian, whorls of beady Lunan wire, a picture in tempera on a crinkle-cracked thick round of quartz that had filled a starship porthole, a Sumerian inscription chiseled into a brick from an atomic oven.

There are a lot of things in the Gallery and I can always find some I haven't ever seen before. It gets you, as I say, thinking about the guys that made them and their thoughts and the far times and places they came from, and sometimes, when I'm feeling low, I'll come and look at them so I'll feel still lower and get inspired to kick myself back into a good temper. It's the only history of the Place there is and it doesn't change a great deal, because the things in it and the feelings that went into them resist the Change Winds better than anything else.

Right now, Erich's witty lecture was bouncing off the big ears I hide under my pageboy bob and I was thinking how awful it is that for us that there's not only change but Change. You don't know from one minute to the next whether a mood or idea you've got is really new or just welling up into you because the past has been altered by the Spiders or Snakes.

Change Winds can blow not only death but anything short of it, down to the featheriest fancy. They blow thousands of times faster than time moves, but no one can say how much faster or how far one of them will travel or what damage it'll do or how soon it'll damp out. The Big Time isn't the little time.

And then, for the Demons, there's the fear that our personality will just fade and someone else climb into the driver's seat and us not even know. Of course, we Demons are supposed to be able to remember through Change and in spite of it; that's why we are Demons and not Ghosts like the other Doublegangers, or merely Zombies or Unborn and nothing more, and as Beau truly said, there aren't any great men among us-and blamed few of the masses, either-we're a rare sort of people and that's why the Spiders have to Recruit us where they find us without caring about our previous knowledge and background, a Foreign Legion of time, a strange kind of folk, bright but always in the background, with built-in nostalgia and cynicism, as adaptable as Centaurian shape-changers but with memories as long as a Lunan's six arms, a kind of Change People, you might say, the cream of the damned.

But sometimes I wonder if our memories are as good as we think they are and if the whole past wasn't once entirely different from anything we remember, and we've forgotten that we forgot.

As I say, the Gallery gets you feeling real low, and so now I said to myself, "Back to your lousy little commandant, kid," and gave myself a stiff boot.

Erich was holding up a green bowl with gold dolphins or spaceships on it and saying, "And, to my mind, this proves that Etruscan art is derived from Egyptian. Don't you agree, Bruce?"

Bruce looked up, all smiles from Lili, and said, "What was that, dear chap?"

Erich's forehead got dark as the Door and I was glad the hussars had parked their sabers along with their shakos, but before he could even get out a Jerry cussword, Doc breezed up in that plateau-state of drunkenness so like hypnotized sobriety, moving as if he were on a dolly, ghosted the bowl out of Erich's hand, said, "A beautiful specimen of Middle Systemic Venusian. When Eightaitch finished it, he told me you couldn't look at it and not feel the waves of the Northern Venusian Shallows rippling around your hoofs. But it might look better inverted. I wonder. Who are you, young officer? *Nichevo*," and he carefully put the bowl back on its shelf and rolled on.

It's a fact that Doc knows the Art Gallery better than any of us, really by heart, he being the oldest inhabitant, though he maybe picked a bad time to show off his knowledge. Erich was going to take out after him, but I said, "Nix, *Kamerad*, remember gloves and sugar," and he contented himself with complaining, "That *nichevo* —it's so gloomy and hopeless, *ungeheuerlich*. I tell you, *Liebchen*, they shouldn't have Russians working for the Spiders, not even as Entertainers."

I grinned at him and squeezed his hand. "Not much entertainment in Doc these days, is there?" I agreed.

He grinned back at me a shade sheepishly and his face smoothed and his blue eyes looked sweet again for a second and he said, "I shouldn't want to claw out at people that way, Greta, but at times I am just a jealous old man," which is not entirely true, as he isn't a day over thirty-three, although his hair is nearly white.

Our lovers had drifted on a few steps until they were almost fading into the Surgery screen. It was the last spot I would have picked for the formal preliminaries to a little British smooching, but Lili probably didn't share my prejudices, though I remembered she'd told me she'd served a brief hitch in an Arachnoid Field Hospital before being transferred to the Place.

But she couldn't have had anything like the experience I'd had during my short and sour career as a Spider nurse, when I'd acquired my best-hated nightmare and flopped completely (jobwise, but on the floor, too) at seeing a doctor flick a switch and a being, badly injured but human, turn into a long cluster of glistening strange fruit-ugh, it always makes me want to toss my cookies and my buttons. And to think that dear old Daddy Anton wanted his Greta chile to be a doctor.

Well, I could see this wasn't getting me anywhere I wanted to go, and after all there was a party going on.

Doc was babbling something at a great rate to Sid —I just hoped Doc wouldn't get inspired to go into his animal imitations, which sound pretty fierce and once seriously offended some recuperating ETs.

Maud was demonstrating to Mark a 23rd Century two-step and Beau sat down at the piano and improvised softly on her rhythm.

As the deep-thrumming relaxing notes hit us, Erich's face brightened and he dragged me over. Pleasantly soon I had my feet off the diamond-rough floor, which we don't carpet because most of the ETs, the dear boys, like it hard, and I was shouldering back deep into the couch nearest the piano, with cushions all around me and a fresh drink in my hand, while my Nazi boy friend was getting ready to discharge his *Weltschmerz* as song, which didn't alarm me too much, as his baritone is passable.

Things felt real good, like the Maintainer was just idling to keep the Place in existence and moored to the cosmos, not exerting itself at all or at most taking an occasional lazy paddle stroke. At times the Place's loneliness can be happy and comfortable.

Then Beau raised an eyebrow at Erich, who nodded, and next thing they were launched into a song we all know, though I've never found out where it originally came from. This time it made me think of Lili, and I wondered why-and why it's a tradition at Recuperation Stations to call the new girl Lili, though in this case it happened to be her real name.

Standing in the Doorway just outside of space,
Winds of Change blow 'round you but don't touch your face;
You smile as you whisper tenderly,
"Please cross to me, Recuperee;
The operation's over, come in and close the Door."

Chapter 4
Sos from Nowhere

De Bailhache, Fresca, Mrs. Cammel, whirled
Beyond the circuit of the shuddering Bear
In fractured atoms.

—Eliot

I realized the piano had deserted Erich and I cranked my head up and saw Beau, Maud and Sid streaking for the control divan. The Major Maintainer was blinking emergency-green and fast, but the code was plain enough for even me to recognize the Spider distress call and for a second I felt just sick. Then Erich blew out his reserve breath in the middle of "Door" and I gave myself another of those helpful mental boots at the base of the spine and we hurried after them toward the center of the Place along with Mark.

The blinks faded as we got there and Sid told us not to move because we were making shadows. He glued an eye to the telltale and we held still as statues as he caressed the dials like he was making love.

One sensitive hand flicked out past the Introversion switch over to the Minor Maintainer and right away the Place was dark as your soul and there was nothing for me but Erich's arm and the knowledge that Sid was nursing a green light I couldn't even see, although my eyes had plenty time to accommodate.

Then the green light finally came back very slowly and I could see the dear reliable old face-the green-gold beard making him look like a merman-and then the telltale flared bright and Sid flicked on the Place lights and I leaned back.

"That nails them, lads, whoever and whenever they may be. Get ready for a pick-up."

Beau, who was closest of course, looked at him sharply. Sid shrugged uneasily. "Meseemed at first it was from our own globe a thousand years before our Lord, but that indication flickered and faded like witchfire. As it is, the call comes from something smaller than the Place and certes adrift from the cosmos. Meseemed too at one point I knew the fist of the caller-an antipodean atomicist named Benson-Carter —but that likewise changed."

Beau said, "We're not in the right phase of the cosmos-Places rhythm for a pick-up, are we, sir?"

Sid answered, "Ordinarily not, boy."

Beau continued, "I didn't think we had any pick-ups scheduled. Or stand-by orders."

Sid said, "We haven't."

Mark's eyes glowed. He tapped Erich on the shoulder. "An octavian denarius against ten Reichsmarks it is a Snake trap."

Erich's grin showed his teeth. "Make it first through the Door next operation and I'm on."

It didn't take that to tell me things were serious, or the thought that there's always a first time for bumping into something from really outside the cosmos. The Snakes have broken our code more than once. Maud was quietly serving out weapons and Doc was helping her. Only Bruce and Lili stood off. But they were watching.

The telltale brightened. Sid reached toward the Maintainer, saying, "All right, my hearties. Remember, through this Doorway pass the fishiest finaglers in and out of the cosmos."

The Door appeared to the left and above where it should be and darkened much too fast. There was a gust of stale salt seawind, if that makes sense, but no stepped-up Change Winds

I could tell-and I had been bracing myself against them. The Door got inky and there was a flicker of gray fur whips and a flash of copper flesh and gilt and something dark and a clump of hoofs and Erich was sighting a stun gun across his left forearm, and then the Door had vanished like that and a tentacled silvery Lunan and a Venusian satyr were coming straight toward us.

The Lunan was hugging a pile of clothes and weapons. The satyr was helping a wasp-waisted woman carry a heavy-looking bronze chest. The woman was wearing a short skirt and high-collared bolero jacket of leather so dark brown it was almost black. She had a two-horned *petsofu* hairdress and she was boldly gilded here and there and wore sandals and copper anklets and wristlets-one of them a copper-plated Caller-and from her wide copper belt hung a short-handled double-headed ax. She was dark-complexioned and her forehead and chin receded, but the effect was anything but weak; she had a face like a beautiful arrowhead-and a familiar one, by golly!

But before I could say, "Kabysia Labrys," Maud shrilly beat me to it with, "It's Kaby with two friends. Break out a couple of Ghostgirls."

And then I saw it really was old-home week because I recognized my Lunan boy friend Ilhilihis, and in the midst of all the confusion I got a nice kick out of knowing I was getting so I could tell the personality of one silver-furred muzzle from another.

They reached the control divan and Illy dumped his load and the others let down the chest, and Kaby staggered but shook off the two ETs when they started to support her, and she looked daggers at Sid when he tried to do the same, although she's his "sweet Keftian friend" he'd mentioned to Bruce.

She leaned straight-armed on the divan and took two gasping breaths so deep that the ridges of her spine showed through her brown-skinned waist, and then she threw up her head and commanded, "Wine!"

While Beau was rushing it, Sid tried to take her hand again, saying, "Sweetling, I'd never heard you call before and knew not this pretty little fist," but she ripped out, "Save your comfort for the Lunan," and I looked and saw-Hey, Zeus! —that one of Ilhilihis' six tentacles was lopped off halfway.

That was for me, and, going to him, I fast briefed myself: "Remember, he only weighs fifty pounds for all he's seven feet high; he doesn't like low sounds or to be grabbed; the two legs aren't tentacles and don't act the same; uses them for long walks, tentacles for leaps; uses tentacles for close vision too and for manipulation, of course; extended, they mean he's at ease; retracted, on guard or nervous; sharply retracted, disgusted; greeting —"

Just then, one of them swept across my face like a sweet-smelling feather duster and I said, "Illy, man, it's been a lot of sleeps," and brushed my fingers across his muzzle. It still took a little self-control not to hug him, and I did reach a little cluckingly for his lopped tentacle, but he wafted it away from me and the little voice-box belted to his side squeaked, "Naughty, naughty. Papa will fix his little old self. Greta girl, ever bandaged even a Terra octopus?"

I had, an intelligent one from around a quarter billion A.D., but I didn't tell him so. I stood and let him talk to the palm of my hand with one of his tentacles —I don't savvy feather-talk but it feels good, though I've often wondered who taught him English-and watched him use a couple others to whisk a sort of Lunan band-aid out of his pouch and cap his wound with it.

Meanwhile, the satyr knelt over the bronze chest, which was decorated with little death's heads and crosses with hoops at the top and swastikas, but looking much older than Nazi, and the satyr said to Sid, "Quick thinkin, Gov, when ya saw the Door comin in high n softened up gravty unner it, but cud I hav sum hep now?"

Sid touched the Minor Maintainer and we all got very light and my stomach did a flip-flop while the satyr piled on the chest the clothes and weapons that Illy had been carrying and pranced off with it all and carefully put it down at the end of the bar. I decided the satyr's English instructor must have been quite a character, too. Wish I'd met him-her-it.

Sid thought to ask Illy if he wanted Moon-normal gravity in one sector, but my boy likes to mix, and being such a lightweight, Earth-normal gravity doesn't bother him. As he said to me once, "Would Jovian gravity bother a beetle, Greta girl?"

I asked Illy about the satyr and he squeaked that his name was Sevensee and that he'd never met him before this operation. I knew the satyrs were from a billion years in the future, just as the Loonies were from a billion in the past, and I thought-Kreesed us! —but it must have been a real big or emergency-like operation to have the Spiders using those two for it, with two billion years between them —a time-difference that gives you a feeling of awe for a second, you know.

I started to ask Illy about it, but just then Beau came scampering back from the bar with a big red-and-black earthenware goblet of wine-we try to keep a variety of drinking tools in stock so folks will feel more at home. Kaby grabbed it from him and drained most of it in one swallow and then smashed it on the floor. She does things like that, though Sid's tried to teach her better. Then she stared at what she was thinking about until the whites showed all around her eyes and her lips pulled way back from her teeth and she looked a lot less human than the two ETs, just like a fury. Only a time traveler knows how like the wild murals and engravings of them some of the ancients can look.

My hair stood up at the screech she let out. She smashed a fist into the divan and cried, "Goddess! Must I see Crete destroyed, revived, and now destroyed again? It is too much for your servant."

Personally, I thought she could stand anything.

There was a rush of questions at what she said about Crete —I asked one of them, for the news certainly frightened me-but she shot up her arm straight for silence and took a deep breath and began.

"In the balance hung the battle. Rowing like black centipedes, the Dorian hulls bore down on our outnumbered ships. On the bright beach, masked by rocks, Sevensee and I stood by the needle gun, ready to give the black hulls silent wounds. Beside us was Ilhilihis, suited as a sea monster. But then ...then..."

Then I saw she wasn't altogether the iron babe, for her voice broke and she started to shake and to sob rackingly, although her face was still a mask of rage, and she threw up the wine. Sid stepped in and made her stop, which I think he'd been wanting to do all along.

Chapter 5
Sid Insists on Ghostgirls

> Whenever I take up a newspaper and read it, I fancy I see ghosts creeping between the lines. There must be ghosts all over the world. They must be as countless as the grains of the sands, it seems to me.
>
> —Ibsen

My Elizabethan boy friend put his fists on his hips and laid down the law to us as if we were a lot of nervous children who'd been playing too hard.

"Look you, masters, this is a Recuperation Station and I am running it as such. A plague of all operations! I care not if the frame of things disjoints and the whole Change World goes to ruin, but you, warrior maid, are going to rest and drink more wine slowly before you tell your tale and your colleagues are going to be properly companioned. No questions, anyone. Beau, and you love us, give us a lively tune."

Kaby relaxed a little and let him put his hand carefully against her back in token of support and she said grudgingly, "All right, Fat Belly."

Then, so help me, to the tune of the Muskrat Ramble, which I'd taught Beau, we got girls for those two ETs and everybody properly paired up.

Right here I want to point out that a lot of the things they say in the Change World about Recuperation Stations simply aren't so-and anyway they always leave out nine-tenths of it. The Soldiers that come through the Door are looking for a good time, sure, but they're hurt real bad too, every one of them, deep down in their minds and hearts, if not always in their bodies or so you can see it right away.

Believe me, a temporal operation is no joke, and to start with, there isn't one person in a hundred who can endure to be cut from his lifeline and become a really wide-awake Double-ganger—a Demon, that is-let alone a Soldier. What does a badly hurt and mixed-up creature need who's been fighting hard? *One individual* to look out for him and feel for him and patch him up, and it helps if the one is of the opposite sex-that's something that goes beyond species.

There's your basis for the Place and the wild way it goes about its work, and also for most other Recuperation Stations or Entertainment Spots. The name Entertainer can be misleading, but I like it. She's got to be a lot more than a good party girl-or boy-though she's got to be that too. She's got to be a nurse and a psychologist and an actress and a mother and a practical ethnologist and a lot of things with longer names-and a reliable friend.

None of us are all those things perfectly or even near it. We just try. But when the call comes, Entertainers have to forget grudges and gripes and envies and jealousies-and remember, they're lively people with sharp emotions-because there isn't any time then for anything but *help and don't ask who!*

And, deep inside her, a good Entertainer doesn't care who. Take the way it shaped up this time. It was pretty clear to me I ought to shift to Illy, although I wasn't quite easy in my mind about leaving Erich, because the Lunan was a long time from home and, after all, Erich was among anthropoids. Ilhilihis needed someone who was *simpatico*.

I like Illy and not just because he is a sort of tall cross between a spider monkey and a persian cat-though that is a handsome combo when you come to think of it. I like him for himself. So when he came in all lopped and shaky after a mean operation, I was the right person to look out for him. Now I've made my little speech and know-nothings in the Change World can go on making their bum jokes. But I ask you, how could an arrangement between Illy and me be anything but Platonic?

We might have had some octopoid girls and nymphs in stock-Sid couldn't be sure until he checked-but Ilhilihis and Sevensee voted for real people and I knew Sid saw it their way. Maud squeezed Mark's hand and tripped over to Sevensee ("Those are sharp hoofs you got, man" —she's picked up some of my language, like she has everything else), though Beau did frown over his shoulder at Lili from the piano, maybe to argue that she ought to take on the ET, as Mark had been a real casualty and could use live nursing. But it was plain as day to anybody but Beau that Bruce and Lili were a big thing and the last to be disturbed.

Erich acted stiffly hurt at losing me, but I knew he wasn't. He thinks he has a great technique with Ghostgirls and he likes to show it off, and he really is pretty slick at it, if you go for that sort of thing and-yang my yin! —who doesn't at times?

And when Sid formally wafted the Countess out of Stores —a real blonde stunner in a white satin hobble skirt with a white egret swaying up from her tiny hat, way ahead of Maud and Lili and me when it came to looks, though transparent as cigarette smoke-and when Erich clicked his heels and bowed over her hand and proudly conducted her to a couch, black Svengali to her Trilby, and started to German-talk some life into her with much head cocking and toothy smiling and a flow of witty flattery, and when she began to flirt back and the dream look in her eyes sharpened hungrily and focused on him-well, then I knew that Erich was happy and felt he was doing proud by the *Reichswehr*. No, my little commandant wasn't worrying me on that score.

Mark had drawn a Greek hetaera, name of Phryne; I suppose not the one who maybe still does the famous courtroom striptease back in Athens, and he was waking her up with little sips of his scotch and soda, though, from some looks he'd flashed, I got the idea Kaby was the kid he really went for. Sid was coaxing the fighting gal to take some high-energy bread and olives along with the wine, and, for a wonder, Doc seemed to be carrying on an animated and rational conversation with Sevensee and Maud, maybe comparing notes on the Northern Venusian Shallows, and Beau had got on to Panther Rag, and Bruce and Lili were leaning on the piano, smiling very appreciatively, but talking to each other a mile a minute.

Illy turned back from inspecting them all and squeaked, "Animals with clothes are so refreshing, dahling! Like you're all carrying banners!"

Maybe he had something there, though my banners were kind of Ash Wednesday, a charcoal gray sweater and skirt. He looked at my mouth with a tentacle to see how I was smiling and he squeaked softly, "Do I seem dull and commonplace to you, Greta girl, because I haven't got banners? Just another Zombie from a billion years in your past, as gray and lifeless as Luna is today, not as when she was a real dreamy sister planet simply bursting with air and water and feather forests. Or am I as strangely interesting to you as you are to me, girl from a billion years in my future?"

"Illy, you're sweet," I told him, giving him a little pat. I noticed his fur was still vibrating nervously and I decided the heck with Sid's orders, I'm going to pump him about what he was doing with Kaby and the satyr. Couldn't have him a billion years from home and bottled up, too. Besides, I was curious.

Chapter 6
Crete Circa 1300 B.C.

> Maiden, Nymph, and Mother are the eternal royal Trinity of the island, and the Goddess, who is worshipped there in each of these aspects, as New Moon, Full Moon, and Old Moon, is the sovereign Deity.
>
> —Graves

Kaby pushed back at Sid some seconds of bread and olives, and, when he raised his bushy eyebrows, gave him a curt nod that meant she knew what she was doing. She stood up and sort of took a position. All the talk quieted down fast, even Bruce's and Lili's. Kaby's face and voice weren't strained now, but they weren't relaxed either.

"Woe to Spider! Woe to Cretan! Heavy is the news I bring you. Bear it bravely, like strong women. When we got the gun unlimbered, I heard seaweed fry and crackle. We three leaped behind the rock wall, saw our gun grow white as sunlight in a heat-ray of the Serpents! Natch, we feared we were outnumbered and I called upon my Caller."

I don't know how she does it, but she does–in English too. That is, when she figures she's got something important to report, and maybe she needs a little time to get ready.

Beau claims that all the ancients fit their thoughts into measured lines as naturally as we pick a word that will do, but I'm not sure how good the Vicksburg language department is. Though why I should wonder about things like that when I've got Kaby spouting the stuff right in front of me, I don't know.

"But I didn't die there, kiddos. I still hoped to hurt the Greek ships, maybe with the Snake's own heat gun. So I quick tried to outflank them. My two comrades crawled beside me–they are males, but they have courage. Soon we spied the ambush-setters. They were Snakes and they were many, filthily disguised as Cretans."

There was an indignant murmur at this, for our cutthroat Change War has its code, the Soldiers tell me. Being an Entertainer, I don't have to say what I think.

"They had seen us when we saw them," Kaby swept on, "and they loosed a killing volley. Heat- and knife-rays struck about us in a storm of wind and fire, and the Lunan lost a feeler, fighting for Crete's Triple Goddess. So we dodged behind a sand hill, steered our flight back toward the water. It was awful, what we saw there: Crete's brave ships all sunk or sinking, blue sky sullied by their death-smoke. Once again the Greeks had licked us! —aided by the filthy Serpents.

"Round our wrecks, their black ships scurried, like black beetles, filth their diet, yet this day they dine on heroes. On the quiet sunlit beach there, I could feel a Change Gale blowing, working changes deep inside me, aches and pains that were a stranger's. Half my memories were doubled, half my lifeline crooked and twisted, three new moles upon my sword-hand. Goddess, Goddess, Triple Goddess —"

Her voice wavered and Sid reached out a hand, but she straightened her back.

"Triple Goddess, give me courage to tell everything that happened. We ran down into the water, hoping to escape by diving. We had hardly gotten under when the heat-rays hit above us, turning all the cool green surface to a roaring white inferno. But as I believe I told you, I was calling on my Caller, and a Door now opened to us, deep below the deadly steam-clouds. We dived in like frightened minnows and a lot of water with us."

Off Chicago's Gold Coast, Dave once gave me a lesson in skin-diving and, remembering it, I got a flash of Kaby's Door in the dark depths.

"For a moment, all was chaos. Then the Door slammed shut behind us. We'd been picked up in time's nick by–an Express Room of our Spiders! —sloshing two feet deep in water, much more cramped for space than this Place. It was manned by a magician, an old coot named Benson-Carter. He dispelled the water quickly and reported on his Caller. We'd got dry, were feeling human, Illy here had shed his swimsuit, when we looked at the Maintainer. It was glowing, changing, melting! And when Benson-Carter touched it, he fell backward–death was in him. Then the Void began to darken, narrow, shrink and close around us, so I called upon my Caller–without wasting time, let me tell you!

"We can't say for sure what was it slowly squeezed that sweet Express Room, but we fear the dirty Snakes have found a way to find our Places and attack outside the cosmos! —found the Spiderweb that links us in the Void's gray less-than-nothing."

No murmur this time. This reaction was genuine; we'd been hit where we lived and I could see everybody was scared as sick as I was. Except maybe Bruce and Lili, who were still holding hands and beaming gently. I decided they were the kind that love makes brave, which it doesn't do to me. It just gives me two people to worry about.

"I can see you dig our feelings," Kaby continued. "This thing scared the pants off of us. If we could have, we'd have even Introverted the Maintainer, broken all the ties that bind us, chanced it incommunicado. But the little old Maintainer was a seething red-hot puddle filled with bubbles big as handballs. We sat tight and watched the Void close. I kept calling on my Caller."

I squeezed my eyes shut, but that made it easier to see the three of them with the Void shutting down on them. (Was ours still behaving? Yes, Bibi Miriam.) Poetry or no poetry, it got me.

"Benson-Carter, lying dying, also thought the Snakes had done it. And he knew that death was in him, so he whispered me his mission, giving me precise instructions: how to press the seven death's hands, starting lockside counterclockwise, one, three, five, six, two, four, seven, then you have a half an hour; after you have pressed the seven, do not monkey with the buttons–get out fast and don't stop moving."

I wasn't getting this part and I couldn't see that anyone else was, though Bruce was whispering to Lili. I remembered seeing skulls engraved on the bronze chest. I looked at Illy and he nodded a tentacle and spread two to say, I guessed, that yes, Benson-Carter had said something like that, but no, Illy didn't know much about it.

"All these things and more he whispered," Kaby went on, "with the last gasps of his life-force, telling all his secret orders–for he'd not been sent to get us, he was on a separate mission, when he heard my SOSs. Sid, it's you he was to contact, as the first leg of his mission, pick up from you three black hussars, death's-head Demons, daring Soldiers, then to wait until the Places next match rhythm with the cosmos-matter of two mealtimes, barely–and to tune in northern Egypt in the age of the last Caesar, in the year of Rome's swift downfall, there to start an operation in a battle near a city named for Thrace's Alexander, there to change the course of battle, blow sky-high the stinking Serpents, all their agents, all their Zombies!

"Goddess, pardon, now I savvy how you've guided my least footstep, when I thought you'd gone and left me–for I flubbed your three-mole signal. We've found Sid's Place, that's the first leg, and I see the three black hussars, and we've brought with us the weapon and the Parthian disguises, salvaged from the doomed Express Room when your Door appeared in time's nick, and the Room around us closing spewed us through before it vanished with the corpse of Benson-Carter. Triple Goddess, draw the milk now from the womanhood I flaunt here and inject the blackest hatred! Vengeance now upon the Serpents, vengeance sweet in northern Egypt, for your island, Crete, Goddess! —and a victory for the Spiders! Goddess, Goddess, we can swing it!"

The roar that made me try to stop my ears with my shoulders didn't come from Kaby-she'd spoken her piece-but from Sid. The dear boy was purple enough to make me want to remind him you can die of high blood pressure just as easy in the Change World.

"Dump me with ops! 'Sblood, I'll not endure it! Is this a battle post? They'll be mounting operations from field hospitals next. Kabysia Labrys, thou art mad to suggest it. And what's this prattle of locks, clocks, and death's heads, buttons and monkeys? This brabble, this farrago, this hocus-pocus! And where's the weapon you prate of? In that whoreson bronze casket, I suppose."

She nodded, looking blank and almost a little shy as poetic possession faded from her. Her answer came like its faltering last echo.

"It is nothing but a tiny tactical atomic bomb."

Chapter 7
Time to Think

> After about 0.1 millisecond (one ten-thousandth part of a second) has elapsed, the radius of the ball of fire is some 45 feet, and the temperature is then in the vicinity of 300,000 degrees Centigrade. At this instant, the luminosity, as observed at a distance of 100,000 yards (5.7 miles), is approximately 100 times that of the sun as seen at the earth's surface ... the ball of fire expands very rapidly to its maximum radius of 450 feet within less than a second from the explosion.

> —Los Alamos

Brother, that was all we needed to make everybody but Kaby and the two ETs start yelping at once, me included. It may seem strange that Change People, able to whiz through time and space and roust around outside the cosmos and knowing at least by hearsay of weapons a billion years in the future, like the Mindbomb, should panic at being shut in with a little primitive mid-20th Century gadget. Well, they feel the same as atomic scientists would feel if a Bengal tiger were brought into their laboratory, neither more nor less scared.

I'm a moron at physics, but I do know the Fireball is bigger than the Place. Remember that, besides the bomb, we'd recently been presented with a lot of other fears we hadn't had time to cope with, especially the business of the Snakes having learned how to get at our Places and melt the Maintainers and collapse them. Not to mention the general impression-first Saint Petersburg, then Crete-that the whole Change War was going against the Spiders.

Yet, in a free corner of my mind, I was shocked at how badly we were all panicking. It made me admit what I didn't like to: that we were all in pretty much the same state as Doc, except that the bottle didn't happen to be our out.

And had the rest of us been controlling our drinking so well lately?

Maud yelled, "Jettison it!" and pulled away from the satyr and ran from the bronze chest. Beau, harking back to what they'd thought of doing in the Express Room when it was too late, hissed, "Sirs, we must Introvert," and vaulted over the piano bench and legged it for the control divan. Erich seconded him with a white-faced *"Gott in Himmel, ja!"* from beside the surly, forgotten Countess, holding, by its slim stem, an empty, rose-stained wine glass.

I felt my mind flinch, because Introverting a Place is several degrees worse than foxholing. It's supposed not only to keep the Door tight shut, but also to lock it so even the Change Winds can't get through-cut the Place loose from the cosmos altogether.

I'd never talked with anyone from a Place that had been Introverted.

Mark dumped Phryne off his lap and ran after Maud. The Greek Ghostgirl, quite solid now, looked around with sleepy fear and fumbled her apple-green chiton together at the throat. She wrenched my attention away from everyone else for a moment, and I couldn't help wondering whether the person or Zombie back in the cosmos, from whose lifeline the Ghost has been taken, doesn't at least have strange dreams or thoughts when something like this happens.

Sid stopped Beau, though he almost got bowled over doing it, and he held the gambler away from the Maintainer in a bear hug and bellowed over his shoulders, "Masters, are you mad? Have you lost your wits? Maud! Mark! Marcus! Magdalene! On your lives, unhand that casket!"

Maud had swept the clothes and bows and quivers and stuff off it and was dragging it out from the bar toward the Door sector, so as to dump it through fast when we got one, I guess, while Mark acted as if he were trying to help her and wrestle it away from her at the same time.

They kept on as if they hadn't heard a word Sid said, with Mark yelling, "Let go, *meretrix*! This holds Rome's answer to Parthia on the Nile."

Kaby watched them as if she wanted to help Mark but scorned to scuffle with a mere-well, Mark had said it in Latin, I guess-call girl.

Then, on the top of the bronze chest, I saw those seven lousy skulls starting at the lock as plain as if they'd been under a magnifying glass, though ordinarily they'd have been a vague circle to my eyes at the distance, and I lost my mind and started to run in the opposite direction, but Illy whipped three tentacles around me, gentle-like, and squeaked, "Easy now, Greta girl, don't you be doing it, too. Hold still or Papa spank. My, my, but you two-leggers can whirl about when you have a mind to."

My stampede had carried his featherweight body a couple of yards, but it stopped me and I got my mind back, partly.

"Unhand it, I say!" Sid repeated without accomplishing anything, and he released Beau, though he kept a hand near the gambler's shoulder.

Then my fat friend from Lynn Regis looked real distraught at the Void and blustered at no one in particular, "'Sdeath, think you I'd mutiny against my masters, desert the Spiders, go to ground like a spent fox and pull my hole in after me? A plague of such cowardice! Who suggests it? Introversion's no mere last-ditch device. Unless ordered, supervised and sanctioned, it means the end. And what if I'd Introverted ere we got Kaby's call for succor, hey?"

His warrior maid nodded with harsh approval and he noticed it and shook his free hand at her and scolded her, "Not that I say yea to your mad plan for that Devil's casket, you half-clad lackwit. And yet to jettison....Oh, ye gods, ye gods —" he wiped his hand across his face — "grant me a minute in which I may think!"

Thinking time wasn't an item even on the strictly limited list at the moment, although Sevensee, squatting dourly on his hairy haunches where Maud had left him, threw in a dead-pan "Thas tellin em, Gov."

Then Doc at the bar stood up tall as Abe Lincoln in his top hat and shawl and 19th Century duds and raised an unwavering arm for silence and said something that sounded like: "Introversh, inversh, glovsh," and then his enunciation switched to better than perfect as he continued, "I know to an absolute certainty what we must do."

It showed me how rabbity we were that the Place got quiet as a church while we all stopped whatever we were doing and waited breathless for a poor drunk to tell us how to save ourselves.

He said something like, "Inversh ... bosh ..." and held our eyes for a moment longer. Then the light went out of his and he slobbered out a "Nichevo" and slid an arm far along the bar for a bottle and started to pour it down his throat without stopping sliding.

Before he completed his collapse to the floor, in the split second while our attention was still focused on the bar, Bruce vaulted up on top of it, so fast it was almost like he'd popped up from nowhere, though I'd seen him start from behind the piano.

"I've a question. Has anyone here triggered that bomb?" he said in a voice that was very clear and just loud enough. "So it can't go off," he went on after just the right pause, his easy grin and brisk manner putting more heart into me all the time. "What's more, if it were to be triggered, we'd still have half an hour. I believe you said it had that long a fuse?"

He stabbed a finger at Kaby. She nodded.

"Right," he said. "It'd have to be that long for whoever plants it in the Parthian camp to get away. There's another safety margin.

"Second question. Is there a locksmith in the house?"

For all Bruce's easiness, he was watching us like a golden eagle and he caught Beau's and Maud's affirmatives before they had a chance to explain or hedge them and said, "That's very good. Under certain circumstances, you two'd be the ones to go to work on the chest. But before we consider that, there's Question Three: Is anyone here an atomics technician?"

That one took a little conversation to straighten out, Illy having to explain that, yes, the Early Lunans had atomic power-hadn't they blasted the life off their planet with it and made all those ghastly craters? —but no, he wasn't a technician exactly, he was a "thinger" (I thought at first his squeakbox was lisping); what was a thinger? —well, a thinger was someone who manipulated things in a way that was truly impossible to describe, but no, you couldn't possibly thing atomics; the idea was quite ridiculous, so he couldn't be an atomics thinger; the term was worse than a contradiction, well, really! —while Sevensee, from his two-thousand-millennia advantage of the Lunan, grunted to the effect that his culture didn't rightly use any kind of power, but just sort of moved satyrs and stuff by wrestling space-time around, "or think em roun ef we hafta. Can't think em in the Void, tho, wus luck. Hafta have —I dunno wut. Dun havvit anyhow."

"So we don't have an A-tech," Bruce summed up, "which makes it worse than useless, down-right dangerous, to tamper with the chest. We wouldn't know what to do if we did get inside safely. One more question." He directed it toward Sid. "How long before we can jettison anything?"

Sid, looking a shade jealous, yet mostly grateful for the way Bruce had calmed his chickens, started to explain, but Bruce didn't seem to be taking any chance of losing his audience, and as soon as Sid got to the word "rhythm," he pulled the answer away from him.

"In brief, not until we can effectively tune in on the cosmos again. Thank you, Master Lessingham. That's at least five hours-two mealtimes, as the Cretan officer put it," and he threw Kaby a quick soldierly smile. "So, whether the bomb goes to Egypt or elsewhere, there's not a thing we can do about it for five hours. All right then!"

His smile blinked out like a light and he took a couple of steps up and down the bar, as if measuring the space he had. Two or three cocktail glasses sailed off and popped, but he didn't seem to notice them and we hardly did either. It was creepy the way he kept staring from one to another of us. We had to look up. Behind his face, with the straight golden hair flirting around it, was only the Void.

"All right then," he repeated suddenly. "We're twelve Spiders and two Ghosts, and we've time for a bit of a talk, and we're all in the same bloody boat, fighting the same bloody war, so we'll all know what we're talking about. I raised the subject a while back, but I was steamed up about a glove, and it was a big jest. All right! But now the gloves are off!"

Bruce ripped them out of his belt where they'd been tucked and slammed them down on the bar, to be kicked off the next time he paced back and forth, and it wasn't funny.

"Because," he went right on, "I've been getting a completely new picture of what this Spiders' war has been doing to each one of us. Oh, it's jolly good sport to slam around in space and time and then have a rugged little party outside both of them when the operation's over. It's sweet to know there's no cranny of reality so narrow, no privacy so intimate or sacred, no wall of was or will be strong enough, that we can't shoulder in. Knowledge is a glamorous thing, sweeter than lust or gluttony or the passion of fighting and including all three, the ultimate insatiable hunger, and it's great to be Faust, even in a pack of other Fausts.

"It's sweet to jigger reality, to twist the whole course of a man's life or a culture's, to ink out his or its past and scribble in a new one, and be the only one to know and gloat over the changes-hah! killing men or carrying off women isn't in it for glutting the sense of power. It's sweet to feel the Change Winds blowing through you and know the pasts that were and the past that is and the pasts that may be. It's sweet to wield the Atropos and cut a Zombie or Unborn out of his lifeline and look the Doubleganger in the face and see the Resurrection-glow in it and Recruit a brother, welcome a newborn fellow Demon into our ranks and decide whether he'll best fit as Soldier, Entertainer, or what.

"Or he can't stand Resurrection, it fries or freezes him, and you've got to decide whether to return him to his lifeline and his Zombie dreams, only they'll be a little grayer and horrider than they were before, or whether, if she's got that tantalizing something, to bring her shell along for a Ghostgirl-that's sweet, too. It's even sweet to have Change Death poised over your neck, to know that the past isn't the precious indestructible thing you've been taught it was, to know that there's no certainty about the future either, whether there'll even be one, to know that no part of reality is holy, that the cosmos itself may wink out like a flicked switch and God be not and nothing left but nothing!"

He threw out his arms against the Void. "And knowing all that, it's doubly sweet to come through the Door into the Place and be out of the worst of the Change Winds and enjoy a well-earned Recuperation and share the memories of all these sweetnesses I've been talking about, and work out all the fascinating feelings you've been accumulating back in the cosmos, layer by black layer, in the company of and with the help of the best bloody little band of fellow Fausts and Faustines going!

"Oh, it's a sweet life, all right, but I'm asking you —" and here his eyes stabbed us again, one by one, fast —"I'm asking you what it's done to us. I've been getting a completely new picture, as I said, of what my life was and what it could have been if there'd been changes of the sort that even we Demons can't make, and what my life is. I've been watching how we've all been responding to things just now, to the news of Saint Petersburg and to what the Cretan officer told beautifully-only it wasn't beautiful what she had to tell-and mostly to that bloody box of bomb. And I'm simply asking each one of you, what's happened to you?"

He stopped his pacing and stuck his thumbs in his belt and seemed to be listening to the wheels turning in at least eleven other heads-only I stopped mine pretty quick, with Dave and Father and the Rape of Chicago coming up out of the dark on the turn and Mother and the Indiana Dunes and Jazz Limited just behind them, followed by the unthinkable thing the Spider doctor had flicked into existence when I flopped as a nurse, because I can't stand that to be done to my mind by anybody but myself.

I stopped them by using the old infallible Entertainers' gimmick, a fast survey of the most interesting topic there is-other people's troubles.

Offhand, Beau looked as if he had most troubles, shamed by his boss and his girl given her heart to a Soldier; he was hugging them to himself very quiet.

I didn't stop for the two ETs-they're too hard to figure-or for Doc; nobody can tell whether a fallen-down drunk's at the black or bright end of his cycle; you just know it's cycling.

Maud ought to be suffering as much as Beau, called names and caught out in a panic, which always hurts her because she's plus three hundred years more future than the rest of us and figures she ought to be that much wiser, which she isn't always-not to mention she's over fifty years old, though her home-century cosmetic science keeps her looking and acting teenage most of the time. She'd backed away from the bronze chest so as not to stand out, and now Lili came from behind the piano and stood beside her.

Lili had the opposite of troubles, a great big glow for Bruce, proud as a promised princess watching her betrothed. Erich frowned when he saw her, for he seemed proud too, proud of the way his *Kamerad* had taken command of us panicky whacks *Führer*-fashion. Sid still looked mostly grateful and inclined to let Bruce keep on talking.

Even Kaby and Mark, those two dragons hot for battle, standing a little in front and to one side of us by the bronze chest, like its guardians, seemed willing to listen. They made me realize one reason Sid had for letting Bruce run on, although the path his talk was leading us down was flashing with danger signals: When it was over, there'd still be the problem of what to do with the bomb, and a real opposition shaping up between Soldiers and Entertainers, and Sid was hoping a solution would turn up in the meantime or at least was willing to put off the evil day.

But beyond all that, and like the rest of us, I could tell from the way Sid was squinting his browy eyes and chewing his beardy lip that he was shaken and moved by what Bruce had said. This New Boy had dipped into our hearts and counted our kicks so beautifully, better than most of us could have done, and then somehow turned them around so that we had to think of what messes and heels and black sheep and lost lambs we were-well, we wanted to keep on listening.

Chapter 8
A Place to Stand

Give me a place to stand, and I will move the world.

—Archimedes

Bruce's voice had a faraway touch and he was looking up left at the Void as he said, "Have you ever really wondered why the two sides of this war are called the Snakes and the Spiders? Snakes may be clear enough-you always call the enemy something dirty. But Spiders-our name for ourselves? Bear with me, Ilhilihis; I know that no being is created dirty or malignant by Nature, but this is a matter of anthropoid feelings and folkways. Yes, Mark, I know that some of your legions have nicknames like the Drunken Lions and the Snails, and that's about as insulting as calling the British Expeditionary Force the Old Contemptibles.

"No, you'd have to go to bands of vicious youths in cities slated for ruin to find a habit of naming like ours, and even they would try to brighten up the black a bit. But simply-Spiders. And Snakes, for that's their name for themselves too, you know. Spiders and Snakes. What are our masters, that we give them names like that?"

It gave me the shivers and set my mind working in a dozen directions and I couldn't stop it, although it made the shivers worse.

Illy beside me now—I'd never given it a thought before, but he did have eight legs of a sort, and I remembered thinking of him as a spider monkey, and hadn't the Lunans had wisdom and atomic power and a billion years in which to get the Change War rolling?

Or suppose, in the far future, Terra's own spiders evolved intelligence and a cruel cannibal culture. They'd be able to keep their existence secret. I had no idea of who or what would be on Earth in Sevensee's day, and wouldn't it be perfect black hairy poisoned spider-mentality to spin webs secretly through the world of thought and all of space and time?

And Beau-wasn't there something real Snaky about him, the way he moved and all?

Spiders and Snakes. *Spinne und Schlange*, as Erich called them. S & S. But SS stood for the Nazi *Schutzstaffel*, the Black Shirts, and what if some of those cruel, crazy Jerries had discovered time travel and—I brought myself up with a jerk and asked myself, "Greta, how nuts can you get?"

From where he was on the floor, the front of the bar his sounding board, Doc shrieked up at Bruce like one of the damned from the pit, "Don't speak against the Spiders! Don't blaspheme! They can hear the Unborn whisper. Others whip only the skin, but they whip the naked brain and heart," and Erich called out, "That's enough, Bruce!"

But Bruce didn't spare him a look and said, "But whatever the Spiders are and no matter how much whip they use, it's plain as the telltale on the Maintainer that the Change War is not only going against them, but getting away from them. Dwell for a bit on the current flurry of stupid slugging and panicky anachronism, when we all know that anachronism is what gets the Change Winds out of control. This punch-drunk pounding on the Cretan-Dorian fracas as if it were the only battle going and the only way to work things. Whisking Constantine from Britain to the Bosporus by rocket, sending a pocket submarine back to sail with the Armada against Drake's woodensides —I'll wager you hadn't heard those! And now, to save Rome, an atomic bomb.

"Ye gods, they could have used Greek fire or even dynamite, but a fission weapon.... I leave you imagine what gaps and scars that will make in what's left of history-the smothering of Greece and the vanishment of Provence and the troubadours and the Papacy's Irish Captivity won't be in it!"

The cut on his cheek had opened again and was oozing a little, but he didn't pay any attention to it, and neither did we, as his lips thinned in irony and he said, "But I'm forgetting that this is a cosmic war and that the Spiders are conducting operations on billions, trillions of planets and inhabited gas clouds through millions of ages and that we're just one little world-one little solar system, Sevensee-and we can hardly expect our inscrutable masters, with all their pressing preoccupations and far-flung responsibilities, to be especially understanding or tender in their treatment of our pet books and centuries, our favorite prophets and periods, or unduly concerned about preserving any of the trifles that we just happen to hold dear.

"Perhaps there are some sentimentalists who would rather die forever than go on living in a world without the *Summa*, the Field Equations, *Process and Reality*, *Hamlet*, Matthew, Keats, and the *Odyssey*, but our masters are practical creatures, ministering to the needs of those rugged souls who want to go on living no matter what."

Erich's "Bruce, I'm telling you that's enough," was lost in the quickening flow of the New Boy's words. "I won't spend much time on the minor signs of our major crack-up —the canceling of leaves, the sharper shortages, the loss of the Express Room, the use of Recuperation Stations for ops and all the other frantic patchwork-last operation but one, we were saddled with three Soldiers from outside the Galaxy and, no fault of theirs, they were no earthly use. Such little things might happen at a bad spot in any war and are perhaps only local. But there's a big thing."

He paused again, to let us wonder, I guess. Maud must have worked her way over to me, for I felt her dry little hand on my arm and she whispered out of the side of her mouth, "What do we do now?"

"We listen," I told her the same way. I felt a little impatient with her need to be doing something about things.

She cocked a gold-dusted eyebrow at me and murmured, "You, too?"

I didn't get to ask her me, too, what? Crush on Bruce? Nuts! —because just then Bruce's voice took up again in the faraway range.

"Have you ever asked yourselves how many operations the fabric of history can stand before it's all stitches, whether too much Change won't one day wear out the past? And the present and the future, too, the whole bleeding business. Is the law of the Conservation of Reality any more than a thin hope given a long name, a prayer of theoreticians? Change Death is as certain as Heat Death, and far faster. Every operation leaves reality a bit cruder, a bit uglier, a bit more makeshift, and a whole lot less rich in those details and feelings that are our heritage, like the crude penciled sketch on canvas when you've stripped off the paint.

"If that goes on, won't the cosmos collapse into an outline of itself, then nothing? How much thinning can reality stand, having more and more Doublegangers cut out of it? And there's another thing about every operation-it wakes up the Zombies a little more, and as its Change Winds die, it leaves them a little more disturbed and nightmare-ridden and frazzled. Those of you who have been on operations in heavily worked-over temporal areas will know what I mean-that look they give you out of the sides of their eyes as if to say, 'You again? For Christ's sake, go away. We're the dead. We're the ones who don't want to wake up, who don't want to be Demons and hate to be Ghosts. Stop torturing us.'"

I looked around at the Ghostgirls; I couldn't help it. They'd somehow got together on the control divan, facing us, their backs to the Maintainers. The Countess had dragged along the bottle of wine Erich had fetched her earlier and they were passing it back and forth. The Countess had a big rose splotch across the ruffled white lace of her blouse.

Bruce said, "There'll come a day when all the Zombies and all the Unborn wake up and go crazy together and figuratively come marching at us in their numberless hordes, saying, 'We've had enough.'"

But I didn't turn back to Bruce right away. Phryne's chiton had slipped off one shoulder and she and the Countess were sitting sagged forward, elbows on knees, legs spread-at least, as far as the Countess's hobble skirt would let her-and swayed toward each other a little. They were still surprisingly solid, although they hadn't had any personal attention for a half hour, and they were looking up over my head with half-shut eyes and they seemed, so help me, to be listening to what Bruce was saying and maybe hearing some of it.

"We make a careful distinction between Zombies and Unborn, between those troubled by our operations whose lifelines lie in the past and those whose lifelines lie in the future. But is there any distinction any longer? Can we tell the difference between the past and the future? Can we any longer locate the now, the real now of the cosmos? The Places have their own nows, the now of the Big Time we're on, but that's different and it's not made for real living.

"The Spiders tell us that the real now is somewhere in the last half of the 20th Century, which means that several of us here are also alive in the cosmos, have lifelines along which the now is traveling. But do you swallow that story quite so easily, Ilhilihis, Sevensee? How does it strike the servants of the Triple Goddess? The Spiders of Octavian Rome? The Demons of Good Queen Bess? The gentlemen Zombies of the Greater South? Do the Unborn man the starships, Maud?

"The Spiders also tell us that, although the fog of battle makes the now hard to pin down precisely, it will return with the unconditional surrender of the Snakes and the establishment of cosmic peace, and roll on as majestically toward the future as before, quickening the continuum with its passage. Do you really believe that? Or do you believe, as I do, that we've used up all the future as well as the past, wasted it in premature experience, and that we've had the real now smudged out of existence, stolen from us forever, the precious now of true growth, the child-moment in which all life lies, the moment like a newborn baby that is the only home for hope there is?"

He let that start to sink in, then took a couple of quick steps and went on, his voice rising over Erich's "Bruce, for the last time —" and seeming to pick up a note of hope from the very word he had used, "But although things look terrifyingly black, there remains a chance-the slimmest chance, but still a chance-of saving the cosmos from Change Death and restoring reality's richness and giving the Ghosts good sleep and perhaps even regaining the real now. We have the means right at hand. What if the power of time traveling were used not for war and destruction, but for healing, for the mutual enrichment of the ages, for quiet communication and growth, in brief, to bring a peace message —"

But my little commandant is quite an actor himself and knows a wee bit about the principles of scene-stealing, and he was not going to let Bruce drown him out as if he were just another extra playing a Voice from the Mob. He darted across our front, between us and the bar, took a running leap, and landed bang on the bloody box of bomb.

A bit later, Maud was silently showing me the white ring above her elbow where I'd grabbed her and Illy was teasing a clutch of his tentacles out of my other hand and squeaking reproachfully, "Greta girl, don't ever do that."

Erich was standing on the chest and I noticed that his boots carefully straddled the circle of skulls, and I should have known anyway you could hardly push them in the right order by jumping on them, and he was pointing at Bruce and saying, "—and that means mutiny, my young sir. *Um Gottes willen*, Bruce, listen to me and step down before you say anything worse. I'm older than you, Bruce. Mark's older. Trust in your *Kameraden*. Guide yourself by their knowledge."

He had got my attention, but I had much rather have him black my eye.

"You older than me?" Bruce was grinning. "When your twelve-years' advantage was spent in soaking up the wisdom of a race of sadistic dreamers gone paranoid, in a world whose thought-stream had already been muddied by one total war? Mark older than me? When all his ideas and loyalties are those of a wolf pack of unimaginative sluggers two thousand years younger than I am? Either of you older because you have more of the killing cynicism that is all the wisdom the Change World ever gives you? Don't make me laugh!

"I'm an Englishman, and I come from an epoch when total war was still a desecration and the flowers and buds of thoughts not yet whacked off or blighted. I'm a poet and poets are wiser than anyone because they're the only people who have the guts to think and feel at the same time. Right, Sid? When I talk to all of you about a peace message, I want you to think about it concretely in terms of using the Places to bring help across the mountains of time when help is really needed, not to bring help that's undeserved or knowledge that's premature or contaminating, sometimes not to bring anything at all, but just to check with infinite tenderness and concern that everything's safe and the glories of the universe unfolding as they were intended to —"

"Yes, you are a poet, Bruce," Erich broke in. "You can tootle soulfully on the flute and make us drip tears. You can let out the stops on the big organ pipes and make us tremble as if at Jehovah's footsteps. For the last twenty minutes, you have been giving us some very *charmante* poetry. But what are you? An Entertainer? Or are you a Soldier?"

Right then — I don't know what it was, maybe Sid clearing his throat — I could sense our feelings beginning to turn against Bruce. I got the strangest feeling of reality clamping down and bright colors going dull and dreams vanishing. Yet it was only then I also realized how much Bruce had moved us, maybe some of us to the verge of mutiny, even. I was mad at Erich for what he was doing, but I couldn't help admiring his cockiness.

I was still under the spell of Bruce's words and the more-than-words behind them, but then Erich would shift around a bit and one of his heels would kick near the death's-head pushbuttons and I wanted to stamp with spike heels on every death's-head button on his uniform. I didn't know exactly what I felt yet.

"Yes, I'm a Soldier," Bruce told him, "and I hope you won't ever have to worry about my courage, because it's going to take more courage than any operation we've ever planned, ever dreamed of, to carry the peace message to the other Places and to the wound-spots of the cosmos. Perhaps it will be a fast wicket and we'll be bowled down before we score a single run, but who cares? We may at least see our real masters when they come to smash us, and for me that will be a deep satisfaction. And we may do some smashing of our own."

"So you're a Soldier," Erich said, his smile showing his teeth. "Bruce, I'll admit that the half-dozen operations you've been on were rougher than anything I drew in my first hundred sleeps. For that, I am all honest sympathy. But that you should let them get you into such a state that love and a girl can turn you upside down and start you babbling about peace messages —"

"Yes, by God, love and a girl have changed me!" Bruce shouted at him, and I looked around at Lili and I remembered Dave saying, "I'm going to Spain," and I wondered if anything would ever again make my face flame like that. "Or, rather, they've made me stand up for what I've believed in all along. They've made me —"

"*Wunderbar*," Erich called and began to do a little sissy dance on the bomb that set my teeth on edge. He bent his wrists and elbows at arty angles and stuck out a hip and ducked his head simperingly and blinked his eyes very fast. "Will you invite me to the wedding, Bruce? You'll have to get another best man, but I will be the flower girl and throw pretty little posies to all the distinguished guests. Here, Mark. Catch, Kaby. One for you, Greta. *Danke schön. Ach, zwei Herzen in dreivierteltakt ... ta-ta ... ta-ta ... ta-ta-ta-ta-ta...*"

"What the hell do you think a woman is?" Bruce raged. "Something to mess around with in your spare time?"

46

Erich kept on humming "Two Hearts in Waltz Time" —and jigging around to it, damn him-but he slipped in a nod to Bruce and a "Precisely." So I knew where I stood, but it was no news to me.

"Very well," Bruce said, "let's leave this Brown Shirt *maricón* to amuse himself and get down to business. I made all of you a proposal and I don't have to tell you how serious it is or how serious Lili and I are about it. We not only must infiltrate and subvert other Places, which luckily for us are made for infiltration, we also must make contact with the Snakes and establish working relationships with their Demons at our level as one of our first steps."

That stopped Erich's jig and got enough of a gasp from some of us to make it seem to come from practically everybody. Erich used it to work a change of pace.

"Bruce! We've let you carry this foolery further than we should. You seem to have the idea that because anything goes in the Place-dueling, drunkenness, *und so weiter* —you can say what you have and it will all be forgotten with the hangover. Not so. It is true that among such a set of monsters and free spirits as ourselves, and working as secret agents to boot, there cannot be the obvious military discipline that would obtain in a Terran army.

"But let me tell you, Bruce, let me grind it home into you-Sid and Kaby and Mark will bear me out in this, as officers of equivalent rank-that the Spider line of command stretches into and through this Place just as surely as the word of *der Führer* rules Chicago. And as I shouldn't have to emphasize to you, Bruce, the Spiders have punishments that would make my countrymen in Belsen and Buchenwald-well, pale a little. So while there is still a shadow of justification for our interpreting your remarks as utterly tasteless clowning —"

"Babble on," Bruce said, giving him a loose downward wave of his hand without looking. "I made you people a proposal." He paused. "How do you stand, Sidney Lessingham?"

Then I felt my legs getting weak, because Sid didn't answer right away. The old boy swallowed and started to look around at the rest of us. Then the feeling of reality clamping down got something awful, because he didn't look around, but straightened his back a little. Just then, Mark cut in fast.

"It grieves me, Bruce, but I think you are possessed. Erich, he must be confined."

Kaby nodded, almost absently. "Confine or kill the coward, whichever is easier, whip the woman, and let's get on to the Egyptian battle."

"Indeed, yes," Mark said. "I died in it. But now perhaps no longer."

Kaby said to him, "I like you, Roman."

Bruce was smiling, barely, and his eyes were moving and fixing. "You, Ilhilihis?"

Illy's squeak box had never sounded mechanical to me before, but it did as he answered, "I'm a lot deeper into borrowed time than the rest of you, tra-la-la, but Papa still loves living. Include me very much out, Brucie."

"Miss Davies?"

Beside me, Maud said flatly, "Do you think I'm a fool?" Beyond her, I saw Lili and I thought, "My God, I might look as proud if I were in her shoes, but I sure as hell wouldn't look as confident."

Bruce's eyes hadn't quite come to Beau when the gambler spoke up. "I have no cause to like you, sir, rather the opposite. But this Place has come to bore me more than Boston and I have always found it difficult to resist a long shot. A very long one, I fear. I am with you, sir."

There was a pain in my chest and a roaring in my ears and through it I heard Sevensee grunting, " —sicka these lousy Spiders. Deal me in."

And then Doc reared up in front of the bar and he'd lost his hat and his hair was wild and he grabbed an empty fifth by the neck and broke the bottom of it all jagged against the bar and he waved it and screeched, "*Ubivaytye Pauki —i Nyemetzi!*"

And right behind his words, Beau sang out fast the English of it, "Kill the Spiders-and the Germans!"

And Doc didn't collapse then, though I could see he was hanging onto the bar tight with his other hand, and the Place got stiller, inside and out, than I've ever known it, and Bruce's eyes were finally moving back toward Sid.

But the eyes stopped short of Sid and I heard Bruce say, "Miss Forzane?" and I thought, "That's funny," and I started to look around at the Countess, and felt all the eyes and I realized, "Hey, that's me! But this can't happen to me. To the others, yes, but not to me. I just work here. Not to Greta, no, no, no!"

But it had, and the eyes didn't let go, and the silence and the feeling of reality were Godawful, and I said to myself, "Greta, you've got to say something, if only a suitable four-letter word," and then suddenly I knew what the silence was like. It was like that of a big city if there were some way of shutting off all the noise in one second. It was like Erich's singing when the piano had deserted him. It was as if the Change Winds should ever die completely ... and I knew beforehand what had happened when I turned my back on them all.

The Ghostgirls were gone. The Major Maintainer hadn't merely been switched to Introvert. It was gone, too.

Chapter 9
A Locked Room

"We examined the moss between the bricks, and found it undisturbed."

"You looked among D——'s papers, of course, and into the books of the library?"

"Certainly; we opened every package and parcel; we not only opened every book, but we turned over every leaf in each volume...."

—Poe

Three hours later, Sid and I plumped down on the couch nearest the kitchen, though too tired to want to eat for a while yet. A tighter search than I could ever have cooked up had shown that the Maintainer was not in the Place.

Of course it had to be in the Place, as we kept telling each other for the first two hours. It had to be, if circumstances and the theories we lived by in the Change World meant anything. A Maintainer is what maintains a Place. The Minor Maintainer takes care of oxygen, temperature, humidity, gravity, and other little life-cycle and matter-cycle things generally, but it's the Major Maintainer that keeps the walls from buckling and the ceiling from falling in. It is little, but oh my, it does so much.

It doesn't work by wires or radio or anything complicated like that. It just hooks into local space-time.

I have been told that its inside working part is made up of vastly tough, vastly hard giant molecules, each one of which is practically a vest-pocket cosmos in itself. Outside, it looks like a portable radio with a few more dials and some telltales and switches and plug-ins for earphones and a lot of other sensory thingumajigs.

But the Maintainer was gone and the Void hadn't closed in, yet. By this time, I was so fagged, I didn't care much whether it did or not.

One thing for sure, the Maintainer had been switched to Introvert before it was spirited away or else its disappearance automatically produced Introversion, take your choice, because we sure were Introverted-real nasty martinet-schoolmaster grip of reality on my thoughts that I knew, without trying, liquor wouldn't soften, not a breath of Change Wind, absolutely stifling, and the gray of the Void seeming so much inside my head that I think I got a glimmering of what the science boys mean when they explain to me that the Place is a kind of interweaving of the material and the mental—a Giant Monad, one of them called it.

Anyway, I said to myself, "Greta, if this is Introversion, I want no part of it. It is not nice to be cut adrift from the cosmos and know it. A lifeboat in the middle of the Pacific and a starship between galaxies are not in it for loneliness."

I asked myself why the Spiders had ever equipped Maintainers with Introversion switches anyway, when we couldn't drill with them and weren't supposed to use them except in an emergency so tight that it was either Introvert or surrender to the Snakes, and for the first time the obvious explanation came to me:

Introversion must be the same as scuttling, its main purpose to withhold secrets and materiel from the enemy. It put a place into a situation from which even the Spider high command couldn't rescue it, and there was nothing left but to sink down, down (out? up?), down into the Void.

If that was the case, our chances of getting back were about those of my being a kid again playing in the Dunes on the Small Time.

I edged a little closer to Sid and sort of squunched under his shoulder and rubbed my cheek against the smudged, gold-worked gray velvet. He looked down and I said, "A long way to Lynn Regis, eh, Siddy?"

"Sweetling, thou spokest a mouthful," he said. He knows very well what he is doing when he mixes his language that way, the wicked old darling.

"Siddy," I said, "why this gold-work? It'd be a lot smoother without it."

"Marry, men must prick themselves out and, 'faith I know not, but it helps if there's metal in it."

"And girls get scratched." I took a little sniff. "But don't put this doublet through the cleaner yet. Until we get out of the woods, I want as much you around as possible."

"Marry, and why should I?" he asked blankly, and I think he wasn't fooling me. The last thing time travelers find out is how they do or don't smell. Then his face clouded and he looked as though he wanted to squunch under my shoulder. "But 'faith, sweetling, your forest has a few more trees than Sherwood."

"Thou saidst it," I agreed, and wondered about the look. He oughtn't to be interested in my girlishness now. I knew I was a mess, but he had stuck pretty close to me during the hunt and you never can tell. Then I remembered that he was the other one who hadn't declared himself when Bruce was putting it to us, and it probably troubled his male vanity. Not me, though —I was still grateful to the Maintainer for getting me out of that spot, whatever other it had got us all into. It seemed ages ago.

We'd all jumped to the conclusion that the two Ghostgirls had run away with the Maintainer, I don't know where or why, but it looked so much that way. Maud had started yipping about how she'd never trusted Ghosts and always known that some day they'd start doing things on their own, and Kaby had got it firmly fixed in her head, right between the horns, that Phryne, being a Greek, was the ringleader and was going to wreak havoc on us all.

But when we were checking Stores the first time, I had noticed that the Ghostgirl envelopes looked flat. Ectoplasm doesn't take up much space when it's folded, but I had opened one anyway, then another, and then called for help.

Every last envelope was empty. We had lost over a thousand Ghostgirls, Sid's whole stock.

Well, at least it proved what none of us had ever seen or heard of being demonstrated: that there is a spooky link —a sort of Change Wind contact-between a Ghost and its lifeline; and when that umbilicus, I've heard it called, is cut, the part away from the lifeline dies.

Interesting, but what had bothered me was whether we Demons were going to evaporate too, because we are as much Doublegangers as the Ghosts and our apron strings had been cut just as surely. We're more solid, of course, but that would only mean we'd take a little longer. Very logical.

I remember I had looked up at Lili and Maud-us girls had been checking the envelopes; it's one of the proprieties we frequently maintain and anyway, if men check them, they're apt to trot out that old wheeze about "instant women" which I'm sick to death of hearing, thank you.

Anyway, I had looked up and said, "It's been nice knowing you," and Lili had said, "Twenty-three, skiddoo," and Maud had said, "Here goes nothing," and we had shook hands all around.

We figured that Phryne and the Countess had faded at the same time as the other Ghostgirls, but an idea had been nibbling at me and I said, "Siddy, do you suppose it's just barely possible that, while we were all looking at Bruce, those two Ghostgirls would have been able to work the Maintainer and get a Door and lam out of here with the thing?"

"Thou speakst my thoughts, sweetling. All weighs against it: Imprimis, 'tis well known that Ghosts cannot lay plots or act on them. Secundo, the time forbade getting a Door. Tercio-and here's the real meat of it-the Place folds without the Maintainer. Quadro, 'twere folly to depend on not one of-how many of us? ten, elf-not looking around in all the time it would have taken them —"

"I looked around once, Siddy. They were drinking and they had got to the control divan under their own power. Now when was that? Oh, yes, when Bruce was talking about Zombies."

"Yes, sweetling. And as I was about to cap my argument with quinquo when you 'gan prattle, I could have sworn none could touch the Maintainer, much less work it and purloin it, without my certain knowledge. Yet..."

"Eftsoons yet," I seconded him.

Somebody must have got a door and walked out with the thing. It certainly wasn't in the Place. The hunt had been a lulu. Something the size of a portable typewriter is not easy to hide and we had been inside everything from Beau's piano to the renewer link of the Refresher.

We had even fluoroscoped everybody, though it had made Illy writhe like a box of worms, as he'd warned us; he said it tickled terribly and I insisted on smoothing his fur for five minutes afterward, although he was a little standoffish toward me.

Some areas, like the bar, kitchen and Stores, took a long while, but we were thorough. Kaby helped Doc check Surgery: since she last made the Place, she has been stationed in a Field Hospital (it turns out the Spiders actually are mounting operations from them) and learned a few nice new wrinkles.

However, Doc put in some honest work on his own, though, of course, every check was observed by at least three people, not including Bruce or Lili. When the Maintainer vanished, Doc had pulled out of his glassy-eyed drunk in a way that would have surprised me if I hadn't seen it happen to him before, but when we finished Surgery and got on to the Art Gallery, he had started to putter and I noticed him hold out his coat and duck his head and whip out a flask and take a swig and by now he was well on his way toward another peak.

The Art Gallery had taken time too, because there's such a jumble of strange stuff, and it broke my heart but Kaby took her ax and split a beautiful blue woodcarving of a Venusian medusa because, although there wasn't a mark in the paw-polished surface, she claimed it was just big enough. Doc cried a little and we left him fitting the pieces together and mooning over the other stuff.

After we'd finished everything else, Mark had insisted on tackling the floor. Beau and Sid both tried to explain to him how this is a one-sided Place, that there is nothing, but nothing, under the floor; it just gets a lot harder than the diamonds crusting it as soon as you get a quarter inch down-that being the solid equivalent of the Void. But Mark was knuckle-headed (like all Romans, Sid assured me on the q.t.) and broke four diamond-plus drills before he was satisfied.

Except for some trick hiding places, that left the Void, and things don't vanish if you throw them at the Void-they half melt and freeze forever unless you can fish them out. Back of the Refresher, at about eye-level, are three Venusian coconuts that a Hittite strongman threw there during a major brawl. I try not to look at them because they are so much like witch heads they give me the woolies. The parts of the Place right up against the Void have strange spatial properties which one of the gadgets in Surgery makes use of in a way that gives me the worse woolies, but that's beside the point.

During the hunt, Kaby and Erich had used their Callers as direction finders to point out the Maintainer, just as they're used in the cosmos to locate the Door-and sometimes in the Big

Places, people tell me. But the Callers only went wild-like a compass needle whirling around without stopping-and nobody knew what that meant.

The trick hiding places were the Minor Maintainer, a cute idea, but it is no bigger than the Major and has its own mysterious insides and had obviously kept on doing its own work, so that was out for several reasons, and the bomb chest, though it seemed impossible for anyone to have opened it, granting they knew the secret of its lock, even before Erich jumped on it and put it in the limelight double. But when you've ruled out everything else, the word impossible changes meaning.

Since time travel is our business, a person might think of all sorts of tricks for sending the Maintainer into the past or future, permanently or temporarily. But the Place is strictly on the Big Time and everybody that should know tells me that time traveling *through* the Big Time is out. It's this way: the Big Time is a train, and the Little Time is the countryside and we're on the train, unless we go out a Door, and as Gertie Stein might put it, you can't time travel through the time you time travel in when you time travel.

I'd also played around with the idea of some fantastically obvious hiding place, maybe something that several people could pass back and forth between them, which would mean a conspiracy, and, of course, if you assume a big enough conspiracy, you can explain anything, including the cosmos itself. Still, I'd got a sort of shell-game idea about the Soldiers' three big black shakos and I hadn't been satisfied until I'd got the three together and looked in them all at the same time.

"Wake up, Greta, and take something. I can't stand here forever." Maud had brought us a tray of hearty snacks from then and yon, and I must say they were tempting; she whips up a mean hors d'oeuvre.

I looked them over and said, "Siddy, I want a hot dog."

"And I want a venison pasty! Out upon you, you finical jill, you o'erscrupulous jade, you whimsic and tyrannous poppet!"

I grabbed a handful and snuggled back against him.

"Go on, call me some more, Siddy," I told him. "Real juicy ones."

Chapter 10
Motives and Opportunities

My thought, whose murder yet is but fantastical,
Shakes so my single state of man that function
Is smother'd in surmise, and nothing is
But what is not.

—Macbeth

My big bad waif from King's Lynn had set the tray on his knees and started to wolf the food down. The others were finishing up. Erich, Mark and Kaby were having a quietly furious argument I couldn't overhear at the end of the bar nearest the bronze chest, and Illy was draped over the piano like a real octopus, listening in.

Beau and Sevensee were pacing up and down near the control divan and throwing each other a word now and then. Beyond them, Bruce and Lili were sitting on the opposite couch from us, talking earnestly about something. Maud had sat down at the other end of the bar and was knitting-it's one of the habits like chess and quiet drinking, or learning to talk by squeak box, that we pick up to pass the time in the Place in the long stretches between parties. Doc was fiddling around the Gallery, picking things up and setting them down, still managing to stay on his feet at any rate.

Lili and Bruce stood up, still gabbing intensely at each other, and Illy began to pick out with one tentacle a little tune in the high keys that didn't sound like anything on God's earth. "Where do they get all the energy?" I wondered.

As soon as I asked myself that, I knew the answer and I began to feel the same way myself. It wasn't energy; it was nerves, pure and simple.

Change is like a drug, I realized-you get used to the facts never staying the same, and one picture of the past and future dissolving into another maybe not very different but still different, and your mind being constantly goosed by strange moods and notions, like nightclub lights of shifting color with weird shadows between shining right on your brain.

The endless swaying and jogging is restful, like riding on a train.

You soon get to like the movement and to need it without knowing, and when it suddenly stops and you're just you and the facts you think from and feel from are exactly the same when you go back to them-boy, that's rough, as I found out now.

The instant we got Introverted, everything that ordinarily leaks into the Place, wake or sleep, had stopped coming, and we were nothing but ourselves and what we meant to each other and what we could make of that, an awfully lonely, scratchy situation.

I decided I felt like I'd been dropped into a swimming pool full of cement and held under until it hardened.

I could understand the others bouncing around a bit. It was a wonder they didn't hit the Void. Maud seemed to be standing it the best; maybe she'd got a little preparation from the long watches between stars; and then she is older than all of us, even Sid, though with a small "o" in "older."

The restless work of the search for the Maintainer had masked the feeling, but now it was beginning to come full force. Before the search, Bruce's speech and Erich's interruptions had done a passable masking job too. I tried to remember when I'd first got the feeling and decided it was after Erich had jumped on the bomb, about the time he mentioned poetry. Though I couldn't be sure. Maybe the Maintainer had been Introverted even earlier, when I'd turned to look at the Ghostgirls. I wouldn't have known. Nuts!

Believe me, I could feel that hardened cement on every inch of me. I remembered Bruce's beautiful picture of a universe without Big Change and decided it was about the worst idea going. I went on eating, though I wasn't so sure now it was a good idea to keep myself strong.

"Does the Maintainer have an Introversion telltale? Siddy!"

"'Sdeath, chit, and you love me, speak lower. Of a sudden, I feel not well, as if I'd drunk a butt of Rhenish and slept inside it. Marry yes, blue. In short flashes, saith the manual. Why ask'st thou?"

"No reason. God, Siddy, what I'd give for a breath of Change Wind."

"Thou can'st say that eftsoons," he groaned. I must have looked pretty miserable myself, for he put his arm around my shoulders and whispered gruffly, "Comfort thyself, sweetling, that while we suffer thus sorely, we yet cannot die the Change Death."

"What's that?" I asked him.

I didn't want to bounce around like the others. I had a suspicion I'd carry it too far. So, to keep myself from going batty, I started to rework the business of who had done what to the Maintainer.

During the hunt, there had been some pretty wild suggestions tossed around as to its disappearance or at least its Introversion: a feat of Snake science amounting to sorcery; the Spider high command bunkering the Places from above, perhaps in reaction to the loss of the Express Room, in such a hurry that they hadn't even time to transmit warnings; the hand of the Late Cosmicians, those mysterious hypothetical beings who are supposed to have successfully resisted the extension of the Change War into the future much beyond Sevensee's epoch-unless the Late Cosmicians are the ones fighting the Change War.

One thing these suggestions had steered very clear of was naming any one of us as a suspect, whether acting as Snake spy, Spider political police, agent of-who knows, after Bruce? —a secret Change World Committee of Public Safety or Spider revolutionary underground, or strictly on our own. Just as no one had piped a word, since the Maintainer had been palmed, about the split between Erich's and Bruce's factions.

Good group thinking probably, to sink differences in the emergency, but that didn't apply to what I did with my own thoughts.

Who wanted to escape so bad they'd Introvert the Place, cutting off all possible contact and communication either way with the cosmos and running the very big risk of not getting back to the cosmos at all?

Leaving out what had happened since Bruce had arrived and stirred things up, Doc seemed to me to have the strongest motive. He knew that Sid couldn't keep covering up for him forever and that Spider punishments for derelictions of duty are not just the clink of a firing squad, as Erich had reminded us. But Doc had been flat on the floor in front of the bar from the time Bruce had jumped on top of it, though I certainly hadn't had my eye on him every second.

Beau? Beau had said he was bored with the Place at a time when what he said counted, so he'd hardly lock himself in it maybe forever, not to mention locking Bruce in with himself and the babe he had a yen for.

Sid loves reality, Changing or not, and every least thing in it, people especially, more than any man or woman I've ever known-he's like a big-eyed baby who wants to grab every object and put it in his mouth-and it was hard to imagine him ever cutting himself off from the cosmos.

Maud, Kaby, Mark and the two ETs? None of them had any motive I knew of, though Sevensee's being from the very far future did tie in with that idea about the Late Cosmicians, and there did seem to be something developing between the Cretan and the Roman that could make them want to be Introverted together.

"Stick to the facts, Greta," I reminded myself with a private groan.

That left Erich, Bruce, Lili and myself.

Erich, I thought-now we're getting somewhere. The little commandant has the nervous system of a coyote and the courage of a crazy tomcat, and if he thought it would help him settle his battle with Bruce better to be locked in with him, he'd do it in a second.

But even before Erich had danced on the bomb, he'd been heckling Bruce from the crowd. Still, there would have been time between heckles for him to step quietly back from us, Introvert the Maintainer and ... well, that was nine-tenths of the problem.

If I was the guilty party, I was nuts and that was the best explanation of all. Gr-r-r!

Bruce's motives seemed so obvious, especially the mortal (or was it immortal?) danger he'd put himself in by inciting mutiny, that it seemed a shame he'd been in full view on the bar so long. Surely, if the Maintainer had been Introverted before he jumped on the bar, we'd all have noticed the flashing blue telltale. For that matter, I'd have noticed it when I looked back at the Ghostgirls-if it worked as Sid claimed, and he said he had never seen it in operation, just read in the manual-oh, 'sdeath!

But Bruce didn't need opportunity, as I'm sure all the males in the Place would have told me right off, because he had Lili to pull the job for him and she had as much opportunity as any of the rest of us. Myself, I have large reservations to this woman-putty-in-the-hands-of-the-man-she-loves-madly theory, but I had to admit there was something to be said for it in this case, and it had seemed quite natural to me when the rest of us had decided, by unspoken agreement, that neither Lili's nor Bruce's checks counted when we were hunting for the Maintainer.

That took care of all of us and left only the mysterious stranger, intruding somehow through a Door (how'd he get it without using our Maintainer?) or from an unimaginable hiding place or straight out of the Void itself. I know that last is impossible-nothing can step out of nothing-but if anything ever looked like it was specially built for something not at all nice to come looming out of, it's the Void-misty, foggily churning, slimy gray....

"Wait a second," I told myself, "and hang onto this, Greta. It should have smacked you in the face at the start."

Whatever came out of the Void, or, more to the point, whoever slipped back from our crowd to the Maintainer, Bruce would have seen them. He was looking at the Maintainer past our heads the whole time, and whatever happened to it, he saw it.

Erich wouldn't have, even after he was on the bomb, because he'd been stagewise enough to face Bruce most of the time to build up his role as tribune of the people.

But Bruce would have-unless he got so caught up in what he was saying....

No, kid, a Demon is always an actor, no matter how much he believes in what he's saying, and there never was an actor yet who wouldn't instantly notice a member of the audience starting to walk out on his big scene.

So Bruce knew, which made him a better actor than I'd have been willing to grant, since it didn't look as if anyone else had thought of what had just occurred to me, or they'd have gone over and put it to him.

Not me, though —I don't work that way. Besides, I didn't feel up to it-Nervy Anna enfold me, I felt like pure hell.

"Maybe," I told myself encouragingly, "the Place is Hell," but added, "Be your age, Greta-be a real rootless, ruleless, ruthless twenty-nine."

Chapter 11
The Western Front, 1917

The barrage roars and lifts. Then, clumsily bowed
With bombs and guns and shovels and battle gear,
Men jostle and climb to meet the bristling fire.
Lines of gray, muttering faces, masked with fear,
They leave their trenches, going over the top,
While time ticks blank and busy on their wrists

—Sassoon

"Please don't, Lili."

"I shall, my love."

"Sweetling, wake up! Hast the shakes?"

I opened my eyes a little and lied to Siddy with a smile and locked my hands together tight and watched Bruce and Lili quarrel nobly near the control divan and wished I had a great love to blur my misery and provide me with a passable substitute for Change Winds.

Lili won the argument, judging from the way she threw her head back and stepped away from Bruce's arms while giving him a proud, tender smile. He walked off a few steps; praise be, he didn't shrug his shoulders at us like an old husband, though his nerves were showing and he didn't seem to be standing Introversion well at all, as who of us were?

Lili rested a hand on the head of the control divan and pressed her lips together and looked around at us, mostly with her eyes. She'd wound a gray silk bandeau around her bangs. Her short gray silk dress without a waistline made her look, not so much like a flapper, though she looked like that all right, as like a little girl, except the neckline was scooped low enough to show she wasn't.

Her gaze hesitated and then stopped at me and I got a sunk feeling of what was coming, because women are always picking on me for an audience. Besides, Sid and I were the centrist party of two in our fresh-out-of-the-shell Place politics.

She took a deep breath and stuck out her chin and said in a voice that was even a little higher and Britisher than she usually uses, "We girls have often cried, 'Shut the Door!' But now the Door is jolly well shut for keeps!"

I knew I'd guessed right and I felt crawly with embarrassment, because I know about this love business of thinking you're the other person and trying to live their life-and grab their glory, though you don't know that-and carry their message for them, and how it can foul things up. Still, I couldn't help admitting what she said wasn't too bad a start-unpleasantly apt to be true, at any rate.

"My fiance believes we may yet be able to open the Door. I do not. He thinks it is a bit premature to discuss the peculiar pickle in which we all find ourselves. I do not."

There was a rasp of laughter from the bar. The militarists were reacting. Erich stepped out, looking very happy. "So now we have to listen to women making speeches," he called. "What is this Place, anyhow? Sidney Lessingham's Saturday Evening Sewing Circle?"

Beau and Sevensee, who'd stopped their pacing halfway between the bar and the control divan, turned toward Erich, and Sevensee looked a little burlier, a little more like half a horse, than satyrs in mythology book illustrations. He stamped-medium hard, I'd say-and said, "Ahh, go flya kite." I'd found out he'd learned English from a Demon who'd been a longshoreman with syndicalist-anarchist sympathies. Erich shut up for a moment and stood there grinning, his hands on his hips.

Lili nodded to the satyr and cleared her throat, looking scared. But she didn't speak; I could see she was thinking and feeling something, and her face got ugly and haggard, as if she were in a Change Wind that hadn't reached me yet, and her mouth went into a snarl to fight tears, but some spurted out, and when she did speak her voice was an octave lower and it wasn't just London talking but New York too.

"I don't know how Resurrection felt to you people, because I'm new and I loathe asking questions, but to me it was pure torture and I wished only I'd had the courage to tell Suzaku, 'I wish to remain a Zombie, if you don't mind. I'd rather the nightmares.' But I accepted Resurrection because I've been taught to be polite and because there is the Demon in me I don't understand that always wishes to live, and I found that I still felt like a Zombie, although I could flit about, and that I still had the nightmares, except they'd grown a deal vivider.

"I was a young girl again, seventeen, and I suppose every woman wishes to be seventeen, but I wasn't seventeen inside my head —I was a woman who had died of Bright's disease in New York in 1929 and also, because a Big Change blew my lifeline into a new drift, a woman who had died of the same disease in Nazi-occupied London in 1955, but rather more slowly because, as you can fancy, the liquor was in far shorter supply. I had to live with both those sets of memories and the Change World didn't blot them out any more than I'm told it does those of any Demon, and it didn't even push them into the background as I'd hoped it would.

"When some Change Fellow would say to me, 'Hallo, beautiful, how about a smile?' or 'That's a posh frock, kiddo,' I'd be back at Bellevue looking down at my swollen figure and the light getting like spokes of ice, or in that dreadful gin-steeped Stepney bedroom with Phyllis coughing herself to death beside me, or at best, for a moment, a little girl in Glamorgan looking at the Roman road and wondering about the wonderful life that lay ahead."

I looked at Erich, remembering he had a long nasty future back in the cosmos himself, and at any rate he wasn't smiling, and I thought maybe he's getting a little humility, knowing someone else has two of those futures, but I doubted it.

"Because, you see," Lili kept forcing it out, "all my three lives I'd been a girl who fell in love with a great young poet she'd never met, the voice of the new youth and all youth, and she'd told her first big lie to get in the Red Cross and across to France to be nearer him, and it was all danger and dark magics and a knight in armor, and she pictured how she'd find him wounded but not seriously, with a little bandage around his head, and she'd light a fag for him and smile lightly, never letting him guess what she felt, but only being her best self and watching to see if that made something happen to him....

"And then the Boche machine guns cut him down at Passchendaele and there couldn't ever have been bandages big enough and the girl stayed seventeen inside and messed about and tried to be wicked, though she wasn't very good at that, and to drink, and she had a bit more talent there, though drinking yourself to death is not nearly as easy as it sounds, even with a kidney weakness to help. But she turned the trick.

"Then a cock crows. She wakes with a tearing start from the gray dreams of death that fill her lifeline. It's cold daybreak. There's the smell of a French farm. She feels her ankles and they're not at all like huge rubber boots filled with water. They're not swollen the least bit. They're young legs.

"There's a little window and the tops of a row of trees that may be poplars when there's more light, and what there is shows cots like her own and heads under blankets, and hanging uniforms make large shadows and a girl is snoring. There's a very distant rumble and it moves the window a bit. Then she remembers they're Red Cross girls many, many kilometers from Passchendaele and that Bruce Marchant is going to die at dawn today.

"In a few more minutes, he's going over the top where there's a crop-headed machine-gunner in field gray already looking down the sights and swinging the gun a bit. But she isn't going to die today. She's going to die in 1929 and 1955.

"And just as she's going mad, there's a creaking and out of the shadows tiptoes a Jap with a woman's hairdo and the whitest face and the blackest eyebrows. He's wearing a rose robe and a black sash which belts to his sides two samurai swords, but in his right hand he has a strange silver pistol. And he smiles at her as if they were brother and sister and lovers at the same time and he says, 'Voulez-vous vivre, mademoiselle?' and she stares and he bobs his head and says, 'Missy wish live, yes, no?'"

Sid's paw closed quietly around my shaking hands. It always gets me to hear about anyone's Resurrection, and although mine was crazier, it also had the Krauts in it. I hoped she wouldn't go through the rest of the formula and she didn't.

"Five minutes later, he's gone down a stairs more like a ladder to wait below and she's dressing in a rush. Her clothes resist a little, as if they were lightly gummed to the hook and the stained wall, and she hates to touch them. It's getting lighter and her cot looks as if someone were still sleeping there, although it's empty, and she couldn't bring herself to put her hand on the place if her new life depended on it.

"She climbs down and her long skirt doesn't bother her because she knows how to swing it. Suzaku conducts her past a sentry who doesn't see them and a puffy-faced farmer in a smock coughing and spitting the night out of his throat. They cross the farmyard and it's filled with rose light and she sees the sun is up and she knows that Bruce Marchant has just bled to death.

"There's an empty open touring car chugging loudly, waiting for someone; it has huge muddy wheels with wooden spokes and a brass radiator that says 'Simplex.' But Suzaku leads her past it to a dunghill and bows apologetically and she steps through a Door."

I heard Erich say to the others at the bar, "How touching! Now shall I tell everyone about my operation?" But he didn't get much of a laugh.

"That's how Lilian Foster came into the Change World with its steel-engraved nightmares and its deadly pace and deadlier lassitudes. I was more alive than I ever had been before, but it was the kind of life a corpse might get from unending electrical shocks and I couldn't summon any purpose or hope and Bruce Marchant seemed farther away than ever.

"Then, not six hours ago, a Soldier in a black uniform came through the Door and I thought, 'It can't be, but it does look like his photographs,' and then I thought I heard someone say the name Bruce, and then he shouted as if to all the world that he was Bruce Marchant, and I knew there was a Resurrection beyond Resurrection, a true resurrection. Oh, Bruce —"

She looked at him and he was crying and smiling and all the young beauty flooded back into her face, and I thought, "It has to be Change Winds, but it can't be. Face it without slobbering, Greta-there's something that works bigger miracles than Change."

And she went on, "And then the Change Winds died when the Snakes vaporized the Maintainer or the Ghostgirls Introverted it and all three of them vanished so swiftly and silently that even Bruce didn't notice-those are the best explanations I can summon and I fancy one of them is true. At all events, the Change Winds died and my past and even my futures became something I could bear lightly, because I have someone to bear them with me, and because at last I have a true future stretching out ahead of me, an unknown future which I shall create by living. Oh, don't you see that all of us have it now, this big opportunity?"

"Hussa for Sidney's suffragettes and the W.C.T.U.!" Erich cheered. "Beau, will you play us a medley of 'Hearts and Flowers' and 'Onward, Christian Soldiers'? I'm deeply moved, Lili. Where do the rest of us queue up for the Great Love Affair of the Century?"

Chapter 12
A Big Opportunity

> Now is a bearable burden. What buckles the back is the added weight of the past's mistakes and the future's fears.
>
> I had to learn to close the front door to tomorrow and the back door to yesterday and settle down to here and now.
>
> —Anonymous

Nobody laughed at Erich's screwball sarcasms and still I thought, "Yes, perish his hysterical little gray head, but he's half right-Lili's got the big thing now and she wants to serve it up to the rest of us on a platter, only love doesn't cook and cut that way."

Those weren't bad ideas she had about the Maintainer, though, especially the one about the Ghostgirls doing the Introverting-it would explain why there couldn't be Introversion drill, the manual stuff about blue flashes being window-dressing, and something disappearing without movement or transition is the sort of thing that might not catch the attention-and I guess they gave the others something to think about too, for there wasn't any follow-up to Erich's frantic sniping.

But I honestly didn't see where there was this big opportunity being stuck away in a gray sack in the Void and I began to wonder and I got the strangest feeling and I said to myself, "Hang onto your hat, Greta. It's hope."

"The dreadful thing about being a Demon is that you have all time to range through," Lili was saying with a smile. "You can never shut the back door to yesterday or the front door to tomorrow and simply live in the present. But now that's been done for us: the Door is shut, we need never again rehash the past or the future. The Spiders and Snakes can never find us, for who ever heard of a Place that was truly lost being rescued? And as those in the know have told me, Introversion is the end as far as those outside are concerned. So we're safe from the Spiders and Snakes, we need never be slaves or enemies again, and we have a Place in which to live our new lives, the Place prepared for us from the beginning."

She paused. "Surely you understand what I mean? Sidney and Beauregard and Dr. Pyeshkov are the ones who explained it to me. The Place is a balanced aquarium, just like the cosmos. No one knows how many ages of Big Time it has been in use, without a bit of new material being brought in-only luxuries and people-and not a bit of waste cast off. No one knows how many more ages it may not sustain life. I never heard of Minor Maintainers wearing out. We have all the future, all the security, anyone can hope for. We have a Place to live together."

You know, she was dead right and I realized that all the time I'd had the conviction in the back of my mind that we were going to suffocate or something if we didn't get a Door open pretty quick. I should have known differently, if anybody should, because I'd once been in the Place without a Door for as long as a hundred sleeps during a foxhole stretch of the Change War and we'd had to start cycling our food and it had been okay.

And then, because it is also the way my mind works, I started to picture in a flash the consequences of our living together all by ourselves like Lili said.

I began to pair people off; I couldn't help it. Let's see, four women, six men, two ETs.

"Greta," I said, "you're going to be Miss Polly Andry for sure. We'll have a daily newspaper and folk-dancing classes, we'll shut the bar except evenings, Bruce'll keep a rhymed history of the Place."

I even thought, though I knew this part was strictly silly, about schools and children. I wondered what Siddy's would look like, or my little commandant's. "Don't go near the Void, dears." Of course that would be specially hard on the two ETs, but Sevensee at least wasn't so different and the genetics boys had made some wonderful advances and Maud ought to know about them and there were some amazing gadgets in Surgery when Doc sobered up. The patter of little hoofs ...

"My fiance spoke to you about carrying a peace message to the rest of the cosmos," Lili added, "and bringing an end to the Big Change, and healing all the wounds that have been made in the Little Time."

I looked at Bruce. His face was set and strained, as will happen to the best of them when a girl starts talking about her man's business, and I don't know why, but I said to myself, "She's crucifying him, she's nailing him to his purpose as a woman will, even when there's not much point to it, as now."

And Lili went on, "It was a wonderful thought, but now we cannot carry or send any message and I believe it is too late in any event for a peace message to do any good. The cosmos is too raveled by change, too far gone. It will dissolve, fade, 'leave not a rack behind.' We're the survivors. The torch of existence has been put in our hands.

"We may already be all that's left in the cosmos, for have you thought that the Change Winds may have died at their source? We may never reach another cosmos, we may drift forever in the Void, but who of us has been Introverted before and who knows what we can or cannot do? We're a seed for a new future to grow from. Perhaps all doomed universes cast off seeds like this Place. It's a seed, it's an embryo, let it grow."

She looked swiftly at Bruce and then at Sid and she quoted, "'Come, my friends, 'tis not too late to seek a newer world'."

I squeezed Sid's hand and I started to say something to him, but he didn't know I was there; he was listening to Lili quote Tennyson with his eyes entranced and his mouth open, as if he were imagining new things to put into it–oh, Siddy!

And then I saw the others were looking at her the same way. Ilhilihis was seeing finer feather forests than long-dead Luna's grow. The greenhouse child Maud ap-Ares Davies was stowing away on a starship bound for another galaxy, or thinking how different her life might have been, the children she might have had, if she'd stayed on the planets and out of the Change World. Even Erich looked as though he might be blitzing new universes, and Mark subduing them, for an eight-legged *Führer-imperator*. Beau was throbbing up a wider Mississippi in a bigger-than-life sidewheeler.

Even I —well, I wasn't dreaming of a Greater Chicago. "Let's not go hog-wild on this sort of thing," I told myself, but I did look up at the Void and I got a shiver because I imagined it drawing away and the whole Place starting to grow.

"I truly meant what I said about a seed," Lili went on slowly. "I know, as you all do, that there are no children in the Change World, that there cannot be, that we all become instantly sterile, that what they call a curse is lifted from us girls and we are no longer in bondage to the moon."

She was right, all right–if there's one thing that's been proved a million times in the Change World, it's that.

"But we are no longer in the Change World," Lili said softly, "and its limitations should no longer apply to us, including that one. I feel deeply certain of it, but —" she looked around slowly —"we are four women here and I thought one of us might have a surer indication."

My eyes followed hers around like anybody's would. In fact, everybody was looking around except Maud, and she had the silliest look of surprise on her face and it stayed there, and then, very carefully, she got down from the bar stool with her knitting. She looked at the half-finished pink bra with the long white needles stuck in it and her eyes bugged bigger yet, as if she were expecting it to turn into a baby sweater right then and there. Then she walked across the Place to Lili and stood beside her. While she was walking, the look of surprise changed to a quiet smile. The only other thing she did was throw her shoulders back a little.

I was jealous of her for a second, but it was a double miracle for her, considering her age, and I couldn't grudge her that. And to tell the truth, I was a little frightened, too. Even with Dave, I'd been bothered about this business of having babies.

Yet I stood up with Siddy —I couldn't stop myself and I guess he couldn't either-and hand in hand we walked to the control divan. Beau and Sevensee were there and Bruce, of course, and then, so help me, those Soldiers to the death, Kaby and Mark, started over from the bar and I couldn't see anything in their eyes about the greater glory of Crete and Rome, but something, I think, about each other, and after a moment Illy slowly detached himself from the piano and followed, lightly trailing his tentacles on the floor.

I couldn't exactly see him hoping for little Illies in this company, unless it was true what the jokes said about Lunans, but maybe he was being really disinterested and maybe he wasn't; maybe he was simply figuring that Illy ought to be on the side with the biggest battalions.

I heard dragging footsteps behind us and here came Doc from the Gallery, carrying in his folded arms an abstract sculpture as big as a newborn baby. It was an agglomeration of perfect shiny gray spheres the size of golf balls, shaping up to something like a large brain, but with holes showing through here and there. He held it out to us like an infant to be admired and worked his lips and tongue as if he were trying very hard to say something, though not a word came out that you could understand, and I thought, "Maxey Aleksevich may be speechless drunk and have all sorts of holes in his head, but he's got the right instincts, bless his soulful little Russian heart."

We were all crowded around the control divan like a football team huddling. The Peace Packers, it came to me. Sevensee would be fullback or center and Illy left end-what a receiver! The right number, too. Erich was alone at the bar, but now even he —"Oh, no, this can't be," I thought-even he came toward us. Then I saw that his face was working the worst ever. He stopped halfway and managed to force a smile, but it was the worst, too. "That's my little commandant," I thought, "no team spirit."

"So now Lili and Bruce-yes, and *Grossmutterchen* Maud-have their little nest," he said, and he wouldn't have had to push his voice very hard to get a screech. "But what are the rest of us supposed to be-cowbirds?"

He crooked his neck and flapped his hands and croaked, "Cuc-koo! Cuc-koo!" And I said to myself, "I often thought you were crazy, boy, but now I know."

"*Teufelsdreck!* —yes, Devil's dirt! —but you all seem to be infected with this dream of children. Can't you see that the Change World is the natural and proper end of evolution? —a period of enjoyment and measuring, an ultimate working out of things, which women call destruction —'Help, I'm being raped!' 'Oh, what are they doing to my children?' —but which men know as fulfillment.

"You're given good parts in *Götterdämmerung* and you go up to the author and tap him on the shoulder and say, 'Excuse me, Herr Wagner, but this Twilight of the Gods is just a bit morbid. Why don't you write an opera for me about the little ones, the dear little blue-eyed curly-tops? A plot? Oh, boy meets girl and they settle down to breed, something like that.'

"Devil's dirt doubled and damned! Have you thought what life will be like without a Door to go out of to find freedom and adventure, to measure your courage and keenness? Do you want to grow long gray beards hobbling around this asteroid turned inside out? Putter around indoors to the end of your days, mooning about little baby cosmoses? —incidentally, with a live bomb for company. The cave, the womb, the little gray home in the nest-is that what you want? It'll grow? Oh, yes, like the city engulfing the wild wood, a proliferation of *Kinder, Kirche, Küche* —I should live so long!

"Women! —how I hate their bright eyes as they look at me from the fireside, bent-shouldered, rocking, deeply happy to be old, and say, 'He's getting weak, he's giving out, soon I'll have to put him to bed and do the simplest things for him.' Your filthy Triple Goddess, Kaby, the birther, bride, and burier of man! Woman, the enfeebler, the fetterer, the crippler! Woman! —and the curly-headed little cancers she wants!"

He lurched toward us, pointing at Lili. "I never knew one who didn't want to cripple a man if you gave her the chance. Cripple him, swaddle him, clip his wings, grind him to sausage to mold another man, hers, a doll man. You hid the Maintainer, you little smother-hen, so you could have your nest and your Brucie!"

He stopped, gasping, and I expected someone to bop him one on the schnozzle, and I think he did, too. I turned to Bruce and he was looking, I don't know how, sorry, guilty, anxious, angry, shaken, inspired, all at once, and I wished people sometimes had simple suburban re-actions like magazine stories.

Then Erich made the mistake, if it was one, of turning toward Bruce and slowly staggering toward him, pawing the air with his hands as if he were going to collapse into his arms, and saying, "Don't let them get you, Bruce. Don't let them tie you down. Don't let them clip you-your words or your deeds. You're a Soldier. Even when you talked about a peace message, you talked about doing some smashing of your own. No matter what you think and feel, Bruce, no matter how much lying you do and how much you hide, you're really not on their side."

That did it.

It didn't come soon enough or, I think, in the right spirit to please me, but I will say it for Bruce that he didn't muck it up by tipping or softening his punch. He took one step forward and his shoulders spun and his fist connected sweet and clean.

As he did it, he said only one word, "Loki!" and darn if that didn't switch me back to a campfire in the Indiana Dunes and my mother telling me out of the Elder Saga about the malicious, sneering, all-spoiling Norse god and how, when the other gods came to trap him in his hideaway by the river, he was on the point of finishing knotting a mysterious net big enough, I had imagined, to snare the whole universe, and that if they'd come a minute later, he would have.

Erich was stretched on the floor, his head hitched up, rubbing his jaw and glaring at Bruce. Mark, who was standing beside me, moved a little and I thought he was going to do something, maybe even clobber Bruce in the old spirit of you can't do that to my buddy, but he just shook his head and said, "*Omnia vincit amor.*" I nudged him and said, "Meaning?" and he said, "Love licks everything."

I'd never have expected it from a Roman, but he was half right at any rate. Lili had her victory: Bruce clearing the field for the marriage by laying out the woman-hating boy friend who would be trying to get him to go out nights. At that moment, I think Bruce wanted Lili and a life with her more than he wanted to reform the Change World. Sure, us women have our little victories-until the legions come or the Little Corporal draws up his artillery or the Panzers roar down the road.

Erich scrambled to his feet and stood there in a half-slump, half-crouch, still rubbing his jaw and glaring at Bruce over his hand, but making no move to continue the fight, and I studied his face and said to myself, "If he can get a gun, he's going to shoot himself, I know."

Bruce started to say something and hesitated, like I would have in his shoes, and just then Doc got one of his unpredictable inspirations and went weaving out toward Erich, holding out the sculpture and making deaf-and-dumb noises like he had to us. Erich looked at him as if he were going to kill him, and then grabbed the sculpture and swung it up over his head and smashed it down on the floor, and for a wonder, it didn't shatter. It just skidded along in one piece and stopped inches from my feet.

That thing not breaking must have been the last straw for Erich. I swear I could see the red surge up through his eyes toward his brain. He swung around into the Stores sector and ran the few steps between him and the bronze bomb chest.

Everything got very slow motion for me, though I didn't do any moving. Almost every man started out after Erich. Bruce didn't, though, and Siddy turned back after the first surge forward, while Illy squunched down for a leap, and it was between Sevensee's hairy shanks and Beau's scissoring white pants that I saw that under-the-microscope circle of death's heads and watched Erich's finger go down on them in the order Kaby had given: one, three, five, six, two, four, seven. I was able to pray seven distinct times that he'd make a mistake.

He straightened up. Illy landed by the box like a huge silver spider and his tentacles whipped futilely across its top. The others surged to a frightened halt around them.

Erich's chest was heaving, but his voice was cool and collected as he said, "You mentioned something about our having a future, Miss Foster. Now you can make that more specific. Unless we get back to the cosmos and dump this box, or find a Spider A-tech, or manage to call headquarters for guidance on disarming the bomb, we have a future exactly thirty minutes long."

Chapter 13
The Tiger is Loose

But whence he was, or of what wombe ybore,
Of beasts, or of the earth, I have not red:
But certes was with milke of wolves and tygres fed.

—Spenser

I guess when they really push the button or throw the switch or spring the trap or focus the beam or what have you, you don't faint or go crazy or anything else convenient. I didn't. Everything, everybody, every move that was made, every word that was spoken, was painfully real to me, like a hand twisting and squeezing things deep inside me, and I saw every least detail spotlighted and magnified like I had the seven skulls.

Erich was standing beyond the bomb chest; little smiles were ruffling his lips. I'd never seen him look so sharp. Illy was beside him, but not on his side, you understand. Mark, Sevensee and Beau were around the chest to the nearer side. Beau had dropped to a knee and was scanning the chest minutely, terror-under-control making him bend his head a little closer than he needed to for clear vision, but with his hands locked together behind his back, I guess to restrain the impulse to push any and everything that looked like a disarming button.

Doc was sprawled face down on the nearest couch, out like a light, I suppose.

Us four girls were still by the control divan. With Kaby, that surprised me, because she didn't look scared or frozen, but almost as intensely alive as Erich.

Sid had turned back, as I'd said, and had one hand stretched out toward but not touching the Minor Maintainer, and a look on his beardy face as if he were calling down death and destruction on every boozy rogue who had ever gone up from King's Lynn to Cambridge and London, and I realized why: if he'd thought of the Minor Maintainer a second sooner, he could have pinned Erich down with heavy gravity before he could touch the buttons.

Bruce was resting one hand on the head of the control divan and was looking toward the group around the chest, toward Erich, I think, as if Erich had done something rather wonderful for him, though I can't imagine myself being tickled at being included in anybody's suicide surprise party. Bruce looked altogether too dreamy, Brahma blast him, for someone who must have the same steel-spiked thought in his head that I know darn well the rest of us had: that in twenty-nine minutes or so, the Place would be a sun in a bag.

Erich was the first to get down to business, as I'd have laid any odds he would be. He had the jump on us and he wasn't going to lose it.

"Well, when are you going to start getting Lili to tell us where she hid the Maintainer? It has to be her-she was too certain it was gone forever when she talked. And Bruce must have seen from the bar who took the Maintainer, and who would he cover up for but his girl?"

There he was plagiarizing my ideas, but I guess I was willing to sign them over to him in full if he got us the right pail of water for that time-bomb.

He glanced at his wrist. "According to my Caller, you have twenty-nine and a half minutes, including the time it will take to get a Door or contact headquarters. When are you going to get busy on the girl?"

Bruce laughed a little-deprecatingly, so help me, and started toward him. "Look here, old man," he said, "there's no need to trouble Lili, or to fuss with headquarters, even if you could. Really not at all. Not to mention that your surmises are quite unfounded, old chap, and I'm a bit surprised at your advancing them. But that's quite all right because, as it happens, I'm an atomics technician and I even worked on that very bomb. To disarm it, you just have to fiddle a bit with some of the ankhs, those hoopy little crosses. Here, let me —"

Allah il allah, but it must have struck everybody as it did me as being just too incredible an assertion, too bloody British a bare-faced bluff, for Erich didn't have to say a word; Mark and Sevensee grabbed Bruce by the arms, one on each side, as he stooped toward the bronze chest, and they weren't gentle about it. Then Erich spoke.

"Oh, no, Bruce. Very sporting of you to try to cover up for your girl friend, but we aren't going to let ourselves be blown to stripped atoms twenty-eight minutes too soon while you monkey with the buttons, the very thing Benson-Carter warned against, and pray for a guess-work miracle. It's too thin, Bruce, when you come from 1917 and haven't been on the Big Time for a hundred sleeps and were calling for an A-tech yourself a few hours ago. Much too thin. Bruce, something is going to happen that I'm afraid you won't like, but you're going to have to put up with it. That is, unless Miss Foster decides to be cooperative."

"I say, you fellows, let me go," Bruce demanded, struggling experimentally. "I know it's a bit thick to swallow and I did give you the wrong impression calling for an A-tech, but I just wanted to capture your attention then; I didn't want to have to work on the bomb. Really, Erich, would they have ordered Benson-Carter to pick us up unless one of us were an A-tech? They'd be sure to include one in the bally operation."

"When they're using patchwork tactics?" Erich grinningly quoted back at him.

Kaby spoke up beside me and said, "Benson-Carter was a magician of matter and he was going on the operation disguised as an old woman. We have the cloak and hood with the other garments," and I wondered how this cold fish of a she-officer could be the same girl who was giving Mark slurpy looks not ten minutes ago.

"Well?" Erich asked, glancing at his Caller and then swinging his eyes around at us as if there must be some of the old *Wehrmacht* iron somewhere. We all found ourselves looking at Lili and she was looking so sharp herself, so ready to jump and so at bay, that it was all *I* needed, at any rate, to make Erich's theory about the Maintainer a rock-bottom certainty.

Bruce must have realized the way our minds were working, for he started to struggle in earnest and at the same time called, "For God's sake, don't do anything to Lili! Let me loose, you idiots! Everything's true I told you—I can save you from that bomb. Sevensee, you took my side against the Spiders; you've nothing to lose. Sid, you're an Englishman. Beau, you're a gentleman and you love her, too-for God's sake, stop them!"

Beau glanced up over his shoulder at Bruce and the others surging around close to his ankles and he had on his poker face. Sid I could tell was once more going through the purgatory of decision. Beau reached his own decision first and I'll say it for him that he acted on it fast and intelligently. Right from his kneeling position and before he'd even turned his head quite back, he jumped Erich.

But other things in this cosmos besides Man can pick sides and act fast. Illy landed on Beau midway and whipped his tentacles around him tight and they went wobbling around like a drunken white-and-silver barber pole. Beau got his hands each around a tentacle, and at the same time his face began to get purple, and I winced at what they were both going through.

Maybe Sevensee had a hoof in Sid's purgatory, because Bruce shook loose from the satyr and tried to knock out Mark, but the Roman twisted his arm and kept him from getting in a good punch.

Erich didn't make a move to mix into either fight, which is my little commandant all over. Using his fists on anybody but me is beneath him.

Then Sid made his choice, but there was no way for me to tell what it was, for, as he reached for the Minor Maintainer, Kaby contemptuously snatched it away from his hands and gave him a knee in the belly that doubled me up in sympathy and sent him sprawling on his knees toward the fighters. On the return, Kaby gave Lili, who'd started to grab too, an effortless backhand smash that set her down on the divan.

Erich's face lit up like an electric sign and he kept his eyes fixed on Kaby.

She crouched a little, carrying her weight on the balls of her feet and firmly cradling the Minor Maintainer in her left arm, like a basketball captain planning an offensive. Then she waved her free hand decisively to the right. I didn't get it, but Erich did and Mark too, for Erich jumped for the Refresher sector and Mark let go of Bruce and followed him, ducking around Sevensee's arms, who was coming back into the fight on which side I don't know. Illy un-whipped from Beau and copied Erich and Mark with one big spring.

Then Kaby twisted a dial as far as it would go and Bruce, Beau, Sevensee and poor Siddy were slammed down and pinned to the floor by about eight gravities.

It should have been lighter near us —I hoped it was, but you couldn't tell from watching Siddy; he went flat on his face, spread-eagled, one hand stretched toward me so close, I could have touched it (but not let go!), and his mouth was open against the floor and he was gasping through a corner of it and I could see his spine trying to sink through his belly. Bruce just managed to get his head and one shoulder up a bit, and they all made me think of a Doré illustration of the *Inferno* where the cream of the damned are frozen up to their necks in ice in the innermost circle of Hell.

The gravity didn't catch me, although I could feel it in my left arm. I was mostly in the Refresher sector, but I dropped down flat too, partly out of a crazy compassion I have, but mostly because I didn't want to take a chance of having Kaby knock me down.

Erich, Mark and Illy had got clear and they headed toward us. Maud picked the moment to make her play; she hadn't much choice of times, if she wanted to make one. The Old Girl was looking it for once, but I guess the thought of her miracle must have survived alongside the fear of sacked sun and must have meant a lot to her, for she launched out fast, all set to straight-arm Kaby into the heavy gravity and grab the Minor Maintainer with the other hand.

Chapter 14
"Now Will You Talk?"

Like diamonds, we are cut with our own dust.

—Webster

Cretans have eyes under their back hair, or let's face it, Entertainers aren't Soldiers. Kaby weaved to one side and flicked a helpful hand and poor old Maud went where she'd been going to send Kaby. It sickened me to see the gravity take hold and yank her down.

I could have jumped up and made it four in a row for Kaby, but I'm not a bit brave when things like my life are at stake.

Lili was starting to get up, acting a little dazed. Kaby gently pushed her down again and quietly said, "Where is it?" and then hauled off and slapped her across the face. What got me was the matter-of-fact way Kaby did it. I can understand somebody getting mad and socking someone, or even deliberately working up a rage so as to be able to do something nasty, but this cold-blooded way turns my stomach.

Lili looked as if half her face were about to start bleeding, but she didn't look dazed any more and her jaw set. Kaby grabbed Lili's pearl necklace and twisted it around her neck and it broke and the pearls went bouncing around like ping-pong balls, so Kaby yanked down Lili's gray silk bandeau until it was around the neck and tightened that. Lili started to choke through her tight-pressed lips. Erich, Mark and Illy had come up and crowded around, but they seemed to be content with the job Kaby was doing.

"Listen, slut," she said, "we have no time. You have a healing room in this place. I can work the things."

"Here it comes," I thought, wishing I could faint. On top of everything, on top of death even, they had to drag in the nightmare personally stylized for me, the horror with my name on it. I wasn't going to be allowed to blow up peacefully. They weren't satisfied with an A-bomb. They had to write my private hell into the script.

"There is a thing called an Invertor," Kaby said exactly as I'd known she would, but as I didn't really hear it just then —a mental split I'll explain in a moment. "It opens you up so they can cure your insides without cutting your skin or making you bleed anywhere. It turns the big parts of you inside out, but not the blood tubes. All your skin-your eyes, ears, nose, toes, all of it-becoming the lining of a little hole that's half-filled with your hair.

"Meantime, your insides are exposed for whatever the healer wants to do to them. You live for a while on the air inside the hole. First the healer gives you an air that makes you sleep, or you go mad in about fifty heartbeats. We'll see what ten heartbeats do to you without the sleepy air. Now will you talk?"

I hadn't been listening to her, though, not the real me, or I'd have gone mad without getting the treatment. I once heard Doc say your liver is more mysterious and farther away from you than the stars, because although you live with your liver all your life, you never see it or learn to point to it instinctively, and the thought of someone messing around with that intimate yet unknown part of you is just too awful.

I knew I had to do something quick. Hell, at the first hint of Introversion, before Kaby had even named it, Illy had winced so that his tentacles were all drawn up like fat feather-sausages. Erich had looked at him questioningly, but that lousy Looney had un-endeared himself to me by squeaking, "Don't mind me, I'm just sensitive. Get on with the girl. Make her tell."

Yes, I knew I had to do something, and here on the floor that meant thinking hard and in high gear about something else. The screwball sculpture Erich had tried to smash was a foot from my nose and I saw a faint trail of white stuff where it had skidded. I reached out and touched the trail; it was finely gritty, like powdered glass. I tipped up the sculpture and the part on which it had skidded wasn't marred at all, not even dulled; the gray spheres were as glisteningly bright as ever. So I knew the trail was diamond dust rubbed off the diamonds in the floor by something even harder.

That told me the sculpture was something special and maybe Doc had had a real idea in his pickled brain when he'd been pushing the thing at all of us and trying to tell us something. He hadn't managed to say anything then, but he had earlier when he'd been going to tell us what to do about the bomb, and maybe there was a connection.

I twisted my memory hard and let it spring back and I got "Inversh ... bosh ..." Bosh, indeed! Bosh and inverse bosh to all boozers, Russki or otherwise.

So I quick tried the memory trick again and this time I got "glovsh" and then I grasped and almost sneezed on diamond dust as I watched the pieces fit themselves together in my mind like a speeded-up movie reel.

It all hung on that black right-hand hussar's glove Lili had produced for Bruce. Only she couldn't have found it in Stores, because we'd searched every fractional pigeonhole later on and there hadn't been any gloves there, not even the left-hand mate there would have been. Also, Bruce had had two left-hand gloves to start with, and we had been through the whole Place with a fine-tooth comb, and there had been only the two black gloves on the floor where Bruce had kicked them off the bar-those two and those two only, the left-hand glove he'd brought from outside and the right-hand glove Lili had produced for him.

So a left-hand glove had disappeared-the last I'd seen of it, Lili had been putting it on her tray-and a right-hand glove had appeared. Which could only add up to one thing: Lili had turned the left-hand glove into an identical right. She couldn't have done it by turning it inside out the ordinary way, because the lining was different.

But as I knew only too sickeningly well, there was an extraordinary way to turn things inside out, things like human beings. You merely had to put them on the Invertor in Surgery and flick the switch for full Inversion.

Or you could flick it for partial Inversion and turn something into a perfect three-dimensional mirror image of itself, just what a right-hand glove is of a left. Rotation through the fourth dimension, the science boys call it; I've heard of it being used in surgery on the highly asymmetric Martians, and even to give a socially impeccable right hand to a man who'd lost one, by turning an amputated right arm into an amputated left.

Ordinarily, nothing but live things are ever Inverted in Surgery and you wouldn't think of doing it to an inanimate object, especially in a Place where the Doc's a drunk and the Surgery hasn't been used for hundreds of sleeps.

But when you've just fallen in love, you think of wonderful crazy things to do for people. Drunk with love, Lili had taken Bruce's extra left-hand glove into Surgery, partially Inverted it, and got a right-hand glove to give him.

What Doc had been trying to say with his "Inversh ... bosh ..." was "Invert the box," meaning we should put the bronze chest through full Inversion to get at the bomb inside to disarm it. Doc too had got the idea from Lili's trick with the glove. What an inside-out tactical atomic bomb would look like, I could not imagine and did not particularly care to see. I might have to, though, I realized.

But the fast-motion film was still running in my head. Later on, Lili had decided like I had that her lover was going to lose out in his plea for mutiny unless she could give him a really captive audience-and maybe, even then, she had been figuring on creating the nest for Bruce's chicks and ... all those other things we'd believed in for a while. So she'd taken the

Major Maintainer and remembered the glove, and not many seconds later, she had set down on a shelf of the Art Gallery an object that no one would think of questioning-except someone who knew the Gallery by heart.

I looked at the abstract sculpture a foot from my nose, at the clustered gray spheres the size of golf balls. I had known that the inside of the Maintainer was made up of vastly tough, vastly hard giant molecules, but I hadn't realized they were quite *that* big.

I said to myself, "Greta, this is going to give you a major psychosis, but you're the one who has to do it, because no one is going to listen to your deductions when they're all practically living on negative time already."

I got up as quietly as if I were getting out of a bed I shouldn't have been in-there are some things Entertainers are good at-and Kaby was just saying "you go mad in about fifty heartbeats." Everybody on their feet was looking at Lili. Sid seemed to have moved, but I had no time for him except to hope he hadn't done anything that might attract attention to me.

I stepped out of my shoes and walked rapidly to Surgery-there's one good thing about this hardest floor anywhere, it doesn't creak. I walked through the Surgery screen that is like a wall of opaque, odorless cigarette smoke and I concentrated on remembering my snafued nurse's training, and before I had time to panic, I had the sculpture positioned on the gleaming table of the Invertor.

I froze for a moment when I reached for the Inversion switch, thinking of the other time and trying to remember what it had been that bothered me so much about an inside-out brain being bigger and not having eyes, but then I either thumbed my nose at my nightmare or kissed my sanity good-by, I don't know which, and twisted the switch all the way over, and there was the Major Maintainer winking blue about three times a second as nice as you could want it.

It must have been working as sweet and steady as ever, all the time it was Inverted, except that, being inside out, it had hocused the direction finders.

Chapter 15
Lord Spider

black legged spiders
with red hearts of hell

—marquis

"Jesu!" I turned and Sid's face was sticking through the screen like a tinted bas-relief hanging on a gray wall and I got the impression he had peered unexpectedly through a slit in an arras into Queen Elizabeth's bedroom.

He didn't have any time to linger on the sensation, even if he'd wanted to, for an elbow with a copper band thrust through the screen and dug his ribs and Kaby marched Lili in by the neck. Erich, Mark and Illy were right behind. They caught the blue flashes and stopped dead, staring at the long-lost. Erich spared me one look which seemed to say, so you did it, not that it matters. Then he stepped forward and picked it up and held it solidly to his left side in the double right-angle made by fingers, forearm and chest, and reached for the Introversion switch with a look on his face as if he were opening a fifth of whisky.

The blue light died and Change Winds hit me like a stiff drink that had been a long, long time in coming, like a hot trumpet note out of nowhere.

I felt the changing pasts blowing through me, and the uncertainties whistling past, and ice-stiff reality softening with all its duties and necessities, and the little memories shredding away and dancing off like autumn leaves, leaving maybe not even ghosts behind, and all the crazy moods like Mardi Gras dancers pouring down an evening street, and something inside me had the nerve to say it didn't care whether Greta Forzane's death was riding in those Winds because they felt so good.

I could tell it was hitting the others the same way. Even battered, tight-lipped Lili seemed to be saying, you're making me drink the stuff and I hate you for it, but I do love it. I guess we'd all had the worry that even finding and Extroverting the Maintainer wouldn't put us back in touch with the cosmos and give us those Winds we hate and love.

The thing that cut through to us as we stood there glowing was not the thought of the bomb, though that would have come in a few seconds more, but Sid's voice. He was still standing in the screen, except that now his face was out the other side and we could just see parts of his gray-doubleted back, but, of course, his "Jesu!" came through the screen as if it weren't there.

At first I couldn't figure out who he could be talking to, but I swear I never heard his voice so courtly obsequious before, so strong and yet so filled with awe and an under-note of, yes, sheer terror.

"Lord, I am filled from top to toe with confusion that you should so honor my poor Place," he said. "Poor say I and mine, when I mean that I have ever busked it faithfully for you, not dreaming that you would ever condescend ...yet knowing that your eye was certes ever upon me ...though I am but as a poor pinch of dust adrift between the suns ...I abase myself. Prithee, how may I serve thee, sir? I know not e'en how most suitably to address thee, Lord ...King ... Emperor Spider!"

I felt like I was getting very small, but not a bit less visible, worse luck, and even with the Change Winds inside me to give me courage, I thought this was really too much, coming on top of everything else; it was simply unfair.

At the same time, I realized it was to be expected that the big bosses would have been watching us with their unblinking beady black eyes ever since we had Introverted waiting to pounce if we should ever come out of it. I tried to picture what was on the other side of the screen and I didn't like the assignment.

But in spite of being petrified, I had a hard time not giggling, like the zany at graduation exercises, at the way the other ones in Surgery were taking it.

I mean the Soldiers. They each stiffened up like they had the old ramrod inside them, and their faces got that important look, and they glanced at each other and the floor without lowering their heads, as if they were measuring the distance between their feet and mentally chalking alternate sets of footprints to step into. The way Erich and Kaby held the Major and Minor Maintainers became formal; the way they checked their Callers and nodded reassuringly was positively esoteric. Even Illy somehow managed to look as if he were on parade.

Then from beyond the screen came what was, under the circumstances, the worst noise I've ever heard, a seemingly wordless distant-sounding howling and wailing, with a note of menace that made me shake, although it also had a nasty familiarity about it I couldn't place. Sid's voice broke into it, loud, fast and frightened.

"Your pardon, Lord, I did not think ... certes, the gravity ... I'll attend to it on the instant." He whipped a hand and half a head back through the screen, but without looking back and snapped his fingers, and before I could blink, Kaby had put the Minor Maintainer in his hand.

Sid went completely out of sight then and the howling stopped, and I thought that if that was the way a Lord Spider expressed his annoyance at being subjected to incorrect gravity, I hoped the bosses wouldn't start any conversations with me.

Erich pursed his lips and threw the other Soldiers a nod and the four of them marched through the screen as if they'd drilled a lifetime for this moment. I had the wild idea that Erich might give me his arm, but he strode past me as if I were ... an Entertainer.

I hesitated a moment then, but I had to see what was happening outside, even if I got eaten up for it. Besides, I had a bit of the thought that if these formalities went on much longer, even a Lord Spider was going to discover just how immune he was to confined atomic blast.

I walked through the screen with Lili beside me.

The Soldiers had stopped a few feet in front of it. I looked around ahead for whatever it was going to turn out to be, prepared to drop a curtsy or whatever else, bar nothing, that seemed expected of me.

I had a hard time spotting the beast. Some of the others seemed to be having trouble too. I saw Doc weaving around foolishly by the control divan, and Bruce and Beau and Sevensee and Maud on their feet beyond it, and I wondered whether we were dealing with an invisible monster; ought to be easy enough for the bosses to turn a simple trick like invisibility.

Then I looked sharply left where everyone else, even glassy-eyed Doc, was coming to look, into the Door sector, only there wasn't any monster there or even a Door, but just Siddy holding the Minor Maintainer and grinning like when he is threatening to tickle me, only more fiendishly.

"Not a move, masters," he cried, his eyes dancing, "or I'll pin the pack of you down, marry and amen I will. It is my firm purpose to see the Place blasted before I let this instrument out of my hands again."

My first thought was, "'Sblood but Siddy is a real actor! I don't care if he didn't study under anyone later than Burbage, that just proves how good Burbage is."

Sid had convinced us not only that the real Spiders had arrived, but earlier that the gravity in the edge of Stores had been a lot heavier than it actually was. He completely fooled all those Soldiers, including my swelled-headed victorious little commandant, and I kind of filed away the timing of that business of reaching out the hand and snapping the fingers without looking, it was so good.

"Beauregard!" Sid called. "Get to the Major Maintainer and call headquarters. But don't come through Door, marry go by Refresher. I'll not trust a single Demon of you in this sector with me until much more has been shown and settled."

"Siddy, you're wonderful," I said, starting toward him. "As soon as I got the Maintainer unsnarled and looked around and saw your sweet old face —"

"Back, tricksy trull! Not the breadth of one scarlet toenail nearer me, you Queen of Sleights and High Priestess of Deception!" he bellowed. "You least of all do I trust. Why you hid the Maintainer, I know not, 'faith, but later you'll discover the truth to me or I'll have your gizzard."

I could see there was going to have to be a little explaining.

Doc, touched off, I guess, by Sid waving his hand at me, threw back his head and let off one of those shuddery Siberian wolf-howls he does so blamed well. Sid waved toward him sharply and he shut up, beaming toothily, but at least I knew who was responsible for the Spider wail of displeasure that Sid had either called for or more likely got as a gift of the gods and used in his act.

Beau came circling around fast and Erich shoved the Major Maintainer into his hands without making any fuss. The four Soldiers were looking pretty glum after losing their grand review.

Beau dumped some junk off one of the Art Gallery's sturdy taborets and set the Major Maintainer on it carefully but fast, and quickly knelt in front of it and whipped on some earphones and started to tune. The way he did it snatched away from me my inward glory at my big Inversion brainwave so fast, I might never have had it, and there was nothing in my mind again but the bronze bomb chest.

I wondered if I should suggest Inverting the thing, but I said to myself, "Uh-uh, Greta, you got no diploma to show them and there probably isn't time to try two things, anyway."

Then Erich for once did something I wanted him to, though I didn't care for its effect on my nerves, by looking at his Caller and saying quietly, "Nine minutes to go, if Place time and cosmic time are synching."

Beau was steady as a rock and working adjustments so fine that I couldn't even see his fingers move.

Then, at the other end of the Place, Bruce took a few steps toward us. Sevensee and Maud followed a bit behind him. I remembered Bruce was another of our nuts with a private program for blowing up the place.

"Sidney," he called, and then, when he'd got Sid's attention, "Remember, Sidney, you and I both came down to London from Peterhouse."

I didn't get it. Then Bruce looked toward Erich with a devil-may-care challenge and toward Lili as if he were asking her forgiveness for something. I couldn't read her expression; the bruises were blue on her throat and her cheek was puffy.

Then Bruce once more shot Erich that look of challenge and he spun and grabbed Sevensee by a wrist and stuck out a foot-even half-horses aren't too sharp about infighting, I guess, and the satyr had every right to feel at least as confused as I felt-and sent him stumbling into Maud, and the two of them tumbled to the floor in a jumble of hairy legs and pearl-gray frock. Bruce raced to the bomb chest.

Most of us yelled, "Stop him, Sid, pin him down," or something like that —I know I did because I was suddenly sure that he'd been asking Lili's pardon for blowing the two of them up-and all the rest of us too, the love-blinded stinker.

Sid had been watching him all the time and now he lifted his hand to the Minor Maintainer, but then he didn't touch any of the dials, just watched and waited, and I thought, "Shaitan shave us! Does Siddy want in on death, too? Ain't he satisfied with all he knows about life?"

Bruce had knelt and was twisting some things on the front of the chest, and it was all as bright as if he were under a bank of Klieg lights, and I was telling myself I wouldn't know anything when the fireball fired, and not believing it, and Sevensee and Maud had got unscrambled and were starting for Bruce, and the rest of us were yelling at Sid, except that Erich was just looking at Bruce very happily, and Sid was still not doing anything, and it was unbearable except just then I felt the little arteries start to burst in my brain like a string of fire-crackers and the old aorta pop, and for good measure, a couple of valves come unhinged in my ticker, and I was thinking, "Well, now I know what it's like to die of heart failure and high blood pressure," and having a last quiet smile at having cheated the bomb, when Bruce jumped up and back from the chest.

"That does it!" he announced cheerily. "She's as safe as the Bank of England."

Sevensee and Maud stopped themselves just short of knocking him down and I said to myself, "Hey, let's get a move on! I thought heart attacks were fast."

Before anyone else could speak, Beau did. He had turned around from the Major Maintainer and pulled aside one of the earphones.

"I got headquarters," he said crisply. "They told me how to disarm the bomb —I merely said I thought we ought to know. What did you do, sir?" he called to Bruce.

"There's a row of four ankhs just below the lock. The first to your left you give a quarter turn to the right, the second a quarter turn to the left, same for the fourth, and you don't touch the third."

"That is it, sir," Beau confirmed.

The long silence was too much for me; I guess I must have the shortest span for unspoken relief going. I drew some nourishment out of my restored arteries into my brain cells and yelled, "Siddy, I know I'm a tricksy trull and the High Vixen of all Foxes, but what the Hell is Peterhouse?"

"The oldest college at Cambridge," he told me rather coolly.

Chapter 16
The Possibility-Binders

"Familiar with infinite universe sheafs and open-ended postulate systems? —the notion that everything is possible-and I mean everything-and everything has happened. *Everything.*"

—Heinlein

An hour later, I was nursing a weak highball and a black eye in the sleepy-time darkness on the couch farthest from the piano, half watching the highlighted party going on around it and the bar, while the Place waited for rendezvous with Egypt and the Battle of Alexandria.

Sid had swept all our outstanding problems into one big bundle and, since his hand held the joker of the Minor Maintainer, he had settled them all as high-handedly as if they'd been those of a bunch of schoolkids.

It amounted to this:

We'd been Introverted when most of the damning things had happened, so presumably only we knew about them, and we were all in so deep one way or another that we'd all have to keep quiet to protect our delicate complexions.

Well, Erich's triggering the bomb did balance rather neatly Bruce's incitement to mutiny, and there was Doc's drinking, while everybody who had declared for the peace message had something to hide. Mark and Kaby I felt inclined to trust anywhere, Maud for sure, and Erich in this particular matter, damn him. Illy I didn't feel at all easy about, but I told myself there always has to be a fly in the ointment—a darn big one this time, and furry.

Sid didn't mention his own dirty linen, but he knew we knew he'd flopped badly as boss of the Place and only recouped himself by that last-minute flimflam.

Remembering Sid's trick made me think for a moment about the real Spiders. Just before I snuck out of Surgery, I'd had a vivid picture of what they must look like, but now I couldn't get it again. It depressed me, not being able to remember-oh, I probably just imagined I'd had a picture, like a hophead on a secret-of-the-universe kick. Me ever find out anything about the Spiders? —except for nervous notions like I'd had during the recent fracas? —what a laugh!

The funniest thing (ha-ha!) was that I had ended up the least-trusted person. Sid wouldn't give me time to explain how I'd deduced what had happened to the Maintainer, and even when Lili spoke up and admitted hiding it, she acted so bored I don't think everybody believed her-although she did spill the realistic detail that she hadn't used partial Inversion on the glove; she'd just turned it inside out to make it a right and then done a full Inversion to get the lining back inside.

I tried to get Doc to confirm that he'd reasoned the thing out the same way I had, but he said he had been blacked out the whole time, except during the first part of the hunt, and he didn't remember having any bright ideas at all. Right now, he was having Maud explain to him twice, in detail, everything that had happened. I decided that it was going to take a little more work before my reputation as a great detective was established.

I looked over the edge of the couch and just made out in the gloom one of Bruce's black gloves. It must have been kicked there. I fished it up. It was the right-hand one. My big clue, and was I sick of it! Got mittens, God forbid! I slung it away and, like a lurking octopus, Illy shot up a tentacle from the next couch, where I hadn't known he was resting, and snatched the glove like it was a morsel of underwater garbage. These ETs can seem pretty shuddery non-human at times.

I thought of what a cold-blooded, skin-saving louse Illy had been, and about Sid and his easy suspicions, and Erich and my black eye, and how, as usual, I'd got left alone in the end. My men!

Bruce had explained about being an A-tech. Like a lot of us, he'd had several widely different jobs during his first weeks in the Change World and one of them had been as secretary to a group of the minor atomics boys from the Manhattan-Project-Earth-Satellite days. I gathered he'd also absorbed some of his bothersome ideas from them. I hadn't quite decided yet what species of heroic heel he belonged to, but he was thick with Mark and Erich again. Everybody's men!

Sid didn't have to argue with anybody; all the wild compulsions and mighty resolves were dead now, anyway until they'd had a good long rest. I sure could use one myself, I knew.

The party at the piano was getting wilder. Lili had been dancing the black bottom on top of it and now she jumped down into Sid's and Sevensee's arms, taking a long time about it. She'd been drinking a lot and her little gray dress looked about as innocent on her as diapers would on Nell Gwyn. She continued her dance, distributing her marks of favor equally between Sid, Erich and the satyr. Beau didn't mind a bit, but serenely pounded out "Tonight's the Night" —which she'd practically shouted to him not two minutes ago.

I was glad to be out of the party. Who can compete with a highly experienced, utterly disillusioned seventeen-year-old really throwing herself away for the first time?

Something touched my hand. Illy had stretched a tentacle into a furry wire to return me the black glove, although he ought to have known I didn't want it. I pushed it away, privately calling Illy a washed-out moronic tarantula, and right away I felt a little guilty. What right had I to be critical of Illy? Would my own character have shown to advantage if I'd been locked in with eleven octopoids a billion years away? For that matter, where did I get off being critical of anyone?

Still, I was glad to be out of the party, though I kept on watching it. Bruce was drinking alone at the bar. Once Sid had gone over to him and they'd had one together and I'd heard Bruce reciting from Rupert Brooke those deliberately corny lines, "For England's the one land, I know, Where men with Splendid Hearts may go; and Cambridgeshire, of all England, The Shire for Men who Understand;" and I'd remembered that Brooke too had died young in World War One and my ideas had got fuzzy. But mostly Bruce was just calmly drinking by himself. Every once in a while Lili would look at him and stop dead in her dancing and laugh.

I'd figured out this Bruce-Lili-Erich business as well as I cared to. Lili had wanted the nest with all her heart and nothing else would ever satisfy her, and now she'd go to hell her own way and probably die of Bright's disease for a third time in the Change World. Bruce hadn't wanted the nest or Lili as much as he wanted the Change World and the chances it gave for Soldierly cavorting and poetic drunks; Lili's seed wasn't his idea of healing the cosmos; maybe he'd make a real mutiny some day, but more likely he'd stick to bar-room epics.

His and Lili's infatuation wouldn't die completely, no matter how rancid it looked right now. The real-love angle might go, but Change would magnify the romance angle and it might seem to them like a big thing of a sort if they met again.

Erich had his *Kamerad*, shaped to suit him, who'd had the guts and cleverness to disarm the bomb he'd had the guts to trigger. You have to hand it to Erich for having the nerve to put us all in a situation where we'd have to find the Maintainer or fry, but I don't know anything disgusting enough to hand to him.

I had tried a while back. I had gone up behind him and said, "Hey, how's my wicked little commandant? Forgotten your *und so weiter?*" and as he turned, I clawed my nails and slammed him across the cheek. That's how I got the black eye. Maud wanted to put an electronic leech on it, but I took the old handkerchief in ice water. Well, at any rate Erich had his scratches to match Bruce's, not as deep, but four of them, and I told myself maybe they'd get infected —I hadn't washed my hands since the hunt. Not that Erich doesn't love scars.

Mark was the one who helped me up after Erich knocked me down.

"You got any omnias for that?" I snapped at him.

"For what?" Mark asked.

"Oh, for everything that's been happening to us," I told him disgustedly.

He seemed to actually think for a moment and then he said, "*Omnia mutantur, nihil interit.*"

"Meaning?" I asked him.

He said, "All things change, but nothing is really lost."

It would be a wonderful philosophy to stand with against the Change Winds. Also damn silly. I wondered if Mark really believed it. I wished I could. Sometimes I come close to thinking it's a lot of baloney trying to be any decent kind of Demon, even a good Entertainer. Then I tell myself, "That's life, Greta. You've got to love through it somehow." But there are times when some of these cookies are not too easy to love.

Something brushed the palm of my hand again. It was Illy's tentacle, with the tendrils of the tip spread out like a little bush. I started to pull my hand away, but then I realized the Loon was simply lonely. I surrendered my hand to the patterned gossamer pressures of feather-talk.

Right away I got the words, "Feeling lonely, Greta girl?"

It almost floored me, I tell you. Here I was understanding feather-talk, which I just didn't, and I was understanding it in English, which didn't make sense at all.

For a second, I thought Illy must have spoken, but I knew he hadn't, and for a couple more seconds I thought he was working telepathy on me, using the feather-talk as cues. Then I tumbled to what was happening: he was playing English on my palm like on the keyboard of his squeakbox, and since I could play English on a squeakbox myself, my mind translated automatically.

Realizing this almost gave my mind stage fright, but I was too fagged to be hocused by self-consciousness. I just lay back and let the thoughts come through. It's good to have someone talk to you, even an underweight octopus, and without the squeaks Illy didn't sound so silly; his phrasing was soberer.

"Feeling sad, Greta girl, because you'll never understand what's happening to us all," Illy asked me, "because you'll never be anything but a shadow fighting shadows-and trying to love shadows in between the battles? It's time you understood we're not really fighting a war at all, although it looks that way, but going through a kind of evolution, though not exactly the kind Erich had in mind.

"Your Terran thought has a word for it and a theory for it—a theory that recurs on many worlds. It's about the four orders of life: Plants, Animals, Men and Demons. Plants are energy-binders—they can't move through space or time, but they can clutch energy and transform it. Animals are space-binders—they can move through space. Man (Terran or ET, Lunan or non-Lunan) is a time-binder—he has memory.

"Demons are the fourth order of evolution, possibility-binders—they can make all of what might be part of what is, and that is their evolutionary function. Resurrection is like the metamorphosis of a caterpillar into a butterfly: a third-order being breaks out of the chrysalis of its lifeline into fourth-order life. The leap from the ripped cocoon of an unchanging reality is like the first animal's leap when he ceases to be a plant, and the Change World is the core of meaning behind the many myths of immortality.

"All evolution looks like a war at first-octopoids against monopoids, mammals against reptiles. And it has a necessary dialectic: there must be the thesis-we call it Snake-and the antithesis-Spider-before there can be the ultimate synthesis, when all possibilities are fully realized in one ultimate universe. The Change War isn't the blind destruction it seems.

76

"Remember that the Serpent is your symbol of wisdom and the Spider your sign for patience. The two names are rightly frightening to you, for all high existence is a mixture of horror and delight. And don't be surprised, Greta girl, at the range of my words and thoughts; in a way, I've had a billion years to study Terra and learn her languages and myths.

"Who are the real Spiders and Snakes, meaning who were the first possibility-binders? Who was Adam, Greta girl? Who was Cain? Who were Eve and Lilith?

"In binding all possibility, the Demons also bind the mental with the material. All fourth-order beings live inside and outside all minds, throughout the whole cosmos. Even this Place is, after its fashion, a giant brain: its floor is the brainpan, the boundary of the Void is the cortex of gray matter-yes, even the Major and Minor Maintainers are analogues of the pineal and pituitary glands, which in some form sustain all nervous systems.

"There's the real picture, Greta girl."

The feather-talk faded out and Illy's tendril tips merged into a soft pad on which I fingered, "Thanks, Daddy Longlegs."

Chewing over in my mind what Illy had just told me, I looked back at the gang around the piano. The party seemed to be breaking up; at least some of them were chopping away at it. Sid had gone to the control divan and was getting set to tune in Egypt. Mark and Kaby were there with him, all bursting with eagerness and the vision of tanks on ranks of mounted Zombie bowmen going up in a mushroom cloud; I thought of what Illy had told me and I managed a smile-seems we've got to win and lose all the battles, every which way.

Mark had just put on his Parthian costume, groaning cheerfully, "Trousers again!" and was striding around under a hat like a fur-lined ice-cream cone and with the sleeves of his metal-stuffed candys flapping over his hands. He waved a short sword with a heart-shaped guard at Bruce and Erich and told them to get a move on.

Kaby was going along on the operation wearing the old-woman disguise intended for Benson-Carter. I got a half-hearted kick out of knowing she was going to have to cover that chest and hobble.

Bruce and Erich weren't taking orders from Mark just yet. Erich went over and said something to Bruce at the bar, and Bruce got down and went over with Erich to the piano, and Erich tapped Beau on the shoulder and leaned over and said something to him, and Beau nodded and yanked "Limehouse Blues" to a fast close and started another piece, something slow and nostalgic.

Erich and Bruce waved to Mark and smiled, as if to show him that whether he came over and stood with them or not, the legate and the lieutenant and the commandant were very much together. And while Sevensee hugged Lili with a simple enthusiasm that made me wonder why I've wasted so much imagination on genetic treatments for him, Erich and Bruce sang:

"*To the legion of the lost ones, to the cohort of the damned,*
To our brothers in the tunnels outside time,
Sing three Change-resistant Zombies, raised from death and robot-crammed,
And Commandos of the Spiders —
Here's to crime!
We're three blind mice on the wrong time-track,
Hush-hush-hush!
We've lost our now and will never get back,
Hush-hush-hush!
Change Commandos out on the spree,
Damned through all possibility,
Ghostgirls, think kindly on such as we,
Hush-hush-hush!"

While they were singing, I looked down at my charcoal skirt and over at Maud and Lili and I thought, "Three gray hustlers for three black hussars, that's our speed." Well, I'd never thought of myself as a high-speed job, winning all the races —I wouldn't feel comfortable that way. Come to think of it, we've got to lose and win all the races in the long run, the way the course is laid out.

I fingered to Illy, "That's the picture, all right, Spider boy."

The Creature from Cleveland Depths

Here is a modern tale of an inner-directed sorcerer and an outer-directed sorcerer's apprentice… a tale of— The Creature from Cleveland Depths

"Come on, Gussy," Fay prodded quietly, "quit stalking around like a neurotic bear and suggest something for my invention team to work on. I enjoy visiting you and Daisy, but I can't stay aboveground all night."

"If being outside the shelters makes you nervous, don't come around any more," Gusterson told him, continuing to stalk. "Why doesn't your invention team think of something to invent? Why don't you? Hah!" In the "Hah!" lay triumphant condemnation of a whole way of life.

"We do," Fay responded imperturbably, "but a fresh viewpoint sometimes helps."

"I'll say it does! Fay, you burglar, I'll bet you've got twenty people like myself you milk for free ideas. First you irritate their bark and then you make the rounds every so often to draw off the latex or the maple gloop."

Fay smiled. "It ought to please you that society still has a use for you outre inner-directed types. It takes something to make a junior executive stay aboveground after dark, when the missiles are on the prowl."

"Society can't have much use for us or it'd pay us something," Gusterson sourly asserted, staring blankly at the tankless TV and kicking it lightly as he passed on.

"No, you're wrong about that, Gussy. Money's not the key goad with you inner-directeds. I got that straight from our Motivations chief."

"Did he tell you what we should use instead to pay the grocer? A deep inner sense of achievement, maybe? Fay, why should I do any free thinking for Micro Systems?"

"I'll tell you why, Gussy. Simply because you get a kick out of insulting us with sardonic ideas. If we take one of them seriously, you think we're degrading ourselves, and that pleases you even more. Like making someone laugh at a lousy pun."

Gusterson held still in his roaming and grinned. "That the reason, huh? I suppose my suggestions would have to be something in the line of ultra-subminiaturized computers, where one sinister fine-etched molecule does the work of three big bumbling brain cells?"

"Not necessarily. Micro Systems is branching out. Wheel as free as a rogue star. But I'll pass along to Promotion your one molecule-three brain cell sparkler. It's a slight exaggeration, but it's catchy."

"I'll have my kids watch your ads to see if you use it and then I'll sue the whole underworld." Gusterson frowned as he resumed his stalking. He stared puzzledly at the antique TV. "How about inventing a plutonium termite?" he said suddenly. "It would get rid of those stockpiles that are worrying you moles to death."

Fay grimaced noncommittally and cocked his head.

"Well, then, how about a beauty mask? How about that, hey? I don't mean one to repair a woman's complexion, but one she'd wear all the time that'd make her look like a 17-year-old sexpot. That'd end *her* worries."

"Hey, that's for me," Daisy called from the kitchen. "I'll make Gusterson suffer. I'll make him crawl around on his hands and knees begging my immature favors."

"No, you won't," Gusterson called back. "You having a face like that would scare the kids. Better cancel that one, Fay. Half the adult race looking like Vina Vidarsson is too awful a thought."

"Yah, you're just scared of making a million dollars," Daisy jeered.

"I sure am," Gusterson said solemnly, scanning the fuzzy floor from one murky glass wall to the other, hesitating at the TV. "How about something homey now, like a flock of little prickly cylinders that roll around the floor collecting lint and flub? They'd work by electricity, or at a pinch cats could bat 'em around. Every so often they'd be automatically herded together and the lint cleaned off the bristles."

"No good," Fay said. "There's no lint underground and cats are *verboten*. And the above-ground market doesn't amount to more moneywise than the state of Southern Illinois. Keep it grander, Gussy, and more impractical-you can't sell people merely useful ideas." From his hassock in the center of the room he looked uneasily around. "Say, did that violet tone in the glass come from the high Cleveland hydrogen bomb or is it just age and ultraviolet, like desert glass?"

"No, somebody's grandfather liked it that color," Gusterson informed him with happy bitterness. "I like it too-the glass, I mean, not the tint. People who live in glass houses can see the stars-especially when there's a window-washing streak in their germ-plasm."

"Gussy, why don't you move underground?" Fay asked, his voice taking on a missionary note. "It's a lot easier living in one room, believe me. You don't have to tramp from room to room hunting things."

"I like the exercise," Gusterson said stoutly.

"But I bet Daisy'd prefer it underground. And your kids wouldn't have to explain why their father lives like a Red Indian. Not to mention the safety factor and insurance savings and a crypt church within easy slidewalk distance. Incidentally, we see the stars all the time, better than you do-by repeater."

"Stars by repeater," Gusterson murmured to the ceiling, pausing for God to comment. Then, "No, Fay, even if I could afford it-and stand it —I'm such a bad-luck Harry that just when I got us all safely stowed at the N minus 1 sublevel, the Soviets would discover an earthquake bomb that struck from below, and I'd have to follow everybody back to the treetops. *Hey! How about bubble homes in orbit around earth?* Micro Systems could subdivide the world's most spacious suburb and all you moles could go ellipsing. Space is as safe as there is: no air, no shock waves. Free fall's the ultimate in restfulness-great health benefits. Commute by rocket-or better yet stay home and do all your business by TV-telephone, or by waldo if it were that sort of thing. Even pet your girl by remote control-she in her bubble, you in yours, whizzing through vacuum. Oh, damn-damn-*damn-damn*-DAMN!"

He was glaring at the blank screen of the TV, his big hands clenching and unclenching.

"Don't let Fay give you apoplexy-he's not worth it," Daisy said, sticking her trim head in from the kitchen, while Fay inquired anxiously, "Gussy, what's the matter?"

"Nothing, you worm!" Gusterson roared, "Except that an hour ago I forgot to tune in on the only TV program I've wanted to hear this year —*Finnegans Wake* scored for English, Gaelic and brogue. Oh, damn-*damn*-DAMN!"

"Too bad," Fay said lightly. "I didn't know they were releasing it on flat TV too."

"Well, they were! Some things are too damn big to keep completely underground. And I had to forget! I'm always doing it —I miss everything! Look here, you rat," he blatted suddenly at Fay, shaking his finger under the latter's chin, "I'll tell you what you can have that ignorant team of yours invent. They can fix me up a mechanical secretary that I can feed orders into and that'll remind me when the exact moment comes to listen to TV or phone somebody or mail in a story or write a letter or pick up a magazine or look at an eclipse or a new orbiting station or fetch the kids from school or buy Daisy a bunch of flowers or whatever it is. It's got to be something that's always with me, not something I have to go and consult or that I can get sick of and put down somewhere. And it's got to remind me forcibly enough so that I take notice and don't just shrug it aside, like I sometimes do even when Daisy reminds me of things. That's what your stupid team can invent for me! If they do a good job, I'll pay 'em as much as fifty dollars!"

"That doesn't sound like anything so very original to me," Fay commented coolly, leaning back from the wagging finger. "I think all senior executives have something of that sort. At least, their secretary keeps some kind of file...."

"I'm not looking for something with spiked falsies and nylons up to the neck," interjected Gusterson, whose ideas about secretaries were a trifle lurid. "I just want a mech reminder-that's all!"

"Well, I'll keep the idea in mind," Fay assured him, "along with the bubble homes and beauty masks. If we ever develop anything along those lines, I'll let you know. If it's a beauty mask, I'll bring Daisy a pilot model-to use to scare strange kids." He put his watch to his ear. "Good lord, I'm going to have to cut to make it underground before the main doors close. Just ten minutes to Second Curfew! 'By, Gus. 'By, Daze."

Two minutes later, living room lights out, they watched Fay's foreshortened antlike figure scurrying across the balding ill-lit park toward the nearest escalator.

Gusterson said, "Weird to think of that big bright space-poor glamor basement stretching around everywhere underneath. Did you remind Smitty to put a new bulb in the elevator?"

"The Smiths moved out this morning," Daisy said tonelessly. "They went underneath."

"Like cockroaches," Gusterson said. "Cockroaches leavin' a sinkin' apartment building. Next the ghosts'll be retreatin' to the shelters."

"Anyhow, from now on we're our own janitors," Daisy said.

He nodded. "Just leaves three families besides us loyal to this glass death trap. Not countin' ghosts." He sighed. Then, "You like to move below, Daisy?" he asked softly, putting his arm lightly across her shoulders. "Get a woozy eyeful of the bright lights and all for a change? Be a rat for a while? Maybe we're getting too old to be bats. I could scrounge me a company job and have a thinking closet all to myself and two secretaries with stainless steel breasts. Life'd be easier for you and a lot cleaner. And you'd sleep safer."

"That's true," she answered and paused. She ran her fingertip slowly across the murky glass, its violet tint barely perceptible against a cold dim light across the park. "But somehow," she said, snaking her arm around his waist, "I don't think I'd sleep happier-or one bit excited."

Three weeks later Fay, dropping in again, handed to Daisy the larger of the two rather small packages he was carrying.

"It's a so-called beauty mask," he told her, "complete with wig, eyelashes, and wettable velvet lips. It even breathes-pinholed elastiskin with a static adherence-charge. But Micro Systems had nothing to do with it, thank God. Beauty Trix put it on the market ten days ago and it's already started a teen-age craze. Some boys are wearing them too, and the police are yipping at Trix for encouraging transvestism with psychic repercussions."

"Didn't I hear somewhere that Trix is a secret subsidiary of Micro?" Gusterson demanded, rearing up from his ancient electric typewriter. "No, you're not stopping me writing, Fay-it's the gut of evening. If I do any more I won't have any juice to start with tomorrow. I got another of my insanity thrillers moving. A real id-teaser. In this one not only all the characters are crazy but the robot psychiatrist too."

"The vending machines are jumping with insanity novels," Fay commented. "Odd they're so popular."

Gusterson chortled. "The only way you outer-directed moles will accept individuality any more even in a fictional character, without your superegos getting seasick, is for them to be crazy. Hey, Daisy! Lemme see that beauty mask!"

But his wife, backing out of the room, hugged the package to her bosom and solemnly shook her head.

"A hell of a thing," Gusterson complained, "not even to be able to see what my stolen ideas look like."

"I got a present for you too," Fay said. "Something you might think of as a royalty on all the inventions someone thought of a little ahead of you. Fifty dollars by your own evaluation." He held out the smaller package. "Your tickler."

"My *what?*" Gusterson demanded suspiciously.

"Your tickler. The mech reminder you wanted. It turns out that the file a secretary keeps to remind her boss to do certain things at certain times is called a tickler file. So we named this a tickler. Here."

Gusterson still didn't touch the package. "You mean you actually put your invention team to work on that nonsense?"

"Well, what do you think? Don't be scared of it. Here, I'll show you."

As he unwrapped the package, Fay said, "It hasn't been decided yet whether we'll manufacture it commercially. If we do, I'll put through a voucher for you-for 'development consultation' or something like that. Sorry no royalty's possible. Davidson's squad had started to work up the identical idea three years ago, but it got shelved. I found it on a snoop through the closets. There! Looks rich, doesn't it?"

On the scarred black tabletop was a dully gleaming silvery object about the size and shape of a cupped hand with fingers merging. A tiny pellet on a short near-invisible wire led off from it. On the back was a punctured area suggesting the face of a microphone; there was also a window with a date and time in hours and minutes showing through and next to that four little buttons in a row. The concave underside of the silvery "hand" was smooth except for a central area where what looked like two little rollers came through.

"It goes on your shoulder under your shirt," Fay explained, "and you tuck the pellet in your ear. We might work up bone conduction on a commercial model. Inside is an ultra-slow fine-wire recorder holding a spool that runs for a week. The clock lets you go to any place on the 7-day wire and record a message. The buttons give you variable speed in going there, so you don't waste too much time making a setting. There's a knack in fingering them efficiently, but it's easily acquired."

Fay picked up the tickler. "For instance, suppose there's a TV show you want to catch tomorrow night at twenty-two hundred." He touched the buttons. There was the faintest whirring.

The clock face blurred briefly three times before showing the setting he'd mentioned. Then Fay spoke into the punctured area: "Turn on TV Channel Two, you big dummy!" He grinned over at Gusterson. "When you've got all your instructions to yourself loaded in, you synchronize with the present moment and let her roll. Fit it on your shoulder and forget it. Oh, yes, and it literally does tickle you every time it delivers an instruction. That's what the little rollers are for. Believe me, you can't ignore it. Come on, Gussy, take off your shirt and try it out. We'll feed in some instructions for the next ten minutes so you get the feel of how it works."

"I don't want to," Gusterson said. "Not right now. I want to sniff around it first. My God, it's small! Besides everything else it does, does it think?"

"Don't pretend to be an idiot, Gussy! You know very well that even with ultra-sub-micro nothing quite this small can possibly have enough elements to do any thinking."

Gusterson shrugged. "I don't know about that. I think bugs think."

Fay groaned faintly. "Bugs operate by instinct, Gussy," he said. "A patterned routine. They do not scan situations and consequences and then make decisions."

"I don't expect bugs to make decisions," Gusterson said. "For that matter I don't like people who go around alla time making decisions."

"Well, you can take it from me, Gussy, that this tickler is just a miniaturized wire recorder and clock...and a tickler. It doesn't do anything else."

"Not yet, maybe," Gusterson said darkly. "Not this model. Fay, I'm serious about bugs thinking. Or if they don't exactly think, they feel. They've got an interior drama. An inner glow. They're conscious. For that matter, Fay, I think all your really complex electronic computers are conscious too."

"Quit kidding, Gussy."

"Who's kidding?"

"You are. Computers simply aren't alive."

"What's alive? A word. I think computers are conscious, at least while they're operating. They've got that inner glow of awareness. They sort of...well...meditate."

"Gussy, computers haven't got any circuits for meditating. They're not programmed for mystical lucubrations. They've just got circuits for solving the problems they're on."

"Okay, you admit they've got problem-solving circuits-like a man has. I say if they've got the equipment for being conscious, they're conscious. What has wings, flies."

"Including stuffed owls and gilt eagles and dodoes-and wood-burning airplanes?"

"Maybe, under some circumstances. There *was* a wood-burning airplane. Fay," Gusterson continued, wagging his wrists for emphasis, "I really think computers are conscious. They just don't have any way of telling us that they are. Or maybe they don't have any *reason* to tell us, like the little Scotch boy who didn't say a word until he was fifteen and was supposed to be deaf and dumb."

"Why didn't he say a word?"

"Because he'd never had anything to say. Or take those Hindu fakirs, Fay, who sit still and don't say a word for thirty years or until their fingernails grow to the next village. If Hindu fakirs can do that, computers can!"

Looking as if he were masticating a lemon, Fay asked quietly, "Gussy, did you say you're working on an insanity novel?"

Gusterson frowned fiercely. "Now you're kidding," he accused Fay. "The dirty kind of kidding, too."

"I'm sorry," Fay said with light contrition. "Well, now you've sniffed at it, how about trying on Tickler?" He picked up the gleaming blunted crescent and jogged it temptingly under Gusterson's chin.

"Why should I?" Gusterson asked, stepping back. "Fay, I'm up to my ears writing a book. The last thing I want is something interrupting me to make me listen to a lot of junk and do a lot of useless things."

"But, dammit, Gussy! It was all your idea in the first place!" Fay blatted. Then, catching himself, he added, "I mean, you were one of the first people to think of this particular sort of instrument."

"Maybe so, but I've done some more thinking since then." Gusterson's voice grew a trifle solemn. "Inner-directed worthwhile thinkin'. Fay, when a man forgets to do something, it's because he really doesn't want to do it or because he's all roiled up down in his unconscious. He ought to take it as a danger signal and investigate the roiling, not hire himself a human or mech reminder."

"Bushwa," Fay retorted. "In that case you shouldn't write memorandums or even take notes."

"Maybe I shouldn't," Gusterson agreed lamely. "I'd have to think that over too."

"Ha!" Fay jeered. "No, I'll tell you what your trouble is, Gussy. You're simply scared of this contraption. You've loaded your skull with horror-story nonsense about machines sprouting minds and taking over the world-until you're even scared of a simple miniaturized and clocked recorder." He thrust it out.

"Maybe I am," Gusterson admitted, controlling a flinch. "Honestly, Fay, that thing's got a gleam in its eye as if it had ideas of its own. Nasty ideas."

"Gussy, you nut, it hasn't *got* an eye."

"Not now, no, but it's got the gleam-the eye may come. It's the Cheshire cat in reverse. If you'd step over here and look at yourself holding it, you could see what I mean. But I don't think computers *sprout* minds, Fay. I just think they've *got* minds, because they've got the mind elements."

"Ho, ho!" Fay mocked. "Everything that has a material side has a mental side," he chanted. "Everything that's a body is also a spirit. Gussy, that dubious old metaphysical dualism went out centuries ago."

"Maybe so," Gusterson said, "but we still haven't anything but that dubious dualism to explain the human mind, have we? It's a jelly of nerve cells and it's a vision of the cosmos. If that isn't dualism, what is?"

"I give up. Gussy, are you going to try out this tickler?"

"No!"

"But dammit, Gussy, we made it just for you! —practically."

"Sorry, but I'm not coming near the thing."

"Zen come near me," a husky voice intoned behind them. "Tonight I vant a man."

Standing in the door was something slim in a short silver sheath. It had golden bangs and the haughtiest snub-nosed face in the world. It slunk toward them.

"My God, Vina Vidarsson!" Gusterson yelled.

"Daisy, that's terrific," Fay applauded, going up to her.

She bumped him aside with a swing of her hips, continuing to advance. "Not you, Ratty," she said throatily. "I vant a real man."

"Fay, I suggested Vina Vidarsson's face for the beauty mask," Gusterson said, walking around his wife and shaking a finger. "Don't tell me Trix just happened to think of that too."

"What else could they think of?" Fay laughed. "This season sex means VV and nobody else." An odd little grin flicked his lips, a tic traveled up his face and his body twitched slightly. "Say, folks, I'm going to have to be leaving. It's exactly fifteen minutes to Second Curfew. Last time I had to run and I got heartburn. When *are* you people going to move downstairs? I'll leave Tickler, Gussy. Play around with it and get used to it. 'By now."

"Hey, Fay," Gusterson called curiously, "have you developed absolute time sense?"

Fay grinned a big grin from the doorway-almost too big a grin for so small a man. "I didn't need to," he said softly, patting his right shoulder. "My tickler told me."

He closed the door behind him.

As side-by-side they watched him strut sedately across the murky chilly-looking park, Guster-son mused, "So the little devil had one of those nonsense-gadgets on all the time and I never no-ticed. Can you beat that?" Something drew across the violet-tinged stars a short bright line that quickly faded. "What's that?" Gusterson asked gloomily. "Next to last stage of missile-here?"

"Won't you settle for an old-fashioned shooting star?" Daisy asked softly. The (wettable) velvet lips of the mask made even her natural voice sound different. She reached a hand back of her neck to pull the thing off.

"Hey, don't do that," Gusterson protested in a hurt voice. "Not for a while anyway."

"Hokay!" she said harshly, turning on him. "Zen down on your knees, dog!"

III

It was a fortnight and Gusterson was loping down the home stretch on his 40,000-word insanity novel before Fay dropped in again, this time promptly at high noon.

Normally Fay cringed his shoulders a trifle and was inclined to slither, but now he strode aggressively, his legs scissoring in a fast, low goosestep. He whipped off the sunglasses that all moles wore topside by day and began to pound Gusterson on the back while calling boisterously, "How are you, Gussy Old Boy, Old Boy?"

Daisy came in from the kitchen to see why Gusterson was choking. She was instantly grabbed and violently bussed to the accompaniment of, "Hiya, Gorgeous! Yum-yum! How about ad-libbing that some weekend?"

She stared at Fay dazedly, rasping the back of her hand across her mouth, while Gusterson yelled, "Quit that! What's got into you, Fay? Have they transferred you out of R & D to Company Morale? Do they line up all the secretaries at roll call and make you give them an eight-hour energizing kiss?"

"Ha, wouldn't you like to know?" Fay retorted. He grinned, twitched jumpingly, held still a moment, then hustled over to the far wall. "Look out there," he rapped, pointing through the violet glass at a gap between the two nearest old skyscraper apartments. "In thirty seconds you'll see them test the new needle bomb at the other end of Lake Erie. It's educational." He began to count off seconds, vigorously semaphoring his arm. "...Two...three...Gussy, I've put through a voucher for two yards for you. Budgeting squawked, but I pressured 'em."

Daisy squealed, "Yards! —are those dollar thousands?" while Gusterson was asking, "Then you're marketing the tickler?"

"Yes. Yes," Fay replied to them in turn. "...Nine...ten..." Again he grinned and twitched. "Time for noon Com-staff," he announced staccato. "Pardon the hush box." He whipped a pancake phone from under his coat, clapped it over his face and spoke fiercely but inaudibly into it, continuing to semaphore. Suddenly he thrust the phone away. "Twenty-nine...thirty... Thar she blows!"

An incandescent streak shot up the sky from a little above the far horizon and a doubly dazzling point of light appeared just above the top of it, with the effect of God dotting an "i".

"Ha, that'll skewer espionage satellites like swatting flies!" Fay proclaimed as the portent faded. "Bracing! Gussy, where's your tickler? I've got a new spool for it that'll razzle-dazzle you."

"I'll bet," Gusterson said drily. "Daisy?"

"You gave it to the kids and they got to fooling with it and broke it."

"No matter," Fay told them with a large sidewise sweep of his hand. "Better you wait for the new model. It's a six-way improvement."

"So I gather," Gusterson said, eyeing him speculatively. "Does it automatically inject you with cocaine? A fix every hour on the second?"

"Ha-ha, joke. Gussy, it achieves the same effect without using any dope at all. Listen: a tickler reminds you of your duties and opportunities-your chances for happiness and success! What's the obvious next step?"

"Throw it out the window. By the way, how do you do that when you're underground?"

"We have hi-speed garbage boosts. The obvious next step is you give the tickler a heart. It not only tells you, it warmly persuades you. It doesn't just say, 'Turn on the TV Channel Two, Joyce program,' it *brills* at you, 'Kid, Old Kid, race for the TV and flip that Two Switch! There's a great show coming through the pipes this second plus ten-you'll enjoy the hell out of yourself! Grab a ticket to ecstasy!'"

"My God," Gusterson gasped, "are those the kind of jolts it's giving you now?"

"Don't you get it, Gussy? You never load your tickler except when you're feeling buoyantly enthusiastic. You don't just tell yourself what to do hour by hour next week, you sell yourself on it. That way you not only make doubly sure you'll obey instructions but you constantly reinoculate yourself with your own enthusiasm."

"I can't stand myself when I'm that enthusiastic," Gusterson said. "I feel ashamed for hours afterwards."

"You're warped-all this lonely sky-life. What's more, Gussy, think how still more persuasive some of those instructions would be if they came to a man in his best girl's most bedroomy voice, or his doctor's or psycher's if it's that sort of thing-or Vina Vidarsson's! By the way, Daze, don't wear that beauty mask outside. It's a grand misdemeanor ever since ten thousand teen-agers rioted through Tunnel-Mart wearing them. And VV's sueing Trix."

"No chance of that," Daisy said. "Gusterson got excited and bit off the nose." She pinched her own delicately.

"I'd no more obey my enthusiastic self," Gusterson was brooding, "than I'd obey a Napoleon drunk on his own brandy or a hopped-up St. Francis. Reinoculated with my own enthusiasm? I'd die just like from snake-bite!"

"Warped, I said," Fay dogmatized, stamping around. "Gussy, having the instructions persuasive instead of neutral turned out to be only the opening wedge. The next step wasn't so obvious, but I saw it. Using subliminal verbal stimuli in his tickler, a man can be given constant supportive euphoric therapy 24 hours a day! And it makes use of all that empty wire. We've revived the ideas of a pioneer dynamic psycher named Dr. Coué. For instance, right now my tickler is saying to me-in tones too soft to reach my conscious mind, but do they stab into the unconscious! —'Day by day in every way I'm getting sharper and sharper.' It alternates that with 'gutsier and gutsier' and...well, forget that. Coué mostly used 'better and better' but that seems too general. And every hundredth time it says them out loud and the tickler gives me a brush-just a faint cootch-to make sure I'm keeping in touch."

"That third word-pair," Daisy wondered, feeling her mouth reminiscently. "Could I guess?"

Gusterson's eyes had been growing wider and wider. "Fay," he said, "I could no more use my mind for anything if I knew all that was going on in my inner ear than if I were being brushed down with brooms by three witches. Look here," he said with loud authority, "you got to stop all this-it's crazy. Fay, if Micro'll junk the tickler, I'll think you up something else to invent-something real good."

"Your inventing days are over," Fay brilled gleefully. "I mean, you'll never equal your masterpiece."

"How about," Gusterson bellowed, "an anti-individual guided missile? The physicists have got small-scale antigravity good enough to float and fly something the size of a hand grenade. I can smell that even though it's a back-of-the-safe military secret. Well, how about keying such a missile to a man's finger-prints —or brainwaves, maybe, or his unique smell! —so it can spot and follow him around then target in on him, without harming anyone else? Long-distance assassination-and the stinkingest gets it! Or you could simply load it with some disgusting goo and key it to teen-agers as a group-that'd take care of them. Fay, doesn't it give you a rich warm kick to think of my midget missiles buzzing around in your tunnels, seeking out evil-doers, like a swarm of angry wasps or angelic bumblebees?"

"You're not luring me down any side trails," Fay said laughingly. He grinned and twitched, then hurried toward the opposite wall, motioning them to follow. Outside, about a hundred yards beyond the purple glass, rose another ancient glass-walled apartment skyscraper. Beyond, Lake Erie rippled glintingly.

"Another bomb-test?" Gusterson asked.

Fay pointed at the building. "Tomorrow," he announced, "a modern factory, devoted solely to the manufacture of ticklers, will be erected on that site."

"You mean one of those windowless phallic eyesores?" Gusterson demanded. "Fay, you people aren't even consistent. You've got all your homes underground. Why not your factories?"

"Sh! Not enough room. And night missiles are scarier."

"I know that building's been empty for a year," Daisy said uneasily, "but how —?"

"Sh! Watch! *Now!*"

The looming building seemed to blur or fuzz for a moment. Then it was as if the lake's bright ripples had invaded the old glass a hundred yards away. Wavelets chased themselves up and down the gleaming walls, became higher, higher...and then suddenly the glass cracked all over to tiny fragments and fell away, to be followed quickly by fragmented concrete and plastic and plastic piping, until all that was left was the nude steel framework, vibrating so rapidly as to be almost invisible against the gleaming lake.

Daisy covered her ears, but there was no explosion, only a long-drawn-out low crash as the fragments hit twenty floors below and dust whooshed out sideways.

"Spectacular!" Fay summed up. "Knew you'd enjoy it. That little trick was first conceived by the great Tesla during his last fruity years. Research discovered it in his biog-we just made the dream come true. A tiny resonance device you could carry in your belt-bag attunes itself to the natural harmonic of a structure and then increases amplitude by tiny pushes exactly in time. Just like soldiers marching in step can break down a bridge, only this is as if it were being done by one marching ant." He pointed at the naked framework appearing out of its own blur and said, "We'll be able to hang the factory on that. If not, we'll whip a mega-current through it and vaporize it. No question the micro-resonator is the neatest sweetest wrecking device going. You can expect a lot more of this sort of efficiency now that mankind has the tickler to enable him to use his full potential. What's the matter, folks?"

Daisy was staring around the violet-walled room with dumb mistrust. Her hands were trembling.

"You don't have to worry," Fay assured her with an understanding laugh. "This building's safe for a month more at least." Suddenly he grimaced and leaped a foot in the air. He raised a clawed hand to scratch his shoulder but managed to check the movement. "Got to beat it, folks," he announced tersely. "My tickler gave me the grand cootch."

"Don't go yet," Gusterson called, rousing himself with a shudder which he immediately explained: "I just had the illusion that if I shook myself all my flesh and guts would fall off my shimmying skeleton, Brr! Fay, before you and Micro go off half cocked, I want you to know there's one insuperable objection to the tickler as a mass-market item. The average man or woman won't go to the considerable time and trouble it must take to load a tickler. He simply hasn't got the compulsive orderliness and willingness to plan that it requires."

"We thought of that weeks ago," Fay rapped, his hand on the door. "Every tickler spool that goes to market is patterned like wallpaper with one of five designs of suitable subliminal supportive euphoric material. 'Ittier and ittier,' 'viriler and viriler' —you know. The buyer is robot-interviewed for an hour, his personalized daily routine laid out and thereafter templated on his weekly spool. He's strongly urged next to take his tickler to his doctor and psycher for further instruction-imposition. We've been working with the medical profession from the start. They love the tickler because it'll remind people to take their medicine on the dot...and rest and eat and go to sleep just when and how doc says. This is a big operation, Gussy —a biiiiiig operation! 'By!"

Daisy hurried to the wall to watch him cross the park. Deep down she was a wee bit worried that he might linger to attach a micro-resonator to *this* building and she wanted to time him. But Gusterson settled down to his typewriter and began to bat away.

"I want to have another novel started," he explained to her, "before the ant marches across this building in about four and a half weeks...or a million sharp little gutsy guys come swarming out of the ground and heave it into Lake Erie."

Early next morning windowless walls began to crawl up the stripped skyscraper between them and the lake. Daisy pulled the black-out curtains on that side. For a day or two longer their thoughts and conversations were haunted by Gusterson's vague sardonic visions of a horde of tickler-energized moles pouring up out of the tunnels to tear down the remaining trees, tank the atmosphere and perhaps somehow dismantle the stars-at least on this side of the world-but then they both settled back into their customary easy-going routines. Gusterson typed. Daisy made her daily shopping trip to a little topside daytime store and started painting a mural on the floor of the empty apartment next theirs but one.

"We ought to lasso some neighbors," she suggested once. "I need somebody to hold my brushes and admire. How about you making a trip below at the cocktail hours, Gusterson, and picking up a couple of girls for a starter? Flash the old viriler charm, cootch them up a bit, emphasize the delights of high living, but make sure they're compatible roommates. You could pick up that two-yard check from Micro at the same time."

"You're an immoral money-ravenous wench," Gusterson said absently, trying to dream of an insanity beyond insanity that would make his next novel a real id-rousing best-vender.

"If that's your vision of me, you shouldn't have chewed up the VV mask."

"I'd really prefer you with green stripes," he told her. "But stripes, spots, or sun-bathing, you're better than those cocktail moles."

Actually both of them acutely disliked going below. They much preferred to perch in their eyrie and watch the people of Cleveland Depths, as they privately called the local sub-suburb, rush up out of the shelters at dawn to work in the concrete fields and windowless factories, make their daytime jet trips and freeway jaunts, do their noon-hour and coffee-break guerrilla practice, and then go scurrying back at twilight to the atomic-proof, brightly lit, vastly exciting, claustrophobic caves.

Fay and his projects began once more to seem dreamlike, though Gusterson did run across a cryptic advertisement for ticklers in *The Manchester Guardian*, which he got daily by facsimile. Their three children reported similar ads, of no interest to young fry, on the TV and one afternoon they came home with the startling news that the monitors at their subsurface school had been issued ticklers. On sharp interrogation by Gusterson, however, it appeared that these last were not ticklers but merely two-way radios linked to the school police station transmitter.

"Which is bad enough," Gusterson commented later to Daisy. "But it'd be even dirtier to think of those clock-watching superegos being strapped to kids' shoulders. Can you imagine Huck Finn with a tickler, tellin' him when to tie up the raft to a tow-head and when to take a swim?"

"I bet Fay could," Daisy countered. "When's he going to bring you that check, anyhow? Iago wants a jetcycle and I promised Imogene a Vina Kit and then Claudius'll have to have something."

Gusterson scowled thoughtfully. "You know, Daze," he said, "I got a feeling Fay's in the hospital, all narcotized up and being fed intravenously. The way he was jumping around last time, that tickler was going to cootch him to pieces in a week."

As if to refute this intuition, Fay turned up that very evening. The lights were dim. Something had gone wrong with the building's old transformer and, pending repairs, the two remaining occupied apartments were making do with batteries, which turned bright globes to mysterious amber candles and made Gusterson's ancient typewriter operate sluggishly.

Fay's manner was subdued or at least closely controlled and for a moment Gusterson thought he'd shed his tickler. Then the little man came out of the shadows and Gusterson saw the large bulge on his right shoulder.

"Yes, we had to up it a bit sizewise," Fay explained in clipped tones. "Additional super-features. While brilliantly successful on the whole, the subliminal euphorics were a shade too effective. Several hundred users went hoppity manic. We gentled the cootch and qualified the subliminals-you know, 'Day by day in every way I'm getting sharper *and more serene*' —but a stabilizing influence was still needed, so after a top-level conference we decided to combine Tickler with Moodmaster."

"My God," Gusterson interjected, "do they have a machine now that does that?"

"Of course. They've been using them on ex-mental patients for years."

"I just don't keep up with progress," Gusterson said, shaking his head bleakly. "I'm falling behind on all fronts."

"You ought to have your tickler remind you to read Science Service releases," Fay told him. "Or simply instruct it to scan the releases and-no, that's still in research." He looked at Gusterson's shoulder and his eyes widened. "You're not wearing the new-model tickler I sent you," he said accusingly.

"I never got it," Gusterson assured him. "Postmen deliver top-side mail and parcels by throwing them on the high-speed garbage boosts and hoping a tornado will blow them to the right addresses." Then he added helpfully, "Maybe the Russians stole it while it was riding the whirlwinds."

"That's not a suitable topic for jesting," Fay frowned. "We're hoping that Tickler will mobilize the full potential of the Free World for the first time in history. Gusterson, you are going to have to wear a ticky-tick. It's becoming impossible for a man to get through modern life without one."

"Maybe I will," Gusterson said appeasingly, "but right now tell me about Moodmaster. I want to put it in my new insanity novel."

Fay shook his head. "Your readers will just think you're behind the times. If you use it, underplay it. But anyhow, Moodmaster is a simple physiotherapy engine that monitors bloodstream chemicals and body electricity. It ties directly into the bloodstream, keeping blood, sugar, et cetera, at optimum levels and injecting euphrin or depressin as necessary-and occasionally a touch of extra adrenaline, as during work emergencies."

"Is it painful?" Daisy called from the bedroom.

"Excruciating," Gusterson called back. "Excuse it, please," he grinned at Fay. "Hey, didn't I suggest cocaine injections last time I saw you?"

"So you did," Fay agreed flatly. "Oh by the way, Gussy, here's that check for a yard I promised you. Micro doesn't muzzle the ox."

"Hooray!" Daisy cheered faintly.

"I thought you said it was going to be for two." Gusterson complained.

"Budgeting always forces a last-minute compromise," Fay shrugged. "You have to learn to accept those things."

"I love accepting money and I'm glad any time for three feet," Daisy called agreeably. "Six feet might make me wonder if I weren't an insect, but getting a yard just makes me feel like a gangster's moll."

"Want to come out and gloat over the yard paper, Toots, and stuff it in your diamond-embroidered net stocking top?" Gusterson called back.

"No, I'm doing something to that portion of me just now. But hang onto the yard, Gusterson."

"Aye-aye, Cap'n," he assured her. Then, turning back to Fay, "So you've taken the Dr. Coué repeating out of the tickler?"

"Oh, no. Just balanced it off with depressin. The subliminals are still a prime sales-point. All the tickler features are cumulative, Gussy. You're still underestimating the scope of the device."

"I guess I am. What's this 'work-emergencies' business? If you're using the tickler to inject drugs into workers to keep them going, that's really just my cocaine suggestion modernized and I'm putting in for another thou. Hundreds of years ago the South American Indians chewed coca leaves to kill fatigue sensations."

"That so? Interesting-and it proves priority for the Indians, doesn't it? I'll make a try for you, Gussy, but don't expect anything." He cleared his throat, his eyes grew distant and, turning his head a little to the right, he enunciated sharply, "Pooh-Bah. Time: Inst oh five. One oh five seven. Oh oh. Record: Gussy coca thou budget. Cut." He explained, "We got a voice-cued setter now on the deluxe models. You can record a memo to yourself without taking off your shirt. Incidentally, I use the ends of the hours for trifle-memos. I've already used up the fifty-nines and eights for tomorrow and started on the fifty-sevens."

"I understood most of your memo," Gusterson told him gruffly. "The last 'Oh oh' was for seconds, wasn't it? Now I call that crude-why not microseconds too? But how do you remember where you've made a memo so you don't rerecord over it? After all, you're rerecording over the wallpaper all the time."

"Tickler beeps and then hunts for the nearest information-free space."

"I see. And what's the Pooh-Bah for?"

Fay smiled. "Cut. My password for activating the setter, so it won't respond to chance numerals it overhears."

"But why Pooh-Bah?"

Fay grinned. "Cut. And you a writer. It's a literary reference, Gussy. Pooh-Bah (cut!) was Lord High Everything Else in *The Mikado*. He had a little list and nothing on it would ever be missed."

"Oh, yeah," Gusterson remembered, glowering. "As I recall it, all that went on that list was the names of people who were slated to have their heads chopped off by Ko-Ko. Better watch your step, Shorty. It may be a back-handed omen. Maybe all those workers you're puttin' ticklers on to pump them full of adrenaline so they'll overwork without noticin' it will revolt and come out some day choppin' for your head."

"Spare me the Marxist mythology," Fay protested. "Gussy, you've got a completely wrong slant on Tickler. It's true that most of our mass sales so far, bar government and army, have been to large companies purchasing for their employees —"

"Ah-ha!"

" —but that's because there's nothing like a tickler for teaching a new man his job. It tells him from instant to instant what he must do-while he's already on the job and without disturbing other workers. Magnetizing a wire with a job pattern is the easiest thing going. And you'd be astonished what the subliminals do for employee morale. It's this way, Gussy: most people are too improvident and unimaginative to see in advance the advantages of ticklers. They buy one because the company strongly suggests it and payment is on easy installments withheld from salary. They find a tickler makes the work day go easier. The little fellow perched on your shoulder is a friend exuding comfort and good advice. The first thing he's set to say is 'Take it easy, pal.'"

"Within a week they're wearing their tickler 24 hours a day-and buying a tickler for the wife, so she'll remember to comb her hair and smile real pretty and cook favorite dishes."

"I get it, Fay," Gusterson cut in. "The tickler is the newest fad for increasing worker efficiency. Once, I read somewheres, it was salt tablets. They had salt-tablet dispensers everywhere, even in air-conditioned offices where there wasn't a moist armpit twice a year and the gals sweat only champagne. A decade later people wondered what all those dusty white pills were for. Sometimes they were mistook for tranquilizers. It'll be the same way with ticklers. Somebody'll open a musty closet and see jumbled heaps of these gripping-hand silvery gadgets gathering dust curls and —"

"They will not!" Fay protested vehemently. "Ticklers are not a fad-they're history-changers, they're Free-World revolutionary! Why, before Micro Systems put a single one on the market, we'd made it a rule that every Micro employee had to wear one! If that's not having supreme confidence in a product —"

"Every employee except the top executives, of course," Gusterson interrupted jeeringly. "And that's not demoting you, Fay. As the R & D chief most closely involved, you'd naturally have to show special enthusiasm."

"But you're wrong there, Gussy," Fay crowed. "Man for man, our top executives have been more enthusiastic about their personal ticklers than any other class of worker in the whole outfit."

Gusterson slumped and shook his head. "If that's the case," he said darkly, "maybe mankind deserves the tickler."

"I'll say it does!" Fay agreed loudly without thinking. Then, "Oh, can the carping, Gussy. Tickler's a great invention. Don't deprecate it just because you had something to do with its genesis. You're going to have to get in the swim and wear one."

"Maybe I'd rather drown horribly."

"Can the gloom-talk too! Gussy, I said it before and I say it again, you're just scared of this new thing. Why, you've even got the drapes pulled so you won't have to look at the tickler factory."

"Yes, I am scared," Gusterson said. "Really sca...AWP!"

Fay whirled around. Daisy was standing in the bedroom doorway, wearing the short silver sheath. This time there was no mask, but her bobbed hair was glitteringly silvered, while her legs, arms, hands, neck, face-every bit of her exposed skin-was painted with beautifully even vertical green stripes.

"I did it as a surprise for Gusterson," she explained to Fay. "He says he likes me this way. The green glop's supposed to be smudgeproof."

Gusterson did not comment. His face had a rapt expression. "I'll tell you why your tickler's so popular, Fay," he said softly. "It's not because it backstops the memory or because it boosts the ego with subliminals. It's because it takes the hook out of a guy, it takes over the job of withstanding the pressure of living. See, Fay, here are all these little guys in this subterranean rat race with atomic-death squares and chromium-plated reward squares and enough money if you pass Go almost to get to Go again-and a million million rules of the game to keep in mind. Well, here's this one little guy and every morning he wakes up there's all these things he's got to keep in mind to do or he'll lose his turn three times in a row and maybe a terrible black rook in iron armor'll loom up and bang him off the chessboard. But now, look, now he's got his tickler and he tells his sweet silver tickler all these things and the tickler's got to remember them. Of course he'll have to do them eventually but meanwhile the pressure's off him, the hook's out of his short hairs. He's shifted the responsibility...."

"Well, what's so bad about that?" Fay broke in loudly. "What's wrong with taking the pressure off little guys? Why shouldn't Tickler be a super-ego surrogate? Micro's Motivations chief noticed that positive feature straight off and scored it three pluses. Besides, it's nothing but a gaudy way of saying that Tickler backstops the memory. Seriously, Gussy, what's so bad about it?"

"I don't know," Gusterson said slowly, his eyes still far away. "I just know it feels bad to me." He crinkled his big forehead. "Well for one thing," he said, "it means that a man's taking orders from something else. He's got a kind of master. He's sinking back into a slave psychology."

"He's only taking orders from himself," Fay countered disgustedly. "Tickler's just a mech reminder, a notebook, in essence no more than the back of an old envelope. It's no master."

"Are you absolutely sure of that?" Gusterson asked quietly.

"Why, Gussy, you big oaf—" Fay began heatedly. Suddenly his features quirked and he twitched. "'Scuse me, folks," he said rapidly, heading for the door, "but my tickler told me I gotta go."

"Hey Fay, don't you mean you told your tickler to tell you when it was time to go?" Gusterson called after him.

Fay looked back in the doorway. He wet his lips, his eyes moved from side to side. "I'm not quite sure," he said in an odd strained voice and darted out.

Gusterson stared for some seconds at the pattern of emptiness Fay had left. Then he shivered. Then he shrugged. "I must be slipping," he muttered. "I never even suggested something for him to invent." Then he looked around at Daisy, who was still standing poker-faced in her doorway.

"Hey, you look like something out of the Arabian Nights," he told her. "Are you supposed to be anything special? How far do those stripes go, anyway?"

"You could probably find out," she told him coolly. "All you have to do is kill me a dragon or two first."

He studied her. "My God," he said reverently, "I really have all the fun in life. What do I do to deserve this?"

"You've got a big gun," she told him, "and you go out in the world with it and hold up big companies and take yards and yards of money away from them in rolls like ribbon and bring it all home to me."

"Don't say that about the gun again," he said. "Don't whisper it, don't even think it. I've got one, dammit-thirty-eight caliber, yet-and I don't want some psionic monitor with two-way clairaudience they haven't told me about catching the whisper and coming to take the gun away from us. It's one of the few individuality symbols we've got left."

Suddenly Daisy whirled away from the door, spun three times so that her silvered hair stood out like a metal coolie hat, and sank to a curtsey in the middle of the room.

"I've just thought of what I am," she announced, fluttering her eyelashes at him. "I'm a sweet silver tickler with green stripes."

V

Next day Daisy cashed the Micro check for ten hundred silver smackers, which she hid in a broken radionic coffee urn. Gusterson sold his insanity novel and started a new one about a mad medic with a hiccupy hysterical chuckle, who gimmicked Moodmasters to turn mental patients into nymphomaniacs, mass murderers and compulsive saints. But this time he couldn't get Fay out of his mind, or the last chilling words the nervous little man had spoken.

For that matter, he couldn't blank the underground out of his mind as effectively as usually. He had the feeling that a new kind of mole was loose in the burrows and that the ground at the foot of their skyscraper might start humping up any minute.

Toward the end of one afternoon he tucked a half dozen newly typed sheets in his pocket, shrouded his typer, went to the hatrack and took down his prize: a miner's hard-top cap with electric headlamp.

"Goin' below, Cap'n," he shouted toward the kitchen.

"Be back for second dog watch," Daisy replied. "Remember what I told you about lassoing me some art-conscious girl neighbors."

"Only if I meet a piebald one with a taste for Scotch-or maybe a pearl gray biped jaguar with violet spots," Gusterson told her, clapping on the cap with a We-Who-Are-About-To-Die gesture.

Halfway across the park to the escalator bunker Gusterson's heart began to tick. He resolutely switched on his headlamp.

As he'd known it would, the hatch robot whirred an extra and higher-pitched ten seconds when it came to his topside address, but it ultimately dilated the hatch for him, first handing him a claim check for his ID card.

Gusterson's heart was ticking like a sledgehammer by now. He hopped clumsily onto the escalator, clutched the moving guard rail to either side, then shut his eyes as the steps went over the edge and became what felt like vertical. An instant later he forced his eyes open, unclipped a hand from the rail and touched the second switch beside his headlamp, which instantly began to blink whitely, as if he were a civilian plane flying into a nest of military jobs.

With a further effort he kept his eyes open and flinchingly surveyed the scene around him. After zigging through a bombproof half-furlong of roof, he was dropping into a large twilit cave. The blue-black ceiling twinkled with stars. The walls were pierced at floor level by a dozen archways with busy niche stores and glowing advertisements crowded between them. From the archways some three dozen slidewalks curved out, tangenting off each other in a bewildering multiple cloverleaf. The slidewalks were packed with people, traveling motionless like purposeful statues or pivoting with practiced grace from one slidewalk to another, like a thousand toreros doing veronicas.

The slidewalks were moving faster than he recalled from his last venture underground and at the same time the whole pedestrian concourse was quieter than he remembered. It was as if the five thousand or so moles in view were all listening-for what? But there was something else that had changed about them —a change that he couldn't for a moment define, or unconsciously didn't want to. Clothing style? No...My God, they weren't all wearing identical monster masks? No...Hair color?...Well....

He was studying them so intently that he forgot his escalator was landing. He came off it with a heel-jarring stumble and bumped into a knot of four men on the tiny triangular hold-still. These four at least sported a new style-wrinkle: ribbed gray shoulder-capes that made them look as if their heads were poking up out of the center of bulgy umbrellas or giant mushrooms.

One of them grabbed hold of Gusterson and saved him from staggering onto a slidewalk that might have carried him to Toledo.

"Gussy, you dog, you must have esped I wanted to see you," Fay cried, patting him on the elbows. "Meet Davidson and Kester and Hazen, colleagues of mine. We're all Micro-men." Fay's companions were staring strangely at Gusterson's blinking headlamp. Fay explained rapidly, "Mr. Gusterson is an insanity novelist. You know, I-D."

"Inner-directed spells *id*," Gusterson said absently, still staring at the interweaving crowd beyond them, trying to figure out what made them different from last trip. "Creativity fuel. Cranky. Explodes through the parietal fissure if you look at it cross-eyed."

"Ha-ha," Fay laughed. "Well, boys, I've found my man. How's the new novel perking, Gussy?"

"Got my climax, I think," Gusterson mumbled, still peering puzzledly around Fay at the slide-standers. "Moodmaster's going to come alive. Ever occur to you that 'mood' is 'doom' spelled backwards? And then...." He let his voice trail off as he realized that Kester and Davidson and Hazen had made their farewells and were sliding into the distance. He reminded himself wryly that nobody ever wants to hear an author talk-he's much too good a listener to be wasted that way. Let's see, was it that everybody in the crowd had the same facial expression...? Or showed symptoms of the same disease...?

"I was coming to visit you, but now you can pay me a call," Fay was saying. "There are two matters I want to —"

Gusterson stiffened. "My God, *they're all hunchbacked!*" he yelled.

"Shh! Of course they are," Fay whispered reprovingly. "They're all wearing their ticklers. But you don't need to be insulting about it."

"*I'm gettin' out o' here.*" Gusterson turned to flee as if from five thousand Richard the Thirds.

"Oh no you're not," Fay amended, drawing him back with one hand. Somehow, underground, the little man seemed to carry more weight. "You're having cocktails in my thinking box. Besides, climbing a down escaladder will give you a heart attack."

In his home habitat Gusterson was about as easy to handle as a rogue rhinoceros, but away from it-and especially if underground-he became more like a pliable elephant. All his bones dropped out through his feet, as he described it to Daisy. So now he submitted miserably as Fay surveyed him up and down, switched off his blinking headlamp ("That coalminer caper is corny, Gussy.") and then-surprisingly-rapidly stuffed his belt-bag under the right shoulder of Gusterson's coat and buttoned the latter to hold it in place.

"So you won't stand out," he explained. Another swift survey. "You'll do. Come on, Gussy. I got lots to brief you on." Three rapid paces and then Gusterson's feet would have gone out from under him except that Fay gave him a mighty shove. The small man sprang onto the slidewalk after him and then they were skimming effortlessly side by side.

Gusterson felt frightened and twice as hunchbacked as the slidestanders around him-morally as well as physically.

Nevertheless he countered bravely, "I got things to brief *you* on. I got six pages of cautions on ti —"

"Shh!" Fay stopped him. "Let's use my hushbox."

He drew out his pancake phone and stretched it so that it covered both their lower faces, like a double yashmak. Gusterson, his neck pushing into the ribbed bulge of the shoulder cape so he could be cheek to cheek with Fay, felt horribly conspicuous, but then he noticed that none of the slidestanders were paying them the least attention. The reason for their abstraction occurred to him. They were listening to their ticklers! He shuddered.

"I got six pages of caution on ticklers," he repeated into the hot, moist quiet of the pancake phone. "I typed 'em so I wouldn't forget 'em in the heat of polemicking. I want you to read every word. Fay, I've had it on my mind ever since I started wondering whether it was you or your tickler made you duck out of our place last time you were there. I want you to —"

"Ha-ha! All in good time." In the pancake phone Fay's laugh was brassy. "But I'm glad you've decided to lend a hand, Gussy. This thing is moving faaaasst. Nationwise, adult underground ticklerization is 90 per cent complete."

"I don't believe that," Gusterson protested while glaring at the hunchbacks around them. The slidewalk was gliding down a low glow-ceiling tunnel lined with doors and advertisements.

Rapt-eyed people were pirouetting on and off. "A thing just can't develop that fast, Fay. It's against nature."

"Ha, but we're not in nature, we're in culture. The progress of an industrial scientific culture is geometric. It goes n-times as many jumps as it takes. More than geometric-exponential. Confidentially, Micro's Math chief tells me we're currently on a fourth-power progress curve trending into a fifth."

"You mean we're goin' so fast we got to watch out we don't bump ourselves in the rear when we come around again?" Gusterson asked, scanning the tunnel ahead for curves. "Or just shoot straight up to infinity?"

"Exactly! Of course most of the last power and a half is due to Tickler itself. Gussy, the tickler's already eliminated absenteeism, alcoholism and aboulia in numerous urban areas-and that's just one letter of the alphabet! If Tickler doesn't turn us into a nation of photo-memory constant-creative-flow geniuses in six months, I'll come live topside."

"You mean because a lot of people are standing around glassy-eyed listening to something mumbling in their ear that it's a good thing?"

"Gussy, you don't know progress when you see it. Tickler is the greatest invention since language. Bar none, it's the greatest instrument ever devised for integrating a man into all phases of his environment. Under the present routine a newly purchased tickler first goes to government and civilian defense for primary patterning, then to the purchaser's employer, then to his doctor-psycher, then to his local bunker captain, then to *him*. *Everything* that's needful for a man's welfare gets on the spools. Efficiency cubed! Incidentally, Russia's got the tickler now. Our dip-satellites have photographed it. It's like ours except the Commies wear it on the left shoulder... but they're two weeks behind us developmentwise and they'll never close the gap!"

Gusterson reared up out of the pancake phone to take a deep breath. A sulky-lipped sylph-figured girl two feet from him twitched-medium cootch, he judged-then fumbled in her belt-bag for a pill and popped it in her mouth.

"Hell, the tickler's not even efficient yet about little things," Gusterson blatted, diving back into the privacy-yashmak he was sharing with Fay. "Whyn't that girl's doctor have the Mood-master component of her tickler inject her with medicine?"

"Her doctor probably wants her to have the discipline of pill-taking —or the exercise," Fay answered glibly. "Look sharp now. Here's where we fork. I'm taking you through Micro's postern."

A ribbon of slidewalk split itself from the main band and angled off into a short alley. Guster-son hardly felt the constant-speed juncture as they crossed it. Then the secondary ribbon speeded up, carrying them at about 30 feet a second toward the blank concrete wall in which the alley ended. Gusterson prepared to jump, but Fay grabbed him with one hand and with the other held up toward the wall a badge and a button. When they were about ten feet away the wall whipped aside, then whipped shut behind them so fast that Gusterson wondered mo-mentarily if he still had his heels and the seat of his pants.

Fay, tucking away his badge and pancake phone, dropped the button in Gusterson's vest pocket. "Use it when you leave," he said casually. "That is, if you leave."

Gusterson, who was trying to read the Do and Don't posters papering the walls they were passing, started to probe that last sinister supposition, but just then the ribbon slowed, a swing-ing door opened and closed behind them and they found themselves in a luxuriously furnished thinking box measuring at least eight feet by five.

"Hey, this is something," Gusterson said appreciatively to show he wasn't an utter yokel. Then, drawing on research he'd done for period novels, "Why, it's as big as a Pullman car compartment, or a first mate's cabin in the War of 1812. You really must rate."

Fay nodded, smiled wanly and sat down with a sigh on a compact overstuffed swivel chair. He let his arms dangle and his head sink into his puffed shoulder cape. Gusterson stared at him. It was the first time he could ever recall the little man showing fatigue.

"Tickler currently does have one serious drawback," Fay volunteered. "It weighs 28 pounds. You feel it when you've been on your feet a couple of hours. No question we're going to give the next model that antigravity feature you mentioned for pursuit grenades. We'd have had it in this model except there were so many other things to be incorporated." He sighed again. "Why, the scanning and decision-making elements alone tripled the mass."

"Hey," Gusterson protested, thinking especially of the sulky-lipped girl, "do you mean to tell me all those other people were toting two stone?"

Fay shook his head heavily. "They were all wearing Mark 3 or 4. I'm wearing Mark 6," he said, as one might say, "I'm carrying the genuine Cross, not one of the balsa ones."

But then his face brightened a little and he went on. "Of course the new improved features make it more than worth it...and you hardly feel it at all at night when you're lying down...and if you remember to talcum under it twice a day, no sores develop...at least not very big ones...."

Backing away involuntarily, Gusterson felt something prod his right shoulderblade. Ripping open his coat, he convulsively plunged his hand under it and tore out Fay's belt-bag...and then set it down very gently on the top of a shallow cabinet and relaxed with the sigh of one who has escaped a great, if symbolic, danger. Then he remembered something Fay had mentioned. He straightened again.

"Hey, you said it's got scanning and decision-making elements. That means your tickler thinks, even by your fancy standards. And if it thinks, it's conscious."

"Gussy," Fay said wearily, frowning, "all sorts of things nowadays have S&DM elements. Mail sorters, missiles, robot medics, high-style mannequins, just to name some of the Ms. They 'think,' to use that archaic word, but it's neither here nor there. And they're certainly not conscious."

"Your tickler thinks," Gusterson repeated stubbornly, "just like I warned you it would. It sits on your shoulder, ridin' you like you was a pony or a starved St. Bernard, and now it thinks."

"Suppose it does?" Fay yawned. "What of it?" He gave a rapid sinuous one-sided shrug that made it look for a moment as if his left arm had three elbows. It stuck in Gusterson's mind, for he had never seen Fay use such a gesture and he wondered where he'd picked it up. Maybe imitating a double-jointed Micro Finance chief? Fay yawned again and said, "Please, Gussy, don't disturb me for a minute or so." His eyes half closed.

Gusterson studied Fay's sunken-cheeked face and the great puff of his shoulder cape.

"Say, Fay," he asked in a soft voice after about five minutes, "are you meditating?"

"Why, no," Fay responded, starting up and then stifling another yawn. "Just resting a bit. I seem to get more tired these days, somehow. You'll have to excuse me, Gussy. But what made you think of meditation?"

"Oh, I just got to wonderin' in that direction," Gusterson said. "You see, when you first started to develop Tickler, it occurred to me that there was one thing about it that might be real good even if you did give it S&DM elements. It's this: having a mech secretary to take charge of his obligations and routine in the real world might allow a man to slide into the other world, the world of thoughts and feelings and intuitions, and sort of ooze around in there and accomplish things. Know any of the people using Tickler that way, hey?"

"Of course not," Fay denied with a bright incredulous laugh. "Who'd want to loaf around in an imaginary world and take a chance of *missing out on what his tickler's doing?* —I mean, on what his tickler has in store for him-what he's *told* his tickler to have in store for him."

Ignoring Gusterson's shiver, Fay straightened up and seemed to brisken himself. "Ha, that little slump did me good. A tickler *makes* you rest, you know-it's one of the great things about it. Pooh-Bah's kinder to me than I ever was to myself." He buttoned open a tiny refrigerator and took out two waxed cardboard cubes and handed one to Gusterson. "Martini? Hope you don't mind drinking from the carton. Cheers. Now, Gussy old pal, there are two matters I want to take up with you —"

"Hold it," Gusterson said with something of his old authority. "There's something I got to get off my mind first." He pulled the typed pages out of his inside pocket and straightened them. "I told you about these," he said. "I want you to read them before you do anything else. Here."

Fay looked toward the pages and nodded, but did not take them yet. He lifted his hands to his throat and unhooked the clasp of his cape, then hesitated.

"You wear that thing to hide the hump your tickler makes?" Gusterson filled in. "You got better taste than those other moles."

"Not to hide it, exactly," Fay protested, "but just so the others won't be jealous. I wouldn't feel comfortable parading a free-scanning decision-capable Mark 6 tickler in front of people who can't buy it-until it goes on open sale at twenty-two fifteen tonight. Lot of shelterfolk won't be sleeping tonight. They'll be queued up to trade in their old tickler for a Mark 6 almost as good as Pooh-Bah."

He started to jerk his hands apart, hesitated again with an oddly apprehensive look at the big man, then whirled off the cape.

Gusterson sucked in such a big gasp that he hiccuped. The right shoulder of Fay's jacket and shirt had been cut away. Thrusting up through the neatly hemmed hole was a silvery gray hump with a one-eyed turret atop it and two multi-jointed metal arms ending in little claws.

It looked like the top half of a pseudo-science robot—a squat evil child robot, Gusterson told himself, which had lost its legs in a railway accident-and it seemed to him that a red fleck was moving around imperceptibly in the huge single eye.

"I'll take that memo now," Fay said coolly, reaching out his hand. He caught the rustling sheets as they slipped from Gusterson's fingers, evened them up very precisely by tapping them on his knee... and then handed them over his shoulder to his tickler, which clicked its claws around either margin and then began rather swiftly to lift the top sheet past its single eye at a distance of about six inches.

"The first matter I want to take up with you, Gussy," Fay began, paying no attention whatsoever to the little scene on his shoulder, " —or warn you about, rather-is the imminent ticklerization of schoolchildren, geriatrics, convicts and topsiders. At three zero zero tomorrow ticklers become mandatory for all adult shelterfolk. The mop-up operations won't be long in coming-in fact, these days we find that the square root of the estimated time of a new development is generally the best time estimate. Gussy, I strongly advise you to start wearing a tickler now. And Daisy and your moppets. If you heed my advice, your kids will have the jump on your class. Transition and conditioning are easy, since Tickler itself sees to it."

Pooh-Bah leafed the first page to the back of the packet and began lifting the second past his eye —a little more swiftly than the first.

"I've got a Mark 6 tickler all warmed up for you," Fay pressed, "and a shoulder cape. You won't feel one bit conspicuous." He noticed the direction of Gusterson's gaze and remarked, "Fascinating mechanism, isn't it? Of course 28 pounds are a bit oppressive, but then you have to remember it's only a way-station to free-floating Mark 7 or 8."

Pooh-Bah finished page two and began to race through page three.

"But I wanted you to read it," Gusterson said bemusedly, staring.

"Pooh-Bah will do a better job than I could," Fay assured him. "Get the gist without losing the chaff."

"But dammit, it's all about him," Gusterson said a little more strongly. "He won't be objective about it."

"A better job," Fay reiterated, "and more fully objective. Pooh-Bah's set for full precis. Stop worrying about it. He's a dispassionate machine, not a fallible, emotionally disturbed human misled by the will-o'-the-wisp of consciousness. Second matter: Micro Systems is impressed by your contributions to Tickler and will recruit you as a senior consultant with a salary and thinking box as big as my own, family quarters to match. It's an unheard-of high start. Gussy, I think you'd be a fool —"

He broke off, held up a hand for silence, and his eyes got a listening look. Pooh-Bah had finished page six and was holding the packet motionless. After about ten seconds Fay's face broke into a big fake smile. He stood up, suppressing a wince, and held out his hand. "Gussy," he said loudly, "I am happy to inform you that all your fears about Tickler are so much thistledown. My word on it. There's nothing to them at all. Pooh-Bah's precis, which he's just given to me, proves it."

"Look," Gusterson said solemnly, "there's one thing I want you to do. Purely to humor an old friend. But I want you to do it. *Read that memo yourself.*"

"Certainly I will, Gussy," Fay continued in the same ebullient tones. "I'll read it —" he twitched and his smile disappeared —"a little later."

"Sure," Gusterson said dully, holding his hand to his stomach. "And now if you don't mind, Fay, I'm goin' home. I feel just a bit sick. Maybe the ozone and the other additives in your shelter air are too heady for me. It's been years since I tramped through a pine forest."

"But Gussy! You've hardly got here. You haven't even sat down. Have another martini. Have a seltzer pill. Have a whiff of oxy. Have a —"

"No, Fay, I'm going home right away. I'll think about the job offer. *Remember to read that memo.*"

"I will, Gussy, I certainly will. You know your way? The button takes you through the wall. 'By, now."

He sat down abruptly and looked away. Gusterson pushed through the swinging door. He tensed himself for the step across onto the slowly-moving reverse ribbon. Then on a impulse he pushed ajar the swinging door and looked back inside.

Fay was sitting as he'd left him, apparently lost in listless brooding. On his shoulder Pooh-Bah was rapidly crossing and uncrossing its little metal arms, tearing the memo to smaller and smaller shreds. It let the scraps drift slowly toward the floor and oddly writhed its three-elbowed left arm...and then Gusterson knew from whom, or rather from what, Fay had copied his new shrug.

When Gusterson got home toward the end of the second dog watch, he slipped aside from Daisy's questions and set the children laughing with a graphic enactment of his slidestanding technique and a story about getting his head caught in a thinking box built for a midget physicist. After supper he played with Imogene, Iago and Claudius until it was their bedtime and thereafter was unusually attentive to Daisy, admiring her fading green stripes, though he did spend a while in the next apartment, where they stored their outdoor camping equipment.

But the next morning he announced to the children that it was a holiday-the Feast of St. Gusterson-and then took Daisy into the bedroom and told her everything.

When he'd finished she said, "This is something I've got to see for myself."

Gusterson shrugged. "If you think you've got to. I say we should head for the hills right now. One thing I'm standing on: the kids aren't going back to school."

"Agreed," Daisy said. "But, Gusterson, we've lived through a lot of things without leaving home altogether. We lived through the Everybody-Six-Feet-Underground-by-Christmas campaign and the Robot Watchdog craze, when you got your left foot half chewed off. We lived through the Venomous Bats and Indoctrinated Saboteur Rats and the Hypnotized Monkey Paratrooper scares. We lived through the Voice of Safety and Anti-Communist Somno-Instruction and Rightest Pills and Jet-Propelled Vigilantes. We lived through the Cold-Out, when you weren't supposed to turn on a toaster for fear its heat would be a target for prowl missiles and when people with fevers were unpopular. We lived through —"

Gusterson patted her hand. "You go below," he said. "Come back when you've decided this is different. Come back as soon as you can anyway. I'll be worried about you every minute you're down there."

When she was gone-in a green suit and hat to minimize or at least justify the effect of the faded stripes-Gusterson doled out to the children provender and equipment for a camping expedition to the next floor. Iago led them off in stealthy Indian file. Leaving the hall door open Gusterson got out his .38 and cleaned and loaded it, meanwhile concentrating on a chess problem with the idea of confusing a hypothetical psionic monitor. By the time he had hid the revolver again he heard the elevator creaking back up.

Daisy came dragging in without her hat, looking as if she'd been concentrating on a chess problem for hours herself and just now given up. Her stripes seemed to have vanished; then Gusterson decided this was because her whole complexion was a touch green.

She sat down on the edge of the couch and said without looking at him, "Did you tell me, Gusterson, that everybody was quiet and abstracted and orderly down below, especially the ones wearing ticklers, meaning pretty much everybody?"

"I did," he said. "I take it that's no longer the case. What are the new symptoms?"

She gave no indication. After some time she said, "Gusterson, do you remember the Doré illustrations to the *Inferno*? Can you visualize the paintings of Hieronymous Bosch with the hordes of proto-Freudian devils tormenting people all over the farmyard and city square? Did you ever see the Disney animations of Moussorgsky's witches' sabbath music? Back in the foolish days before you married me, did that drug-addict girl friend of yours ever take you to a genuine orgy?"

"As bad as that, hey?"

She nodded emphatically and all of a sudden shivered violently. "Several shades worse," she said. "If they decide to come topside —" She shot up. "Where are the kids?"

"Upstairs campin' in the mysterious wilderness of the 21st floor," Gusterson reassured her. "Let's leave 'em there until we're ready to —"

He broke off. They both heard the faint sound of thudding footsteps.

"They're on the stairs," Daisy whispered, starting to move toward the open door. "But are they coming from up or down?"

"It's just one person," judged Gusterson, moving after his wife. "Too heavy for one of the kids."

The footsteps doubled in volume and came rapidly closer. Along with them there was an agonized gasping. Daisy stopped, staring fearfully at the open doorway. Gusterson moved past her. Then he stopped too.

Fay stumbled into view and would have fallen on his face except he clutched both sides of the doorway halfway up. He was stripped to the waist. There was a little blood on his shoulder. His narrow chest was arching convulsively, the ribs standing out starkly, as he sucked in oxygen to replace what he'd burned up running up twenty flights. His eyes were wild.

"They've taken over," he panted. Another gobbling breath. "Gone crazy." Two more gasps. "Gotta stop 'em."

His eyes filmed. He swayed forward. Then Gusterson's big arms were around him and he was carrying him to the couch.

Daisy came running from the kitchen with a damp cool towel. Gusterson took it from her and began to mop Fay off. He sucked in his own breath as he saw that Fay's right ear was raw and torn. He whispered to Daisy, "Look at where the thing savaged him."

The blood on Fay's shoulder came from his ear. Some of it stained a flush-skin plastic fitting that had two small valved holes in it and that puzzled Gusterson until he remembered that Moodmaster tied into the bloodstream. For a second he thought he was going to vomit.

The dazed look slid aside from Fay's eyes. He was gasping less painfully now. He sat up, pushing the towel away, buried his face in his hands for a few seconds, then looked over the fingers at the two of them.

"I've been living in a nightmare for the last week," he said in a taut small voice, "knowing the thing had come alive and trying to pretend to myself that it hadn't. Knowing it was taking charge of me more and more. Having it whisper in my ear, over and over again, in a cracked little rhyme that I could only hear every hundredth time, 'Day by day, in every way, you're learning to listen... and *obey*. Day by day —'"

His voice started to go high. He pulled it down and continued harshly, "I ditched it this morning when I showered. It let me break contact to do that. It must have figured it had complete control of me, mounted or dismounted. I think it's telepathic, and then it did some, well, rather unpleasant things to me late last night. But I pulled together my fears and my will and I ran for it. The slidewalks were chaos. The Mark 6 ticklers showed some purpose, though I couldn't tell you what, but as far as I could see the Mark 3s and 4s were just cootching their mounts to death-Chinese feather torture. Giggling, gasping, choking... gales of mirth. People are dying of laughter... ticklers!... the irony of it! It was the complete lack of order and sanity and that let me get topside. There were things I saw —" Once again his voice went shrill. He clapped his hand to his mouth and rocked back and forth on the couch.

Gusterson gently but firmly laid a hand on his good shoulder. "Steady," he said. "Here, swallow this."

Fay shoved aside the short brown drink. "We've got to stop them," he cried. "Mobilize the topsiders-contact the wilderness patrols and manned satellites-pour ether in the tunnel airpumps-invent and crash-manufacture missiles that will home on ticklers without harming humans-SOS Mars and Venus-dope the shelter water supply-do something! Gussy, you don't realize what people are going through down there every second."

"I think they're experiencing the ultimate in outer-directedness," Gusterson said gruffly.

"Have you no heart?" Fay demanded. His eyes widened, as if he were seeing Gusterson for the first time. Then, accusingly, pointing a shaking finger: "*You invented the tickler, George Gusterson! It's all your fault! You've got to do something about it!*"

Before Gusterson could retort to that, or begin to think of a reply, or even assimilate the full enormity of Fay's statement, he was grabbed from behind and frog-marched away from Fay and something that felt remarkably like the muzzle of a large-caliber gun was shoved in the small of his back.

Under cover of Fay's outburst a huge crowd of people had entered the room from the hall-eight, to be exact. But the weirdest thing about them to Gusterson was that from the first instant he had the impression that only one mind had entered the room and that it did not reside in any of the eight persons, even though he recognized three of them, but in something that they were carrying.

Several things contributed to this impression. The eight people all had the same blank expression-watchful yet empty-eyed. They all moved in the same slithery crouch. And they had all taken off their shoes. Perhaps, Gusterson thought wildly, they believed he and Daisy ran a Japanese flat.

Gusterson was being held by two burly women, one of them quite pimply. He considered stamping on her toes, but just at that moment the gun dug in his back with a corkscrew movement.

The man holding the gun on him was Fay's colleague Davidson. Some yards beyond Fay's couch, Kester was holding a gun on Daisy, without digging it into her, while the single strange man holding Daisy herself was doing so quite decorously—a circumstance which afforded Gusterson minor relief, since it made him feel less guilty about not going berserk.

Two more strange men, one of them in purple lounging pajamas, the other in the gray uniform of a slidewalk inspector, had grabbed Fay's skinny upper arms, one on either side, and were lifting him to his feet, while Fay was struggling with such desperate futility and gibbering so pitifully that Gusterson momentarily had second thoughts about the moral imperative to go berserk when menaced by hostile force. But again the gun dug into him with a twist.

Approaching Fay face-on was the third Micro-man Gusterson had met yesterday-Hazen. It was Hazen who was carrying-quite reverently or solemnly-or at any rate very carefully the object that seemed to Gusterson to be the mind of the little storm troop presently desecrating the sanctity of his own individual home.

All of them were wearing ticklers, of course-the three Micro-men the heavy emergent Mark 6s with their clawed and jointed arms and monocular cephalic turrets, the rest lower-numbered Marks of the sort that merely made Richard-the-Third humps under clothing.

The object that Hazen was carrying was the Mark 6 tickler Gusterson had seen Fay wearing yesterday. Gusterson was sure it was Pooh-Bah because of its air of command, and because he would have sworn on a mountain of Bibles that he recognized the red fleck lurking in the back of its single eye. And Pooh-Bah alone had the aura of full conscious thought. Pooh-Bah alone had mana.

It is not good to see an evil legless child robot with dangling straps bossing-apparently by telepathic power-not only three objects of its own kind and five close primitive relatives, but also eight human beings...and in addition throwing into a state of twitching terror one miserable, thin-chested, half-crazy research-and-development director.

Pooh-Bah pointed a claw at Fay. Fay's handlers dragged him forward, still resisting but more feebly now, as if half-hypnotized or at least cowed.

Gusterson grunted an outraged, "Hey!" and automatically struggled a bit, but once more the gun dug in. Daisy shut her eyes, then firmed her mouth and opened them again to look.

Seating the tickler on Fay's shoulder took a little time, because two blunt spikes in its bottom had to be fitted into the valved holes in the flush-skin plastic disk. When at last they plunged home Gusterson felt very sick indeed-and then even more so, as the tickler itself poked a tiny pellet on a fine wire into Fay's ear.

The next moment Fay had straightened up and motioned his handlers aside. He tightened the straps of his tickler around his chest and under his armpits. He held out a hand and someone gave him a shoulderless shirt and coat. He slipped into them smoothly, Pooh-Bah dexterously using its little claws to help put its turret and body through the neatly hemmed holes. The small storm troop looked at Fay with deferential expectation. He held still for a moment, as if thinking, and then walked over to Gusterson and looked him in the face and again held still.

Fay's expression was jaunty on the surface, agonized underneath. Gusterson knew that he wasn't thinking at all, but only listening for instructions from something that was whispering on the very threshold of his inner ear.

"Gussy, old boy," Fay said, twitching a depthless grin, "I'd be very much obliged if you'd answer a few simple questions." His voice was hoarse at first but he swallowed twice and corrected that. "What exactly did you have in mind when you invented ticklers? What exactly are they supposed to be?"

"Why, you miserable —" Gusterson began in a kind of confused horror, then got hold of himself and said curtly, "They were supposed to be mech reminders. They were supposed to record memoranda and —"

Fay held up a palm and shook his head and again listened for a space. Then, "That's how ticklers were supposed to be of use to humans," he said. "I don't mean that at all. I mean how ticklers were supposed to be of use to themselves. Surely you had some notion." Fay wet his lips. "If it's any help," he added, "keep in mind that it's not Fay who's asking this question, but Pooh-Bah."

Gusterson hesitated. He had the feeling that every one of the eight dual beings in the room was hanging on his answer and that something was boring into his mind and turning over his next thoughts and peering at and under them before he had a chance to scan them himself. Pooh-Bah's eye was like a red searchlight.

"Go on," Fay prompted. "What were ticklers supposed to be-for themselves?"

"Nothin'," Gusterson said softly. "Nothin' at all."

He could feel the disappointment well up in the room-and with it a touch of something like panic.

This time Fay listened for quite a long while. "I hope you don't mean that, Gussy," he said at last very earnestly. "I mean, I hope you hunt deep and find some ideas you forgot, or maybe never realized you had at the time. Let me put it to you differently. What's the place of ticklers in the natural scheme of things? What's their aim in life? Their special reason? Their genius? Their final cause? What gods should ticklers worship?"

But Gusterson was already shaking his head. He said, "I don't know anything about that at all."

Fay sighed and gave simultaneously with Pooh-Bah the now-familiar triple-jointed shrug. Then the man briskened himself. "I guess that's as far as we can get right now," he said. "Keep thinking, Gussy. Try to remember something. You won't be able to leave your apartment — I'm setting guards. If you want to see me, tell them. Or just think-In due course you'll be questioned further in any case. Perhaps by special methods. Perhaps you'll be ticklerized. That's all. Come on, everybody, let's get going."

The pimply woman and her pal let go of Gusterson, Daisy's man loosed his decorous hold, Davidson and Kester sidled away with an eye behind them and the little storm troop trudged out.

Fay looked back in the doorway. "I'm sorry, Gussy," he said and for a moment his old self looked out of his eyes. "I wish I could —" A claw reached for his ear, a spasm of pain crossed his face, he stiffened and marched off. The door shut.

Gusterson took two deep breaths that were close to angry sobs. Then, still breathing stentorously, he stamped into the bedroom.

"What —?" Daisy asked, looking after him.

He came back carrying his .38 and headed for the door.

"What are you up to?" she demanded, knowing very well.

"I'm going to blast that iron monkey off Fay's back if it's the last thing I do!"

She threw her arms around him.

"Now lemme go," Gusterson growled. "I gotta be a man one time anyway."

As they struggled for the gun, the door opened noiselessly, Davidson slipped in and deftly snatched the weapon out of their hands before they realized he was there. He said nothing, only smiled at them and shook his head in sad reproof as he went out.

Gusterson slumped. "I *knew* they were all psionic," he said softly. "I just got out of control now-that last look Fay gave us." He touched Daisy's arm. "Thanks, kid."

He walked to the glass wall and looked out desultorily. After a while he turned and said, "Maybe you better be with the kids, hey? I imagine the guards'll let you through."

Daisy shook her head. "The kids never come home until supper. For the next few hours they'll be safer without me."

Gusterson nodded vaguely, sat down on the couch and propped his chin on the base of his palm. After a while his brow smoothed and Daisy knew that the wheels had started to turn inside and the electrons to jump around-except that she reminded herself to permanently cross out those particular figures of speech from her vocabulary.

After about half an hour Gusterson said softly, "I think the ticklers are so psionic that it's as if they just had one mind. If I were with them very long I'd start to be part of that mind. Say something to one of them and you say it to all."

Fifteen minutes later: "They're not crazy, they're just newborn. The ones that were creating a cootching chaos downstairs were like babies kickin' their legs and wavin' their eyes, tryin' to see what their bodies could do. Too bad their bodies are us."

Ten minutes more: "I gotta do something about it. Fay's right. It's all my fault. He's just the apprentice; I'm the old sorcerer himself."

Five minutes more, gloomily: "Maybe it's man's destiny to build live machines and then bow out of the cosmic picture. Except the ticklers need us, dammit, just like nomads need horses."

Another five minutes: "Maybe somebody could dream up a purpose in life for ticklers. Even a religion-the First Church of Pooh-Bah Tickler. But I hate selling other people spiritual ideas and that'd still leave ticklers parasitic on humans...."

As he murmured those last words Gusterson's eyes got wide as a maniac's and a big smile reached for his ears. He stood up and faced himself toward the door.

"What are you intending to do now?" Daisy asked flatly.

"I'm merely goin' out an' save the world," he told her. "I may be back for supper and I may not."

Davidson pushed out from the wall against which he'd been resting himself and his two-stone tickler and moved to block the hall. But Gusterson simply walked up to him. He shook his hand warmly and looked his tickler full in the eye and said in a ringing voice, "Ticklers should have bodies of their own!" He paused and then added casually, "Come on, let's visit your boss."

Davidson listened for instructions and then nodded. But he watched Gusterson warily as they walked down the hall.

In the elevator Gusterson repeated his message to the second guard, who turned out to be the pimply woman, now wearing shoes. This time he added, "Ticklers shouldn't be tied to the frail bodies of humans, which need a lot of thoughtful supervision and drug-injecting and can't even fly."

Crossing the park, Gusterson stopped a hump-backed soldier and informed him, "Ticklers gotta cut the apron string and snap the silver cord and go out in the universe and find their own purposes." Davidson and the pimply woman didn't interfere. They merely waited and watched and then led Gusterson on.

On the escaladder he told someone, "It's cruel to tie ticklers to slow-witted snaily humans when ticklers can think and live…ten thousand times as fast," he finished, plucking the figure from the murk of his unconscious.

By the time they got to the bottom, the message had become, "Ticklers should have a planet of their own!"

They never did catch up with Fay, although they spent two hours skimming around on slide-walks, under the subterranean stars, pursuing rumors of his presence. Clearly the boss tickler (which was how they thought of Pooh-bah) led an energetic life. Gusterson continued to deliver his message to all and sundry at 30-second intervals. Toward the end he found himself doing it in a dreamy and forgetful way. His mind, he decided, was becoming assimilated to the communal telepathic mind of the ticklers. It did not seem to matter at the time.

After two hours Gusterson realized that he and his guides were becoming part of a general movement of people, a flow as mindless as that of blood corpuscles through the veins, yet at the same time dimly purposeful-at least there was the feeling that it was at the behest of a mind far above.

The flow was topside. All the slidewalks seemed to lead to the concourses and the escaladders. Gusterson found himself part of a human stream moving into the tickler factory adjacent to his apartment-or another factory very much like it.

Thereafter Gusterson's awarenesses were dimmed. It was as if a bigger mind were doing the remembering for him and it were permissible and even mandatory for him to dream his way along. He knew vaguely that days were passing. He knew he had work of a sort: at one time he was bringing food to gaunt-eyed tickler-mounted humans working feverishly in a production line-human hands and tickler claws working together in a blur of rapidity on silvery mechanisms that moved along jumpily on a great belt; at another he was sweeping piles of metal scraps and garbage down a gray corridor.

Two scenes stood out a little more vividly.

A windowless wall had been knocked out for twenty feet. There was blue sky outside, its light almost hurtful, and a drop of many stories. A file of humans were being processed. When one of them got to the head of the file his (or her) tickler was ceremoniously unstrapped from his shoulder and welded onto a silvery cask with smoothly pointed ends. The result was something that looked-at least in the case of the Mark 6 ticklers-like a stubby silver submarine, child size. It would hum gently, lift off the floor and then fly slowly out through the big blue gap. Then the next tickler-ridden human would step forward for processing.

The second scene was in a park, the sky again blue, but big and high with an argosy of white clouds. Gusterson was lined up in a crowd of humans that stretched as far as he could see, row on irregular row. Martial music was playing. Overhead hovered a flock of little silver submarines, lined up rather more orderly in the air than the humans were on the ground. The music rose to a heart-quickening climax. The tickler nearest Gusterson gave (as if to say, "And now-who knows?") a triple-jointed shrug that stung his memory. Then the ticklers took off straight up on their new and shining bodies. They became a flight of silver geese...of silver midges...and the humans around Gusterson lifted a ragged cheer....

That scene marked the beginning of the return of Gusterson's mind and memory. He shuffled around for a bit, spoke vaguely to three or four people he recalled from the dream days, and then headed for home and supper-three weeks late, and as disoriented and emaciated as a bear coming out of hibernation.

Six months later Fay was having dinner with Daisy and Gusterson. The cocktails had been poured and the children were playing in the next apartment. The transparent violet walls brightened, then gloomed, as the sun dipped below the horizon.

Gusterson said, "I see where a spaceship out beyond the orbit of Mars was holed by a tickler. I wonder where the little guys are headed now?"

Fay started to give a writhing left-armed shrug, but stopped himself with a grimace.

"Maybe out of the solar system altogether," suggested Daisy, who'd recently dyed her hair fire-engine red and was wearing red leotards.

"They got a weary trip ahead of them," Gusterson said, "unless they work out a hyper-Einsteinian drive on the way."

Fay grimaced again. He was still looking rather peaked. He said plaintively, "Haven't we heard enough about ticklers for a while?"

"I guess so," Gusterson agreed, "but I get to wondering about the little guys. They were so serious and intense about everything. I never did solve their problem, you know. I just shifted it onto other shoulders than ours. No joke intended," he hurried to add.

Fay forbore to comment. "By the way, Gussy," he said, "have you heard anything from the Red Cross about that world-saving medal I nominated you for? I know you think the whole concept of world-saving medals is ridiculous, especially when they started giving them to all heads of state who didn't start atomic wars while in office, but —"

"Nary a peep," Gusterson told him. "I'm not proud, Fay. I could use a few world-savin' medals. I'd start a flurry in the old-gold market. But I don't worry about those things. I don't have time to. I'm busy these days thinkin' up a bunch of new inventions."

"Gussy!" Fay said sharply, his face tightening in alarm, "Have you forgotten your promise?"

"'Course not, Fay. My new inventions aren't for Micro or any other firm. They're just a legitimate part of my literary endeavors. Happens my next insanity novel is goin' to be about a mad inventor."

The Night of the Long Knives

Chapter 1

Any man who saw you, or even heard your footsteps must be ambushed, stalked and killed, whether needed for food or not. Otherwise, so long as his strength held out, he would be on your trail.

—The Twenty-Fifth Hour,
by Herbert Best

I was one hundred miles from Nowhere-and I mean that literally-when I spotted this girl out of the corner of my eye. I'd been keeping an extra lookout because I still expected the other undead bugger left over from the murder party at Nowhere to be stalking me.

I'd been following a line of high-voltage towers all canted over at the same gentlemanly tipsy angle by an old blast from the Last War. I judged the girl was going in the same general direction and was being edged over toward my course by a drift of dust that even at my distance showed dangerous metallic gleams and dark humps that might be dead men or cattle.

She looked slim, dark topped, and on guard. Small like me and like me wearing a scarf loosely around the lower half of her face in the style of the old buckaroos.

We didn't wave or turn our heads or give the slightest indication we'd seen each other as our paths slowly converged. But we were intensely, minutely watchful —I knew I was and she had better be.

Overhead the sky was a low dust haze, as always. I don't remember what a high sky looks like. Three years ago I think I saw Venus. Or it may have been Sirius or Jupiter.

The hot smoky light was turning from the amber of midday to the bloody bronze of evening.

The line of towers I was following showed the faintest spread in the direction of their canting-they must have been only a few miles from blast center. As I passed each one I could see where the metal on the blast side had been eroded-vaporized by the original blast, mostly smoothly, but with welts and pustules where the metal had merely melted and run. I supposed the lines the towers carried had all been vaporized too, but with the haze I couldn't be sure, though I did see three dark blobs up there that might be vultures perching.

From the drift around the foot of the nearest tower a human skull peered whitely. That is rather unusual. Years later now you still see more dead bodies with the meat on them than skeletons. Intense radiation has killed their bacteria and preserved them indefinitely from decay, just like the packaged meat in the last advertisements. In fact such bodies are one of the signs of a really hot drift-you avoid them. The vultures pass up such poisonously hot carrion too-they've learned their lesson.

Ahead some big gas tanks began to loom up, like deformed battleships and flat-tops in a smoke screen, their prows being the juncture of the natural curve of the off-blast side with the massive concavity of the on-blast side.

None of the three other buggers and me had had too clear an idea of where Nowhere had been-hence, in part, the name-but I knew in a general way that I was somewhere in the Death-lands between Porter County and Ouachita Parish, probably much nearer the former.

It's a real mixed-up America we've got these days, you know, with just the faintest trickle of a sense of identity left, like a guy in the paddedest cell in the most locked up ward in the whole loony bin. If a time traveler from mid Twentieth Century hopped forward to it across the few intervening years and looked at a map of it, if anybody has a map of it, he'd think that the map had run-that it had got some sort of disease that had swollen a few tiny parts beyond all bounds, paper tumors, while most of the other parts, the parts he remembered carrying names in such big print and showing such bold colors, had shrunk to nothingness.

To the east he'd see Atlantic Highlands and Savannah Fortress. To the west, Walla Walla Territory, Pacific Palisades, and Los Alamos-and there he'd see an actual change in the coastline, I'm told, where three of the biggest stockpiles of fusionables let go and opened Death Valley to the sea-so that Los Alamos is closer to being a port. Centrally he'd find Porter County and Manteno Asylum surprisingly close together near the Great Lakes, which are tilted and spilled out a bit toward the southwest with the big quake. South-centrally: Ouachita Parish inching up the Mississippi from old Louisiana under the cruel urging of the Fisher Sheriffs.

Those he'd find and a few, a very few other places, including a couple I suppose I haven't heard of. Practically all of them would surprise him-no one can predict what scraps of a blasted nation are going to hang onto a shred of organization and ruthlessly maintain it and very slowly and very jealously extend it.

But biggest of all, occupying practically all the map, reducing all those swollen localities I've mentioned back to tiny blobs, bounding most of America and thrusting its jetty pseudopods everywhere, he'd see the great inkblot of the Deathlands. I don't know how else than by an area of solid, absolutely unrelieved black you'd represent the Deathlands with its multicolored radioactive dusts and its skimpy freightage of lonely Deathlanders, each bound on his murderous, utterly pointless, but utterly absorbing business-an area where names like Nowhere, It, Anywhere, and the Place are the most natural thing in the world when a few of us decide to try to pad down together for a few nervous months or weeks.

As I say, I was somewhere in the Deathlands near Manteno Asylum.

The girl and me were getting closer now, well within pistol or dart range though beyond any but the most expert or lucky knife throw. She wore boots and a weathered long-sleeved shirt and jeans. The black topping was hair, piled high in an elaborate coiffure that was held in place by twisted shavings of bright metal. A fine bug-trap, I told myself.

In her left hand, which was closest to me, she carried a dart gun, pointed away from me, across her body. It was the kind of potent tiny crossbow you can't easily tell whether the spring is loaded. Back around on her left hip a small leather satchel was strapped to her belt. Also on the same side were two sheathed knives, one of which was an oddity-it had no handle, just the bare tang. For nothing but throwing, I guessed.

I let my own left hand drift a little closer to my Banker's Special in its open holster-Ray Baker's great psychological weapon, though (who knows?) the two .38 cartridges it contained might actually fire. The one I'd put to the test at Nowhere had, and very lucky for me.

She seemed to be hiding her right arm from me. Then I spotted the weapon it held, one you don't often see, a stevedore's hook. She *was* hiding her right hand, all right, she had the long sleeve pulled down over it so just the hook stuck out. I asked myself if the hand were perhaps covered with radiation scars or sores or otherwise disfigured. We Deathlanders have our vanities. I'm sensitive about my baldness.

Then she let her right arm swing more freely and I saw how short it was. She had no right hand. The hook was attached to the wrist stump.

I judged she was about ten years younger than me. I'm pushing forty, I think, though some people have judged I'm younger. No way of my knowing for sure. In this life you forget trifles like chronology.

Anyway, the age difference meant she would have quicker reflexes. I'd have to keep that in mind.

The greenishly glinting dust drift that I'd judged she was avoiding swung closer ahead. The girl's left elbow gave a little kick to the satchel on her hip and there was a sudden burst of irregular ticks that almost made me start. I steadied myself and concentrated on thinking whether I should attach any special significance to her carrying a Geiger counter. Naturally it wasn't the sort of thinking that interfered in any way with my watchfulness-you quickly lose the habit of that kind of thinking in the Deathlands or you lose something else.

It could mean she was some sort of greenhorn. Most of us old-timers can visually judge the heat of a dust drift or crater or rayed area more reliably than any instrument. Some buggers claim they just feel it, though I've never known any of the latter too eager to navigate in unfamiliar country at night-which you'd think they'd be willing to do if they could feel heat blind.

But she didn't look one bit like a tenderfoot-like for instance some citizeness newly banished from Manteno. Or like some Porter burgher's unfaithful wife or troublesome girlfriend whom he'd personally carted out beyond the ridges of cleaned-out hot dust that help guard such places, and then abandoned in revenge or from boredom-and they call themselves civilized, those cultural queers!

No, she looked like she *belonged* in the Deathlands. But then why the counter?

Her eyes might be bad, real bad. I didn't think so. She raised her boot an extra inch to step over a little jagged fragment of concrete. No.

Maybe she was just a born double-checker, using science to back up knowledge based on experience as rich as my own or richer. I've met the super-careful type before. They mostly get along pretty well, but they tend to be a shade too slow in the clutches.

Maybe she was *testing* the counter, planning to use it some other way or trade it for something.

Maybe she made a practice of traveling by night! Then the counter made good sense. But then why use it by day? Why reveal it to me in any case?

Was she trying to convince me that she was a greenhorn? Or had she hoped that the sudden noise would throw me off guard? But who would go to the trouble of carrying a Geiger counter for such devious purposes? And wouldn't she have waited until we got closer before trying the noise gambit?

Think-shmink —it gets you nowhere!

She kicked off the counter with another bump of her elbow and started to edge in toward me faster. I turned the thinking all off and gave my whole mind to watchfulness.

Soon we were barely more than eight feet apart, almost within lunging range without even the preliminary one-two step, and still we hadn't spoken or looked straight at each other, though being that close we'd had to cant our heads around a bit to keep each other in peripheral vision. Our eyes would be on each other steadily for five or six seconds, then dart forward an instant to check for rocks and holes in the trail we were following in parallel. A cultural queer from one of the "civilized" places would have found it funny, I suppose, if he'd been able to watch us perform in an arena or from behind armor glass for his exclusive pleasure.

The girl had eyebrows as black as her hair, which in its piled-up and metal-knotted savagery called to mind African queens despite her typical pale complexion-very little ultraviolet gets through the dust. From the inside corner of her right eye socket a narrow radiation scar ran up between her eyebrows and across her forehead at a rakish angle until it disappeared under a sweep of hair at the upper left corner of her forehead.

I'd been smelling her, of course, for some time.

I could even tell the color of her eyes now. They were blue. It's a color you never see. Almost no dusts have a bluish cast, there are few blue objects except certain dark steels, the sky never gets very far away from the orange range, though it is green from time to time, and water reflects the sky.

Yes, she had blue eyes, blue eyes and that jaunty scar, blue eyes and that jaunty scar and a dart gun and a steel hook for a right hand, and we were walking side by side, eight feet apart, not an inch closer, still not looking straight at each other, still not saying a word, and I realized that the initial period of unadulterated watchfulness was over, that I'd had adequate opportunity to inspect this girl and size her up, and that night was coming on fast, and that here I was, once again, back with *the problem of the two urges*.

I could try either to kill her or go to bed with her.

I know that at this point the cultural queers (and certainly our imaginary time traveler from mid Twentieth Century) would make a great noise about not understanding and not believing in the genuineness of the simple urge to murder that governs the lives of us Deathlanders. Like detective-story pundits, they would say that a man or woman murders for gain, or concealment of crime, or from thwarted sexual desire or outraged sexual possessiveness-and maybe they would list a few other "rational" motives-but not, they would say, just for the simple sake of murder, for the sure release and relief it gives, for the sake of wiping out one recognizable bit more (the closest bit we can, since those of us with the courage or lazy rationality to wipe out ourselves have long since done so) —wiping out one recognizable bit more of the whole miserable, unutterably disgusting human mess. Unless, they would say, a person is completely insane, which is actually how all outsiders view us Deathlanders. They can think of us in no other way.

I guess cultural queers and time travelers simply *don't* understand, though to be so blind it seems to me that they have to overlook much of the history of the Last War and of the subsequent years, especially the mushrooming of crackpot cults with a murder tinge: the werewolf gangs, the Berserkers and Amuckers, the revival of Shiva worship and the Black Mass, the machine wreckers, the kill-the-killers movements, the new witchcraft, the Unholy Creepers, the Unconsciousers, the radioactive blue gods and rocket devils of the Atomites, and a dozen other groupings clearly prefiguring Deathlander psychology. Those cults had all been as unpredictable as Thuggee or the Dancing Madness of the Middle Ages or the Children's Crusade, yet they had happened just the same.

But cultural queers are good at overlooking things. They have to be, I suppose. They think they're humanity growing again. Yes, despite their laughable warpedness and hysterical crippledness, they actually believe-each howlingly different community of them-that they're the new Adams and Eves. They're all excited about themselves and whether or not they wear fig leaves. They don't carry with them, twenty-four hours a day, like us Deathlanders do, the burden of all that was forever lost.

Since I've gone this far I'll go a bit further and make the paradoxical admission that even us Deathlanders don't really understand our urge to murder. Oh, we have our rationalizations of it, just like everyone has of his ruling passion-we call ourselves junkmen, scavengers, gangrene surgeons; we sometimes believe we're doing the person we kill the ultimate kindness, yes and get slobbery tearful about it afterwards; we sometimes tell ourselves we've finally found and are rubbing out the one man or woman who was responsible for everything; we talk, mostly to ourselves, about the aesthetics of homicide; we occasionally admit, but only each to himself alone, that we're just plain nuts.

But we don't really understand our urge to murder, we only *feel* it.

At the hateful sight of another human being, we feel it begins to grow in us until it becomes an overpowering impulse that jerks us, like a puppet is jerked by its strings, into the act itself or its attempted commission.

Like I was feeling it grow in me now as we did this parallel deathmarch through the reddening haze, me and this girl and our problem. This girl with the blue eyes and the jaunty scar.

The problem of the *two* urges, I said. The other urge, the sexual, is one that I know all cultural queers (and certainly our time traveler) would claim to know all about. Maybe they do. But I wonder if they understand how intense it can be with us Deathlanders when it's the only release (except maybe liquor and drugs, which we seldom can get and even more rarely dare use) —the only complete release, even though a brief one, from the overpowering loneliness and from the tyranny of the urge to kill.

To embrace, to possess, to glut lust on, yes even briefly to love, briefly to shelter in-that was good, that was a relief and release to be treasured.

But it couldn't last. You could draw it out, prop it up perhaps for a few days, for a month even (though sometimes not for a single night) —you might even start to talk to each other a little, after a while-but it could never last. The glands always tire, if nothing else.

Murder was the only *final* solution, the only *permanent* release. Only us Deathlanders know how good it feels. But then after the kill the loneliness would come back, redoubled, and after a while I'd meet another hateful human...

Our problem of the two urges. As I watched this girl slogging along parallel to me, as I kept constant watch on her of course, I wondered how *she* was feeling the two urges. Was she attracted to the ridgy scars on my cheeks half revealed by my scarf? —to me they have a pleasing symmetry. Was she wondering how my head and face looked without the black felt skullcap low-visored over my eyes? Or was she thinking mostly of that hook swinging into my throat under the chin and dragging me down?

I couldn't tell. She looked as poker-faced as I was trying to.

For that matter, I asked myself, how was *I* feeling the two urges? —how was I feeling them as I watched this girl with the blue eyes and the jaunty scar and the arrogantly thinned lips that asked to be smashed, and the slender throat? —and I realized that there was no way to describe that, not even to myself. I could only feel the two urges grow in me, side by side, like monstrous twins, until they would simply be too big for my taut body and one of them would have to get out fast.

I don't know which one of us started to slow down first, it happened so gradually, but the dust puffs that rise from the ground of the Deathlands under even the lightest treading became smaller and smaller around our steps and finally vanished altogether, and we were standing still. Only then did I notice the obvious physical trigger for our stopping. An old freeway ran at right angles across our path. The shoulder by which we'd approached it was sharply eroded, so that the pavement, which even had a shallow cave eroded under it, was a good three feet above the level of our path, forming a low wall. From where I'd stopped I could almost reach out and touch the rough-edged smooth-topped concrete. So could she.

We were right in the midst of the gas tanks now, six or seven of them towered around us, squeezed like beer cans by the decade-old blast but their metal looking sound enough until you became aware of the red light showing through in odd patterns of dots and dashes where vaporization or later erosion had been complete. Almost but not quite lace-work. Just ahead of us, right across the freeway, was the six-storey skeletal structure of an old cracking plant, sagged like the power towers away from the blast and the lower storeys drifted with piles and ridges and smooth gobbets of dust.

The light was getting redder and smokier every minute.

With the cessation of the physical movement of walking, which is always some sort of release for emotions, I could feel the twin urges growing faster in me. But that was all right, I told myself-this was the crisis, as she must realize too, and that should key us up to bear the urges a little longer without explosion.

I was the first to start to turn my head. For the first time I looked straight into her eyes and she into mine. And as always happens at such times, a third urge appeared abruptly, an urge momentarily as strong as the other two-the urge to speak, to tell and ask all about it. But even as I started to phrase the first crazily happy greeting, my throat lumped, as I'd known it would, with the awful melancholy of all that was forever lost, with the uselessness of any communication, with the impossibility of recreating the past, our individual pasts, any pasts. And as it always does, the third urge died.

I could tell she was feeling that ultimate pain just like me. I could see her eyelids squeeze down on her eyes and her face lift and her shoulders go back as she swallowed hard.

She was the first to start to lay aside a weapon. She took two sidewise steps toward the freeway and reached her whole left arm further across her body and laid the dart gun on the concrete and drew back her hand from it about six inches. At the same time looking at me hard-fiercely angrily, you'd say-across her left shoulder. She had the experienced duelist's trick of seeming to look into my eyes but actually focussing on my mouth. I was using the same gimmick myself-it's tiring to look straight into another person's eyes and it can put you off guard.

My left side was nearest the wall so I didn't for the moment have the problem of reaching across my body. I took the same sidewise steps she had and using just two fingers, very gingerly —*disarmingly*, I hoped —I lifted my antique firearm from its holster and laid it on the concrete and drew back my hand from it all the way. Now it was up to her again, or should be. Her hook was going to be quite a problem, I realized, but we needn't come to it right away.

She temporized by successively unsheathing the two knives at her left side and laying them beside the dart gun. Then she stopped and her look told me plainly that it was up to me.

Now I am a bugger who believes in carrying *one perfect knife* —otherwise, I know for a fact, you'll go knife-happy and end up by weighing yourself down with dozens, literally. So I am naturally very reluctant to get out of touch in any way with Mother, who is a little rusty along the sides but made of the toughest and most sharpenable alloy steel I've ever run across.

Still, I was most curious to find out what she'd do about that hook, so I finally laid Mother on the concrete beside the .38 and rested my hands lightly on my hips, all ready to enjoy myself-at least I hoped I gave that impression.

She smiled, it was almost a nice smile-by now we'd let our scarves drop since we weren't raising any more dust-and then she took hold of the hook with her left hand and started to unscrew it from the leather-and-metal base fitting over her stump.

Of course, I told myself. And her second knife, the one without a grip, must be that way so she could screw its tang into the base when she wanted a knife on her right hand instead of a hook. I ought to have guessed.

I grinned my admiration of her mechanical ingenuity and immediately unhitched my knapsack and laid it beside my weapons. Then a thought occurred to me. I opened the knapsack and moving my hand slowly and very openly so she'd have no reason to suspect a ruse, I drew out a blanket and, trying to show her both sides of it in the process, as if I were performing some damned conjuring trick, dropped it gently on the ground between us.

She unsnapped the straps on her satchel that fastened it to her belt and laid it aside and then she took off her belt too, slowly drawing it through the wide loops of weathered denim. Then she looked meaningfully at my belt.

I had to agree with her. Belts, especially heavy-buckled ones like ours, can be nasty weapons. I removed mine. Simultaneously each belt joined its corresponding pile of weapons and other belongings.

She shook her head, not in any sort of negation, and ran her fingers into the black hair at several points, to show me it hid no weapon, then looked at me questioningly. I nodded that I was satisfied —I hadn't seen anything run out of it, by the way. Then she looked up at my black skullcap and she raised her eyebrows and smiled again, this time with a spice of mocking anticipation.

In some ways I hate to part with that headpiece more than I do with Mother. Not really because of its sandwiched lead-mesh inner lining-if the rays haven't baked my brain yet they never will and I'm sure that the patches of lead mesh sewed into my pants over my loins give a lot more practical protection. But I was getting real attracted to this girl by now and there are times when a person must make a sacrifice of his vanity. I whipped off my stylish black felt and tossed it on my pile and dared her to laugh at my shiny egg top.

Strangely she didn't even smile. She parted her lips and ran her tongue along the upper one. I gave an eager grin in reply, an incautiously wide one, and she saw my plates flash.

My plates are something rather special though they are by no means unique. Back toward the end of the Last War, when it was obvious to any realist how bad things were going to be, though not how strangely terrible, a number of people, like myself, had all their teeth jerked and replaced with durable plates. I went some of them one better. My plates were stainless steel biting and chewing ridges, smooth continuous ones that didn't attempt to copy individual teeth. A person who looks closely at a slab of chewing tobacco, say, I offer him will be puzzled by the smoothly curved incision, made as if by a razor blade mounted on the arm of a compass. Magnetic powder buried in my gums makes for a real nice fit.

This sacrifice was worse than my hat and Mother combined, but I could see the girl expected me to make it and would take no substitutes, and in this attitude I had to admit that she showed very sound judgment, because I keep the incisor parts of those plates filed to razor sharpness. I have to be careful about my tongue and lips but I figure it's worth it. With my dental scimitars I can in a wink bite out a chunk of throat and windpipe or jugular, though I've never had occasion to do so yet.

For the first minute it made me feel like an old man, a real dodderer, but by now the attraction this girl had for me was getting irrational. I carefully laid the two plates on top of my knapsack.

In return, as a sort of reward you might say, she opened her mouth wide and showed me what was left of her own teeth-about two-thirds of them, a patchwork of tartar and gold.

We took off our boots, pants and shirts, she watching very suspiciously —I knew she'd been skeptical of my carrying only one knife.

Oddly perhaps, considering how touchy I am about my baldness, I felt no sensitivity about revealing the lack of hair on my chest and in fact a sort of pride in displaying the slanting radiation scars that have replaced it, though they are crawling keloids of the ugliest, bumpiest sort. I guess to me such scars are tribal insignia-one-man and one-woman tribes of course. No question but that the scar on the girl's forehead had been the first focus of my desire for her and it still added to my interest.

By now we weren't staying as perfectly on guard or watching each other's clothing for concealed weapons as carefully as we should —I know I wasn't. It was getting dark fast, there wasn't much time left, and the other interest was simply becoming too great.

We were still automatically careful about how we did things. For instance the way we took off our pants was like ballet, simultaneously crouching a little on the left foot and whipping the right leg out of its sheath in one movement, all ready to jump without tripping ourselves if the other person did anything funny, and then skinning down the left pants-leg with a movement almost as swift.

But as I say it was getting too late for perfect watchfulness, in fact for any kind of effective watchfulness at all. The complexion of the whole situation was changing in a rush. The possibilities of dealing or receiving death-along with the chance of the minor indignity of cannibalism, which some of us practice-were suddenly gone, all gone. It was going to be all right this time, I was telling myself. This was the time it would be different, this was the time love would last, this was the time lust would be the firm foundation for understanding and trust, this time there would be really safe sleeping. This girl's body would be home for me, a beautiful tender inexhaustibly exciting home, and mine for her, for always.

As she threw off her shirt, the last darkly red light showed me another smooth slantwise scar, this one around her hips, like a narrow girdle that has slipped down a little on one side.

Chapter 2

Murder most foul, as in the best it is;

But this most foul, strange and unnatural.

—Hamlet

When I woke the light was almost full amber and I could feel no flesh against mine, only the blanket under me. I very slowly rolled over and there she was, sitting on the corner of the blanket not two feet from me, combing her long black hair with a big, wide-toothed comb she'd screwed into the leather-and-metal cap over her wrist stump.

She'd put on her pants and shirt, but the former were rolled up to her knees and the latter, though tucked in, wasn't buttoned.

She was looking at me, contemplating me you might say, quite dreamily but with a faint, easy smile.

I smiled back at her.

It was lovely.

Too lovely. There had to be something wrong with it.

There was. Oh, nothing big. Just a solitary trifle-nothing worth noticing really.

But the tiniest solitary things can sometimes be the most irritating, like *one* mosquito.

When I'd first rolled over she'd been combing her hair straight back, revealing a wedge of baldness following the continuation of her forehead scar deep back across her scalp. Now with a movement that was swift though not hurried-looking she swept the mass of her hair forward and to the left, so that it covered the bald area. Also her lips straightened out.

I was hurt. She shouldn't have hidden her bit of baldness, it was something we had in common, something that brought us closer. And she shouldn't have stopped smiling at just that moment. Didn't she realize I loved that blaze on her scalp just as much as any other part of her, that she no longer had any need to practice vanity in front of me?

Didn't she realize that as soon as she stopped smiling, her contemplative stare became an insult to me? What right had she to stare, critically I felt sure, at my bald head? What right had she to know about the nearly-healed ulcer on my left shin? —that was a piece of information worth a man's life in a fight. What right had she to cover up, anyways, while I was still naked? She ought to have waked me up so that we could have got dressed as we'd undressed, together. There were lots of things wrong with her manners.

Oh, I know that if I'd been able to think calmly, maybe if I'd just had some breakfast or a little coffee inside me, or even if there'd been some hot breakfast to eat at that moment, I'd have recognized my irritation for the irrational, one-mosquito surge of negative feeling that it was.

Even without breakfast, if I'd just had the knowledge that there was a reasonably secure day ahead of me in which there'd be an opportunity for me to straighten out my feelings, I wouldn't have been irked, or at least being irked wouldn't have bothered me terribly.

But a sense of security is an even rarer commodity in the Deathlands than a hot breakfast.

Given just the ghost of a sense of security and/or some hot breakfast, I'd have told myself that she was merely being amusingly coquettish about her bald streak and her hair, that it was natural for a woman to try to preserve some mystery about herself in front of the man she beds with.

But you get leery of any kind of mystery in the Deathlands. It makes you frightened and angry, like it does an animal. Mystery is for cultural queers, strictly. The only way for two people to get along together in the Deathlands, even for a while, is never to hide anything and never to make a move that doesn't have an immediate clear explanation. You can't talk, you see, certainly not at first, and so you can't explain anything (most explanations are just lies and dreams, anyway), so you have to be doubly careful and explicit about everything you do.

This girl wasn't being either. Right now, on top of her other gaucheries, she was unscrewing the comb from her wrist-an unfriendly if not quite a hostile act, as anyone must admit.

Understand, please, I wasn't *showing* any of these negative reactions of mine any more than she was showing hers, except for her stopping smiling. In fact *I hadn't* stopped smiling, I was playing the game to the hilt.

But inside me everything was stewed up and the other urge had come back and presently it would begin to grow again. That's the trouble, you know, with sex as a solution to the problem of the two urges. It's fine while it lasts but it wears itself out and then you're back with Urge Number One and you have nothing left to balance it with.

Oh, I wouldn't kill this girl today, I probably wouldn't seriously think of killing her for a month or more, but Old Urge Number One would be there and growing, mostly under cover, all the time. Of course there were things I could do to slow its growth, lots of little gimmicks, in fact —I was pretty experienced at this business.

For instance, I could take a shot at talking to her pretty soon. For a catchy starter, I could tell her about Nowhere, how these five other buggers and me found ourselves independently skulking along after this scavenging expedition from Porter, how we naturally joined forces in that situation, how we set a pitfall for their alky-powered jeep and wrecked it and them, how when our haul turned out to be unexpectedly big the four of us left from the kill chummied up and padded down together and amused each other for a while and played games, you might say. Why, at one point we even had an old crank phonograph going and read some books. And, of course, how when the loot gave out and the fun wore off, we had our murder party and I survived along with, I think, a bugger named Jerry-at any rate, he was gone when the blood stopped spurting, and I'd had no stomach for tracking him, though I probably should have.

And in return she could tell me how she had killed off her last set of girlfriends, or boyfriends, or friend, or whatever it was.

After that, we could have a go at exchanging news, rumors and speculations about local, national and world events. Was it true that Atlantic Highlands had planes of some sort or were they from Europe? Were they actually crucifying the Deathlanders around Walla Walla or only nailing up their dead bodies as dire warnings to others such? Had Manteno made Christianity compulsory yet, or were they still tolerating Zen Buddhists? Was it true that Los Alamos had been completely wiped out by plague, but the area taboo to Deathlanders because of the robot guards they'd left behind-metal guards eight feet tall who tramped across the white sands, wailing? Did they still have free love in Pacific Palisades? Did she know there'd been a pitched battle fought by expeditionary forces from Ouachita and Savannah Fortress? Over the loot of Birmingham, apparently, after yellow fever had finished off that principality. Had she rooted out any "observers" lately? —some of the "civilized" communities, the more "scientific" ones, try to maintain a few weather stations and the like in the Deathlands, camouflaging them elaborately and manning them with one or two impudent characters to whom we give a hard time if we uncover them. Had she heard the tale that was going around that South America and the French Riviera had survived the Last War absolutely untouched? —and the obviously ridiculous rider that they had blue skies there and saw stars every third night? Did she think that subsequent conditions were showing that the Earth actually had plunged into an interstellar dust cloud coincidentally with the start of the Last War (the dust cloud used as a cover for the first attacks, some said) or did she still hold with the majority that the dust was solely of atomic origin with a little help from volcanoes and dry spells? How many green sunsets had she seen in the last year?

After we'd chewed over those racy topics and some more like them, and incidentally got bored with guessing and fabricating, we might, if we felt especially daring and conversation were going particularly well, even take a chance on talking a little about our childhoods, about how things were before the Last War (though she was almost too young for that) —about the *little* things we remembered-the big things were much too dangerous topics to venture on and sometimes even the little memories could suddenly twist you up as if you'd swallowed lye.

But after that there wouldn't be anything left to talk about. Anything you'd risk talking about, that is. For instance, no matter how long we talked, it was very unlikely that we'd either of us tell the other anything complete or very accurate about how we lived from day to day, about our techniques of surviving and staying sane or at least functional-that would be too imprudent, it would go too much against the grain of any player of the murder game. Would I tell her, or anyone, about how I worked the ruses of playing dead and disguising myself as a woman, about my trick of picking a path just before dark and then circling back to it by a pre-surveyed route, about the chess games I played with myself, about the bottle of green, terribly hot-looking powder I carried to sprinkle behind me to bluff off pursuers? A fat chance of my revealing things like that!

And when all the talk was over, what would it have gained us? Our minds would be filled with a lot of painful stuff better kept buried-meaningless hopes, scraps of vicarious living in "cultured" communities, memories that were nothing but melancholy given concrete form. The melancholy is easiest to bear when it's the diffused background for everything; and all garbage is best kept in the can. Oh yes, our talking would have gained us a few more days of infatuation, of phantom security, but those we could have-almost as many of them, at any rate-without talking.

For instance things were smoothing over already between her and me again and I no longer felt quite so irked. She'd replaced the comb with an inoffensive-looking pair of light pliers and was doing up her hair with the metal shavings. And I was acting as if content to watch her, as in a way I was. I'd still made no move to get dressed.

She looked real sweet, you know, primping herself that way. Her face was a little flat, but it was young, and the scar gave it just the fillip it needed.

But what was going on behind that forehead right now, I asked myself? I felt real psychic this morning, my mind as clear as a bottle of White Rock you find miraculously unbroken in a blasted tavern, and the answers to the question I'd asked myself came effortlessly.

She was telling herself she'd got herself a man again, a man who was adequate in the primal clutch (I gave myself that pat on the back), and that she wouldn't have to be plagued and have her safety endangered by *that* kind of mind-dulling restlessness and yearning for a while.

She was lightly playing around with ideas about how she'd found a home and a protector, knowing she was kidding herself, that it was the most gimcracky feminine make-believe, but enjoying it just the same.

She was sizing me up, deciding in detail just what I went for in a woman, what whetted my interest, so she could keep that roused as long as seemed desirable or prudent to her to continue our relation.

She was kicking herself, only lightly to begin with, because she hadn't taken any precautions-because we who've escaped hot death against all reasonable expectations by virtue of some incalculable resistance to the ills of radioactivity, quite often find we've escaped sterility too. If she should become pregnant, she was telling herself, then she had a real sticky business ahead of her where no man could be trusted for a second.

And because she was thinking of this and because she was obviously a realistic Deathlander, she was reminding herself that a woman is basically less impulsive and daring and resourceful than a man and so had always better be sure she gets in the first blow. She would be thinking that I was a realist myself and a smart man, one able to understand her predicament quite clearly-and because of that a much sooner danger to her. She was feeling Old Number One Urge starting to grow in her again and wondering whether it mightn't be wisest to give it the hot-house treatment.

That is the trouble with a clear mind. For a little while you see things as they really are and you can accurately predict how they're going to shape the future ... and then suddenly you realize you've predicted yourself a week or a month into the future and you can't live the intervening time any more because you've already imagined it in detail. People who live in communities, even the cultural queers of our maimed era, aren't much bothered by it-there must be some sort of blinkers they hand you out along with the key to the city-but in the Deathlands it's a fairly common phenomenon and there's no hiding from it.

Me and my clear mind! —once again it had done me out of days of fun, changed a thoroughly-explored love affair into a one night stand. Oh, there was no question about it, this girl and I were finished, right this minute, as of now, because she was just as psychic as I was this morning and had sensed every last thing that I'd been thinking.

With a movement smooth enough not to look rushed I swung into a crouch. She was on her knees faster than that, her left hand hovering over the little set of tools for her stump, which like any good mechanic she'd lined up neatly on the edge of the blanket-the hook, the comb, a long telescoping fork, a couple of other items, and the knife. I'd grabbed a handful of blanket, ready to jerk it from under her. She'd seen that I'd grabbed it. Our gazes dueled.

There was a high-pitched whine over our heads! Quite loud from the start, though it sounded as if it were very deep up in the haze. It swiftly dropped in pitch and volume.

The top of the skeletal cracking plant across the freeway glowed with St. Elmo's fire! Three times it glowed that way, so bright we could see the violet-blue flames of it reaching up despite the full amber daylight.

The whine died away but in the last moment, paradoxically, it seemed to be coming closer!

This shared threat-for any unexpected event is a threat in the Deathlands and a mysterious event doubly so-put a stop to our murder game. The girl and I were buddies again, buddies to be relied on in a pinch, for the duration of the threat at least. No need to say so or to reassure each other of the fact in any way, it was taken for granted. Besides, there was no time. We had to use every second allowed us in getting ready for whatever was coming.

First I grabbed up Mother. Then I relieved myself-fear made it easy. Then I skinned into my pants and boots, slapped in my teeth, thrust the blanket and knapsack into the shallow cave under the edge of the freeway, looking around me all the time so as not to be surprised from any quarter.

Meanwhile the girl had put on her boots, located her dart gun, unscrewed the pliers from her stump, put the knife in, and was arranging her scarf so it made a sling for the maimed arm —I wondered why but had no time to waste guessing, even if I'd wanted to, for at that moment a small dull silver plane, beetle-shaped more than anything else, loomed out of the haze beyond the cracking plant and came silently drifting down toward us.

The girl thrust her satchel into the cave and along with it her dart gun. I caught her idea and tucked Mother into my pants behind my back.

I'd thought from the first glimpse of it that the plane was disabled —I guess it was its silence that gave me the idea. This theory was confirmed when one of its very stubby wings or vanes touched a corner pillar of the cracking plant. The plane was moving in too slow a glide to be wrecked, in fact it was moving in a slower glide than I would have believed possible-but then it's many years since I have seen a plane in flight.

It wasn't wrecked but the little collision spun it around twice in a lazy circle and it landed on the freeway with a scuffing noise not fifty feet from us. You couldn't exactly say it had crashed in, but it stayed at an odd tilt. It looked crippled all right.

An oval door in the plane opened and a man dropped lightly out on the concrete. And what a man! He was nearer seven feet tall than six, close-cropped blond hair, face and hands richly tanned, the rest of him covered by trim garments of a gleaming gray. He must have weighed as much as the two of us together, but he was beautifully built, muscular yet supple-seeming. His face looked brightly intelligent and even-tempered and kind.

Yes, kind! —damn him! It wasn't enough that his body should fairly glow with a health and vitality that was an insult to our seared skins and stringy muscles and ulcers and half-rotted stomachs and half-arrested cancers, he had to look kind too-the sort of man who would put

120

you to bed and take care of you, as if you were some sort of interesting sick fox, and maybe even say a little prayer for you, and all manner of other abominations.

I don't think I could have endured my fury standing still. Fortunately there was no need to. As if we'd rehearsed the whole thing for hours, the girl and I scrambled up onto the freeway and scurried toward the man from the plane, cunningly swinging away from each other so that it would be harder for him to watch the two of us at once, but not enough to make it obvious that we attended an attack from two quarters.

We didn't run though we covered the ground as fast as we dared-running would have been too much of a give-away too, and the Pilot, which was how I named him to myself, had a strange-looking small gun in his right hand. In fact the way we moved was part of our act —I dragged one leg as if it were crippled and the girl faked another sort of limp, one that made her approach a series of half curtsies. Her arm in the sling was all twisted, but at the same time she was accidently showing her breasts —I remember thinking *you won't distract this breed bull that way, sister, he probably has a harem of six-foot heifers.* I had my head thrown back and my hands stretched out supplicatingly. Meanwhile the both of us were babbling a blue streak. I was rapidly croaking something like, "Mister for God's sake save my pal he's hurt a lot worse'n I am not a hundred yards away he's dyin' mister he's dyin' o' thirst his tongue's black'n all swole up oh save him mister save my pal he's not a hundred yards away he's dyin' mister dyin' —" and she was singsonging an even worse rigamarole about how "they" were after us from Porter and going to crucify us because we believed in science and how they'd already impaled her mother and her ten-year-old sister and a lot more of the same.

It didn't matter that our stories didn't fit or make sense, the babble had a convincing tone and getting us closer to this guy, which was all that counted. He pointed his gun at me and then I could see him hesitate and I thought exultingly *it's a lot of healthy meat you got there, mister, but it's tame meat, mister, tame!*

He compromised by taking a step back and sort of hooting at us and waving us off with his left hand, as if we were a couple of stray dogs.

It was greatly to our advantage that we'd acted without hesitation, and I don't think we'd have been able to do that except that we'd been all set to kill each other when he dropped in. Our muscles and nerves and minds were keyed for instant ruthless attack. And some "civilized" people still say that the urge to murder doesn't contribute to self-preservation!

We were almost close enough now and he was steeling himself to shoot and I remember wondering for a split second what his damn gun did to you, and then me and the girl had started the alternation routine. I'd stop dead, as if completely cowed by the threat of his weapon, and as he took note of it she'd go in a little further, and as his gaze shifted to her she'd stop dead and I'd go in another foot and then try to make my halt even more convincing as his gaze darted back to me. We worked it perfectly, our rhythm was beautiful, as if we were old dancing partners, though the whole thing was absolutely impromptu.

Still, I honestly don't think we'd ever have got to him if it hadn't been for the distraction that came just then to help us. I could tell, you see, that he'd finally steeled himself and we still weren't quite close enough. He wasn't as tame as I'd hoped. I reached behind me for Mother, determined to do a last-minute rush and leap anyway, when there came this sick scream.

I don't know how else to describe it briefly. It was a scream, feminine for choice, it came from some distance and the direction of the old cracking plant, it had a note of anguish and warning, yet at the same time it was weak and almost faltering you might say and squeaky at the end, as if it came from a person half dead and a throat choked with phlegm. It had all those qualities or a wonderful mimicking of them.

And it had quite an effect on our boy in gray for in the act of shooting me down he started to turn and look over his shoulder.

Oh, it didn't altogether stop him from shooting me. He got me partly covered again as I was in the middle of my lunge. I found out what his gun did to you. My right arm, which was the part he'd covered, just went dead and I finished my lunge slamming up against his iron knees, like a highschool kid trying to block out a pro footballer, with the knife slipping uselessly away from my fingers.

But in the blessed meanwhile the girl had lunged too, not with a slow slash, thank God, but with a high, slicing thrust aimed arrow-straight for a point just under his ear.

She connected and a fan of blood sprayed her full in the face.

I grabbed my knife with my left hand as it fell, scrambled to my feet, and drove the knife at his throat in a round-house swing that happened to come handiest at the time. The point went through his flesh like nothing and jarred against his spine with a violence that I hoped would shock into nervous insensibility the stoutest medulla oblongata and prevent any dying reprisals on his part.

I got my wish, in large part. He swayed, straightened, dropped his gun, and fell flat on his back, giving his skull a murderous crack on the concrete for good measure. He lay there and after a half dozen gushes the bright blood quit pumping strongly out of his neck.

Then came the part that was like a dying reprisal, though obviously not being directed by him as of now. And come to think of it, it may have had its good points.

The girl, who was clearly a most cool-headed cuss, snatched for his gun where he'd dropped it, to make sure she got it ahead of me. She snatched, yes-and then jerked back, letting off a sizable squeal of pain, anger, and surprise.

Where we'd seen his gun hit the concrete there was now a tiny incandescent puddle. A rill of blood snaked out from the pool around his head and touched the whitely glowing puddle and a jet of steam sizzled up.

Somehow the gun had managed to melt itself in the moment of its owner dying. Well, at any rate that showed it hadn't contained any gunpowder or ordinary chemical explosives, though I already knew it operated on other principles from the way it had been used to paralyze me. More to the point, it showed that the gun's owner was the member of a culture that believed in taking very complete precautions against its gadgets falling into the hands of strangers.

But the gun fusing wasn't quite all. As the girl and me shifted our gaze from the puddle, which was cooling fast and now glowed red like the blood-as we shifted our gaze back from the puddle to the dead man, we saw that at three points (points over where you'd expect pockets to be) his gray clothing had charred in small irregularly shaped patches from which threads of black smoke were twisting upward.

Just at that moment, so close as to make me jump in spite of years of learning to absorb shocks stoically-right at my elbow it seemed to (the girl jumped too, I may say) —a voice said, "Done a murder, hey?"

Advancing briskly around the skewily grounded plane from the direction of the cracking plant was an old geezer, a seasoned, hard-baked Deathlander if I ever saw one. He had a shock of bone-white hair, the rest of him that showed from his weathered gray clothing looked fried by the sun's rays and others to a stringy crisp, and strapped to his boots and weighing down his belt were a good dozen knives.

Not satisfied with the unnerving noise he'd made already, he went on brightly, "Neat job too, I give you credit for that, but why the hell did you have to set the guy afire?"

Chapter 3

We are always, thanks to our human nature, potential criminals. None of us stands outside humanity's black collective shadow.
—The Undiscovered Self,
by Carl Jung

Ordinarily scroungers who hide around on the outskirts until the killing's done and then come in to share the loot get what they deserve-wordless orders, well backed up, to be on their way at once. Sometimes they even catch an after-clap of the murder urge, if it hasn't all been expended on the first victim or victims. Yet they *will* do it, trusting I suppose to the irresistible glamor of their personalities. There were several reasons why we didn't at once give Pop this treatment.

In the first place we didn't neither of us have our distance weapons. My revolver and her dart gun were both tucked in the cave back at the edge of the freeway. And there's one bad thing about a bugger so knife-happy he lugs them around by the carload-he's generally good at tossing them. With his dozen or so knives Pop definitely outgunned us.

Second, we were both of us without the use of an arm. That's right, the both of us. My right arm still dangled like a string of sausages and I couldn't yet feel any signs of it coming undead. While she'd burned her fingers badly grabbing at the gun —I could see their red-splotched tips now as she pulled them out of her mouth for a second to wipe the Pilot's blood out of her eyes. All she had was her stump with the knife screwed to it. Me, I can throw a knife left-handed if I have to, but you bet I wasn't going to risk Mother that way.

Then I'd no sooner heard Pop's voice, breathy and a little high like an old man's will get, than it occurred to me that he must have been the one who had given the funny scream that had distracted the Pilot's attention and let us get him. Which incidentally made Pop a quick thinker and imaginative to boot, and meant that he'd helped on the killing.

Besides all that, Pop did not come in fawning and full of extravagant praise, as most scroungers will. He just assumed equality with us right from the start and he talked in an absolutely matter-of-fact way, neither praising nor criticizing one bit-too damn matter-of-fact and open, for that matter, to suit my taste, but then I have heard other buggers say that some old men are apt to get talkative, though I had never worked with or run into one myself. Old people are very rare in the Deathlands, as you might imagine.

So the girl and me just scowled at him but did nothing to stop him as he came along. Near us, his extra knives would be no advantage to him.

"Hum," he said, "looks a lot like a guy I murdered five years back down Los Alamos way. Same silver monkey suit and almost as tall. Nice chap too-was trying to give me something for a fever I'd faked. That his gun melted? My man didn't smoke after I gave him his quietus, but then it turned out he didn't have any metal on him. I wonder if this chap —" He started to kneel down by the body.

"Hands off, Pop!" I gritted at him. That was how we started calling him Pop.

"Why sure, sure," he said, staying there on one knee. "I won't lay a finger on him. It's just that I've heard the Alamosers have it rigged so that any metal they're carrying melts when they die, and I was wondering about this boy. But he's all yours, friend. By the way, what's your name, friend?"

"Ray," I snarled. "Ray Baker." I think the main reason I told him was that I didn't want him calling me "friend" again. "You talk too much, Pop."

"I suppose I do, Ray," he agreed. "What's your name, lady?"

The girl just sort of hissed at him and he grinned at me as if to say, "Oh, women!" Then he said, "Why don't you go through his pockets, Ray? I'm real curious."

"Shut up," I said, but I felt that he'd put me on the spot just the same. I was curious about the guy's pockets myself, of course, but I was also wondering if Pop was alone or if he had somebody with him, and whether there was anybody else in the plane or not-things like that, too many things. At the same time I didn't want to let on to Pop how useless my right arm was-if I'd just get a twinge of feeling in that arm, I knew I'd feel a lot more confident fast. I knelt down across the body from him, started to lay Mother aside and then hesitated.

The girl gave me an encouraging look, as if to say, "I'll take care of the old geezer." On the strength of her look I put down Mother and started to pry open the Pilot's left hand, which was clenched in a fist that looked a mite too big to have nothing inside it.

The girl started to edge behind Pop, but he caught the movement right away and looked at her with a grin that was so knowing and yet so friendly, and yet so pitying at the same time-with the pity of the old pro for even the seasoned amateur-that in her place I think I'd have blushed myself, as she did now ... through the streaks of the Pilot's blood.

"You don't have to worry none about me, lady," he said, running a hand through his white hair and incidentally touching the pommel of one of the two knives strapped high on the back of his jacket so he could reach one over either shoulder. "I quit murdering some years back. It got to be too much of a strain on my nerves."

"Oh yeah?" I couldn't help saying as I pried up the Pilot's index finger and started on the next. "Then why the stab-factory, Pop?"

"Oh you mean those," he said, glancing down at his knives. "Well, the fact is, Ray, I carry them to impress buggers dumber than you and the lady here. Anybody wants to think I'm still a practicing murderer I got no objections. Matter of sentiment, too, I just hate to part with them-they bring back important memories. And then-you won't believe this, Ray, but I'm going to tell you just the same-guys just up and give me their knives and I doubly hate to part with a gift."

I wasn't going to say "Oh yeah?" again or "Shut up!" either, though I certainly wished I could turn off Pop's spigot, or thought I did. Then I felt a painful tingling shoot down my right arm. I smiled at Pop and said, "Any other reasons?"

"Yep," he said. "Got to shave and I might as well do it in style. A new blade every day in the fortnight is twice as good as the old ads. You know, it makes you keep a knife in fine shape if you shave with it. What you got there, Ray?"

"You were wrong, Pop," I said. "He did have some metal on him that didn't melt."

I held up for them to see the object I'd extracted from his left fist: a bright steel cube measuring about an inch across each side, but it felt lighter than if it were solid metal. Five of the faces looked absolutely bare. The sixth had a round button recessed in it.

From the way they looked at it neither Pop nor the girl had the faintest idea of what it was. I certainly hadn't.

"Had he pushed the button?" the girl asked. Her voice was throaty but unexpectedly refined, as if she'd done no talking at all, not even to herself, since coming to the Deathlands and so retained the cultured intonations she'd had earlier, whenever and wherever that had been. It gave me a funny feeling, of course, because they were the first words I'd heard her speak.

"Not from the way he was holding it," I told her. "The button was pointed up toward his thumb but the thumb was on the outside of his fingers." I felt an unexpected satisfaction at having expressed myself so clearly and I told myself not to get childish.

The girl slitted her eyes. "Don't you push it, Ray," she said.

"Think I'm nuts?" I told her, meanwhile sliding the cube into the smaller pocket of my pants, where it fit tight and wouldn't turn sideways and the button maybe get pressed by accident. The tingling in my right arm was almost unbearable now, but I was getting control over the muscles again.

"Pushing that button," I added, "might melt what's left of the plane, or blow us all up." It never hurts to emphasize that you may have another weapon in your possession, even if it's just a suicide bomb.

"There was a man pushed another button once," Pop said softly and reflectively. His gaze went far out over the Deathlands and took in a good half of the horizon and he slowly shook his head. Then his face brightened. "Did you know, Ray," he said, "that I actually met that man? Long afterwards. You don't believe me, I know, but I actually did. Tell you about it some other time."

I almost said, "Thanks, Pop, for sparing me at least for a while," but I was afraid that would set him off again. Besides, it wouldn't have been quite true. I've heard other buggers tell the yarn of how they met (and invariably rubbed out) the actual guy who pushed the button or buttons that set the fusion missiles blasting toward their targets, but I felt a sudden curiosity as to what Pop's version of the yarn would be. Oh well, I could ask him some other time, if we both lived that long. I started to check the Pilot's pockets. My right hand could help a little now.

"Those look like mean burns you got there, lady," I heard Pop tell the girl. He was right. There were blisters easy to see on three of the fingertips. "I've got some salve that's pretty good," he went on, "and some clean cloth. I could put on a bandage for you if you wanted. If your hand started to feel poisoned you could always tell Ray here to slip a knife in me."

Pop was a cute gasser, you had to admit. I reminded myself that it was Pop's business to play up to the both of us, charm being the secret weapon of all scroungers.

The girl gave a harsh little laugh. "Very well," she said, "but we will use my salve, I know it works for me." And she started to lead Pop to where we'd hidden our things.

"I'll go with you," I told them, standing up.

It didn't look like we were going to have any more murders today-Pop had got through the preliminary ingratiations pretty well and the girl and me had had our catharsis-but that would be no excuse for any such stupidity as letting the two of them get near my .38.

Strolling to the cave and back I eased the situation a bit more by saying, "That scream you let off, Pop, really helped. I don't know what gave you the idea, but thanks."

"Oh that," he said. "Forget about it."

"I won't," I told him. "You may say you've quit killing, but helped on a do-in today."

"Ray," he said a little solemnly, "if it'll make you feel any happier, I'll take a bit of the responsibility for every murder that's been done since the beginning of time."

I looked at him for a while. Then, "Pop, you're not by any chance the religious type?" I asked suddenly.

"Lord, no," he told us.

That struck me as a satisfactory answer. God preserve me from the religious type! We have quite a few of those in the Deathlands. It generally means that they try to convert you to something before they kill you. Or sometimes afterwards.

We completed our errands. I felt a lot more secure with Old Financier's Friend strapped to my middle. Mother is wonderful but she is not enough.

I dawdled over inspecting the Pilot's pockets, partly to give my right hand time to come back all the way. And to tell the truth I didn't much enjoy the job —a corpse, especially such a handsome cadaver as this, just didn't go with Pop's brand of light patter.

Pop did up the girl's hand in high style, bandaging each finger separately and then persuading her to put on a big left-hand work glove he took out of his small pack.

"Lost the right," he explained, "which was the only one I ever used anyway. Never knew until now why I kept this. How does it feel, Alice?"

I might have known he'd worm her name out of her. It occurred to me that Pop's ideas of scrounging might extend to Alice's favors. The urge doesn't die out when you get old, they tell me. Not completely.

He'd also helped her replace the knife on her stump with the hook.

By that time I'd poked into all the Pilot's pockets I could get at without stripping him and found nothing but three irregularly shaped blobs of metal, still hot to the touch. Under the charred spots, of course.

I didn't want the job of stripping him. Somebody else could do a little work, I told myself. I've been bothered by bodies before (as who hasn't, I suppose?) but this one was really beginning to make me sick. Maybe I was cracking up, it occurred to me. Murder is a very wearing business, as all Deathlanders know, and although some crack earlier than others, all crack in the end.

I must have been showing how I was feeling because, "Cheer up, Ray," Pop said. "You and Alice have done a big murder —I'd say the subject was six foot ten-so you ought to be happy. You've drawn a blank on his pockets but there's still the plane."

"Yeah, that's right," I said, brightening a little. "There's still the stuff in the plane." I knew there were some items I couldn't hope for, like .38 shells, but there'd be food and other things.

"Nuh-uh," Pop corrected me. "I said *the plane*. You may have thought it's wrecked, but I don't. Have you taken a real gander at it? It's worth doing, believe me."

I jumped up. My heart was suddenly pounding. I was glad of an excuse to get away from the body, but there was a lot more in my feelings than that. I was filled with an excitement to which I didn't want to give a name because it would make the let-down too great.

One of the wide stubby wings of the plane, raking downward so that its tip almost touched the concrete, had hidden the undercarriage of the fuselage from our view. Now, coming around the wing, I saw that *there was no undercarriage.*

I had to drop to my hands and knees and scan around with my cheek next to the concrete before I'd believe it. *The "wrecked" plane was at all points at least six inches off the ground.*

I got to my feet again. I was shaking. I wanted to talk but I couldn't. I grabbed the leading edge of the wing to stop from falling. The whole body of the plane gave a fraction of an inch and then resisted my leaning weight with lazy power, just like a gyroscope.

"Antigravity," I croaked, though you couldn't have heard me two feet. Then my voice came back. "Pop, Alice! They got antigravity! Antigravity-and it's working!"

Alice had just come around the wing and was facing me. She was shaking too and her face was white like I knew mine was. Pop was politely standing off a little to one side, watching us curiously. "Told you you'd won a real prize," he said in his matter-of-fact way.

Alice wet her lips. "Ray," she said, "we can get away."

Just those four words, but they did it. Something in me unlocked-no, exploded describes it better.

"We can go places!" I almost shouted.

"Beyond the dust," she said. "Mexico City. South America!" She was forgetting the Death-lander's cynical article of belief that the dust never ends, but then so was I. It makes a difference whether or not you've got a means of doing something.

"Rio!" I topped her with. "The Indies. Hong Kong. Bombay. Egypt. Bermuda. The French Riviera!"

"Bullfights and clean beds," she burst out with. "Restaurants. Swimming pools. Bathrooms!"

"Skindiving," I took it up with, as hysterical as she was. "Road races and roulette tables."

"Bentleys and Porsches!"

"Aircoups and DC4s and Comets!"

"Martinis and hashish and ice cream sodas!"

"Hot food! Fresh coffee! Gambling, smoking, dancing, music, drinks!" I was going to add *women*, but then I thought of how hard-bitten little Alice would look beside the dream creatures I had in mind. I tactfully suppressed the word but I filed the idea away.

I don't think either of us knew exactly what we were saying. Alice in particular I don't believe was old enough to have experienced almost any of the things the words referred to. They were mysterious symbols of long-interdicted delights spewing out of us.

"Ray," Alice said, hurrying to me, "let's get aboard."

"Yes," I said eagerly and then I saw a little problem. The door to the plane was a couple of feet above our heads. Whoever hoisted himself up first-or got hoisted up, as would have to be the case with Alice on account of her hand-would be momentarily at the other's mercy. I guess it occurred to Alice too because she stopped and looked at me. It was a little like the old teaser about the fox, the goose, and the corn.

Maybe, too, we were both a little scared the plane was booby-trapped.

Pop solved the problem in the direct way I might have expected of him by stepping quietly between us, giving a light leap, catching hold of the curving sill, chinning himself on it, and scrambling up into the plane so quickly that we'd hardly have had time to do anything about it if we'd wanted to. Pop couldn't be much more than a bantamweight, even with all his knives. The plane sagged an inch and then swung up again.

As Pop disappeared from view I backed off, reaching for my .38, but a moment later he stuck out his head and grinned down at us, resting his elbows on the sill.

"Come on up," he said. "It's quite a place. I promise not to push any buttons 'til you get here, though there's whole regiments of them."

I grinned back at Pop and gave Alice a boost up. She didn't like it, but she could see it had to be her next. She hooked onto the sill and Pop caught hold of her left wrist below the big glove and heaved.

Then it was my turn. I didn't like it. I didn't like the idea of those two buggers poised above me while my hands were helpless on the sill. But I thought *Pop's a nut. You can trust a nut, at least a little ways, though you can't trust nobody else.* I heaved myself up. It was strange to feel the plane giving and then bracing itself like something alive. It seemed to have no trouble accepting our combined weight, which after all was hardly more than half again the Pilot's.

Inside the cabin was pretty small but as Pop had implied, oh my! Everything looked soft and smoothly curved, like you imagine your insides being, and almost everything was a restfully dull silver. The general shape of it was something like the inside of an egg. Forward, which was the larger end, were a couple of screens and a wide viewport and some small dials and the button brigades Pop had mentioned, lined up like blank typewriter keys but enough for writing Chinese.

Just aft of the instrument panel were two very comfortable-looking strange low seats. They seemed to be facing backwards until I realized they were meant to be knelt into. The occupant, I could see, would sort of sprawl forward, his hands free for button-pushing and such. There were spongy chinrests.

Aft was a tiny instrument panel and a kind of sideways seat, not nearly so fancy. The door by which we'd entered was to the side, a little aft.

I didn't see any indications of cabinets or fixed storage spaces of any kinds, but somehow stuck to the walls here and there were quite a few smooth blobby packages, mostly dull silver too, some large, some small-valises and handbags, you might say.

All in all, it was a lovely cabin and, more than that, it seemed lived in. It looked as if it had been shaped for, and maybe by one man. It had a personality you could feel, a strong but warm personality of its own.

Then I realized whose personality it was. I almost got sick-so close to it I started telling myself it must be something antigravity did to your stomach.

But it was all too interesting to let you get sick right away. Pop was poking into two of the large mound-shaped cases that were sitting loose and open on the right-hand seat, as if ready for emergency use. One had a folded something with straps on it that was probably a parachute. The second had I judged a thousand or more of the inch cubes such as I'd pried out of the Pilot's hand, all neatly stacked in a cubical box inside the soft outer bag. You could see the one-cube gap where he'd taken the one.

I decided to take the rest of the bags off the walls and open them, if I could figure out how. The others had the same idea, but Alice had to take off her hook and put on her pliers, before she could make progress. Pop helped her. There was room enough for us to do these things without crowding each other too closely.

By the time Alice was set to go I'd discovered the trick of getting the bags off. You couldn't pull them away from the wall no matter what force you used, at least I couldn't, and you couldn't even slide them straight along the walls, but if you just gave them a gentle counterclockwise twist they came off like nothing. Twisting them clockwise glued them back on. It was very strange, but I told myself that if these boys could generate antigravity fields they could create screwy fields of other sorts.

It also occurred to me to wonder if "these boys" came from Earth. The Pilot had looked human enough, but these accomplishments didn't —not by my standards for human achievement in the Age of the Deaders. At any rate I had to admit to myself that my pet term "cultural queer" did not describe to my own satisfaction members of a culture which could create things like this cabin. Not that I liked making the admission. It's hard to admit an exception to a pet gripe against things.

The excitement of getting down and opening the Christmas packages saved me from speculating too much along these or any other lines.

I hit a minor jackpot right away. In the same bag were a compass, a catalytic pocket lighter, a knife with a saw-tooth back edge that made my affection for Mother waver, a dust mask, what looked like a compact water-filtration unit, and several other items adding up to a deluxe Deathlands Survival Kit.

There were some goggles in the kit I didn't savvy until I put them on and surveyed the landscape out the viewport. A nearby dust drift I knew to be hot glowed green as death in the slightly smoky lenses. Wow! Those specs had Geiger counters beat a mile and I privately bet myself they worked at night. I stuck them in my pocket quick.

We found bunches of tiny electronics parts —I think they were; spools of magnetic tape, but nothing to play it on; reels of very narrow film with frames much too small to see anything at all unmagnified; about three thousand cigarettes in unlabeled transparent packs of twenty-we lit up quick, using my new lighter; a picture book that didn't make much sense because the views might have been of tissue sections or starfields, we couldn't quite decide, and there were no captions to help; a thin book with ricepaper pages covered with Chinese characters —that was a puzzler; a thick book with nothing but columns of figures, all zeros and ones and nothing else; some tiny chisels; and a mouth organ. Pop, who'd make a point of just helping in the hunt, appropriated that last item —I might have known he would, I told myself. Now we could expect "Turkey in the Straw" at odd moments.

Alice found a whole bag of what were women's things judging from the frilliness of the garments included. She set aside some squeeze-packs and little gadgets and elastic items right away, but she didn't take any of the clothes. I caught her measuring some kind of transparent chemise against herself when she thought we weren't looking; it was for a girl maybe six sizes bigger.

And we found food. Cans of food that was heated up inside by the time you got the top rolled off, though the outside could still be cool to the touch. Cans of boneless steak, boneless chops, cream soup, peas, carrots, and fried potatoes-they weren't labeled at all but you could generally guess the contents from the shape of the can. Eggs that heated when you touched them and were soft-boiled evenly and barely firm by the time you had the shell broke. And small plastic bottles of strong coffee that heated up hospitably too-in this case the tops did a five-second hesitation in the middle of your unscrewing them.

At that point as you can imagine we let the rest of the packages go and had ourselves a feast. The food ate even better than it smelled. It was real hard for me not to gorge.

Then as I was slurping down my second bottle of coffee I happened to look out the viewport and see the Pilot's body and the darkening puddle around it and the coffee began to taste, well, not bad, but sickening. I don't think it was guilty conscience. Deathlanders outgrow those if they ever have them to start with; loners don't keep consciences-it takes cultures to give you those and make them work. Artistic inappropriateness is the closest I can come to describing what bothered me. Whatever it was, it made me feel lousy for a minute.

About the same time Alice did an odd thing with the last of *her* coffee. She slopped it on a rag and used it to wash her face. I guess she'd caught a reflection of herself with the blood smears. She didn't eat any more after that either. Pop kept on chomping away, a slow feeder and appreciative.

To be doing something I started to inspect the instrument panel and right away I was all excited again. The two screens were what got me. They showed shadowy maps, one of North America, the other of the World. The first one was a whole lot like the map I'd been imagining earlier-faint colors marked the small "civilized" areas including one in Eastern Canada and another in Upper Michigan that must be "countries" I didn't know about, and the Deathlands were real dark just as I'd always maintained they should be!

South of Lake Michigan was a brightly luminous green point that must be where we were, I decided. And for some reason the colored areas representing Los Alamos and Atlantic Highlands were glowing brighter than the others-they had an active luminosity. Los Alamos was blue, Atla-Hi violet. Los Alamos was shown having more territory than I expected. Savannah Fortress for that matter was a whole *lot* bigger than I'd have made it, pushing out pseudopods west and northeast along the coast, though its red didn't have the extra glow. But its growth-pattern reeked of imperialism.

The World screen showed dim color patches too, but for the moment I was more interested in the other.

The button armies marched right up to the lower edge of the screens and right away I got the crazy hunch that they were connected with spots on the map. Push the button for a certain spot and the plane would go there! Why, one button even seemed to have a faint violet nimbus around it (or else my eyes were going bad) as if to say, "Push me and we go to Atlantic Highlands."

A crazy notion as I say and no sensible way to handle a plane's navigation according to any standards I could imagine, but then as I've also said this plane didn't seem to be designed according to any standards but rather in line with one man's ideas, including his whims.

At any rate that was my hunch about the buttons and the screens. It tantalized rather than helped, for the only button that seemed to be marked in any way was the one (guessing by color) for Atlantic Highlands, and I certainly didn't want to go there. Like Alamos, Atla-Hi has the reputation for being a mysteriously dangerous place. Not openly mean and death-on-Deathlanders like Walla Walla or Porter, but buggers who swing too close to Atla-Hi have a way of never turning up again. You never expect to see again two out of three buggers who pass in the night, but for three out of three to keep disappearing is against statistics.

Alice was beside me now, scanning things over too, and from the way she frowned and what not I gathered she had caught my hunch and also shared my puzzlement.

Now was the time, all right, when we needed an instruction manual and not one in Chinese neither!

Pop swallowed a mouthful and said, "Yep, now'd be a good time to have him back for a minute, to explain things a bit. Oh, don't take offense, Ray, I know how it was for you and for you too, Alice. I know the both of you *had* to murder him, it wasn't a matter of free choice, it's the way us Deathlanders are built. Just the same, it'd be nice to have a way of killing 'em and keeping them on hand at the same time. I remember feeling that way after murdering the Alamoser I told you about. You see, I come down with the very fever I'd faked and almost died of it, while the man who could have cured me easy wouldn't do nothing but perfume the landscape with the help of a gang of anaerobic bacteria. Stubborn single-minded cuss!"

The first part of that oration started up my sickness again and irked me not a little. Dammit, what right had Pop to talk about how all us Deathlanders *had to* kill (which was true enough and by itself would have made me cotton to him) if as he'd claimed earlier *he'd* been able to quit killing? Pop was, an old hypocrite, I told myself-he'd helped murder the Pilot, he'd admitted as much-and Alice and me'd be better off if we bedded the both of them down together. But then the second part of what Pop said so made me want to feel pleasantly sorry for myself and laugh at the same time that I forgave the old geezer. Practically everything Pop said had that reassuring touch of insanity about it.

So it was Alice who said, "Shut up, Pop" —and rather casually at that-and she and me went on to speculate and then to argue about which buttons we ought to push, if any and in what order.

"Why not just start anywhere and keep pushing 'em one after another? —you're going to have to eventually, may as well start now," was Pop's light-hearted contribution to the discussion. "Got to take some chances in this life." He was sitting in the back seat and still nibbling away like a white-topped mangy old squirrel.

Of course Alice and me knew more than that. We kept making guesses as to how the buttons worked and then backing up our guesses with hot language. It was a little like two savages trying to decide how to play chess by looking at the pieces. And then the old escape-to-paradise theme took hold of us again and we studied the colored blobs on the World screen, trying to decide which would have the fanciest accommodations for blase ex-murderers. On the North America screen too there was an intriguing pink patch in southern Mexico that seemed to take in old Mexico City and Acapulco too.

"Quit talking and start pushing," Pop prodded us. "This way you're getting nowhere fast. I can't stand hesitation, it riles my nerves."

Alice thought you ought to push ten buttons at once, using both hands, and she was working out patterns for me to try. But I was off on a kick about how we should darken the plane to see if any of the other buttons glowed beside the one with the Atla-Hi violet.

"Look here, you killed a big man to get this plane," Pop broke in, coming up behind me. "Are you going to use it for discussion groups or are you going to fly it?"

"Quiet," I told him. I'd got a new hunch and was using the dark glasses to scan the instrument panel. They didn't show anything.

"Dammit, I can't stand this any more," Pop said and reached a hand and arm between us and brought it down on about fifty buttons, I'd judge.

The other buttons just went down and up, but the Atla-Hi button went down and stayed down.

The violet blob of Atla-Hi on the screen got even brighter in the next few moments.

The door closed with a tiny thud.

We took off.

Chapter 4

Any man who deals in murder, must have very incorrect ways of think-
ing, and truly inaccurate principles.
—*Thomas de Quincey in*
Murder Considered as One of the Fine Arts

For that matter we took off *fast* with the plane swinging to beat hell. Alice and me was in the two kneeling seats and we hugged them tight, but Pop was loose and sort of rattled around the cabin for a while-and serve him right!

On one of the swings I caught a glimpse of the seven dented gas tanks, looking like dull crescents from this angle through the orange haze and getting rapidly smaller as they hazed out.

After a while the plane levelled off and quit swinging, and a while after that my image of the cabin quit swinging too. Once again I just managed to stave off the vomits, this time the vomits from natural causes. Alice looked very pale around the gills and kept her face buried in the chinrest of her chair.

Pop ended up right in our faces, sort of spread-eagled against the instrument panel. In get-ting himself off it he must have braced his hands against half the buttons at one time or another and I noticed that none of them went down a fraction. They were *locked*. It had probably happened automatically when the Atla-Hi button got pushed.

I'd have stopped him messing around in that apish way, but with the ultra-queasy state of my stomach I lacked all ambition and was happy just not to be smelling him so close.

I still wasn't taking too great an interest in things as I idly watched the old geezer rummaging around the cabin for something that got misplaced in the shake-up. Eventually he found it —a small almond-shaped can. He opened it. Sure enough it turned out to have almonds in it. He fitted himself in the back seat and munched them one at a time. Ish!

"Nothing like a few nuts to top off with," he said cheerfully.

I could have cut his throat even more cheerfully, but the damage had been done and you think twice before you kill a person in close quarters when you aren't absolutely sure you'll be able to dispose of the body. How did I know I'd be able to open the door? I remember philosophizing that Pop ought at least to have broke an arm so he'd be as badly off as Alice and me (though for that matter my right arm was fully recovered now) but he was all in one piece. There's no justice in events, that's for sure.

The plane ploughed along silently through the orange soup, though there was really no way to tell it was moving now-until a skewy spindle shape loomed up ahead and shot back over the viewport. I think it was a vulture. I don't know how vultures manage to operate in the haze, which ought to cancel their keen eyesight, but they do. It shot past *fast*.

Alice lifted her face out of the sponge stuff and began to study the buttons again. I heaved myself up and around a little and said, "Pop, Alice and me are going to try to work out how this plane navigates. This time we don't want no interference." I didn't say a word more about what he'd done. It never does to hash over stupidities.

"That's perfectly fine, go right ahead," he told me. "I feel calm as a kitten now we're going somewheres. That's all that ever matters with me." He chuckled a bit and added, "You got to admit I gave you and Alice something to work with," but then he had the sense to shut up tight.

We weren't so chary of pushing buttons this time, but ten minutes or so convinced us that you couldn't push any of the buttons any more, they *were* all locked down-all locked except for maybe one, which we didn't try at first for a special reason.

We looked for other controls-sticks, levers, pedals, finger-holes and the like. There weren't any. Alice went back and tried the buttons on Pop's minor console. They were locked too. Pop looked interested but didn't say a word.

We realized in a general way what had happened, of course. Pushing the Atla-Hi button had set us on some kind of irreversible automatic. I couldn't imagine the why of gimmicking a plane's controls like that, unless maybe to keep loose children or prisoners from being able to mess things up while the pilot took a snooze, but there were a lot of whys to this plane that didn't seem to have any standard answers.

The business of taking off on irreversible automatic had happened so neatly that I naturally wondered whether Pop might not know more about navigating this plane than he let on, a whole lot more in fact, and the seemingly idiotic petulance of his pushing all the buttons have been a shrewd cover for pushing the Atla-Hi button. But if Pop had been acting he'd been acting beautifully, with a serene disregard for the chances of breaking his own neck. I decided this was a possibility I could think about later and maybe act on then, after Alice and me had worked through the more obvious stuff.

The reason we hadn't tried the one button yet was that it showed a green nimbus, just like the Atla-Hi button had had a violet nimbus. Now there was no green on either of the screens except for the tiny green star that I had figured stood for the plane and it didn't make sense to go where we already were. And if it meant some other place, some place not shown on the screens, you bet we weren't going to be too quick about deciding to go there. It might not be on Earth.

Alice expressed it by saying, "My namesake was always a little too quick at responding to those DRINK ME cues."

I suppose she thought she was being cryptic, but I fooled her. "*Alice in Wonderland?*" I asked. She nodded, and gave me a little smile, not at all like one of the EAT ME smiles she'd given me last evening.

It is funny how crazily happy a little touch of the intellectual past like that can make you feel-and how horribly uncomfortable a moment later.

We both started to study the North America screen again and almost at once we realized that it had changed in one small particular. The green star had twinned. Where there had been one point of green light there were now two, very close together like the double star in the handle of the Dipper. We watched it for a while. The distance between the two stars grew perceptibly greater. We watched it for a while longer, considerably longer. It became clear that the position of the more westerly star on the screen was fixed, while the more easterly star was moving east toward Atla-Hi with about the speed of the tip of the minute hand on a wrist watch (two inches an hour, say). The pattern began to make sense.

I figured it this way: the moving star must stand for the plane, the other green dot must stand for where the plane had just been. For some reason the spot on the freeway by the old cracking plant was recognized as a marked locality by the screen. Why I don't know. It reminded me of the old "X Marks the Spot" of newspaper murders, but that would be getting very fancy. Anyway the spot we'd just taken off from was so marked and in that case the button with the green nimbus...

"Hold tight, everybody," I said to Alice, grudgingly including Pop in my warning. "I got to try it."

I gripped my seat with my knees and one arm and pushed the green button. It pushed.

The plane swung around in a level loop, not too tight to disturb the stomach much, and steadied out again.

I couldn't judge how far we'd swung but Alice and me watched the green stars and after about a minute she said, "They're getting closer," and a little while later I said, "Yeah, for sure."

I scanned the board. The green button-the cracking-plant button, to call it that-was locked down of course. The Atla-Hi button was up, glowing violet. All the other buttons were still up and *locked* up —I tried them all again.

It was clear as day used to be. We could either go to Atla-Hi or we could go back where we'd started from. There was no third possibility.

It was a little hard to take. You think of a plane as freedom, as something that will carry you anywhere in the world you choose to go, especially any paradise, and then you find yourself worse limited than if you'd stayed on the ground-at least that was the way it was happening to us.

But Alice and me were realists. We knew it wouldn't help to wail. We were up against another of those "two" problems, the problem of two destinations, and we had to choose ours.

If we go back, I thought, *we can trek on somewhere-anywhere-richer by the loot from the plane, especially that Survival Kit. Trek on with some loot we'll mostly never understand and with the knowledge that we are leaving a plane that can fly, that we are shrinking back from an unknown adventure.*

Also if we go back there's something else we'll have to face, something we'll have to live with for a little while at least that won't be nice to live with after this cozily personal cabin, something that shouldn't bother me at all but, dammit, it does.

Alice made the decision for us and at the same time showed she was thinking about the same thing as me.

"I don't want to have to smell him, Ray," she said. "I am not going back to keep company with that filthy corpse. I'd rather anything than that." And she pushed the Atla-Hi button again and as the plane started to swing she looked at me defiantly as if to say I'd reverse the course again over her dead body.

"Don't tense up," I told her. "I want a new shake of the dice myself."

"You know, Alice," Pop said reflectively, "it was the smell of my Alamoser got to me too. I just couldn't bear it. I couldn't get away from it because my fever had me pinned down, so there was nothing left for me to do but go crazy. No Atla-Hi for me, just Bug-land. My mind died, though not my memory. By the time I'd got my strength back I'd started to be a new bugger. I didn't know no more about living than a newborn babe, except I knew I couldn't go back-go back to murdering and all that. My new mind knew that much though otherwise it was just a blank. It was all very funny."

"And then I suppose," Alice cut in, her voice corrosive with sarcasm, "you hunted up a wandering preacher, or perhaps a kindly old hermit who lived on hot manna, and he showed you the blue sky!"

"Why no, Alice," Pop said. "I told you I don't go for religion. As it happens, I hunted me up a couple of murderers, guys who were worse cases then myself but who'd wanted to quit because it wasn't getting them nowhere and who'd found, I'd heard, a way of quitting, and the three of us had a long talk together."

"And they told you the great secret of how to live in the Deathlands without killing," Alice continued acidly. "Drop the nonsense, Pop. It can't be done."

"It's hard, I'll grant you," Pop said. "You have to go crazy or something almost as bad-in fact, maybe going crazy is the easiest way. But it can be done and, in the long run, murder is even harder."

I decided to interrupt this idle chatter. Since we were now definitely headed for Atla-Hi and there was nothing to do until we got there, unless one of us got a brainstorm about the controls, it was time to start on the less obvious stuff I'd tabled in my mind.

"Why are you on this plane, Pop?" I asked sharply. "What do you figure on getting out of Alice and me? —and I don't mean the free meals."

He grinned. His teeth were white and even-plates, of course. "Why, Ray," he said, "I was just giving Alice the reason. I like to talk to murderers, practicing murderers preferred. I need to —*have* to talk to 'em, to keep myself straight. Otherwise I might start killing again and I'm not up to that any more."

"Oh, so you get your kicks at second hand, you old peeper," Alice put in but, "Quit lying, Pop," I said. "About having quit killing, for one thing. In my books, which happen to be the old books in this case, the accomplice is every bit as guilty as the man with the slicer. You helped us kill the Pilot by giving that funny scream and you know it."

"Who says I did?" Pop countered, rearing up a little. "I never said so. I just said, 'Forget it.'" He hesitated a moment, studying me. Then he said, "I wasn't the one gave that scream. In fact, I'd have stopped it if I'd been able."

"Who did then?"

Again he studied me as he hesitated. "I'm not telling," he said, settling back.

"Pop!" I said, sharp again. "Buggers who pad together tell everything."

"Oh yeah," he agreed, smiling. "I remember saying that to quite a few guys in my day. It's a very restful comradely sentiment. I killed every last one of 'em, too."

"You may have, Pop," I granted, "but we're two to one."

"So you are," he agreed softly, looking the both of us over. I knew what he was thinking—that Alice still had just her pliers on and that in these close quarters his knives were as good as my gun.

"Give me your right hand, Alice," I said. Without taking my eyes off Pop I reached the knife without a handle out of her belt and then I started to unscrew the pliers out of her stump.

"Pop," I said as I did so, "you may have quit killing for all I know. I mean you may have quit killing clean decent Deathland style. But I don't believe one bit of that guff about having to talk to murderers to keep your mind sweet. Furthermore —"

"It's true though," he interrupted. "I got to keep myself reminded of how lousy it feels to be a murderer."

"So?" I said. "Well, here's one person who believes you've got a more practical reason for being on this plane. Pop, what's the bounty Atla-Hi gives you for every Deathlander you bring in? What would it be for two live Deathlanders? And what sort of reward would they pay for a lost plane brought in? Seems to me they might very well make you a citizen for that."

"Yes, even give you your own church," Alice added with a sort of wicked gaiety. I squeezed her stump gently to tell her let me handle it.

"Why, I guess you can believe that if you want to," Pop said and let out a soft breath. "Seems to me you need a lot of coincidences and happenstances to make that theory hold water, but you sure can believe it if you want to. I got no way, Ray, to prove to you I'm telling the truth except to say I am."

"Right," I said and then I threw the next one at him real fast. "What's more, Pop, weren't you traveling in this plane to begin with? That cuts a happenstance. Didn't you hop out while we were too busy with the Pilot to notice and just *pretend* to be coming from the cracking plant? Weren't the buttons locked because you were the Pilot's prisoner?"

Pop creased his brow thoughtfully. "It could have been that way," he said at last. "Could have been-according to the evidence as you saw it. It's quite a bright idea, Ray. I can almost see myself skulking in this cabin, while you and Alice —"

"You were skulking somewhere," I said. I finished screwing in the knife and gave Alice back her hand. "I'll repeat it, Pop," I said. "We're two to one. You'd better talk."

"Yes," Alice added, disregarding my previous hint. "You may have given up fighting, Pop, but I haven't. Not fighting, nor killing, nor anything in between those two. Any least thing." My girl was being her most pantherish.

"Now who says I've given up *fighting*?" Pop demanded, rearing a little again. "You people assume too much, it's a dangerous habit. Before we have any trouble and somebody squawks about me cheating, let's get one thing straight. If anybody jumps me I'll try to disable them, I'll try to hurt them in any way short of killing, and that means hamstringing and rabbit-punching and everything else. Every least thing, Alice. And if they happen to die while I'm honestly just trying to hurt them in a way short of killing, then I won't grieve too much. My conscience will be reasonably clear. Is that understood?"

I had to admit that it was. Pop might be lying about a lot of things, but I just didn't believe he was lying about this. And I already knew Pop was quick for his age and strong enough. If Alice and me jumped him now there'd be blood let six different ways. You can't jump a man who has a dozen knives easy to hand and not expect that to happen, two to one or not. We'd get him in the end but it would be gory.

"And now," Pop said quietly, "I *will* talk a little if you don't mind. Look here, Ray ...Alice ... the two of you are confirmed murderers, I know you wouldn't tell me nothing different, and being such you both know that there's nothing in murder in the long run. It satisfies a hunger and maybe gets you a little loot and it lets you get on to the next killing. But that's all, absolutely all. Yet you got to do it because it's the way you're built. The urge is there, it's an overpowering urge, and you got nothing to oppose it with. You feel the Big Grief and the Big Resentment, the dust is eating at your bones, you can't stand the city squares-the Porterites and Mantenors and such-because you know they're whistling in the dark and it's a dirty tune, so you go on killing. But if there were a decent practical way to quit, you'd take it. At least I think you would. When you still thought this plane could take you to Rio or Europe you felt that way, didn't you? You weren't planning to go there as murderers, were you? You were going to leave your trade behind."

It was pretty quiet in the cabin for a couple of seconds. Then Alice's thin laugh sliced the silence. "We were dreaming then," she said. "We were out of our heads. But now you're talking about practical things, as you say. What do you expect us to do if we quit our trade, as you call it-go into Walla Walla or Ouachita and give ourselves up? I might lose more than my right hand at Ouachita this time-that was just on suspicion."

"Or Atla-Hi," I added meaningfully. "Are you expecting us to admit we're murderers when we get to Atla-Hi, Pop?"

The old geezer smiled and thinned his eyes. "Now that wouldn't accomplish much, would it? Most places they'd just string you up, maybe after tickling your pain nerves a bit, or if it was Manteno they might put you in a cage and feed you slops and pray over you, and would that help you or anybody else? If a man or woman quits killing there's a lot of things he's got to straighten out-first his own mind and feelings, next he's got to do what he can to make up for the murders he's done-help the next of kin if any and so on-then he's got to carry the news to other killers who haven't heard it yet. He's got no time to waste being hanged. Believe me, he's got work lined up for him, work that's got to be done mostly in the Deathlands, and it's the sort of work the city squares can't help him with one bit, because they just don't understand us murderers and what makes us tick. We have to do it ourselves."

"Hey, Pop," I cut in, getting a little interested in the argument (there wasn't anything else to get interested in until we got to Atla-Hi or Pop let down his guard), "I dig you on the city squares (I call 'em cultural queers) and what sort of screwed-up fatheads they are, but just the same for a man to quit killing he's got to quit lone-wolfing it. He's got to belong to a community, he's got to have a culture of some sort, no matter how disgusting or nutsy."

"Well," Pop said, "don't us Deathlanders have a culture? With customs and folkways and all the rest? A very tight little culture, in fact. Nutsy as all get out, of course, but that's one of the beauties of it."

"Oh sure," I granted him, "but it's a culture based on murder and devoted wholly to murder. Murder is our way of life. That gets your argument nowhere, Pop."

"Correction," he said. "Or rather, re-interpretation." And now for a little while his voice got less old-man harsh and yet bigger somehow, as if it were more than just Pop talking. "Every culture," he said, "is a way of growth as well as a way of life, because the first law of life is growth. Our Deathland culture is devoted to growing *through* murder *away from* murder. That's my thought. It's about the toughest way of growth anybody was ever asked to face up to, but it's a way of growth just the same. A lot bigger and fancier cultures never could figure out the answer to the problem of war and killing —we know that, all right, we inhabit their grandest failure. Maybe us Deathlanders, working with murder every day, unable to pretend that it isn't part of every one of us, unable to put it out of our minds like the city squares do-maybe us Deathlanders are the ones to do that little job."

"But hell, Pop," I objected, getting excited in spite of myself, "even if we got a culture here in the Deathlands, a culture that can grow, it ain't a culture that can deal with repentant murderers. In a *real* culture a murderer feels guilty and confesses and then he gets hanged or imprisoned a long time and that squares things for him and everybody. You need religion and courts and hangmen and screws and all the rest of it. I don't think it's enough for a man just to say he's sorry and go around glad-handing other killers —*that* isn't going to be enough to wipe out his sense of guilt."

Pop squared his eyes at mine. "Are you so fancy that you have to have a sense of guilt, Ray?" he demanded. "Can't you just see when something's lousy? A sense of guilt's a luxury. Of course it's not enough to say you're sorry-you're going to have to spend a good part of the rest of your life making up for what you've done ... and what you will do, too! But about hanging and prisons-was it ever proved those were the right thing for murderers? As for religion now-some of us who've quit killing are religious and a lot of us (me included) aren't; and some of the ones that are religious figure (maybe because there's no way for them to get hanged) that they're damned eternally-but that doesn't stop them doing good work. I ask you now, is any little thing like being damned eternally a satisfactory excuse for behaving like a complete rat?"

That did it, somehow. That last statement of Pop's appealed so much to me and was completely crazy at the same time, that I couldn't help warming up to him. Don't get me wrong, I didn't really fall for his line of chatter at all, but I found it fun to go along with it-so long as the plane was in this shuttle situation and we had nothing better to do.

Alice seemed to feel the same way. I guess any bugger that could kid religion the way Pop could got a little silver star in her books. Bronze, anyway.

Right away the atmosphere got easier. To start with we asked Pop to tell us about this "us" he kept mentioning and he said it was some dozens (or hundreds-nobody had accurate figures) of killers who'd quit and went nomading around the Deathlands trying to recruit others and help those who wanted to be helped. They had semi-permanent meeting places where they tried to get together at pre-arranged dates, but mostly they kept on the go, by twos and threes or-more rarely-alone. They were all men so far, at least Pop hadn't heard of any women members, but-he assured Alice earnestly-he would personally guarantee that there would be no objections to a girl joining up. They had recently taken to calling themselves Murderers Anonymous, after some pre-war organization Pop didn't know the original purpose of. Quite a few of them had slipped and gone back to murdering again, but some of these had come back after a while, more determined than ever to make a go of it.

"We welcomed 'em, of course," Pop said. "We welcome everybody. Everybody that's a genuine murderer, that is, and says he wants to quit. Guys that aren't blooded yet we draw the line at, no matter how fine they are."

Also, "We have a lot of fun at our meetings," Pop assured us. "You never saw such high times. Nobody's got a right to go glooming around or pull a long face just because he's done a killing or two. Religion or no religion, pride's a sin."

Alice and me ate it all up like we was a couple of kids and Pop was telling us fairy tales. That's what it all was, of course, a fairy tale —a crazy mixed-up fairy tale. Alice and me knew there could be no fellowship of Deathlanders like Pop was describing-it was impossible as blue sky-but it gave us a kick to pretend to ourselves for a while to believe in it.

Pop could talk forever, apparently, about murder and murderers and he had a bottomless bag of funny stories on the same topic and character vignettes-the murderers who were forever wanting their victims to understand and forgive them, the ones who thought of themselves as little kings with divine rights of dispensing death, the ones who insisted on laying down (chastely) beside their finished victims and playing dead for a couple of hours, the ones who weren't so chaste, the ones who could only do their killings when they were dressed a certain way (and the troubles they had with their murder costumes), the ones who could only kill people with certain traits or of a certain appearance (red-heads, say, or people who read books, or who couldn't carry tunes, or who used bad language), the ones who always mixed sex and murder and the ones who believed that murder was contaminated by the least breath of sex, the sticklers and the Sloppy Joes, the artists and the butchers, the ax- and stiletto-types, the *compulsives* and the *repulsives*-honestly, Pop's portraits from life added up to a Dance of Death as good as anything the Middle Ages ever produced and they ought to have been illustrated like those by some great artist. Pop told us a lot about his own killings too. Alice and me was interested, but neither of us wasn't tempted into making parallel revelations about ourselves. Your private life's your own business, I felt, as close as your guts, and no joke's good enough to justify revealing a knot of it.

Not that we talked about nothing but murder while we were bulleting along toward Atla-Hi. The conversation was free-wheeling and we got onto all sorts of topics. For instance, we got to talking about the plane and how it flew itself-or levitated itself, rather. I said it must generate an antigravity field that was keyed to the body of the plane but nothing else, so that *we* didn't feel lighter, nor any of the objects in the cabin-it just worked on the dull silvery metal-and I proved my point by using Mother to shave a little wisp of metal off the edge of the control board. The curlicue stayed in the air wherever you put it and when you moved it you could feel the faintest sort of gyroscopic resistance. It was very strange.

Pop pointed out it was a little like magnetism. A germ riding on an iron filing that was traveling toward the pole of a big magnet wouldn't feel the magnetic pull-it wouldn't be operating on him, only on the iron-but just the same the germ'd be carried along with the filing and feel its acceleration and all, provided he could hold on-but for that purpose you could imagine a tiny cabin in the filing. "That's what we are," Pop added. "Three germs, jumbo size."

Alice wanted to know why an antigravity plane should have even the stubbiest wings or a jet for that matter, for we remembered now we'd noticed the tubes, and I said it was maybe just a reserve system in case the antigravity failed and Pop guessed it might be for extra-fast battle maneuvering or even for operating outside the atmosphere (which hardly made sense, as I proved to him).

"If we're a battle plane, where's our guns?" Alice asked. None of us had an answer.

We remembered the noise the plane had made before we saw it. It must have been using its jets then. "And do you suppose," Pop asked, "that it was something from the antigravity that made electricity flare out of the top of the cracking plant? Like to have scared the pants off me!" No answer to that either.

Now was a logical time, of course, to ask Pop what he knew about the cracking plant and just who had done the scream if not him, but I figured he still wouldn't talk; as long as we were acting friendly there was no point in spoiling it.

We guessed around a little, though, about where the plane came from. Pop said Alamos, I said Atla-Hi, Alice said why not from both, why couldn't Alamos and Atla-Hi have some sort of treaty and the plane be traveling from the one to the other. We agreed it might be. At least it fitted with the Atla-Hi violet and the Alamos blue being brighter than the other colors.

"I just hope we got some sort of anti-collision radar," I said. I guessed we had, because twice we'd jogged in our course a little, maybe to clear the Alleghenies. The easterly green star was by now getting pretty close to the violet blot of Atla-Hi. I looked out at the orange soup, which was *one* thing that hadn't changed a bit so far, and I got to wishing like a baby that it wasn't there and to thinking how it blanketed the whole Earth (stars over the Riviera? —don't make me laugh!) and I heard myself asking, "Pop, did you rub out that guy that pushed the buttons for all this?"

"Nope," Pop answered without hesitation, just as if it hadn't been four hours or so since he'd mentioned the point. "Nope, Ray. Fact is I welcomed him into our little fellowship about six months back. This is *his* knife here, this horn-handle in my boot, though he never killed with it. He claimed he'd been tortured for years by the thought of the millions and millions he'd killed with blast and radiation, but now he was finding peace at last because he was where he belonged, with the murderers, and could start to do something about it. Several of the boys didn't want to let him in. They claimed he wasn't a real murderer, doing it by remote control, no matter how many he bumped off."

"I'd have been on their side," Alice said, thinning her lips.

"Yep," Pop continued, "they got real hot about it. *He* got hot too and all excited and offered to go out and kill somebody with his bare hands right off, or try to (he's a skinny little runt), if that's what he had to do to join. We argued it over, I pointed out that we let ex-soldiers count the killings they'd done in service, and that we counted poisonings and booby traps and such too-which are remote-control killings in a way-so eventually we let him in. He's doing good work. We're fortunate to have him."

"Do you think he's really the guy who pushed the buttons?" I asked Pop.

"How should I know?" Pop replied. "He claims to be."

I was going to say something about people who faked confessions to get a little easy glory, as compared to the guys who were really guilty and would sooner be chopped up than talk about it, but at that moment a fourth voice started talking in the plane. It seemed to be coming out of the violet patch on the North America screen. That is, it came from the general direction of the screen at any rate and my mind instantly tied it to the violet patch at Atla-Hi. It gave us a fright, I can tell you. Alice grabbed my knee with her pliers (she changed again), harder than she'd intended, I suppose, though I didn't let out a yip—I was too defensively frozen.

The voice was talking a language I didn't understand at all that went up and down the scale like atonal music.

"Sounds like Chinese," Pop whispered, giving me a nudge.

"It *is* Chinese. Mandarin," the screen responded instantly in the purest English-at least that was how I'd describe it. Practically Boston. "Who are you? And where is Grayl? Come in, Grayl."

I knew well enough who Grayl must be-or rather, have been. I looked at Pop and Alice. Pop grinned, maybe a mite feebly this time, I thought, and gave me a look as if to say, "You want to handle it?"

I cleared my throat. Then, "We've taken over for Grayl," I said to the screen.

"Oh." The screen hesitated, just barely. Then, "Do any of 'you' speak Mandarin?"

I hardly bothered to look at Pop and Alice. "No," I said.

"Oh." Again a tiny pause. "Is Grayl aboard the plane?"

"No." I said.

"Oh. Incapacitated in some way, I suppose?"

"Yes," I said, grateful for the screen's tactfulness, unintentional or not.

"But you have taken over for him?" the screen pressed.

"Yes," I said, swallowing. I didn't know what I was getting us into, things were moving too fast, but it seemed the merest sense to act cooperative.

"I'm very glad of that," the screen said with something in its tone that made me feel funny—I guess it was sincerity. Then it said, "Is the —" and hesitated, and started again with "Are the blocks aboard?"

I thought. Alice pointed at the stuff she dumped out of the other seat. I said. "There's a box with a thousand or so one-inch underweight steel cubes in it. Like a child's blocks, but with buttons in them. Alongside a box with a parachute."

"That's what I mean," the screen said and somehow, maybe because whoever was talking was trying to hide it, I caught a note of great relief.

"Look," the screen said, more rapidly now, "I don't know how much you know, but we may have to work very fast. You aren't going to be able to deliver the steel cubes to us directly. In fact you aren't going to be able to land in Atlantic Highlands at all. We're sieged in by planes and ground forces of Savannah Fortress. All our aircraft, such as haven't been destroyed, are pinned down. You're going to have to parachute the blocks to a point as near as possible to one of our ground parties that's made a sortie. We'll give you a signal. I hope it will be later-nearer here, that is-but it may be sooner. Do you know how to fight the plane you're in? Operate its armament?"

"No," I said, wetting my lip.

"Then that's the first thing I'd best teach you. Anything you see in the haze from now on will be from Savannah. You must shoot it down."

Chapter 5

And we are here as on a darkling plain
Swept with confused alarms of struggle and flight,

Where ignorant armies clash by night.

—Dover Beach,
by Matthew Arnold

I am not going to try to describe point by point all that happened the next half hour because there was too much of it and it involved all three of us, sometimes doing different things at the same time, and although we were told a lot of things, we were seldom if ever told the why of them, and through it all was the constant impression that we were dealing with human beings (I almost left out the "human" and I'm still not absolutely sure whether I shouldn't) of vastly greater scope-and probably intelligence too-than ourselves.

And that was just the *basic* confusion, to give it a name. After a while the situation got more difficult, as I'll try to tell in due course.

To begin with, it was extremely weird to plunge from a rather leisurely confab about a fairy-tale fellowship of non-practicing murderers into a shooting war between a violet blob and a dark red puddle on a shadowy fluorescent map. The voice didn't throw any great shining lights on this topic, because after the first-and perhaps unguarded-revelation, we learned little more of the war between Atla-Hi and Savannah Fortress and nothing of the reasons behind it. Presumably Savannah was the aggressor, reaching out north after the conquest of Birmingham, but even that was just a guess. It is hard to describe how shadowy it all felt to me; there were some minutes while my mind kept mixing up the whole thing with what I'd read long ago about the Civil War: Savannah was Lee, Atla-Hi was Grant, and we had been dropped spang into the middle of the second Battle of the Wilderness.

Apparently the Savannah planes had some sort of needle ray as part of their armament-at any rate I was warned to watch out for "swinging lines in the haze, like straight strings of pink stars" and later told to aim at the sources of such lines. And naturally I guessed that the steel cubes must be some crucial weapon for Atla-Hi, or ammunition for a weapon, or parts for some essential instrument like a giant computer, but the voice ignored my questions on that point and didn't fall into the couple of crude conversational traps I tried to set. We were to drop the cubes when told, that was all. Pop had the box of them closed again and rigged to the parachute-he took over that job because Alice and me were busy with other things when the instructions on that came through-and he was told how to open the door of the plane for the drop (you just held your hand steadily on a point beside the door), but, as I say, that was all.

Naturally it occurred to me that once we had made the drop, Atla-Hi would have no more use for us and might simply let us be destroyed by Savannah or otherwise-perhaps *want* us to be destroyed-so that it might be wisest for us to refuse to make the drop when the signal came and hang onto those myriad steel cubes as our only bargaining point. Still, I could see no advantage to refusing *before* the signal came. I'd have liked to discuss the point with Alice and maybe Pop too, but apparently everything we said, even whispered, could be overheard by Atla-Hi. (We never did determine, incidentally, whether Atla-Hi could *see* into the cabin of the plane also. I don't believe they could, though they sure had it bugged for sound.)

All in all, we found out almost nothing about Atla-Hi. In fact, three witless germs traveling in a cabin in an iron filing wasn't a bad description of us at all. As I often say of my deductive faculties-think-shmink! But Atla-Hi (always meaning, of course, the personality behind the voice from the screen) found out all it wanted about us-and apparently knew a good deal to start with. For one thing, they must have been tracking our plane for some time, because they guessed it was on automatic and that we could reverse its course but nothing else. Though they seemed under the impression that we could reverse its course to Los Alamos, not the cracking plant. Here obviously I did get a nugget of new data, though it was just about the only one. For a moment the voice from the screen got real unguarded-anxious as it asked, "Do you know if it is true that they have stopped dying at Los Alamos, or are they merely broadcasting that to cheer us up?"

I answered, "Oh yes, they're all fine," to that, but I couldn't have made it very convincing, because the next thing I knew the voice was getting me to admit that we'd only boarded the plane somewhere in the Central Deathlands. I even had to describe the cracking plant and freeway and gas tanks—I couldn't think of a lie that mightn't get us into as much trouble as the truth-and the voice said, "Oh, did Grayl stay there?" and I said, "Yes," and braced myself to do some more admitting, or some heavy lying, as the inspiration took me.

But the voice continued to skirt around the question of what exactly had happened to Grayl. I guess they knew well enough we'd bumped him off, but didn't bring it up because they needed our cooperation-they were handling us like children or savages, you see.

One pretty amazing point-Atla-Hi apparently knew something about Pop's fairy-tale fellowship of non-practicing murderers, because when he had to speak up, while he was getting instructions on preparing the stuff for the drop, the voice said, "Excuse me, but you sound like one of those M. A. boys."

Murderers Anonymous, Pop had said some of their boys called their unorganized organization.

"Yep, I am," Pop admitted uncomfortably.

"Well, a word of advice then, or perhaps I only mean gossip," the screen said, for once getting on a side track. "Most of our people do not believe you are serious about it, although you may think that you are. Our skeptics (which includes all but a very few of us) split quite evenly between those who think that the M. A. spirit is a terminal psychotic illusion and those who believe it is an elaborate ruse in preparation for some concerted attack on cities by Deathlanders."

"Can't say that I blame the either of them," was Pop's only comment. "I think I'm nuts myself and a murderer forever." Alice glared at him for that admission, but it seemed to do us no damage. Pop really did seem out of his depth though during this part of our adventure, more out of his depth than even Alice and me—I mean, as if he could only really function in the Deathland with Deathlanders and wanted to get anything else over quickly.

I think one reason Pop was that way was that he was feeling very intensely something I was feeling myself: a sort of sadness and bewilderment that beings as smart as the voice from the screen sounded should still be fighting wars. Murder, as you must know by now, I can understand and sympathize with deeply, but war? —no!

Oh, I can understand cultural queers fighting city squares and even get a kick out of it and whoop 'em on, but these Atla-Hi and Alamos folk seemed a different sort of cat altogether (though I'd only come to that point of view today) —the kind of cat that ought to have outgrown war or thought its way around it. Maybe Savannah Fortress had simply forced the war on them and they had to defend themselves. I hadn't contacted any Savannans-they might be as blood-simple as the Porterites. Still, I don't know that it's always a good excuse that somebody else forced you into war. That sort of justification can keep on until the end of time. But who's a germ to judge?

A minute later I was feeling doubly like a germ and a very lowly one, because the situation had just got more difficult and depressing too-the thing had happened that I said I'd tell you about in due course.

The voice was just repeating its instructions to Pop on making the drop, when it broke off of a sudden and a second voice came in, a deep voice with a sort of European accent (not Chinese, oddly)—not talking *to* us, I think, but to the first voice and overlooking or not caring that we could hear.

"*Also* tell them," the second voice said, "that we will blow them out of the sky the instant they stop obeying us! If they should hesitate to make the drop or if they should put a finger on the button that reverses their course, then —*pouf!* Such brutes understand only the language of force. *Also* warn them that the blocks are atomic grenades that will blow them out of the sky too if—"

"Dr. Kovalsky, will you permit me to point out—" the first voice interrupted, getting as close to expressing irritation as I imagine it ever allowed itself to do. Then both voices cut off abruptly and the screen was silent for ten seconds or so. I guess the first voice thought it wasn't nice for us to overhear Atla-Hi bickering with itself, even if the second voice didn't give a damn (any more than a farmer would mind the pigs overhearing him squabble with his hired man; of course this guy seemed to overlook that we were killer-pigs, but there wasn't anything we could do in that line just now except get burned up).

When the screen came on again, it was just the first voice talking once more, but it had something to say that was probably the result of a rapid conference and compromise.

"Attention, everyone! I wish to inform you that the plane in which you are traveling can be exploded-melted in the air, rather-if we activate a certain control at this end. We will *not* do so, now or subsequently, if you make the drop when we give the signal and if you remain on your present course until then. Afterwards you will be at liberty to reverse your course and escape as best you may. Let me re-emphasize that when you told me you had taken over for Grayl I accepted that assertion in full faith and still so accept it. Is that all fully understood?"

We all told him "Yes," though I don't imagine we sounded very happy about it, even Pop. However I did get that funny feeling again that the voice was being really sincere-an illusion, I supposed, but still a comforting one.

Now while all these things were going on, believe it or not, and while the plane continued to bullet through the orange haze-which hadn't shown any foreign objects in it so far, thank God, even vultures, let alone "straight strings of pink stars" —I was receiving a cram course in gunnery! (Do you wonder I don't try to tell this part of my story consecutively?)

It turned out that Alice had been brilliantly right about one thing: if you pushed some of the buttons simultaneously in patterns of five they unlocked and you could play on them like organ keys. Two sets of five keys, played properly, would rig out a sight just in front of the viewport and let you aim and fire the plane's main gun in any forward direction. There was a rearward firing gun too, that you aimed by changing over the World Screen to a rear-view TV window, but we didn't get around to mastering that one. In fact, in spite of my special talents it was all I could do to achieve a beginner's control over the main gun, and I wouldn't have managed even that except that Alice, from the thinking she'd been doing about patterns of five, was quick at understanding from the voice's descriptions which buttons were meant. She couldn't work them herself of course, what with her stump and burnt hand, but she could point them out for me.

After twenty minutes of drill I was a gunner of sorts, sprawled in the right-hand kneeling seat and intently scanning the onrushing orange haze which at last was beginning to change toward the bronze of evening. If something showed up in it I'd be able to make a stab at getting a shot in. Not that I knew what my gun fired-the voice wasn't giving away any unnecessary data.

Naturally I had asked why didn't the voice teach me to fly the plane so that I could maneuver in case of attack, and naturally the voice had told me it was out of the question-much too difficult and besides they wanted us on a known course so they could plan better for the drop and recovery. (I think maybe the voice would have given me some hints-and maybe even told me more about the steel cubes too and how much danger we were in from them-if it hadn't been for the second voice, which presumably had issued from a being who was keeping watch to make sure among other things that the first voice didn't get soft-hearted.)

So there I was being a front gunner. Actually a part of me was getting a big bang out of it-from antique Banker's Special to needle cannon (or whatever it was) —but at the same time another part of me was disgusted with the idea of acting like I belonged to a live culture (even a smart, unqueer one) and working in a war (even just so as to get out of it fast), while a third part of me-one that I normally keep down-was very simply horrified.

Pop was back by the door with the box and 'chute, ready to make the drop.

Alice had no duties for the moment, but she'd suddenly started gathering up food cans and packing them in one bag —I couldn't figure out at first what she had in mind. Orderly house-wife wouldn't be exactly my description of her occupational personality.

Then of course everything had to happen at once.

The voice said, "Make the drop!"

Alice crossed to Pop and thrust out the bag of cans toward him, writhing her lips in silent "talk" to tell him something. She had a knife in her burnt hand too.

But I didn't have time to do any lip-reading, because just then a glittering pink asterisk showed up in the darkening haze ahead —a whole half dozen straight lines spreading out from a blank central spot, as if a super-fast gigantic spider had laid in the first strands of its web.

Wind whistled as the door of the plane started to open.

I fought to center my sight on the blank central spot, which drifted toward the left.

One of the straight lines grew dazzlingly bright.

I heard Alice whisper fiercely, "Drop *these!*" and the part of my mind that couldn't be applied to gunnery instantly deduced that she'd had some last-minute inspiration about dropping a bunch of cans instead of the steel cubes.

I got the sight centered and held down the firing combo. The thought flashed to me: *it's a city you're firing at, not a plane,* and I flinched.

The dazzlingly pink line dipped down toward me.

Behind me, the sound of a struggle. Alice snarling and Pop giving a grunt.

Then all at once a scream from Alice, a big whoosh of wind, a flash way ahead (where I'd aimed), a spatter of hot metal inside the cabin, a blinding spot in the middle of the World Screen, a searing beam inches from my neck, an electric shock that lifted me from my seat and ripped at my consciousness!

When I came to (if I really ever was out-seconds later, at most) there were no more pink lines. The haze was just its disgustingly tawny evening self with black spots that were only after-images. The cabin stunk of ozone, but wind funneling through a hole in the one-time World Screen was blowing it out fast enough-Savannah had gotten in one lick, all right. And we were falling, the plane was swinging down like a crippled bird —I could feel it and there was no use kidding myself.

But staring at the control panel wouldn't keep us from crashing if that was in the cards. I looked around and there were Pop and Alice glaring at each other across the closing door. He looked mean. She looked agonized and was pressing her burnt hand into her side with her elbow as if he'd stamped on the hand, maybe. I didn't see any blood though. I didn't see the box and 'chute either, though I did see Alice's bag of groceries. I guessed Pop had made the drop.

Now, it occurred to me, was a bully time for Voice Two to melt the plane-if he hadn't already tried. My first thought had been that the spatter of hot metal had come from the Savannah craft spitting us, but there was no way to be sure.

I looked around at the viewport in time to see rocks and stunted trees jump out of the haze. *Good old Ray,* I thought, *always in at the death.* But just then the plane took a sickening bounce, as if its antigravity had only started to operate within yards of the ground. Another lurching fall and another bounce, less violent. A couple of repetitions of that, each one a little gentler, and then we were sort of bumping along on an even keel with the rocks and such sliding past fast about a hundred feet below, I judged. We'd been spoiled for altitude work, it seemed, but we could still cripple along in some sort of low-power repulsion field.

I looked at the North America screen and the buttons, wondering if I should start us back west again or leave us set on Atla-Hi and see what the hell happened-at the moment I hardly cared what else Savannah did to us. I needn't have wasted the mental energy. The decision was made for me. As I watched, the Atla-Hi button jumped up by itself and the button for the cracking plant went down and there was some extra bumping as we swung around.

Also, the violet patch of Atla-Hi went real dim and the button for it no longer had a violet nimbus. The Los Alamos blue went dull too. The cracking-plant dot glowed a brighter green-that was all.

All except for one thing. As the violet dimmed I thought I heard Voice One very faintly (not as if speaking directly but as if the screen had heard and remembered-not a voice but the fluorescent ghost of one): "Thank you and good luck!"

Chapter 6

Many a man has dated his ruin from some murder or other that perhaps
he thought little of at the time.

—Thomas de Quincey

"And a long merry siege to you, sir, and roast rat for Christmas!" I responded, very out loud
and rather to my surprise.

"War! How I hate war!"—that was what Pop exploded with. He didn't exactly dance in
senile rage-he was still keeping too sharp a watch on Alice-but his voice sounded that way.

"Damn you, Pop!" Alice contributed. "And you too, Ray! We might have pulled something,
but you had to go obedience-happy." Then her anger got the better of her grammar, or maybe
Pop and me was corrupting it. "Damn the both of you!" she finished.

It didn't make much sense, any of it. We were just cutting loose, I guess, after being scared
to say anything for the last half hour.

I said to Alice, "I don't know what you could have pulled, except the chain on us." To Pop I
remarked, "You may hate war, but you sure helped that one along. Those grenades you dropped
will probably take care of a few hundred Savannans."

"That's what you always say about me, isn't it?" he snapped back. "But I don't suppose I
should expect any kinder interpretation of my motives." To Alice he said, "I'm sorry I had to
slap your burnt fingers, sister, but you can't say I didn't warn you about my low-down tactics."
Then to me again: "I *do* hate war, Ray. It's just murder on a bigger scale, though some of the
boys give me an argument there."

"Then why don't you go preach against war in Atla-Hi and Savannah?" Alice demanded,
still very hot but not quite so bitter.

"Yeah, Pop, how about it?" I seconded.

"Maybe I should," he said, thoughtful all at once. "They sure need it." Then he
grinned. "Hey, how'd this sound: HEAR THE WORLD-FAMOUS MURDERER POP
TRUMBULL TALK AGAINST WAR. WEAR YOUR STEEL THROAT PROTECTORS.
Pretty good, hey?"

We all laughed at that, grudgingly at first, then with a touch of wholeheartedness. I think
we all recognized that things weren't going to be very cheerful from here on in and we'd better
not turn up our noses at the feeblest fun.

"I guess I didn't have anything very bright in mind," Alice admitted to me, while to Pop she
said, "All right, I forgive you for the present."

"Don't!" Pop said with a shudder. "I hate to think of what happened to the last bugger
made the mistake of forgiving me."

We looked around and took stock of our resources. It was time we did. It was getting dark
fast, although we were chasing the sun, and there weren't any cabin lights coming on and we
sure didn't know of any way of getting any.

We wadded a couple of satchels into the hole in the World Screen without trying to probe
it. After a while it got warmer again in the cabin and the air a little less dusty. Presently it
started to get too smoky from the cigarettes we were burning, but that came later.

We screwed off the walls the few storage bags we hadn't inspected. They didn't contain
nothing of consequence, not even a flashlight.

I had one last go at the buttons, though there weren't any left with nimbuses on them-the
darker it got, the clearer that was. Even the Atla-Hi button wouldn't push now that it had
lost its violet halo. I tried the gunnery patterns, figuring to put in a little time taking pot
shots at any mountains that turned up, but the buttons that had been responding so well a few
minutes ago refused to budge. Alice suggested different patterns, but none of them worked.
That console was really locked-maybe the shot from Savannah was partly responsible, though
Atla-Hi remote-locking things was explanation enough.

"The buggers!" I said. "They didn't have to tie us up *this* tight. Going east we at least had a choice-forward or back. Now we got none."

"Maybe we're just as well off," Pop said. "If Atla-Hi had been able to do anything more for us-that is, if they hadn't been sieged in, I mean-they'd sure as anything have pulled us in. Pull the plane in, I mean, and picked us out of it-with a big pair of tweezers, likely as not. And contrary to your flattering opinion of my preaching (which by the way none of the religious boys in my outfit share-they call me 'that misguided old atheist'), I don't think none of us would go over big at Atla-Hi."

We had to agree with him there. I couldn't imagine Pop or Alice or even me cutting much of a figure (even if we weren't murder-pariahs) with the pack of geniuses that seemed to make up the Atla-Alamos crowd. The Double-A Republics, to give them a name, might have their small-brain types, but somehow I didn't think so. There must be more than one Edison-Einstein, it seemed to me, back of antigravity and all the wonders in this plane and the other things we'd gotten hints of. Also, Grayl had seemed bred for brains as well as size, even if us small mammals had cooked his goose. And none of the modern "countries" had more than a few thousand population yet, I was pretty sure, and that hardly left room for a dumbbell class. Finally, too, I got hold of a memory I'd been reaching for the last hour-how when I was a kid I'd read about some scientists who learned to talk Mandarin just for kicks. I told Alice and Pop.

"And if *that's* the average Atla-Alamoser's idea of mental recreation," I said, "well, you can see what I mean."

"I'll grant you they got a monopoly of brains," Pop agreed. "Not sense, though," he added doggedly.

"Intellectual snobs," was Alice's comment. "I know the type and I detest it." ("You *are* sort of intellectual, aren't you?" Pop told her, which fortunately didn't start a riot.)

Still, I guess all three of us found it fun to chew over a bit the new slant we'd gotten on two (in a way, three) of the great "countries" of the modern world. (And as long as we thought of it as fun, we didn't have to admit the envy and wistfulness that was behind our wisecracks.)

I said, "We've always figured in a general way that Alamos was the remains of a community of scientists and technicians. Now we know the same's true of the Atla-Hi group. They're the Brookhaven survivors."

"Manhattan Project, don't you mean?" Alice corrected.

"Nope, that was in Colorado Springs," Pop said with finality.

I also pointed out that a community of scientists would educate for technical intelligence, maybe breed for it too. And being a group picked for high I. Q. to begin with, they might make startlingly fast progress. You could easily imagine such folk, unimpeded by the boobs, creating a wonder world in a couple of generations.

"They got their troubles though," Pop reminded me and that led us to speculating about the war we'd dipped into. Savannah Fortress, we knew, was supposed to be based on some big atomic plants on the river down that way, but its culture seemed to have a fiercer ingredient than Atla-Alamos. Before we knew it we were, musing almost romantically about the plight of Atla-Hi, besieged by superior and (it was easy to suppose) barbaric forces, and maybe distant Los Alamos in a similar predicament-Alice reminded me how the voice had asked if they were still dying out there. For a moment I found myself fiercely proud that I had been able to strike a blow against evil aggressors. At once, of course, then, the revulsion came.

"This is a hell of a way," I said, "for three so-called realists to be mooning about things."

"Yes, especially when your heroes kicked us out," Alice agreed.

Pop chuckled. "Yep," he said, "they even took Ray's artillery away from him."

"You're wrong there, Pop," I said, sitting up. "I still got one of the grenades-the one the pilot had in his fist." To tell the truth I'd forgotten all about it and it bothered me a little now to feel it snugged up in my pocket against my hip bone where the skin is thin.

"You believe what that old Dutchman said about the steel cubes being atomic grenades?" Pop asked me.

"I don't know," I said, "He sure didn't sound enthusiastic about telling us the truth about anything. But for that matter he sounded mean enough to tell the truth figuring we'd think it was a lie. Maybe this *is* some sort of baby A-bomb with a fuse timed like a grenade." I got it out and hefted it. "How about I press the button and drop it out the door? Then we'll know." I really felt like doing it-restless, I guess.

"Don't be a fool, Ray," Alice said.

"Don't tense up, I won't," I told her. At the same time I made myself the little promise that if I ever got to feeling restless, that is, restless and *bad*, I'd just go ahead and punch the button and see what happened-sort of leave my future up to the gods of the Deathlands, you might say.

"What makes you so sure it's a weapon?" Pop asked.

"What else would it be," I asked him, "that they'd be so hot on getting them in the middle of a war?"

"I don't know for sure," Pop said. "I've made a guess, but I don't want to tell it now. What I'm getting at, Ray, is that your first thought about anything you find-in the world outside or in your own mind-is that it's a weapon."

"Anything worthwhile in your mind is a weapon!" Alice interjected with surprising intensity.

"You see?" Pop said. "That's what I mean about the both of you. That sort of thinking's been going on a long time. Cave man picks up a rock and right away asks himself, 'Who can I brain with this?' Doesn't occur to him for several hundred thousand years to use it to start building a hospital."

"You know, Pop," I said, carefully tucking the cube back in my pocket, "you *are* sort of preachy at times."

"Guess I am," he said. "How about some grub?"

It was a good idea. Another few minutes and we wouldn't have been able to see to eat, though with the cans shaped to tell their contents I guess we'd have managed. It was a funny circumstance that in this wonder plane we didn't even know how to turn on the light-and a good measure of our general helplessness.

We had our little feed and lit up again and settled ourselves. I judged it would be an overnight trip, at least to the cracking plant-we weren't making anything like the speed we had been going east. Pop was sitting in back again and Alice and I lay half hitched around on the kneeling seats, which allowed us to watch each other. Pretty soon it got so dark we couldn't see anything of each other but the glowing tips of the cigarettes and a bit of face around the mouth when the person took a deep drag. They were a good idea, those cigarettes-kept us from having ideas about the other person starting to creep around with a knife in his hand.

The North America screen still glowed dimly and we could watch our green dot trying to make progress. The viewport was dead black at first, then there came the faintest sort of bronze blotch that very slowly shifted forward and down. The Old Moon, of course, going west ahead of us.

After a while I realized what it was like-an old Pullman car (I'd traveled in one once as a kid) or especially the smoker of an old Pullman, very late at night. Our crippled antigravity, working on the irregularities of the ground as they came along below, made the ride rhythmically bumpy, you see. I remembered how lonely and strange that old sleeping car had seemed to me as a kid. This felt the same. I kept waiting for a hoot or a whistle. It was the sort of loneliness that settles in your bones and keeps working at you.

"I recall the first man I ever killed —" Pop started to reminisce softly.

"Shut up!" Alice told him. "Don't you ever talk about anything but murder, Pop?"

"Guess not," he said. "After all, it's the only really interesting topic there is. Do you know of another?"

It was silent in the cabin for a long time after that. Then Alice said, "It was the afternoon before my twelfth birthday when they came into the kitchen and killed my father. He'd been wise, in a way, and had us living at a spot where the bombs didn't touch us or the worst fallout. But he hadn't counted on the local werewolf gang. He'd just been slicing some bread-homemade from our own wheat (Dad was great on back to nature and all) —but he laid down the knife.

"Dad couldn't see any object or idea as a weapon, you see-that was his great weakness. Dad couldn't even see weapons as weapons. Dad had a philosophy of cooperation, that was his name for it, that he was going to explain to people. Sometimes I think he was glad of the Last War, because he believed it would give him his chance.

"But the werewolves weren't interested in philosophy and although their knives weren't as sharp as Dad's they didn't lay them down. Afterwards they had themselves a meal, with me for dessert. I remember one of them used a slice of bread to sop up blood like gravy. And another washed his hands and face in the cold coffee..."

She didn't say anything else for a bit. Pop said softly, "That was the afternoon, wasn't it, that the fallen angels ..." and then just said, "My big mouth."

"You were going to say 'the afternoon they killed God?'" Alice asked him. "You're right, it was. They killed God in the kitchen that afternoon. That's how I know he's dead. Afterwards they would have killed me too, eventually, except —"

Again she broke off, this time to say, "Pop, do you suppose I can have been thinking about myself as the Daughter of God all these years? That that's why everything seems so intense?"

"I don't know," Pop said. "The religious boys say we're all children of God. I don't put much stock in it-or else God sure has some lousy children. Go on with your story."

"Well, they would have killed me too, except the leader took a fancy to me and got the idea of training me up for a Weregirl or She-wolf Deb or whatever they called it."

"That was my first experience of ideas as weapons. He got an idea about me and I used it to kill him. I had to wait three months for my opportunity. I got him so lazy he let me shave him. He bled to death the same way as Dad."

"Hum," Pop commented after a bit, "that was a chiller, all right. I got to remember to tell it to Bill-it was somebody killing his mother that got *him* started. Alice, you had about as good a justification for your first murder as any I remember hearing."

"Yet," Alice said after another pause, with just a trace of the old sarcasm creeping back into her voice, "I don't suppose you think I was right to do it?"

"Right? Wrong? Who knows?" Pop said almost blusteringly. "Sure you were justified in a whole pack of ways. Anybody'd sympathize with you. A man often has fine justification for the first murder he commits. But as you must know, it's not that the first murder's always so bad in itself as that it's apt to start you on a killing spree. Your sense of values gets shifted a tiny bit and never shifts back. But you know all that and who am I to tell you anything, anyway? I've killed men because I didn't like the way they spit. And may very well do it again if I don't keep watching myself and my mind ventilated."

"Well, Pop," Alice said, "I didn't always have such dandy justification for my killings. Last one was a moony old physicist-he fixed me the Geiger counter I carry. A silly old geek —I don't know how he survived so long. Maybe an exile or a runaway. You know, I often attach myself to the elderly do-gooder type like my father was. Or like you, Pop."

Pop nodded. "It's good to know yourself," he said.

There was a third pause and then, although I hadn't exactly been intending to, I said, "Alice had justification for her first murder, personal justification that an ape would understand. I had no personal justification at all for mine, yet I killed about a million people at a modest estimate. You see, I was the boss of the crew that took care of the hydrogen missile ticketed for Moscow, and when the ticket was finally taken up I was the one to punch it. My finger on the firing button, I mean."

I went on, "Yeah, Pop, I was one of the button-pushers. There were really quite a few of us, of course-that's why I get such a laugh out of stories about being or rubbing out the *one* guy who pushed all the buttons."

"That so?" Pop said with only mild-sounding interest. "In that case you ought to know —"

We didn't get to hear right then who I ought to know because I had a fit of coughing and we realized the cigarette smoke was getting just too thick. Pop fixed the door so it was open a crack and after a while the atmosphere got reasonably okay though we had to put up with a low lonely whistling sound.

"Yeah," I continued, "I was the boss of the missile crew and I wore a very handsome uniform with impressive insignia-not the bully old stripes I got on my chest now-and I was very young and handsome myself. We were all very young in that line of service, though a few of the men under me were a little older. Young and dedicated. I remember feeling a very deep and grim-and *clean* —responsibility. But I wonder sometimes just how deep it went or how clean it really was.

"I had an uncle flew in the war they fought to lick fascism, bombardier on a Flying Fortress or something, and once when he got drunk he told me how some days it didn't bother him at all to drop the eggs on Germany; the buildings and people down there seemed just like toys that a kid sets up to kick over, and the whole business about as naive fun as poking an anthill.

"*I* didn't even have to fly over at seven miles what I was going to be aiming at. Only I remember sometimes getting out a map and looking at a certain large dot on it and smiling a little and softly saying, 'Pow!' —and then giving a little conventional shudder and folding up the map quick.

"Naturally we told ourselves we'd never have to do it, fire the thing, I mean, we joked about how after twenty years or so we'd all be given jobs as museum attendants of this same bomb, deactivated at last. But naturally it didn't work out that way. There came the day when our side of the world got hit and the orders started cascading down from Defense Coordinator Bigelow —"

"Bigelow?" Pop interrupted. "Not Joe Bigelow?"

"Joseph A., I believe," I told him, a little annoyed.

"Why he's my boy then, the one I was telling you about-the skinny runt had this horn-handle! Can you beat that?" Pop sounded startlingly happy. "Him and you'll have a lot to talk about when you get together."

I wasn't so sure of that myself, in fact my first reaction was that the opposite would be true. To be honest I was for the first moment more than a little annoyed at Pop interrupting my story of my Big Grief-for it was that to me, make no mistake. Here my story had finally been teased out of me, against all expectation, after decades of repression and in spite of dozens of assorted psychological blocks-and here was Pop interrupting it for the sake of a lot of trivial organizational gossip about Joes and Bills and Georges we'd never heard of and what they'd say or think!

But then all of a sudden I realized that I didn't really care, that it didn't feel like a Big Grief any more, that just starting to tell about it after hearing Pop and Alice tell their stories had purged it of that unnecessary weight of feeling that had made it a millstone around my neck. It seemed to me now that I could look down at Ray Baker from a considerable height (but not an angelic or contemptuously superior height) and ask myself *not* why he had grieved so much-that was understandable and even desirable-but why he had grieved so *uselessly* in such a stuffy little private hell.

And it *would* be interesting to find out how Joseph A. Bigelow had felt.

"How does it feel, Ray, to kill a million people?"

I realized that Alice had asked me the question several seconds back and it was hanging in the air.

"That's just what I've been trying to tell you," I told her and started to explain it all over again-the words poured out of me now. I won't put them down here-it would take too long-but they were honest words as far as I knew and they eased me.

I couldn't get over it: here were us three murderers feeling a trust and understanding and sharing a communion that I wouldn't have believed possible between *any* two or three people in the Age of the Deaders-or in *any* age, to tell the truth. It was against everything I knew of Deathland psychology, but it was happening just the same. Oh, our strange isolation had something to do with it, I knew, and that Pullman-car memory hypnotizing my mind, and our reactions to the voices and violence of Atla-Alamos, but in spite of all that I ranked it as a wonder. I felt an inward freedom and easiness that I never would have believed possible. Pop's little disorganized organization had really got hold of something, I couldn't deny it.

Three treacherous killers talking from the bottoms of their hearts and believing each other! — for it never occurred to me to doubt that Pop and Alice were feeling exactly like I was. In fact, we were all so sure of it that we didn't even mention our communion to each other. Perhaps we were a little afraid we would rub off the bloom. We just enjoyed it.

We must have talked about a thousand things that night and smoked a couple of hundred cigarettes. After a while we started taking little catnaps-we'd gotten too much off our chests and come to feel too tranquil for even our excitement to keep us awake. I remember the first time I dozed waking up with a cold start and grabbing for Mother-and then hearing Pop and Alice gabbing in the dark, and remembering what had happened, and relaxing again with a smile.

Of all things, Pop was saying, "Yep, I imagine Ray must be good to make love to, murderers almost always are, they got the fire. It reminds me of what a guy named Fred told me, one of our boys..."

Mostly we took turns going to sleep, though I think there were times when all three of us were snoozing. About the fifth time I woke up, after some tighter shut-eye, the orange soup was back again outside and Alice was snoring gently in the next seat and Pop was up and had one of his knives out.

He was looking at his reflection in the viewport. His face gleamed. He was rubbing butter into it.

"Another day, another pack of troubles," he said cheerfully.

The tone of his remark jangled my nerves, as that tone generally does early in the morning. I squeezed my eyes. "Where are we?" I asked.

He poked his elbow toward the North America screen. The two green dots were almost one.

"My God, we're practically there," Alice said for me. She'd waked fast, Deathlands style.

"I know," Pop said, concentrating on what he was doing, "but I aim to be shaved before they commence landing maneuvers."

"You think automatic will land us?" Alice asked. "What if we just start circling around?"

"We can figure out what to do when it happens," Pop said, whittling away at his chin. "Until then, I'm not interested. There's still a couple of bottles of coffee in the sack. I've had mine."

I didn't join in this chit-chat because the green dots and Alice's first remark had reminded me of a lot deeper reason for my jangled nerves than Pop's cheerfulness. Night was gone, with its shielding cloak and its feeling of being able to talk forever, and the naked day was here, with its demands for action. It is not so difficult to change your whole view of life when you are flying, or even bumping along above the ground with friends who understand, but soon, I knew, I'd be down in the dust with something I never wanted to see again.

"Coffee, Ray?"

"Yeah, I guess so." I took the bottle from Alice and wondered whether my face looked as glum as hers.

"They shouldn't salt butter," Pop asserted. "It makes it lousy for shaving."

"It was the *best* butter," Alice said.

"Yeah," I said. "The Dormouse, when they buttered the watch."

It may be true that feeble humor is better than none. I don't know.

"What are you two yakking about?" Pop demanded.

"A book we both read," I told him.

"Either of you writers?" Pop asked with sudden interest. "Some of the boys think we should have a book about us. I say it's too soon, but they say we might all die off or something. Whoa, Jenny! Easy does it. Gently, please!"

That last remark was by way of recognizing that the plane had started an authoritative turn to the left. I got a sick and cold feeling. This was it.

Pop sheathed his knife and gave his face a final rub. Alice belted on her satchel. I reached for my knapsack, but I was staring through the viewport, dead ahead.

The haze lightened faintly, three times. I remembered the St. Elmo's fire that had flamed from the cracking plant.

"Pop," I said-almost whined, to be truthful, "why'd the bugger ever have to land here in the first place? He was rushing stuff they needed bad at Atla-Hi —why'd he have to break his trip?"

"That's easy," Pop said. "He was being a bad boy. At least that's my theory. He was supposed to go straight to Atla-Hi, but there was somebody he wanted to check up on first. He stopped here to see his girlfriend. Yep, his girlfriend. She tried to warn him off-that's my explanation of the juice that flared out of the cracking plant and interfered with his landing, though I'm sure she didn't intend the last. By the way, whatever she turned on to give him the warning must still be turned on. But Grayl came on down in spite of it."

Before I could assimilate that, the seven deformed gas tanks materialized in the haze. We got the freeway in our sights and steadied and slowed and kept slowing. The plane didn't graze the cracking plant this time, though I'd have sworn it was going to hit it head on. When I saw we *weren't* going to hit it, I wanted to shut my eyes, but I couldn't.

The stain was black now and the Pilot's body was thicker than I remembered-bloated. But that wouldn't last long. Three or four vultures were working on it.

Chapter 7

Here now in his triumph where all things falter,
Stretched out on the spoils that his own hand spread,
As a god self-slain on his own strange altar,

Death lies dead.

—A Forsaken Garden,
by Charles Swinburne

Pop was first down. Between us we helped Alice. Before joining them I took a last look at the control panel. The cracking plant button was up again and there was a blue nimbus on another button. For Los Alamos, I supposed. I was tempted to push it and get away solo, but then I thought, *nope, there's nothing for me at the other end and the loneliness will be worse than what I got to face here.* I climbed out.

I didn't look at the body, although we were practically on top of it. I saw a little patch of silver off to one side and remembered the gun that had melted. The vultures had waddled off but only a few yards.

"We could kill them," Alice said to Pop.

"Why?" he responded. "Didn't some Hindus use them to take care of dead bodies? Not a bad idea, either."

"Parsees," Alice amplified.

"Yep, Parsees, that's what I meant. Give you a nice clean skeleton in a matter of days."

Pop was leading us past the body toward the cracking plant. I heard the flies buzzing loudly. I felt terrible. I wanted to be dead myself. Just walking along after Pop was an awful effort.

"His girl was running a hidden observation tower here," Pop was saying now. "Weather and all that, I suppose. Or maybe setting up a robot station of some kind. I couldn't tell you about her before, because you were both in a mood to try to rub out anybody remotely connected with the Pilot. In fact, I did my best to lead you astray, letting you think I'd been the one to scream and all. Even now, to be honest about it, I don't know if I'm doing the right thing telling and showing you all this, but a man's got to take some risks whatever he does."

"Say, Pop," I said dully, "isn't she apt to take a shot at us or something?" Not that I'd have minded on my own account. "Or are you and her that good friends?"

"Nope, Ray," he said, "she doesn't even know me. But I don't think she's in a position to do any shooting. You'll see why. Hey, she hasn't even shut the door. That's bad."

He seemed to be referring to a kind of manhole cover standing on its edge just inside the open-walled first story of the cracking plant. He knelt and looked down the hole the cover was designed to close off.

"Well, at least she didn't collapse at the bottom of the shaft," he said. "Come on, let's see what happened." And he climbed into the shaft.

We followed him like zombies. At least that's how I felt. The shaft was about twenty feet deep. There were foot- and hand-holds. It got stuffy right away, and warmer, in spite of the shaft being open at the top.

At the bottom there was a short horizontal passage. We had to duck to get through it. When we could straighten up we were in a large and luxurious bomb-resistant dugout, to give it a name. And it was stuffier and hotter than ever.

There was a lot of scientific equipment around and several small control panels reminding me of the one in the back of the plane. Some of them, I supposed, connected with instruments, weather and otherwise, hidden up in the skeletal structure of the cracking plant. And there were signs of occupancy, a young woman's occupancy-clothes scattered around in a frivolous way, and some small objects of art, and a slightly more than life-size head in clay that I guessed the occupant must have been sculpting. I didn't give that last more than the most fleeting look, strictly unintentional to begin with, because although it wasn't finished I could tell whose head it was supposed to be-the Pilot's.

The whole place was finished in dull silver like the cabin of the plane, and likewise it instantly struck me as having a living personality, partly the Pilot's and partly someone else's —the personality of a marriage. Which wasn't a bit nice, because the whole place smelt of death.

But to tell the truth I didn't give the place more than the quickest look-over, because my attention was rivetted almost at once on a long wide couch with the covers kicked off it and on the body there.

The woman was about six feet tall and built like a goddess. Her hair was blonde and her skin tanned. She was lying on her stomach and she was naked.

She didn't come anywhere near my libido, though. She looked sick to death. Her face, twisted towards us, was hollow-cheeked and flushed. Her eyes, closed, were sunken and dark-circled. She was breathing shallowly and rapidly through her open mouth, gasping now and then.

I got the crazy impression that all the heat in the place was coming from her body, radiating from her fever.

And the whole place stunk of death. Honestly it seemed to me that this dugout was Death's underground temple, the bed Death's altar, and the woman Death's sacrifice. (Had I unconsciously come to worship Death as a god in the Deathlands? I don't really know. There it gets too deep for me.)

No, she didn't come within a million miles of my libido, but there was another part of me that she was eating at...

If guilt's a luxury, then I'm a plutocrat.

...eating at until I was an empty shell, until I had no props left, until I wanted to die then and there, until I figured I had to die...

There was a faint sharp hiss right at my elbow. I looked and found that, unbeknownst to myself, I'd taken the steel cube out of my pocket and holding it snuggled between my first and second fingers I'd punched the button with my thumb just as I'd promised myself I would if I got to really feeling bad.

It goes to show you that you should never give your mind any kind of instructions even half in fun, unless you're prepared to have them carried out whether you approve later or not.

Pop saw what I'd done and looked at me strangely. "So you had to die after all, Ray," he said softly. "Most of us find out we have to, one way or another."

We waited. Nothing happened. I noticed a very faint milky cloud a few inches across hanging in the air by the cube.

Thinking right away of poison gas, I jerked away a little, dispersing the cloud.

"What's that?" I demanded of no one in particular.

"I'd say," said Pop, "that that's something that squirted out of a tiny hole in the side of the cube opposite the button. A hole so nearly microscopic you wouldn't see it unless you looked for it hard. Ray, I don't think you're going to get your baby A-blast, and what's more I'm afraid you've wasted something that's damn valuable. But don't let it worry you. Before I dropped those cubes for Atla-Hi I snagged one."

And darn if he didn't pull the brother of my cube out of his pocket.

"Alice," he said, "I noticed a half pint of whiskey in your satchel when we got the salve. Would you put some on a rag and hand it to me."

Alice looked at him like he was nuts, but while her eyes were looking her pliers and her gloved hand were doing what he told her.

Pop took the rag and swabbed a spot on the sick woman's nearest buttock and jammed the cube against the spot and pushed the button.

"It's a jet hypodermic, folks," he said.

He took the cube away and there was the welt to substantiate his statement.

"Hope we got to her in time," he said. "The plague is tough. Now I guess there's nothing for us to do but wait, maybe for quite a while."

I felt shaken beyond all recognition.

"Pop, you old caveman detective!" I burst out. "When did you get that idea for a steel hospital?" Don't think I was feeling anywhere near that gay. It was reaction, close to hysterical.

Pop was taken aback, but then he grinned. "I had a couple of clues that you and Alice didn't," he said. "I knew there was a very sick woman involved. And I had that bout with Los Alamos fever I told you. They've had a lot of trouble with it, I believe-some say its spores come from outside the world with the cosmic dust-and now it seems to have been carried to Atla-Hi. Let's hope they've found the answer this time. Alice, maybe we'd better start getting some water into this gal."

After a while we sat down and fitted the facts together more orderly. Pop did the fitting mostly. Alamos researchers must have been working for years on the plague as it ravaged intermittently, maybe with mutations and ET tricks to make the job harder. Very recently they'd found a promising treatment (cure, we hoped) and prepared it for rush shipment to Atla-Hi, where the plague was raging too and they were sieged in by Savannah as well. Grayl was picked to fly the serum, or drug or whatever it was. But he knew or guessed that this lone woman observer (because she'd fallen out of radio communication or something) had come down with the plague too and he decided to land some serum for her, probably without authorization.

"How do we know she's his girlfriend?" I asked.

"Or wife," Pop said tolerantly. "Why, there was that bag of woman's stuff he was carrying, frilly things like a man would bring for a woman. Who else'd he be apt to make a special stop for?

"Another thing," Pop said. "He must have been using jets to hurry his trip. We heard them, you know."

That seemed about as close a reconstruction of events as we could get. Strictly hypothetical, of course. Deathlanders trying to figure out what goes on inside a "country" like Atla-Alamos and why are sort of like foxes trying to understand world politics, or wolves the Gothic migrations. Of course we're all human beings, but that doesn't mean as much as it sounds.

Then Pop told us how he'd happened to be on the scene. He'd been doing a "tour of duty", as he called it, when he spotted this woman's observatory and decided to hang around anonymously and watch over her for a few days and maybe help protect her from some dangerous characters that he knew were in the neighborhood.

"Pop, that sounds like a lousy idea to me," I objected. "Risky, I mean. Spying on another person, watching them without their knowing, would be the surest way to stir up in me the idea of murdering them. Safest thing for me to do in that situation would be to turn around and run."

"You probably should," he agreed. "For now, anyway. It's all a matter of knowing your own strength and stage of growth. Me, it helps to give myself these little jobs. And the essence of 'em is that the other person shouldn't know I'm helping."

It sounded like knighthood and pilgrimage and the Boy Scouts all over again-for murderers. Well, why not?

Pop had seen this woman come out of the manhole a couple of times and look around and then go back down and he'd got the impression she was sick and troubled. He'd even guessed she might be coming down with Alamos fever. He'd seen us arrive, of course, and that had bothered him. Then when the plane landed she'd come up again, acting out of her head, but when she'd seen the Pilot and us going for him she'd given that scream and collapsed at the top of the shaft. He'd figured the only thing he could do for her was keep us occupied. Besides, now that he knew for sure we were murderers he'd started to burn with the desire to talk to us and maybe help us quit killing if we seemed to want to. It was only much later, in the middle of our trip, that he began to suspect that the steel cubes were jet hypodermics.

While Pop had been telling us all this, we hadn't been watching the woman so closely. Now Alice called our attention to her. Her skin was covered with fine beads of perspiration, like diamonds.

"That's a good sign," Pop said and Alice started to wipe her off. While she was doing that the woman came to in a groggy sort of way and Pop fed her some thin soup and in the middle of his doing it she dropped off to sleep.

Alice said, "Any other time I would be wild to kill another woman that beautiful. But she has been so close to death that I would feel I was robbing another murderer. I suppose there is more behind the change in my feelings than that, though."

"Yeah, a little, I suppose," Pop said.

I didn't have anything to say about my own feelings. Certainly not out loud. I knew that they had changed and that they were still changing. It was complicated.

After a while it occurred to me and Alice to worry whether we mightn't catch this woman's sickness. It would serve us right, of course, but plague is plague. But Pop reassured us. "Actually I snagged three cubes," he said. "That should take care of you two. I figure I'm immune."

Time wore on. Pop dragged out the harmonica, as I'd been afraid he would, but his playing wasn't too bad. "Tenting Tonight," "When Johnnie Comes Marching Home," and such. We had a meal.

The Pilot's woman woke up again, in her full mind this time or something like it. We were clustered around the bed, smiling a little I suppose and looking inquiring. Being even assistant nurses makes you all concerned about the patient's health and state of mind.

Pop helped her sit up a little. She looked around. She saw me and Alice. Recognition came into her eyes. She drew away from us with a look of loathing. She didn't say a word, but the look stayed.

Pop drew me aside and whispered, "I think it would be a nice gesture if you and Alice took a blanket and went up and sewed him into it. I noticed a big needle and some thread in her satchel." He looked me in the eye and added, "You can't expect this woman to feel any other way toward you, you know. Now or ever."

He was right of course. I gave Alice the high sign and we got out.

No point in dwelling on the next scene. Alice and me sewed up in a blanket a big guy who'd been dead a day and worked over by vultures. That's all.

About the time we'd finished, Pop came up.

"She chased me out," he explained. "She's getting dressed. When I told her about the plane, she said she was going back to Los Alamos. She's not fit to travel, of course, but she's giving herself injections. It's none of our business. Incidentally, she wants to take the body back with her. I told her how we'd dropped the serum and how you and Alice had helped and she listened."

The Pilot's woman wasn't long after Pop. She must have had trouble getting up the shaft, she had a little trouble even walking straight, but she held her head high. She was wearing a dull silver tunic and sandals and cloak. As she passed me and Alice I could see the look of loathing come back into her eyes, and her chin went a little higher. I thought, why shouldn't she want us dead? Right now she probably wants to be dead herself.

Pop nodded to us and we hoisted up the body and followed her. It was almost too heavy a load even for the three of us.

As she reached the plane a silver ladder telescoped down to her from below the door. I thought, *the Pilot must have had it keyed to her some way, so it would let down for her but nobody else. A very lovely gesture.*

The ladder went up after her and we managed to lift the body above our heads, our arms straight, and we walked it through the door of the plane that way, she receiving it.

The door closed and we stood back and the plane took off into the orange haze, us watching it until it was swallowed.

Pop said, "Right now, I imagine you two feel pretty good in a screwed-up sort of way. I know I do. But take it from me, it won't last. A day or two and we're going to start feeling another way, the *old* way, if we don't get busy."

I knew he was right. You don't shake Old Urge Number One anything like that easy.

"So," said Pop, "I got places I want to show you. Guys I want you to meet. And there's things to do, a lot of them. Let's get moving."

So there's my story. Alice is still with me (Urge Number Two is even harder to shake, supposing you wanted to) and we haven't killed anybody lately. (Not since the Pilot, in fact, but it doesn't do to boast.) We're making a stab (my language!) at doing the sort of work Pop does in the Deathlands. It's tough but interesting. I still carry a knife, but I've given Mother to Pop. He has it strapped to him alongside Alice's screw-in blade.

Atla-Hi and Alamos still seem to be in existence, so I guess the serum worked for them generally as it did for the Pilot's Woman; they haven't sent us any medals, but they haven't sent a hangman's squad after us either-which is more than fair, you'll admit. But Savannah, turned back from Atla-Hi, is still going strong: there's a rumor they have an army at the gates of Ouachita right now. We tell Pop he'd better start preaching fast-it's one of our standard jokes.

There's also a rumor that a certain fellowship of Deathlanders is doing surprisingly well, a rumor that there's a new America growing in the Deathlands-an America that never need kill again. But don't put too much stock in it. Not *too* much.

A Hitch in Space

My Space-partner was a good reliable sidekick-but *his* partner was something else!

Once when I was doing a hitch with the Shaulan Space Guard out Scorpio way, my partner Jeff Bogart developed just about the most harmless psychosis you could imagine: he got himself an imaginary companion.

And the imaginary companion turned out to be me.

Well, I'm a pretty nice guy and so having two of me in the ship didn't seem a particularly bad idea. At first. In fact there'd be advantages of it, I thought. For instance, Jeff liked to talk a weary lot ... and the imaginary Joe Hansen could spell me listening to him, while I projected a book or just harkened to the wheels going around in my own head against the faint patter of starlight on the hull.

I met Jeff first at a space-rodeo, oddly enough, but now the two of us were out on a servicing check of the orbital beacons and relays and rescue depots of the five planets of the Shaulan system. A completely routine job, its only drawback that it was lengthy. Our ship was an ionic jeep that looked like a fancy fountain pen, but was very roomy for three men-one of them imaginary.

I caught on to Jeff's little mania by overhearing him talking to me. I'd be coming back from the head or stores or linear accelerator or my bunk, and I'd hear him yakking at me. It embarrassed me the first time, how to go back into the cabin when the other me was there. But I just swam in, and without any transition-strain at all that I could observe Jeff looked around at me, smiling sort of glaze-eyed, and said warmly, "Joe. My buddy Joe. Am I glad they paired us."

If Jeff had a major fault, as opposed to a species of nuttiness, it was that he was strictly a speak-only-good, positive-thinking guy who always deferred to me. Even idolized me, if you can imagine that. He'd give me such fulsome praise I'd be irked ten times an orbit.

Another thing that helped me catch on was that he always called the other me Joseph.

At first I thought the whole thing might be a gag, or maybe a deliberate way of letting off steam against me without violating his always-a-sweet-guy code-like happy husbands cursing in the bathroom-but then came the scrambled eggs.

I'd slept late and when I squinted into the cabin there was Jeff hovering over a plate of yellow fluff and shaking his finger at my empty seat and saying, "Dammit, Joseph, eat your scrambled eggs, I cooked 'em 'specially for you," and when he crawfished out toward the galley a couple seconds later he was saying, "Now you start on those eggs, Joseph, before I get back."

I thought for a bit and then I slid into my place and polished them off.

When he floated in with the coffee he gave me another of those glaze-eyed God-fearing looks-but just a mite disappointed, I thought-and said, "Dammit, Joe, you're perfect! You always clean your plate."

Apparently when I was there, Joseph just didn't exist for Jeff. And vice versa. It was sort of eerie, especially with the hum of space in my ears like a seashell and nobody else for five million miles.

Beginning with the scrambled eggs, I discovered that Jeff didn't exactly idolize Joseph-or even take with him the attitude of "My buddy can do no wrong," like he did with me. I overheard him criticizing Joseph. Reasonably at first; then I heard him chewing him out-next bullying him.

It made me wistful, that last, thinking how good it would feel to be full-bloodedly cursed to my face once in a while instead of all the sweetness and light. And right there I got the idea for some amateur therapy, Shaula-Deva help me.

I waited for a moment when we were both relaxed and then I said, "Jeff, the trouble with you is you're too nice. You ought to criticize things more. For a starter, criticize me. Tell me my faults. Go ahead."

He flushed a little and said, "Dammit, Joe, how can I? You're perfect!"

"No man is perfect, Jeff," I told him solemnly, feeling pretty foolish.

"But you're my buddy I always can trust," he protested, squirming a bit. "I wish you wouldn't talk this way."

"Jeff, you can't trust anybody too far," I said. "Even good guys can do bad things. When I was a boy there was a kid named Harry I practically worshipped. We lived on a pioneer world of Fomalhaut that had good snow, and we'd hitch rides with our sleds off little airscrew planes taking off. We'd each have a long white line on his sled and loop it beforehand around the plane's tail-gear and back to the sled. Then we'd hide. As soon as the pilot got aboard we'd jump on our sleds and each grab the free end of his line and have one comet of a ride, until the plane took off. Then we'd quick let go.

"Well, one frosty morning I let go and nothing happened, except I started to rise. Harry had tied the free end of my line tight to my sled.

"I could have just rolled off, I suppose, but I didn't want to lose my sled or my line either. Luckily I had a sheath knife handy and I used it. I even made a whizeroo of a landing. But ever afterwards my feelings toward Harry—"

"Stop it, please, Joe!" Jeff interrupted, very red in the face and shaking a little. "That boy Harry was utterly evil. And I don't want to hear any more about this, or anything like it, ever again. Understand?"

I told him sure I did. Heck, I could see I'd gone the wrong way about it. I even begged his pardon.

After that I just sweated it out. But I found I couldn't spend much time on books or my thoughts, I'd keep listening for what Jeff was saying to Joseph. And sometimes when he'd pause for Joseph's reply I'd catch myself waiting for the imaginary me to make one. So I took to staying in the same cabin as Jeff as much as I could.

That seemed to make him uncomfortable after a while, though he pretended to glory in it. He'd ask me questions like, "Tell me about life, Joe. So I'll know how to handle myself if we're ever parted."

But the weariest things come to an end, even duty orbits around Shaula. And so the time came when we were servicing our last beacon-outside the planet Shaula-by, it was. Next step would be a fast interplanetary orbit for Base at Shaula-near.

I was out working-on a safety line of course, but suit-jetting around more than I needed to, just for the pure joy of it, so that my suit tank was almost dry. I'd switched my suit radio off for a bit, because, working in space, Jeff had taken to just gabbling to me nervously all the time-maybe because he figured there couldn't be room for Joseph with him in his suit.

I finished up and paused for a last look at the ship. She was sweetly slim from her conical living quarters to the taper-tail of her ionic jet, but she had more junk on her than an amateur asteroid prospector hangs on his suit the first time out. Every duty orbit, fifty scientists come with permission from the Commandant to hang some automatic research gadget on the hull. The craziest one this time was a huge flattened band of gold-plated aluminum, little more than foil-thick, attached crosswise just in front of the tail and sticking out twenty feet on each side. I don't know what it was there for-maybe to measure the effects of space on a Moebius strip-but it looked like a wedding ring that had been stepped on. So Jeff and I called it Trompled Love.

But in spite of the junk, the ship looked mighty sweet against the saffron steppes and baby-blue seas of Shaula-by with Shaula herself, old Lambda Scorpii, flaming warm and wildly beyond, and with "United States" standing out big as life on the ship's living quarters. United States of Shaula, of course.

I was almost dreaming out there, thinking how it hadn't been such a terrible duty after all, when I saw the ship begin to slide past Shaula.

Poking out of her tail, ghostlier than the flame over a cafe royale, was the evil blue glow of her jet. In an instant I'd guessed exactly what had happened and was beating myself on the head for not having anticipated it. Joseph had swum into the cabin right after Jeff. And Jeff had yelled at him. "It's about time, you lazy lunkhead! Everything secure? Okay, I'm switching on the beam!" And I'd probably brought the whole thing about by telling him that damfool sled story-and then sticking to him so close he just had to get rid of me, so as to be with Joseph.

Meanwhile the ship was gathering speed in her sneaky way and the wavy safety line between me and the airlock was starting to straighten.

As you know, an ionic jet's only good space-to-space. It's not for heavy-G work; ours could deliver only one-half G at max and was doing less than one-quarter now. Which meant the ship was starting off slower than most ground cars.

But the beam would fire for hours, building up to a terminal velocity of fifteen miles a second and carrying the ship far, far away from lonely Joe Hansen.

Except that we were tied together, of course.

I was very grateful then for the weeks I'd practiced space-roping, though I'd never won any prizes with it, because without thinking I started to whip my line very carefully. And on the third try, just as it was getting pretty straight, I managed to settle it in a notch in one outside end of Trompled Love. After that I took up strain on the line as gradually as I could, letting it friction through my gloves for as long as I could before putting all my mass on it-because although one-quarter G isn't much, it piles up in a few seconds to quite a jerk. I spread that jerk into several little ones.

Well, the last jerk came and the line didn't part and Trompled Love didn't crumple much, though the Shaula-light showed me several very nasty-looking wrinkles in it. And there I was trailing along after the ship, though out to one side, and feeling about as much strain on the line as if I were hanging from a cliff on the moon, and knowing I was going about five feet a second faster every second.

My idea wanting to be out to the side (and bless my impulses for realizing it was the one important thing!) was to keep my line and myself out of the beam. An ionic jet doesn't look hot from the side. But from straight on it's a lot brighter than an arc light-it's almost as tight as a laser beam-and I didn't want to think about what it would do to me, even trailing as I was a hundred yards aft.

Though of course long before it had ruined me, it would have disintegrated my line.

My being out to the side was putting the ship off balance on its jet and presumably throwing its course toward base and Shaula-near little by little into error. But that was the least of my worries, believe me.

I thought for a bit and remembered I could talk to Jeff over my suit radio. I decided to try it, not without misgivings.

I tongued it on and said, "Jeff. Oh, Jeff. I'm out here. You forgot me."

I was going to say some more, but just then he broke in, angry and so loud it made my helmet ring, with, "Joseph! Did you hear anything then?" A pause, then, "Well, clean the wax out of your ears, stupid, because I did! I think we got an enemy out there!"

Another and longer pause, while my blood curdled a bit thicker, then, "Well, okay, Joseph, I'll go along with you this time. But if I hear the enemy once more, I'm going to suit up and take a rifle and sit in the airlock door until I've potted him."

I tongued the radio off quick, fearful I'd sneeze or something. I had only one faint consolation: Joseph seemed to be a bit on my side, or maybe he was just lazy.

I thought some more, a mite frantic-like now, and after a while I said to myself, *Been going five minutes now, so I'm doing about a quarter of a mile a second-that's fifteen miles a minute, wow! —but out here velocities are purely relative. My suit does a little better than a quarter G full on. Okay. I'll jet to the ship.*

No sooner said than acted on —I was beginning to rely too much on impulse now. The suit jet killed my false weight at once and I was off, mighty careful to aim myself along my line or a little outside it, so as not to wander over into the beam.

Pretty soon the tail and Trompled Love were getting noticeably bigger.

Then a lot bigger.

Then my suit fuel ran out.

I'd built up enough velocity so that I was still gaining on the ship for a few seconds. In fact, I almost made it. My gauntlet was about to close on Trompled Love when the ship started slowly to pull away. Oh, it was frustrating!

I remembered then what I should have a lot earlier, and grabbed for the ship-end of my line so as not to lose the distance I'd gained-and in my haste I knocked it away from me. The only good thing was that I didn't knock it out of the notch.

Now I was losing space to the ship faster and faster. Yet all I could do was reel in the me-end of the line as fast as I could. Suddenly the whole line straightened and gave me a bigger jerk than I'd intended. I could see Trompled Love crumple a little. And I was swinging just a bit, like a pendulum.

I used a glove-friction to spread the rest of the jerk, but still I was at the end of my line and Trompled Love had crumpled a bit more before I was coasting along with the ship again.

My side of Trompled Love was bent back maybe twenty degrees. The eye of the beam shone at me from the tail like a pale blue moon. For quite a while it brightened and dimmed as I tick-tock swung.

Meanwhile I was beating my skull for not having thought earlier of the obvious slow-but-safe way of doing it, instead of that lunatic suit-jetting. I once heard a psychologist say we're mental slaves to power-machinery and I guess he had something.

Clearly all I had to do was climb hand-over-hand up the line to the ship. At moon gravity that would be easy. If I should get tired I only had to clamp on and rest.

So I waited for my emotions to settle a bit, and then I reached along the line and gave a smooth, medium-strength heave.

Maybe there is something to ESP-at least in a devilish sort of way-because I picked the exact moment when Jeff decided to feed the beam more juice.

There was a *big* jerk and I saw Trompled Love crumple a lot, so that it was pointing more than forty-five degrees aft.

Now there was a steady pull on the line like I was hanging from a cliff on Mars. And the eye of the beam was a blue moon not so pale-in fact more like a sizzling blue sun seen through a light fog.

After that I just didn't have the heart to try the climb again. Once I started to draw myself up, very cautious, but on the first handhold I seemed to feel along the line Trompled Love crumpling some more and I quit for good.

I figured that at this boost Jeff would be up to proper speed for Shaula-near in less than two hours. Well, I had suit-oxy and refrigeration for longer than that.

Of course if Jeff decided not to cut the beam on schedule, maybe with the idea of eloping with Joseph to the next solar system-well, I'd discover then whether suit-oxy running out would stimulate me to try the climb again alongside the beam.

(Or I could wait until he got her up near the speed of light, when by the General Theory of Relativity the line ought to be shortened enough so that I could hop aboard if I were sudden enough about it....*No, Joe Hansen, you quit that,* I told myself, *you don't want to die with the gears in your head all stripped.*)

Thinking about the beam got me wondering exactly how close I was to it. I unshipped my suit-antenna and pulled it out to full length-about eight feet-and fished around with it in the direction of the beam.

Nothing seemed to happen to it. It didn't glow or anything; but I suddenly got a little electric shock, and when I drew it back I could see three inches of the tip were gone and the next couple inches were pitted. So much for curiosity.

Next I reattached the antenna to my suit-which turned out to be a lot more troublesome job than unshipping it-and tongued on the radio with the idea of listening in on Jeff.

Right away I heard him say, "Wake up, Joseph! I'm going to tell you your faults again. I got a new way of cataloguing them chronologically. Begin with childhood. You hitched sled-rides on airplanes. That was bad, Joseph, that was against the law. If the man had caught you doing it, if he'd seen you whizzing along there back of him, he'd have had every right to shoot you down in cold blood. Life is hard, Joseph, life is merciless...."

Right then I felt a tickle in my throat.

I tried quick to shut off the radio, but it is remarkably difficult to tongue anything when you have a cough coming. It came out finally in a series of squeaky glubs.

"Snap to, Joseph, and listen hard," I heard Jeff say. "It's started again. Animal noises this time. You know if they make spacesuits for black panthers, Joseph?"

I tongued off the radio quick, before the follow-up cough came.

I didn't have anything left to do now but think. So I thought about Jeff-how there seemed to be one Jeff who hated my guts and another Jeff who idolized me and another Jeff sneaking around in a jungle of sabertooth tigers and ... heck, there was probably a good twenty Jeffs sitting around inside his skull, some in light, some in darkness, but all of them watching each other and arguing together all the time. It was an odd way to think of a personality —a sort of perpetual *Kaffeeklatsch* —but it had its points. Maybe some of the little guys weren't Jeffs at all, but his father and mother and a caveman ancestor or two and maybe some great-great-grandchild butting in now and then from the future....

Well, I saw that speculation was getting out of hand so, taking a tip from Jeff, I began to count my own sins.

It took quite a while. Some of them were pretty interesting reading, almost enough to take my mind off my predicament, but I tired of it finally.

Then I began to count the stars.

It was really the longest two hours plus I ever spent, except maybe the time my first big girl disappeared. But I don't know. The experiences are hard to compare.

I was about halfway through the stars when I went weightless. For an awful instant I thought the line had parted at last, but then I looked toward the ship and saw the bright little moon was gone.

Right away I gave a couple of tugs on the line and began to close slowly with the tail. No trouble at all-actually my only difficulty was resisting the temptation to build up more momentum, which would have resulted in a crash landing.

I softed-in on Trompled Love okay, except there was a big spark. The beam must have charged me good. Then I worked my way to the true hull. After that there were handholds.

Finally I got to a porthole in the living quarters, and I looked in, and there was Jeff jawing away at my empty seat. I put my helmet against the hull and very faintly I heard him say, "Joseph, I'm still worried about the enemy. I keep thinking I hear him or it. I'm going to make us some coffee, so we'll stay real alert. You break out the guns."

I don't suppose anyone ever moved quite so quietly *and* so quickly in a spacesuit as I did then. I got in the airlock, I got her up to pressure, I got unsuited-and all in less than five minutes, I'm sure. Maybe less than four.

I swam to the cabin. It was empty. I slid into my seat just as Jeff floated in with the coffee.

He went real pale when he spotted me. I saw there might be some trouble this time with the Joseph-Joe transition. But I knew the only way to play it was real cool. I nested there in my seat as if I hadn't a worry or urge in the world-though my nerves and throat were just screaming for a squirt of that coffee.

"Joe!" he squeaked at last. "Migod, you gave me an awful scare. I thought you'd done a bunk, I thought, you'd spaced yourself, I kept picturing you outside the ship."

"Why no, Jeff," I answered quietly. "One way or another, I've been in this seat ever since take-off."

His brow wrinkled as he thought about that.

I looked at the board and noticed that our terminal trip-velocity read fifteen miles a second. My, my.

Finally Jeff said, "That's right, you have." And then, just a shade unhappily, "I might have known. You always tell the truth, Joe-you're perfect."

A Pail of Air

*The dark star passed, bringing with it
eternal night and turning history into
incredible myth in a single generation!*

Pa had sent me out to get an extra pail of air. I'd just about scooped it full and most of the warmth had leaked from my fingers when I saw the thing.

You know, at first I thought it was a young lady. Yes, a beautiful young lady's face all glowing in the dark and looking at me from the fifth floor of the opposite apartment, which hereabouts is the floor just above the white blanket of frozen air. I'd never seen a live young lady before, except in the old magazines-Sis is just a kid and Ma is pretty sick and miserable-and it gave me such a start that I dropped the pail. Who wouldn't, knowing everyone on Earth was dead except Pa and Ma and Sis and you?

Even at that, I don't suppose I should have been surprised. We all see things now and then. Ma has some pretty bad ones, to judge from the way she bugs her eyes at nothing and just screams and screams and huddles back against the blankets hanging around the Nest. Pa says it is natural we should react like that sometimes.

When I'd recovered the pail and could look again at the opposite apartment, I got an idea of what Ma might be feeling at those times, for I saw it wasn't a young lady at all but simply a light —a tiny light that moved stealthily from window to window, just as if one of the cruel little stars had come down out of the airless sky to investigate why the Earth had gone away from the Sun, and maybe to hunt down something to torment or terrify, now that the Earth didn't have the Sun's protection.

I tell you, the thought of it gave me the creeps. I just stood there shaking, and almost froze my feet and did frost my helmet so solid on the inside that I couldn't have seen the light even if it had come out of one of the windows to get me. Then I had the wit to go back inside.

Pretty soon I was feeling my familiar way through the thirty or so blankets and rugs Pa has got hung around to slow down the escape of air from the Nest, and I wasn't quite so scared. I began to hear the tick-ticking of the clocks in the Nest and knew I was getting back into air, because there's no sound outside in the vacuum, of course. But my mind was still crawly and uneasy as I pushed through the last blankets-Pa's got them faced with aluminum foil to hold in the heat-and came into the Nest.

Let me tell you about the Nest. It's low and snug, just room for the four of us and our things. The floor is covered with thick woolly rugs. Three of the sides are blankets, and the blankets roofing it touch Pa's head. He tells me it's inside a much bigger room, but I've never seen the real walls or ceiling.

Against one of the blanket-walls is a big set of shelves, with tools and books and other stuff, and on top of it a whole row of clocks. Pa's very fussy about keeping them wound. He says we must never forget time, and without a sun or moon, that would be easy to do.

The fourth wall has blankets all over except around the fireplace, in which there is a fire that must never go out. It keeps us from freezing and does a lot more besides. One of us must always watch it. Some of the clocks are alarm and we can use them to remind us. In the early days there was only Ma to take turns with Pa —I think of that when she gets difficult-but now there's me to help, and Sis too.

It's Pa who is the chief guardian of the fire, though. I always think of him that way: a tall man sitting cross-legged, frowning anxiously at the fire, his lined face golden in its light, and

163

every so often carefully placing on it a piece of coal from the big heap beside it. Pa tells me there used to be guardians of the fire sometimes in the very old days-vestal virgins, he calls them-although there was unfrozen air all around then and you didn't really need one.

He was sitting just that way now, though he got up quick to take the pail from me and bawl me out for loitering-he'd spotted my frozen helmet right off. That roused Ma and she joined in picking on me. She's always trying to get the load off her feelings, Pa explains. He shut her up pretty fast. Sis let off a couple of silly squeals too.

Pa handled the pail of air in a twist of cloth. Now that it was inside the Nest, you could really feel its coldness. It just seemed to suck the heat out of everything. Even the flames cringed away from it as Pa put it down close by the fire.

Yet it's that glimmery white stuff in the pail that keeps us alive. It slowly melts and vanishes and refreshes the Nest and feeds the fire. The blankets keep it from escaping too fast. Pa'd like to seal the whole place, but he can't —building's too earthquake-twisted, and besides he has to leave the chimney open for smoke.

Pa says air is tiny molecules that fly away like a flash if there isn't something to stop them. We have to watch sharp not to let the air run low. Pa always keeps a big reserve supply of it in buckets behind the first blankets, along with extra coal and cans of food and other things, such as pails of snow to melt for water. We have to go way down to the bottom floor for that stuff, which is a mean trip, and get it through a door to outside.

You see, when the Earth got cold, all the water in the air froze first and made a blanket ten feet thick or so everywhere, and then down on top of that dropped the crystals of frozen air, making another white blanket sixty or seventy feet thick maybe.

Of course, all the parts of the air didn't freeze and snow down at the same time.

First to drop out was the carbon dioxide-when you're shoveling for water, you have to make sure you don't go too high and get any of that stuff mixed in, for it would put you to sleep, maybe for good, and make the fire go out. Next there's the nitrogen, which doesn't count one way or the other, though it's the biggest part of the blanket. On top of that and easy to get at, which is lucky for us, there's the oxygen that keeps us alive. Pa says we live better than kings ever did, breathing pure oxygen, but we're used to it and don't notice. Finally, at the very top, there's a slick of liquid helium, which is funny stuff. All of these gases in neat separate layers. Like a pussy caffay, Pa laughingly says, whatever that is.

I was busting to tell them all about what I'd seen, and so as soon as I'd ducked out of my helmet and while I was still climbing out of my suit, I cut loose. Right away Ma got nervous and began making eyes at the entry-slit in the blankets and wringing her hands together-the hand where she'd lost three fingers from frostbite inside the good one, as usual. I could tell that Pa was annoyed at me scaring her and wanted to explain it all away quickly, yet could see I wasn't fooling.

"And you watched this light for some time, son?" he asked when I finished.

I hadn't said anything about first thinking it was a young lady's face. Somehow that part embarrassed me.

"Long enough for it to pass five windows and go to the next floor."

"And it didn't look like stray electricity or crawling liquid or starlight focused by a growing crystal, or anything like that?"

He wasn't just making up those ideas. Odd things happen in a world that's about as cold as can be, and just when you think matter would be frozen dead, it takes on a strange new life. A slimy stuff comes crawling toward the Nest, just like an animal snuffing for heat-that's the liquid helium. And once, when I was little, a bolt of lightning-not even Pa could figure where it came from-hit the nearby steeple and crawled up and down it for weeks, until the glow finally died.

"Not like anything I ever saw," I told him.

He stood for a moment frowning. Then, "I'll go out with you, and you show it to me," he said.

Ma raised a howl at the idea of being left alone, and Sis joined in, too, but Pa quieted them. We started climbing into our outside clothes-mine had been warming by the fire. Pa made them. They have plastic headpieces that were once big double-duty transparent food cans, but they keep heat and air in and can replace the air for a little while, long enough for our trips for water and coal and food and so on.

Ma started moaning again, "I've always known there was something outside there, waiting to get us. I've felt it for years-something that's part of the cold and hates all warmth and wants to destroy the Nest. It's been watching us all this time, and now it's coming after us. It'll get you and then come for me. Don't go, Harry!"

Pa had everything on but his helmet. He knelt by the fireplace and reached in and shook the long metal rod that goes up the chimney and knocks off the ice that keeps trying to clog it. Once a week he goes up on the roof to check if it's working all right. That's our worst trip and Pa won't let me make it alone.

"Sis," Pa said quietly, "come watch the fire. Keep an eye on the air, too. If it gets low or doesn't seem to be boiling fast enough, fetch another bucket from behind the blanket. But mind your hands. Use the cloth to pick up the bucket."

Sis quit helping Ma be frightened and came over and did as she was told. Ma quieted down pretty suddenly, though her eyes were still kind of wild as she watched Pa fix on his helmet tight and pick up a pail and the two of us go out.

———————————————

Pa led the way and I took hold of his belt. It's a funny thing, I'm not afraid to go by myself, but when Pa's along I always want to hold on to him. Habit, I guess, and then there's no denying that this time I was a bit scared.

You see, it's this way. We know that everything is dead out there. Pa heard the last radio voices fade away years ago, and had seen some of the last folks die who weren't as lucky or well-protected as us. So we knew that if there was something groping around out there, it couldn't be anything human or friendly.

Besides that, there's a feeling that comes with it always being night, *cold* night. Pa says there used to be some of that feeling even in the old days, but then every morning the Sun would come and chase it away. I have to take his word for that, not ever remembering the Sun as being anything more than a big star. You see, I hadn't been born when the dark star snatched us away from the Sun, and by now it's dragged us out beyond the orbit of the planet Pluto, Pa says, and taking us farther out all the time.

I found myself wondering whether there mightn't be something on the dark star that wanted us, and if that was why it had captured the Earth. Just then we came to the end of the corridor and I followed Pa out on the balcony.

I don't know what the city looked like in the old days, but now it's beautiful. The starlight lets you see it pretty well-there's quite a bit of light in those steady points speckling the blackness above. (Pa says the stars used to twinkle once, but that was because there was air.) We are on a hill and the shimmery plain drops away from us and then flattens out, cut up into neat squares by the troughs that used to be streets. I sometimes make my mashed potatoes look like it, before I pour on the gravy.

Some taller buildings push up out of the feathery plain, topped by rounded caps of air crystals, like the fur hood Ma wears, only whiter. On those buildings you can see the darker squares of windows, underlined by white dashes of air crystals. Some of them are on a slant, for many of the buildings are pretty badly twisted by the quakes and all the rest that happened when the dark star captured the Earth.

Here and there a few icicles hang, water icicles from the first days of the cold, other icicles of frozen air that melted on the roofs and dripped and froze again. Sometimes one of those icicles will catch the light of a star and send it to you so brightly you think the star has swooped into the city. That was one of the things Pa had been thinking of when I told him about the light, but I had thought of it myself first and known it wasn't so.

He touched his helmet to mine so we could talk easier and he asked me to point out the windows to him. But there wasn't any light moving around inside them now, or anywhere else. To my surprise, Pa didn't bawl me out and tell me I'd been seeing things. He looked all around quite a while after filling his pail, and just as we were going inside he whipped around without warning, as if to take some peeping thing off guard.

I could feel it, too. The old peace was gone. There was something lurking out there, watching, waiting, getting ready.

Inside, he said to me, touching helmets, "If you see something like that again, son, don't tell the others. Your Ma's sort of nervous these days and we owe her all the feeling of safety we can give her. Once-it was when your sister was born—I was ready to give up and die, but your Mother kept me trying. Another time she kept the fire going a whole week all by herself when I was sick. Nursed me and took care of the two of you, too."

"You know that game we sometimes play, sitting in a square in the Nest, tossing a ball around? Courage is like a ball, son. A person can hold it only so long, and then he's got to toss it to someone else. When it's tossed your way, you've got to catch it and hold it tight-and hope there'll be someone else to toss it to when you get tired of being brave."

His talking to me that way made me feel grown-up and good. But it didn't wipe away the thing outside from the back of my mind-or the fact that Pa took it seriously.

It's hard to hide your feelings about such a thing. When we got back in the Nest and took off our outside clothes, Pa laughed about it all and told them it was nothing and kidded me for having such an imagination, but his words fell flat. He didn't convince Ma and Sis any more than he did me. It looked for a minute like we were all fumbling the courage-ball. Something had to be done, and almost before I knew what I was going to say, I heard myself asking Pa to tell us about the old days, and how it all happened.

He sometimes doesn't mind telling that story, and Sis and I sure like to listen to it, and he got my idea. So we were all settled around the fire in a wink, and Ma pushed up some cans to thaw for supper, and Pa began. Before he did, though, I noticed him casually get a hammer from the shelf and lay it down beside him.

It was the same old story as always—I think I could recite the main thread of it in my sleep-though Pa always puts in a new detail or two and keeps improving it in spots.

He told us how the Earth had been swinging around the Sun ever so steady and warm, and the people on it fixing to make money and wars and have a good time and get power and treat each other right or wrong, when without warning there comes charging out of space this dead star, this burned out sun, and upsets everything.

You know, I find it hard to believe in the way those people felt, any more than I can believe in the swarming number of them. Imagine people getting ready for the horrible sort of war they were cooking up. Wanting it even, or at least wishing it were over so as to end their nervousness. As if all folks didn't have to hang together and pool every bit of warmth just to keep alive. And how can they have hoped to end danger, any more than we can hope to end the cold?

Sometimes I think Pa exaggerates and makes things out too black. He's cross with us once in a while and was probably cross with all those folks. Still, some of the things I read in the old magazines sound pretty wild. He may be right.

The dark star, as Pa went on telling it, rushed in pretty fast and there wasn't much time to get ready. At the beginning they tried to keep it a secret from most people, but then the truth came out, what with the earthquakes and floods-imagine, oceans of *unfrozen* water! —and people seeing stars blotted out by something on a clear night. First off they thought it would hit the Sun, and then they thought it would hit the Earth. There was even the start of a rush to get to a place called China, because people thought the star would hit on the other side. But then they found it wasn't going to hit either side, but was going to come very close to the Earth.

Most of the other planets were on the other side of the Sun and didn't get involved. The Sun and the newcomer fought over the Earth for a little while-pulling it this way and that, like two dogs growling over a bone, Pa described it this time-and then the newcomer won and carried us off. The Sun got a consolation prize, though. At the last minute he managed to hold on to the Moon.

That was the time of the monster earthquakes and floods, twenty times worse than anything before. It was also the time of the Big Jerk, as Pa calls it, when all Earth got yanked suddenly, just as Pa has done to me once or twice, grabbing me by the collar to do it, when I've been sitting too far from the fire.

You see, the dark star was going through space faster than the Sun, and in the opposite direction, and it had to wrench the world considerably in order to take it away.

The Big Jerk didn't last long. It was over as soon as the Earth was settled down in its new orbit around the dark star. But it was pretty terrible while it lasted. Pa says that all sorts of cliffs and buildings toppled, oceans slopped over, swamps and sandy deserts gave great sliding surges that buried nearby lands. Earth was almost jerked out of its atmosphere blanket and the air got so thin in spots that people keeled over and fainted-though of course, at the same time, they were getting knocked down by the Big Jerk and maybe their bones broke or skulls cracked.

We've often asked Pa how people acted during that time, whether they were scared or brave or crazy or stunned, or all four, but he's sort of leery of the subject, and he was again tonight. He says he was mostly too busy to notice.

You see, Pa and some scientist friends of his had figured out part of what was going to happen-they'd known we'd get captured and our air would freeze-and they'd been working like mad to fix up a place with airtight walls and doors, and insulation against the cold, and big supplies of food and fuel and water and bottled air. But the place got smashed in the last earthquakes and all Pa's friends were killed then and in the Big Jerk. So he had to start over and throw the Nest together quick without any advantages, just using any stuff he could lay his hands on.

I guess he's telling pretty much the truth when he says he didn't have any time to keep an eye on how other folks behaved, either then or in the Big Freeze that followed-followed very quick, you know, both because the dark star was pulling us away very fast and because Earth's rotation had been slowed in the tug-of-war, so that the nights were ten old nights long.

Still, I've got an idea of some of the things that happened from the frozen folk I've seen, a few of them in other rooms in our building, others clustered around the furnaces in the basements where we go for coal.

In one of the rooms, an old man sits stiff in a chair, with an arm and a leg in splints. In another, a man and woman are huddled together in a bed with heaps of covers over them. You can just see their heads peeking out, close together. And in another a beautiful young lady is sitting with a pile of wraps huddled around her, looking hopefully toward the door, as if waiting for someone who never came back with warmth and food. They're all still and stiff as statues, of course, but just like life.

Pa showed them to me once in quick winks of his flashlight, when he still had a fair supply of batteries and could afford to waste a little light. They scared me pretty bad and made my heart pound, especially the young lady.

Now, with Pa telling his story for the umpteenth time to take our minds off another scare, I got to thinking of the frozen folk again. All of a sudden I got an idea that scared me worse than anything yet. You see, I'd just remembered the face I'd thought I'd seen in the window. I'd forgotten about that on account of trying to hide it from the others.

What, I asked myself, if the frozen folk were coming to life? What if they were like the liquid helium that got a new lease on life and started crawling toward the heat just when you thought its molecules ought to freeze solid forever? Or like the electricity that moves endlessly when it's just about as cold as that? What if the ever-growing cold, with the temperature creeping down the last few degrees to the last zero, had mysteriously wakened the frozen folk to life-not warm-blooded life, but something icy and horrible?

That was a worse idea than the one about something coming down from the dark star to get us.

Or maybe, I thought, both ideas might be true. Something coming down from the dark star and making the frozen folk move, using them to do its work. That would fit with both things I'd seen-the beautiful young lady and the moving, starlike light.

The frozen folk with minds from the dark star behind their unwinking eyes, creeping, crawling, snuffing their way, following the heat to the Nest.

I tell you, that thought gave me a very bad turn and I wanted very badly to tell the others my fears, but I remembered what Pa had said and clenched my teeth and didn't speak.

We were all sitting very still. Even the fire was burning silently. There was just the sound of Pa's voice and the clocks.

And then, from beyond the blankets, I thought I heard a tiny noise. My skin tightened all over me.

Pa was telling about the early years in the Nest and had come to the place where he philosophizes.

"So I asked myself then," he said, "what's the use of going on? What's the use of dragging it out for a few years? Why prolong a doomed existence of hard work and cold and loneliness? The human race is done. The Earth is done. Why not give up, I asked myself-and all of a sudden I got the answer."

Again I heard the noise, louder this time, a kind of uncertain, shuffling tread, coming closer. I couldn't breathe.

"Life's always been a business of working hard and fighting the cold," Pa was saying. "The earth's always been a lonely place, millions of miles from the next planet. And no matter how long the human race might have lived, the end would have come some night. Those things don't matter. What matters is that life is good. It has a lovely texture, like some rich cloth or fur, or the petals of flowers-you've seen pictures of those, but I can't describe how they feel-or the fire's glow. It makes everything else worth while. And that's as true for the last man as the first."

And still the steps kept shuffling closer. It seemed to me that the inmost blanket trembled and bulged a little. Just as if they were burned into my imagination, I kept seeing those peering, frozen eyes.

"So right then and there," Pa went on, and now I could tell that he heard the steps, too, and was talking loud so we maybe wouldn't hear them, "right then and there I told myself that I was going on as if we had all eternity ahead of us. I'd have children and teach them all I could. I'd get them to read books. I'd plan for the future, try to enlarge and seal the Nest. I'd do what I could to keep everything beautiful and growing. I'd keep alive my feeling of wonder even at the cold and the dark and the distant stars."

But then the blanket actually did move and lift. And there was a bright light somewhere behind it. Pa's voice stopped and his eyes turned to the widening slit and his hand went out until it touched and gripped the handle of the hammer beside him.

In through the blanket stepped the beautiful young lady. She stood there looking at us the strangest way, and she carried something bright and unwinking in her hand. And two other faces peered over her shoulders-men's faces, white and staring.

Well, my heart couldn't have been stopped for more than four or five beats before I realized she was wearing a suit and helmet like Pa's homemade ones, only fancier, and that the men were, too-and that the frozen folk certainly wouldn't be wearing those. Also, I noticed that the bright thing in her hand was just a kind of flashlight.

The silence kept on while I swallowed hard a couple of times, and after that there was all sorts of jabbering and commotion.

They were simply people, you see. We hadn't been the only ones to survive; we'd just thought so, for natural enough reasons. These three people had survived, and quite a few others with them. And when we found out *how* they'd survived, Pa let out the biggest whoop of joy.

They were from Los Alamos and they were getting their heat and power from atomic energy. Just using the uranium and plutonium intended for bombs, they had enough to go on for thousands of years. They had a regular little airtight city, with air-locks and all. They even generated electric light and grew plants and animals by it. (At this Pa let out a second whoop, waking Ma from her faint.)

But if we were flabbergasted at them, they were double-flabbergasted at us.

One of the men kept saying, "But it's impossible, I tell you. You can't maintain an air supply without hermetic sealing. It's simply impossible."

That was after he had got his helmet off and was using our air. Meanwhile, the young lady kept looking around at us as if we were saints, and telling us we'd done something amazing, and suddenly she broke down and cried.

They'd been scouting around for survivors, but they never expected to find any in a place like this. They had rocket ships at Los Alamos and plenty of chemical fuel. As for liquid oxygen, all you had to do was go out and shovel the air blanket at the top *level*. So after they'd got things going smoothly at Los Alamos, which had taken years, they'd decided to make some trips to likely places where there might be other survivors. No good trying long-distance radio signals, of course, since there was no atmosphere to carry them around the curve of the Earth.

Well, they'd found other colonies at Argonne and Brookhaven and way around the world at Harwell and Tanna Tuva. And now they'd been giving our city a look, not really expecting to find anything. But they had an instrument that noticed the faintest heat waves and it had told them there was something warm down here, so they'd landed to investigate. Of course we hadn't heard them land, since there was no air to carry the sound, and they'd had to investigate around quite a while before finding us. Their instruments had given them a wrong steer and they'd wasted some time in the building across the street.

By now, all five adults were talking like sixty. Pa was demonstrating to the men how he worked the fire and got rid of the ice in the chimney and all that. Ma had perked up wonderfully and was showing the young lady her cooking and sewing stuff, and even asking about how the women dressed at Los Alamos. The strangers marveled at everything and praised it to the skies. I could tell from the way they wrinkled their noses that they found the Nest a bit smelly, but they never mentioned that at all and just asked bushels of questions.

In fact, there was so much talking and excitement that Pa forgot about things, and it wasn't until they were all getting groggy that he looked and found the air had all boiled away in the pail. He got another bucket of air quick from behind the blankets. Of course that started them all laughing and jabbering again. The newcomers even got a little drunk. They weren't used to so much oxygen.

Funny thing, though —I didn't do much talking at all and Sis hung on to Ma all the time and hid her face when anybody looked at her. I felt pretty uncomfortable and disturbed myself, even about the young lady. Glimpsing her outside there, I'd had all sorts of mushy thoughts, but now I was just embarrassed and scared of her, even though she tried to be nice as anything to me.

I sort of wished they'd all quit crowding the Nest and let us be alone and get our feelings straightened out.

And when the newcomers began to talk about our all going to Los Alamos, as if that were taken for granted, I could see that something of the same feeling struck Pa and Ma, too. Pa got very silent all of a sudden and Ma kept telling the young lady, "But I wouldn't know how to act there and I haven't any clothes."

The strangers were puzzled like anything at first, but then they got the idea. As Pa kept saying, "It just doesn't seem right to let this fire go out."

Well, the strangers are gone, but they're coming back. It hasn't been decided yet just what will happen. Maybe the Nest will be kept up as what one of the strangers called a "survival school." Or maybe we will join the pioneers who are going to try to establish a new colony at the uranium mines at Great Slave Lake or in the Congo.

Of course, now that the strangers are gone, I've been thinking a lot about Los Alamos and those other tremendous colonies. I have a hankering to see them for myself.

You ask me, Pa wants to see them, too. He's been getting pretty thoughtful, watching Ma and Sis perk up.

"It's different, now that we know others are alive," he explains to me. "Your mother doesn't feel so hopeless any more. Neither do I, for that matter, not having to carry the whole responsibility for keeping the human race going, so to speak. It scares a person."

I looked around at the blanket walls and the fire and the pails of air boiling away and Ma and Sis sleeping in the warmth and the flickering light.

"It's not going to be easy to leave the Nest," I said, wanting to cry, kind of. "It's so small and there's just the four of us. I get scared at the idea of big places and a lot of strangers."

He nodded and put another piece of coal on the fire. Then he looked at the little pile and grinned suddenly and put a couple of handfuls on, just as if it was one of our birthdays or Christmas.

"You'll quickly get over that feeling son," he said. "The trouble with the world was that it kept getting smaller and smaller, till it ended with just the Nest. Now it'll be good to have a real huge world again, the way it was in the beginning."

I guess he's right. You think the beautiful young lady will wait for me till I grow up? I'll be twenty in only ten years.

The Moon is Green

Anybody who wanted to escape death could, by paying a very simple price-denial of life!

"Effie! What the devil are you up to?"

Her husband's voice, chopping through her mood of terrified rapture, made her heart jump like a startled cat, yet by some miracle of feminine self-control her body did not show a tremor.

Dear God, she thought, *he mustn't see it. It's so beautiful, and he always kills beauty.*

"I'm just looking at the Moon," she said listlessly. "It's green."

Mustn't, mustn't see it. And now, with luck, he wouldn't. For the face, as if it also heard and sensed the menace in the voice, was moving back from the window's glow into the outside dark, but slowly, reluctantly, and still faunlike, pleading, cajoling, tempting, and incredibly beautiful.

"Close the shutters at once, you little fool, and come away from the window!"

"Green as a beer bottle," she went on dreamily, "green as emeralds, green as leaves with sunshine striking through them and green grass to lie on." She couldn't help saying those last words. They were her token to the face, even though it couldn't hear.

"Effie!"

She knew what that last tone meant. Wearily she swung shut the ponderous lead inner shutters and drove home the heavy bolts. That hurt her fingers; it always did, but he mustn't know that.

"You know that those shutters are not to be touched! Not for five more years at least!"

"I only wanted to look at the Moon," she said, turning around, and then it was all gone-the face, the night, the Moon, the magic-and she was back in the grubby, stale little hole, facing an angry, stale little man. It was then that the eternal thud of the air-conditioning fans and the crackle of the electrostatic precipitators that sieved out the dust reached her consciousness again like the bite of a dentist's drill.

"Only wanted to look at the Moon!" he mimicked her in falsetto. "Only wanted to die like a little fool and make me that much more ashamed of you!" Then his voice went gruff and professional. "Here, count yourself."

She silently took the Geiger counter he held at arm's length, waited until it settled down to a steady ticking slower than a clock-due only to cosmic rays and indicating nothing dangerous-and then began to comb her body with the instrument. First her head and shoulders, then out along her arms and back along their under side. There was something oddly voluptuous about her movements, although her features were gray and sagging.

The ticking did not change its tempo until she came to her waist. Then it suddenly spurted, clicking faster and faster. Her husband gave an excited grunt, took a quick step forward, froze. She goggled for a moment in fear, then grinned foolishly, dug in the pocket of her grimy apron and guiltily pulled out a wristwatch.

He grabbed it as it dangled from her fingers, saw that it had a radium dial, cursed, heaved it up as if to smash it on the floor, but instead put it carefully on the table.

"You imbecile, you incredible imbecile," he softly chanted to himself through clenched teeth, with eyes half closed.

She shrugged faintly, put the Geiger counter on the table, and stood there slumped.

He waited until the chanting had soothed his anger, before speaking again. He said quietly, "I do suppose you still realize the sort of world you're living in?"

She nodded slowly, staring at nothingness. Oh, she realized, all right, realized only too well. It was the world that hadn't realized. The world that had gone on stockpiling hydrogen bombs. The world that had put those bombs in cobalt shells, although it had promised it wouldn't, because the cobalt made them much more terrible and cost no more. The world that had started throwing those bombs, always telling itself that it hadn't thrown enough of them yet to make the air really dangerous with the deadly radioactive dust that came from the cobalt. Thrown them and kept on throwing until the danger point, where air and ground would become fatal to all human life, was approached.

Then, for about a month, the two great enemy groups had hesitated. And then each, unknown to the other, had decided it could risk one last gigantic and decisive attack without exceeding the danger point. It had been planned to strip off the cobalt cases, but someone forgot and then there wasn't time. Besides, the military scientists of each group were confident that the lands of the other had got the most dust. The two attacks came within an hour of each other.

After that, the Fury. The Fury of doomed men who think only of taking with them as many as possible of the enemy, and in this case-they hoped-all. The Fury of suicides who know they have botched up life for good. The Fury of cocksure men who realize they have been outsmarted by fate, the enemy, and themselves, and know that they will never be able to improvise a defense when arraigned before the high court of history-and whose unadmitted hope is that there will be no high court of history left to arraign them. More cobalt bombs were dropped during the Fury than in all the preceding years of the war.

After the Fury, the Terror. Men and women with death sifting into their bones through their nostrils and skin, fighting for bare survival under a dust-hazed sky that played fantastic tricks with the light of Sun and Moon, like the dust from Krakatoa that drifted around the world for years. Cities, countryside, and air were alike poisoned, alive with deadly radiation.

The only realistic chance for continued existence was to retire, for the five or ten years the radiation would remain deadly, to some well-sealed and radiation-shielded place that must also be copiously supplied with food, water, power, and a means of air-conditioning.

Such places were prepared by the far-seeing, seized by the stronger, defended by them in turn against the desperate hordes of the dying ... until there were no more of those.

After that, only the waiting, the enduring. A mole's existence, without beauty or tenderness, but with fear and guilt as constant companions. Never to see the Sun, to walk among the trees-or even know if there were still trees.

Oh, yes, she realized what the world was like.

"You understand, too, I suppose, that we were allowed to reclaim this ground-level apartment only because the Committee believed us to be responsible people, and because I've been making a damn good showing lately?"

"Yes, Hank."

"I thought you were eager for privacy. You want to go back to the basement tenements?"

God, no! Anything rather than that fetid huddling, that shameless communal sprawl. And yet, was this so much better? The nearness to the surface was meaningless; it only tantalized. And the privacy magnified Hank.

She shook her head dutifully and said, "No, Hank."

"Then why aren't you careful? I've told you a million times, Effie, that glass is no protection against the dust that's outside that window. The lead shutter must never be touched! If you make one single slip like that and it gets around, the Committee will send us back to the lower levels without blinking an eye. And they'll think twice before trusting me with any important jobs."

"I'm sorry, Hank."

"Sorry? What's the good of being sorry? The only thing that counts is never to make a slip! Why the devil do you do such things, Effie? What drives you to it?"

She swallowed. "It's just that it's so dreadful being cooped up like this," she said hesitatingly, "shut away from the sky and the Sun. I'm just hungry for a little beauty."

"And do you suppose I'm not?" he demanded. "Don't you suppose I want to get outside, too, and be carefree and have a good time? But I'm not so damn selfish about it. I want my children to enjoy the Sun, and my children's children. Don't you see that that's the all-important thing and that we have to behave like mature adults and make sacrifices for it?"

"Yes, Hank."

He surveyed her slumped figure, her lined and listless face. "You're a fine one to talk about hunger for beauty," he told her. Then his voice grew softer, more deliberate. "You haven't forgotten, have you, Effie, that until last month the Committee was so concerned about your sterility? That they were about to enter my name on the list of those waiting to be allotted a free woman? Very high on the list, too!"

She could nod even at that one, but not while looking at him. She turned away. She knew very well that the Committee was justified in worrying about the birth rate. When the community finally moved back to the surface again, each additional healthy young person would be an asset, not only in the struggle for bare survival, but in the resumed war against Communism which some of the Committee members still counted on.

It was natural that they should view a sterile woman with disfavor, and not only because of the waste of her husband's germ-plasm, but because sterility might indicate that she had suffered more than the average from radiation. In that case, if she did bear children later on, they would be more apt to carry a defective heredity, producing an undue number of monsters and freaks in future generations, and so contaminating the race.

Of course she understood it. She could hardly remember the time when she didn't. Years ago? Centuries? There wasn't much difference in a place where time was endless.

His lecture finished, her husband smiled and grew almost cheerful.

"Now that you're going to have a child, that's all in the background again. Do you know, Effie, that when I first came in, I had some very good news for you? I'm to become a member of the Junior Committee and the announcement will be made at the banquet tonight." He cut short her mumbled congratulations. "So brighten yourself up and put on your best dress. I want the other Juniors to see what a handsome wife the new member has got." He paused. "Well, get a move on!"

She spoke with difficulty, still not looking at him. "I'm terribly sorry, Hank, but you'll have to go alone. I'm not well."

He straightened up with an indignant jerk. "There you go again! First that infantile, inexcusable business of the shutters, and now this! No feeling for my reputation at all. Don't be ridiculous, Effie. You're coming!"

"Terribly sorry," she repeated blindly, "but I really can't. I'd just be sick. I wouldn't make you proud of me at all."

"Of course you won't," he retorted sharply. "As it is, I have to spend half my energy running around making excuses for you-why you're so odd, why you always seem to be ailing, why you're always stupid and snobbish and say the wrong thing. But tonight's really important, Effie. It will cause a lot of bad comment if the new member's wife isn't present. You know how just a hint of sickness starts the old radiation-disease rumor going. You've *got* to come, Effie."

She shook her head helplessly.

"Oh, for heaven's sake, come on!" he shouted, advancing on her. "This is just a silly mood. As soon as you get going, you'll snap out of it. There's nothing really wrong with you at all."

He put his hand on her shoulder to turn her around, and at his touch her face suddenly grew so desperate and gray that for a moment he was alarmed in spite of himself.

"Really?" he asked, almost with a note of concern.

She nodded miserably.

"Hmm!" He stepped back and strode about irresolutely. "Well, of course, if that's the way it is ..." He checked himself and a sad smile crossed his face. "So you don't care enough about your old husband's success to make one supreme effort in spite of feeling bad?"

Again the helpless headshake. "I just can't go out tonight, under any circumstances." And her gaze stole toward the lead shutters.

He was about to say something when he caught the direction of her gaze. His eyebrows jumped. For seconds he stared at her incredulously, as if some completely new and almost unbelievable possibility had popped into his mind. The look of incredulity slowly faded, to be replaced by a harder, more calculating expression. But when he spoke again, his voice was shockingly bright and kind.

"Well, it can't be helped naturally, and I certainly wouldn't want you to go if you weren't able to enjoy it. So you hop right into bed and get a good rest. I'll run over to the men's dorm to freshen up. No, really, I don't want you to have to make any effort at all. Incidentally, Jim Barnes isn't going to be able to come to the banquet either-touch of the old 'flu, he tells me, of all things."

He watched her closely as he mentioned the other man's name, but she didn't react noticeably. In fact, she hardly seemed to be hearing his chatter.

"I got a bit sharp with you, I'm afraid, Effie," he continued contritely. "I'm sorry about that. I was excited about my new job and I guess that was why things upset me. Made me feel let down when I found you weren't feeling as good as I was. Selfish of me. Now you get into bed right away and get well. Don't worry about me a bit. I know you'd come if you possibly could. And I know you'll be thinking about me. Well, I must be off now."

He started toward her, as if to embrace her, then seemed to think better of it. He turned back at the doorway and said, emphasizing the words, "You'll be completely alone for the next four hours." He waited for her nod, then bounced out.

She stood still until his footsteps died away. Then she straightened up, walked over to where he'd put down the wristwatch, picked it up and smashed it hard on the floor. The crystal shattered, the case flew apart, and something went *zing!*

She stood there breathing heavily. Slowly her sagged features lifted, formed themselves into the beginning of a smile. She stole another look at the shutters. The smile became more definite. She felt her hair, wet her fingers and ran them along her hairline and back over her ears. After wiping her hands on her apron, she took it off. She straightened her dress, lifted her head with a little flourish, and stepped smartly toward the window.

Then her face went miserable again and her steps slowed.

No, it couldn't be, and it won't be, she told herself. It had been just an illusion, a silly romantic dream that she had somehow projected out of her beauty-starved mind and given a moment's false reality. There couldn't be anything alive outside. There hadn't been for two whole years.

And if there conceivably were, it would be something altogether horrible. She remembered some of the pariahs-hairless, witless creatures, with radiation welts crawling over their bodies like worms, who had come begging for succor during the last months of the Terror-and been shot down. How they must have hated the people in refuges!

But even as she was thinking these things, her fingers were caressing the bolts, gingerly drawing them, and she was opening the shutters gently, apprehensively.

No, there couldn't be anything outside, she assured herself wryly, peering out into the green night. Even her fears had been groundless.

But the face came floating up toward the window. She started back in terror, then checked herself.

174

For the face wasn't horrible at all, only very thin, with full lips and large eyes and a thin proud nose like the jutting beak of a bird. And no radiation welts or scars marred the skin, olive in the tempered moonlight. It looked, in fact, just as it had when she had seen it the first time.

For a long moment the face stared deep, deep into her brain. Then the full lips smiled and a half-clenched, thin-fingered hand materialized itself from the green darkness and rapped twice on the grimy pane.

Her heart pounding, she furiously worked the little crank that opened the window. It came unstuck from the frame with a tiny explosion of dust and a *zing* like that of the watch, only louder. A moment later it swung open wide and a puff of incredibly fresh air caressed her face and the inside of her nostrils, stinging her eyes with unanticipated tears.

The man outside balanced on the sill, crouching like a faun, head high, one elbow on knee. He was dressed in scarred, snug trousers and an old sweater.

"Is it tears I get for a welcome?" he mocked her gently in a musical voice. "Or are those only to greet God's own breath, the air?"

He swung down inside and now she could see he was tall. Turning, he snapped his fingers and called, "Come, puss."

A black cat with a twisted stump of a tail and feet like small boxing gloves and ears almost as big as rabbits' hopped clumsily in view. He lifted it down, gave it a pat. Then, nodding familiarly to Effie, he unstrapped a little pack from his back and laid it on the table.

She couldn't move. She even found it hard to breathe.

"The window," she finally managed to get out.

He looked at her inquiringly, caught the direction of her stabbing finger. Moving without haste, he went over and closed it carelessly.

"The shutters, too," she told him, but he ignored that, looking around.

"It's a snug enough place you and your man have," he commented. "Or is it that this is a free-love town or a harem spot, or just a military post?" He checked her before she could answer. "But let's not be talking about such things now. Soon enough I'll be scared to death for both of us. Best enjoy the kick of meeting, which is always good for twenty minutes at the least." He smiled at her rather shyly. "Have you food? Good, then bring it."

She set cold meat and some precious canned bread before him and had water heating for coffee. Before he fell to, he shredded a chunk of meat and put it on the floor for the cat, which left off its sniffing inspection of the walls and ran up eagerly mewing. Then the man began to eat, chewing each mouthful slowly and appreciatively.

From across the table Effie watched him, drinking in his every deft movement, his every cryptic quirk of expression. She attended to making the coffee, but that took only a moment. Finally she could contain herself no longer.

"What's it like up there?" she asked breathlessly. "Outside, I mean."

He looked at her oddly for quite a space. Finally, he said flatly, "Oh, it's a wonderland for sure, more amazing than you tombed folk could ever imagine. A veritable fairyland." And he quickly went on eating.

"No, but really," she pressed.

Noting her eagerness, he smiled and his eyes filled with playful tenderness. "I mean it, on my oath," he assured her. "You think the bombs and the dust made only death and ugliness. That was true at first. But then, just as the doctors foretold, they changed the life in the seeds and loins that were brave enough to stay. Wonders bloomed and walked." He broke off suddenly and asked, "Do any of you ever venture outside?"

"A few of the men are allowed to," she told him, "for short trips in special protective suits, to hunt for canned food and fuels and batteries and things like that."

"Aye, and those blind-souled slugs would never see anything but what they're looking for," he said, nodding bitterly. "They'd never see the garden where a dozen buds blossom where one

175

did before, and the flowers have petals a yard across, with stingless bees big as sparrows gently supping their nectar. Housecats grown spotted and huge as leopards (not little runts like Joe Louis here) stalk through those gardens. But they're gentle beasts, no more harmful than the rainbow-scaled snakes that glide around their paws, for the dust burned all the murder out of them, as it burned itself out.

"I've even made up a little poem about that. It starts, 'Fire can hurt me, or water, or the weight of Earth. But the dust is my friend.' Oh, yes, and then the robins like cockatoos and squirrels like a princess's ermine! All under a treasure chest of Sun and Moon and stars that the dust's magic powder changes from ruby to emerald and sapphire and amethyst and back again. Oh, and then the new children —"

"You're telling the truth?" she interrupted him, her eyes brimming with tears. "You're not making it up?"

"I am not," he assured her solemnly. "And if you could catch a glimpse of one of the new children, you'd never doubt me again. They have long limbs as brown as this coffee would be if it had lots of fresh cream in it, and smiling delicate faces and the whitish teeth and the finest hair. They're so nimble that I —a sprightly man and somewhat enlivened by the dust-feel like a cripple beside them. And their thoughts dance like flames and make me feel a very imbecile.

"Of course, they have seven fingers on each hand and eight toes on each foot, but they're the more beautiful for that. They have large pointed ears that the Sun shines through. They play in the garden, all day long, slipping among the great leaves and blooms, but they're so swift that you can hardly see them, unless one chooses to stand still and look at you. For that matter, you have to look a bit hard for all these things I'm telling you."

"But it is true?" she pleaded.

"Every word of it," he said, looking straight into her eyes. He put down his knife and fork. "What's your name?" he asked softly. "Mine's Patrick."

"Effie," she told him.

He shook his head. "That can't be," he said. Then his face brightened. "Euphemia," he exclaimed. "That's what Effie is short for. Your name is Euphemia." As he said that, looking at her, she suddenly felt beautiful. He got up and came around the table and stretched out his hand toward her.

"Euphemia —" he began.

"Yes?" she answered huskily, shrinking from him a little, but looking up sideways, and very flushed.

"Don't either of you move," Hank said.

The voice was flat and nasal because Hank was wearing a nose respirator that was just long enough to suggest an elephant's trunk. In his right hand was a large blue-black automatic pistol.

They turned their faces to him. Patrick's was abruptly alert, shifty. But Effie's was still smiling tenderly, as if Hank could not break the spell of the magic garden and should be pitied for not knowing about it.

"You little —" Hank began with an almost gleeful fury, calling her several shameful names. He spoke in short phrases, closing tight his unmasked mouth between them while he sucked in breath through the respirator. His voice rose in a crescendo. "And not with a man of the community, but a pariah! *A pariah!*"

"I hardly know what you're thinking, man, but you're quite wrong," Patrick took the opportunity to put in hurriedly, conciliatingly. "I just happened to be coming by hungry tonight, a lonely tramp, and knocked at the window. Your wife was a bit foolish and let kindheartedness get the better of prudence —"

"Don't think you've pulled the wool over my eyes, Effie," Hank went on with a screechy laugh, disregarding the other man completely. "Don't think I don't know why you're suddenly going to have a child after four long years."

At that moment the cat came nosing up to his feet. Patrick watched him narrowly, shifting his weight forward a little, but Hank only kicked the animal aside without taking his eyes off them.

"Even that business of carrying the wristwatch in your pocket instead of on your arm," he went on with channeled hysteria. "A neat bit of camouflage, Effie. Very neat. And telling me it was my child, when all the while you've been seeing him for months!"

"Man, you're mad; I've not touched her!" Patrick denied hotly though still calculatingly, and risked a step forward, stopping when the gun instantly swung his way.

"Pretending you were going to give me a healthy child," Hank raved on, "when all the while you knew it would be-either in body or germ plasm —a thing like *that*!"

He waved his gun at the malformed cat, which had leaped to the top of the table and was eating the remains of Patrick's food, though its watchful green eyes were fixed on Hank.

"I should shoot him down!" Hank yelled, between sobbing, chest-racking inhalations through the mask. "I should kill him this instant for the contaminated pariah he is!"

All this while Effie had not ceased to smile compassionately. Now she stood up without haste and went to Patrick's side. Disregarding his warning, apprehensive glance, she put her arm lightly around him and faced her husband.

"Then you'd be killing the bringer of the best news we've ever had," she said, and her voice was like a flood of some warm sweet liquor in that musty, hate-charged room. "Oh, Hank, forget your silly, wrong jealousy and listen to me. Patrick here has something wonderful to tell us."

Hank stared at her. For once he screamed no reply. It was obvious that he was seeing for the first time how beautiful she had become, and that the realization jolted him terribly.

"What do you mean?" he finally asked unevenly, almost fearfully.

"I mean that we no longer need to fear the dust," she said, and now her smile was radiant. "It never really did hurt people the way the doctors said it would. Remember how it was with me, Hank, the exposure I had and recovered from, although the doctors said I wouldn't at first-and without even losing my hair? Hank, those who were brave enough to stay outside, and who weren't killed by terror and suggestion and panic-they adapted to the dust. They changed, but they changed for the better. Everything —"

"Effie, he told you lies!" Hank interrupted, but still in that same agitated, broken voice, cowed by her beauty.

"Everything that grew or moved was purified," she went on ringingly. "You men going outside have never seen it, because you've never had eyes for it. You've been blinded to beauty, to life itself. And now all the power in the dust has gone and faded, anyway, burned itself out. That's true, isn't it?"

She smiled at Patrick for confirmation. His face was strangely veiled, as if he were calculating obscure changes. He might have given a little nod; at any rate, Effie assumed that he did, for she turned back to her husband.

"You see, Hank? We can all go out now. We need never fear the dust again. Patrick is a living proof of that," she continued triumphantly, standing straighter, holding him a little tighter. "Look at him. Not a scar or a sign, and he's been out in the dust for years. How could he be this way, if the dust hurt the brave? Oh, believe me, Hank! Believe what you see. Test it if you want. Test Patrick here."

"Effie, you're all mixed up. You don't know —" Hank faltered, but without conviction of any sort.

"Just test him," Effie repeated with utter confidence, ignoring-not even noticing-Patrick's warning nudge.

"All right," Hank mumbled. He looked at the stranger dully. "Can you count?" he asked.

Patrick's face was a complete enigma. Then he suddenly spoke, and his voice was like a fencer's foil-light, bright, alert, constantly playing, yet utterly on guard.

"Can I count? Do you take me for a complete simpleton, man? Of course I can count!"

"Then count yourself," Hank said, barely indicating the table.

"Count myself, should I?" the other retorted with a quick facetious laugh. "Is this a kindergarten? But if you want me to, I'm willing." His voice was rapid. "I've two arms, and two legs, that's four. And ten fingers and ten toes-you'll take my word for them? —that's twenty-four. A head, twenty-five. And two eyes and a nose and a mouth —"

"With this, I mean," Hank said heavily, advanced to the table, picked up the Geiger counter, switched it on, and handed it across the table to the other man.

But while it was still an arm's length from Patrick, the clicks began to mount furiously, until they were like the chatter of a pigmy machine gun. Abruptly the clicks slowed, but that was only the counter shifting to a new scaling circuit, in which each click stood for 512 of the old ones.

With those horrid, rattling little volleys, fear cascaded into the room and filled it, smashing like so much colored glass all the bright barriers of words Effie had raised against it. For no dreams can stand against the Geiger counter, the Twentieth Century's mouthpiece of ultimate truth. It was as if the dust and all the terrors of the dust had incarnated themselves in one dread invading shape that said in words stronger than audible speech, "Those were illusions, whistles in the dark. This is reality, the dreary, pitiless reality of the Burrowing Years."

Hank scuttled back to the wall. Through chattering teeth he babbled, "... enough radioactives ... kill a thousand men ... freak ... a freak ..." In his agitation he forgot for a moment to inhale through the respirator.

Even Effie-taken off guard, all the fears that had been drilled into her twanging like piano wires-shrank from the skeletal-seeming shape beside her, held herself to it only by desperation.

Patrick did it for her. He disengaged her arm and stepped briskly away. Then he whirled on them, smiling sardonically, and started to speak, but instead looked with distaste at the chattering Geiger counter he held between fingers and thumb.

"Have we listened to this racket long enough?" he asked.

Without waiting for an answer, he put down the instrument on the table. The cat hurried over to it curiously and the clicks began again to mount in a minor crescendo. Effie lunged for it frantically, switched it off, darted back.

"That's right," Patrick said with another chilling smile. "You do well to cringe, for I'm death itself. Even in death I could kill you, like a snake." And with that his voice took on the tones of a circus barker. "Yes, I'm a freak, as the gentleman so wisely said. That's what one doctor who dared talk with me for a minute told me before he kicked me out. He couldn't tell me why, but somehow the dust doesn't kill me. Because I'm a freak, you see, just like the men who ate nails and walked on fire and ate arsenic and stuck themselves through with pins. Step right up, ladies and gentlemen-only not too close! —and examine the man the dust can't harm. Rappaccini's child, brought up to date; his embrace, death!

"And now," he said, breathing heavily, "I'll get out and leave you in your damned lead cave."

He started toward the window. Hank's gun followed him shakingly.

"Wait!" Effie called in an agonized voice. He obeyed. She continued falteringly, "When we were together earlier, you didn't act as if..."

"When we were together earlier, I wanted what I wanted," he snarled at her. "You don't suppose I'm a bloody saint, do you?"

"And all the beautiful things you told me?"

"That," he said cruelly, "is just a line I've found that women fall for. They're all so bored and so starved for beauty-as *they* generally put it."

"Even the garden?" Her question was barely audible through the sobs that threatened to suffocate her.

He looked at her and perhaps his expression softened just a trifle.

"What's outside," he said flatly, "is just a little worse than either of you can imagine." He tapped his temple. "The garden's all here."

"You've killed it," she wept. "You've killed it in me. You've both killed everything that's beautiful. But you're worse," she screamed at Patrick, "because he only killed beauty once, but you brought it to life just so you could kill it again. Oh, I can't stand it! I won't stand it!" And she began to scream.

Patrick started toward her, but she broke off and whirled away from him to the window, her eyes crazy.

"You've been lying to us," she cried. "The garden's there. I know it is. But you don't want to share it with anyone."

"No, no, Euphemia," Patrick protested anxiously. "It's hell out there, believe me. I wouldn't lie to you about it."

"Wouldn't lie to me!" she mocked. "Are you afraid, too?"

With a sudden pull, she jerked open the window and stood before the blank green-tinged oblong of darkness that seemed to press into the room like a menacing, heavy, wind-urged curtain.

At that Hank cried out a shocked, pleading, "Effie!"

She ignored him. "I can't be cooped up here any longer," she said. "And I won't, now that I know. I'm going to the garden."

Both men sprang at her, but they were too late. She leaped lightly to the sill, and by the time they had flung themselves against it, her footsteps were already hurrying off into the darkness.

"Effie, come back! Come back!" Hank shouted after her desperately, no longer thinking to cringe from the man beside him, or how the gun was pointed. "I love you, Effie. Come back!"

Patrick added his voice. "Come back, Euphemia. You'll be safe if you come back right away. Come back to your home."

No answer to that at all.

They both strained their eyes through the greenish murk. They could barely make out a shadowy figure about half a block down the near-black canyon of the dismal, dust-blown street, into which the greenish moonlight hardly reached. It seemed to them that the figure was scooping something up from the pavement and letting it sift down along its arms and over its bosom.

"Go out and get her, man," Patrick urged the other. "For if I go out for her, I warn you I won't bring her back. She said something about having stood the dust better than most, and that's enough for me."

But Hank, chained by his painfully learned habits and by something else, could not move.

And then a ghostly voice came whispering down the street, chanting, "Fire can hurt me, or water, or the weight of Earth. But the dust is my friend."

Patrick spared the other man one more look. Then, without a word, he vaulted up and ran off.

Hank stood there. After perhaps a half minute he remembered to close his mouth when he inhaled. Finally he was sure the street was empty. As he started to close the window, there was a little *mew.*

He picked up the cat and gently put it outside. Then he did close the window, and the shutters, and bolted them, and took up the Geiger counter, and mechanically began to count himself.

Later Than You Think

It's much later. The question is ... how late?

Obviously the Archeologist's study belonged to an era vastly distant from today. Familiar similarities here and there only sharpened the feeling of alienage. The sunlight that filtered through the windows in the ceiling had a wan and greenish cast and was augmented by radiation from some luminous material impregnating the walls and floor. Even the wide desk and the commodious hassocks glowed with a restful light. Across the former were scattered metal-backed wax tablets, styluses, and a pair of large and oddly formed spectacles. The crammed bookcases were not particularly unusual, but the books were bound in metal and the script on their spines would have been utterly unfamiliar to the most erudite of modern linguists. One of the books, lying open on a hassock, showed leaves of a thin, flexible, rustless metal covered with luminous characters. Between the bookcases were phosphorescent oil paintings, mainly of sea bottoms, in somber greens and browns. Their style, neither wholly realistic nor abstract, would have baffled the historian of art.

A blackboard with large colored crayons hinted equally at the schoolroom and the studio.

In the center of the room, midway to the ceiling, hung a fish with irridescent scales of breathtaking beauty. So invisible was its means of support that-also taking into account the strange paintings and the greenish light-one would have sworn that the object was to create an underwater scene.

The Explorer made his entrance in a theatrical swirl of movement. He embraced the Archeologist with a warmth calculated to startle that crusty old fellow. Then he settled himself on a hassock, looked up and asked a question in a speech and idiom so different from any we know that it must be called another means of communication rather than another language. The import was, "Well, what about it?"

If the Archeologist were taken aback, he concealed it. His expression showed only pleasure at being reunited with a long-absent friend.

"What about what?" he queried.

"About your discovery!"

"What discovery?" The Archeologist's incomprehension was playful.

The Explorer threw up his arms. "Why, what else but your discovery, here on Earth, of the remains of an intelligent species? It's the find of the age! Am I going to have to coax you? Out with it!"

"I didn't make the discovery," the other said tranquilly. "I only supervised the excavations and directed the correlation of material. *You* ought to be doing the talking. *You're* the one who's just returned from the stars."

"Forget that." The Explorer brushed the question aside. "As soon as our spaceship got within radio range of Earth, they started to send us a continuous newscast covering the period of our absence. One of the items, exasperatingly brief, mentioned your discovery. It captured my imagination. I couldn't wait to hear the details." He paused, then confessed, "You get so eager out there in space —a metal-filmed droplet of life lost in immensity. You rediscover your emotions...." He changed color, then finished rapidly, "As soon as I could decently get away, I came straight to you. I wanted to hear about it from the best authority-yourself."

The Archeologist regarded him quizzically. "I'm pleased that you should think of me and my work, and I'm very happy to see you again. But admit it now, isn't there something a bit odd about your getting so worked up over this thing? I can understand that after your long absence from Earth, any news of Earth would seem especially important. But isn't there an additional reason?"

The Explorer twisted impatiently. "Oh, I suppose there is. Disappointment, for one thing. We were hoping to get in touch with intelligent life out there. We were specially trained in techniques for establishing mental contact with alien intelligent life forms. Well, we found some planets with life upon them, all right. But it was primitive life, not worth bothering about."

Again he hesitated embarrassedly. "Out there you get to thinking of the preciousness of intelligence. There's so little of it, and it's so lonely. And we so greatly need intercourse with another intelligent species to give depth and balance to our thoughts. I suppose I set too much store by my hopes of establishing a contact." He paused. "At any rate, when I heard that what we were looking for, you had found here at home-even though dead and done for —I felt that at least it was something. I was suddenly very eager. It is odd, I know, to get so worked up about an extinct species-as if my interest could mean anything to them now-but that's the way it hit me."

Several small shadows crossed the windows overhead. They might have been birds, except they moved too slowly.

"I think I understand," the Archeologist said softly.

"So get on with it and tell me about your discovery!" the Explorer exploded.

"I've already told you that it wasn't my discovery," the Archeologist reminded him. "A few years after your expedition left, there was begun a detailed resurvey of Earth's mineral resources. In the course of some deep continental borings, one party discovered a cache-either a very large box or a rather small room-with metallic walls of great strength and toughness. Evidently its makers had intended it for the very purpose of carrying a message down through the ages. It proved to contain artifacts; models of buildings, vehicles, and machines, objects of art, pictures, and books-hundreds of books, along with elaborate pictorial dictionaries for interpreting them. So now we even understand their languages."

"Languages?" interrupted the Explorer. "That's queer. Somehow one thinks of an alien species as having just one language."

"Like our own, this species had several, though there were some words and symbols that were alike in all their languages. These words and symbols seem to have come down unchanged from their most distant prehistory."

The Explorer burst out, "I am not interested in all that dry stuff! Give me the wet! What were they like? How did they live? What did they create? What did they want?"

The Archeologist gently waved aside the questions. "All in good time. If I am to tell you everything you want to know, I must tell it my own way. Now that you are back on Earth, you will have to reacquire those orderly and composed habits of thought which you have partly lost in the course of your wild interstellar adventurings."

"Curse you, I think you're just trying to tantalize me."

The Archeologist's expression showed that this was not altogether untrue. He casually fondled an animal that had wriggled up onto his desk, and which looked rather more like an eel than a snake. "Cute little brute, isn't it?" he remarked. When it became apparent that the Explorer wasn't to be provoked into another outburst, he continued, "It became my task to interpret the contents of the cache, to reconstruct its makers' climb from animalism and savagery to civilization, their rather rapid spread across the world's surface, their first fumbling attempts to escape from the Earth."

"They had spaceships?"

"It's barely possible. I rather hope they did, since it would mean the chance of a survival else-where, though the negative results of your expedition rather lessen that." He went on, "The cache was laid down when they were first attempting space flight, just after their discovery of atomic power, in the first flush of their youth. It was probably created in a kind of exuberant fan-cifulness, with no serious belief that it would ever serve the purpose for which it was intended." He looked at the Explorer strangely. "If I am not mistaken, we have laid down similar caches."

After a moment the Archeologist continued, "My reconstruction of their history, subsequent to the laying down of the cache, has been largely hypothetical. I can only guess at the reasons for their decline and fall. Supplementary material has been very slow in coming in, though we are still making extensive excavations at widely separated points. Here are the last reports." He tossed the Explorer a small metal-leaf pamphlet. It flew with a curiously slow motion.

"That's what struck me so queer right from the start," the Explorer observed, putting the pamphlet aside after a glance. "If these creatures were relatively advanced, why haven't we learned about them before? They must have left so many things-buildings, machines, engineer-ing projects, some of them on a large scale. You'd think we'd be turning up traces everywhere."

"I have four answers to that," the Archeologist replied. "The first is the most obvious. Time. Geologic ages of it. The second is more subtle. What if we should have been looking in the wrong place? I mean, what if the creatures occupied a very different portion of the Earth than our own? Third, it's possible that atomic energy, out of control, finished the race and destroyed its traces. The present distribution of radioactive compounds throughout the Earth's surface lends some support to this theory.

"Fourth," he went on, "it's my belief that when an intelligent species begins to retrogress, it tends to destroy, or, rather, debase all the things it has laboriously created. Large buildings are torn down to make smaller ones. Machines are broken up and worked into primitive tools and weapons. There is a kind of unraveling or erasing. A cultural Second Law of Thermodynamics begins to operate, whereby the intellect and all its works are gradually degraded to the lowest level of meaning and creativity."

"But why?" The Explorer sounded anguished. "Why should any intelligent species end like that? I grant the possibility of atomic power getting out of hand, though one would have thought they'd have taken the greatest precautions. Still, it could happen. But that fourth answer-it's morbid."

"Cultures and civilizations die," said the Archeologist evenly. "That has happened repeatedly in our own history. Why not species? An individual dies-and is there anything intrinsically more terrible in the death of a species than in the death of an individual?"

He paused. "With respect to the members of this one species, I think that a certain tem-peramental instability hastened their end. Their appetites and emotions were not sufficiently subordinated to their understanding and to their sense of drama-their enjoyment of the com-edy and tragedy of existence. They were impatient and easily incapacitated by frustration. They seem to have been singularly guilty in their pleasures, behaving either like gloomy moralists or gluttons.

"Because of taboos and an overgrown possessiveness," he continued, "each individual tended to limit his affection to a tiny family; in many cases he focused his love on himself alone. They set great store by personal prestige, by the amassing of wealth and the exercise of power. Their notable capacity for thought and manipulative activity was expended on things rather than per-sons or feelings. Their technology outstripped their psychology. They skimped fatally when it came to hard thinking about the purpose of life and intellectual activity, and the means for preserving them."

Again the slow shadows drifted overhead.

"And finally," the Archeologist said, "they were a strangely haunted species. They seem to have been obsessed by the notion that others, greater than themselves, had prospered before them and then died, leaving them to rebuild a civilization from ruins. It was from those others that they thought they derived the few words and symbols common to all their languages."

"Gods?" mused the Explorer.

The Archeologist shrugged. "Who knows?"

The Explorer turned away. His excitement had visibly evaporated, leaving behind a cold and miserable residue of feeling. "I am not sure I want to hear much more about them," he said. "They sound too much like us. Perhaps it was a mistake, my coming here. Pardon me, old friend, but out there in space even *our* emotions become undisciplined. Everything becomes indescribably poignant. Moods are tempestuous. You shift in an instant from zenith to nadir-and remember, out there you can see both.

"I was very eager to hear about this lost species," he added in a sad voice. "I thought I would feel a kind of fellowship with them across the eons. Instead, I touch only corpses. It reminds me of when, out in space, there looms up before your prow, faint in the starlight, a dead sun. They were a young race. They thought they were getting somewhere. They promised themselves an eternity of effort. And all the while there was wriggling toward them out of that future for which they yearned ...oh, it's so completely futile and unfair."

"I disagree," the Archeologist said spiritedly. "Really, your absence from Earth has unsettled you even more than I first surmised. Look at the matter squarely. Death comes to everything in the end. Our past is strewn with our dead. That species died, it's true. But what they achieved, they achieved. What happiness they had, they had. What they did in their short span is as significant as what they might have done had they lived a billion years. The present is always more important than the future. And no creature can have all the future-it must be shared, left to others."

"Maybe so," the Explorer said slowly. "Yes, I guess you're right. But I still feel a horrible wistfulness about them, and I hug to myself the hope that a few of them escaped and set up a colony on some planet we haven't yet visited." There was a long silence. Then the Explorer turned back. "You old devil," he said in a manner that showed his gayer and more boisterous mood had returned, though diminished, "you still haven't told me anything definite about them."

"So I haven't," replied the Archeologist with guileful innocence. "Well, they were vertebrates."

"Oh?"

"Yes. What's more, they were mammals."

"Mammals? I was expecting something different."

"I thought you were."

The Explorer shifted. "All this matter of evolutionary categories is pretty cut-and-dried. Even a knowledge of how they looked doesn't mean much. I'd like to approach them in a more intimate way. How did they think of themselves? What did they call themselves? I know the word won't mean anything to me, but it will give me a feeling-of recognition."

"I can't say the word," the Archeologist told him, "because I haven't the proper vocal equipment. But I know enough of their script to be able to write it for you as they would have written it. Incidentally, it is one of those words common to all their languages, that they attributed to an earlier race of beings."

The Archeologist extended one of his eight tentacles toward the blackboard. The suckers at its tip firmly grasped a bit of orange crayon. Another of his tentacles took up the spectacles and adjusted them over his three-inch protruding pupils.

The eel-like glittering pet drifted back into the room and nosed curiously about the crayon as it traced:

RAT

Nice Girl with Five Husbands

Adventure is relative to one's previous experience. Sometimes, in fact, you can't even be sure you're having or not having one!

To be given paid-up leisure and find yourself unable to create is unpleasant for any artist. To be stranded in a cluster of desert cabins with a dozen lonely people in the same predicament only makes it worse. So Tom Dorset was understandably irked with himself and the Tosker-Brown Vacation Fellowships as he climbed with the sun into the valley of red stones. He accepted the chafing of his camera strap against his shoulder as the nagging of conscience. He agreed with the disparaging hisses of the grains of sand rutched by his sneakers, and he wished that the occasional breezes, which faintly echoed the same criticisms, could blow him into a friendlier, less jealous age.

He had no way of knowing that just as there are winds that blow through space, so there are winds that blow through time. Such winds may be strong or weak. The strong ones are rare and seldom blow for short distances, or more of us would know about them. What they pick up is almost always whirled far into the future or past.

This has happened to people. There was Ambrose Bierce, who walked out of America and existence, and there are thousands of others who have disappeared without a trace, though many of these may not have been caught up by time tornadoes and I do not know if a time gale blew across the deck of the *Marie Celeste*.

Sometimes a time wind is playful, snatching up an object, sporting with it for a season and then returning it unharmed to its original place. Sometimes we may be blown about by whimsical time winds without realizing it. Memory, for example, is a tiny time breeze, so weak that it can ripple only the mind.

A very few time winds are like the monsoon, blowing at fixed intervals, first in one direction, then the other. Such a time wind blows near a balancing rock in a valley of red stones in the American Southwest. Every morning at ten o'clock, it blows a hundred years into the future; every afternoon at two, it blows a hundred years into the past.

Quite a number of people have unwittingly seen time winds in operation. There are misty spots on the sea's horizon and wavery patches over desert sands. There are mirages and will o' the wisps and ice blinks. And there are dust devils, such as Tom Dorset walked into near the balancing rock.

It seemed to him no more than a spiteful upgust of sand, against which he closed his eyes until the warm granules stopped peppering the lids. He opened them to see the balancing rock had silently fallen and lay a quarter buried—no, that couldn't be, he told himself instantly. He had been preoccupied; he must have passed the balancing rock and held its image in his mind.

Despite this rationalization he was quite shaken. The strap of his camera slipped slowly down his arm without his feeling it. And just then there stepped around the giant bobbin of the rock an extraordinarily pretty girl with hair the same pinkish copper color.

She was barefoot and wearing a pale blue playsuit rather like a Grecian tunic. But most important, as she stood there toeing his rough shadow in the sand, there was a complete naturalness about her, an absence of sharp edges, as if her personality had weathered without aging, just as the valley seemed to have taken another step toward eternity in the space of an instant.

She must have assumed something of the same gentleness in him, for her faint surprise faded and she asked him, as easily as if he were a friend of five years' standing, "Tell now, do you think a woman can love just one man? All her life? And a man just one woman?"

Tom Dorset made a dazed sound.

His mind searched wildly.

"I do," she said, looking at him as calmly as at a mountain. "I think a man and woman can be each other's world, like Tristan and Isolde or Frederic and Catherine. Those old authors were wise. I don't see why on earth a girl has to spread her love around, no matter how enriching the experiences may be."

"You know, I agree with you," Tom said, thinking he'd caught her idea-it was impossible not to catch her casualness. "I think there's something cheap about the way everybody's supposed to run after sex these days."

"I don't mean that exactly. Tenderness is beautiful, but —" She pouted. "A big family can be vastly crushing. I wanted to declare today a holiday, but they outvoted me. Jock said it didn't chime with our mood cycles. But I was angry with them, so I put on my clothes —"

"Put on —?"

"To make it a holiday," she explained bafflingly. "And I walked here for a tantrum." She stepped out of Tom's shadow and hopped back. "Ow, the sand's getting hot," she said, rubbing the grains from the pale and uncramped toes.

"You go barefoot a lot?" Tom guessed.

"No, mostly digitals," she replied and took something shimmering from a pocket at her hip and drew it on her foot. It was a high-ankled, transparent moccasin with five separate toes. She zipped it shut with the speed of a card trick, then similarly gloved the other foot. Again the metal-edged slit down the front seemed to close itself.

"I'm behind on the fashions," Tom said, curious. They were walking side by side now, the way she'd come and he'd been going. "How does that zipper work?"

"Magnetic. They're on all my clothes. Very simple." She parted her tunic to the waist, then let it zip together.

"Clever," Tom remarked with a gulp. There seemed no limits to this girl's naturalness.

"I see you're a button man," she said. "You actually believe it's possible for a man and woman to love just each other?"

His chuckle was bitter. He was thinking of Elinore Murphy at Tosker-Brown and a bit about cold-faced Miss Tosker herself. "I sometimes wonder if it's possible for anyone to love anyone."

"You haven't met the right girls," she said.

"Girl," he corrected.

She grinned at him. "You'll make me think you really are a monogamist. What group do you come from?"

"Let's not talk about that," he requested. He was willing to forego knowing how she'd guessed he was from an art group, if he could be spared talking about the Vacation Fellowships and those nervous little cabins.

"My group's very nice on the whole," the girl said, "but at times they can be nefandously exasperating. Jock's the worst, quietly guiding the rest of us like an analyst. How I loathe that man! But Larry's almost as bad, with his shame-faced bumptiousness, as if we'd all sneaked off on a joyride to Venus. And there's Jokichi at the opposite extreme, forever scared he won't distribute his affection equally, dividing it up into mean little packets like candy for jealous children who would scream if they got one chewy less. And then there's Sasha and Ernest —"

"Who are you talking about?" Tom asked.

"My husbands." She shook her head dolefully. "To find five more difficult men would be positively Martian."

Tom's mind backtracked frantically, searching all conversations at Tosker-Brown for gossip about cultists in the neighborhood. It found nothing and embarked on a wider search. There were the Mormons (was that the word that had sounded like Martian?) but it wasn't the Mormon husbands who were plural. And then there was Oneida (weren't husbands and wives both plural there?) but that was 19th century New England.

"Five husbands?" he repeated. She nodded. He went on, "Do you mean to say five men have got you alone somewhere up here?"

"To be sure not," she replied. "There are my kwives."

"Kwives?"

"Co-wives," she said more slowly. "They can be fascinerously exasperating, too."

Tom's mind did some more searching. "And yet you believe in monogamy?"

She smiled. "Only when I'm having tantrums. It was civilized of you to agree with me."

"But I actually do believe in monogamy," he protested.

She gave his hand a little squeeze. "You are nice, but let's rush now. I've finished my tantrum and I want you to meet my group. You can fresh yourself with us."

As they hurried across the heated sands, Tom Dorset felt for the first time a twinge of uneasiness. There was something about this girl, more than her strange clothes and the odd words she used now and then, something almost-though ghosts don't wear digitals-spectral.

They scrambled up a little rise, digging their footgear into the sand, until they stood on a long flat. And there, serpentining around two great clumps of rock, was a many-windowed adobe ranch house with a roof like fresh soot.

"Oh, they've put on their clothes," his companion exclaimed with pleasure. "They've decided to make it a holiday after all."

Tom spotted a beard in the group swarming out to meet them. Its cultish look gave him a momentary feeling of superiority, followed by an equally momentary apprehension-the five husbands were certainly husky. Then both feelings were swallowed up in the swirl of introduction.

He told his own name, found that his companion's was Lois Wolver, then smiling faces began to bob toward his, his hands were shaken, his cheeks were kissed, he was even spun around like blind man's bluff, so that he lost track of the husbands and failed to attach Mary, Rachel, Simone and Joyce to the right owners.

He did notice that Jokichi was an Oriental with a skin as tight as enameled china, and that Rachel was a tall slim Negro girl. Also someone said, "Joyce isn't a Wolver, she's just visiting."

He got a much clearer impression of the clothes than the names. They were colorful, costly-looking, and mostly Egyptian and Cretan in inspiration. Some of them would have been quite immodest, even compared to Miss Tosker's famous playsuits, except that the wearers didn't seem to feel so.

"There goes the middle-morning rocket!" one of them eagerly cried.

Tom looked up with the rest, but his eyes caught the dazzling sun. However, he heard a faint roaring that quickly sank in volume and pitch, and it reminded him that the Army had a rocket testing range in this area. He had little interest in science, but he hadn't known they were on a daily schedule.

"Do you suppose it's off the track?" he asked anxiously.

"Not a chance," someone told him-the beard, he thought. The assurance of the tones gave him a possible solution. Scientists came from all over the world these days and might have all sorts of advanced ideas. This could be a group working at a nearby atomic project and leading its peculiar private life on the side.

As they eddied toward the house he heard Lois remind someone, "But you finally did declare it a holiday," and a husband who looked like a gay pharaoh respond, "I had another see at the mood charts and I found a subtle surge I'd missed."

Meanwhile the beard (a black one) had taken Tom in charge. Tom wasn't sure of his name, but he had a tan skin, a green sarong, and a fiercely jovial expression. "The swimming pool's around there, the landing spot's on the other side," he began, then noticed Tom gazing at the sooty roof. "Sun power cells," he explained proudly. "They store all the current we need."

Tom felt his idea confirmed. "Wonder you don't use atomic power," he observed lightly.

The beard nodded. "We've been asked that. Matter of esthetics. Why waste sunlight or use hard radiations needlessly? Of course, you might feel differently. What's your group, did you say?"

"Tosker-Brown," Tom told him, adding when the beard frowned, "the Fellowship people, you know."

"I don't," the beard confessed. "Where are you located?"

Tom briefly described the ranch house and cabins at the other end of the valley.

"Comic, I can't place it." The beard shrugged. "Here come the children."

A dozen naked youngsters raced around the ranch house, followed by a woman in a vaguely African dress open down the sides.

"Yours?" Tom asked.

"Ours," the beard answered.

"C'est un homme!"

"Regardez des vêtements!"

"No need to practice, kids; this is a holiday," the beard told them. "Tom, Helen," he said, introducing the woman with the air-conditioned garment. "Her turn today to companion die Kinder."

One of the latter rapped on the beard's knee. "May we show the stranger our things?" Instantly the others joined in pleading. The beard shot an inquiring glance at Tom, who nodded. A moment later the small troupe was hurrying him toward a spacious lean-to at the end of the ranch house. It was chuckful of strange toys, rocks and plants, small animals in cages and out, and the oddest model airplanes, or submarines. But Tom was given no time to look at any one thing for long.

"See my crystals? I grew them."

"Smell my mutated gardenias. Tell now, isn't there a difference?" There didn't seem to be, but he nodded.

"Look at my squabbits." This referred to some long-eared white squirrels nibbling carrots and nuts.

"Here's my newest model spaceship, a DS-57-B. Notice the detail." The oldest boy shoved one of the submarine affairs in his face.

Tom felt like a figure that is being tugged about in a rococo painting by wide pink ribbons in the chubby hands of naked cherubs. Except that these cherubs were slim and tanned, fantastically energetic, and apparently of depressingly high IQ. (What these scientists did to children!) He missed Lois and was grateful for the single little girl solemnly skipping rope in a corner and paying no attention to him.

The odd lingo she repeated stuck in his mind: "Gik-lo, I-o, Rik-o, Gis-so. Gik-lo, I-o...."

Suddenly the air was filled with soft chimes. "Lunch," the children shouted and ran away.

Tom followed at a soberer pace along the wall of the ranch house. He glanced in the huge windows, curious about the living and sleeping arrangements of the Wolvers, but the panes were strangely darkened. Then he entered the wide doorway through which the children had scampered and his curiosity turned to wonder.

A resilient green floor that wasn't flat, but sloped up toward the white of the far wall like a breaking wave. Chairs like giants' hands tenderly cupped. Little tables growing like mushrooms and broad-leafed plants out of the green floor. A vast picture window showing the red rocks.

Yet it was the wood-paneled walls that electrified his artistic interest. They blossomed with fruits and flowers, deep and poignantly carved in several styles. He had never seen such work.

190

He became aware of a silence and realized that his hosts and hostesses were smiling at him from around a long table. Moved by a sudden humility, he knelt and unlaced his sneakers and added them to the pile of sandals and digitals by the door. As he rose, a soft and comic piping started and he realized that beyond the table the children were lined up, solemnly puffing at little wooden flutes and recorders. He saw the empty chair at the table and went toward it, conscious for the moment of nothing but his dusty feet.

He was disappointed that Lois wasn't sitting next to him, but the food reminded him that he was hungry. There was a charming little steak, striped black and brown with perfection, and all sorts of vegetables and fruits, one or two of which he didn't recognize.

"Flown from Africa," someone explained to him.

These sly scientists, he thought, living behind their security curtain in the most improbable world!

When they were sitting with coffee and wine, and the children had finished their concert and were busy at another table, he asked, "How do you manage all this?"

Jock, the gay pharaoh, shrugged. "It's not difficult."

Rachel, the slim Negro, chuckled in her throat. "We're just people, Tom."

He tried to phrase his question without mentioning money. "What do you all do?"

"Jock's a uranium miner," Larry (the beard) answered, briskly taking over. "Rachel's an algae farmer. I'm a rocket pilot. Lois —"

Although pleased at this final confirmation of his guess, Tom couldn't help feeling a surge of uneasiness. "Sure you should be telling me these things?"

Larry laughed. "Why not? Lois and Jokichi have been exchange-workers in China the last six months."

"Mostly digging ditches," Jokichi put in with a smile.

" —and Sasha's in an assembly plant. Helen's a psychiatrist. Oh, we just do ordinary things. Now we're on grand vacation."

"Grand vacation?"

"When all of us have a vacation together," Larry explained. "What do you do?"

"I'm an artist," Tom said, taking out a cigaret.

"But what else?" Larry asked.

Tom felt an angry embarrassment. "Just an artist," he mumbled, cigaret in mouth, digging in his pockets for a match.

"Hold on," said Joyce beside him and pointed a silver pencil at the tip of the cigaret. He felt a faint thrill in his lips and then started back, coughing. The cigaret was lighted.

"Please mutate my poppy seeds, Mommy." A little girl had darted to Joyce from the children's table.

"You're a very dirty little girl," Joyce told her without reproof. "Hold them out." She briefly directed the silver pencil at the clay pellets on the grimy little palm. The little girl shivered delightedly. "I love ultrasonics, they feel so funny." She scampered off.

Tom cleared his throat. "I must say I'm tremendously impressed with the wood carvings. I'd like to photograph them. Oh, Lord!"

"What's the matter?" Rachel asked.

"I lost my camera somewhere."

"Camera?" Jokichi showed interest. "You mean one for stills?"

"Yes."

"What kind?"

"A Leica," Tom told him.

Jokichi seemed impressed. "That is interesting. I've never seen one of those old ones."

"Tom's a button man," Lois remarked by way of explanation, apparently. "Was the camera in a brown case? You dropped it where we met. We can get it later."

"Good, I'd really like to take those pictures," Tom said. "Incidentally, who did the carvings?"

"We did," Jock said. "Together."

Tom was grateful that the scamper of the children out of the room saved him from having to reply. He couldn't think of anything but a grunt of astonishment.

The conversation split into a group of chats about something called a psych machine, trips to Russia, the planet Mars, and several artists Tom had never heard of. He wanted to talk to Lois, but she was one of the group gabbling about Mars like children. He felt suddenly uneasy and out of things, and neither Rachel's deprecating remarks about her section of the wood carvings nor Joyce's interesting smiles helped much. He was glad when they all began to get up. He wandered outside and made his way to the children's lean-to, feeling very depressed.

Once again he was the center of a friendly naked cluster, except for the same solemn-faced little girl skipping rope. A rather malicious but not very hopeful whim prompted him to ask the youngest, "What's one and one?"

"Ten," the shaver answered glibly. Tom felt pleased.

"It could also be two," the oldest boy remarked.

"I'll say," Tom agreed. "What's the population of the world?"

"About seven hundred million."

Tom nodded noncommittally and, grabbing at the first long word that he thought of, turned to the eldest girl. "What's poliomyelitis?"

"Never heard of it," she said.

The solemn little girl kept droning the same ridiculous chant: "Gik-lo, I-o, Rik-o, Gis-so."

His ego eased, Tom went outside and there was Lois.

"What's the matter?" she asked.

"Nothing," he said.

She took his hand. "Have we pushed ourselves at you too much? Has our jabbering bothered you? We're a loud-mouthed family and I didn't think to ask if you were loning."

"Loning?"

"Solituding."

"In a way," he said. They didn't speak for a moment. Then, "Are you happy, Lois, in your life here?" he asked.

Her smile was instant. "Of course. Don't you like my group?"

He hesitated. "They make me feel rather no good," he said, and then admitted, "but in a way I'm more attracted to them than any people I've ever met."

"You are?" Her grip on his hand tightened. "Then why don't you stay with us for a while? I like you. It's too early to propose anything, but I think you have a quality our group lacks. You could see how you fit in. And there's Joyce. She's just visiting, too. You wouldn't have to lone unless you wanted."

Before he could think, there was a rhythmic rush of feet and the Wolvers were around them.

"We're swimming," Simone announced.

Lois looked at Tom inquiringly. He smiled his willingness, started to mention he didn't have trunks, then realized that wouldn't be news here. He wondered whether he would blush.

Jock fell in beside him as they rounded the ranch house. "Larry's been telling me about your group at the other end of the valley. It's comic, but I've whirled down the valley a dozen times and never spotted any sort of place there. What's it like?"

"A ranch house and several cabins."

Jock frowned. "Comic I never saw it." His face cleared. "How about whirling over there? You could point it out to me."

"It's really there," Tom said uneasily. "I'm not making it up."

"Of course," Jock assured him. "It was just an idea."

"We could pick up your camera on the way," Lois put in.

The rest of the group had turned back from the huge oval pool and the dark blue and flashing thing beyond it, and stood gay-colored against the pool's pale blue shimmer.

"How about it?" Jock asked them. "A whirl before we bathe?"

Two or three said yes besides Lois, and Jock led the way toward the helicopter that Tom now saw standing beyond the pool, its beetle body as blue as a scarab, its vanes flashing silver.

The others piled in. Tom followed as casually as he could, trying to suppress the pounding of his heart. "Wonder you don't go by rocket," he remarked lightly.

Jock laughed. "For such a short trip?"

The vanes began to thrum. Tom sat stiffly, gripping the sides of the seat, then realized that the others had sunk back lazily in the cushions. There was a moment of strain and they were falling ahead and up. Looking out the side, Tom saw for a moment the sooty roof of the ranch house and the blue of the pool and the pinkish umber of tanned bodies. Then the helicopter lurched gently around. Without warning a miserable uneasiness gripped him, a desire to cling mixed with an urge to escape. He tried to convince himself it was fear of the height.

He heard Lois tell Jock, "That's the place, down by that rock that looks like a wrecked spaceship."

The helicopter began to fall forward. Tom felt Lois' hand on his.

"You haven't answered my question," she said.

"What?" he asked dully.

"Whether you'll stay with us. At least for a while."

He looked at her. Her smile was a comfort. He said, "If I possibly can."

"What could possibly stop you?"

"I don't know," he answered abstractedly.

"You're strange," Lois told him. "There's a weight of sadness in you. As if you lived in a less happy age. As if it weren't 2050."

"Twenty?" he repeated, awakening from his thoughts with a jerk. "What's the time?" he asked anxiously.

"Two," Jock said. The word sounded like a knell.

"You need cheering," Lois announced firmly.

Amid a whoosh of air rebounding from earth, they jounced gently down. Lois vaulted out. "Come on," she said.

Tom followed her. "Where?" he asked stupidly, looking around at the red rocks through the settling sand cloud stirred by the vanes.

"Your camera," she told him, laughing. "Over there. Come on, I'll race you."

He started to run with her and then his uneasiness got beyond his control. He ran faster and faster. He saw Lois catch her foot on a rock and go down sprawling, but he couldn't stop. He ran desperately around the rock and into a gust of up-whirling sand that terrified him with its suddenness. He tried to escape from the stinging, blinding gust, but there was the nightmarish fright that his wild strides were carrying him nowhere.

Then the sand settled. He stopped running and looked around him. He was standing by the balancing rock. He was gasping. At his feet the rusty brown leather of the camera case peeped from the sand. Lois was nowhere in sight. Neither was the helicopter. The valley seemed different, rawer-one might almost have said younger.

Hours after dark he trailed into Tosker-Brown. Curtained lights still glowed from a few cabins. He was footsore, bewildered, frightened. All afternoon and through the twilight and into the moonlit evening that turned the red rocks black, he had searched the valley. Nowhere had he been able to find the soot-roofed ranch house of the Wolvers. He hadn't even been able to locate the rock like a giant bobbin where he'd met Lois.

During the next days he often returned to the valley. But he never found anything. And he never happened to be near the balancing rock when the time winds blew at ten and two, though once or twice he did see dust devils. Then he went away and eventually forgot.

In his casual reading he ran across popular science articles describing the binary system of numbers used in electronic calculating machines, where one and one make ten. He always skipped them. And more than once he saw the four equations expressing Einstein's generalized theory of gravitation:

$$\text{``g}\underset{\underset{\text{+}}{\downarrow}\text{--}}{i}K; \ell_{=0}; \Gamma_{i=0}; R_{ik=0}; \varphi, \underset{s}{\overset{is}{v}}{=0}\text{''}!$$

He never connected them with the little girl's chant: "Gik-lo, I-o, Rik-o, Gis-so."

No Great Magic

The troupers of the Big Time
lack no art to sway a crowd —
or to change all history!

I

> To bring the dead to life
> Is no great magic.
> Few are wholly dead:
> Blow on a dead man's embers
> And a live flame will start.
> —Graves

I dipped through the filmy curtain into the boys' half of the dressing room and there was Sid sitting at the star's dressing table in his threadbare yellowed undershirt, the lucky one, not making up yet but staring sternly at himself in the bulb-framed mirror and experimentally working his features a little, as actors will, and kneading the stubble on his fat chin.

I said to him quietly, "Siddy, what are we putting on tonight? Maxwell Anderson's *Elizabeth the Queen* or Shakespeare's *Macbeth*? It says *Macbeth* on the callboard, but Miss Nefer's getting ready for Elizabeth. She just had me go and fetch the red wig."

He tried out a few eyebrow rears-right, left, both together-then turned to me, sucking in his big gut a little, as he always does when a gal heaves into hailing distance, and said, "Your pardon, sweetling, what sayest thou?"

Sid always uses that kook antique patter backstage, until I sometimes wonder whether I'm in Central Park, New York City, nineteen hundred and three quarters, or somewhere in Southwark, Merry England, fifteen hundred and same. The truth is that although he loves every last fat part in Shakespeare and will play the skinniest one with loyal and inspired affection, he thinks Willy S. penned Falstaff with nobody else in mind but Sidney J. Lessingham. (And no accent on the ham, please.)

I closed my eyes and counted to eight, then repeated my question.

He replied, "Why, the Bard's tragical history of the bloody Scot, certes." He waved his hand toward the portrait of Shakespeare that always sits beside his mirror on top of his reserve makeup box. At first that particular picture of the Bard looked too nancy to me —a sort of peeping-tom schoolteacher-but I've grown used to it over the months and even palsy-feeling.

He didn't ask me why I hadn't asked Miss Nefer my question. Everybody in the company knows she spends the hour before curtain-time getting into character, never parting her lips except for that purpose-or to bite your head off if you try to make the most necessary conversation.

"Aye, 'tiz *Macbeth* tonight," Sid confirmed, returning to his frowning-practice: left eyebrow up, right down, reverse, repeat, rest. "And I must play the ill-starred Thane of Glamis."

I said, "That's fine, Siddy, but where does it leave us with Miss Nefer? She's already thinned her eyebrows and beaked out the top of her nose for Queen Liz, though that's as far as she's got. A beautiful job, the nose. Anybody else would think it was plastic surgery instead of putty. But it's going to look kind of funny on the Thaness of Glamis."

Sid hesitated a half second longer than he usually would —I thought, *his timing's off tonight* —and then he harrumphed and said, "Why, Iris Nefer, decked out as Good Queen Bess, will speak a prologue to the play —a prologue which I have myself but last week writ." He owled his eyes. "'Tis an experiment in the new theater."

I said, "Siddy, prologues were nothing new to Shakespeare. He had them on half his other plays. Besides, it doesn't make sense to use Queen Elizabeth. She was dead by the time he whipped up *Macbeth*, which is all about witchcraft and directed at King James."

He growled a little at me and demanded, "Prithee, how comes it your peewit-brain bears such a ballast of fusty book-knowledge, chit?"

I said softly, "Siddy, you don't camp in a Shakespearean dressing room for a year, tete-a-teting with some of the wisest actors ever, without learning a little. Sure I'm a mental case, a poor little A & A existing on your sweet charity, and don't think I don't appreciate it, but —"

"A-*and*-A, thou sayest?" he frowned. "Methinks the gladsome new forswearers of sack and ale call themselves AA."

"Agoraphobe and Amnesiac," I told him. "But look, Siddy, I was going to sayest that I do know the plays. Having Queen Elizabeth speak a prologue to *Macbeth* is as much an anachronism as if you put her on the gantry of the British moonship, busting a bottle of champagne over its schnozzle."

"Ha!" he cried as if he'd caught me out. "And saying there's a new Elizabeth, wouldn't that be the bravest advertisement ever for the Empire? —perchance rechristening the pilot, copilot and astrogator Drake, Hawkins and Raleigh? And the ship *The Golden Hind*? Tilly fally, lady!"

He went on, "My prologue an anachronism, quotha! The groundlings will never mark it. Think'st thou wisdom came to mankind with the stenchful rocket and the sundered atomy? More, the Bard himself was topfull of anachronism. He put spectacles on King Lear, had clocks tolling the hour in Caesar's Rome, buried that Roman 'stead o' burning him and gave Czechoslovakia a seacoast. Go to, doll."

"Czechoslovakia, Siddy?"

"Bohemia, then, what skills it? Leave me now, sweet poppet. Go thy ways. I have matters of import to ponder. There's more to running a repertory company than reading the footnotes to Furness."

Martin had just slouched by calling the Half Hour and looking in his solemnity, sneakers, levis and dirty T-shirt more like an underage refugee from Skid Row than Sid's newest recruit, assistant stage manager and hardest-worked juvenile-though for once he'd remembered to shave. I was about to ask Sid who was going to play Lady Mack if Miss Nefer wasn't, or, if she were going to double the roles, shouldn't I help her with the change? She's a slow dresser and the Elizabeth costumes are pretty realistically stayed. And she would have trouble getting off that nose, I was sure. But then I saw that Siddy was already slapping on the alboline to keep the grease paint from getting into his pores.

Greta, you ask too many questions, I told myself. *You get everybody riled up and you rack your own poor ricketty little mind*; and I hied myself off to the costumery to settle my nerves.

The costumery, which occupies the back end of the dressing room, is exactly the right place to settle the nerves and warm the fancies of any child, including an unraveled adult who's saving what's left of her sanity by pretending to be one. To begin with there are the regular costumes for Shakespeare's plays, all jeweled and spangled and brocaded, stage armor, great Roman togas with weights in the borders to make them drape right, velvets of every color to rest your cheek against and dream, and the fantastic costumes for the other plays we favor; Ibsen's *Peer Gynt*, Shaw's *Back to Methuselah* and Hilliard's adaptation of Heinlein's *Children of Methuselah*, the Capek brothers' *Insect People*, O'Neill's *The Fountain*, Flecker's *Hassan*, *Camino Real*, *Children of the Moon*, *The Beggar's Opera*, *Mary of Scotland*, *Berkeley Square*, *The Road to Rome*.

There are also the costumes for all the special and variety performances we give of the plays: *Hamlet* in modern dress, *Julius Caesar* set in a dictatorship of the 1920's, *The Taming of the Shrew* in caveman furs and leopard skins, where Petruchio comes in riding a dinosaur, *The Tempest* set on another planet with a spaceship wreck to start it off *Karrumph!* —which means a half dozen spacesuits, featherweight but looking ever so practical, and the weirdest sort of extraterrestrial-beast outfits for Ariel and Caliban and the other monsters.

Oh, I tell you the stuff in the costumery ranges over such a sweep of space and time that you sometimes get frightened you'll be whirled up and spun off just anywhere, so that you have to clutch at something very real to you to keep it from happening and to remind you where you *really* are-as I did now at the subway token on the thin gold chain around my neck (Siddy's first gift to me that I can remember) and chanted very softly to myself, like a charm or a prayer, closing my eyes and squeezing the holes in the token: "Columbus Circle, Times Square, Penn Station, Christopher Street...."

But you don't ever get *really* frightened in the costumery. Not exactly, though your goose-hairs get wonderfully realistically tingled and your tummy chilled from time to time-because you know it's all make-believe, a lifesize doll world, a children's dress-up world. It gets you thinking of far-off times and scenes as *pleasant* places and not as black hungry mouths that might gobble you up and keep you forever. It's always safe, always *just in the theatre, just on the stage*, no matter how far it seems to plunge and roam ... and the best sort of therapy for a pot-holed mind like mine, with as many gray ruts and curves and gaps as its cerebrum, that can't remember one single thing before this last year in the dressing room and that can't ever push its shaking body out of that same motherly fatherly room, except to stand in the wings for a scene or two and watch the play until the fear gets too great and the urge to take just one peek at *the audience* gets too strong ... and I remember what happened the two times I *did* peek, and I have to come scuttling back.

The costumery's good occupational therapy for me, too, as my pricked and calloused finger-tips testify. I think I must have stitched up or darned half the costumes in it this last twelve-month, though there are so many of them that I swear the drawers have accordion pleats and the racks extend into the fourth dimension-not to mention the boxes of props and the shelves of scripts and prompt-copies and other books, including a couple of encyclopedias and the many thick volumes of Furness's *Variorum Shakespeare*, which as Sid had guessed I'd been boning up on. Oh, and I've sponged and pressed enough costumes, too, and even refitted them to newcomers like Martin, ripping up and resewing seams, which can be a punishing job with heavy materials.

In a less sloppily organized company I'd be called wardrobe mistress, I guess. Except that to anyone in show business that suggests a crotchety old dame with lots of authority and scissors hanging around her neck on a string. Although I got my crochets, all right, I'm not that old. Kind of childish, in fact. As for authority, everybody outranks me, even Martin.

Of course to somebody *outside* show business, wardrobe mistress might suggest a yummy gal who spends her time dressing up as Nell Gwyn or Anitra or Mrs. Pinchwife or Cleopatra or even Eve (we got a legal costume for it) and inspiring the boys. I've tried that once or twice. But Siddy frowns on it, and if Miss Nefer ever caught me at it I think she'd whang me.

And in a normaller company it would be the wardrobe room, too, but costumery is my infantile name for it and the actors go along with my little whims.

I don't mean to suggest our company is completely crackers. To get as close to Broadway even as Central Park you got to have something. But in spite of Sid's whip-cracking there is a comforting looseness about its efficiency-people trade around the parts they play without fuss, the bill may be changed a half hour before curtain without anybody getting hysterics, nobody gets fired for eating garlic and breathing it in the leading lady's face. In short, we're a team. Which is funny when you come to think of it, as Sid and Miss Nefer and Bruce and Maudie are British (Miss Nefer with a touch of Eurasian blood, I romance); Martin and Beau and me are American (at least I *think* I am) while the rest come from just everywhere.

Besides my costumery work, I fetch things and run inside errands and help the actresses dress and the actors too. The dressing room's very coeducational in a halfway respectable way. And every once in a while Martin and I police up the whole place, me skittering about with dustcloth and wastebasket, he wielding the scrub-brush and mop with such silent grim efficiency that it always makes me nervous to get through and duck back into the costumery to collect myself.

Yes, the costumery's a great place to quiet your nerves or improve your mind or even dream your life away. But this time I couldn't have been there eight minutes when Miss Nefer's Eliz-abeth-angry voice came skirling, "Girl! Girl! Greta, where is my ruff with silver trim?" I laid my hands on it in a flash and loped it to her, because Old Queen Liz was known to slap even her Maids of Honor around a bit now and then and Miss Nefer is a bear on getting into character—a real Paul Muni.

She was all made up now, I was happy to note, at least as far as her face went—I hate to see that spooky eight-spoked faint tattoo on her forehead (I've sometimes wondered if she got it acting in India or Egypt maybe).

Yes, she was already all made up. This time she'd been going extra heavy on the burrowing-into-character bit, I could tell right away, even if it was only for a hacked-out anachronistic prologue. She signed to me to help her dress without even looking at me, but as I got busy I looked at *her* eyes. They were so cold and sad and lonely (maybe because they were so far away from her eyebrows and temples and small tight mouth, and so shut away from each other by that ridge of nose) that I got the creeps. Then she began to murmur and sigh, very softly at first, then loudly enough so I got the sense of it.

"Cold, so cold," she said, still seeing things far away though her hands were working smoothly with mine. "Even a gallop hardly fires my blood. Never was such a Januarius, though there's no snow. Snow will not come, or tears. Yet my brain burns with the thought of Mary's death-warrant unsigned. There's my particular hell!—to doom, perchance, all future queens, or leave a hole for the Spaniard and the Pope to creep like old worms back into the sweet apple of England. Philip's tall black crooked ships massing like sea-going fortresses south-away—cragged castles set to march into the waves. Parma in the Lowlands! And all the while my bright young idiot gentlemen spurting out my treasure as if it were so much water, as if gold pieces were a glut of summer posies. Oh, alackanight!"

And I thought, *Cry Iced!—that's sure going to be one tyrannosaur of a prologue. And how you'll ever shift back to being Lady Mack beats me. Greta, if this is what it takes to do just a bit part, you'd better give up your secret ambition of playing walk-ons some day when your nerves heal.*

She was really getting to me, you see, with that characterization. It was as if I'd managed to go out and take a walk and sat down in the park outside and heard the President talking to himself about the chances of war with Russia and realized he'd sat down on a bench with its back to mine and only a bush between. You see, here we were, two females undignifiedly twisted together, at the moment getting her into that crazy crouch-deep bodice that's like a big icecream cone, and yet here at the same time was Queen Elizabeth the First of England, three hundred and umpty-ump years dead, coming back to life in a Central Park dressing room. It shook me.

She looked so much the part, you see-even without the red wig yet, just powdered pale makeup going back to a quarter of an inch from her own short dark bang combed and netted back tight. The age too. Miss Nefer can't be a day over forty-well, forty-two at most-but now she looked and talked and felt to my hands dressing her, well, at least a dozen years older. I guess when Miss Nefer gets into character she does it with each molecule.

That age point fascinated me so much that I risked asking her a question. Probably I was figuring that she couldn't do me much damage because of the positions we happened to be in at the moment. You see, I'd started to lace her up and to do it right I had my knee against the tail of her spine.

"How old, I mean how young might your majesty be?" I asked her, innocently wonderingly like some dumb serving wench.

For a wonder she didn't somehow swing around and clout me, but only settled into character a little more deeply.

"Fifty-four winters," she replied dismally. " 'Tiz Januarius of Our Lord's year One Thousand and Five Hundred and Eighty and Seven. I sit cold in Greenwich, staring at the table where Mary's death warrant waits only my sign manual. If I send her to the block, I open the doors to future, less official regicides. But if I doom her not, Philip's armada will come inching up the Channel in a season, puffing smoke and shot, and my English Catholics, thinking only of

Mary Regina, will rise and i' the end the Spaniard will have all. All history would alter. That must not be, even if I'm damned for it! And yet ... and yet...."

A bright blue fly came buzzing along (the dressing room has *some* insect life) and slowly circled her head rather close, but she didn't even flicker her eyelids.

"I sit cold in Greenwich, going mad. Each afternoon I ride, praying for some mischance, some prodigy, to wash from my mind away the bloody question for some little space. It skills not what: a fire, a tree a-failing, Davison or e'en Eyes Leicester tumbled with his horse, an assassin's ball clipping the cold twigs by my ear, a maid crying rape, a wild boar charging with dipping tusks, news of the Spaniard at Thames' mouth or, more happily, a band of strolling actors setting forth some new comedy to charm the fancy or some great unheard-of tragedy to tear the heart-though that were somewhat much to hope for at this season and place, even if Southwark be close by."

The lacing was done. I stood back from her, and really she looked so much like Elizabeth painted by Gheeraerts or on the Great Seal of Ireland or something-though the ash-colored plush dress trimmed in silver and the little silver-edge ruff and the black-silver tinsel-cloth cloak lined with white plush hanging behind her looked most like a winter riding costume-and her face was such a pale frozen mask of Elizabeth's inward tortures, that I told myself, *Oh, I got to talk to Siddy again, he's made some big mistake, the lardy old lackwit. Miss Nefer just can't be figuring on playing in Macbeth tonight.*

As a matter of fact I was nerving myself to ask *her* all about it direct, though it was going to take some real nerve and maybe be risking broken bones or at least a flayed cheek to break the ice of that characterization, when who should come by calling the Fifteen Minutes but Martin. He looked so downright goofy that it took my mind off Nefer-in-character for all of eight seconds.

His levied bottom half still looked like *The Lower Depths*. Martin is Village Stanislavsky rather than Ye Olde English Stage Traditions. But above that ... well, all it really amounted to was that he was stripped to the waist and had shaved off the small high tuft of chest hair and was wearing a black wig that hung down in front of his shoulders in two big braids heavy with silver hoops and pins. But just the same those simple things, along with his tarpaper-solarium tan and habitual poker expression, made him look so like an American Indian that I thought, *Hey Zeus! —he's all set to play Hiawatha, or if he'd just cover up that straight-line chest, a frowny Pocahontas.* And I quick ran through what plays with Indian parts we do and could only come up with *The Fountain*.

I mutely goggled my question at him, wiggling my hands like guppy fins, but he brushed me off with a solemn mysterious smile and backed through the curtain. I thought, *nobody can explain this but Siddy,* and I followed Martin.

History does not move in one current,
like the wind across bare seas,
but in a thousand streams and eddies,
like the wind over a broken landscape.
—Cary

The boys' half of the dressing room (two-thirds really) was bustling. There was the smell of spirit gum and Max Factor and just plain men. Several guys were getting dressed or un-, and Bruce was cussing Bloody-something because he'd just burnt his fingers unwinding from the neck of a hot electric bulb some crepe hair he'd wound there to dry after wetting and stretching it to turn it from crinkly to straight for his Banquo beard. Bruce is always getting to the theater late and trying shortcuts.

But I had eyes only for Sid. So help me, as soon as I saw him they bugged again. *Greta*, I told myself, *you're going to have to send Martin out to the drugstore for some anti-bug powder.* "For the roaches, boy?" "No, for the eyes."

Sid was made up and had his long mustaches and elf-locked Macbeth wig on-and his corset too. I could tell by the way his waist was sucked in before he saw me. But instead of dark kilts and that bronze-studded sweat-stained leather battle harness that lets him show off his beefy shoulders and the top half of his heavily furred chest-and which really does look great on Macbeth in the first act when he comes in straight from battle-but instead of that he was wearing, so help me, red tights cross-gartered with strips of gold-blue tinsel-cloth, a green doublet gold-trimmed and to top it a ruff, and he was trying to fit onto his front a bright silvered cuirass that would have looked just dandy maybe on one of the Pope's Swiss Guards.

I thought, *Siddy, Willy S. ought to reach out of his portrait there and bop you one on the koko for contemplating such a crazy-quilt desecration of just about his greatest and certainly his most atmospheric play.*

Just then he noticed me and hissed accusingly, "There thou art, slothy minx! Spring to and help stuff me into this monstrous chest-kettle."

"Siddy, what *is* all this?" I demanded as my hands automatically obeyed. "Are you going to play *Macbeth* for laughs, except maybe leaving the Porter a serious character? You think you're Red Skelton?"

"What monstrous brabble is this, you mad bitch?" he retorted, grunting as I bear-hugged his waist, shouldering the cuirass to squeeze it home.

"The clown costumes on all you men," I told him, for now I'd noticed that the others were in rainbow hues, Bruce a real eye-buster in yellow tights and violet doublet as he furiously bushed out and clipped crosswise sections of beard and slapped them on his chin gleaming brown with spirit gum. "I haven't seen any eight-inch polka-dots yet but I'm sure I will."

Suddenly a big grin split Siddy's face and he laughed out loud at me, though the laugh changed to a gasp as I strapped in the cuirass three notches too tight. When we'd got that adjusted he said, "I' faith thou slayest me, pretty witling. Did I not tell you this production is an experiment, a novelty? We shall but show *Macbeth* as it might have been costumed at the court of King James. In the clothes of the day, but gaudier, as was then the stage fashion. Hold, dove, I've somewhat for thee." He fumbled his grouch bag from under his doublet and dipped finger and thumb in it, and put in my palm a silver model of the Empire State Building, charm bracelet size, and one of the new Kennedy dimes.

As I squeezed those two and gloated my eyes on them, feeling securer and happier and friendlier for them though I didn't at the moment want to, I thought, *Well, Siddy's right about that, at least I've read they used to costume the plays that way, though I don't see how Shakespeare stood it. But it was dirty of them all not to tell me beforehand.*

But that's the way it is. Sometimes I'm the butt as well as the pet of the dressing room, and considering all the breaks I get I shouldn't mind. I smiled at Sid and went on tiptoes and necked out my head and kissed him on a powdery cheek just above an aromatic mustache. Then I wiped the smile off my face and said, "Okay, Siddy, play Macbeth as Little Lord Fauntleroy or Baby Snooks if you want to. I'll never squeak again. But the Elizabeth prologue's still an anachronism. And-this is the thing I came to tell you, Siddy-Miss Nefer's not getting ready for any measly prologue. She's set to play Queen Elizabeth all night and tomorrow morning too. Whatever you think, she doesn't know we're doing *Macbeth*. But who'll do Lady Mack if she doesn't? And Martin's not dressing for Malcolm, but for the Son of the Last of the Mohicans, I'd say. What's more —"

You know, something I said must have annoyed Sid, for he changed his mood again in a flash. "Shut your jaw, you crook brained cat, and begone!" he snarled at me. "Here's curtain time close upon us, and you come like a wittol scattering your mad questions like the crazed Ophelia her flowers. Begone, I say!"

"Yessir," I whipped out softly. I skittered off toward the door to the stage, because that was the easiest direction. I figured I could do with a breath of less grease-painty air. Then, "Oh, Greta," I heard Martin call nicely.

He'd changed his levis for black tights, and was stepping into and pulling up around him a very familiar dress, dark green and embroidered with silver and stage-rubies. He'd safety-pinned a folded towel around his chest-to make a bosom of sorts, I realized.

He armed into the sleeves and turned his back to me. "Hook me up, would you?" he entreated.

Then it hit me. They had no actresses in Shakespeare's day, they used boys. And the dark green dress was so familiar to me because —

"Martin," I said, halfway up the hooks and working fast-Miss Nefer's costume fitted him fine. "You're going to play —?"

"Lady Macbeth, yes," he finished for me. "Wish me courage, will you Greta? Nobody else seems to think I need it."

I punched him half-heartedly in the rear. Then, as I fastened the last hooks, my eyes topped his shoulder and I looked at our faces side by side in the mirror of his dressing table. His, in spite of the female edging and him being at least eight years younger than me, I think, looked wise, poised, infinitely resourceful with power in reserve, very very real, while mine looked like that of a bewildered and characterless child ghost about to scatter into air-and the edges of my charcoal sweater and skirt, contrasting with his strong colors, didn't dispel that last illusion.

"Oh, by the way, Greta," he said, "I picked up a copy of *The Village Times* for you. There's a thumbnail review of our *Measure for Measure*, though it mentions no names, darn it. It's around here somewhere...."

But I was already hurrying on. Oh, it was logical enough to have Martin playing Mrs. Macbeth in a production styled to Shakespeare's own times (though pedantically over-authentic, I'd have thought) and it really did answer all my questions, even why Miss Nefer could sink herself wholly in Elizabeth tonight if she wanted to. But it meant that I must be missing so much of what was going on right around me, in spite of spending 24 hours a day in the dressing room, or at most in the small adjoining john or in the wings of the stage just outside the dressing room door, that it scared me. Siddy telling everybody, "*Macbeth* tonight in Elizabethan costume, boys and girls," sure, that I could have missed-though you'd have thought he'd have asked my help on the costumes.

But Martin getting up in Mrs. Mack. Why, someone must have held the part on him twenty-eight times, cueing him, while he got the lines. And there must have been at least a couple of run-through rehearsals to make sure he had all the business and stage movements down pat, and Sid and Martin would have been doing their big scenes every backstage minute they could spare with Sid yelling, "Witling! Think'st *that's* a wifely buss?" and Martin would have been droning his lines last time he scrubbed and mopped....

Greta, they're hiding things from you, I told myself.

Maybe there was a 25th hour nobody had told me about yet when they did all the things they didn't tell me about.

Maybe they were things they didn't dare tell me because of my top-storey weakness.

I felt a cold draft and shivered and I realized I was at the door to the stage.

I should explain that our stage is rather an unusual one, in that it can face two ways, with the drops and set pieces and lighting all capable of being switched around completely. To your left, as you look out the dressing-room door, is an open-air theater, or rather an open-air place for the audience —a large upward-sloping glade walled by thick tall trees and with benches for over two thousand people. On that side the stage kind of merges into the grass and can be made to look part of it by a green groundcloth.

To your right is a big roofed auditorium with the same number of seats.

The whole thing grew out of the free summer Shakespeare performances in Central Park that they started back in the 1950's.

The Janus-stage idea is that in nice weather you can have the audience outdoors, but if it rains or there's a cold snap, or if you want to play all winter without a single break, as we've been doing, then you can put your audience in the auditorium. In that case, a big accordion-pleated wall shuts off the out of doors and keeps the wind from blowing your backdrop, which is on that side, of course, when the auditorium's in use.

Tonight the stage was set up to face the outdoors, although that draft felt mighty chilly.

I hesitated, as I always do at the door to the stage-though it wasn't the actual stage lying just ahead of me, but only backstage, the wings. You see, I always have to fight the feeling that if I go out the dressing room door, go out just eight steps, the world will change while I'm out there and I'll never be able to get back. It won't be New York City any more, but Chicago or Mars or Algiers or Atlanta, Georgia, or Atlantis or Hell and I'll never be able to get back to that lovely warm womb with all the jolly boys and girls and all the costumes smelling like autumn leaves.

Or, especially when there's a cold breeze blowing, I'm afraid that *I'll* change, that I'll grow wrinkled and old in eight footsteps, or shrink down to the witless blob of a baby, or forget altogether who I am —

—or, it occurred to me for the first time now, *remember* who I am. Which might be even worse.

Maybe that's what I'm afraid of.

I took a step back. I noticed something new just beside the door: a high-legged, short-keyboard piano. Then I saw that the legs were those of a table. The piano was just a box with yellowed keys. Spinet? Harpsichord?

"Five minutes, everybody," Martin quietly called out behind me.

I took hold of myself. Greta, I told myself-also for the first time, *you know that some day you're really going to have to face this thing, and not just for a quick dip out and back either. Better get in some practice.*

I stepped through the door.

Beau and Doc were already out there, made up and in costume for Ross and King Duncan. They were discreetly peering past the wings at the gathering audience. Or at the place where the audience ought to be gathering, at any rate-sometimes the movies and girlie shows and brainheavy beatnik bruhahas outdraw us altogether. Their costumes were the same kooky colorful ones as the others'. Doc had a mock-ermine robe and a huge gilt papier-mache crown. Beau was carrying a ragged black robe and hood over his left arm-he doubles the First Witch.

As I came up behind them, making no noise in my black sneakers, I heard Beau say, "I see some rude fellows from the City approaching. I was hoping we wouldn't get any of those. How should they scent us out?"

Brother, I thought, *where do you expect them to come from if not the City? Central Park is bounded on three sides by Manhattan Island and on the fourth by the Eighth Avenue Subway. And Brooklyn and Bronx boys have got pretty sharp scenters. And what's it get you insulting the woiking and non-woiking people of the woild's greatest metropolis? Be grateful for any audience you get, boy.*

But I suppose Beau Lassiter considers anybody from north of Vicksburg a "rude fellow" and is always waiting for the day when the entire audience will arrive in carriage and democrat wagons.

Doc replied, holding down his white beard and heavy on the mongrel Russo-German accent he miraculously manages to suppress on stage except when "Vot does it matter? Ve don't convinze zem, ve don't convinze nobody. *Nichevo.*"

Maybe, I thought, *Doc shares my doubts about making Macbeth plausible in rainbow pants.*

Still unobserved by them, I looked between their shoulders and got the first of my shocks.

It wasn't night at all, but afternoon. A dark cold lowering afternoon, admittedly. But afternoon all the same.

Sure, between shows I sometimes forget whether it's day or night, living inside like I do. But getting matinees and evening performances mixed is something else again.

It also seemed to me, although Beau was leaning in now and I couldn't see so well, that the glade was smaller than it should be, the trees closer to us and more irregular, and I couldn't see the benches. That was Shock Two.

Beau said anxiously, glancing at his wrist, "I wonder what's holding up the Queen?"

Although I was busy keeping up nerve-pressure against the shocks, I managed to think. *So he knows about Siddy's stupid Queen Elizabeth prologue too. But of course he would. It's only me they keep in the dark. If he's so smart he ought to remember that Miss Nefer is always the last person on stage, even when she opens the play.*

And then I thought I heard, through the trees, the distant drumming of horses' hoofs and the sound of a horn.

Now they do have horseback riding in Central Park and you can hear auto horns there, but the hoofbeats don't drum that wild way. And there aren't so many riding together. And no auto horn I ever heard gave out with that sweet yet imperious *ta-ta-ta-TA*.

I must have squeaked or something, because Beau and Doc turned around quickly, blocking my view, their expressions half angry, half anxious.

I turned too and ran for the dressing room, for I could feel one of my mind-wavery fits coming on. At the last second it had seemed to me that the scenery was getting skimpier, hardly more than thin trees and bushes itself, and underfoot feeling more like ground than a ground cloth, and overhead not theater roof but gray sky. *Shock Three and you're out, Greta*, my umpire was calling.

I made it through the dressing room door and nothing there was wavering or dissolving, praised be Pan. Just Martin standing with his back to me, alert, alive, poised like a cat inside that green dress, the prompt book in his right hand with a finger in it, and from his left hand long black tatters swinging-telling me he'd still be doubling Second Witch. And he was hissing, "Places, please, everybody. On stage!"

With a sweep of silver and ash-colored plush, Miss Nefer came past him, for once leading the last-minute hurry to the stage. She had on the dark red wig now. For me that crowned her characterization. It made me remember her saying, "My brain burns." I ducked aside as if she were majesty incarnate.

And then she didn't break her own precedent. She stopped at the new thing beside the door and poised her long white skinny fingers over the yellowed keys, and suddenly I remembered what it was called: a virginals.

She stared down at it fiercely, evilly, like a witch planning an enchantment. Her face got the secret fiendish look that, I told myself, the real Elizabeth would have had ordering the deaths of Ballard and Babington, or plotting with Drake (for all they say she didn't) one of his raids, that long long forefinger tracing crooked courses through a crabbedly drawn map of the Indies and she smiling at the dots of cities that would burn.

Then all her eight fingers came flickering down and the strings inside the virginals began to twang and hum with a high-pitched rendering of Grieg's "In the Hall of the Mountain King."

Then as Sid and Bruce and Martin rushed past me, along with a black swooping that was Maud already robed and hooded for Third Witch, I beat it for my sleeping closet like Peer Gynt himself dashing across the mountainside away from the cave of the Troll King, who only wanted to make tiny slits in his eyeballs so that forever afterwards he'd see reality just a little differently. And as I ran, the master-anachronism of that menacing mad march music was shrilling in my ears.

III

Sound a dumbe shew. Enter the three fatall sisters, with a rocke, a threed, and a pair of sheeres.

—Old Play

My sleeping closet is just a cot at the back end of the girls' third of the dressing room, with a three-panel screen to make it private.

When I sleep I hang my outside clothes on the screen, which is pasted and thumbtacked all over with the New York City stuff that gives me security: theater programs and restaurant menus, clippings from the *Times* and the *Mirror*, a torn-out picture of the United Nations building with a hundred tiny gay paper flags pasted around it, and hanging in an old hairnet a home-run baseball autographed by Willie Mays. Things like that.

Right now I was jumping my eyes over that stuff, asking it to keep me located and make me safe, as I lay on my cot in my clothes with my knees drawn up and my fingers over my ears so the louder lines from the play wouldn't be able to come nosing back around the trunks and tables and bright-lit mirrors and find me. Generally I like to listen to them, even if they're sort of sepulchral and drained of overtones by their crooked trip. But they're always tense-making. And tonight (I mean this afternoon) —no!

It's funny I should find security in mementos of a city I daren't go out into-no, not even for a stroll through Central Park, though I know it from the Pond to Harlem Meer-the Met Museum, the Menagerie, the Ramble, the Great Lawn, Cleopatra's Needle and all the rest. But that's the way it is. Maybe I'm like Jonah in the whale, reluctant to go outside because the whale's a terrible monster that's awful scary to look in the face and might really damage you gulping you a second time, yet reassured to know you're living in the stomach of that particular monster and not a seventeen tentacled one from the fifth planet of Aldebaran.

It's really true, you see, about me actually living in the dressing room. The boys bring me meals: coffee in cardboard cylinders and doughnuts in little brown grease-spotted paper sacks and malts and hamburgers and apples and little pizzas, and Maud brings me raw vegetables-carrots and parsnips and little onions and such, and watches to make sure I exercise my molars grinding them and get my vitamins. I take spit-baths in the little john. Architects don't seem to think actors ever take baths, even when they've browned themselves all over playing Pindarus the Parthian in *Julius Caesar*. And all my shut-eye is caught on this little cot in the twilight of my NYC screen.

You'd think I'd be terrified being alone in the dressing room during the wee and morning hours, let alone trying to sleep then, but that isn't the way it works out. For one thing, there's apt to be someone sleeping in too. Maudie especially. And it's my favorite time too for costume-mending and reading the *Variorum* and other books, and for just plain way-out dreaming. You see, the dressing room is the one place I really do feel safe. Whatever is out there in New York that terrorizes me, I'm pretty confident that it can never get in here.

Besides that, there's a great big bolt on the inside of the dressing room door that I throw whenever I'm all alone after the show. Next day they buzz for me to open it.

It worried me a bit at first and I had asked Sid, "But what if I'm so deep asleep I don't hear and you have to get in fast?" and he had replied, "Sweetling, a word in your ear: our own Beauregard Lassiter is the prettiest picklock unjailed since Jimmy Valentine and Jimmy Dale. I'll not ask where he learned his trade, but 'tis sober truth, upon my honor."

And Beau had confirmed this with a courtly bow, murmuring, "At your service, Miss Greta."

"How do you jigger a big iron bolt through a three-inch door that fits like Maudie's tights?" I wanted to know.

"He carries lodestones of great power and divers subtle tools," Sid had explained for him.

I don't know how they work it so that some Traverse-Three cop or park official doesn't find out about me and raise a stink. Maybe Sid just throws a little more of the temperament he uses to keep most outsiders out of the dressing-room. We sure don't get any janitors or scrubwomen, as Martin and I know only too well. More likely he squares someone. I do get the impression all the company's gone a little way out on a limb letting me stay here-that the directors of our theater wouldn't like it if they found out about me.

In fact, the actors are all so good about helping me and putting up with my antics (though they have their own, Danu digs!) that I sometimes think I must be related to one of them —a distant cousin or sister-in-law (or wife, my God!), because I've checked our faces side by side in the mirrors often enough and I can't find any striking family resemblances. Or maybe I was even an actress in the company. The least important one. Playing the tiniest roles like Lucius in *Caesar* and Bianca in *Othello* and one of the little princes in *Dick the Three Eyes* and Fleance and the Gentlewoman in *Macbeth*, though me doing even that much acting strikes me to laugh.

But whatever I am in that direction-if I'm anything-not one of the actors has told me a word about it or dropped the least hint. Not even when I beg them to tell me or try to trick them into it, presumably because it might revive the shock that gave me agoraphobia and amnesia in the first place, and maybe this time knock out my entire mind or at least smash the new mouse-in-a-hole consciousness I've made for myself.

I guess they must have got by themselves a year ago and talked me over and decided my best chance for cure or for just bumping along half happily was staying in the dressing room rather than being sent home (funny, could I have another?) or to a mental hospital. And then they must have been cocky enough about their amateur psychiatry and interested enough in me (the White Horse knows why) to go ahead with a program almost any psychiatrist would be bound to yike at.

I got so worried about the set up once and about the risks they might be running that, gritting down my dread of the idea, I said to Sid, "Siddy, shouldn't I see a doctor?"

He looked at me solemnly for a couple of seconds and then said, "Sure, why not? Go talk to Doc right now," tipping a thumb toward Doc Pyeskov, who was just sneaking back into the bottom of his makeup box what looked like a half pint from the flask I got. I did, incidentally. Doc explained to me Kraepelin's classification of the psychoses, muttering, as he absentmindedly fondled my wrist, that in a year or two he'd be a good illustration of Korsakov's Syndrome.

They've all been pretty darn good to me in their kooky ways, the actors have. Not one of them has tried to take advantage of my situation to extort anything out of me, beyond asking me to sew on a button or polish some boots or at worst clean the wash bowl. Not one of the boys has made a pass I didn't at least seem to invite. And when my crush on Sid was at its worst he shouldered me off by getting polite-something he only is to strangers. On the rebound I hit Beau, who treated me like a real Southern gentleman.

All this for a stupid little waif, whom anyone but a gang of sentimental actors would have sent to Bellevue without a second thought or feeling. For, to get disgustingly realistic, my most plausible theory of me is that I'm a stage-struck girl from Iowa who saw her twenties slipping away and her sanity too, and made the dash to Greenwich Village, and went so ape on Shakespeare after seeing her first performance in Central Park that she kept going back there night after night (Christopher Street, Penn Station, Times Square, Columbus Circle-see?) and hung around the stage door, so mousy but open-mouthed that the actors made a pet of her.

And then something very nasty happened to her, either down at the Village or in a dark corner of the Park. Something so nasty that it blew the top of her head right off. And she ran to the only people and place where she felt she could ever again feel safe. And she showed them the top of her head with its singed hair and its jagged ring of skull and they took pity.

My least plausible theory of me, but the one I like the most, is that I was born in the dressing room, cradled in the top of a flat theatrical trunk with my ears full of Shakespeare's lines before I ever said "Mama," let alone lamped a TV; hush-walked when I cried by whoever was off stage, old props my first toys, trying to eat crepe hair my first indiscretion, sticks of grease-paint my first crayons. You know, I really wouldn't be bothered by crazy fears about New York changing and the dressing room shifting around in space and time, if I could be sure I'd always be able to stay in it and that the same sweet guys and gals would always be with me and that the shows would always go on.

This show was sure going on, it suddenly hit me, for I'd let my fingers slip off my ears as I sentimentalized and wish-dreamed and I heard, muted by the length and stuff of the dressing room, the slow beat of a drum and then a drum note in Maudie's voice taking up that beat as she warned the other two witches, "A drum, a drum! Macbeth doth come."

Why, I'd not only missed Sid's history-making-and-breaking Queen Elizabeth prologue (kicking myself that I had, now it was over), I'd also missed the short witch scene with its famous "Fair is foul and foul is fair," the Bloody Sergeant scene where Duncan hears about Macbeth's victory, and we were well into the second witch scene, the one on the blasted heath where Macbeth gets it predicted to him he'll be king after Duncan and is tempted to speculate about hurrying up the process.

I sat up. I did hesitate a minute then, my fingers going back toward my ears, because *Macbeth* is specially tense-making and when I've had one of my mind-wavery fits I feel weak for a while and things are blurry and uncertain. Maybe I'd better take a couple of the barbiturate sleeping pills Maudie manages to get for me and-but *No, Greta*, I told myself, *you want to watch this show, you want to see how they do in those crazy costumes. You especially want to see how Martin makes out. He'd never forgive you if you didn't.*

So I walked to the other end of the empty dressing room, moving quite slowly and touching the edges here and there, the words of the play getting louder all the time. By the time I got to the door Bruce-Banquo was saying to the witches, "If you can look into the seeds of time, And say which grain will grow and which will not,"—those lines that stir anyone's imagination with their veiled vision of the universe.

The overall lighting was a little dim (afternoon fading already?—a *late* matinee?) and the stage lights flickery and the scenery still a little spectral-flimsy. Oh, my mind-wavery fits can be lulus! But I concentrated on the actors, watching them through the entrance-gaps in the wings. They were solid enough.

Giving a solid performance, too, as I decided after watching that scene through and the one after it where Duncan congratulates Macbeth, with never a pause between the two scenes in true Elizabethan style. Nobody was laughing at the colorful costumes. After a while I began to accept them myself.

Oh, it was a different *Macbeth* than our company usually does. Louder and faster, with shorter pauses between speeches, the blank verse at times approaching a chant. But it had a lot of real guts and everybody was just throwing themselves into it, Sid especially.

The first Lady Macbeth scene came. Without exactly realizing it I moved forward to where I'd been when I got my three shocks. Martin is so intent on his career and making good that he has me the same way about it.

The Thaness started off, as she always does, toward the opposite side of the stage and facing a little away from me. Then she moved a step and looked down at the stage-parchment letter in her hands and began to read it, though there was nothing on it but scribble, and my heart sank because the voice I heard was Miss Nefer's. I thought (and almost said out loud) *Oh, dammit, he funked out, or Sid decided at the last minute he couldn't trust him with the part. Whoever got Miss Nefer out of the ice cream cone in time?*

Then she swung around and I saw that no, my God, it *was* Martin, no mistaking. He'd been using her voice. When a person first does a part, especially getting up in it without much rehearsing, he's bound to copy the actor he's been hearing doing it. And as I listened on, I realized it was fundamentally Martin's own voice pitched a trifle high, only some of the intonations and rhythms were Miss Nefer's. He was showing a lot of feeling and intensity too and real Martin-type poise. *You're off to a great start, kid,* I cheered inwardly. *Keep it up!*

Just then I looked toward the audience. Once again I almost squeaked out loud. For out there, close to the stage, in the very middle of the reserve section, was a carpet spread out. And sitting in the middle of it on some sort of little chair, with what looked like two charcoal braziers smoking to either side of her, was Miss Nefer with a string of extras in Elizabethan hats with cloaks pulled around them.

For a second it really threw me because it reminded me of the things I'd seen or thought I'd seen the couple of times I'd sneaked a peek through the curtain-hole at the audience in the indoor auditorium.

It hardly threw me for more than a second, though, because I remembered that the characters who speak Shakespeare's prologues often stay on stage and sometimes kind of join the audience and even comment on the play from time to time-Christopher Sly and attendant lords in *The Shrew,* for one. Sid had just copied and in his usual style laid it on thick.

Well, bully for you, Siddy, I thought, *I'm sure the witless New York groundlings will be thrilled to their cold little toes knowing they're sitting in the same audience as Good Queen Liz and attendant courtiers. And as for you, Miss Nefer,* I added a shade invidiously, *you just keep on sitting cold in Central Park, warmed by dry-ice smoke from braziers, and keep your mouth shut and everything'll be fine. I'm sincerely glad you'll be able to be Queen Elizabeth all night long. Just so long as you don't try to steal the scene from Martin and the rest of the cast, and the real play.*

I suppose that camp chair will get a little uncomfortable by the time the Fifth Act comes tramping along to that drumbeat, but I'm sure you're so much in character you'll never feel it.

One thing though: just don't scare me again pretending to work witchcraft-with a virginals or any other way.

Okay?

Swell.

Me, now, I'm going to watch the play.

... to dream of new dimensions,
Cheating checkmate
by painting the king's robe
So that he slides like a queen;
—Graves

I swung back to the play just at the moment Lady Mack soliloquizes, "Come to my woman's breasts. And take my milk for gall, you murdering ministers." Although I knew it was just folded towel Martin was touching with his fingertips as he lifted them to the top half of his green bodice, I got carried away, he made it so real. I decided boys can play girls better than people think. Maybe they should do it a little more often, and girls play boys too.

Then Sid-Macbeth came back to his wife from the wars, looking triumphant but scared because the murder-idea's started to smoulder in him, and she got busy fanning the blaze like any other good little *hausfrau* intent on her husband rising in the company and knowing that she's the power behind him and that when there are promotions someone's always got to get the axe. Sid and Martin made this charming little domestic scene so natural yet gutsy too that I wanted to shout hooray. Even Sid clutching Martin to that ridiculous pot-chested cuirass didn't have one note of horseplay in it. Their bodies spoke. It was the McCoy.

After that, the play began to get real good, the fast tempo and exaggerated facial expressions actually helping it. By the time the Dagger Scene came along I was digging my fingernails into my sweaty palms. Which was a good thing-my eating up the play, I mean-because it kept me from looking at the audience again, even taking a fast peek. As you've gathered, audiences bug me. All those people out there in the shadows, watching the actors in the light, all those silent voyeurs as Bruce calls them. Why, they might be anything. And sometimes (to my mind-wavery sorrow) I think they are. Maybe crouching in the dark out there, hiding among the others, is the one who did the nasty thing to me that tore off the top of my head.

Anyhow, if I so much as glance at the audience, I begin to get ideas about it-and sometimes even if I don't, as just at this moment I thought I heard horses restlessly pawing hard ground and one whinny, though that was shut off fast. *Krishna kressed us!* I thought, *Skiddy can't have hired horses for Nefer-Elizabeth much as he's a circus man at heart. We don't have that kind of money. Besides —*

But just then Sid-Macbeth gasped as if he were sucking in a bucket of air. He'd shed the cuirass, fortunately. He said, "Is this a dagger which I see before me, the handle toward my hand?" and the play hooked me again, and I had no time to think about or listen for anything else. Most of the offstage actors were on the other side of the stage, as that's where they make their exits and entrances at this point in the Second Act. I stood alone in the wings, watching the play like a bug, frightened only of the horrors Shakespeare had in mind when he wrote it.

Yes, the play was going great. The Dagger Scene was terrific where Duncan gets murdered offstage, and so was the part afterwards where hysteria mounts as the crime's discovered.

But just at this point I began to catch notes I didn't like. Twice someone was late on entrance and came on as if shot from a cannon. And three times at least Sid had to throw someone a line when they blew up-in the clutches Sid's better than any prompt book. It began to look as if the play were getting out of control, maybe because the new tempo was so hot.

But they got through the Murder Scene okay. As they came trooping off, yelling "Well contented," most of them on my side for a change, I went for Sid with a towel. He always sweats like a pig in the Murder Scene. I mopped his neck and shoved the towel up under his doublet to catch the dripping armpits.

Meanwhile he was fumbling around on a narrow table where they lay props and costumes for quick changes. Suddenly he dug his fingers into my shoulder, enough to catch my attention at this point, meaning I'd show bruises tomorrow, and yelled at me under his breath, "And you love me, our crows and robes. Presto!"

I was off like a flash to the costumery. There were Mr. and Mrs. Mack's king-and-queen robes and stuff hanging and sitting just where I knew they'd have to be.

I snatched them up, thinking, *Boy, they made a mistake when they didn't tell about this special performance*, and I started back like Flash Two.

As I shot out the dressing room door the theater was very quiet. There's a short low-pitched scene on stage then, to give the audience a breather. I heard Miss Nefer say loudly (it had to be loud to get to me from even the front of the audience): "'Tis a good bloody play, Eyes," and some voice I didn't recognize reply a bit grudgingly, "There's meat in it and some poetry too, though rough-wrought." She went on, still as loudly as if she owned the theater, "'Twill make Master Kyd bite his nails with jealousy-ha, ha!"

Ha-ha yourself, you scene-stealing witch, I thought, as I helped Sid and then Martin on with their royal outer duds. But at the same time I knew Sid must have written those lines himself to go along with his prologue. They had the unmistakable rough-wrought Lessingham touch. Did he really expect the audience to make anything of that reference to Shakespeare's predecessor Thomas Kyd of *The Spanish Tragedy* and the lost *Hamlet*? And if they knew enough to spot that, wouldn't they be bound to realize the whole Elizabeth-Macbeth tie-up was anachronistic? But when Sid gets an inspiration he can be very bull-headed.

Just then, while Bruce-Banquo was speaking his broody low soliloquy on stage, Miss Nefer cut in again loudly with, "Aye, Eyes, a good bloody play. Yet somehow, methinks —I know not how —I've heard it before." Whereupon Sid grabbed Martin by the wrist and hissed, "Did'st hear? Oh, I like not that," and I thought, *Oh-ho, so now she's beginning to ad-lib.*

Well, right away they all went on stage with a flourish, Sid and Martin crowned and hand in hand. The play got going strong again. But there were still those edge-of-control undercurrents and I began to be more uneasy than caught up, and I had to stare consciously at the actors to keep off a wavery-fit.

Other things began to bother me too, such as all the doubling.

Macbeth's a great play for doubling. For instance, anyone except Macbeth or Banquo can double one of the Three Witches-or one of the Three Murderers for that matter. Normally we double at least one or two of the Witches and Murderers, but this performance there'd been more multiple-parting than I'd ever seen. Doc had whipped off his Duncan beard and thrown on a brown smock and hood to play the Porter with his normal bottle-roughened accents. Well, a drunk impersonating a drunk, pretty appropriate. But Bruce was doing the next-door-to-impossible double of Banquo and Macduff, using a ringing tenor voice for the latter and wearing in the murder scene a helmet with dropped visor to hide his Banquo beard. He'd be able to tear it off, of course, after the Murderers got Banquo and he'd made his brief appearance as a bloodied-up ghost in the Banquet Scene. I asked myself, *My God, has Siddy got all the other actors out in front playing courtiers to Elizabeth-Nefer? Wasting them that way? The whoreson rogue's gone nuts!*

But really it was plain frightening, all that frantic doubling and tripling with its suggestion that the play (and the company too, Freya forfend) was becoming a ricketty patchwork illusion with everybody racing around faster and faster to hide the holes. And the scenery-wavery stuff and the warped Park-sounds were scary too. I was actually shivering by the time Sid got to: "Light thickens; and the crow Makes wing to the rooky wood: Good things of day begin to droop and drowse; Whiles night's black agents to their preys do rouse." Those graveyard lines didn't help my nerves any, of course. Nor did thinking I heard Nefer-Elizabeth say from the audience, rather softly for her this time, "Eyes, I have heard that speech, I know not where. Think you 'tiz stolen?"

Greta, I told myself, *you need a miltown before the crow makes wing through your kooky head.*

I turned to go and fetch me one from my closet. And stopped dead.

Just behind me, pacing back and forth like an ash-colored tiger in the gloomy wings, looking daggers at the audience every time she turned at that end of her invisible cage, but ignoring me completely, was Miss Nefer in the Elizabeth wig and rig.

Well, I suppose I should have said to myself, *Greta, you imagined that last loud whisper from the audience. Miss Nefer's simply unkinked herself, waved a hand to the real audience and come back stage. Maybe Sid just had her out there for the first half of the play. Or maybe she just couldn't stand watching Martin give such a bang-up performance in her part of Lady Mack.*

Yes, maybe I should have told myself something like that, but somehow all I could think then-and I thought it with a steady mounting shiver-was, *We got two Elizabeths. This one is our witch Nefer. I know. I dressed her. And I know that devil-look from the virginals. But if this is our Elizabeth, the company Elizabeth, the stage Elizabeth ... who's the other?*

And because I didn't dare to let myself think of the answer to that question, I dodged around the invisible cage that the ash-colored skirt seemed to ripple against as the Tiger Queen turned and I ran into the dressing room, my only thought to get behind my New York City Screen.

Even little things are turning out to be great things and becoming intensely interesting.

Have you ever thought about the properties of numbers?

—The Maiden

Lying on my cot, my eyes crosswise to the printing, I looked from a pink Algonquin menu to a pale green New Amsterdam program, with a tiny doll of Father Knickerbocker dangling between them on a yellow thread. Really they weren't covering up much of anything. A ghostly hole an inch and a half across seemed to char itself in the program. As if my eye were right up against it, I saw in vivid memory what I'd seen the two times I'd dared a peek through the hole in the curtain: a bevy of ladies in masks and Nell Gwyn dresses and men in King Charles knee-breeches and long curled hair, and the second time a bunch of people and creatures just wild: all sorts and colors of clothes, humans with hoofs for feet and antennae springing from their foreheads, furry and feathery things that had more arms than two and in one case that many heads-as if they were dressed up in our *Tempest, Peer Gynt* and *Insect People* costumes and some more besides.

Naturally I'd had mind-wavery fits both times. Afterwards Sid had wagged a finger at me and explained that on those two nights we'd been giving performances for people who'd arranged a costume theater-party and been going to attend a masquerade ball, and 'zounds, when would I learn to guard my half-patched pate?

I don't know, I guess never, I answered now, quick looking at a Giants pennant, a Korvette ad, a map of Central Park, my Willie Mays baseball and a Radio City tour ticket. That was eight items I'd looked at this trip without feeling any inward improvement. They weren't reassuring me at all.

The blue fly came slowly buzzing down over my screen and I asked it, "What are you looking for? A spider?" when what should I hear coming back through the dressing room straight toward my sleeping closet but Miss Nefer's footsteps. No one else walks that way.

She's going to do something to you, Greta, I thought. *She's the maniac in the company. She's the one who terrorized you with the boning knife in the shrubbery, or sicked the giant tarantula on you at the dark end of the subway platform, or whatever it was, and the others are covering up for. She's going to smile the devil-smile and weave those white twig-fingers at you, all eight of them. And Birnam Wood'll come to Dunsinane and you'll be burnt at the stake by men in armor or drawn and quartered by eight-legged monkeys that talk or torn apart by wild centaurs or whirled through the roof to the moon without being dressed for it or sent burrowing into the past to stifle in Iowa 1948 or Egypt 4,008 B.C. The screen won't keep her out.*

Then a head of hair pushed over the screen. But it was black-bound-with-silver, Brahma bless us, and a moment later Martin was giving me one of his rare smiles.

I said, "Marty, do something for me. Don't ever use Miss Nefer's footsteps again. Her voice, okay, if you have to. But not the footsteps. Don't ask me why, just don't."

Martin came around and sat on the foot of my cot. My legs were already doubled up. He straightened out his blue-and-gold skirt and rested a hand on my black sneakers.

"Feeling a little wonky, Greta?" he asked. "Don't worry about me. Banquo's dead and so's his ghost. We've finished the Banquet Scene. I've got lots of time."

I just looked at him, queerly I guess. Then without lifting my head I asked him, "Martin, tell me the truth. Does the dressing room move around?"

I was talking so low that he hitched a little closer, not touching me anywhere else though.

"The Earth's whipping around the sun at 20 miles a second," he replied, "and the dressing room goes with it."

I shook my head, my cheek scrubbing the pillow, "I mean ... shifting," I said. "By itself."

"How?" he asked.

"Well," I told him, "I've had this idea-it's just a sort of fancy, remember-that if you wanted to time-travel and, well, do things, you could hardly pick a more practical machine than a dressing room and sort of stage and half-theater attached, with actors to man it. Actors can fit in anywhere. They're used to learning new parts and wearing strange costumes. Heck, they're even used to traveling a lot. And if an actor's a bit strange nobody thinks anything of it-he's almost expected to be foreign, it's an asset to him."

"And a theater, well, a theater can spring up almost anywhere and nobody ask questions, except the zoning authorities and such and they can always be squared. Theaters come and go. It happens all the time. They're transitory. Yet theaters are crossroads, anonymous meeting places, anybody with a few bucks or sometimes nothing at all can go. And theaters attract important people, the sort of people you might want to do something to. Caesar was stabbed in a theater. Lincoln was shot in one. And...."

My voice trailed off. "A cute idea," he commented.

I reached down to his hand on my shoe and took hold of his middle finger as a baby might.

"Yeah," I said, "But Martin, is it true?"

He asked me gravely, "What do you think?"

I didn't say anything.

"How would you like to work in a company like that?" he asked speculatively.

"I don't really know," I said.

He sat up straighter and his voice got brisk. "Well, all fantasy aside, how'd you like to work in this company?" He asked, lightly slapping my ankle. "On the stage, I mean. Sid thinks you're ready for some of the smaller parts. In fact, he asked me to put it to you. He thinks you never take him seriously."

"Pardon me while I gasp and glow," I said. Then, "Oh Marty, I can't really imagine myself doing the tiniest part."

"Me neither, eight months ago," he said. "Now, look. Lady Macbeth."

"But Marty," I said, reaching for his finger again, "you haven't answered my question. About whether it's true."

"Oh that!" he said with a laugh, switching his hand to the other side. "Ask me something else."

"Okay," I said, "why am I bugged on the number eight? Because I'm permanently behind a private 8-ball?"

"Eight's a number with many properties," he said, suddenly as intently serious as he usually is. "The corners of a cube."

"You mean I'm a square?" I said. "Or just a brick? You know, 'She's a brick.'"

"But eight's most curious property," he continued with a frown, "is that lying on its side it signifies infinity. So eight erect is really —" and suddenly his made-up, naturally solemn face got a great glow of inspiration and devotion —"Infinity Arisen!"

Well, I don't know. You meet quite a few people in the theater who are bats on numerology, they use it to pick stage-names. But I'd never have guessed it of Martin. He always struck me as the skeptical, cynical type.

"I had another idea about eight," I said hesitatingly. "Spiders. That 8-legged asterisk on Miss Nefer's forehead —" I suppressed a shudder.

"You don't like her, do you?" he stated.

"I'm afraid of her," I said.

"You shouldn't be. She's a very great woman and tonight she's playing an infinitely more difficult part than I am. No, Greta," he went on as I started to protest, "believe me, you don't understand anything about it at this moment. Just as you don't understand about spiders, fearing them. They're the first to climb the rigging and to climb ashore too. They're the web-weavers, the line-throwers, the connectors, Siva and Kali united in love. They're the double mandala, the beginning and the end, infinity mustered and on the march —"

"They're also on my New York screen!" I squeaked, shrinking back across the cot a little and pointing at a tiny glinting silver-and-black thing mounting below my Willy-ball.

Martin gently caught its line on his finger and lifted it very close to his face. "Eight eyes too," he told me. Then, "Poor little god," he said and put it back.

"Marty? Marty?" Sid's desperate stage-whisper rasped the length of the dressing room.

Martin stood up. "Yes, Sid?"

Sid's voice stayed a whisper but went from desperate to ferocious. "You villainous elf-skin! Know you not the Cauldron Scene's been playing a hundred heartbeats? 'Tis 'most my entrance and we still mustering only two witches out of three! Oh, you nott-pated starveling!"

Before Sid had got much more than half of that out, Martin had slipped around the screen, raced the length of the dressing room, and I'd heard a lusty thwack as he went out the door. I couldn't help grinning, though with Martin racked by anxieties and reliefs over his first time as Lady Mack, it was easy to understand it slipping his mind that he was still doubling Second Witch.

VI

I will vault credit
and affect high pleasures
Beyond death.
—Ferdinand

I sat down where Martin had been, first pushing the screen far enough to the side for me to see the length of the dressing room and notice anyone coming through the door and any blurs moving behind the thin white curtain shutting off the boys' two-thirds.

I'd been going to think. But instead I just sat there, experiencing my body and the room around it, steadying myself or maybe readying myself. I couldn't tell which, but it was nothing to think about, only to feel. My heartbeat became a very faint, slow, solid throb. My spine straightened.

No one came in or went out. Distantly I heard Macbeth and the witches and the apparitions talk.

Once I looked at the New York Screen, but all the stuff there had grown stale. No protection, no nothing.

I reached down to my suitcase and from where I'd been going to get a miltown I took a dexedrine and popped it in my mouth. Then I started out, beginning to shake.

When I got to the end of the curtain I went around it to Sid's dressing table and asked Shakespeare, "Am I doing the right thing, Pop?" But he didn't answer me out of his portrait. He just looked sneaky-innocent, like he knew a lot but wouldn't tell, and I found myself think of a little silver-framed photo Sid had used to keep there too of a cocky German-looking young actor with "Erich" autographed across it in white ink. At least I supposed he was an actor. He looked a little like Erich von Stroheim, but nicer yet somehow nastier too. The photo had used to upset me, I don't know why. Sid must have noticed it, for one day it was gone.

I thought of the tiny black-and-silver spider crawling across the remembered silver frame, and for some reason it gave me the cold creeps.

Well, this wasn't doing me any good, just making me feel dismal again, so I quickly went out. In the door I had to slip around the actors coming back from the Cauldron Scene and the big bolt nicked my hip.

Outside Maud was peeling off her Third Witch stuff to reveal Lady Macduff beneath. She twitched me a grin.

"How's it going?" I asked.

"Okay, I guess," she shrugged. "What an audience! Noisy as highschool kids."

"How come Sid didn't have a boy do your part?" I asked.

"He goofed, I guess. But I've battened down my bosoms and playing Mrs. Macduff as a boy."

"How does a girl do that in a dress?" I asked.

"She sits stiff and thinks pants," she said, handing me her witch robe. "'Scuse me now. I got to find my children and go get murdered."

I'd moved a few steps nearer the stage when I felt the gentlest tug at my hip. I looked down and saw that a taut black thread from the bottom of my sweater connected me with the dressing room. It must have snagged on the big bolt and unraveled. I moved my body an inch or so, tugging it delicately to see what it felt like and I got the answers: Theseus's clew, a spider's line, an umbilicus.

I reached down close to my side and snapped it with my fingernails. The black thread leaped away. But the dressing room door didn't vanish, or the wings change, or the world end, and I didn't fall down.

After that I just stood there for quite a while, feeling my new freedom and steadiness, letting my body get used to it. I didn't do any thinking. I hardly bothered to study anything around me, though I did notice that there were more bushes and trees than set pieces, and that the flickery lightning was simply torches and that Queen Elizabeth was in (or back in) the audience. Sometimes letting your body get used to something is all you should do, or maybe can do.

And I did smell horse dung.

When the Lady Macduff Scene was over and the Chicken Scene well begun, I went back to the dressing room. Actors call it the Chicken Scene because Macduff weeps in it about "all my pretty chickens and their dam," meaning his kids and wife, being murdered "at one fell swoop" on orders of that chickenyard-raiding "hell-kite" Macbeth.

Inside the dressing room I steered down the boys' side. Doc was putting on an improbable-looking dark makeup for Macbeth's last faithful servant Seyton. He didn't seem as boozy-woozy as usual for Fourth Act, but just the same I stopped to help him get into a chain-mail shirt made of thick cord woven and silvered.

In the third chair beyond, Sid was sitting back with his corset loosened and critically survey-ing Martin, who'd now changed to a white wool nightgown that clung and draped beautifully, but not particularly enticingly, on him and his folded towel, which had slipped a bit.

From beside Sid's mirror, Shakespeare smiled out of his portrait at them like an intelligent big-headed bug.

Martin stood tall, spread his arms rather like a high priest, and intoned, *"Amici! Romani! Populares!"*

I nudged Doc. "What goes on now?" I whispered.

He turned a bleary eye on them. "I think they are rehearsing *Julius Caesar* in Latin." He shrugged. "It begins the oration of Antony."

"But why?" I asked. Sid does like to put every moment to use when the performance-fire is in people, but this project seemed pretty far afield-hyper-pedantic. Yet at the same time I felt my scalp shivering as if my mind were jumping with speculations just below the surface.

Doc shook his head and shrugged again.

Sid shoved a palm at Martin and roared softly, "'Sdeath, boy, thou'rt not playing a Roman statua but a Roman! Loosen your knees and try again."

Then he saw me. Signing Martin to stop, he called, "Come hither, sweetling." I obeyed quickly. He gave me a fiendish grin and said, "Thou'st heard our proposal from Martin. What sayest thou, wench?"

This time the shiver was in my back. It felt good. I realized I was grinning back at him, and I knew what I'd been getting ready for the last twenty minutes.

"I'm on," I said. "Count me in the company."

Sid jumped up and grabbed me by the shoulders and hair and bussed me on both cheeks. It was a little like being bombed.

"Prodigious!" he cried. "Thou'lt play the Gentlewoman in the Sleepwalking Scene tonight. Martin, her costume! Now sweet wench, mark me well." His voice grew grave and old. "When was it she last walked?"

The new courage went out of me like water down a chute. "But Siddy, I can't start *tonight*," I protested, half pleading, half outraged.

"Tonight or never! 'Tis an emergency-we're short-handed." Again his voice changed. "When was it she last walked?"

"But Siddy, I don't *know* the part."

"You must. You've heard the play twenty times this year past. When was it she last walked?"

Martin was back and yanking down a blonde wig on my head and shoving my arms into a light gray robe.

"I've never studied *the lines*," I squeaked at Sidney.

"Liar! I've watched your lips move a dozen nights when you watched the scene from the wings. Close your eyes, girl! Martin, unhand her. Close your eyes, girl, empty your mind, and listen, listen only. When was it she last walked?"

In the blackness I heard myself replying to that cue, first in a whisper, then more loudly, then full-throated but grave, "Since his majesty went into the field, I have seen her rise from her bed, throw her nightgown upon her, unlock her closet, take forth —"

"Bravissimo!" Siddy cried and bombed me again. Martin hugged his arm around my shoulders too, then quickly stooped to start hooking up my robe from the bottom.

"But that's only the first lines, Siddy," I protested.

"They're enough!"

"But Siddy, what if I blow up?" I asked.

"Keep your mind empty. You won't. Further, I'll be at your side, doubling the Doctor, to prompt you if you pause."

That ought to take care of two of me, I thought. Then something else struck me. "But Siddy," I quavered, "how do I play the Gentlewoman as a boy?"

"Boy?" he demanded wonderingly. "Play her without falling down flat on your face and I'll be past measure happy!" And he smacked me hard on the fanny.

Martin's fingers were darting at the next to the last hook. I stopped him and shoved my hand down the neck of my sweater and got hold of the subway token and the chain it was on and yanked. It burned my neck but the gold links parted. I started to throw it across the room, but instead I smiled at Siddy and dropped it in his palm.

"The Sleepwalking Scene!" Maud hissed insistently to us from the door.

I know death hath ten thousand several doors
For men to take their exits, and 'tis found
They go on such strange geometrical hinges,
You may open them both ways.
—The Duchess

There is this about an actor on stage: he can see the audience but he can't *look* at them, unless he's a narrator or some sort of comic. I wasn't the first (Grendel groks!) and only scared to death of becoming the second as Siddy walked me out of the wings onto the stage, over the groundcloth that felt so much like ground, with a sort of interweaving policeman-grip on my left arm.

Sid was in a dark gray robe looking like some dismal kind of monk, his head so hooded for the Doctor that you couldn't see his face at all.

My skull was pulse-buzzing. My throat was squeezed dry. My heart was pounding. Below that my body was empty, squirmy, electricity-stung, yet with the feeling of wearing ice cold iron pants.

I heard as if from two million miles, "When was it she last walked?" and then an iron bell somewhere tolling the reply —I guess it had to be my voice coming up through my body from my iron pants: "Since his majesty went into the field —" and so on, until Martin had come on stage, stary-eyed, a white scarf tossed over the back of his long black wig and a flaring candle two inches thick gripped in his right hand and dripping wax on his wrist, and started to do Lady Mack's sleepwalking half-hinted confessions of the murders of Duncan and Banquo and Lady Macduff.

So here is what I saw then without looking, like a vivid scene that floats out in front of your mind in a reverie, hovering against a background of dark blur, and sort of flashes on and off as you think, or in my case act. All the time, remember, with Sid's hand hard on my wrist and me now and then tolling Shakespearan language out of some lightless storehouse of memory I'd never known was there to belong to me.

There was a medium-size glade in a forest. Through the half-naked black branches shone a dark cold sky, like ashes of silver, early evening.

The glade had two horns, as it were, narrowing back to either side and going off through the forest. A chilly breeze was blowing out of them, almost enough to put out the candle. Its flame rippled.

Rather far back in the horn to my left, but not very far, were clumped two dozen or so men in dark cloaks they huddled around themselves. They wore brimmed tallish hats and pale stuff showing at their necks. Somehow I assumed that these men must be the "rude fellows from the City" I remembered Beau mentioning a million or so years ago. Although I couldn't see them very well, and didn't spend much time on them, there was one of them who had his hat off or excitedly pushed way back, showing a big pale forehead. Although that was all the conscious impression I had of his face, he seemed frighteningly familiar.

In the horn to my right, which was wider, were lined up about a dozen horses, with grooms holding tight every two of them, but throwing their heads back now and then as they strained against the reins, and stamping their front hooves restlessly. Oh, they frightened me, I tell you, that line of two-foot-long glossy-haired faces, writhing back their upper lips from teeth wide as piano keys, every horse of them looking as wild-eyed and evil as Fuseli's steed sticking its head through the drapes in his picture "The Nightmare."

To the center the trees came close to the stage. Just in front of them was Queen Elizabeth sitting on the chair on the spread carpet, just as I'd seen her out there before; only now I could see that the braziers were glowing and redly high-lighting her pale cheeks and dark red hair and the silver in her dress and cloak. She was looking at Martin-Lady Mack-most intently, her mouth grimaced tight, twisting her fingers together.

Standing rather close around her were a half dozen men with fancier hats and ruffs and wide-flaring riding gauntlets.

Then, through the trees and tall leafless bushes just behind Elizabeth, I saw an identical Elizabeth-face floating, only this one was smiling a demonic smile. The eyes were open very wide. Now and then the pupils darted rapid glances from side to side.

There was a sharp pain in my left wrist and Sid whisper-snarling at me, "Accustomed action!" out of the corner of his shadowed mouth.

I tolled on obediently, "It is an accustomed action with her, to seem thus washing her hands: I have known her continue in this a quarter of an hour."

Martin had set down the candle, which still flared and guttered, on a little high table so firm its thin legs must have been stabbed into the ground. And he was rubbing his hands together slowly, continually, tormentedly, trying to get rid of Duncan's blood which Mrs. Mack knows in her sleep is still there. And all the while as he did it, the agitation of the seated Elizabeth grew, the eyes flicking from side to side, hands writhing.

He got to the lines, "Here's the smell of blood still: all the perfumes of Arabia will not sweeten this little hand. Oh, oh, oh!"

As he wrung out those soft, tortured sighs, Elizabeth stood up from her chair and took a step forward. The courtiers moved toward her quickly, but not touching her, and she said loudly, "Tis the blood of Mary Stuart whereof she speaks-the pails of blood that will gush from her chopped neck. Oh, I cannot endure it!" And as she said that last, she suddenly turned about and strode back toward the trees, kicking out her ash-colored skirt. One of the courtiers turned with her and stooped toward her closely, whispering something. But although she paused a moment, all she said was, "Nay, Eyes, stop not the play, but follow me not! Nay, I say leave me, Leicester!" And she walked into the trees, he looking after her.

Then Sid was kicking my ankle and I was reciting something and Martin was taking up his candle again without looking at it saying with a drugged agitation, "To bed; to bed; there's knocking at the gate."

Elizabeth came walking out of the trees again, her head bowed. She couldn't have been in them ten seconds. Leicester hurried toward her, hand anxiously outstretched.

Martin moved offstage, torturedly yet softly wailing, "What's done cannot be undone."

Just then Elizabeth flicked aside Leicester's hand with playful contempt and looked up and she was smiling the devil-smile. A horse whinnied like a trumpeted snicker.

As Sid and I started our last few lines together I intoned mechanically, letting words free-fall from my mind to my tongue. All this time I had been answering Lady Mack in my thoughts, *That's what you think, sister.*

God cannot effect that anything which is past should not have been.

It is more impossible than rising the dead.

—Summa Theologica

The moment I was out of sight of the audience I broke away from Sid and ran to the dressing room. I flopped down on the first chair I saw, my head and arms trailed over its back, and I almost passed out. It wasn't a mind-wavery fit. Just normal faint.

I couldn't have been there long-well, not very long, though the battle-rattle and alarums of the last scene were echoing tinnily from the stage-when Bruce and Beau and Mark (who was playing Malcolm, Martin's usual main part) came in wearing their last-act stage-armor and carrying between them Queen Elizabeth flaccid as a sack. Martin came after them, stripping off his white wool nightgown so fast that buttons flew. I thought automatically, *I'll have to sew those.*

They laid her down on three chairs set side by side and hurried out. Unpinning the folded towel, which had fallen around his waist, Martin walked over and looked down at her. He yanked off his wig by a braid and tossed it at me.

I let it hit me and fall on the floor. I was looking at that white queenly face, eyes open and staring sightless at the ceiling, mouth open a little too with a thread of foam trailing from the corner, and at that ice-cream-cone bodice that never stirred. The blue fly came buzzing over my head and circled down toward her face.

"Martin," I said with difficulty, "I don't think I'm going to like what we're doing."

He turned on me, his short hair elfed, his fists planted high on his hips at the edge of his black tights, which now were all his clothes.

"You knew!" he said impatiently. "You knew you were signing up for more than acting when you said, 'Count me in the company.'"

Like a legged sapphire the blue fly walked across her upper lip and stopped by the thread of foam.

"But Martin ... changing the past ... dipping back and killing the real queen ... replacing her with a double —"

His dark brows shot up. "The real-You think this is the real Queen Elizabeth?" He grabbed a bottle of rubbing alcohol from the nearest table, gushed some on a towel stained with greasepaint and, holding the dead head by its red hair (no, wig-the real one wore a wig too) scrubbed the forehead.

The white cosmetic came away, showing sallow skin and on it a faint tattoo in the form of an "S" styled like a yin-yang symbol left a little open.

"Snake!" he hissed. "Destroyer! The arch-enemy, the eternal opponent! God knows how many times people like Queen Elizabeth have been dug out of the past, first by Snakes, then by Spiders, and kidnapped or killed and replaced in the course of our war. This is the first big operation I've been on, Greta. But I know that much."

My head began to ache. I asked, "If she's an enemy double, why didn't she know a performance of Macbeth in her lifetime was an anachronism?"

"Foxholed in the past, only trying to hold a position, they get dulled. They turn half zombie. Even the Snakes. Even our people. Besides, she almost did catch on, twice when she spoke to Leicester."

"Martin," I said dully, "if there've been all these replacements, first by them, then by us, what's happened to the *real* Elizabeth?"

He shrugged. "God knows."

I asked softly, "But does He, Martin? Can He?"

He hugged his shoulders in, as if to contain a shudder. "Look, Greta," he said, "it's the Snakes who are the warpers and destroyers. We're restoring the past. The Spiders are trying to keep things as first created. We only kill when we must."

I shuddered then, for bursting out of my memory came the glittering, knife-flashing, night-shrouded, bloody image of my lover, the Spider soldier-of-change Erich von Hohenwald, dying in the grip of a giant silver spider, or spider-shaped entity large as he, as they rolled in a tangled ball down a flight of rocks in Central Park.

But the memory-burst didn't blow up my mind, as it had done a year ago, no more than snapping the black thread from my sweater had ended the world. I asked Martin, "Is that what the Snakes say?"

"Of course not! They make the same claims we do. But somewhere, Greta, you have to *trust*." He put out the middle finger of his hand.

I didn't take hold of it. He whirled it away, snapping it against his thumb.

"You're still grieving for that carrion there!" he accused me. He jerked down a section of white curtain and whirled it over the stiffening body. "If you must grieve, grieve for Miss Nefer! Exiled, imprisoned, locked forever in the past, her mind pulsing faintly in the black hole of the dead and gone, yearning for Nirvana yet nursing one lone painful patch of consciousness. And only to hold a fort! Only to make sure Mary Stuart is executed, the Armada licked, and that all the other consequences flow on. The Snakes' Elizabeth let Mary live ... and England die ... and the Spaniard hold North America to the Great Lakes and New Scandinavia."

Once more he put out his middle finger.

"All right, all right," I said, barely touching it. "You've convinced me."

"Great!" he said. "'By for now, Greta. I got to help strike the set."

"That's good," I said. He loped out.

I could hear the skirling sword-clashes of the final fight to the death of the two Macks, Duff and Beth. But I only sat there in the empty dressing room pretending to grieve for a devil-smiling snow tiger locked in a time-cage and for a cute sardonic German killed for insubordination that *I* had reported ... but really grieving for a girl who for a year had been a rootless child of the theater with a whole company of mothers and fathers, afraid of nothing more than subway bogies and Park and Village monsters.

As I sat there pitying myself beside a shrouded queen, a shadow fell across my knees. I saw stealing through the dressing room a young man in worn dark clothes. He couldn't have been more than twenty-three. He was a frail sort of guy with a weak chin and big forehead and eyes that saw everything. I knew at one he was the one who had seemed familiar to me in the knot of City fellows.

He looked at me and I looked from him to the picture sitting on the reserve makeup box by Siddy's mirror. And I began to tremble.

He looked at it too, of course, as fast as I did. And then he began to tremble too, though it was a finer-grained tremor than mine.

The sword-fight had ended seconds back and now I heard the witches faintly wailing, "Fair is foul, and foul is fair —" Sid has them echo that line offstage at the end to give a feeling of prophecy fulfilled.

Then Sid came pounding up. He's the first finished, since the fight ends offstage so Macduff can carry back a red-necked papier-mache head of him and show it to the audience. Sid stopped dead in the door.

Then the stranger turned around. His shoulders jerked as he saw Sid. He moved toward him just two or three steps at a time, speaking at the same time in breathy little rushes.

Sid stood there and watched him. When the other actors came boiling up behind him, he put his hands on the doorframe to either side so none of them could get past. Their faces peered around him.

And all this while the stranger was saying, "What may this mean? Can such things be? Are all the seeds of time ... wetted by some hell-trickle ... sprouted at once in their granary? Speak ... speak! You played me a play ... that I am writing in my secretest heart. Have you disjointed the frame of things ... to steal my unborn thoughts? Fair is foul indeed. Is all the world a stage? Speak, I say! Are you not my friend Sidney James Lessingham of King's Lynn ... singed by time's fiery wand ... sifted over with the ashes of thirty years? Speak, are you not he? Oh, there are more things in heaven and earth ... aye, and perchance hell too ... Speak, I charge you!"

And with that he put his hands on Sid's shoulders, half to shake him, I think, but half to keep from falling over. And for the one time I ever saw it, glib old Siddy had nothing to say.

He worked his lips. He opened his mouth twice and twice shut it. Then, with a kind of desperation in his face, he motioned the actors out of the way behind him with one big arm and swung the other around the stranger's narrow shoulders and swept him out of the dressing room, himself following.

The actors came pouring in then, Bruce tossing Macbeth's head to Martin like a football while he tugged off his horned helmet, Mark dumping a stack of shields in the corner, Maudie pausing as she skittered past me to say, "Hi Gret, great you're back," and patting my temple to show what part of me she meant. Beau went straight to Sid's dressing table and set the portrait aside and lifted out Sid's reserve makeup box.

"The lights, Martin!" he called.

Then Sid came back in, slamming and bolting the door behind him and standing for a moment with his back against it, panting.

I rushed to him. Something was boiling up inside me, but before it could get to my brain I opened my mouth and it came out as, "Siddy, you can't fool me, that was no dirty S-or-S. I don't care how much he shakes and purrs, or shakes a spear, or just plain shakes-Siddy, that was Shakespeare!"

"Aye, girl, I think so," he told me, holding my wrists together. "They can't find dolls to double men like that-or such is my main hope." A big sickly grin came on his face. "Oh, gods," he demanded, "with what words do you talk to a man whose speech you've stolen all your life?"

I asked him, "Sid, were we *ever* in Central Park?"

He answered, "Once-twelve months back. A one-night stand. They came for Erich. You flipped."

He swung me aside and moved behind Beau. All the lights went out.

Then I saw, dimly at first, the great dull-gleaming jewel, covered with dials and green-glowing windows, that Beau had lifted from Sid's reserve makeup box. The strongest green glow showed his intent face, still framed by the long glistening locks of the Ross wig, as he kneeled before the thing-Major Maintainer, I remembered it was called.

"When now? Where?" Beau tossed impatiently to Sid over his shoulder.

"The forty-fourth year before our Lord's birth!" Sid answered instantly. "Rome!"

Beau's fingers danced over the dials like a musician's, or a safe-cracker's. The green glow flared and faded flickeringly.

"There's a storm in that vector of the Void."

"Circle it," Sid ordered.

"There are dark mists every way."

"Then pick the likeliest dark path!"

I called through the dark, "Fair is foul, and foul is fair, eh, Siddy?"

"Aye, chick," he answered me. "'Tis all the rule we have!"

Appointment in Tomorrow

Is it possible to have a world without moral values?
Or does lack of morality become a moral value, also?

The first angry rays of the sun–which, startlingly enough, still rose in the east at 24 hour intervals–pierced the lacy tops of Atlantic combers and touched thousands of sleeping Americans with unconscious fear, because of their unpleasant similarity to the rays from World War III's atomic bombs.

They turned to blood the witch-circle of rusty steel skeletons around Inferno in Manhattan. Without comment, they pointed a cosmic finger at the tarnished brass plaque commemorating the martyrdom of the Three Physicists after the dropping of the Hell Bomb. They tenderly touched the rosy skin and strawberry bruises on the naked shoulders of a girl sleeping off a drunk on the furry and radiantly heated floor of a nearby roof garden. They struck green magic from the glassy blot that was Old Washington. Twelve hours before, they had revealed things as eerily beautiful, and as ravaged, in Asia and Russia. They pinked the white walls of the Colonial dwelling of Morton Opperly near the Institute for Advanced Studies; upstairs they slanted impartially across the Pharoahlike and open-eyed face of the elderly physicist and the ugly, sleep-surly one of young Willard Farquar in the next room. And in nearby New Washington they made of the spire of the Thinkers' Foundation a blue and optimistic glory that outshone White House, Jr.

It was America approaching the end of the Twentieth Century. America of juke-box burlesque and your local radiation hospital. America of the mask-fad for women and Mystic Christianity. America of the off-the-bosom dress and the New Blue Laws. America of the Endless War and the loyalty detector. America of marvelous Maizie and the monthly rocket to Mars. America of the Thinkers and (a few remembered) the Institute. "Knock on titanium," "Whadya do for black-outs," "Please, lover, don't think when I'm around," America, as combat-shocked and crippled as the rest of the bomb-shattered planet.

Not one impudent photon of the sunlight penetrated the triple-paned, polarizing windows of Jorj Helmuth's bedroom in the Thinker's Foundation, yet the clock in his brain awakened him to the minute, or almost. Switching off the Educational Sandman in the midst of the phrase, "...applying tensor calculus to the nucleus," he took a deep, even breath and cast his mind to the limits of the world and his knowledge. It was a somewhat shadowy vision, but, he noted with impartial approval, definitely less shadowy than yesterday morning.

Employing a rapid mental scanning technique, he next cleared his memory chains of false associations, including those acquired while asleep. These chores completed, he held his finger on a bedside button, which rotated the polarizing window panes until the room slowly filled with a muted daylight. Then, still flat on his back, he turned his head until he could look at the remarkably beautiful blonde girl asleep beside him.

Remembering last night, he felt a pang of exasperation, which he instantly quelled by taking his mind to a higher and dispassionate level from which he could look down on the girl and even himself as quaint, clumsy animals. Still, he grumbled silently, Caddy might have had enough consideration to clear out before he awoke. He wondered if he shouldn't have used his hypnotic control of the girl to smooth their relationship last night, and for a moment the word that would send her into deep trance trembled on the tip of his tongue. But no, that special power of his over her was reserved for far more important purposes.

Pumping dynamic tension into his 20-year-old muscles and confidence into his 60-year-old mind, the 40-year-old Thinker rose from bed. No covers had to be thrown off; the nuclear heating unit made them unnecessary. He stepped into his clothing-the severe tunic, tights and sockassins of the modern business man. Next he glanced at the message tape beside his phone, washed down with ginger ale a vita-amino-enzyme tablet, and walked to the window. There, gazing along the rows of newly planted mutant oaks lining Decontamination Avenue, his smooth face broke into a smile.

It had come to him, the next big move in the intricate game making up his life-and mankind's. Come to him during sleep, as so many of his best decisions did, because he regularly employed the time-saving technique of somno-thought, which could function at the same time as somno-learning.

He set his who?-where? robot for "Rocket Physicist" and "Genius Class." While it worked, he dictated to his steno-robot the following brief message:

Dear Fellow Scientist:

A project is contemplated that will have a crucial bearing on man's future in deep space. Ample non-military Government funds are available. There was a time when professional men scoffed at the Thinkers. Then there was a time when the Thinkers perforce neglected the professional men. Now both times are past. May they never return! I would like to consult you this afternoon, three o'clock sharp, Thinkers' Foundation I.

Jorj Helmuth

Meanwhile the who?-where? had tossed out a dozen cards. He glanced through them, hesitated at the name "Willard Farquar," looked at the sleeping girl, then quickly tossed them all into the addresso-robot and plugged in the steno-robot.

The buzz-light blinked green and he switched the phone to audio.

"The President is waiting to see Maizie, sir," a clear feminine voice announced. "He has the general staff with him."

"Martian peace to him," Jorj Helmuth said. "Tell him I'll be down in a few minutes."

Huge as a primitive nuclear reactor, the great electronic brain loomed above the knot of hush-voiced men. It almost filled a two-story room in the Thinkers' Foundation. Its front was an orderly expanse of controls, indicators, telltales, and terminals, the upper ones reached by a chair on a boom.

Although, as far as anyone knew, it could sense only the information and questions fed into it on a tape, the human visitors could not resist the impulse to talk in whispers and glance uneasily at the great cryptic cube. After all, it had lately taken to moving some of its own controls-the permissible ones-and could doubtless improvise a hearing apparatus if it wanted to.

For this was the thinking machine beside which the Marks and Eniacs and Maniacs and Maddidas and Minervas and Mimirs were less than Morons. This was the machine with a million times as many synapses as the human brain, the machine that remembered by cutting delicate notches in the rims of molecules (instead of kindergarten paper-punching or the Coney Island shimmying of columns of mercury). This was the machine that had given instructions on building the last three-quarters of itself. This was the goal, perhaps, toward which fallible human reasoning and biased human judgment and feeble human ambition had evolved.

This was the machine that really thought —a million-plus!

This was the machine that the timid cyberneticists and stuffy professional scientists had said could not be built. Yet this was the machine that the Thinkers, with characteristic Yankee push, *had* built. And nicknamed, with characteristic Yankee irreverence and girl-fondness, "Maizie."

Gazing up at it, the President of the United States felt a chord plucked within him that hadn't been sounded for decades, the dark and shivery organ chord of his Baptist childhood. Here, in a strange sense, although his reason rejected it, he felt he stood face to face with the living God: infinitely stern with the sternness of reality, yet infinitely just. No tiniest error or wilful misstep could ever escape the scrutiny of this vast mentality. He shivered.

The grizzled general-there was also one who was gray-was thinking that this was a very odd link in the chain of command. Some shadowy and usually well-controlled memories from World War II faintly stirred his ire. Here he was giving orders to a being immeasurably more intelligent than himself. And always orders of the "Tell me how to kill that man" rather than the "Kill that man" sort. The distinction bothered him obscurely. It relieved him to know that Maizie had built-in controls which made her always the servant of humanity, or of humanity's right-minded leaders-even the Thinkers weren't certain which.

The gray general was thinking uneasily, and, like the President, at a more turbid level, of the resemblance between Papal infallibility and the dictates of the machine. Suddenly his bony wrists began to tremble. He asked himself: Was this the Second Coming? Mightn't an incarnation be in metal rather than flesh?

The austere Secretary of State was remembering what he'd taken such pains to make everyone forget: his youthful flirtation at Lake Success with Buddhism. Sitting before his *guru*, his teacher, feeling the Occidental's awe at the wisdom of the East, or its pretense, he had felt a little like this.

The burly Secretary of Space, who had come up through United Rockets, was thanking his stars that at any rate the professional scientists weren't responsible for this job. Like the grizzled general, he'd always felt suspicious of men who kept telling you how to do things, rather than doing them themselves. In World War III he'd had his fill of the professional physicists, with their eternal taint of a misty sort of radicalism and free-thinking. The Thinkers were better-more disciplined, more human. They'd called their brain-machine Maizie, which helped take the curse off her. Somewhat.

The President's Secretary, a paunchy veteran of party caucuses, was also glad that it was the Thinkers who had created the machine, though he trembled at the power that it gave them over the Administration. Still, you could do business with the Thinkers. And nobody (not even the Thinkers) could do business (that sort of business) with Maizie!

Before that great square face with its thousands of tiny metal features, only Jorj Helmuth seemed at ease, busily entering on the tape the complex Questions of the Day that the high officials had handed him: logistics for the Endless War in Pakistan, optimum size for next year's sugar-corn crop, current thought trends in average Soviet minds-profound questions, yet many of them phrased with surprising simplicity. For figures, technical jargon, and layman's language were alike to Maizie; there was no need to translate into mathematical shorthand, as with the lesser brain-machines.

The click of the taper went on until the Secretary of State had twice nervously fired a cigaret with his ultrasonic lighter and twice quickly put it away. No one spoke.

Jorj looked up at the Secretary of Space. "Section Five, Question Four-whom would that come from?"

The burly man frowned. "That would be the physics boys, Opperly's group. Is anything wrong?"

Jorj did not answer. A bit later he quit taping and began to adjust controls, going up on the boom-chair to reach some of them. Eventually he came down and touched a few more, then stood waiting.

From the great cube came a profound, steady purring. Involuntarily the six officials backed off a bit. Somehow it was impossible for a man to get used to the sound of Maizie starting to think.

Jorj turned, smiling. "And now, gentlemen, while we wait for Maizie to celebrate, there should be just enough time for us to watch the takeoff of the Mars rocket." He switched on a giant television screen. The others made a quarter turn, and there before them glowed the rich ochres and blues of a New Mexico sunrise and, in the middle distance, a silvery mighty spindle.

Like the generals, the Secretary of Space suppressed a scowl. Here was something that ought to be spang in the center of his official territory, and the Thinkers had locked him completely out of it. That rocket there-just an ordinary Earth satellite vehicle commandeered from the Army, but equipped by the Thinkers with Maizie-designed nuclear motors capable of the Mars journey and more. The first spaceship-and the Secretary of Space was not in on it!

Still, he told himself, Maizie had decreed it that way. And when he remembered what the Thinkers had done for him in rescuing him from breakdown with their mental science, in rescuing the whole Administration from collapse he realized he had to be satisfied. And that was without taking into consideration the amazing additional mental discoveries that the Thinkers were bringing down from Mars.

"Lord," the President said to Jorj as if voicing the Secretary's feeling, "I wish you people could bring a couple of those wise little devils back with you this trip. Be a good thing for the country."

Jorj looked at him a bit coldly. "It's quite unthinkable," he said. "The telepathic abilities of the Martians make them extremely sensitive. The conflicts of ordinary Earth minds would impinge on them psychotically, even fatally. As you know, the Thinkers were able to contact them only because of our degree of learned mental poise and errorless memory-chains. So for the present it must be our task alone to glean from the Martians their astounding mental skills. Of course, some day in the future, when we have discovered how to armor the minds of the Martians —"

"Sure, I know," the President said hastily. "Shouldn't have mentioned it, Jorj."

Conversation ceased. They waited with growing tension for the great violet flames to bloom from the base of the silvery shaft.

Meanwhile the question tape, like a New Year's streamer tossed out a high window into the night, sped on its dark way along spinning rollers. Curling with an intricate aimlessness curiously like that of such a streamer, it tantalized the silvery fingers of a thousand relays, saucily evaded the glances of ten thousand electric eyes, impishly darted down a narrow black alleyway of memory banks, and, reaching the center of the cube, suddenly emerged into a small room where a suave fat man in shorts sat drinking beer.

He flipped the tape over to him with practiced finger, eyeing it as a stockbroker might have studied a ticker tape. He read the first question, closed his eyes and frowned for five seconds. Then with the staccato self-confidence of a hack writer, he began to tape out the answer.

For many minutes the only sounds were the rustle of the paper ribbon and the click of the taper, except for the seconds the fat man took to close his eyes, or to drink or pour beer. Once, too, he lifted a phone, asked a concise question, waited half a minute, listened to an answer, then went back to the grind.

Until he came to Section Five, Question Four. That time he did his thinking with his eyes open.

The question was: "Does Maizie stand for Maelzel?"

He sat for a while slowly scratching his thigh. His loose, persuasive lips tightened, without closing, into the shape of a snarl.

Suddenly he began to tape again.

"Maizie does not stand for Maelzel. Maizie stands for amazing, humorously given the form of a girl's name. Section Six, Answer One: The mid-term election viewcasts should be spaced as follows...."

But his lips didn't lose the shape of a snarl.

Five hundred miles above the ionosphere, the Mars rocket cut off its fuel and slumped gratefully into an orbit that would carry it effortlessly around the world at that altitude. The pilot unstrapped himself and stretched, but he didn't look out the viewport at the dried-mud disc that was Earth, cloaked in its haze of blue sky. He knew he had two maddening months ahead of him in which to do little more than that. Instead, he unstrapped Sappho.

Used to free fall from two previous experiences, and loving it, the fluffy little cat was soon bounding about the cabin in curves and gyrations that would have made her the envy of all back-alley and parlor felines on the planet below. A miracle cat in the dream world of free fall. For a long time she played with a string that the man would toss out lazily. Sometimes she caught the string on the fly, sometimes she swam for it frantically.

After a while the man grew bored with the game. He unlocked a drawer and began to study the details of the wisdom he would discover on Mars this trip-priceless spiritual insights that would be balm to war-battered mankind.

The cat carefully selected a spot three feet off the floor, curled up on the air, and went to sleep.

Jorj Helmuth snipped the emerging answer tape into sections and handed each to the appropriate man. Most of them carefully tucked theirs away with little more than a glance, but the Secretary of Space puzzled over his.

"Who the devil would Maelzel be?" he asked.

A remote look came into the eyes of the Secretary of State. "Edgar Allen Poe," he said frowningly, with eyes half-closed.

The grizzled general snapped his fingers. "Sure! Maelzel's Chess player. Read it when I was a kid. About an automaton that was supposed to play chess. Poe proved it hid a man inside it."

The Secretary of Space frowned. "Now what's the point in a fool question like that?"

"You said it came from Opperly's group?" Jorj asked sharply.

The Secretary of Space nodded. The others looked at the two men puzzledly.

"Who would that be?" Jorj pressed. "The group, I mean."

The Secretary of Space shrugged. "Oh, the usual little bunch over at the Institute. Hindeman, Gregory, Opperly himself. Oh, yes, and young Farquar."

"Sounds like Opperly's getting senile," Jorj commented coldly. "I'd investigate."

The Secretary of Space nodded. He suddenly looked tough. "I will. Right away."

Sunlight striking through French windows spotlighted a ballet of dust motes untroubled by air-conditioning. Morton Opperly's living room was well-kept but worn and quite behind the times. Instead of reading tapes there were books; instead of steno-robots, pen and ink; while in place of a four by six TV screen, a Picasso hung on the wall. Only Opperly knew that the painting was still faintly radioactive, that it had been riskily so when he'd smuggled it out of his bomb-singed apartment in New York City.

The two physicists fronted each other across a coffee table. The face of the elder was cadaverous, large-eyed, and tender-fined down by a long life of abstract thought. That of the younger was forceful, sensuous, bulky as his body, and exceptionally ugly. He looked rather like a bear.

Opperly was saying, "So when he asked who was responsible for the Maelzel question, I said I didn't remember." He smiled. "They still allow me my absent-mindedness, since it nourishes their contempt. Almost my sole remaining privilege." The smile faded. "Why do you keep on teasing the zoo animals, Willard?" he asked without rancor. "I've maintained many times that we shouldn't truckle to them by yielding to their demand that we ask Maizie questions.

You and the rest have overruled me. But then to use those questions to convey veiled insults isn't reasonable. Apparently the Secretary of Space was bothered enough about this last one to pay me a 'copter call within twenty minutes of this morning's meeting at the Foundation. Why do you do it, Willard?"

The features of the other convulsed unpleasantly. "Because the Thinkers are charlatans who must be exposed," he rapped out. "We know their Maizie is no more than a tealeaf-reading fake. We've traced their Mars rockets and found they go nowhere. We know their Martian mental science is bunk."

"But we've already exposed the Thinkers very thoroughly," Opperly interposed quietly. "You know the good it did."

Farquar hunched his Japanese-wrestler shoulders. "Then it's got to be done until it takes."

Opperly studied the bowl of mutated flowers by the coffee pot. "I think you just want to tease the animals, for some personal reason of which you probably aren't aware."

Farquar scowled. "We're the ones in the cages."

Opperly continued his inspection of the flowers' bells. "All the more reason not to poke sticks through the bars at the lions and tigers strolling outside. No, Willard, I'm not counseling appeasement. But consider the age in which we live. It wants magicians." His voice grew especially tranquil. "A scientist tells people the truth. When times are good-that is, when the truth offers no threat-people don't mind. But when times are very, very bad...." A shadow darkened his eyes. "Well, we all know what happened to —" And he mentioned three names that had been household words in the middle of the century. They were the names on the brass plaque dedicated to the martyred three physicists.

He went on, "A magician, on the other hand, tells people what they wish were true-that perpetual motion works, that cancer can be cured by colored lights, that a psychosis is no worse than a head cold, that they'll live forever. In good times magicians are laughed at. They're a luxury of the spoiled wealthy few. But in bad times people sell their souls for magic cures, and buy perpetual motion machines to power their war rockets."

Farquar clenched his fist. "All the more reason to keep chipping away at the Thinkers. Are we supposed to beg off from a job because it's difficult and dangerous?"

Opperly shook his head. "We're to keep clear of the infection of violence. In my day, Willard, I was one of the Frightened Men. Later I was one of the Angry Men and then one of the Minds of Despair. Now I'm convinced that all my reactions were futile."

"Exactly!" Farquar agreed harshly. "You reacted. You didn't act. If you men who discovered atomic energy had only formed a secret league, if you'd only had the foresight and the guts to use your tremendous bargaining position to demand the power to shape mankind's future...."

"By the time you were born, Willard," Opperly interrupted dreamily, "Hitler was merely a name in the history books. We scientists weren't the stuff out of which cloak-and-dagger men are made. Can you imagine Oppenheimer wearing a mask or Einstein sneaking into the Old White House with a bomb in his briefcase?" He smiled. "Besides, that's not the way power is seized. New ideas aren't useful to the man bargaining for power-only established facts or lies are."

"Just the same, it would have been a good thing if you'd had a little violence in you."

"No," Opperly said.

"I've got violence in me," Farquar announced, shoving himself to his feet.

Opperly looked up from the flowers. "I think you have," he agreed.

"But what are we to do?" Farquar demanded. "Surrender the world to charlatans without a struggle?"

Opperly mused for a while. "I don't know what the world needs now. Everyone knows Newton as the great scientist. Few remember that he spent half his life muddling with alchemy, looking for the philosopher's stone. Which Newton did the world need then?"

"Now you are justifying the Thinkers!"

"No, I leave that to history."

"And history consists of the actions of men," Farquar concluded. "I intend to act. The Thinkers are vulnerable, their power fantastically precarious. What's it based on? A few lucky guesses. Faith-healing. Some science hocus-pocus, on the level of those juke-box burlesque acts between the strips. Dubious mental comfort given to a few nerve-torn neurotics in the Inner Cabinet-and their wives. The fact that the Thinkers' clever stage-managing won the President a doubtful election. The erroneous belief that the Soviets pulled out of Iraq and Iran because of the Thinkers' Mind Bomb threat. A brain-machine that's just a cover for Jan Tregarron's guesswork. Oh, yes, and that hogwash of 'Martian wisdom.' All of it mere bluff! A few pushes at the right times and points are all that are needed-and the Thinkers know it! I'll bet they're terrified already, and will be more so when they find that we're gunning for them. Eventually they'll be making overtures to us, turning to us for help. You wait and see."

"I am thinking again of Hitler," Opperly interposed quietly. "On his first half dozen big steps, he had nothing but bluff. His generals were against him. They knew they were in a cardboard fort. Yet he won every battle, until the last. Moreover," he pressed on, cutting Farquar short, "the power of the Thinkers isn't based on what they've got, but on what the world hasn't got-peace, honor, a good conscience...."

The front-door knocker clanked. Farquar answered it. A skinny old man with a radiation scar twisting across his temple handed him a tiny cylinder. "Radiogram for you, Willard." He grinned across the hall at Opperly. "When are you going to get a phone put in, Mr. Opperly?"

The physicist waved to him. "Next year, perhaps, Mr. Berry."

The old man snorted with good-humored incredulity and trudged off.

"What did I tell you about the Thinkers making overtures?" Farquar chortled suddenly. "It's come sooner than I expected. Look at this."

He held out the radiogram, but the older man didn't take it. Instead he asked, "Who's it from? Tregarron?"

"No, from Helmuth. There's a lot of sugar corn about man's future in deep space, but the real reason is clear. They know that they're going to have to produce an actual nuclear rocket pretty soon, and for that they'll need our help."

"An invitation?"

Farquar nodded. "For this afternoon." He noticed Opperly's anxious though distant frown. "What's the matter?" he asked. "Are you bothered about my going? Are you thinking it might be a trap-that after the Maelzel question they may figure I'm better rubbed out?"

The older man shook his head. "I'm not afraid for your life, Willard. That's yours to risk as you choose. No, I'm worried about other things they might do to you."

"What do you mean?" Farquar asked.

Opperly looked at him with a gentle appraisal. "You're a strong and vital man, Willard, with a strong man's prides and desires." His voice trailed off for a bit. Then, "Excuse me, Willard, but wasn't there a girl once? A Miss Arkady?"

Farquar's ungainly figure froze. He nodded curtly, face averted.

"And didn't she go off with a Thinker?"

"If girls find me ugly, that's their business," Farquar said harshly, still not looking at Opperly. "What's that got to do with this invitation?"

Opperly didn't answer the question. His eyes got more distant. Finally he said, "In my day we had it a lot easier. A scientist was an academician, cushioned by tradition."

Willard snorted. "Science had already entered the era of the police inspectors, with laboratory directors and political appointees stifling enterprise."

"Perhaps," Opperly agreed. "Still, the scientist lived the safe, restricted, highly respectable life of a university man. He wasn't exposed to the temptations of the world."

Farquar turned on him. "Are you implying that the Thinkers will somehow be able to buy me off?"

"Not exactly."

"You think I'll be persuaded to change my aims?" Farquar demanded angrily.

Opperly shrugged his helplessness. "No, I don't think you'll change your aims."

Clouds encroaching from the west blotted the parallelogram of sunlight between the two men.

As the slideway whisked him gently along the corridor toward his apartment, Jorj was thinking of his spaceship. For a moment the silver-winged vision crowded everything else out of his mind.

Just think, a spaceship with sails! He smiled a bit, marveling at the paradox.

Direct atomic power. Direct utilization of the force of the flying neutrons. No more ridiculous business of using a reactor to drive a steam engine, or boil off something for a jet exhaust-processes that were as primitive and wasteful as burning gunpowder to keep yourself warm.

Chemical jets would carry his spaceship above the atmosphere. Then would come the thrilling order, "Set sail for Mars!" The vast umbrella would unfold and open out around the stern, its rear or Earthward side a gleaming expanse of radioactive ribbon perhaps only an atom thick and backed with a material that would reflect neutrons. Atoms in the ribbon would split, blasting neutrons astern at fantastic velocities. Reaction would send the spaceship hurtling forward.

In airless space, the expanse of sails would naturally not retard the ship. More radioactive ribbon, manufactured as needed in the ship itself, would feed out onto the sail as that already there became exhausted.

A spaceship with direct nuclear drive-and he, a Thinker, had conceived it completely except for the technical details! Having strengthened his mind by hard years of somno-learning, mind-casting, memory-straightening, and sensory training, he had assured himself of the executive power to control the technicians and direct their specialized abilities. Together they would build the true Mars rocket.

But that would only be a beginning. They would build the true Mind Bomb. They would build the true Selective Microbe Slayer. They would discover the true laws of ESP and the inner life. They would even-his imagination hesitated a moment, then strode boldly forward-build the true Maizie!

And then ... then the Thinkers would be on even terms with the scientists. Rather, they'd be far ahead. No more deception.

He was so exalted by this thought that he almost let the slideway carry him past his door. He stepped inside and called, "Caddy!" He waited a moment, then walked through the apartment, but she wasn't there.

Confound the girl, he couldn't help thinking. This morning, when she should have made herself scarce, she'd sprawled about sleeping. Now, when he felt like seeing her, when her presence would have added a pleasant final touch to his glowing mood, she chose to be absent. He really should use his hypnotic control on her, he decided, and again there sprang into his mind the word —a pet form of her name-that would send her into obedient trance.

No, he told himself again, that was to be reserved for some moment of crisis or desperate danger, when he would need someone to strike suddenly and unquestioningly for himself and mankind. Caddy was merely a wilful and rather silly girl, incapable at present of understanding the tremendous tensions under which he operated. When he had time for it, he would train her up to be a fitting companion without hypnosis.

Yet the fact of her absence had a subtly disquieting effect. It shook his perfect self-confidence just a fraction. He asked himself if he'd been wise in summoning the rocket physicists without consulting Tregarron.

But this mood, too, he conquered quickly. Tregarron wasn't his boss, but just the Thinker's most clever salesman, an expert in the mumbo-jumbo so necessary for social control in this chaotic era. He himself, Jorj Helmuth, was the real leader in theoretics and all-over strategy, the mind behind the mind behind Maizie.

He stretched himself on the bed, almost instantly achieved maximum relaxation, turned on the somno-learner, and began the two hour rest he knew would be desirable before the big conference.

Jan Tregarron had supplemented his shorts with pink coveralls, but he was still drinking beer. He emptied his glass and lifted it a lazy inch. The beautiful girl beside him refilled it without a word and went on stroking his forehead.

"Caddy," he said reflectively, without looking at her, "there's a little job I want you to do. You're the only one with the proper background. The point is: it will take you away from Jorj for some time."

"I'd welcome it," she said with decision. "I'm getting pretty sick of watching his push-ups and all his other mind and muscle stunts. And that damn somno-learner of his keeps me awake."

Tregarron smiled. "I'm afraid Thinkers make pretty sad sweethearts."

"Not all of them," she told him, returning his smile tenderly.

He chuckled. "It's about one of those rocket physicists in the list you brought me. A fellow named Willard Farquar."

Caddy didn't say anything, but she stopped stroking his forehead.

"What's the matter?" he asked. "You knew him once, didn't you?"

"Yes," she replied and then added, with surprising feeling, "The big, ugly ape!"

"Well, he's an ape whose services we happen to need. I want you to be our contact girl with him."

She took her hands away from his forehead. "Look, Jan," she said, "I wouldn't like this job."

"I thought he was very sweet on you once."

"Yes, as he never grew tired of trying to demonstrate to me. The clumsy, overgrown, bumbling baby! The man's disgusting, Jan. His approach to a woman is a child wanting candy and enraged because Mama won't produce it on the instant. I don't mind Jorj-he's just a pipsqueak and it amuses me to see how he frustrates himself. But Willard is...."

"...a bit frightening?" Tregarron finished for her.

"No!"

"Of course you're not afraid," Tregarron purred. "You're our beautiful, clever Caddy, who can do anything she wants with any man, and without whose...."

"Look, Jan, this is different —" she began agitatedly.

"...and without whose services we'd have got exactly nowhere. Clever, subtle Caddy, whose most charming attainment in the ever-appreciative eyes of Papa Jan is her ability to handle every man in the neatest way imaginable and without a trace of real feeling. Kitty Kaddy, who...."

"Very well," she said with a sigh. "I'll do it."

"Of course you will," Jan said, drawing her hands back to his forehead. "And you'll begin right away by getting into your nicest sugar-and-cream war clothes. You and I are going to be the welcoming committee when that ape arrives this afternoon."

"But what about Jorj? He'll want to see Willard."

"That'll be taken care of," Jan assured her.

"And what about the other dozen rocket physicists Jorj asked to come?"

"Don't worry about them."

The President looked inquiringly at his secretary across his littered desk in his homey study at White House, Jr. "So Opperly didn't have any idea how that odd question about Maizie turned up in Section Five?"

His secretary settled his paunch and shook his head. "Or claimed not to. Perhaps he's just the absent-minded prof, perhaps something else. The old feud of the physicists against the Thinkers may be getting hot again. There'll be further investigation."

The President nodded. He obviously had something uncomfortable on his mind. He said uneasily, "Do you think there's any possibility of it being true?"

"What?" asked the secretary guardedly.

"That peculiar hint about Maizie."

The secretary said nothing.

"Mind you, I don't think there is," the President went on hurriedly, his face assuming a sorrowful scowl. "I owe a lot to the Thinkers, both as a private person and as a public figure. Lord, a man has to lean on *something* these days. But just supposing it were true —" he hesitated, as before uttering blasphemy —"that there was a man inside Maizie, what could we do?"

The secretary said stolidly, "The Thinkers won our last election. They chased the Commies out of Iran. We brought them into the Inner Cabinet. We've showered them with public funds." He paused. "We couldn't do a damn thing."

The President nodded with equal conviction, and, not very happily, summed up: "So if anyone should go up against the Thinkers-and I'm afraid I wouldn't want to see that happen, whatever's true-it would have to be a scientist."

Willard Farquar felt his weight change the steps under his feet into an escalator. He cursed under his breath, but let them carry him, a defiant hulk, up to the tall and mystic blue portals, which silently parted when he was five meters away. The escalator changed to a slideway and carried him into a softly gleaming, high-domed room rather like the antechamber of a temple.

"Martian peace to you, Willard Farquar," an invisible voice intoned. "You have entered the Thinkers' Foundation. Please remain on the slideway."

"I want to see Jorj Helmuth," Willard growled loudly.

The slideway carried him into the mouth of a corridor and paused. A dark opening dilated on the wall. "May we take your hat and coat?" a voice asked politely. After a moment the request was repeated, with the addition of, "Just pass them through."

Willard scowled, then fought his way out of his shapeless coat and passed it and his hat through in a lump. Instantly the opening contracted, imprisoning his wrists, and he felt his hands being washed on the other side of the wall.

He gave a great jerk which failed to free his hands from the snugly padded gyves. "Do not be alarmed," the voice advised him. "It is only an esthetic measure. As your hands are laved, invisible radiations are slaughtering all the germs in your body, while more delicate emanations are producing a benign rearrangement of your emotions."

The rather amateurish curses Willard was gritting between his teeth became more sulfurous. His sensations told him that a towel of some sort was being applied to his hands. He wondered if he would be subjected to a face-washing and even greater indignities. Then, just before his wrists were released, he felt-for a moment only, but unmistakably-the soft touch of a girl's hand.

234

That touch, like the mysterious sweet chink of a bell in darkness, brought him a sudden feeling of excitement, wonder.

Yet the feeling was as fleeting as that caused by a lurid advertisement, for as the slideway began to move again, carrying him past a series of depth-pictures and inscriptions celebrating the Thinkers' achievements, his mood of bitter exasperation returned doubled. This place, he told himself, was a plague spot of the disease of magic in an enfeebled and easily infected world. He reminded himself that he was not without resources-the Thinkers must fear or need him, whether because of the Maelzel question or the necessity of producing a nuclear power spaceship. He felt his determination to smash them reaffirmed.

The slideway, having twice turned into an escalator, veered toward an opalescent door, which opened as silently as the one below. The slideway stopped at the threshold. Momentum carried him a couple of steps into the room. He stopped and looked around.

The place was a sybarite's modernistic dream. Sponge-carpeting thick as a mattress and topped with down. Hassocks and couches that looked butter-soft. A domed ceiling of deep glossy blue mimicking the night sky, with the constellations tooled in silver. A wall of niches crammed with statuettes of languorous men, women, beasts. A self-service bar with a score of golden spigots. A depth-TV-screen simulating a great crystal ball. Here and there barbaric studs of hammered gold that might have been push-buttons. A low table set for three with exquisite ware of crystal and gold. An ever-changing scent of resins and flowers.

A smiling fat man clad in pearl gray sports clothes came through one of the curtained archways. Willard recognized Jan Tregarron from his pictures, but did not at once offer to speak to him. Instead he let his gaze wander with an ostentatious contempt around the crammed walls, take in the bar and the set table with its many wine glasses, and finally return to his host.

"And where," he asked with harsh irony, "are the dancing girls?"

The fat man's eyebrows rose. "In there," he said innocently, indicating the second archway. The curtains parted.

"Oh, I *am* sorry," the fat man apologized. "There seems to be only one on duty. I hope that isn't too much at variance with your tastes."

She stood in the archway, demure and lovely in an off-the-bosom frock of pale blue skylon edged in mutated mink. She was smiling the first smile that Willard had ever had from her lips.

"Mr. Willard Farquar," the fat man murmured, "Miss Arkady Simms."

Jorj Helmuth turned from the conference table with its dozen empty chairs to the two mousily pretty secretaries.

"No word from the door yet, Master," one of them ventured to say.

Jorj twisted in his chair, though hardly uncomfortably, since it was a beautiful pneumatic job. His nervousness at having to face the twelve rocket physicists —a feeling which, he had to admit, had been unexpectedly great-was giving way to impatience.

"What's Willard Farquar's phone?" he asked sharply.

One of the secretaries ran through a clutch of desk tapes, then spent some seconds whispering into her throat-mike and listening to answers from the soft-speaker.

"He lives with Morton Opperly, who doesn't have one," she finally told Jorj in scandalized tones.

"Let me see the list," Jorj said. Then, after a bit, "Try Dr. Welcome's place."

This time there were results. Within a quarter of a minute he was handed a phone which he hung expertly on his shoulder.

"This is Dr. Asa Welcome," a reedy voice told him.

"This is Helmuth of the Thinkers' Foundation," Jorj said icily. "Did you get my communication?"

The reedy voice became anxious and placating. "Why, yes, Mr. Helmuth, I did. Very glad to get it too. Sounded most interesting. Very eager to come. But...."

"Yes?"

"Well, I was just about to hop in my 'copter-my son's 'copter-when the other note came."

"What other note?"

"Why, the note calling the meeting off."

"I sent no other note!"

The other voice became acutely embarrassed. "But I considered it to be from you ... or just about the same thing. I really think I had the right to assume that."

"How was it signed?" Jorj rapped.

"Mr. Jan Tregarron."

Jorj broke the connection. He didn't move until a low sound shattered his abstraction and he realized that one of the girls was whispering a call to the door. He handed back the phone and dismissed them. They went in a rustle of jackets and skirtlets, hesitating at the doorway but not quite daring to look back.

He sat motionless a minute longer. Then his hand crept fretfully onto the table and pushed a button. The room darkened and a long section of wall became transparent, revealing a dozen silvery models of spaceships, beautifully executed. He quickly touched another; the models faded and the opposite wall bloomed with an animated cartoon that portrayed with charming humor and detail the designing and construction of a neutron-drive spaceship. A third button, and a depth-picture of deep star-speckled space opened behind the cartoon, showing a section of Earth's surface and in the far distance the tiny ruddy globe of Mars. Slowly a tiny rocket rose from the section of Earth and spread its silvery sails.

He switched off the pictures, keeping the room dark. By a faint table light he dejectedly examined his organizational charts for the neutron-drive project, the long list of books he had boned up on by somno-learning, the concealed table of physical constants and all sorts of other crucial details about rocket physics —a cleverly condensed encyclopedic "pony" to help out his memory on technical points that might have arisen in his discussion with the experts.

He switched out all the lights and slumped forward, blinking his eyes and trying to swallow the lump in his throat. In the dark his memory went seeping back, back, to the day when his math teacher had told him, very superciliously, that the marvelous fantasies he loved to read and hoarded by his bed weren't real science at all, but just a kind of lurid pretense. He had so wanted to be a scientist, and the teacher's contempt had cast a damper on his ambition.

And now that the conference was canceled, would he ever know that it wouldn't have turned out the same way today? That his somno-learning hadn't taken? That his "pony" wasn't good enough? That his ability to handle people extended only to credulous farmer Presidents and mousy girls in skirtlets? Only the test of meeting the experts would have answered those questions.

Tregarron was the one to blame! Tregarron with his sly tyrannical ways, Tregarron with his fear of losing the future to men who really understood theoretics and could handle experts. Tregarron, so used to working by deception that he couldn't see when it became a fault and a crime. Tregarron, who must now be shown the light ... or, failing that, against whom certain steps must be taken.

For perhaps half an hour Jorj sat very still, thinking. Then he turned to the phone and, after some delay, got his party.

"What is it now, Jorj?" Caddy asked impatiently. "Please don't bother me with any of your moods, because I'm tired and my nerves are on edge."

He took a breath. When steps may have to be taken, he thought, one must hold an agent in readiness. "Caddums," he intoned hypnotically, vibrantly. "Caddums...."

The voice at the other end had instantly changed, become submissive, sleepy, suppliant. "Yes, Master?"

Morton Opperly looked up from the sheet of neatly penned equations at Willard Farquar, who had somehow acquired a measure of poise. He neither lumbered restlessly nor grimaced. He removed his coat with a certain dignity and stood solidly before his mentor. He smiled. Granting that he was a bear, one might guess he had just been fed.

"You see?" he said. "They didn't hurt me."

"They didn't hurt you?" Opperly asked softly.

Willard slowly shook his head. His smile broadened.

Opperly put down his pen, folded his hands. "And you're as determined as ever to expose and smash the Thinkers?"

"Of course!" The menacing growl came back into the bear's voice, except that it was touched with a certain pleased luxuriousness. "Only from now on I won't be teasing the zoo animals, and I won't embarrass you by asking any more Maelzel questions. I have reached the objective at which those tactics were aimed. After this I shall bore from within."

"Bore from within," Opperly repeated, frowning. "Now where have I heard that phrase before?" His brow cleared. "Oh, yes," he said listlessly. "Do I understand that you are becoming a Thinker, Willard?"

The other gave him a faintly pitying smile and stretched himself on the couch, gazed at the ceiling. All his movements were deliberate, easy.

"Certainly. That's the only realistic way to smash them. Rise high in their councils. Outtrick all their trickeries. Organize a fifth column. Then *strike!*"

"The end justifying the means, of course," Opperly said.

"Of course. As surely as the desire to stand up justifies your disturbing the air over your head. All action in this world is nothing but means."

Opperly nodded abstractedly. "I wonder if anyone else ever became a Thinker for those same reasons. I wonder if being a Thinker doesn't simply mean that you've decided you have to use lies and tricks as your chief method."

Willard shrugged. "Could be." There was no longer any doubt about the pitying quality of his smile.

Opperly stood up, squaring together his papers. "So you'll be working with Helmuth?"

"Not Helmuth. Tregarron." The bear's smile became cruel. "I'm afraid that Helmuth's career as a Thinker is going to have quite a setback."

"Helmuth," Opperly mused. "Morgenschein once told me a bit about him. A man of some idealism, despite his affiliations. Best of a bad lot. Incidentally, is he the one with whom...."

"...Miss Arkady Simms ran off?" Willard finished without any embarrassment. "Yes, that was Helmuth. But that's all going to be changed now."

Opperly nodded. "Good-by, Willard," he said.

Willard quickly heaved himself up on an elbow. Opperly looked at him for about five seconds, then, without a word, walked out of the room.

The only obvious furnishings in Jan Tregarron's office were a flat-topped desk and a few chairs. Tregarron sat behind the desk, the top of which was completely bare. He looked almost bored, except that his little eyes were smiling. Jorj Helmuth sat across the desk from him, a few feet back, erect and grim-faced, while shadowy in the muted light, Caddy stood against the wall behind Tregarron. She still wore the fur-trimmed skylon frock she'd put on that afternoon. She took no part in the conversation, seemed almost unaware of it.

"So you just went ahead and canceled the conference without consulting me?" Jorj was saying.

"You called it without consulting me." Tregarron playfully wagged a finger. "Shouldn't do that sort of thing, Jorj."

"But I tell you I was completely prepared. I was absolutely sure of my ground."

"I know, I know," Tregarron said lightly. "But it's not the right time for it. I'm the best judge of that."

"When will be the right time?"

Tregarron shrugged. "Look here, Jorj," he said, "every man should stick to his trade, to his forte. Technology isn't ours."

Jorj's lips thinned. "But you know as well as I do that we are going to have to have a nuclear spaceship and actually go to Mars someday."

Tregarron lifted his eyebrows. "Are we?"

"Yes! Just as we're going to have to build a real Maizie. Everything we've done until now have been emergency measures."

"Really?"

Jorj stared at him. "Look here, Jan," he said, gripping his knees with his hands, "you and I are going to have to talk things through."

"Are you quite sure of that?" Jan's voice was very cool. "I have a feeling that it might be best if you said nothing and accepted things as they are."

"No!"

"Very well." Tregarron settled himself in his chair.

"I helped you organize the Thinkers," Jorj said, and waited. "At least, I was your first partner."

Tregarron barely nodded.

"Our basic idea was that the time had come to apply science to the life of man on a large scale, to live rationally and realistically. The only things holding the world back from this all-important step were the ignorance, superstition, and inertia of the average man, and the stuffiness and lack of enterprise of the academic scientists-their worship of facts, even when facts were clearly dangerous.

"Yet we knew that in their deepest hearts the average man and the professionals were both on our side. They wanted the new world visualized by science. They wanted the simplifications and conveniences, the glorious adventures of the human mind and body. They wanted the trips to Mars and into the depths of the human psyche, they wanted the robots and the thinking machines. All they lacked was the nerve to take the first big step-and that was what we supplied.

"It was no time for half measures, for slow and sober plodding. The world was racked by wars and neurosis, in danger of falling into the foulest hands. What was needed was a tremendous and thrilling appeal to the human imagination, an Earth-shaking affirmation of the power of science for good.

"But the men who provided that appeal and affirmation couldn't afford to be cautious. They wouldn't check and double check. They couldn't wait for the grudging and jealous approval of the professionals. They had to use stunts, tricks, fakes —*anything to get over the big point*. Once that had been done, once mankind was headed down the new road, it would be easy enough to give the average man the necessary degree of insight to heal the breach with the professionals, to make good in actuality what had been made good only in pretense.

"Have I stated our position fairly?"

Tregarron's eyes were hooded. "You're the one who's telling it."

"On those general assumptions we established our hold on susceptible leaders and the mob," Jorj went on. "We built Maizie and the Mars rocket and the Mind Bomb. We discovered the wisdom of the Martians. We *sold* the people on the science that the professionals had been too high-toned to advertise or bring into the market place.

"But now that we've succeeded, now that we've made the big point, now that Maizie and Mars and science do rule the average human imagination, the time has come to take the second big step, to let accomplishment catch up with imagination, to implement fantasy with fact.

"Do you suppose I'd ever have gone into this with you, if it hadn't been for the thought of that second big step? Why, I'd have felt dirty and cheap, a mere charlatan-except for the sure conviction that someday everything would be set right. I've devoted my whole life to that conviction, Jan. I've studied and disciplined myself, using every scientific means at my disposal, so that I wouldn't be found lacking when the day came to heal the breach between the Thinkers and the professionals. I've trained myself to be the perfect liaison man for the job.

"Jan, the day's come and I'm the man. I know you've been concentrating on other aspects of our work; you haven't had time to keep up with my side of it. But I'm sure that as soon as you see how carefully I've prepared myself, how completely practical the neutron-drive rocket project is, you'll beg me to go ahead!"

Tregarron smiled at the ceiling for a moment. "Your general idea isn't so bad, Jorj, but your time scale is out of whack and your judgment is a joke. Oh, yes. Every revolutionary wants to see the big change take place in his lifetime. Tcha! It's as if he were watching evolutionary vaudeville and wanted the Ape-to-Man Act over in twenty minutes.

"Time for the second big step? Jorj, the average man's exactly what he was ten years ago, except that he's got a new god. More than ever he thinks of Mars as a Hollywood paradise, with wise men and yummy princesses. Maizie is Mama magnified a million times. As for professional scientists, they're more jealous and stuffy than ever. All they'd like to do is turn the clock back to a genteel dream world of quiet quadrangles and caps and gowns, where every commoner bows to the passing scholar.

"Maybe in ten thousand years we'll be ready for the second big step. Maybe. Meanwhile, as should be, the clever will rule the stupid for their own good. The realists will rule the dreamers. Those with free hands will rule those who have deliberately handcuffed themselves with taboos.

"Secondly, your judgment. Did you actually think you could have bossed those professionals, kept your mental footing in the intellectual melee? You a nuclear physicist? A rocket scientist? Why, it's—Take it easy now, boy, and listen to me. They'd have torn you to pieces in twenty minutes and glad of the chance! You baffle me, Jorj. You know that Maizie and the Mars rocket and all that are fakes, yet you believe in your somno-learning and consciousness-expansion and optimism-pumping like the veriest yokel. I wouldn't be surprised to hear you'd taken up ESP and hypnotism. I think you should take stock of yourself and get a new slant. It's overdue."

He leaned back. Jorj's face had become a mask. His eyes did not flicker from Tregarron's, yet there was a subtle change in his expression. Behind Tregarron, Caddy swayed as if in a sudden gust of intangible wind and took a silent step forward from the wall.

"That's your honest opinion?" Jorj asked, very quietly.

"It's more than that," Tregarron told him, just as unmelodramatically. "It's orders."

Jorj stood up purposefully. "Very well," he said. "In that case I have to tell you that —"

Casually, but with no wasted motion, Tregarron slipped an ultrasonic pistol from under the desk and laid it on the empty top.

"No," he said, "let me tell you something. I was afraid this would happen and I made preparations. If you've studied your Nazi, Fascist and Soviet history, you know what happens to old revolutionaries who don't move with the times. But I'm not going to be too harsh. I have a couple of the boys waiting outside. They'll take you by 'copter to the field, then by jet to New Mex. Bright and early tomorrow morning, Jorj, you're leaving on a trip to Mars."

Jorj hardly reacted to the words. Caddy was two steps nearer Tregarron.

"I decided Mars would be the best place for you," the fat man continued. "The robot controls will be arranged so that your 'visit' to Mars lasts two years. Perhaps in that time you will have learned wisdom, such as realizing that the big liar must never fall for his own big lie.

"Meanwhile, there will have to be a replacement for you. I have in mind a person who may prove peculiarly worthy to occupy your position, with all its perquisites. A person who seems to understand that force and desire are the motive powers of life, and that anyone who believes the big lie proves himself strictly a jerk."

Caddy was standing behind Tregarron now, her half-closed, sleepy eyes fixed on Jorj's.

"His name is Willard Farquar. You see, I too believe in cooperating with the scientists, Jorj, but by subversion rather than conference. My idea is to offer the hand of friendship to a selected few of them—the hand of friendship with a nice big bribe in it." He smiled. "You were a good man, Jorj, for the early days, when we needed a publicist with catchy ideas about Mind Bombs, ray guns, plastic helmets, fancy sweaters, space brassieres, and all that other corn. Now we can afford a soldier."

Jorj moistened his lips.

"We'll have a neat explanation of what's happened to you. Callers will be informed that you've gone on an extended visit to imbibe the wisdom of the Martians."

Jorj whispered, "Caddums."

Caddy leaned forward. Her arms snaked down Tregarron's, as if to imprison his wrists. But instead she reached out and took the ultrasonic pistol and put it in Tregarron's right hand. Then she looked up at Jorj with eyes that were very bright.

She said very sweetly and sympathetically, "Poor Superman."

Bread Overhead

The Staff of Life suddenly and
disconcertingly sprouted wings
—and mankind had to eat crow!

As a blisteringly hot but guaranteed weather-controlled future summer day dawned on the Mississippi Valley, the walking mills of Puffy Products ("Spike to Loaf in One Operation!") began to tread delicately on their centipede legs across the wheat fields of Kansas.

The walking mills resembled fat metal serpents, rather larger than those Chinese paper dragons animated by files of men in procession. Sensory robot devices in their noses informed them that the waiting wheat had reached ripe perfection.

As they advanced, their heads swung lazily from side to side, very much like snakes, gobbling the yellow grain. In their throats, it was threshed, the chaff bundled and burped aside for pickup by the crawl trucks of a chemical corporation, the kernels quick-dried and blown along into the mighty chests of the machines. There the tireless mills ground the kernels to flour, which was instantly sifted, the bran being packaged and dropped like the chaff for pickup. A cluster of tanks which gave the metal serpents a decidedly humpbacked appearance added water, shortening, salt and other ingredients, some named and some not. The dough was at the same time infused with gas from a tank conspicuously labeled "Carbon Dioxide" ("No Yeast Creatures in Your Bread!").

Thus instantly risen, the dough was clipped into loaves and shot into radionic ovens forming the midsections of the metal serpents. There the bread was baked in a matter of seconds, a fierce heat-front browning the crusts, and the piping-hot loaves sealed in transparent plastic bearing the proud Puffyloaf emblem (two cherubs circling a floating loaf) and ejected onto the delivery platform at each serpent's rear end, where a cluster of pickup machines, like hungry piglets, snatched at the loaves with hygienic claws.

A few loaves would be hurried off for the day's consumption, the majority stored for winter in strategically located mammoth deep freezes.

But now, behold a wonder! As loaves began to appear on the delivery platform of the first walking mill to get into action, they did not linger on the conveyor belt, but rose gently into the air and slowly traveled off down-wind across the hot rippling fields.

The robot claws of the pickup machines clutched in vain, and, not noticing the difference, proceeded carefully to stack emptiness, tier by tier. One errant loaf, rising more sluggishly than its fellows, was snagged by a thrusting claw. The machine paused, clumsily wiped off the injured loaf, set it aside-where it bobbed on one corner, unable to take off again-and went back to the work of storing nothingness.

A flock of crows rose from the trees of a nearby shelterbelt as the flight of loaves approached. The crows swooped to investigate and then suddenly scattered, screeching in panic.

The helicopter of a hangoverish Sunday traveler bound for Wichita shied very similarly from the brown fliers and did not return for a second look.

A black-haired housewife spied them over her back fence, crossed herself and grabbed her walkie-talkie from the laundry basket. Seconds later, the yawning correspondent of a regional newspaper was jotting down the lead of a humorous news story which, recalling the old flying-saucer scares, stated that now apparently bread was to be included in the mad aerial tea party.

The congregation of an open-walled country church, standing up to recite the most familiar of Christian prayers, had just reached the petition for daily sustenance, when a sub-flight of the loaves, either forced down by a vagrant wind or lacking the natural buoyancy of the rest, came coasting silently as the sunbeams between the graceful pillars at the altar end of the building.

Meanwhile, the main flight, now augmented by other bread flocks from scores and hundreds of walking mills that had started work a little later, mounted slowly and majestically into the cirrus-flecked upper air, where a steady wind was blowing strongly toward the east.

About one thousand miles farther on in that direction, where a cluster of stratosphere-tickling towers marked the location of the metropolis of NewNew York, a tender scene was being enacted in the pressurized penthouse managerial suite of Puffy Products. Megera Winterly, Secretary in Chief to the Managerial Board and referred to by her underlings as the Blonde Icicle, was dealing with the advances of Roger ("Racehorse") Snedden, Assistant Secretary to the Board and often indistinguishable from any passing office boy.

"Why don't you jump out the window, Roger, remembering to shut the airlock after you?" the Golden Glacier said in tones not unkind. "When are your high-strung, thoroughbred nerves going to accept the fact that I would never consider marriage with a business inferior? You have about as much chance as a starving Ukrainian kulak now that Moscow's clapped on the interdict."

Roger's voice was calm, although his eyes were feverishly bright, as he replied, "A lot of things are going to be different around here, Meg, as soon as the Board is forced to admit that only my quick thinking made it possible to bring the name of Puffyloaf in front of the whole world."

"Puffyloaf could do with a little of that," the business girl observed judiciously. "The way sales have been plummeting, it won't be long before the Government deeds our desks to the managers of Fairy Bread and asks us to take the Big Jump. But just where does your quick thinking come into this, Mr. Snedden? You can't be referring to the helium-that was Rose Thinker's brainwave."

She studied him suspiciously. "You've birthed another promotional bumble, Roger. I can see it in your eyes. I only hope it's not as big a one as when you put the Martian ambassador on 3D and he thanked you profusely for the gross of Puffyloaves, assuring you that he'd never slept on a softer mattress in all his life on two planets."

"Listen to me, Meg. Today-yes, today! —you're going to see the Board eating out of my hand."

"Hah! I guarantee you won't have any fingers left. You're bold enough now, but when Mr. Gryce and those two big machines come through that door —"

"Now wait a minute, Meg —"

"Hush! They're coming now!"

Roger leaped three feet in the air, but managed to land without a sound and edged toward his stool. Through the dilating iris of the door strode Phineas T. Gryce, flanked by Rose Thinker and Tin Philosopher.

The man approached the conference table in the center of the room with measured pace and gravely expressionless face. The rose-tinted machine on his left did a couple of impulsive pirouettes on the way and twittered a greeting to Meg and Roger. The other machine quietly took the third of the high seats and lifted a claw at Meg, who now occupied a stool twice the height of Roger's.

"Miss Winterly, please-our theme."

The Blonde Icicle's face thawed into a little-girl smile as she chanted bubblingly:

"Made up of tiny wheaten motes
And reinforced with sturdy oats,
It rises through the air and floats —
The bread on which all Terra dotes!"

"Thank You, Miss Winterly," said Tin Philosopher. "Though a purely figurative statement, that bit about rising through the air always gets me-here." He rapped his midsection, which gave off a high musical *clang*.

"Ladies —" he inclined his photocells toward Rose Thinker and Meg —"and gentlemen. This is a historic occasion in Old Puffy's long history, the inauguration of the helium-filled loaf ('So Light It Almost Floats Away!') in which that inert and heaven-aspiring gas replaces old-fashioned carbon dioxide. Later, there will be kudos for Rose Thinker, whose bright relays genius-sparked the idea, and also for Roger Snedden, who took care of the details.

"By the by, Racehorse, that was a brilliant piece of work getting the helium out of the government-they've been pretty stuffy lately about their monopoly. But first I want to throw wide the casement in your minds that opens on the Long View of Things."

Rose Thinker spun twice on her chair and opened her photocells wide. Tin Philosopher coughed to limber up the diaphragm of his speaker and continued:

"Ever since the first cave wife boasted to her next-den neighbor about the superior paleness and fluffiness of her tortillas, mankind has sought lighter, whiter bread. Indeed, thinkers wiser than myself have equated the whole upward course of culture with this poignant quest. Yeast was a wonderful discovery-for its primitive day. Sifting the bran and wheat germ from the flour was an even more important advance. Early bleaching and preserving chemicals played their humble parts.

"For a while, barbarous faddists-blind to the deeply spiritual nature of bread, which is recognized by all great religions-held back our march toward perfection with their hair-splitting insistence on the vitamin content of the wheat germ, but their case collapsed when tasteless colorless substitutes were triumphantly synthesized and introduced into the loaf, which for flawless purity, unequaled airiness and sheer intangible goodness was rapidly becoming mankind's supreme gustatory experience."

"I wonder what the stuff tastes like," Rose Thinker said out of a clear sky.

"I wonder what taste tastes like," Tin Philosopher echoed dreamily. Recovering himself, he continued:

"Then, early in the twenty-first century, came the epochal researches of Everett Whitehead, Puffyloaf chemist, culminating in his paper 'The Structural Bubble in Cereal Masses' and making possible the baking of airtight bread twenty times stronger (for its weight) than steel and of a lightness that would have been incredible even to the advanced chemist-bakers of the twentieth century —a lightness so great that, besides forming the backbone of our own promotion, it has forever since been capitalized on by our conscienceless competitors of Fairy Bread with their enduring slogan: 'It Makes Ghost Toast'."

"That's a beaut, all right, that ecto-dough blurb," Rose Thinker admitted, bugging her photocells sadly. "Wait a sec. How about? —

"There'll be bread
Overhead
When you're dead —
It is said."

Phineas T. Gryce wrinkled his nostrils at the pink machine as if he smelled her insulation smoldering. He said mildly, "A somewhat unhappy jingle, Rose, referring as it does to the end of the customer as consumer. Moreover, we shouldn't overplay the figurative 'rises through the air' angle. What inspired you?"

She shrugged. "I don't know-oh, yes, I do. I was remembering one of the workers' songs we machines used to chant during the Big Strike —

> "Work and pray,
> Live on hay.
> You'll get pie
> In the sky
> When you die —
> It's a lie!

"I don't know why we chanted it," she added. "We didn't want pie-or hay, for that matter. And machines don't pray, except Tibetan prayer wheels."

Phineas T. Gryce shook his head. "Labor relations are another topic we should stay far away from. However, dear Rose, I'm glad you keep trying to outjingle those dirty crooks at Fairy Bread." He scowled, turning back his attention to Tin Philosopher. "I get whopping mad, Old Machine, whenever I hear that other slogan of theirs, the discriminatory one —'Untouched by Robot Claws.' Just because they employ a few filthy androids in their factories!"

Tin Philosopher lifted one of his own sets of bright talons. "Thanks, P.T. But to continue my historical resume, the next great advance in the baking art was the substitution of purified carbon dioxide, recovered from coal smoke, for the gas generated by yeast organisms indwelling in the dough and later killed by the heat of baking, their corpses remaining *in situ*. But even purified carbon dioxide is itself a rather repugnant gas, a product of metabolism whether fast or slow, and forever associated with those life processes which are obnoxious to the fastidious."

Here the machine shuddered with delicate clinkings. "Therefore, we of Puffyloaf are taking today what may be the ultimate step toward purity: we are aerating our loaves with the noble gas helium, an element which remains virginal in the face of all chemical temptations and whose slim molecules are eleven times lighter than obese carbon dioxide-yes, noble uncontaminable helium, which, if it be a kind of ash, is yet the ash only of radioactive burning, accomplished or initiated entirely on the Sun, a safe 93 million miles from this planet. Let's have a cheer for the helium loaf!"

Without changing expression, Phineas T. Gryce rapped the table thrice in solemn applause, while the others bowed their heads.

"Thanks, T.P.," P.T. then said. "And now for the Moment of Truth. Miss Winterly, how is the helium loaf selling?"

The business girl clapped on a pair of earphones and whispered into a lapel mike. Her gaze grew abstracted as she mentally translated flurries of brief squawks into coherent messages. Suddenly a single vertical furrow creased her matchlessly smooth brow.

"It isn't, Mr. Gryce!" she gasped in horror. "Fairy Bread is outselling Puffyloaves by an infinity factor. So far this morning, *there has not been one single delivery of Puffyloaves to any sales spot*! Complaints about non-delivery are pouring in from both walking stores and sessile shops."

"Mr. Snedden!" Gryce barked. "What bug in the new helium process might account for this delay?"

Roger was on his feet, looking bewildered. "I can't imagine, sir, unless-just possibly-there's been some unforeseeable difficulty involving the new metal-foil wrappers."

"Metal-foil wrappers? Were *you* responsible for those?"

"Yes, sir. Last-minute recalculations showed that the extra lightness of the new loaf might be great enough to cause drift during stackage. Drafts in stores might topple sales pyramids. Metal-foil wrappers, by their added weight, took care of the difficulty."

"And you ordered them without consulting the Board?"

"Yes, sir. There was hardly time and —"

"Why, you fool! I noticed that order for metal-foil wrappers, assumed it was some sub-secretary's mistake, and canceled it last night!"

Roger Snedden turned pale. "You canceled it?" he quavered. "And told them to go back to the lighter plastic wrappers?"

"Of course! Just what is behind all this, Mr. Snedden? *What* recalculations were you trusting, when our physicists had demonstrated months ago that the helium loaf was safely stackable in light airs and gentle breezes-winds up to Beaufort's scale 3. *Why* should a change from heavier to lighter wrappers result in complete non-delivery?"

Roger Snedden's paleness became tinged with an interesting green. He cleared his throat and made strange gulping noises. Tin Philosopher's photocells focused on him calmly, Rose Thinker's with unfeigned excitement. P.T. Gryce's frown grew blacker by the moment, while Megera Winterly's Venus-mask showed an odd dawning of dismay and awe. She was getting new squawks in her earphones.

"Er ...ah ...er...." Roger said in winning tones. "Well, you see, the fact is that I...."

"Hold it," Meg interrupted crisply. "Triple-urgent from Public Relations, Safety Division. Tulsa-Topeka aero-express makes emergency landing after being buffeted in encounter with vast flight of objects first described as brown birds, although no failures reported in airway's electronic anti-bird fences. After grounding safely near Emporia-no fatalities-pilot's windshield found thinly plastered with soft white-and-brown material. Emblems on plastic wrappers embedded in material identify it incontrovertibly as an undetermined number of Puffyloaves cruising at three thousand feet!"

Eyes and photocells turned inquisitorially upon Roger Snedden. He went from green to Puffyloaf white and blurted: "All right, I did it, but it was the only way out! Yesterday morning, due to the Ukrainian crisis, the government stopped sales and deliveries of all strategic stockpiled materials, including helium gas. Puffy's new program of advertising and promotion, based on the lighter loaf, was already rolling. There was only one thing to do, there being only one other gas comparable in lightness to helium. I diverted the necessary quantity of hydrogen gas from the Hydrogenated Oils Section of our Magna-Margarine Division and substituted it for the helium."

"You substituted ...hydrogen ...for the ...helium?" Phineas T. Gryce faltered in low mechanical tones, taking four steps backward.

"Hydrogen is twice as light as helium," Tin Philosopher remarked judiciously.

"And many times cheaper-did you know that?" Roger countered feebly. "Yes, I substituted hydrogen. The metal-foil wrapping would have added just enough weight to counteract the greater buoyancy of the hydrogen loaf. But —"

"So, when this morning's loaves began to arrive on the delivery platforms of the walking mills...." Tin Philosopher left the remark unfinished.

"Exactly," Roger agreed dismally.

"Let me ask you, Mr. Snedden," Gryce interjected, still in low tones, "if you expected people to jump to the kitchen ceiling for their Puffybread after taking off the metal wrapper, or reach for the sky if they happened to unwrap the stuff outdoors?"

"Mr. Gryce," Roger said reproachfully, "you have often assured me that what people do with Puffybread after they buy it is no concern of ours."

"I seem to recall," Rose Thinker chirped somewhat unkindly, "that dictum was created to answer inquiries after Roger put the famous sculptures-in-miniature artist on 3D and he testified that he always molded his first attempts from Puffybread, one jumbo loaf squeezing down to approximately the size of a peanut."

Her photocells dimmed and brightened. "Oh, boy-hydrogen! The loaf's unwrapped. After a while, in spite of the crust-seal, a little oxygen diffuses in. An explosive mixture. Housewife in curlers and kimono pops a couple slices in the toaster. Boom!"

The three human beings in the room winced.

Tin Philosopher kicked her under the table, while observing, "So you see, Roger, that the non-delivery of the hydrogen loaf carries some consolations. And I must confess that one aspect of the affair gives me great satisfaction, not as a Board Member but as a private machine. You have at last made a reality of the 'rises through the air' part of Puffybread's theme. They can't ever take that away from you. By now, half the inhabitants of the Great Plains must have observed our flying loaves rising high."

Phineas T. Gryce shot a frightened look at the west windows and found his full voice.

"Stop the mills!" he roared at Meg Winterly, who nodded and whispered urgently into her mike.

"A sensible suggestion," Tin Philosopher said. "But it comes a trifle late in the day. If the mills are still walking and grinding, approximately seven billion Puffyloaves are at this moment cruising eastward over Middle America. Remember that a six-month supply for deep-freeze is involved and that the current consumption of bread, due to its matchless airiness, is eight and one-half loaves per person per day."

Phineas T. Gryce carefully inserted both hands into his scanty hair, feeling for a good grip. He leaned menacingly toward Roger who, chin resting on the table, regarded him apathetically.

"Hold it!" Meg called sharply. "Flock of multiple-urgents coming in. News Liaison: information bureaus swamped with flying-bread inquiries. Aero-expresslines: Clear our airways or face law suit. U. S. Army: Why do loaves flame when hit by incendiary bullets? U. S. Customs: If bread intended for export, get export license or face prosecution. Russian Consulate in Chicago: Advise on destination of bread-lift. And some Kansas church is accusing us of a hoax inciting to blasphemy, of faking miracles —I don't know *why*."

The business girl tore off her headphones. "Roger Snedden," she cried with a hysteria that would have dumfounded her underlings, "you've brought the name of Puffyloaf in front of the whole world, all right! Now do something about the situation!"

Roger nodded obediently. But his pallor increased a shade, the pupils of his eyes disappeared under the upper lids, and his head burrowed beneath his forearms.

"Oh, boy," Rose Thinker called gayly to Tin Philosopher, "this looks like the start of a real crisis session! Did you remember to bring spare batteries?"

Meanwhile, the monstrous flight of Puffyloaves, filling midwestern skies as no small fliers had since the days of the passenger pigeon, soared steadily onward.

Private fliers approached the brown and glistening bread-front in curiosity and dipped back in awe. Aero-expresslines organized sightseeing flights along the flanks. Planes of the government forestry and agricultural services and 'copters bearing the Puffyloaf emblem hovered on the fringes, watching developments and waiting for orders. A squadron of supersonic fighters hung menacingly above.

The behavior of birds varied considerably. Most fled or gave the loaves a wide berth, but some bolder species, discovering the minimal nutritive nature of the translucent brown objects, attacked them furiously with beaks and claws. Hydrogen diffusing slowly through the crusts had now distended most of the sealed plastic wrappers into little balloons, which ruptured, when pierced, with disconcerting *pops*.

Below, neck-craning citizens crowded streets and back yards, cranks and cultists had a field day, while local and national governments raged indiscriminately at Puffyloaf and at each other.

Rumors that a fusion weapon would be exploded in the midst of the flying bread drew angry protests from conservationists and a flood of telefax pamphlets titled "H-Loaf or H-bomb?"

Stockholm sent a mystifying note of praise to the United Nations Food Organization.

Delhi issued nervous denials of a millet blight that no one had heard of until that moment and reaffirmed India's ability to feed her population with no outside help except the usual.

Radio Moscow asserted that the Kremlin would brook no interference in its treatment of the Ukrainians, jokingly referred to the flying bread as a farce perpetrated by mad internationalists inhabiting Cloud Cuckoo Land, added contradictory references to airborne bread booby-trapped by Capitalist gangsters, and then fell moodily silent on the whole topic.

Radio Venus reported to its winged audience that Earth's inhabitants were establishing food depots in the upper air, preparatory to taking up permanent aerial residence "such as we have always enjoyed on Venus."

New York made feverish preparations for the passage of the flying bread. Tickets for sight-seeing space in skyscrapers were sold at high prices; cold meats and potted spreads were hawked to viewers with the assurance that they would be able to snag the bread out of the air and enjoy a historic sandwich.

Phineas T. Gryce, escaping from his own managerial suite, raged about the city, demanding general cooperation in the stretching of great nets between the skyscrapers to trap the errant loaves. He was captured by Tin Philosopher, escaped again, and was found posted with oxygen mask and submachine gun on the topmost spire of Puffyloaf Tower, apparently determined to shoot down the loaves as they appeared and before they involved his company in more trouble with Customs and the State Department.

Recaptured by Tin Philosopher, who suffered only minor bullet holes, he was given a series of mild electroshocks and returned to the conference table, calm and clear-headed as ever.

But the bread flight, swinging away from a hurricane moving up the Atlantic coast, crossed a clouded-in Boston by night and disappeared into a high Atlantic overcast, also thereby evading a local storm generated by the Weather Department in a last-minute effort to bring down or at least disperse the H-loaves.

Warnings and counterwarnings by Communist and Capitalist governments seriously interfered with military trailing of the flight during this period and it was actually lost in touch with for several days.

At scattered points, seagulls were observed fighting over individual loaves floating down from the gray roof-that was all.

A mood of spirituality strongly tinged with humor seized the people of the world. Ministers sermonized about the bread, variously interpreting it as a call to charity, a warning against gluttony, a parable of the evanescence of all earthly things, and a divine joke. Husbands and wives, facing each other across their walls of breakfast toast, burst into laughter. The mere sight of a loaf of bread anywhere was enough to evoke guffaws. An obscure sect, having as part of its creed the injunction "Don't take yourself so damn seriously," won new adherents.

The bread flight, rising above an Atlantic storm widely reported to have destroyed it, passed unobserved across a foggy England and rose out of the overcast only over Mittel-europa. The loaves had at last reached their maximum altitude.

The Sun's rays beat through the rarified air on the distended plastic wrappers, increasing still further the pressure of the confined hydrogen. They burst by the millions and tens of millions. A high-flying Bulgarian evangelist, who had happened to mistake the up-lever for the east-lever in the cockpit of his flier and who was the sole witness of the event, afterward described it as "the foaming of a sea of diamonds, the crackle of God's knuckles."

By the millions and tens of millions, the loaves coasted down into the starving Ukraine. Shaken by a week of humor that threatened to invade even its own grim precincts, the Kremlin made a sudden about-face. A new policy was instituted of communal ownership of the produce of communal farms, and teams of hunger-fighters and caravans of trucks loaded with pumpernickel were dispatched into the Ukraine.

World distribution was given to a series of photographs showing peasants queueing up to trade scavenged Puffyloaves for traditional black bread, recently aerated itself but still extra solid by comparison, the rate of exchange demanded by the Moscow teams being twenty Puffyloaves to one of pumpernickel.

Another series of photographs, picturing chubby workers' children being blown to bits by booby-trapped bread, was quietly destroyed.

Congratulatory notes were exchanged by various national governments and world organizations, including the Brotherhood of Free Business Machines. The great bread flight was over, though for several weeks afterward scattered falls of loaves occurred, giving rise to a new folk-lore of manna among lonely Arabian tribesmen, and in one well-authenticated instance in Tibet, sustaining life in a party of mountaineers cut off by a snow slide.

Back in NewNew York, the managerial board of Puffy Products slumped in utter collapse around the conference table, the long crisis session at last ended. Empty coffee cartons were scattered around the chairs of the three humans, dead batteries around those of the two machines. For a while, there was no movement whatsoever. Then Roger Snedden reached out wearily for the earphones where Megera Winterly had hurled them down, adjusted them to his head, pushed a button and listened apathetically.

After a bit, his gaze brightened. He pushed more buttons and listened more eagerly. Soon he was sitting tensely upright on his stool, eyes bright and lower face all a-smile, muttering terse comments and questions into the lapel mike torn from Meg's fair neck.

The others, reviving, watched him, at first dully, then with quickening interest, especially when he jerked off the earphones with a happy shout and sprang to his feet.

"Listen to this!" he cried in a ringing voice. "As a result of the worldwide publicity, Puffy-loaves are outselling Fairy Bread three to one-and that's just the old carbon-dioxide stock from our freezers! It's almost exhausted, but the government, now that the Ukrainian crisis is over, has taken the ban off helium and will also sell us stockpiled wheat if we need it. We can have our walking mills burrowing into the wheat caves in a matter of hours!

"But that isn't all! The far greater demand everywhere is for Puffyloaves that will actually float. Public Relations, Child Liaison Division, reports that the kiddies are making their mothers' lives miserable about it. If only we can figure out some way to make hydrogen non-explosive or the helium loaf float just a little —"

"I'm sure we can take care of that quite handily," Tin Philosopher interrupted briskly. "Puffy-loaf has kept it a corporation secret-even you've never been told about it-but just before he went crazy, Everett Whitehead discovered a way to make bread using only half as much flour as we do in the present loaf. Using this secret technique, which we've been saving for just such an emergency, it will be possible to bake a helium loaf as buoyant in every respect as the hydrogen loaf."

"Good!" Roger cried. "We'll tether 'em on strings and sell 'em like balloons. No mother-child shopping team will leave the store without a cluster. Buying bread balloons will be the big event of the day for kiddies. It'll make the carry-home shopping load lighter too! I'll issue orders at once —"

He broke off, looking at Phineas T. Gryce, said with quiet assurance, "Excuse me, sir, if I seem to be taking too much upon myself."

"Not at all, son; go straight ahead," the great manager said approvingly. "You're" —he laughed in anticipation of getting off a memorable remark —"rising to the challenging situation like a genuine Puffyloaf."

Megera Winterly looked from the older man to the younger. Then in a single leap she was upon Roger, her arms wrapped tightly around him.

"My sweet little ever-victorious, self-propelled monkey wrench!" she crooned in his ear. Roger looked fatuously over her soft shoulder at Tin Philosopher who, as if moved by some similar feeling, reached over and touched claws with Rose Thinker.

This, however, was what he telegraphed silently to his fellow machine across the circuit so completed:

"Good-o, Rosie! That makes another victory for robot-engineered world unity, though you almost gave us away at the start with that 'bread overhead' jingle. We've struck another blow against the next world war, in which–as we know only too well! —we machines would suffer the most. Now if we can only arrange, say, a fur-famine in Alaska and a migration of long-haired Siberian lemmings across Behring Straits ...we'd have to swing the Japanese Current up there so it'd be warm enough for the little fellows....Anyhow, Rosie, with a spot of help from the Brotherhood, those humans will paint themselves into the peace corner yet."

Meanwhile, he and Rose Thinker quietly watched the Blonde Icicle melt.

Bullet with His Name

Before passing judgment, just ask yourself
one question: Would you like answering for
humanity any better than Ernie Meeker did?

The Invisible Being shifted his anchorage a bit in Earth's gravitational field, which felt like a push rather than a pull to him, and said, "This featherless biped seems to satisfy Galaxy Center's requirements. I'd say he's a suitable recipient for the Gifts."

His Coadjutor, equally invisible and negatively massed, chewed that over. "Mature by his length and mass. Artificial plumage neither overly gaudy nor utterly drab indicating median social level, which is confirmed by the size of his bachelor nest. Inward maps of his environment not fantastically inaccurate. Feelings reasonably meshed-at least neither volcanic nor frozen. Thoughts and values in reasonable order. Yes, I agree, a satisfactory test subject. Except...."

"Except what?"

"Except we can never be sure of that 'reasonable' part."

"Of course not! Thank your stars *that's* beyond the reach of Galaxy Center's keenest telepathy, or even ours on the spot. Otherwise you and I'd be out of a job."

"And have to scheme up some other excuse for free-touring the Cosmos with backtracking permitted."

"Exactly!" The Being and his Coadjutor understood each other very well and were the best of friends. "Well, how many Gifts would you suggest for the test?"

"How about two Little and one Big?" the Coadjutor ventured.

"Umm ... statistically adequate but spiritually unsatisfying. Remember, the fate of his race hangs on his reactions to them. I'd be inclined to increase your suggestion by one each and add a Great."

"No-at least I question the last. After all, the Great Gifts aren't as important, really, as the Big Gifts. Besides...."

"Besides what? Come on, spit it out!" The Invisible Being was the bluff, blunt type.

"Well," said his less hearty but unswervingly honest companion, "I'm always afraid that you'll use the granting of a Great Gift as an excuse for some sardonic trick-that you'll put a sting in its tail."

"And why shouldn't I, if I want to? Snakes have stings in their tails (or do they on this planet?) and I'm a sort of snake. If he fails the test, he fails. And aren't both of us malicious, plaguing spirits, eager to knock holes in the inward armor of provincial entities? It's in the nature of our job. But we can argue about that in due course. What Little Gifts would you suggest?"

"That's something I want to talk about. Many of the Little Gifts are already well within his race's reach, if not his. After all, they've already got atomic power."

"Which as you very well know scores them nothing one way or the other on a Galaxy Center test. We're agreed on the nature and the number of our Gifts-three Little, two Big, and one Great?"

"Yes," his Coadjutor responded resignedly.

"And we're agreed on our subject?"

"Yes to that too."

"All right, then, let's get started. This isn't the only solar system we have to visit on this circuit."

Ernie Meeker-of Chicago, Illinois, U.S. of A., Occident, Terra, Sol, Starswarm 37, Rim Sector, Milky Way Galaxy-rubbed his chin and slanted across the street to a drugstore.

"Package of blades. Double edge. Five. Cheapest."

At one point during the transaction, the clerk lost sight of the tiny packet he'd placed on the coin-whitened glass between them. He gave a suspicious look, as if the customer had palmed them.

Ernie blinked. After a moment, he pointed toward the center of the counter.

"There they are," he said, dropping a coin beside them.

The clerk's face didn't get any less suspicious. Customer who could sneak something without your seeing could sneak it back the same way. He rang up the sale and closed the register fast.

Ernie Meeker went home and shaved. Five days-and-shaves-later, he pushed the first blade, uncomfortably dull now, through the tiny slot beside the bathroom mirror. He unwrapped the second blade from the packet.

Five shaves later, he cut himself under the chin with the second blade, although he was drawing it as gently through his soaped beard as if it were only his second shave with it, or at most his third. He looked at it sourly and checked the packet. Wouldn't have been the first time he'd absentmindedly changed blades ahead of schedule.

But there were still three blades in their waxed wrappings.

Maybe, he thought, he'd still had one of the blades from the last packet and shuffled it into this series.

Or maybe-although the manufacturers undoubtedly had inspectors to prevent it from happening-he'd got a decent blade for once.

Two or three shaves later, it still seemed as sharp as ever, or almost so.

"Funny thing," he remarked to Bill at lunch, "sometimes you get a blade that shaves a lot better. Looks exactly like the others, but shaves better. Or worse sometimes, of course."

"And sometimes," his office mate said, "you wear out a blade fast by not soaking your beard enough. For me, one shave with a stiff beard and the blade's through. On the other hand, if you're careful to soak your beard real good-four, five minutes at least-have the water steaming hot, get the soap really into it, one blade can last a long time."

"That's true, all right," Ernie agreed, trying to remember how well he had been soaking his beard lately. Shaving was a good topic for light conversation, warm and agreeable, like most bathroom and kitchen topics.

But next morning in the bathroom, looking at the reflection of his unremarkable face, there was something chilly in his feelings that he couldn't quite analyze. He flipped his razor open and suspiciously studied the bright metal wafer, then flipped it closed with an irritated shrug.

As he shaved, it occurred to him that a good detective-story murder method would be to substitute a very sharp razor blade for one the victim knew was extremely dull. He'd whip it across his throat, putting a lot of muscle into the stroke to get through the tangle, and —urrk!

Ridiculous, of course. Wouldn't work except with a straight razor. Wouldn't even work with a straight razor, unless ...oh, well.

He told himself the blade was noticeably duller today.

Next morning, he was still using the freak blade, but with a persistent though very slight uneasiness. Things should behave as you expected them to, in accordance with their flimsy souls, he told himself at the barely conscious level. Men should die, hearts should break, girls should tell, nations perish, curtains get dirty, milk sour ...and razor blades grow dull. It was the comfortable, expected, reassuring way.

He told himself the blade was duller still. Just a bit.

The third morning, face lathered, he flipped open the razor and lifted it out.

"You're through," he said to it silently. "I've had the experience before of getting bum shaves by trying to save a penny by pretending to myself that a wornout blade was still sharp enough, when it obviously couldn't be. Or maybe —" he grinned a little wryly —"maybe I'd almost get one more shave out of you and then you'd fall to pieces like the Wonderful One Horse Shay and leave me with a chin full of steel porcupine quills. No, thanks."

So Ernie Meeker pushed through the little slot beside the mirror and heard tinkle faintly down and away the first of the Little Gifts, the Everlasting Razor Blade. One hundred and fifty thousand years later, it turned up, bright and shining, in the midst of a small knob of red iron oxide excavated by an archeological expedition of multi-brachs from Antares Gamma. Those wise history-mad beings handed it about wonderingly, from tentacle to impatient tentacle.

That day, Ernie felt a little sick, somehow. After dinner, he decided it was the Thuringer sausage he'd eaten at lunch. He hurried up to the bathroom with a spoon, but as he clutched the box of bicarbonate of soda, preparatory to plunging the spoon into it, it seemed to him that the box said distinctly, in a small inward-outward voice:

"No, no, no!"

Ernie sat down suddenly on the toilet seat. The spoon rattled against the porcelain finish of the washbowl as he laid it down. He held the box firmly in both hands and studied it.

Size, shape, materials, blue color, closure, etc., were exactly as they should be. But the white lettering on the blue background read:

AQUEOUS FUEL CATALYST

Dissociates H_2O into hemi-quasi-stable H and O, furnishing a serviceable fuel-and-oxydizer mix for most motorcycles, automobiles, trucks, motorboats, airplanes, stationary motors, torque-twisters, translators, and rockets (exhaust velocity up to 6000 meters per second). Operates safely within and outside of all normal atmospheres. No special adaptor needed on oxygenizer-atmosphere motors.

Directions: Place one pinch in fuel tank, fill with water. Add water as needed.

A-F Catalyst should generally be renewed when objective tests show fuel quality has deteriorated 50 per cent.

U.S. and Foreign Patents Pending

After reading that several times, with suitable mind-checking and eye-testing in between, Ernie took up a little of the white powder on the end of a nailfile. He had thought of tasting it, but had instantly abandoned the notion and even refrained from sniffing the stuff-after all, the human body is mostly water.

After reducing the quantity several times, he gingerly dumped at most four or five grains on the flat edge of the washbowl and then used the broad end of the nailfile to maneuver a large bead of water over to the almost invisible white deposit. He closed the box, put it and the nailfile carefully on the window ledge, lit a match and touched it to the drop, at the last moment ducking his head a little below the level of the washbowl.

Nothing happened. After a moment, he slowly withdrew the match, shaking it out, and looked. There was nothing to see. He reached out to touch the stupid squashed ovoid of water.

Ouch! He withdrew his fingers much faster than the match, shook them more sharply. Something was there, all right. Heat. Heat enough to hurt.

He cautiously explored the boundaries of the heat. It became noticeable about eighteen inches above the drop and almost an inch to each side-an invisible slim vertical cylinder. Crouching close, eyes level with the top of the washbowl, he could make out the flame —a thin finger of crinkled light.

He noticed that a corner of the drop was seething-but only a corner, as if the heat were sharply bounded in that direction and perhaps as if the catalyst were only transforming the water to fuel a bit at a time.

He reached up and tugged off the light. Now he could see the flame-ghostly, about four inches high, hardly thicker than a string, and colored not blue but pale green. A spectral green needle. He blew at it softly. It shimmied gracefully, but not, he thought, as much as the flame of a match or candle. It had character.

He switched on the light. The drop was more than half gone now; the part that was left was all seething. And the bathroom was markedly warmer.

"Ernie! Are you going to be much longer?"

The knock hadn't been loud and his widowed sister's voice was more apologetic than peremptory, but he jumped, of course.

"I am testing something," he started to say and changed it mid-way. It came out, "I am be out in a minute."

He turned off the light again. The flame was a little shorter now and it shrank as he watched, about a quarter inch a second. As soon as it died, he switched on the light. The drop was gone.

He scrubbed off the spot with a dry washrag, on second thought put a dab of vaseline on the washrag, scrubbed the spot again with that-he didn't like to think of even a grain of the powder getting in the drains or touching any water. He folded the washrag, tucked it in his pocket, put the blue box-after a final check of the lettering-in his other coat pocket, and opened the door.

"I was taking some bicarb," he told his sister. "Thuringer sausage at lunch."

She nodded absently.

Sleep refused even to flirt with Ernie, his mind was full of so many things, especially calculations involving the distance between his car and the house and the length of the garden hose. In desperation, as the white hours accumulated and his thoughts began to squirm, he grabbed up the detective story he'd bought at the corner newsstand. He had read thirty pages before he realized that he was turning them as rapidly as he could focus just once on each facing page.

He jumped out of bed. My God, he thought, at that rate he'd finish the book under three minutes and here it wasn't even two o'clock yet!

He selected the thickest book on the shelf, an overpoweringly dull historical treatise in small print. He turned two pages, three, then closed it with a clap and looked at the wall with frightened eyes. Ernie Meeker had discovered, inside the birthday box that was himself, the first of the Big Gifts.

The trouble was that in that wee-hour, lonely bedroom, it didn't seem like a gift at all. How would he ever keep himself in books, he wondered, if he read them so fast? And think how full to bursting his mind would get-right now, the seven pages of fine-print history were churning in it, vividly clear, along with the first chapters of the new detective story. If he kept on absorbing information that fast, he'd have to be revising all his opinions and beliefs every couple of days at least-maybe every couple of hours.

It seemed a dreadful, literally maddening prospect-his mind would ultimately become a universe of squirming macaroni. Even the wallpaper he was staring at, which imitated the grain of wood, had in an instant become so fully part of his consciousness that he felt he could turn his back on it right now and draw a picture of it correct to the tiniest detail. But who would ever want to do such a thing, or want to be able to?

It was an abnormal, dangerous, temporary sensitivity, he told himself, generated by the excitement of the crazy discovery he'd made in the bathroom. Like the thoughts of a drowning man, riffling an infinity-paneled adventure-comic of his life as he bolts his last rough ration of air. Or like the feeling a psychotic must have that he's on the verge of visualizing the whole universe, having its ultimate secrets patter down into the palm of his outstretched hand-just before the walls close in.

Ernie Meeker was not a drinking man, then. A pint had stood a week on his closet shelf and only been diminished three shots. But now he did a good job on the sturdy remainder.

Pretty soon the unbearable, edge-of-doom clarity in his mind faded, the universe-macaroni cooked down to a thick white soup uniform as fog, and the words of the detective story were sliding into his mind individually, or at most in strings of three and four. Which, if it wasn't as it ideally should be in an ambitious man's mind, was at least darn comfortable.

He had not rejected the Big Gift of Page-at-a-Glance Reading. Not quite. But he had dislocated for tonight at least the imposed nervous field on which it depended.

For want of a better place, Ernie dropped the rubber tube from the bathtub spray into the scrub bucket half full of odorous pink fluid and stared doubtfully at the uncapped gas tank. The tank had been almost empty when he'd last driven his car, he knew, because he'd been waiting until payday to gas up. Now he had used the tube to siphon out what he could of the remainder (he still could taste the stuff!) and he'd emptied the fuel line and carburetor, more or less.

Further than that, in the way of engine hygiene, Ernie's strictly kitchen mechanics did not go, but he felt that a catalyst used in pinches shouldn't be too particular about contaminants. Besides, the directions on the box hadn't said anything about cleaning the fuel tank, had they?

He hesitated. At his feet, the garden hose gurgled noisily over the curb into the gutter; it had vindicated his midnight estimate, proving just long enough. He looked uneasily up and down the dawning street and was relieved to find it still empty. He wished fervently, not for the first time this Saturday morning, that he had a garage. Then he sighed, squared his shoulders a little, and lifted the box out of his pocket.

Making to check the directions the umpteenth time, he received a body blow. The white lettering on the box had disappeared. The box didn't proclaim itself sodium bicarbonate again-there was just no lettering at all, only blue background. He turned it over several times.

Right there died his tentative plan of eventually sharing his secret with some friend who knew more than himself about motors (he hadn't decided anyway who that would be). It would be just too silly to approach anyone he knew with a more-than-wild story and featureless blue box.

For a moment, he came very close to dropping the box between the wide-set bars of the street drain and pouring the pink gas back in the tank. It had hit him, in a way for the first time, just how *crazy* this all was, how jarringly implausible even on such hypotheses as practical jokes, secret product perhaps military, or mad inventor (except himself).

For how the devil should the stuff get into his bathroom disguised as bicarb? That circumstance seemed beyond imagination. Green flames ... vanishing letters ... "torque-twisters, translators" ... a box that talked....

At that point, simple faith came to Ernie's rescue: in the same bathroom, he *had* seen the green flame; it had burned his fingers.

Quickly he dipped up a little of the white powder on the edge of a fifty-cent piece, dumped it in the gas tank without quibbling as to quantity, rapped the coin on the edge of the opening, closed and pocketed the blue box, and picked up the spurting hose and jabbed it into the round hole.

His heart was pounding and his breath was coming fast. That had taken real effort. So he was slow in hearing the footsteps behind him.

His neighbor's gate was open and Mr. Jones stood open-mouthed a few feet behind him, all ready for his day's work as streetcar motorman and wearing the dark blue uniform that always made him look for a moment unpleasantly like a policeman.

Ernie swung the hose around, flipping his thumb over the end to make a spray, and nonchalantly began to water the little rectangle of lawn between sidewalk and curb.

The first things he watered were the bottoms of Mr. Jones's pants legs.

Mr. Jones voiced no complaint. He backed off several steps, stared intently at Ernie, rather palely, it seemed to the latter. Then he turned and made off for the streetcar tracks at a very fast shuffle, shaking his feet a little now and then and glancing back several times over his shoulder without slowing down.

Ernie felt light-headed. He decided there was enough water in the gas tank, capped it, and momentarily continued to water the lawn.

"Ernie! Come on in and have breakfast!"

He heeded his sister's call, telling himself it would be a good idea "to give the stuff time to mix" before testing the engine.

He had divined her question and was ready with an answer.

"I've just found out that we're supposed to water our lawns only before seven in the morning or after seven in the evenings. It's the law."

It was the day for their monthly drive out to Wheaton to visit Uncle Fabius. On the whole, Ernie was glad his sister was in the car when he turned the key in the starter-it forced him to be calm and collected, though he didn't feel exactly right about exposing her to the danger of being blown up without first explaining to her the risk. But the motor started right up and began purring powerfully. Ernie's sister commented on it favorably.

Then she went on to ask, "Did you remember to buy gas yesterday?"

"No," he said without thinking; then, realizing his mistake, quickly added, "I'll buy some in Wheaton. There's enough to get us there."

"You didn't think so yesterday," she objected. "You said the tank was nearly empty."

"I was wrong. Look, the gauge shows it's half full."

"But then how ... Ernie, didn't you once tell me the gauge doesn't work?"

"Did I?"

"Yes. Look, there's a station. Why don't you buy gas now?"

"No, I'll wait for Wheaton —I know a place there I can get it cheaper," he insisted, rather lamely, he feared.

His sister looked at him steadily. He settled his head between his shoulders and concentrated on driving. His feeling of excitement was spoiled, but a few minutes of silence brought it back. He thought of the blur of green flashes inside the purring motor. If the passing drivers only knew!

Uncle Fabius, retired perhaps a few years too early and opinionated, was a trial, but he did know something about the automobile industry. Ernie chose a moment when his sister was out of the room to ask if he'd ever heard of a white powder that would turn water into gasoline or some usable fuel.

"Who's been getting at you?" Uncle Fabius demanded sharply, to Ernie's surprise and embarrassment. "That's one of the oldest swindles. They always tell this story about how this man had a white powder or something and demonstrated it once with a pail of water and then disappeared. You're supposed to believe that Detroit or the big oil companies got rid of him. It's just another of those malicious legends, concocted-by Russia, I imagine-to weaken your faith in American Industry, like the everlasting battery or the razor blade that never gets dull. You're looking pale, Ernie-don't tell me you've already put money in this white powder? I suppose someone's approached you with a proposition, though?"

With considerable difficulty, Ernie convinced his uncle that he had "just heard the story from a friend."

"In that case," Uncle Fabius opined, "you can be sure some fuel-powder swindler has been getting at *him*. When you see him-and be sure to make that soon-tell him from me that —" and Uncle Fabius began an impassioned ninety-minute defense of big business, small business, prosperity, America, money, know-how, and a number of other institutions that defended pretty easily, so that the situation was wholly normal when Ernie's sister returned.

As soon as the car pulled away from the curb on their way back to Chicago, she reminded him about the gas.

"Oh, I've already done that," he assured her. "Made a special trip so I wouldn't forget. It was while you were out of the room. Didn't you hear me?"

"No," she said, "I didn't," and she looked at him steadily, as she had that morning. He similarly retreated to driving.

Stopping for a railroad crossing, he braked too hard and the car stalled. His sister grabbed his arm. "I knew that was going to happen," she said. "I knew that for some reason you lied to me when —" The motor, starting readily again, cut short her remark and Ernie didn't press his small triumph by asking her what she was about to say.

To tell the truth, Ernie wasn't feeling as elated about today's fifty-mile drive as he'd imagined he would. Now he thought he could put his finger on the reason: It was the completely ... well, *arbitrary* way in which the white powder had come into his possession.

If he'd concocted it himself, or been given it by a shady promoter, or even seen the box fall out of the pocket of a suspicious-looking man in a trenchcoat, *then* he'd have felt more able to *do* something about it, whether in the general line of starting a fuel-powder company or of going to the F.B.I.

But just having the stuff drop into his hands from the sky, so to speak, as if in a crazy dream, and for that same reason not feeling able to talk about it and assure himself he wasn't going crazy ... oh, it is rough when you can't share things, really rough; not being able to share depressing news corrodes the spirit, but not being able to share exciting news can sometimes be even more corroding.

Maybe, he told himself, he could figure out someone to tell. But who? And how? His mind shied away from the problem, rather decisively.

When he checked the blue box that night, the original sodium bicarbonate lettering had returned with all its humdrum paragraphs. Not one word about exhaust velocities.

From that moment, the fuel-powder became a trial to Ernie rather than a secret glory. He'd wake in the middle of the night doubting that he had ever really read the mind-dizzying lettering, ever really tested the stuff-perhaps he'd bring from sleep the chilling notion that in the dimness and excitement of Saturday morning he'd put the water in some other car's gas tank, perhaps Mr. Jones's. He could usually argue such ideas away, but they kept coming back. And yet he did no more bathroom testing.

Of course the car still ran. He even fueled it once again with the garden hose, sniffing the nozzle to make sure it hadn't somehow got connected to the basement furnace oil-tank. He picked three o'clock in the morning for the act, but nevertheless as he was returning indoors he heard a window in Mr. Jones's house slam loudly. It unsettled him. Coming home the next day, he caught his sister and Mr. Jones consulting about something on the latter's doorsteps, which unsettled him further.

He couldn't decide on a safe place to keep the box and took to carrying it around with him day and night. Bill spotted it once down at the office and by an unhappy coincidence needed some bicarb just then for a troubled stomach. Ernie explained on the spur of the moment that he was using the box to carry plaster of Paris, which involved him in further lies that he felt were quite unconvincing as well as making him appear decidedly eccentric, even butter-brained. Bill took to calling him "the sculptor."

Meanwhile, besides the problem of the white powder, Ernie was having other unsettling experiences, stemming (though of course he didn't know that) from the other Gifts-and not just the Big Gift of Page-at-a-Glance Reading, though that still returned from time to time to shock his consciousness and send him hurrying for a few quick shots.

Like many another car-owning commuter, Ernie found the traffic and parking problems a bit too much for comfort and so used the fast electric train to carry him five times a week to the heart of the city. During those brief, swift, crowded trips Ernie, generally looking steadily out the window at the brown buildings and black stanchions whipping past, enjoyed a kind of anonymity and privacy more refreshing to his spirit than he realized. But now all that had been suddenly changed. People had started to talk to him; total strangers struck up conversations almost every morning and afternoon.

Ernie couldn't figure out the reason and wasn't at all sure he liked it-except for Vivian.

She was the sort of girl Ernie dreamed about, improperly. Tall, blonde and knowing, excitedly curved but armored in a black suit, friendly and funny but given to making almost cruelly deflating remarks, as if the neatly furled short umbrella dangling from her wrist might better be a black dog whip.

She worked in an office too, a fancier one than Ernie's, as he found out from their morning conversations. He hadn't got to the point of asking her to lunch, but he was prodding himself.

Why such a girl should ever have asked him for a match in the first place and then put up with his clumsy babblings on subsequent mornings was a mystery to him. He finally asked her about it in what he hoped was a joking way, though she seemed to know a lot more about joking than he did.

"Don't you know?" she countered. "I mean what makes you attractive to people?"

"Me attractive? No."

"Well, I'll tell you then, Ernie, and I've got to admit it's something quite out of the ordinary. *I've* never noticed it in anyone else. Ernie, I'm sure your knowledge of romantic novels is shamefully deficient, it's clear from your manners, but in the earlier ones-not in style now-the hero is described as tall, manly, broad-shouldered, Anglo-Saxon features, etcetera, etcetera, but there's one thing he always has, something that sounds like poetic over-enthusiasm if you stop to analyze it, a physical impossibility, but that I have to admit you, Ernie, actually have. Flashing eyes."

"Flashing eyes? Me?"

She nodded solemnly. He thought her long straight lips trembled on the verge of a grin, but he couldn't be sure.

"How do you mean, flashing eyes?" he protested. "How *can* eyes flash, except by reflecting light? In that case, I guess they'd seem to 'flash' more if a person opened them wide but kept blinking them a lot. Is that what I do?"

"No, Ernie, though you're doing it now," she told him, shaking her head. "No, Ernie, your eyes just give a tiny flash of their own about every five seconds, like a lighthouse, but barely, *barely* bright enough for another person to notice. It makes you irresistible. Of course I've never seen you in the dark; maybe they wouldn't flash in the dark."

"You're joking."

Vivian frowned a little at that remark, as if she were puzzled herself.

"Well, maybe I am and maybe I'm not," she said. "In any case, don't get conceited about your Flashing Eyes, because I'm sure you'll never know how to take advantage of them."

When he parted from her downtown, pausing a moment to watch her walk away with feline majesty, he muttered "Flashing Eyes!" with a shrug of the shoulders and a skeptical growl. Just the same, he ducked his head as he moved off and he pulled the brim of his hat down sharply.

Afternoons, hurtling home in the five o'clock rush, it was not Vivian but Verna who frequently occupied the seat beside him, taking up rather more space in it than the Panther Princess. Verna was another of his newly acquired and not altogether welcome conversation-pals, along with Jacob the barber, Mr. Willis the druggist and Herman the health-food manufacturer, inventor of Soybean Mush-conquests of his Flashing Eyes or whatever it was.

Verna was stocky, pasty-faced, voluble (with him), coy, and had bad breath-he could see the tiny triangles of pale food between her incisors and canines whenever her conversations became particularly vehement and confidential, which was often. She always had a stack of books hugged to her stomach. She worked in a fur-storage vault, she said, and could snatch quite a bit of time for reading-rather heavy reading, it seemed.

It wasn't very long before Verna was head-over-heels (fearful picture!) infatuated with him. Somehow his friendliness had touched a hidden spring in this ugly, friendless, clumsy girl and for once she had lost her fear of the world's ridicule and opened her hulking heart to another human being. It was touching but rather overpowering, especially since she always opened her mouth too. He learned a great deal about herself, her invalid father, Elizabethan and Restoration poetry, paleontology, an organization known as the Working Girls' Front, Mr. Abrusian, and a brassy Miss Minkin who sounded like a fiendish caricature of Vivian.

He felt that deliberately avoiding Verna would be a dirtier trick than he liked to think himself capable of. Nevertheless there were times when he seriously wished he'd never acquired whatever power it was-except for Vivian, of course. What the devil, he asked himself for the nth time, could that power be?

That night, in the bathroom, the question came back to him and he impulsively switched off the light and looked into the mirror. He gasped and seemed on the point of shrieking out something, but he only grasped the washbowl more tightly and stared into the mirror more intently.

After about a minute, he tugged on the light again. He was pale. He had convinced himself of the actual existence of the phenomenon that was in reality the third of the Little Gifts: Flashing Eyes.

He couldn't notice anything in the light, but in the dark his eyes gave off a faint blue flash about every five seconds, just as Vivian had said, lighting up his cheeks and eyebrows like some comic-book vampire!

It might be attractive by day, when it just registered as an impalpable hint, but it was damn sinister in the dark! It wasn't much, but it was *there* —unless the flashes were inside his head and he was projecting them ... blue ... something called the Purkinje effect? ... but then Vivian had actually seen ... oh, damn!

Suddenly he wildly looked around, a little like a trapped animal. Why did it always have to happen in the *bathroom*, he asked himself-the bicarb, the flame, the blade (if that counted), and now this? Could there be something wrong about the bathroom, something either in the room itself or in his childhood associations?

But neither the bathroom walls nor his minutely searched memory returned an answer.

It was dark in the hall outside and he almost bumped into his sister. He recoiled, stared at her a moment, then threw his hand over his eyes, darted into his bedroom and shut the door.

"Is there something wrong, Ernie?" she called after him.

"Wrong?"

The door muffled his voice. "How do you mean?"

"I mean about your eyes."

"My *eyes*?" It was almost a scream. "What about my eyes?"

"Don't shout, Ernie. I mean are they painful?"

"Painful? Why should they be painful?"

"I really don't know, Ernie." She was being very patient and calm.

"I mean did you *notice* anything about them?" He was trying to be the same without much success.

"Just that you put your hand up to them as if they hurt."

"Oh." Great relief. "Yes, they do smart a little. I guess I've been using them too much. I'm putting some eye-drops in them now."

"Can I help you, Ernie? And shouldn't you see an opto ... ocu ... optha ... I mean an eye doctor?"

Ernie answered "No" to both those questions, but of course it took a lot more lying and improvising and general smoothing out before his sister would even pretend to be satisfied and stop her general nagging for the evening. She was getting uncomfortably cagy and curious lately, addicted to asking such questions out of a blue sky as:

"Ernie, when we were visiting Uncle Fabius, did you actually believe that you went out and bought gas?"

That one momentarily brought Ernie's stammer back, something which hadn't troubled him for years.

And when she wasn't asking questions, her quiet studying of him for long minutes was even more upsetting.

Next morning, on the way to the electric train, Ernie made a purchase at the drugstore. When he sat down beside Vivian, she took one look at him and gave a very deliberate-sounding hollow laugh.

"Black glasses!" she said. "I tell him he's attractive because he has Flashing Eyes and within two days he's wearing black glasses. I suppose I should have guessed it."

"But my eyes hurt," Ernie protested. "Sensitive to sunlight, I think." He wished he could explain to her that he'd bought the glasses not only in case he got caught out at night, but also to convince his sister he hadn't been lying about sore eyes. He hadn't intended to wear them by day and hardly knew why he'd put them on before joining Vivian.

"Spare me your rationalizations," she said. "Your motives are clear to me, Ernie, and they happen to be very commonplace."

She leaned toward him and her voice, little more than a whisper, took on an unexpectedly gloomy, chilling, hopeless tone.

"See these people all around us, Ernie? They're suicides, every one of them. Day by day, in every way, they're killing themselves. People love them, admire them, and it only makes them uneasy. They have abilities and charms by the bushel-yes, they do, even that man with the wen on his neck-and they only try to hide them. The spotlight turns their way and they goof. They think they're running away from failure, but actually they're running away from success."

Ernie looked at them, he couldn't help it, her voice made him, and the ability of Page-at-a-Glance Reading chose that moment to come back to him, only applied to faces instead of letters, and there seemed to be another ability along with it, unclear as yet but frightening. He felt like a very old detective scanning the lineup for the thousandth time.

The black glasses didn't interfere a bit-the dozens of faces in this speeding electric car were suddenly as familiar as the court cards in a deck-and he had the feeling that, like a bunch of pink pasteboards, they were about to be hurled in his face.

My God, he asked himself, flinching, how could you go on living with so many faces so close to you, so completely known? —each street you turned into, each store you entered, each gathering you joined, another deluge of unique features. Ugly, pretty, strong, weak-those words didn't mean anything any more in this drenching of individuality he was getting, and that showed no signs of stopping.

So he hardly heard Vivian saying, "And it's true of you, Ernie-in spades, for your black glasses," and he hardly remembered parting from her, and when he found himself alone he did something unprecedented for him at that time of day-he went to a bar and drank two double whiskies.

The drinks brought the downtown landscape back to normal and stopped the faces printing themselves on his mind, but they left him very disturbed, and the suspiciousness with which he was treated at the office didn't improve that, and Ernie began to wish for ordinariness and commonplaceness in himself more than anything in the whole world. If only, he silently implored, there were some way of junking everything that had happened to him in the past few weeks-except maybe Vivian.

Verna on the train home positively terrified him. She was unusually talkative and engulfing this evening and he thought that if the faces-forever feeling came to him just as she was baring her food-triangles and all, he wouldn't be able to stand it. Somehow, it didn't. Yet the very intensity of his distaste frightened him. Not for the first time, the word "insanity" appeared in his mind, pulsing in pale yellowish-green.

Half a block from home, passing his parked car (with an unconscious little veer of avoidance), he spotted three figures in close conference in front of his house: his sister, a man in dark blue-yes, Mr. Jones, and ...a man in a white coat.

Almost before he knew it, he was in his car and driving away. He truly didn't know what he was going to do, only that he was going to do it, and found a trivial interest in trying to guess what it was going to be. Whatever it was, it was going to dim that yellowish-green word, decrease its type-size, make him a little more able to face the crisis waiting him at home ... or somewhere.

He had a picture of himself getting on an airplane, another of renting a room in a slum, another of stopping the car on a lonely, treeless country road and getting out and looking up to the coldly glimmering Milky Way-why?

That last picture was the most vivid, and when he realized he had actually stopped his car, it was a moment before it would go away. Then he saw he was parked in front of a demolished old apartment building a few blocks from his home. Only yesterday he'd watched the last wall going down. Now, just across the littered sidewalk from him, the old cellar gaped, flimsily guarded in front by a makeshift rail and surrounded on the other three sides by great hillocks of battered bricks. Tomorrow probably (and in fact that was the way it happened) a bulldozer would tumble them forward, filling the cellar with old bricks and brick-dust, leveling the lot.

Now he knew what he was going to do. He unlatched the top over the windshield and pushed the button. Slowly the top folded back over his head, showing the smoke-dark sky, almost night. He hitched up a little in the seat, reached inside his coat, pulled out the blue box he always carried and pitched it into the dark pit across the sidewalk.

He was driving away almost before it landed. Yet through the hum of the motor he thought he heard something call faintly, "Good-by."

The material of the filled-in cellar stayed fairly dry for many years and the atom-bombing, when it finally came, created a partial surface-seal of fused stone over that area. However, the bicarb box fell apart in time; water reached it in little seepings and was accumulated as a non-evaporating fuel-and-oxydizer mix. The amount of this strange fluid grew and grew, eventually invading and filling a now-blind section of the city's old sewer system.

Many tens of thousands of years after that, the buried pool was sensed by the fuel-finders of a spaceship from up Polaris way, which had made an emergency landing on the ruined planet. A well was drilled and the mix pumped up and the centipedal Polarians, scuttling about the bleak landscape, had a fine time trying to explain how such a sophisticated fluid should occur in a seeming state of nature. However, they were grateful to the Cosmic All-Father.

Long before that, Ernie had arrived home in something of a daze. He told himself that he had cast off the most tangible element of his "insanity," but he didn't feel any the better for it. In fact, he felt distinctly apathetic when his sister confronted him and only with an effort did he manage to brace himself for the trial he knew she had in store for him.

"Ernie," she said hesitatingly, "I've come to a decision about something-about a change in our arrangements here, to tell you the truth-and I've gone ahead with it without consulting you. I do hope you won't mind."

"No," he said heavily, "I guess I won't mind."

"I'm doing it partly on Mr. Jones's advice," she added slowly. "As a matter of fact he suggested it."

Ernie nodded. "Yes, I've noticed the two of you conferring together."

"You have? Then maybe you know what I'm talking about."

"Oh, yes." Ernie nodded again and smiled grimly. "The man in white?"

She laughed. "Exactly, the man in white. For a long time, I've thought it was just too much bother for either of us to carry the milk home, and the eggs and my yogurt too. So I decided to have the milkman that Mr. Jones uses make deliveries. Mr. Jones brought him over half an hour ago and it's all arranged. Four quarts a week, one dozen eggs, and yogurt Tuesdays and Fridays."

The Invisible Being and his Coadjutor, backtracking for a checkup, summarized the situation.

The latter said, "So he's already thrown away the Everlasting Cosmetic Knife and the Water Splitter; he seems to be trying to reject the third Little Gift and the first Big One, while he still isn't even conscious of the other two Gifts."

"Cheer up," said the Invisible Being. "It's his life and he's doing what he thinks best."

"Yes," the Coadjutor said, "but he doesn't know he's making these decisions for his race as well as himself. Sometimes I think Galaxy Center makes it too hard for chaps like him. For instance, that trick of having the images on the box fade back to the old ones."

"Nonsense! We have to take all reasonable precautions that our activities remain secret. He knew that the powder worked. He should have had faith."

"Sometimes it takes a lot of faith."

"You're right, it does." The Invisible Being smiled his Cheshire smile. "You feel a lot for these test subjects, don't you? That's fine, but you've got to remember you can't accept the Gifts for them; that's one thing they have to do themselves, however long they take about it. Which reminds me, I think we ought to set up a recorder here to report the final outcome of the test to Galaxy Center."

"Good idea."

"And cheer up, I say. This test isn't over yet and our featherless biped isn't necessarily licked. If he thinks to link up the third Little Gift with the two Big Ones, he has a pretty sweet setup for making psychic progress-and his race will be Galactic Citizens in a jiffy."

"You're right."

"Moreover, it stands to reason he's soon going to become aware of the Great Gift, and that generally gives a person a jolt and makes him think seriously about other things."

"True enough-though I still have the feeling you intend some sardonic trick in conjunction with the Great Gift. Are you sure you're not planning to leave some other setup here along with the recorder? I notice you've got a spare Juxtaposer in the ship and it bothers me."

"That, dear Coadjutor, is my business. Whatever I do, it won't interfere in any way with the fairness of the tests."

"Sometimes I think the tests are *too* fair," the Coadjutor observed. "I'd like to be able to ease them up a bit in special cases."

"Confidentially, my friend, so would I."

The Great Gift announced itself to Ernie next morning at 7:53 sharp, when the Special slowed to forty miles an hour to swing past the platform on which he was waiting for the Express.

One moment he was standing morning-weary on the thick wooden planks, looking down through the quarter-inch gaps between them at the cinders five feet below, vaguely conscious of a woman's white-polka-dotted black skirt on one side of his field of vision and a man's brown shoes and briefcase to the other.

Next moment he was in a small cab under which steel rails were vanishing at an alarming speed, and way ahead he could just make out the platform on which he was standing, and something was hurting his head and he was slumping forward and everything was darkening and the cab was leaping forward more swiftly still.

The third moment he was back on the platform, running furiously to get off it. He didn't care who yelled at him or whom he bumped, so long as it didn't slow him down. The people were just blurs anyway and soon he was beyond them. He took in two strides the short flight of wooden steps leading down off the platform proper and spurted the last sixty feet to the stairs leading down to street level. There he stumbled, recovered himself, and chanced a hasty backward look.

There was a tall man at his heels, hugging a briefcase and panting hard. Then, beyond the tall man, he saw the platform rear up like a wooden caterpillar, spilling people against the bright gray morning sky. There was a cosmic crunch and the battered Special, still coming strong, burst through the upreared platform in a blossoming broken-matchstick crown of planks and beams-and big blue sparks where a writhing power wire, snagged by the uprearing platform, was grounding against the first car.

Ernie ducked his head and plunged down the steps ahead.

(That was how I came to meet Ernie Meeker. I was the tall man. As you can imagine, it's quite strange to be standing in a huddle of fresh-washed morning commuters and have the one beside you close his eyes and slump a little and then take off like a bat out of hell-without a word spoken or a thing happened to explain it. I started to laugh, but then I got the funniest feeling of curiosity and terror and I took off after him. It saved my life.

(Afterward, Ernie and I went back to help with the ghastliness, but pretty soon there were more than enough trainmen, firemen, police, and what not, and we got chased off. We had a couple of drinks together and met a few times after and that's how I got some of this story. But my chief sources of information I am not permitted to disclose.)

As the Invisible Being had predicted, Ernie's first brush with the Great Gift gave him a considerable jolt, though he didn't suspect at first that it was a permanent gift.

He analyzed what had happened, quite reasonably, I believe, as a case of second sight. Somehow his mind had been projected into the brain of the motorman of the Special just at the moment the latter had his stroke (the final official explanation too) and blindly put on more speed instead of reducing it for the approaching curve and station. His second sight saved his life by getting him off the platform before the Special jumped the tracks and ploughed through it.

It certainly gave a jolt to Ernie's habit patterns, as it temporarily did of a great many other people. He started driving his car to work, for one thing, and he took to drinking regularly in the evenings, though not excessively as yet.

He also had the feeling, which he did not try to analyze, that his miraculous escape marked the end of the "strange weeks" in his life, when he'd had such odd illusions or been the victim of such odd circumstances; and, true enough, that first week or so there were no recurrences of his chillingly weird experiences.

But jolts have their infallible Law of Diminishing Effects.

After a few days, Ernie found the traffic and parking problems as nervous and wearisome as ever and he grew envious of the snug commuters meditating luxuriously in their electric coaches. Come the first morning of the third week and he was standing on the rebuilt platform, studying the new planks, ties and rails with a pleasantly morbid interest.

Vivian was not in her accustomed seat nor on the train, as far as he could tell, which did not surprise him, though it disappointed him sharply; the Panther Princess had a stronger hold on his feelings, or at least on his imagination, than he'd realized.

But Verna was on the train home all right; in fact, she gave a small whoop of pleasure when she spotted him. And he had barely sat down beside her when who should come prowling smoothly along but Vivian in a charcoal version of her tailored black armor.

Ernie jumped up and blurted out introductions. Vivian accepted his seat with a certain deliberateness and with a smile that seemed to Ernie to say, "So I'm his morning light-badinage girl, but this is the girl Mr. Meeker goes home with. It's another instance of 'black-glasses' behavior, don't you think? He puts her on whenever he gets afraid he's getting attractive."

The two women started to chat easily enough, however, and shortly Ernie got over his confusion and, smiling down at them from where he swayed in his aisle with his hand lightly touching the back of the seat ahead, was even thinking quite smugly that here in one seat, by gosh, were the woman he wanted and the woman who wanted him. Very interesting to be the man in the middle.

Just at that moment, the power came back to him that made everything feverishly real, expanding his center of attention to his visual horizons, and this time it was only a prelude, for a second gateway opened behind the first —a window into all human hearts and minds, the power of human insight fantastically sharpened and enlarged. He could "read minds," or at least he knew the motives-the core of values and consciousness-of any person he cared to look at. Most especially, he knew the motives of Verna and Vivian almost as if he *were* them.

The big thing about Vivian was her fear-no, her conviction, that she wasn't attractive. Every glance her way knocked a hole in the armor of artificial attractiveness she built around herself, and all the hours she devoted to perfecting it, even the desperate worship she lavished on her body, were all utterly lost. A simple relationship with another human being was unthinkable; her armor got in the way and under her armor she knew she was worthless. A man was sometimes attracted to her armor-never to herself! —but as soon as he started to scrutinize it, it began to tarnish and crumple.

She hoped that other people, men especially, had a trace of her own weaknesses, and she sniped away at them constantly to get under the armor to find out. Ernie was one in a long series of such men. She was actually in love with him, but only as one loves a dream, not the real Ernie at all. Physically he was disgusting to her, like most men.

Verna, on the other hand, had absolute confidence that she was sufficiently attractive for all practical purposes. She wasn't in love with Ernie at all. She wanted to make an intellectual conquest of him, add him to her private Brain Trust, her cultured entourage that won Mr. Abrusian's seldom-tendered admiration and broke Miss Minkin's heart, and finally get Ernie to join the Working Boys' Front. He was one of her projects. If it became tactically necessary during her campaign, she knew that Ernie would be only too happy to jump in bed with her, food-triangles and all.

Now in other circumstances (who really knows?), Ernie might have found the courage to accept Vivian and Verna as they really were and work on from there, ruthlessly discarding his false pictures of them-and of himself. He might conceivably have found the strength to accept all people not as shadowy projections of himself, fabricated targets of his desires and aversions, puppets in his private chess games and circuses, but as complete persons with inexhaustible surprises and contradictions, each a microcosm, a universe-in-little with his or her own earth and stars, spaceflight and crawling, heaven and hell.

But under the present circumstances, Ernie was confused. His knowledge of the real Vivian spoiled completely the titillating picture of the Panther Princess, who might submit to him contemptuously in the end-he needed that sex idol more than he needed truth. As for Verna, her stalwart self-reliance and her accurate appraisal of his own motives and possible future behavior were both unbearably humiliating to him. And the delight of really knowing people was completely outweighed, in his tired spirit, by the thought of the lifetime of work that would be involved in adjusting himself to this new knowledge. It was so much more comfortable to work with stereotypes.

The Express was slowing for his station. Both girls were looking at him puzzledly.

"Good-by, Verna. Good-by, Vivian," he said in a set sort of voice. "This is where I get off."

He moved stiffly toward the door. They watched him go, and turned to each other with a frown.

That evening marked the beginning of Ernie's serious drinking. He never saw either of the V-girls again. He took his car or the bus to work; then, for a short period, he took taxicabs, then he lost his job and was working in another part of the city. He became mixed up with a number of other women and crowds, but they are not part of this or any story.

Among other things, his drinking eventually completely confused his memories of abnormal personal powers with his entirely normal illusions of alcoholic ones. And it also seemed to be blotting out the former. Once, at a party, he bet twenty dollars that his eyes glowed in the dark. Next morning he was relieved to discover, after making several anxious phone calls, that he'd lost his bet.

When he finally pulled out of it, some five years later, because of a growing aversion to liquor that he only understood later, the two Big Gifts of Page-at-a-Glance and Mind Reading were gone forever.

The Great Gift had a more durable lodgment in him. From his alcoholic years, he brought hazy memories of accidents avoided because of sudden wrong-ended visions of onrushing cars, alley rollings missed because he'd seen himself reeling along a block away through the eyes of lounging hoodlums. Now, sober again, he had a clear confirmation of it when he left a banquet on a trumped-up excuse because of a disturbing vision of inexplicable rodlike shapes-and read the next day that a hundred of the guests, of whom four finally died, had come down with bacterial food poisoning. Another time, hiking in dry woods, he'd smelled smoke that his companions couldn't —and persuaded them to turn back, avoiding a disastrous flash fire that broke out soon afterward.

He had to admit to himself that he certainly seemed to have the gift of second sight, warning him against threats to his life.

"All right," he told himself, "so forget it. Gifts are upsetting. Even as a kid, you sweated more about your birthday presents than you ever got fun out of them."

Our story has already jumped five years; now it must jump twenty. Ernie is living with his sister again; while he was drinking, they pulled apart, and now they've once more pulled together. They're having dinner, have arrived at dessert, a big piece of chocolate cake each with satiny thick creamy frosting and filling.

Ernie looks at his piece-and sees himself climbing stairs and clutching at his heart. He thinks of warning his sister, but she's already halfway through her piece. Then she goes on and eats Ernie's.

Ernie's sister didn't get food poisoning, she only got fat, but the incident of the chocolate cake was for Ernie the beginning of a series of peculiar food revulsions and diet experiments that eventually made Ernie instead of his sister the family yogurt-fiend and a regular customer of his old acquaintance, Herman, the health-food manufacturer.

Herman had to admit that Ernie had cooked himself up a pretty good longevity diet for an amateur, though there were some items in it that made the old man shake his head-and he always asserted that Ernie was passing up a good thing in Soybean Mush.

Ernie got his diet tailored to fit his tastes and stuck to it. He had a strong suspicion of what had happened, though he tried not to think about it too often: that his gift of second sight had taken to warning him of the longer-range dangers to his existence; after all, chocolate cake can be as deadly as atomic bombs in the long run.

More years passed. Friends and relatives began to remark quietly to each other that his sister was aging faster. Ernie, they had to admit, was a remarkably well-preserved old gent. Ironic, considering what a drunk he'd been and what strange junk he insisted on eating now.

One day Ernie's self-styled health diet began to pall on him. It didn't revolt him; it merely left him unsatisfied, yet with no yearning for any particular food he could think of. He lived with this yearning for some weeks, meditating on it and trying to guess its nature. Finally he had an inspiration. He headed for Mr. Willis' drugstore.

The bent, silvery-haired man greeted him eagerly; somehow there was a special warmth about the friendships Ernie had made during the "strange weeks" (Verna and Vivian excepted) that put them in a different class from any other of his human relationships.

"Now what can I give you, Ernie?" Mr. Willis asked. "Anything in the place within reason."

"I'll tell you, Bert I'd like to go back in your dispensary-you with me, if you want-and just shop around."

"That's a sort of screwy idea, Ernie. I couldn't sell you any narcotics or sleeping pills, of course-well, maybe a few sleeping pills."

"I wouldn't want any."

"What's the idea, Ernie? Getting interested in chemistry in your old ...You know, Ernie, you just don't look your years."

"Secret of mine. Yes, in a way I've got interested in chemistry."

"Won't talk, eh? I remember, when I first met you, I tagged you for an evening inventor. Well, come on back and shop around. Just don't ask me for *elixer vitae*, *aurum potabile*, or ground philosophers' stone."

"Not unless I see 'em."

Afterward, Bert Willis used to say it was one of the most mystifying experiences of his life. For a good half a day, Ernie Meeker studied the rows of jars, canisters and glass-stoppered bottles, sometimes lifting two down together and contemplating them, one in each hand, as if he could weigh the difference. Often he'd take out a stopper and sniff, and maybe, asking permission of Bert with a glance, take up a dab of some powder and taste it.

"You know that game," Bert would say, "where someone goes out of the room and you all decide on an object, or hide one, and he comes back and tries to find it by telepathy or muscle-reading or something? That was exactly the way Ernie was acting. Dog on a difficult scent."

A couple of times, especially when the customers came in, Bert wanted to chase him out, except that Ernie was such a special friend and Bert was so darn curious about it all himself.

In the end, Ernie made a good twenty purchases, including a mortar and pestle and two poisons for which Bert made him sign, though the amounts were less than a lethal dose.

"Actually none of the chemicals he bought were very dangerous," Bert would say. "And none of them were terribly unusual. The thing about them was that, put together, they just didn't make sense-as a medicine or anything else. Let me see, there was sulphur, bismuth, a bit of mercury, one of the sulfa drugs, a tiny packet of auric chloride, and ...I had 'em all on a list once, but I've lost it."

After that, Ernie always mixed a little grayish paste in his cup of yogurt at suppertime.

Ernie stopped aging altogether.

After his sister's coffin was lowered past the margins of green matting into the ground, Ernie shook hands with the minister, walked Bert Willis and Herman Schover to their car and told them he thought he'd better drive home with some relatives who'd turned up. Actually he just wanted to stay behind a while. It was a beautiful blue-and-white summer day; the tidy suburban cemetery had caught his fancy, and now he felt like a quiet stroll.

Ernie followed his little impulses these days. As he sometimes said, "I figure I've got plenty of time. I just don't feel the pressure like I used to."

The last car chugged away. Ernie stretched and started to stroll, slowly, but not like an old man, now that he was alone. His hair had grown whiter in the last few years and his face a little wrinkled, but that was due to the very judicious use of silvering and theatrical liner-people's comments about his youthfulness had gotten wearisome and would, he knew, eventually become suspicious.

Keeping himself oriented by a white tower at the cemetery gate, he arrived at an area that had no graves as yet, no trees either, just lawn. He made his way to the center of it, where there was a gently swelling hummock, and sat down in the warm crinkly grass, resting his back against the slope. The sky was lovely, enough clouds to be interesting, but a great oval of pure blue just overhead —a pear-shaped gateway to space.

He felt no grief at his sister's death, only the desire to think a bit, have a quiet look at his past and another at the great future.

Alone like this, he dared to face his fate for a moment and admit to himself that, all wishful thinking aside, it really began to look as if he were going to live forever, or at least for a very long time.

Live forever! That was a phrase to give you a chill, he told himself. And what to do, he asked himself, with all that time?

Back in the "strange weeks," he'd have had little trouble in answering that question-if only he'd known then what he did now and realized what was being offered him. For, during his sober decades, Ernie had gradually come to a shrewdly accurate estimate of what had happened to him then. He thought of it in terms of having been offered six Gifts and turned down five of them.

Back in the "strange weeks" and armed with the five rejected Gifts (Page-at-a-Glance and Mind Reading were the only ones that counted, though), he could easily have said, "Live forever by all means! Increase your knowledge and understanding until your mind bursts or is transfigured. Plunge forever into the unending variety of the Cosmos. Open yourself to everything."

But now, equipped to travel only as a snail....

Still, even snails get somewhere. With forever to work with, even four-words-at-a-glance gets you through many, many books. Patient love and dispassionate thought give you human insight in the end, can finally open the tightest shutter on the darkest human heart.

But that would take so very long and Ernie felt tired. Not old, just tired, tired. Best simply to watch the soft clouds-the pear-shaped gateway had become almost circular. To do anything but drift through life, a stereotype among stereotypes, was simply ... too ... much ... work....

At that very moment, as if his thought had summoned the experience into being, another scene filmed over the blue sky and white clouds above him. The sudden humming in his ears —a kind of "audible silence" —informed him that his second sight was at work, warning him of some deadly danger. But this was a more gentle instance of it, for not all his consciousness jumped somewhere else. All through the experience, he was still aware of himself leaning against the grassy hummock, of the restful melancholy of the scene around him, and of the sky overhead. The second scene only superimposed itself on the first.

He was poised many hundreds of miles above the Earth, a ghost-Ernie immune to the airlessness and the Sun's untempered beams. At his back was black night filled with stars. Below him stretched the granulated dry brown of Earth's surface, tinged here and there with green, clumped with white cloud, and everywhere faintly hazed with blue.

Up there in space with him, right at his elbow, so close that he could reach out and touch it, was a tiny silver cylinder about as big as a hazelnut, domed at one end, reflecting sunlight from one point in a way that would have been blinding enough except that Ernie's ghost eyes were immune to brightness.

As he reached out to examine it, the thing darted away from him as if at some imperious summons, like a bit of iron jumping through a magnetic field.

But in spite of its enormous acceleration, Ernie's ghost was able to follow it in its downward plunge. It kept just ahead of his outstretched fingertips.

The brown granules that were Earth's surface grew in size. The tiny metal cylinder began to glow with more than reflected sunlight. It turned red, orange, yellow and then blazing white as atmospheric friction transformed it into a meteor.

Ernie's ghost, immune to friction and incandescence alike, followed it as it dove toward its target-for even though Ernie had never heard of a Juxtaposer and how it brought objects together, he had the feeling, from the dizzy speed of the meteor's plunge, that it yearned for something.

He knew most meteors vaporized or exploded, but this did not, even when Earth's brown surface grew rivers and roads. Suddenly there was a cloudbank ahead; then, in the white, there appeared an almost circular hole toward the very center of which the meteorite plunged.

Everything was happening very fast now, but his ghost senses were able to keep pace. As they plunged through the cloud-ring and the green landscape below grew explosively, he saw the white tower, the trees, the curving drives, and the clearing which was now the target.

There was still time to escape. Lying on the warm grass, with death lancing down from the sky at miles a second, he had merely to roll over.

But it was simply ... too ... much ... work....

Elsewhere near Earth, a recorder sped toward Galaxy Center a message which ended, "Six Gifts tendered, all finally refused. I will now sign off and await pickup with one Juxtaposer."

A little later, a Receiver in Galaxy Center passed the message to a Central Recorder, which filed it in the Starswarm 37 section with this addition: "Spiritual immaturity of Terran bipeds indicated. Advise against enlightenment and admission to Galactic citizenship. Test subject humanely released."

Police, digging into the turf under Ernie's shattered head two days later found the bright bullet, cold now, of course, and untarnished.

"Looks like silver!" one cop said, scratching his head. "Haven't I heard somewhere that the Mafia use silver bullets? So bright, though."

Lieutenant Padilla, later on, lifting the bullet in his forceps to re-examine it for rifling marks, had the same thought about its brightness. By now, however, he knew it was not silver. (What alloy was never satisfactorily determined. Actually it was made of the same substance as the Everlasting Razor Blade.)

This time, although he still found no rifling marks, a tiny dull stretch on the flat end of the cylinder caught his attention. He took up a magnifier and examined it carefully.

A moment later, he put down the magnifier, snatched up the pocketbook found on the dead man and rechecked some cards in it. The bullet dropped from the forceps, rolled a few inches. The lieutenant sat back in his chair, breathing a little hard.

"This is one for the books, all right!" he told himself. "I've heard a lot of people, soldiers especially, talk about such bullets, but I never expected to see one!"

For under the magnifying glass, finely engraved in very tiny letters, he had read the words: ERNEST WENCESLAUS MEEKER.

The Big Engine

Have you found out about the Big
Engine? It's all around us, you
know-can't you hear it even now?

There are all sorts of screwy theories (the Professor said) of what makes the wheels of the world go round. There's a boy in Chicago who thinks we're all of us just the thoughts of a green cat; when the green cat dies we'll all puff to nothing like smoke. There's a man in the west who thinks all women are witches and run the world by conjure magic. There's a man in the east who believes all rich people belong to a secret society that's a lot tighter and tougher than the Mafia and that has a monopoly of power-secrets and pleasure-secrets other people don't dream exist.

Me, I think the wheels of the world just go. I decided that forty years ago and I've never since seen or heard or read anything to make me change my mind.

I was a stoker on a lake boat then (the Professor continued, delicately sipping smoke from his long thin cigarette). I was as stupid as they make them, but I liked to think. Whenever I'd get a chance I'd go to one of the big libraries and make them get me all sorts of books. That was how guys started calling me the Professor. I'd get books on philosophy, metaphysics, science, even religion. I'd read them and try to figure out the world. What was it all about, anyway? Why was I here? What was the point in the whole business of getting born and working and dying? What was the use of it? Why'd it have to go on and on?

And why'd it have to be so complicated?

Why all the building and tearing down? Why'd there have to be cities, with crowded streets and horse cars and cable cars and electric cars and big open-work steel boxes built to the sky to be hung with stone and wood-my closest friend got killed falling off one of those steel boxkites. Shouldn't there be some simpler way of doing it all? Why did things have to be so mixed up that a man like myself couldn't have a single clear decent thought?

More than that, why weren't people a real part of the world? Why didn't they show more honest-to-God response? When you slept with a woman, why was it something you had and she didn't? Why, when you went to a prize fight, were the bruisers only so much meat, and the crowd a lot of little screaming popinjays? Why was a war nothing but blather and blowup and bother? Why'd everybody have to go through their whole lives so dead, doing everything so methodical and prissy like a Sunday School picnic or an orphan's parade?

And then, when I was reading one of the science books, it came to me. The answer was all there, printed out plain to see only nobody saw it. It was just this: Nobody was really alive.

Back of other people's foreheads there weren't any real thoughts or minds, or love or fear, to explain things. The whole universe-stars and men and dirt and worms and atoms, the whole shooting match-was just one great big engine. It didn't take mind or life or anything else to run the engine. It just ran.

Now one thing about science. It doesn't lie. Those men who wrote those science books that showed me the answer, they had no more minds than anybody else. Just darkness in their brains, but because they were machines built to use science, they couldn't help but get the right answers. They were like the electric brains they've got now, but hadn't then, that give out the right answer when you feed in the question. I'd like to feed in the question, "What's Life?" to one of those machines and see what came out. Just figures, I suppose. I read somewhere that if a billion monkeys had typewriters and kept pecking away at them they'd eventually turn out all the Encyclopedia Brittanica in trillions and trillions of years. Well, they've done it all right, and in jig time.

They're doing it now.

A lot of philosophy and psychology books I worked through really fit in beautifully. There was Watson's *Behaviorism* telling how we needn't even assume that people are conscious to explain their actions. There was Leibitz's *Monadology*, with its theory that we're all of us lonely atoms that are completely out of touch and don't effect each other in the slightest, but only seem to ... because all our little clockwork motors were started at the same time in pre-established harmony. We *seem* to be responding to each other, but actually we're just a bunch of wooden-minded puppets. Jerk one puppet up into the flies and the others go on acting as if exactly nothing at all had happened.

So there it was all laid out for me (the Professor went on, carefully pinching out the end of his cigarette). That was why there was no honest-to-God response in people. They were machines.

The fighters were machines made for fighting. The people that watched them were machines for stamping and screaming and swearing. The bankers had banking cogs in their bellies, the crooks had crooked cams. A woman was just a loving machine, all nicely adjusted to give you a good time (sometimes!) but the farthest star was nearer to you than the mind behind that mouth you kissed.

See what I mean? People just machines, set to do a certain job and then quietly rust away. If you kept on being the machine you were supposed to be, well and good. Then your actions fitted with other people's. But if you didn't, if you started doing something else, then the others didn't respond. They just went on doing what was called for.

It wouldn't matter what you did, they'd just go on making the motions they were set to make. They might be set to make love, and you might decide you wanted to fight. They'd go on making love while you fought them. Or it might happen the other way—seems to, more often!

Or somebody might be talking about Edison. And you'd happen to say something about Ingersoll. But he'd just go on talking about Edison.

You were all alone.

Except for a few others—not more than one in a hundred thousand, I guess—who wake up and figure things out. And they mostly go crazy and run themselves to death, or else turn mean. Mostly they turn mean. They get a cheap little kick out of pushing things around that can't push back. All over the world you find them—little gangs of three or four, half a dozen—who've waked up, but just to their cheap kicks. Maybe it's a couple of coppers in 'Frisco, a schoolteacher in K.C., some artists in New York, some rich kids in Florida, some undertakers in London—who've found that all the people walking around are just dead folk and to be treated no decenter, who see how bad things are and get their fun out of making it a little worse. Just a mean *little* bit worse. They don't dare to destroy in a big way, because they know the machine feeds them and tends them, and because they're always scared they'd be noticed by gangs like themselves and wiped out. They haven't the guts to really wreck the whole shebang. But they get a kick out of scribbling their dirty pictures on it, out of meddling and messing with it.

I've seen some of their fun, as they call it, sometimes hidden away, sometimes in the open streets.

You've seen a clerk dressing a figure in a store window? Well, suppose he slapped its face. Suppose a kid stuck pins in a calico pussy-cat, or threw pepper in the eyes of a doll.

No decent live man would have anything to do with nickel sadism or dime paranoia like that. He'd either go back to his place in the machine and act out the part set for him, or else he'd hide away like me and live as quiet as he could, not stirring things up. Like a mouse in a dynamo or an ant in an atomics plant.

(The Professor went to the window and opened it, letting the sour old smoke out and the noises of the city in.)

272

Listen (he said), listen to the great mechanical symphony, the big black combo. The airplanes are the double bass. Have you noticed how you can always hear one nowadays? When one walks out of the sky another walks in.

Presses and pumps round out the bass section. Listen to them rumble and thump! Tonight they've got an old steam locomotive helping. Maybe they're giving a benefit show for the old duffer.

Cars and traffic-they're the strings. Mostly cellos and violas. They purr and wail and whine and keep trying to get out of their section.

Brasses? To me the steel-on-steel of streetcars and El trains always sounds like trumpets and cornets. Strident, metallic, fiery cold.

Hear that siren way off? It's a clarinet. The ship horns are tubas, the diesel horn's an oboe. And that lovely dreadful french horn is an electric saw cutting down the last tree.

But what a percussion section they've got! The big stuff, like streetcar bells jangling, is easy to catch, but you have to really listen to get the subtleties-the buzz of a defective neon sign, the click of a stoplight changing.

Sometimes you do get human voices, I'll admit, but they're not like they are in Beethoven's *Ninth* or Holst's *Planets*.

There's the real sound of the universe (the Professor concluded, shutting the window). That's your heavenly choir. That's the music of the spheres the old alchemists kept listening for-if they'd just stayed around a little longer they'd all have been deafened by it. Oh, to think that Schopenhauer was bothered by the crack of carters' whips!

And now it's time for this mouse to tuck himself in his nest in the dynamo. Good night, gentlemen!

Coming Attraction

Women will always go on trying to attract men...
even when the future seems to have no future!

The coupe with the fishhooks welded to the fender shouldered up over the curb like the nose of a nightmare. The girl in its path stood frozen, her face probably stiff with fright under her mask. For once my reflexes weren't shy. I took a fast step toward her, grabbed her elbow, yanked her back. Her black skirt swirled out.

The big coupe shot by, its turbine humming. I glimpsed three faces. Something ripped. I felt the hot exhaust on my ankles as the big coupe swerved back into the street. A thick cloud like a black flower blossomed from its jouncing rear end, while from the fishhooks flew a black shimmering rag.

"Did they get you?" I asked the girl.

She had twisted around to look where the side of her skirt was torn away. She was wearing nylon tights.

"The hooks didn't touch me," she said shakily. "I guess I'm lucky."

I heard voices around us:

"Those kids! What'll they think up next?"

"They're a menace. They ought to be arrested."

Sirens screamed at a rising pitch as two motor-police, their rocket-assist jets full on, came whizzing toward us after the coupe. But the black flower had become a thick fog obscuring the whole street. The motor-police switched from rocket assists to rocket brakes and swerved to a stop near the smoke cloud.

"Are you English?" the girl asked me. "You have an English accent."

Her voice came shudderingly from behind the sleek black satin mask. I fancied her teeth must be chattering. Eyes that were perhaps blue searched my face from behind the black gauze covering the eyeholes of the mask. I told her she'd guessed right. She stood close to me. "Will you come to my place tonight?" she asked rapidly. "I can't thank you now. And there's something you can help me about."

My arm, still lightly circling her waist, felt her body trembling. I was answering the plea in that as much as in her voice when I said, "Certainly." She gave me an address south of Inferno, an apartment number and a time. She asked me my name and I told her.

"Hey, you!"

I turned obediently to the policeman's shout. He shooed away the small clucking crowd of masked women and barefaced men. Coughing from the smoke that the black coupe had thrown out, he asked for my papers. I handed him the essential ones.

He looked at them and then at me. "British Barter? How long will you be in New York?"

Suppressing the urge to say, "For as short a time as possible," I told him I'd be here for a week or so.

"May need you as a witness," he explained. "Those kids can't use smoke on us. When they do that, we pull them in."

He seemed to think the smoke was the bad thing. "They tried to kill the lady," I pointed out.

He shook his head wisely. "They always pretend they're going to, but actually they just want to snag skirts. I've picked up rippers with as many as fifty skirt-snags tacked up in their rooms. Of course, sometimes they come a little too close."

I explained that if I hadn't yanked her out of the way, she'd have been hit by more than hooks. But he interrupted, "If she'd thought it was a real murder attempt, she'd have stayed here."

I looked around. It was true. She was gone.

"She was fearfully frightened," I told him.

"Who wouldn't be? Those kids would have scared old Stalin himself."

"I mean frightened of more than 'kids.' They didn't look like 'kids.'"

"What did they look like?"

I tried without much success to describe the three faces. A vague impression of viciousness and effeminacy doesn't mean much.

"Well, I could be wrong," he said finally. "Do you know the girl? Where she lives?"

"No," I half lied.

The other policeman hung up his radiophone and ambled toward us, kicking at the tendrils of dissipating smoke. The black cloud no longer hid the dingy facades with their five-year-old radiation flash-burns, and I could begin to make out the distant stump of the Empire State Building, thrusting up out of Inferno like a mangled finger.

"They haven't been picked up so far," the approaching policeman grumbled. "Left smoke for five blocks, from what Ryan says."

The first policeman shook his head. "That's bad," he observed solemnly.

I was feeling a bit uneasy and ashamed. An Englishman shouldn't lie, at least not on impulse.

"They sound like nasty customers," the first policeman continued in the same grim tone. "We'll need witnesses. Looks as if you may have to stay in New York longer than you expect."

I got the point. I said, "I forgot to show you all my papers," and handed him a few others, making sure there was a five dollar bill in among them.

When he handed them back a bit later, his voice was no longer ominous. My feelings of guilt vanished. To cement our relationship, I chatted with the two of them about their job.

"I suppose the masks give you some trouble," I observed. "Over in England we've been reading about your new crop of masked female bandits."

"Those things get exaggerated," the first policeman assured me. "It's the men masking as women that really mix us up. But, brother, when we nab them, we jump on them with both feet."

"And you get so you can spot women almost as well as if they had naked faces," the second policeman volunteered. "You know, hands and all that."

"Especially all that," the first agreed with a chuckle. "Say, is it true that some girls don't mask over in England?"

"A number of them have picked up the fashion," I told him. "Only a few, though-the ones who always adopt the latest style, however extreme."

"They're usually masked in the British newscasts."

"I imagine it's arranged that way out of deference to American taste," I confessed. "Actually, not very many do mask."

The second policeman considered that. "Girls going down the street bare from the neck up." It was not clear whether he viewed the prospect with relish or moral distaste. Likely both.

"A few members keep trying to persuade Parliament to enact a law forbidding all masking," I continued, talking perhaps a bit too much.

The second policeman shook his head. "What an idea. You know, masks are a pretty good thing, brother. Couple of years more and I'm going to make my wife wear hers around the house."

The first policeman shrugged. "If women were to stop wearing masks, in six weeks you wouldn't know the difference. You get used to anything, if enough people do or don't do it."

I agreed, rather regretfully, and left them. I turned north on Broadway (old Tenth Avenue, I believe) and walked rapidly until I was beyond Inferno. Passing such an area of undecontaminated radioactivity always makes a person queasy. I thanked God there weren't any such in England, as yet.

The street was almost empty, though I was accosted by a couple of beggars with faces tunneled by H-bomb scars, whether real or of makeup putty, I couldn't tell. A fat woman held out a baby with webbed fingers and toes. I told myself it would have been deformed anyway and that she was only capitalizing on our fear of bomb-induced mutations. Still, I gave her a seven-and-a-half-cent piece. Her mask made me feel I was paying tribute to an African fetish.

"May all your children be blessed with one head and two eyes, sir."

"Thanks," I said, shuddering, and hurried past her.

"...There's only trash behind the mask, so turn your head, stick to your task: Stay away, stay away-from-the-girls!"

This last was the end of an anti-sex song being sung by some religionists half a block from the circle-and-cross insignia of a femalist temple. They reminded me only faintly of our small tribe of British monastics. Above their heads was a jumble of billboards advertising predigested foods, wrestling instruction, radio handies and the like.

I stared at the hysterical slogans with disagreeable fascination. Since the female face and form have been banned on American signs, the very letters of the advertiser's alphabet have begun to crawl with sex-the fat-bellied, big-breasted capital B, the lascivious double O. However, I reminded myself, it is chiefly the mask that so strangely accents sex in America.

A British anthropologist has pointed out, that, while it took more than 5,000 years to shift the chief point of sexual interest from the hips to the breasts, the next transition to the face has taken less than 50 years. Comparing the American style with Moslem tradition is not valid; Moslem women are compelled to wear veils, the purpose of which is concealment, while American women have only the compulsion of fashion and use masks to create mystery.

Theory aside, the actual origins of the trend are to be found in the anti-radiation clothing of World War III, which led to masked wrestling, now a fantastically popular sport, and that in turn led to the current female fashion. Only a wild style at first, masks quickly became as necessary as brassieres and lipsticks had been earlier in the century.

I finally realized that I was not speculating about masks in general, but about what lay behind one in particular. That's the devil of the things; you're never sure whether a girl is heightening loveliness or hiding ugliness. I pictured a cool, pretty face in which fear showed only in widened eyes. Then I remembered her blonde hair, rich against the blackness of the satin mask. She'd told me to come at the twenty-second hour-ten p.m.

I climbed to my apartment near the British Consulate; the elevator shaft had been shoved out of plumb by an old blast, a nuisance in these tall New York buildings. Before it occurred to me that I would be going out again, I automatically tore a tab from the film strip under my shirt. I developed it just to be sure. It showed that the total radiation I'd taken that day was still within the safety limit. I'm not phobic about it, as so many people are these days, but there's no point in taking chances.

I flopped down on the day bed and stared at the silent speaker and the dark screen of the video set. As always, they made me think, somewhat bitterly, of the two great nations of the world. Mutilated by each other, yet still strong, they were crippled giants poisoning the planet with their dreams of an impossible equality and an impossible success.

I fretfully switched on the speaker. By luck, the newscaster was talking excitedly of the prospects of a bumper wheat crop, sown by planes across a dust bowl moistened by seeded rains. I listened carefully to the rest of the program (it was remarkably clear of Russian telejamming) but there was no further news of interest to me. And, of course, no mention of the Moon, though everyone knows that America and Russia are racing to develop their primary bases into fortresses capable of mutual assault and the launching of alphabet-bombs toward Earth. I myself knew perfectly well that the British electronic equipment I was helping trade for American wheat was destined for use in spaceships.

I switched off the newscast. It was growing dark and once again I pictured a tender, frightened face behind a mask. I hadn't had a date since England. It's exceedingly difficult to become acquainted with a girl in America, where as little as a smile, often, can set one of them yelping for the police-to say nothing of the increasing puritanical morality and the roving gangs that keep most women indoors after dark. And naturally, the masks which are definitely not, as the Soviets claim, a last invention of capitalist degeneracy, but a sign of great psychological insecurity. The Russians have no masks, but they have their own signs of stress.

I went to the window and impatiently watched the darkness gather. I was getting very restless. After a while a ghostly violet cloud appeared to the south. My hair rose. Then I laughed. I had momentarily fancied it a radiation from the crater of the Hell-bomb, though I should instantly have known it was only the radio-induced glow in the sky over the amusement and residential area south of Inferno.

Promptly at twenty-two hours I stood before the door of my unknown girl friend's apartment. The electronic say-who-please said just that. I answered clearly, "Wysten Turner," wondering if she'd given my name to the mechanism. She evidently had, for the door opened. I walked into a small empty living room, my heart pounding a bit.

The room was expensively furnished with the latest pneumatic hassocks and sprawlers. There were some midgie books on the table. The one I picked up was the standard hard-boiled detective story in which two female murderers go gunning for each other.

The television was on. A masked girl in green was crooning a love song. Her right hand held something that blurred off into the foreground. I saw the set had a handie, which we haven't in England as yet, and curiously thrust my hand into the handie orifice beside the screen. Contrary to my expectations, it was not like slipping into a pulsing rubber glove, but rather as if the girl on the screen actually held my hand.

A door opened behind me. I jerked out my hand with as guilty a reaction as if I'd been caught peering through a keyhole.

She stood in the bedroom doorway. I think she was trembling. She was wearing a gray fur coat, white-speckled, and a gray velvet evening mask with shirred gray lace around the eyes and mouth. Her fingernails twinkled like silver.

It hadn't occurred to me that she'd expect us to go out.

"I should have told you," she said softly. Her mask veered nervously toward the books and the screen and the room's dark corners. "But I can't possibly talk to you here."

I said doubtfully, "There's a place near the Consulate...."

"I know where we can be together and talk," she said rapidly. "If you don't mind."

As we entered the elevator I said, "I'm afraid I dismissed the cab."

But the cab driver hadn't gone for some reason of his own. He jumped out and smirkingly held the front door open for us. I told him we preferred to sit in back. He sulkily opened the rear door, slammed it after us, jumped in front and slammed the door behind him.

My companion leaned forward. "Heaven," she said.

The driver switched on the turbine and televisor.

"Why did you ask if I were a British subject?" I said, to start the conversation.

She leaned away from me, tilting her mask close to the window. "See the Moon," she said in a quick, dreamy voice.

"But why, really?" I pressed, conscious of an irritation that had nothing to do with her.

"It's edging up into the purple of the sky."

"And what's your name?"

"The purple makes it look yellower."

Just then I became aware of the source of my irritation. It lay in the square of writhing light in the front of the cab beside the driver.

I don't object to ordinary wrestling matches, though they bore me, but I simply detest watching a man wrestle a woman. The fact that the bouts are generally "on the level," with the man greatly outclassed in weight and reach and the masked females young and personable, only makes them seem worse to me.

"Please turn off the screen," I requested the driver.

He shook his head without looking around. "Uh-uh, man," he said. "They've been grooming that babe for weeks for this bout with Little Zirk."

Infuriated, I reached forward, but my companion caught my arm. "Please," she whispered frightenedly, shaking her head.

I settled back, frustrated. She was closer to me now, but silent and for a few moments I watched the heaves and contortions of the powerful masked girl and her wiry masked opponent on the screen. His frantic scrambling at her reminded me of a male spider.

I jerked around, facing my companion. "Why did those three men want to kill you?" I asked sharply.

The eyeholes of her mask faced the screen. "Because they're jealous of me," she whispered.

"Why are they jealous?"

She still didn't look at me. "Because of him."

"Who?"

She didn't answer.

I put my arm around her shoulders. "Are you afraid to tell me?" I asked. "What *is* the matter?"

She still didn't look my way. She smelled nice.

"See here," I said laughingly, changing my tactics, "you really should tell me something about yourself. I don't even know what you look like."

I half playfully lifted my hand to the band of her neck. She gave it an astonishingly swift slap. I pulled it away in sudden pain. There were four tiny indentations on the back. From one of them a tiny bead of blood welled out as I watched. I looked at her silver fingernails and saw they were actually delicate and pointed metal caps.

"I'm dreadfully sorry," I heard her say, "but you frightened me. I thought for a moment you were going to...."

At last she turned to me. Her coat had fallen open. Her evening dress was Cretan Revival, a bodice of lace beneath and supporting the breasts without covering them.

"Don't be angry," she said, putting her arms around my neck. "You were wonderful this afternoon."

The soft gray velvet of her mask, molding itself to her cheek, pressed mine. Through the mask's lace the wet warm tip of her tongue touched my chin.

"I'm not angry," I said. "Just puzzled and anxious to help."

The cab stopped. To either side were black windows bordered by spears of broken glass. The sickly purple light showed a few ragged figures slowly moving toward us.

The driver muttered, "It's the turbine, man. We're grounded." He sat there hunched and motionless. "Wish it had happened somewhere else."

My companion whispered, "Five dollars is the usual amount."

She looked out so shudderingly at the congregating figures that I suppressed my indignation and did as she suggested. The driver took the bill without a word. As he started up, he put his hand out the window and I heard a few coins clink on the pavement.

My companion came back into my arms, but her mask faced the television screen, where the tall girl had just pinned the convulsively kicking Little Zirk.

"I'm so frightened," she breathed.

Heaven turned out to be an equally ruinous neighborhood, but it had a club with an awning and a huge doorman uniformed like a spaceman, but in gaudy colors. In my sensuous daze I rather liked it all. We stepped out of the cab just as a drunken old woman came down the sidewalk, her mask awry. A couple ahead of us turned their heads from the half revealed face, as if from an ugly body at the beach. As we followed them in I heard the doorman say, "Get along, grandma, and watch yourself."

Inside, everything was dimness and blue glows. She had said we could talk here, but I didn't see how. Besides the inevitable chorus of sneezes and coughs (they say America is fifty per cent allergic these days), there was a band going full blast in the latest robop style, in which an electronic composing machine selects an arbitrary sequence of tones into which the musicians weave their raucous little individualities.

Most of the people were in booths. The band was behind the bar. On a small platform beside them, a girl was dancing, stripped to her mask. The little cluster of men at the shadowy far end of the bar weren't looking at her.

We inspected the menu in gold script on the wall and pushed the buttons for breast of chicken, fried shrimps and two scotches. Moments later, the serving bell tinkled. I opened the gleaming panel and took out our drinks.

The cluster of men at the bar filed off toward the door, but first they stared around the room. My companion had just thrown back her coat. Their look lingered on our booth. I noticed that there were three of them.

The band chased off the dancing girl with growls. I handed my companion a straw and we sipped our drinks.

"You wanted me to help you about something," I said. "Incidentally, I think you're lovely."

She nodded quick thanks, looked around, leaned forward. "Would it be hard for me to get to England?"

"No," I replied, a bit taken aback. "Provided you have an American passport."

"Are they difficult to get?"

"Rather," I said, surprised at her lack of information. "Your country doesn't like its nationals to travel, though it isn't quite as stringent as Russia."

"Could the British Consulate help me get a passport?"

"It's hardly their...."

"Could you?"

I realized we were being inspected. A man and two girls had paused opposite our table. The girls were tall and wolfish-looking, with spangled masks. The man stood jauntily between them like a fox on its hind legs.

My companion didn't glance at them, but she sat back. I noticed that one of the girls had a big yellow bruise on her forearm. After a moment they walked to a booth in the deep shadows.

"Know them?" I asked. She didn't reply. I finished my drink. "I'm not sure you'd like England," I said. "The austerity's altogether different from your American brand of misery."

She leaned forward again. "But I must get away," she whispered.

"Why?" I was getting impatient.

"Because I'm so frightened."

There were chimes. I opened the panel and handed her the fried shrimps. The sauce on my breast of chicken was a delicious steaming compound of almonds, soy and ginger. But something must have been wrong with the radionic oven that had thawed and heated it, for at the first bite I crunched a kernel of ice in the meat. These delicate mechanisms need constant repair and there aren't enough mechanics.

I put down my fork. "What are you really scared of?" I asked her.

For once her mask didn't waver away from my face. As I waited I could feel the fears gathering without her naming them, tiny dark shapes swarming through the curved night outside, converging on the radioactive pest spot of New York, dipping into the margins of the purple. I felt a sudden rush of sympathy, a desire to protect the girl opposite me. The warm feeling added itself to the infatuation engendered in the cab.

"Everything," she said finally.

I nodded and touched her hand.

"I'm afraid of the Moon," she began, her voice going dreamy and brittle as it had in the cab. "You can't look at it and not think of guided bombs."

"It's the same Moon over England," I reminded her.

"But it's not England's Moon any more. It's ours and Russia's. You're not responsible."

I pressed her hand.

"Oh, and then," she said with a tilt of her mask, "I'm afraid of the cars and the gangs and the loneliness and Inferno. I'm afraid of the lust that undresses your face. And —" her voice hushed —"I'm afraid of the wrestlers."

"Yes?" I prompted softly after a moment.

Her mask came forward. "Do you know something about the wrestlers?" she asked rapidly. "The ones that wrestle women, I mean. They often lose, you know. And then they have to have a girl to take their frustration out on. A girl who's soft and weak and terribly frightened. They need that, to keep them men. Other men don't want them to have a girl. Other men want them just to fight women and be heroes. But they must have a girl. It's horrible for her."

I squeezed her fingers tighter, as if courage could be transmitted-granting I had any. "I think I can get you to England," I said.

Shadows crawled onto the table and stayed there. I looked up at the three men who had been at the end of the bar. They were the men I had seen in the big coupe. They wore black sweaters and close-fitting black trousers. Their faces were as expressionless as dopers. Two of them stood above me. The other loomed over the girl.

"Drift off, man," I was told. I heard the other inform the girl: "We'll wrestle a fall, sister. What shall it be? Judo, slapsie or kill-who-can?"

I stood up. There are times when an Englishman simply must be mal-treated. But just then the foxlike man came gliding in like the star of a ballet. The reaction of the other three startled me. They were acutely embarrassed.

He smiled at them thinly. "You won't win my favor by tricks like this," he said.

"Don't get the wrong idea, Zirk," one of them pleaded.

"I will if it's right," he said. "She told me what you tried to do this afternoon. That won't endear you to me, either. Drift."

They backed off awkwardly. "Let's get out of here," one of them said loudly, as they turned. "I know a place where they fight naked with knives."

Little Zirk laughed musically and slipped into the seat beside my companion. She shrank from him, just a little. I pushed my feet back, leaned forward.

"Who's your friend, baby?" he asked, not looking at her.

She passed the question to me with a little gesture. I told him.

"British," he observed. "She's been asking you about getting out of the country? About passports?" He smiled pleasantly. "She likes to start running away. Don't you, baby?" His small hand began to stroke her wrist, the fingers bent a little, the tendons ridged, as if he were about to grab and twist.

"Look here," I said sharply. "I have to be grateful to you for ordering off those bullies, but —"

"Think nothing of it," he told me. "They're no harm except when they're behind steering wheels. A well-trained fourteen-year-old girl could cripple any one of them. Why, even Theda here, if she went in for that sort of thing...." He turned to her, shifting his hand from her wrist to her hair. He stroked it, letting the strands slip slowly through his fingers. "You know I lost tonight, baby, don't you?" he said softly.

I stood up. "Come along," I said to her. "Let's leave."

She just sat there. I couldn't even tell if she was trembling. I tried to read a message in her eyes through the mask.

"I'll take you away," I said to her. "I can do it. I really will."

He smiled at me. "She'd like to go with you," he said. "Wouldn't you, baby?"

"Will you or won't you?" I said to her. She still just sat there.

He slowly knotted his fingers in her hair.

"Listen, you little vermin," I snapped at him, "Take your hands off her."

He came up from the seat like a snake. I'm no fighter. I just know that the more scared I am, the harder and straighter I hit. This time I was lucky. But as he crumpled back, I felt a slap and four stabs of pain in my cheek. I clapped my hand to it. I could feel the four gashes made by her dagger finger caps, and the warm blood oozing out from them.

She didn't look at me. She was bending over little Zirk and cuddling her mask to his cheek and crooning: "There, there, don't feel bad, you'll be able to hurt me afterward."

There were sounds around us, but they didn't come close. I leaned forward and ripped the mask from her face.

I really don't know why I should have expected her face to be anything else. It was very pale, of course, and there weren't any cosmetics. I suppose there's no point in wearing any under a mask. The eye-brows were untidy and the lips chapped. But as for the general expression, as for the feelings crawling and wriggling across it —

Have you ever lifted a rock from damp soil? Have you ever watched the slimy white grubs?

I looked down at her, she up at me. "Yes, you're so frightened, aren't you?" I said sarcastically. "You dread this little nightly drama, don't you? You're scared to death."

And I walked right out into the purple night, still holding my hand to my bleeding cheek. No one stopped me, not even the girl wrestlers. I wished I could tear a tab from under my shirt, and test it then and there, and find I'd taken too much radiation, and so be able to ask to cross the Hudson and go down New Jersey, past the lingering radiance of the Narrows Bomb, and so on to Sandy Hook to wait for the rusty ship that would take me back over the seas to England.

X Marks the Pedwalk

This is how it all began-the terrible
civil strife that devastates our world!

The raggedy little old lady with the big shopping bag was in the exact center of the crosswalk when she became aware of the big black car bearing down on her.

Behind the thick bullet-proof glass its seven occupants had a misty look, like men in a diving bell.

She saw there was no longer time to beat the car to either curb. Veering remorselessly, it would catch her in the gutter.

Useless to attempt a feint and double-back, such as any venturesome child executed a dozen times a day. Her reflexes were too slow.

Polite vacuous laughter came from the car's loudspeaker over the engine's mounting roar.

From her fellow pedestrians lining the curbs came a sigh of horror.

The little old lady dipped into her shopping bag and came up with a big blue-black automatic. She held it in both fists, riding the recoils like a rodeo cowboy on a bucking bronco.

Aiming at the base of the windshield, just as a big-game hunter aims at the vulnerable spine of a charging water buffalo over the horny armor of its lowered head, the little old lady squeezed off three shots before the car chewed her down.

From the right-hand curb a young woman in a wheelchair shrieked an obscenity at the car's occupants.

Smythe-de Winter, the driver, wasn't happy. The little old lady's last shot had taken two members of his car pool. Bursting through the laminated glass, the steel-jacketed slug had traversed the neck of Phipps-McHeath and buried itself in the skull of Horvendile-Harker.

Braking viciously, Smythe-de Winter rammed the car over the right-hand curb. Pedestrians scattered into entries and narrow arcades, among them a youth bounding high on crutches.

But Smythe-de Winter got the girl in the wheelchair.

Then he drove rapidly out of the Slum Ring into the Suburbs, a shred of rattan swinging from the flange of his right fore mudguard for a trophy. Despite the two-for-two casualty list, he felt angry and depressed. The secure, predictable world around him seemed to be crumbling.

While his companions softly keened a dirge to Horvy and Phipps and quietly mopped up their blood, he frowned and shook his head.

"They oughtn't to let old ladies carry magnums," he murmured.

Witherspoon-Hobbs nodded agreement across the front-seat corpse. "They oughtn't to let 'em carry anything. God, how I hate Feet," he muttered, looking down at his shrunken legs. "Wheels forever!" he softly cheered.

The incident had immediate repercussions throughout the city. At the combined wake of the little old lady and the girl in the wheelchair, a fiery-tongued speaker inveighed against the White-Walled Fascists of Suburbia, telling to his hearers, the fabled wonders of old Los Angeles, where pedestrians were sacrosanct, even outside crosswalks. He called for a hobnail march across the nearest lawn-bowling alleys and perambulator-traversed golf courses of the motorists.

At the Sunnyside Crematorium, to which the bodies of Phipps and Horvy had been conveyed, an equally impassioned and rather more grammatical orator reminded his listeners of the legendary justice of old Chicago, where pedestrians were forbidden to carry small arms and anyone with one foot off the sidewalk was fair prey. He broadly hinted that a holocaust, primed if necessary with a few tankfuls of gasoline, was the only cure for the Slums.

Bands of skinny youths came loping at dusk out of the Slum Ring into the innermost sections of the larger doughnut of the Suburbs slashing defenseless tires, shooting expensive watchdogs and scrawling filthy words on the pristine panels of matrons' runabouts which never ventured more than six blocks from home.

Simultaneously squadrons of young suburban motorcycles and scooterites roared through the outermost precincts of the Slum Ring, harrying children off sidewalks, tossing stink-bombs through second-story tenement windows and defacing hovel-fronts with sprays of black paint.

Incident —a thrown brick, a cut corner, monster tacks in the portico of the Auto Club-were even reported from the center of the city, traditionally neutral territory.

The Government hurriedly acted, suspending all traffic between the Center and the Suburbs and establishing a 24-hour curfew in the Slum Ring. Government agents moved only by centipede-car and pogo-hopper to underline the point that they favored neither contending side.

The day of enforced non-movement for Feet and Wheels was spent in furtive vengeful preparations. Behind locked garage doors, machine-guns that fired through the nose ornament were mounted under hoods, illegal scythe blades were welded to oversize hubcaps and the stainless steel edges of flange fenders were honed to razor sharpness.

While nervous National Guardsmen hopped about the deserted sidewalks of the Slum Ring, grim-faced men and women wearing black armbands moved through the webwork of secret tunnels and hidden doors, distributing heavy-caliber small arms and spike-studded paving blocks, piling cobblestones on strategic roof-tops and sapping upward from the secret tunnels to create car-traps. Children got ready to soap intersections after dark. The Committee of Pedestrian Safety, sometimes known as Robespierre's Rats, prepared to release its two carefully hoarded anti-tank guns.

At nightfall, under the tireless urging of the Government, representatives of the Pedestrians and the Motorists met on a huge safety island at the boundary of the Slum Ring and the Suburbs.

Underlings began a noisy dispute as to whether Smythe-de Winter had failed to give a courtesy honk before charging, whether the little old lady had opened fire before the car had come within honking distance, how many wheels of Smythe-de's car had been on the sidewalk when he hit the girl in the wheelchair and so on. After a little while the High Pedestrian and the Chief Motorist exchanged cautious winks and drew aside.

The red writhing of a hundred kerosene flares and the mystic yellow pulsing of a thousand firefly lamps mounted on yellow sawhorses ranged around the safety island illumined two tragic, strained faces.

"A word before we get down to business," the Chief Motorist whispered. "What's the current S.Q. of your adults?"

"Forty-one and dropping," the High Pedestrian replied, his eyes fearfully searching from side to side for eavesdroppers. "I can hardly get aides who are halfway *compos mentis.*"

"Our own Sanity Quotient is thirty-seven," the Chief Motorist revealed. He shrugged helplessly...."The wheels inside my people's heads are slowing down. I do not think they will be speeded up in my lifetime."

"They say Government's only fifty-two," the other said with a matching shrug.

"Well, I suppose we must scrape out one more compromise," the one suggested hollowly, "though I must confess there are times when I think we're all the figments of a paranoid's dream."

Two hours of concentrated deliberations produced the new Wheel-Foot Articles of Agreement. Among other points, pedestrian handguns were limited to a slightly lower muzzle velocity and to .38 caliber and under, while motorists were required to give three honks at one block distance before charging a pedestrian in a crosswalk. Two wheels over the curb changed a traffic kill from third-degree manslaughter to petty homicide. Blind pedestrians were permitted to carry hand grenades.

Immediately the Government went to work. The new Wheel-Foot Articles were loudspeakered and posted. Detachments of police and psychiatric social hoppers centipedaled and pogoed through the Slum Ring, seizing outsize weapons and giving tranquilizing jet-injections to the unruly. Teams of hypnotherapists and mechanics scuttled from home to home in the Suburbs and from garage to garage, in-chanting a conformist serenity and stripping illegal armament from cars. On the advice of a rogue psychiatrist, who said it would channel off aggressions, a display of bull-fighting was announced, but this had to be canceled when a strong protest was lodged by the Decency League, which had a large mixed Wheel-Foot membership.

At dawn, curfew was lifted in the Slum Ring and traffic reopened between the Suburbs and the Center. After a few uneasy moments it became apparent that the *status quo* had been restored.

Smythe-de Winter tooled his gleaming black machine along the Ring. A thick steel bolt with a large steel washer on either side neatly filled the hole the little old lady's slug had made in the windshield.

A brick bounced off the roof. Bullets pattered against the side windows.

Smythe-de ran a handkerchief around his neck under his collar and smiled.

A block ahead children were darting into the street, cat-calling and thumbing their noses. Behind one of them limped a fat dog with a spiked collar.

Smythe-de suddenly gunned his motor. He didn't hit any of the children, but he got the dog.

A flashing light on the dash showed him the right front tire was losing pressure. Must have hit the collar as well! He thumbed the matching emergency-air button and the flashing stopped.

He turned toward Witherspoon-Hobbs and said with thoughtful satisfaction, "I like a normal orderly world, where you always have a little success, but not champagne-heady; a little failure, but just enough to brace you."

Witherspoon-Hobbs was squinting at the next crosswalk. Its center was discolored by a brownish stain ribbon-tracked by tires.

"That's where you bagged the little old lady, Smythe-de," he remarked. "I'll say this for her now: she had spirit."

"Yes, that's where I bagged her," Smythe-de agreed flatly. He remembered wistfully the witchlike face growing rapidly larger, her jerking shoulders in black bombazine, the wild white-circled eyes. He suddenly found himself feeling that this was a very dull day.

Kreativity For Kats

They are the aliens among us-and
their ways and wonders are
stranger than extraterrestrials!

Gummitch peered thoughtfully at the molten silver image of the sun in his little bowl of water on the floor inside the kitchen window. He knew from experience that it would make dark ghost suns swim in front of his eyes for a few moments, and that was mildly interesting. Then he slowly thrust his head out over the water, careful not to ruffle its surface by rough breathing, and stared down at the mirror cat-the Gummitch Double-staring up at him.

Gummitch had early discovered that water mirrors are very different from most glass mirrors. The scentless spirit world behind glass mirrors is an upright one sharing our gravity system, its floor a continuation of the floor in the so-called real world. But the world in a water mirror has reverse gravity. One looks down into it, but the spirit-doubles in it look *up* at one. In a way water mirrors are holes or pits in the world, leading down to a spirit infinity or ghostly nadir.

Gummitch had pondered as to whether, if he plunged into such a pit, he would be sustained by the spirit gravity or fall forever. (It may well be that speculations of this sort account for the caution about swimming characteristic of most cats.)

There was at least one exception to the general rule. The looking glass on Kitty-Come-Here's dressing table also opened into a spirit world of reverse gravity, as Gummitch had discovered when he happened to look into it during one of the regular visits he made to the dressing table top, to enjoy the delightful flowery and musky odors emanating from the fragile bottles assembled there.

But exceptions to general rules, as Gummitch knew well, are only doorways to further knowledge and finer classifications. The wind could not get into the spirit world below Kitty-Come-Here's looking glass, while one of the definitive characteristics of water mirrors is that movement can very easily enter the spirit world below them, rhythmically disturbing it throughout, producing the most surreal effects, and even reducing it to chaos. Such disturbances exist only in the spirit world and are in no way a mirroring of anything in the real world: Gummitch knew that his paw did not change when it flicked the surface of the water, although the image of his paw burst into a hundred flickering fragments. (Both cats and primitive men first deduced that the world in a water mirror is a spirit world because they saw that its inhabitants were easily blown apart by the wind and must therefore be highly tenuous, though capable of regeneration.)

Gummitch mildly enjoyed creating rhythmic disturbances in the spirit worlds below water mirrors. He wished there were some way to bring their excitement and weird beauty into the real world.

On this sunny day when our story begins, the spirit world below the water mirror in his drinking bowl was particularly vivid and bright. Gummitch stared for a while longer at the Gummitch Double and then thrust down his tongue to quench his thirst. Curling swiftly upward, it conveyed a splash of water into his mouth and also flicked a single drop of water into the air before his nose. The sun struck the drop and it flashed like a diamond. In fact, it seemed to Gummitch that for a moment he had juggled the sun on his tongue. He shook his head amazedly and touched the side of the bowl with his paw. The bowl was brimful and a few drops fell out; they also flashed like tiny suns as they fell. Gummitch had a fleeting vision, a momentary creative impulse, that was gone from his mind before he could seize it. He shook his head once more, backed away from the bowl, and then lay down with his head pillowed on his paws to contemplate the matter. The room darkened as the sun went under a cloud and the young golden dark-barred cat looked like a pool of sunlight left behind.

Kitty-Come-Here had watched the whole performance from the door to the dining room and that evening she commented on it to Old Horsemeat.

"He backed away from the water as if it were poison," she said. "They have been putting more chlorine in it lately, you know, and maybe he can taste the fluorides they put in for dental decay."

Old Horsemeat doubted that, but his wife went on, "I can't figure out where Gummitch does his drinking these days. There never seems to be any water gone from his bowl. And we haven't had any cut flowers. And none of the faucets drip."

"He probably does his drinking somewhere outside," Old Horsemeat guessed.

"But he doesn't go outside very often these days," Kitty-Come-Here countered. "Scarface and the Mad Eunuch, you know. Besides, it hasn't rained for weeks. It's certainly a mystery to me where he gets his liquids. Boiling gets the chlorine out of water, doesn't it? I think I'll try him on some tomorrow."

"Maybe he's depressed," Old Horsemeat suggested. "That often leads to secret drinking."

This baroque witticism hit fairly close to the truth. Gummitch *was* depressed-had been depressed ever since he had lost his kittenish dreams of turning into a man, achieving spaceflight, learning and publishing all the secrets of the fourth dimension, and similar marvels. The black cloud of disillusionment at realizing he could only be a cat had lightened somewhat, but he was still feeling dull and unfulfilled.

Gummitch was at that difficult age for he-cats, between First Puberty, when the cat achieves essential maleness, and Second Puberty, when he gets broad-chested, jowly and thick-ruffed, becoming a fully armed sexual competitor. In the ordinary course of things he would have been spending much of his time exploring the outer world, detail-mapping the immediate vicinity, spying on other cats, making cautious approaches to unescorted females and in all ways comporting himself like a fledgling male. But this was prevented by the two burly toms who lived in the houses next door and who, far more interested in murder than the pursuit of mates, had entered into partnership with the sole object of bushwacking Gummitch. Gummitch's household had nicknamed them Scarface and the Mad Eunuch, the latter being one of those males whom "fixing" turns, not placid, but homicidally maniacal. Compared to these seasoned heavyweights, Gummitch was a welterweight at most. Scarface and the Mad Eunuch lay in wait for him by turns just beyond the kitchen door, so that his forays into the outside world were largely reduced to dashes for some hiding hole, followed by long, boring but perilous sieges.

He often wished that old Horsemeat's two older cats, Ashurbanipal and Cleopatra, had not gone to the country to live with Old Horsemeat's mother. They would have shown the evil bushwackers a thing or two!

Because of Scarface and the Mad Eunuch, Gummitch spent most of his time indoors. Since a cat is made for a half-and-half existence-half in the wild forest, half in the secure cave-he took to brooding quite morbidly. He thought over-much of ghost cats in the mirror world and of the Skeleton Cat who starved to death in a locked closet and similar grisly legends. He immersed himself in racial memories, not so much of Ancient Egypt where cats were prized as minions of the lovely cat-goddess Bast and ceremoniously mummified at the end of tranquil lives, as of the Middle Ages, when European mankind waged a genocidal war against felines as being the familiars of witches. (He thought briefly of turning Kitty-Come-Here into a witch, but his hypnotic staring and tentative ritualistic mewing only made her fidgety.) And he devoted more and more time to devising dark versions of the theory of transmigration, picturing cats as Silent Souls, Gagged People of Great Talent, and the like.

He had become too self-conscious to re-enter often the make-believe world of the kitten, yet his imagination remained as active as ever. It was a truly frustrating predicament.

More and more often and for longer periods he retired to meditate in a corrugated cardboard shoebox, open only at one end. The cramped quarters made it easier for him to think. Old Horsemeat called it the Cat Orgone Box after the famed Orgone Energy Accumulators of the late wildcat psychoanalyst Dr. Wilhelm Reich.

If only, Gummitch thought, he could devise some way of objectifying the intimations of beauty that flitted through his darkly clouded mind! Now, on the evening of the sunny day when he had backed away from his water bowl, he attacked the problem anew. He knew he had been fleetingly on the verge of a great idea, an idea involving water, light and movement. An idea he had unfortunately forgotten. He closed his eyes and twitched his nose. I must concentrate, he thought to himself, concentrate....

Next day Kitty-Come-Here remembered her idea about Gummitch's water. She boiled two cupfuls in a spotless enamelware saucepan, letting it cool for half an hour before using it to replace the seemingly offensive water in the young cat's bowl. It was only then she noticed that the bowl had been upset.

She casually assumed that big-footed Old Horsemeat must have been responsible for the accident, or possibly one of the two children-darting Sissy or blundering Baby. She wiped the bowl and filled it with the water she had dechlorinated.

"Come here, Kitty, come here," she called to Gummitch, who had been watching her actions attentively from the dining room door. The young cat stayed where he was. "Oh, well, if you want to be coy," she said, shrugging her shoulders.

There was a mystery about the spilled water. It had apparently disappeared entirely, though the day seemed hardly dry enough for total evaporation. Then she saw it standing in a puddle by the wall fully ten feet away from the bowl. She made a quick deduction and frowned a bit worriedly.

"I never realized the kitchen floor sloped *that* much," she told Old Horsemeat after dinner. "Maybe some beams need to be jacked up in the basement. I'd hate to think of collapsing into it while I cooked dinner."

"I'm sure this house finished all its settling thirty years ago," her husband assured her hurriedly. "That slope's always been there."

"Well, if you say so," Kitty-Come-Here allowed doubtfully.

Next day she found Gummitch's bowl upset again and the remains of the boiled water in a puddle across the room. As she mopped it up, she began to do some thinking without benefit of Concentration Box.

That evening, after Old Horsemeat and Sissy had vehemently denied kicking into the water bowl or stepping on its edge, she voiced her conclusions. "I think *Gummitch* upsets it," she said. "He's rejecting it. It still doesn't taste right to him and he wants to show us."

"Maybe he only likes it after it's run across the floor and got seasoned with household dust and the corpses of germs," suggested Old Horsemeat, who believed most cats were bohemian types.

"I'll have you know I *scrub* that linoleum," Kitty-Come-Here asserted.

"Well, with detergent and scouring powder, then," Old Horsemeat amended resourcefully.

Kitty-Come-Here made a scornful noise. "I still want to know where he gets his liquids," she said. "He's been off milk for weeks, you know, and he only drinks a little broth when I give him that. Yet he doesn't seem dehydrated. It's a real mystery and —"

"Maybe he's built a still in the attic," Old Horsemeat interjected.

" —and I'm going to find the answers," Kitty-Come-Here concluded, ignoring the facetious interruption. "I'm going to find out *where* he gets the water he does drink and *why* he rejects the water I give him. This time I'm going to boil it and put in a pinch of salt. Just a pinch."

"You make animals sound more delicate about food and drink than humans," Old Horsemeat observed.

"They probably are," his wife countered. "For one thing they don't smoke, or drink Martinis. It's my firm belief that animals-cats, anyway-like good food just as much as we do. And the same sort of good food. They don't enjoy canned catfood any more than we would, though they *can* eat it. Just as we could if we had to. I really don't think Gummitch would have such a passion for raw horsemeat except you started him on it so early."

"He probably thinks of it as steak tartare," Old Horsemeat said.

Next day Kitty-Come-Here found her salted offering upset just as the two previous bowls had been.

Such were the beginnings of the Great Spilled Water Mystery that preoccupied the human members of the Gummitch household for weeks. Not every day, but frequently, and sometimes two and three times a day, Gummitch's little bowl was upset. No one ever saw the young cat do it. But it was generally accepted that he was responsible, though for a time Old Horsemeat had theories that he did not voice involving Sissy and Baby.

Kitty-Come-Here bought Gummitch a firm-footed rubber bowl for his water, though she hesitated over the purchase for some time, certain he would be able to taste the rubber. This bowl was found upset just like his regular china one and like the tin one she briefly revived from his kitten days.

All sorts of clues and possibly related circumstances were seized upon and dissected. For instance, after about a month of the mysterious spillings, Kitty-Come-Here announced, "I've been thinking back and as far as I can remember it never happens except on sunny days."

"Oh, Good Lord!" Old Horsemeat reacted.

Meanwhile Kitty-Come-Here continued to try to concoct a kind of water that would be palatable to Gummitch. As she continued without success, her formulas became more fantastic. She quit boiling it for the most part but added a pinch of sugar, a spoonful of beer, a few flakes of oregano, a green leaf, a violet, a drop of vanilla extract, a drop of iodine....

"No wonder he rejects the stuff," Old Horsemeat was tempted to say, but didn't.

Finally Kitty-Come-Here, inspired by the sight of a greenly glittering rack of it at the supermarket, purchased a half gallon of bottled water from a famous spring. She wondered why she hadn't thought of this step earlier-it certainly ought to take care of her haunting convictions about the unpalatableness of chlorine or fluorides. (She herself could distinctly taste the fluorides in the tap water, though she never mentioned this to Old Horsemeat.)

One other development during the Great Spilled Water Mystery was that Gummitch gradually emerged from depression and became quite gay. He took to dancing cat schottisches and gigues impromptu in the living room of an evening and so forgot his dignity as to battle joyously with the vacuum-cleaner dragon when Old Horsemeat used one of the smaller attachments to curry him; the young cat clutched the hairy round brush to his stomach and madly clawed it as it *whuffled* menacingly. Even the afternoon he came home with a shoulder gashed by the Mad Eunuch he seemed strangely light-hearted and debonair.

The Mystery was abruptly solved one sunny Sunday afternoon. Going into the bathroom in her stocking feet, Kitty-Come-Here saw Gummitch apparently trying to drown himself in the toilet. His hindquarters were on the seat but the rest of his body went down into the bowl. Coming closer, she saw that his forelegs were braced against the opposite side of the bowl, just above the water surface, while his head thrust down sharply between his shoulders. She could distinctly hear rhythmic lapping.

To tell the truth, Kitty-Come-Here was rather shocked. She had certain rather fixed ideas about the delicacy of cats. It speaks well for her progressive grounding that she did not shout at Gummitch but softly summoned her husband.

By the time Old Horsemeat arrived the young cat had refreshed himself and was coming out of his "well" with a sudden backward undulation. He passed them in the doorway with a single mew and upward look and then made off for the kitchen.

The blue and white room was bright with sunlight. Outside the sky was blue and the leaves were rustling in a stiff breeze. Gummitch looked back once, as if to make sure his human congeners had followed, mewed again, and then advanced briskly toward his little bowl with the air of one who proposes to reveal all mysteries at once.

Kitty-Come-Here had almost outdone herself. She had for the first time poured him the bottled water, and she had floated a few rose petals on the surface.

Gummitch regarded them carefully, sniffed at them, and then proceeded to fish them out one by one and shake them off his paw. Old Horsemeat repressed the urge to say, "I told you so."

When the water surface was completely free and winking in the sunlight, Gummitch curved one paw under the side of the bowl and jerked.

Half the water spilled out, gathered itself, and then began to flow across the floor in little rushes, a silver ribbon sparkling with sunlight that divided and subdivided and reunited as it followed the slope. Gummitch crouched to one side, watching it intensely, following its progress inch by inch and foot by foot, almost pouncing on the little temporary pools that formed, but not quite touching them. Twice he mewed faintly in excitement.

"He's *playing* with it," Old Horsemeat said incredulously.

"No," Kitty-Come-Here countered wide-eyed, "he's *creating* something. Silver mice. Water-snakes. Twinkling vines."

"Good Lord, you're right," Old Horsemeat agreed. "It's a new art form. Would you call it water painting? Or water sculpture? Somehow I think that's best. As if a sculptor made mobiles out of molten tin."

"It's gone so quickly, though," Kitty-Come-Here objected, a little sadly. "Art ought to last. Look, it's almost all flowed over to the wall now."

"Some of the best art forms are completely fugitive," Old Horsemeat argued. "What about improvisation in music and dancing? What about jam sessions and shadow figures on the wall? Gummitch can always do it again-in fact, he must have been doing it again and again this last month. It's never exactly the same, like waves or fires. But it's beautiful."

"I suppose so," Kitty-Come-Here said. Then coming to herself, she continued, "But I don't think it can be healthy for him to go on drinking water out of the toilet. Really."

Old Horsemeat shrugged. He had an insight about the artistic temperament and the need to dig for inspiration into the smelly fundamentals of life, but it was difficult to express delicately.

Kitty-Come-Here sighed, as if bidding farewell to all her efforts with rose petals and crystalline bottled purity and vanilla extract and the soda water which had amazed Gummitch by faintly spitting and purring at him.

"Oh, well," she said, "I can scrub it out more often, I suppose."

Meanwhile, Gummitch had gone back to his bowl and, using both paws, overset it completely. Now, nose a-twitch, he once more pursued the silver streams alive with suns, refreshing his spirit with the sight of them. He was fretted by no problems about what he was doing. He had solved them all with one of his characteristically sharp distinctions: there was the *sacred* water, the sparklingly clear water to create with, and there was the water with character, the water to *drink*.

Time in the Round

> Poor Butcher suffered more than any dictator
> in history: everybody gave in to him because
> he was so puny and they were so impregnable!

From the other end of the Avenue of Wisdom that led across the Peace Park, a gray, hairless, heavily built dog was barking soundlessly at the towering crystal glory of the Time Theater. For a moment, the effect was almost frightening: a silent picture of the beginning of civilization challenging the end of it. Then a small boy caught up with the dog and it rolled over enthusiastically at his feet and the scene was normal again.

The small boy, however, seemed definitely pre-civilization. He studied the dog coldly and then inserted a thin metal tube under its eyelid and poked. The dog wagged its stumpy tail. The boy frowned, tightened his grip on the tube and jabbed hard. The dog's tail thumped the cushiony pavement and the four paws beat the air. The boy shortened his grip and suddenly jabbed the dog several times in the stomach. The stiff tube rebounded from the gray, hairless hide. The dog's face split in an upside-down grin, revealing formidable ivory fangs across which a long black tongue lolled.

The boy regarded the tongue speculatively and pocketed the metal tube with a grimace of utter disgust. He did not look up when someone called: "Hi, Butch! Sic 'em, Darter, sic 'em!"

A larger small boy and a somewhat older one were approaching across the luxurious, neatly cropped grass, preceded by a hurtling shape that, except for a black hide, was a replica of Butch's gray dog.

Butch shrugged his shoulders resignedly and said in a bored voice: "Kill 'em, Brute."

The gray dog hurled itself on Darter. Jaws gaped to get a hold on necks so short and thick as to be mere courtesy terms. They whirled like a fanged merry-go-round. Three more dogs, one white, one slate blue and one pink, hurried up and tried to climb aboard.

Butch yawned.

"What's the matter?" inquired Darter's master. "I thought you liked dog fights, Butch."

"I do like dog fights," Butch said somberly, without looking around. "I don't like uninj fights. They're just a pretend, like everything else. Nobody gets hurt. And look here, Joggy-and you, too, Hal-when you talk to me, don't just say Butch. It's the Butcher, see?"

"That's not exactly a functional name," Hal observed with the judiciousness of budding maturity, while Joggy said agreeably: "All right, Butcher, I suppose you'd like to have lived way back when people were hurting each other all the time so the blood came out?"

"I certainly would," the Butcher replied. As Joggy and Hal turned back skeptically to watch the fight, he took out the metal tube, screwed up his face in a dreadful frown and jabbed himself in the hand. He squeaked with pain and whisked the tube out of sight.

"A kid can't do anything any more," he announced dramatically. "Can't break anything except the breakables they give him to break on purpose. Can't get dirty except in the dirt-pen —and they graduate him from that when he's two. Can't even be bitten by an uninj-it's contraprogrammed."

"Where'd you ever get so fixated on dirt?" Hal asked in a gentle voice acquired from a robot adolescer.

"I've been reading a book about a kid called Huckleberry Finn," the Butcher replied airily. "A swell book. That guy got dirtier than anything." His eyes became dreamy. "He even ate out of a garbage pail."

"What's a garbage pail?"

293

"I don't know, but it sounds great."

The battling uninjes careened into them. Brute had Darter by the ear and was whirling him around hilariously.

"Aw, *quit* it, Brute," the Butcher said in annoyance.

Brute obediently loosed his hold and returned to his master, paying no attention to his adversary's efforts to renew the fight.

The Butcher looked Brute squarely in the eyes. "You're making too much of a rumpus," he said. "I want to think."

He kicked Brute in the face. The dog squirmed joyously at his feet.

"Look," Joggy said, "you wouldn't hurt an uninj, for instance, would you?"

"How can you hurt something that's uninjurable?" the Butcher demanded scathingly. "An uninj isn't really a dog. It's just a lot of circuits and a micropack bedded in hyperplastic." He looked at Brute with guarded wistfulness.

"I don't know about that," Hal put in. "I've heard an uninj is programmed with so many genuine canine reactions that it practically has racial memory."

"I mean if you *could* hurt an uninj," Joggy amended.

"Well, maybe I wouldn't," the Butcher admitted grudgingly. "But shut up —I want to think."

"About what?" Hal asked with saintly reasonableness.

The Butcher achieved a fearful frown. "When I'm World Director," he said slowly, "I'm going to have warfare again."

"You think so now," Hal told him. "We all do at your age."

"We do not," the Butcher retorted. "I bet *you* didn't."

"Oh, yes, I was foolish, too," the older boy confessed readily. "All newborn organisms are self-centered and inconsiderate and ruthless. They have to be. That's why we have uninjes to work out on, and death games and fear houses, so that our emotions are cleared for adult conditioning. And it's just the same with newborn civilizations. Why, long after atom power and the space drive were discovered, people kept having wars and revolutions. It took ages to condition them differently. Of course, you can't appreciate it this year, but Man's greatest achievement was when he learned to automatically reject all violent solutions to problems. You'll realize that when you're older."

"I will not!" the Butcher countered hotly. "I'm not going to be a sissy." Hal and Joggy blinked at the unfamiliar word. "And what if we were attacked by bloodthirsty monsters from outside the Solar System?"

"The Space Fleet would take care of them," Hal replied calmly. "That's what it's for. Adults aren't conditioned to reject violent solutions to problems where non-human enemies are concerned. Look at what we did to viruses."

"But what if somebody got at us through the Time Bubble?"

"They can't. It's impossible."

"Yes, but suppose they did all the same."

"You've never been inside the Time Theater-you're not old enough yet-so you just can't know anything about it or about the reasons why it's impossible," Hal replied with friendly factuality. "The Time Bubble is just a viewer. You can only look through it, and just into the past, at that. But you can't travel through it because you can't change the past. Time traveling is a lot of kid stuff."

"I don't care," the Butcher asserted obstinately. "I'm still going to have warfare when I'm World Director."

"They'll condition you out of the idea," Hal assured him.

"They will not. I won't let 'em."

"It doesn't matter what you think now," Hal said with finality. "You'll have an altogether different opinion when you're six."

"Well, what if I will?" the Butcher snapped back. "You don't have to keep *telling* me about it, do you?"

The others were silent. Joggy began to bounce up and down abstractedly on the resilient pavement. Hal called in his three uninjes and said in soothing tones: "Joggy and I are going to swim over to the Time Theater. Want to walk us there, Butch?"

Butch scowled.

"How about it, Butch?"

Still Butch did not seem to hear.

The older boy shrugged and said: "Oh, well, how about it-Butcher?"

The Butcher swung around. "They won't let me in the Time Theater. You said so yourself."

"You could walk us over there."

"Well, maybe I will and maybe I won't."

"While you're deciding, we'll get swimming. Come along, Joggy."

Still scowling, the Butcher took a white soapy crayon from the bulging pocket in his silver shorts. Pressed into the pavement, it made a black mark. He scrawled pensively: KEEP ON THE GRASS.

He gazed at his handiwork. No, darn it, that was just what grownups wanted you to do. This grass couldn't be hurt. You couldn't pull it up or tear it off; it hurt your fingers to try. A rub with the side of the crayon removed the sign. He thought for a moment, then wrote: KEEP OFF THE GRASS.

With an untroubled countenance, he sprang up and hurried after the others.

Joggy and the older boy were swimming lazily through the air at shoulder height. In the pavement directly under each of them was a wide, saucer-shaped depression which swam along with them. The uninjes avoided the depressions. Darter was strutting on his hind legs, looking up inquiringly at his master.

"Gimme a ride, Hal, gimme a ride!" the Butcher called. The older boy ignored him. "Aw, gimme a ride, Joggy."

"Oh, all right." Joggy touched the small box attached to the front of his broad metal harness and dropped lightly to the ground. The Butcher climbed on his back. There was a moment of rocking and pitching, during which each boy accused the other of trying to upset them.

Then the Butcher got his balance and they began to swim along securely, though at a level several inches lower. Brute sprang up after his master and was invisibly rebuffed. He retired baffled, but a few minutes later, he was amusing himself by furious futile efforts to climb the hemispherical repulsor field.

Slowly the little cavalcade of boys and uninjes proceeded down the Avenue of Wisdom. Hal amused himself by stroking toward a tree. When he was about four feet from it, he was gently bounced away.

It was really a more tiring method of transportation than walking and quite useless against the wind. True, by rocking the repulsor hemisphere backward, you could get a brief forward push, but it would be nullified when you rocked forward. A slow swimming stroke was the simplest way to make progress.

The general sensation, however, was delightful and levitators were among the most prized of toys.

"There's the Theater," Joggy announced.

"I *know*," the Butcher said irritably.

But even he sounded a little solemn and subdued. From the Great Ramp to the topmost airy finial, the Time Theater was the dream of a god realized in unearthly substance. It imparted the aura of demigods to the adults drifting up and down the ramp.

"My father remembers when there wasn't a Time Theater," Hal said softly as he scanned the facade's glowing charts and maps. "Say, they're viewing Earth, somewhere in Scandinavia around zero in the B.C.-A.D. time scale. It should be interesting."

"Will it be about Napoleon?" the Butcher asked eagerly. "Or Hitler?" A red-headed adult heard and smiled and paused to watch. A lock of hair had fallen down the middle of the Butcher's forehead, and as he sat Joggy like a charger, he did bear a faint resemblance to one of the grim little egomaniacs of the Dawn Era.

"Wrong millennium," Hal said.

"Tamerlane then?" the Butcher pressed. "He killed cities and piled the skulls. Blood-bath stuff. Oh, yes, and Tamerlane was a Scand of the Navies."

Hal looked puzzled and then quickly erased the expression. "Well, even if it is about Tamerlane, you can't see it. How about it, Joggy?"

"They won't let me in, either."

"Yes, they will. You're five years old now."

"But I don't feel any older," Joggy replied doubtfully.

"The feeling comes at six. Don't worry, the usher will notice the difference."

Hal and Joggy switched off their levitators and dropped to their feet. The Butcher came down rather hard, twisting an ankle. He opened his mouth to cry, then abruptly closed it hard, bearing his pain in tight-lipped silence like an ancient soldier-like Stalin, maybe, he thought. The red-headed adult's face twitched in half-humorous sympathy.

Hal and Joggy mounted the Ramp and entered a twilit corridor which drank their faint footsteps and returned pulses of light. The Butcher limped manfully after them, but when he got inside, he forgot his battle injury.

Hal looked back. "Honestly, the usher will stop you."

The Butcher shook his head. "I'm going to think my way in. I'm going to think old."

"You won't be able to fool the usher, Butcher. You under-fives simply aren't allowed in the Time Theater. There's a good reason for it-something dangerous might happen if an under-five got inside."

"Why?"

"I don't exactly know, but something."

"Hah! I bet they're scared we'd go traveling in the Time Bubble and have some excitement."

"They are not. I guess they just know you'd get bored and wander away from your seats and maybe disturb the adults or upset the electronics or something. But don't worry about it, Butcher. The usher will take care of you."

"Shut up—I'm thinking I'm World Director," the Butcher informed them, contorting his face diabolically.

Hal spoke to the uninjes, pointing to the side of the corridor. Obediently four of them lined up.

But Brute was peering down the corridor toward where it merged into a deeper darkness. His short legs stiffened, his neckless head seemed to retreat even further between his powerful shoulders, his lips writhed back to show his gleaming fangs, and a completely unfamiliar sound issued from his throat. A choked, grating sound. A growl. The other uninjes moved uneasily.

"Do you suppose something's the matter with his circuits?" Joggy whispered. "Maybe he's getting racial memories from the Scands."

"Of course not," Hal said irritably.

"Brute, get over there," the Butcher commanded. Unwillingly, eyes still fixed on the blackness ahead, Brute obeyed.

The three boys started on. Hal and Joggy experienced a vaguely electrical tingling that vanished almost immediately. They looked back. The Butcher had been stopped by an invisible wall.

"I told you you couldn't fool the usher," Hal said.

The Butcher hurled himself forward. The wall gave a little, then bounced him back with equal force.

"I bet it'll be a bum time view anyway," the Butcher said, not giving up, but not trying again. "And I still don't think the usher can tell how old you are. I bet there's an over-age teacher spying on you through a hole, and if he doesn't like your looks, he switches on the usher."

But the others had disappeared in the blackness. The Butcher waited and then sat down beside the uninjes. Brute laid his head on his knee and growled faintly down the corridor.

"Take it easy, Brute," the Butcher consoled him. "I don't think Tamerlane was really a Scand of the Navies anyhow."

Two chattering girls hardly bigger than himself stepped through the usher as if it weren't there.

The Butcher grimly slipped out the metal tube and put it to his lips. There were two closely spaced faint *plops* and a large green stain appeared on the bare back of one girl, while purple fluid dripped from the close-cropped hair of the other.

They glared at him and one of them said: "A cub!" But he had his arms folded and wasn't looking at them.

Meanwhile, subordinate ushers had guided Hal and Joggy away from the main entrance to the Time Theater. A sphincter dilated and they found themselves in a small transparent cubicle from which they could watch the show without disturbing the adult audience. They unstrapped their levitators, laid them on the floor and sat down.

The darkened auditorium was circular. Rising from a low central platform was a huge bubble of light, its lower surface somewhat flattened. The audience was seated in concentric rows around the bubble, their keen and compassionate faces dimly revealed by the pale central glow.

But it was the scene within the bubble that riveted the attention of the boys.

Great brooding trees, the trunks of the nearer ones sliced by the bubble's surface, formed the background. Through the dark, wet foliage appeared glimpses of a murky sky, while from the ceiling of the bubble, a ceaseless rain dripped mournfully. A hooded figure crouched beside a little fire partly shielded by a gnarled trunk. Squatting round about were wiry, blue-eyed men with shoulder-length blond hair and full blond beards. They were clothed in furs and metal-studded leather.

Here and there were scattered weapons and armor-long swords glistening with oil to guard them from rust, crudely painted circular shields, and helmets from which curved the horns of beasts. Back and forth, lean, wolflike dogs paced with restless monotony.

Sometimes the men seemed to speak together, or one would rise to peer down the misty forest vistas, but mostly they were motionless. Only the hooded figure, which they seemed to regard with a mingled wonder and fear, swayed incessantly to the rhythm of some unheard chant.

"The Time Bubble has been brought to rest in one of the barbaric cultures of the Dawn Era," a soft voice explained, so casually that Joggy looked around for the speaker, until Hal nudged him sharply, whispering with barely perceptible embarrassment: "Don't do that, Joggy. It's just the electronic interpreter. It senses our development and hears our questions and then it automats background and answers. But it's no more alive than an adolescer or a kinderobot. Got a billion microtapes, though."

The interpreter continued: "The skin-clad men we are viewing in Time in the Round seem to be a group of warriors of the sort who lived by pillage and rapine. The hooded figure is a most unusual find. We believe it to be that of a sorcerer who pretended to control the forces of nature and see into the future."

Joggy whispered: "How is it that we can't see the audience through the other side of the bubble? We can see through this side, all right."

"The bubble only shines light out," Hal told him hurriedly, to show he knew some things as well as the interpreter. "Nothing, not even light, can get into the bubble from outside. The audience on the other side of the bubble sees into it just as we do, only they're seeing the other way-for instance, they can't see the fire because the tree is in the way. And instead of seeing us beyond, they see more trees and sky."

Joggy nodded. "You mean that whatever way you look at the bubble, it's a kind of hole through time?"

"That's right." Hal cleared his throat and recited: "The bubble is the locus of an infinite number of one-way holes, all centering around two points in space-time, one now and one then. The bubble looks completely open, but if you tried to step inside, you'd be stopped-and so would an atom beam. It takes more energy than an atom beam just to maintain the bubble, let alone maneuver it."

"I see, I guess," Joggy whispered. "But if the hole works for light, why can't the people inside the bubble step out of it into our world?"

"Why-er-you see, Joggy —"

The interpreter took over. "The holes are one-way for light, but no-way for matter. If one of the individuals inside the bubble walked toward you, he would cross-section and disappear. But to the audience on the opposite side of the bubble, it would be obvious that he had walked away along the vista down which they are peering."

As if to provide an example, a figure suddenly materialized on their side of the bubble. The wolflike dogs bared their fangs. For an instant, there was only an eerie, distorted, rapidly growing silhouette, changing from blood-red to black as the boundary of the bubble cross-sectioned the intruding figure. Then they recognized the back of another long-haired warrior and realized that the audience on the other side of the bubble had probably seen him approaching for some time.

He bowed to the hooded figure and handed him a small bag.

"More atavistic cubs, big and little! Hold still, Cynthia," a new voice cut in.

Hal turned and saw that two cold-eyed girls had been ushered into the cubicle. One was wiping her close-cropped hair with one hand while mopping a green stain from her friend's back with the other.

Hal nudged Joggy and whispered: "Butch!"

But Joggy was still hypnotized by the Time Bubble.

"Then how is it, Hal," he asked, "that light comes out of the bubble, if the people don't? What I mean is, if one of the people walks toward us, he shrinks to a red blot and disappears. Why doesn't the light coming our way disappear, too?"

"Well-you see, Joggy, it isn't real light. It's —"

Once more the interpreter helped him out.

"The light that comes from the bubble is an isotope. Like atoms of one element, photons of a single frequency also have isotopes. It's more than a matter of polarization. One of these isotopes of light tends to leak futureward through holes in space-time. Most of the light goes down the vistas visible to the other side of the audience. But one isotope is diverted through the walls of the bubble into the Time Theater. Perhaps, because of the intense darkness of the theater, you haven't realized how dimly lit the scene is. That's because we're getting only a single isotope of the original light. Incidentally, no isotopes have been discovered that leak pastward, though attempts are being made to synthesize them."

"Oh, explanations!" murmured one of the newly arrived girls. "The cubs are always angling for them. Apple-polishers!"

"*I* like this show," a familiar voice announced serenely. "They cut anybody yet with those choppers?"

Hal looked down beside him. "Butch! How did you manage to get in?"

"I don't see any blood. Where's the bodies?"

"But how *did* you get in-Butcher?"

The Butcher replied airily: "A red-headed man talked to me and said it certainly was sad for a future dictator not to be able to enjoy scenes of carnage in his youth, so I told him I'd been inside the Time Theater and just come out to get a drink of water and go to the eliminator, but then my sprained ankle had got worse —I kind of tried to get up and fell down again-so he picked me up and carried me right through the usher."

"Butcher, that wasn't honest," Hal said a little worriedly. "You tricked him into thinking you were older and his brain waves blanketed yours, going through the usher. I really *have* heard it's dangerous for you under-fives to be in here."

"The way those cubs beg for babying and get it!" one of the girls commented. "Talk about sex favoritism!" She and her companion withdrew to the far end of the cubicle.

The Butcher grinned at them briefly and concentrated his attention on the scene in the Time Bubble.

"Those big dogs —" he began suddenly. "Brute must have smelled 'em."

"Don't be silly," Hal said. "Smells can't come out of the Time Bubble. Smells haven't any isotopes and —"

"I don't care," the Butcher asserted. "I bet somebody'll figure out someday how to use the bubble for time traveling."

"You can't travel in a point of view," Hal contradicted, "and that's all the bubble is. Besides, some scientists think the bubble isn't real at all, but a —uh —"

"I believe," the interpreter cut in smoothly, "that you're thinking of the theory that the Time Bubble operates by hypermemory. Some scientists would have us believe that all memory is time traveling and that the basic location of the bubble is not space-time at all, but ever-present eternity. Some of them go so far as to state that it is only a mental inability that prevents the Time Bubble from being used for time traveling-just as it may be a similar disability that keeps a robot with the same or even more scopeful memories from being a real man or animal.

"It is because of this minority theory that under-age individuals and other beings with impulsive mentalities are barred from the Time Theater. But do not be alarmed. Even if the minority theory should prove true-and no evidence for it has ever appeared-there are automatically operating safeguards to protect the audience from any harmful consequences of time traveling (almost certainly impossible, remember) in either direction."

"Sissies!" was the Butcher's comment.

"You're rather young to be here, aren't you?" the interpreter inquired.

The Butcher folded his arms and scowled.

The interpreter hesitated almost humanly, probably snatching through a quarter-million microtapes. "Well, you wouldn't have got in unless a qualified adult had certified you as plus-age. Enjoy yourself."

There was no need for the last injunction. The scene within the bubble had acquired a gripping interest. The shaggy warriors were taking up their swords, gathering about the hooded sorcerer. The hood fell back, revealing a face with hawklike, disturbing eyes that seemed to be looking straight out of the bubble at the future.

"This is getting good," the Butcher said, squirming toward the edge of his seat.

"Stop being an impulsive mentality," Hal warned him a little nervously.

"Hah!"

The sorcerer emptied the small bag on the fire and a thick cloud of smoke puffed toward the ceiling of the bubble. A clawlike hand waved wildly. The sorcerer appeared to be expostulating, commanding. The warriors stared uncomprehendingly, which seemed to exasperate the sorcerer.

"That's right," the Butcher approved loudly. "Sock it to 'em!"

"Butcher!" Hal admonished.

Suddenly the bubble grew very bright, as if the Sun had just shone forth in the ancient world, though the rain still dripped down.

"A viewing anomaly has occurred," the interpreter announced. "It may be necessary to collapse the Time Bubble for a short period."

In a frenzy, his ragged robes twisting like smoke, the sorcerer rushed at one of the warriors, pushing him backward so that in a moment he must cross-section.

"Attaboy!" the Butcher encouraged.

Then the warrior was standing outside the bubble, blinking toward the shadows, rain dripping from his beard and furs.

"Oh, *boy!*" the Butcher cheered in ecstasy.

"Butcher, you've done it!" Hal said, aghast.

"I sure did," the Butcher agreed blandly, "but that old guy in the bubble helped me. Must take two to work it."

"Keep your seats!" the interpreter said loudly. "We are energizing the safeguards!"

The warriors inside the bubble stared in stupid astonishment after the one who had disappeared from their view. The sorcerer leaped about, pushing them in his direction.

Abrupt light flooded the Time Theater. The warriors who had emerged from the bubble stiffened themselves, baring their teeth.

"The safeguards are now energized," the interpreter said.

A woman in a short golden tunic stood up uncertainly from the front row of the audience.

The first warrior looked her up and down, took one hesitant step forward, then another, then suddenly grabbed her and flung her over his left shoulder, looking around menacingly and swinging his sword in his right hand.

"I repeat, the safeguards have been fully energized! Keep your seats!" the interpreter enjoined.

In the cubicle, Hal and Joggy gasped, the two girls squeaked, but the Butcher yelled a "Hey!" of disapproval, snatched up something from the floor and darted out through the sphincter.

Here and there in the audience, other adults stood up. The emerged warriors formed a ring of swinging swords and questing eyes. Between their legs their wolfish dogs, emerged with them, crouched and snarled. Then the warriors began to fan out.

"There has been an unavoidable delay in energizing the safeguards," the interpreter said. "Please be patient."

At that moment, the Butcher entered the main auditorium, brandishing a levitator above his head and striding purposefully down the aisle. At his heels, five stocky forms trotted. In a definitely pre-civilization voice, or at least with pre-civilization volume, he bellowed: "Hey, you! You quit that!"

The first warrior looked toward him, gave his left shoulder a shake to quiet his wriggling captive, gave his right shoulder one to supple his sword arm, and waited until the dwarfish challenger came into range. Then his sword swished down in a flashing arc.

Next moment, the Butcher was on his knees and the warrior was staring at him open-mouthed. The sword had rebounded from something invisible an arm's length above the gnomelike creature's head. The warrior backed a step.

300

The Butcher stayed down, crouching half behind an aisle seat and digging for something in his pocket. But he didn't stay quiet. "Sic 'em, Brute!" he shrilled. "Sic 'em, Darter! Sic 'em, Pinkie and Whitie and Blue!" Then he stopped shouting and raised his hand to his mouth.

Growling quite unmechanically, the five uninjes hurled themselves forward and closed with the warrior's wolflike dogs. At the first encounter, Brute and Pinkie were grabbed by the throats, shaken, and tossed a dozen feet. The warriors snarled approval and advanced. But then Brute and Pinkie raced back eagerly to the fight-and suddenly the face of the leading warrior was drenched with scarlet. He blinked and touched his fingers to it, then looked at his hand in horror.

The Butcher spared a second to repeat his command to the uninjes. But already the battle was going against the larger dogs. The latter had the advantage of weight and could toss the smaller dogs like so many foxes. But their terrible fangs did no damage, and whenever an uninj clamped on a throat, that throat was torn out.

Meanwhile, great bloody stains had appeared on the bodies of all the warriors. They drew back in a knot, looking at each other fearfully. That was when the Butcher got to his feet and strode forward, hand clenching the levitator above his head.

"Get back where you belong, you big jerks! And drop that lady!"

The first warrior pointed toward him and hissed something. Immediately, a half dozen swords were smiting at the Butcher.

"We are working to energize the safeguards," the interpreter said in mechanical panic. "Remain patient and in your seats."

The uninjes leaped into the melee, at first tearing more fur than flesh. Swords caught them and sent them spinning through the air. They came yapping back for more. Brute fixed on the first warrior's ankle. He dropped the woman, stamped unavailingly on the uninj, and let out a screech.

Swords were still rebounding from the invisible shield under which the Butcher crouched, making terrible faces at his attackers. They drew back, looked again at their bloodstains, goggled at the demon dogs. At their leader's screech, they broke and plunged back into the Time Bubble, their leader stumbling limpingly after them. There they wasted no time on their own ragged sorcerer. Their swords rose and fell, and no repulsor field stayed them.

"Brute, come back!" the Butcher yelled.

The gray uninj let go his hold on the leader's ankle and scampered out of the Time Bubble, which swiftly dimmed to its original light intensity and then winked out.

For once in their very mature lives, all the adults in the auditorium began to jabber at each other simultaneously.

"We are sorry, but the anomaly has made it necessary to collapse the Time Bubble," the interpreter said. "There will be no viewing until further announcement. Thank you for your patience."

Hal and Joggy caught up with the Butcher just as Brute jumped into his arms and the woman in gold picked him up and hugged him fiercely. The Butcher started to pull away, then grudgingly submitted.

"Cubs!" came a small cold voice from behind Hal and Joggy. "Always playing hero! Say, what's that awful smell, Cynthia? It must have come from those dirty past men."

Hal and Joggy were shouting at the Butcher, but he wasn't listening to them or to the older voices clamoring about "revised theories of reality" and other important things. He didn't even squirm as Brute licked his cheek and the woman in gold planted a big kiss practically on his mouth.

He smiled dreamily and stroked Brute's muzzle and murmured softly: "We came, we saw, we conquered, didn't we, Brute?"

A Bad Day for Sales

Don't wait to "Get 'em while they're hot."
By then, it is too late to get them of all!

The big bright doors of the office building parted with a pneumatic *whoosh* and Robie glided onto Times Square. The crowd that had been watching the fifty-foot-tall girl on the clothing billboard get dressed, or reading the latest news about the Hot Truce scrawl itself in yard-high script, hurried to look.

Robie was still a novelty. Robie was fun. For a little while yet, he could steal the show. But the attention did not make Robie proud. He had no more emotions than the pink plastic giantess, who dressed and undressed endlessly whether there was a crowd or the street was empty, and who never once blinked her blue mechanical eyes. But she merely drew business while Robie went out after it.

For Robie was the logical conclusion of the development of vending machines. All the earlier ones had stood in one place, on a floor or hanging on a wall, and blankly delivered merchandise in return for coins, whereas Robie searched for customers. He was the demonstration model of a line of sales robots to be manufactured by Shuler Vending Machines, provided the public invested enough in stocks to give the company capital to go into mass production.

The publicity Robie drew stimulated investments handsomely. It was amusing to see the TV and newspaper coverage of Robie selling, but not a fraction as much fun as being approached personally by him. Those who were usually bought anywhere from one to five hundred shares, if they had any money and foresight enough to see that sales robots would eventually be on every street and highway in the country.

Robie radared the crowd, found that it surrounded him solidly, and stopped. With a carefully built-in sense of timing, he waited for the tension and expectation to mount before he began talking.

"Say, Ma, he doesn't look like a robot at all," a child said. "He looks like a turtle."

Which was not completely inaccurate. The lower part of Robie's body was a metal hemisphere hemmed with sponge rubber and not quite touching the sidewalk. The upper was a metal box with black holes in it. The box could swivel and duck.

A chromium-bright hoopskirt with a turret on top.

"Reminds me too much of the Little Joe Paratanks," a legless veteran of the Persian War muttered, and rapidly rolled himself away on wheels rather like Robie's.

His departure made it easier for some of those who knew about Robie to open a path in the crowd. Robie headed straight for the gap. The crowd whooped.

Robie glided very slowly down the path, deftly jogging aside whenever he got too close to ankles in skylon or sockassins. The rubber buffer on his hoopskirt was merely an added safeguard.

The boy who had called Robie a turtle jumped in the middle of the path and stood his ground, grinning foxily.

Robie stopped two feet short of him. The turret ducked. The crowd got quiet.

"Hello, youngster," Robie said in a voice that was smooth as that of a TV star, and was, in fact, a recording of one.

The boy stopped smiling. "Hello," he whispered.

"How old are you?" Robie asked.

"Nine. No, eight."

"That's nice," Robie observed. A metal arm shot down from his neck, stopped just short of the boy.

The boy jerked back.

"For you," Robie said.

The boy gingerly took the red polly-lop from the neatly fashioned blunt metal claws, and began to unwrap it.

"Nothing to say?" asked Robie.

"Uh-thank you."

After a suitable pause, Robie continued. "And how about a nice refreshing drink of Poppy Pop to go with your polly-lop?" The boy lifted his eyes, but didn't stop licking the candy. Robie waggled his claws slightly. "Just give me a quarter and within five seconds —"

A little girl wriggled out of the forest of legs. "Give me a polly-lop, too, Robie," she demanded.

"Rita, come back here!" a woman in the third rank of the crowd called angrily.

Robie scanned the newcomer gravely. His reference silhouettes were not good enough to let him distinguish the sex of children, so he merely repeated, "Hello, youngster."

"Rita!"

"Give me a polly-lop!"

Disregarding both remarks, for a good salesman is single-minded and does not waste bait, Robie said winningly, "I'll bet you read *Junior Space Killers*. Now I have here —"

"Uh-uh, I'm a girl. *He* got a polly-lop."

At the word "girl," Robie broke off. Rather ponderously, he said, "I'll bet you read *Gee-Gee Jones, Space Stripper*. Now I have here the latest issue of that thrilling comic, not yet in the stationary vending machines. Just give me fifty cents and within five —"

"Please let me through. I'm her mother."

A young woman in the front rank drawled over her powder-sprayed shoulder, "I'll get her for you," and slithered out on six-inch platform shoes. "Run away, children," she said nonchalantly. Lifting her arms behind her head, she pirouetted slowly before Robie to show how much she did for her bolero half-jacket and her form-fitting slacks that melted into skylon just above the knees. The little girl glared at her. She ended the pirouette in profile.

At this age-level, Robie's reference silhouettes permitted him to distinguish sex, though with occasional amusing and embarrassing miscalls. He whistled admiringly. The crowd cheered.

Someone remarked critically to a friend, "It would go over better if he was built more like a real robot. You know, like a man."

The friend shook his head. "This way it's subtler."

No one in the crowd was watching the newscript overhead as it scribbled, "Ice Pack for Hot Truce? Vanadin hints Russ may yield on Pakistan."

Robie was saying, "...in the savage new glamor-tint we have christened Mars Blood, complete with spray applicator and fit-all fingerstalls that mask each finger completely except for the nail. Just give me five dollars-uncrumpled bills may be fed into the revolving rollers you see beside my arm-and within five seconds —"

"No, thanks, Robie," the young woman yawned.

"Remember," Robie persisted, "for three more weeks, seductivizing Mars Blood will be unobtainable from any other robot or human vendor."

"No, thanks."

Robie scanned the crowd resourcefully. "Is there any gentleman here ..." he began just as a woman elbowed her way through the front rank.

"I told you to come back!" she snapped at the little girl.

"But I didn't get my polly-lop!"

"...who would care to...."

"Rita!"

"Robie cheated. Ow!"

Meanwhile, the young woman in the half bolero had scanned the nearby gentlemen on her own. Deciding that there was less than a fifty per cent chance of any of them accepting the proposition Robie seemed about to make, she took advantage of the scuffle to slither gracefully back into the ranks. Once again the path was clear before Robie.

He paused, however, for a brief recapitulation of the more magical properties of Mars Blood, including a telling phrase about "the passionate claws of a Martian sunrise."

But no one bought. It wasn't quite time. Soon enough silver coins would be clinking, bills going through the rollers faster than laundry, and five hundred people struggling for the privilege of having their money taken away from them by America's first mobile sales robot.

But there were still some tricks that Robie had to do free, and one certainly should enjoy those before starting the more expensive fun.

So Robie moved on until he reached the curb. The variation in level was instantly sensed by his under-scanners. He stopped. His head began to swivel. The crowd watched in eager silence. This was Robie's best trick.

Robie's head stopped swiveling. His scanners had found the traffic light. It was green. Robie edged forward. But then the light turned red. Robie stopped again, still on the curb. The crowd softly *ahhed* its delight.

It was wonderful to be alive and watching Robie on such an exciting day. Alive and amused in the fresh, weather-controlled air between the lines of bright skyscrapers with their winking windows and under a sky so blue you could almost call it dark.

(But way, way up, where the crowd could not see, the sky was darker still. Purple-dark, with stars showing. And in that purple-dark, a silver-green something, the color of a bud, plunged down at better than three miles a second. The silver-green was a newly developed paint that foiled radar.)

Robie was saying, "While we wait for the light, there's time for you youngsters to enjoy a nice refreshing Poppy Pop. Or for you adults-only those over five feet tall are eligible to buy-to enjoy an exciting Poppy Pop fizz. Just give me a quarter or-in the case of adults, one dollar and a quarter; I'm licensed to dispense intoxicating liquors-and within five seconds...."

But that was not cutting it quite fine enough. Just three seconds later, the silver-green bud bloomed above Manhattan into a globular orange flower. The skyscrapers grew brighter and brighter still, the brightness of the inside of the Sun. The windows winked blossoming white fire-flowers.

The crowd around Robie bloomed, too. Their clothes puffed into petals of flame. Their heads of hair were torches.

The orange flower grew, stem and blossom. The blast came. The winking windows shattered tier by tier, became black holes. The walls bent, rocked, cracked. A stony dandruff flaked from their cornices. The flaming flowers on the sidewalk were all leveled at once. Robie was shoved ten feet. His metal hoopskirt dimpled, regained its shape.

The blast ended. The orange flower, grown vast, vanished overhead on its huge, magic beanstalk. It grew dark and very still. The cornice-dandruff pattered down. A few small fragments rebounded from the metal hoopskirt.

Robie made some small, uncertain movements, as if feeling for broken bones. He was hunting for the traffic light, but it no longer shone either red or green.

He slowly scanned a full circle. There was nothing anywhere to interest his reference silhouettes. Yet whenever he tried to move, his under-scanners warned him of low obstructions. It was very puzzling.

The silence was disturbed by moans and a crackling sound, as faint at first as the scampering of distant rats.

A seared man, his charred clothes fuming where the blast had blown out the fire, rose from the curb. Robie scanned him.

"Good day, sir," Robie said. "Would you care for a smoke? A truly cool smoke? Now I have here a yet-unmarketed brand...."

But the customer had run away, screaming, and Robie never ran after customers, though he could follow them at a medium brisk roll. He worked his way along the curb where the man had sprawled, carefully keeping his distance from the low obstructions, some of which writhed now and then, forcing him to jog. Shortly he reached a fire hydrant. He scanned it. His electronic vision, though it still worked, had been somewhat blurred by the blast.

"Hello, youngster," Robie said. Then, after a long pause, "Cat got your tongue? Well, I have a little present for you. A nice, lovely polly-lop.

"Take it, youngster," he said after another pause. "It's for you. Don't be afraid."

His attention was distracted by other customers, who began to rise up oddly here and there, twisting forms that confused his reference silhouettes and would not stay to be scanned properly. One cried, "Water," but no quarter clinked in Robie's claws when he caught the word and suggested, "How about a nice refreshing drink of Poppy Pop?"

The rat-crackling of the flames had become a jungle muttering. The blind windows began to wink fire again.

A little girl marched, stepping neatly over arms and legs she did not look at. A white dress and the once taller bodies around her had shielded her from the brilliance and the blast. Her eyes were fixed on Robie. In them was the same imperious confidence, though none of the delight, with which she had watched him earlier.

"Help me, Robie," she said. "I want my mother."

"Hello, youngster," Robie said. "What would you like? Comics? Candy?"

"Where is she, Robie? Take me to her."

"Balloons? Would you like to watch me blow up a balloon?"

The little girl began to cry. The sound triggered off another of Robie's novelty circuits, a service feature that had brought in a lot of favorable publicity.

"Is something wrong?" he asked. "Are you in trouble? Are you lost?"

"Yes, Robie. Take me to my mother."

"Stay right here," Robie said reassuringly, "and don't be frightened. I will call a policeman." He whistled shrilly, twice.

Time passed. Robie whistled again. The windows flared and roared. The little girl begged, "Take me away, Robie," and jumped onto a little step in his hoopskirt.

"Give me a dime," Robie said.

The little girl found one in her pocket and put it in his claws.

"Your weight," Robie said, "is fifty-four and one-half pounds."

"Have you seen my daughter, have you seen her?" a woman was crying somewhere. "I left her watching that thing while I stepped inside —*Rita!*"

"Robie helped me," the little girl began babbling at her. "He knew I was lost. He even called the police, but they didn't come. He weighed me, too. Didn't you, Robie?"

But Robie had gone off to peddle Poppy Pop to the members of a rescue squad which had just come around the corner, more robotlike in their asbestos suits than he in his metal skin.

Dr Kometevsky's Day

Before science, there was superstition. After
science, there will be ... what? The biggest,
most staggering, most final fact of them all!

"But it's all predicted here! It even names this century for the next reshuffling of the planets."

Celeste Wolver looked up unwillingly at the book her friend Madge Carnap held aloft like a torch. She made out the ill-stamped title, *The Dance of the Planets*. There was no mistaking the time of its origin; only paper from the Twentieth Century aged to that particularly nasty shade of brown. Indeed, the book seemed to Celeste a brown old witch resurrected from the Last Age of Madness to confound a world growing sane, and she couldn't help shrinking back a trifle toward her husband Theodor.

He tried to come to her rescue. "Only predicted in the vaguest way. As I understand it, Kometevsky claimed, on the basis of a lot of evidence drawn from folklore, that the planets and their moons trade positions every so often."

"As if they were playing Going to Jerusalem, or musical chairs," Celeste chimed in, but she couldn't make it sound funny.

"Jupiter was supposed to have started as the outermost planet, and is to end up in the orbit of Mercury," Theodor continued. "Well, nothing at all like that has happened."

"But it's begun," Madge said with conviction. "Phobos and Deimos have disappeared. You can't argue away that stubborn little fact."

That was the trouble; you couldn't. Mars' two tiny moons had simply vanished during a period when, as was generally the case, the eyes of astronomy weren't on them. Just some hundred-odd cubic miles of rock-the merest cosmic flyspecks-yet they had carried away with them the security of a whole world.

Looking at the lovely garden landscape around her, Celeste Wolver felt that in a moment the shrubby hills would begin to roll like waves, the charmingly aimless paths twist like snakes and sink in the green sea, the sparsely placed skyscrapers dissolve into the misty clouds they pierced.

People must have felt like this, she thought, *when Aristarches first hinted and Copernicus told them that the solid Earth under their feet was falling dizzily through space. Only it's worse for us, because they couldn't see that anything had changed. We can.*

"You need something to cling to," she heard Madge say. "Dr. Kometevsky was the only person who ever had an inkling that anything like this might happen. I was never a Kometevskyite before. Hadn't even heard of the man."

She said it almost apologetically. In fact, standing there so frank and anxious-eyed, Madge looked anything but a fanatic, which made it much worse.

"Of course, there are several more convincing alternate explanations...." Theodor began hesitantly, knowing very well that there weren't. If Phobos and Deimos had suddenly disintegrated, surely Mars Base would have noticed something. Of course there was the Disordered Space Hypothesis, even if it was little more than the chance phrase of a prominent physicist pounded upon by an eager journalist. And in any case, what sense of security were you left with if you admitted that moons and planets might explode, or drop through unseen holes in space? So he ended up by taking a different tack: "Besides, if Phobos and Deimos simply shot off somewhere, surely they'd have been picked up by now by 'scope or radar."

"Two balls of rock just a few miles in diameter?" Madge questioned. "Aren't they smaller than many of the asteroids? I'm no astronomer, but I think' I'm right."

And of course she was.

She swung the book under her arm. "Whew, it's heavy," she observed, adding in slightly scandalized tones, "Never been microfilmed." She smiled nervously and looked them up and down. "Going to a party?" she asked.

Theodor's scarlet cloak and Celeste's green culottes and silver jacket justified the question, but they shook their heads.

"Just the normally flamboyant garb of the family," Celeste said, while Theodor explained, "As it happens, we're bound on business connected with the disappearance. We Wolvers practically constitute a sub-committee of the Congress for the Discovery of New Purposes. And since a lot of varied material comes to our attention, we're going to see if any of it correlates with this bit of astronomical sleight-of-hand."

Madge nodded. "Give you something to do, at any rate. Well, I must be off. The Buddhist temple has lent us their place for a meeting." She gave them a woeful grin. "See you when the Earth jumps."

Theodor said to Celeste, "Come on, dear. We'll be late."

But Celeste didn't want to move too fast. "You know, Teddy," she said uncomfortably, "all this reminds me of those old myths where too much good fortune is a sure sign of coming disaster. It was just too much luck, our great-grandparents missing World III and getting the World Government started a thousand years ahead of schedule. Luck like that couldn't last, evidently. Maybe we've gone too fast with a lot of things, like space-flight and the Deep Shaft and —" she hesitated a bit —"complex marriages. I'm a woman. I want complete security. Where am I to find it?"

"In me," Theodor said promptly.

"In you?" Celeste questioned, walking slowly. "But you're just one-third of my husband. Perhaps I should look for it in Edmund or Ivan."

"You angry with me about something?"

"Of course not. But a woman wants her source of security whole. In a crisis like this, it's disturbing to have it divided."

"Well, we are a whole and, I believe, indivisible family," Theodor told her warmly. "You're not suggesting, are you, that we're going to be punished for our polygamous sins by a cosmic catastrophe? Fire from Heaven and all that?"

"Don't be silly. I just wanted to give you a picture of my feeling." Celeste smiled. "I guess none of us realized how much we've come to depend on the idea of unchanging scientific law. Knocks the props from under you."

Theodor nodded emphatically. "All the more reason to get a line on what's happening as quickly as possible. You know, it's fantastically far-fetched, but I think the experience of persons with Extra-Sensory Perception may give us a clue. During the past three or four days there's been a remarkable similarity in the dreams of ESPs all over the planet. I'm going to present the evidence at the meeting."

Celeste looked up at him. "So that's why Rosalind's bringing Frieda's daughter?"

"Dotty is your daughter, too, and Rosalind's," Theodor reminded her.

"No, just Frieda's," Celeste said bitterly. "Of course you may be the father. One-third of a chance."

Theodor looked at her sharply, but didn't comment. "Anyway, Dotty will be there," he said. "Probably asleep by now. All the ESPs have suddenly seemed to need more sleep."

As they talked, it had been growing darker, though the luminescence of the path kept it from being bothersome. And now the cloud rack parted to the east, showing a single red planet low on the horizon.

"Did you know," Theodor said suddenly, "that in *Gulliver's Travels* Dean Swift predicted that better telescopes would show Mars to have two moons? He got the sizes and distances and periods damned accurately, too. One of the few really startling coincidences of reality and literature."

"Stop being eerie," Celeste said sharply. But then she went on, "Those names Phobos and Deimos-they're Greek, aren't they? What do they mean?"

Theodor lost a step. "Fear and Terror," he said unwillingly. "Now don't go taking that for an omen. Most of the mythological names of major and minor ancient gods had been taken-the bodies in the Solar System are named that way, of course-and these were about all that were available."

It was true, but it didn't comfort him much.

I am a God, Dotty was dreaming, *and I want to be by myself and think. I and my god-friends like to keep some of our thoughts secret, but the other gods have forbidden us to.*

A little smile flickered across the lips of the sleeping girl, and the woman in gold tights and gold-spangled jacket leaned forward thoughtfully. In her dignity and simplicity and straight-spined grace, she was rather like a circus mother watching her sick child before she went out for the trapeze act.

I and my god-friends sail off in our great round silver boats, Dotty went on dreaming. *The other gods are angry and scared. They are frightened of the thoughts we may think in secret. They follow us to hunt us down. There are many more of them than of us.*

As Celeste and Theodor entered the committee room, Rosalind Wolver —a glitter of platinum against darkness-came in through the opposite door and softly shut it behind her. Frieda, a fair woman in blue robes, got up from the round table.

Celeste turned away with outward casualness as Theodor kissed his two other wives. She was pleased to note that Edmund seemed impatient too. A figure in close-fitting black, unrelieved except for two red arrows at the collar, he struck her as embodying very properly the serious, fateful temper of the moment.

He took two briefcases from his vest pocket and tossed them down on the table beside one of the microfilm projectors.

"I suggest we get started without waiting for Ivan," he said.

Frieda frowned anxiously. "It's ten minutes since he phoned from the Deep Space Bar to say he was starting right away. And that's hardly a two minutes walk."

Rosalind instantly started toward the outside door.

"I'll check," she explained. "Oh, Frieda, I've set the mike so you'll hear if Dotty calls."

Edmund threw up his hands. "Very well, then," he said and walked over, switched on the picture and stared out moodily.

Theodor and Frieda got out their briefcases, switched on projectors, and began silently checking through their material.

Celeste fiddled with the TV and got a newscast. But she found her eyes didn't want to absorb the blocks of print that rather swiftly succeeded each other, so, after a few moments, she shrugged impatiently and switched to audio.

At the noise, the others looked around at her with surprise and some irritation, but in a few moments they were also listening.

"The two rocket ships sent out from Mars Base to explore the orbital positions of Phobos and Deimos-that is, the volume of space they'd be occupying if their positions had remained normal-report finding masses of dust and larger debris. The two masses of fine debris are moving in the same orbits and at the same velocities as the two vanished moons, and occupy roughly the same volumes of space, though the mass of material is hardly a hundredth that of the moons. Physicists have ventured no statements as to whether this constitutes a confirmation of the Disintegration Hypothesis.

"However, we're mighty pleased at this news here. There's a marked lessening of tension. The finding of the debris-solid, tangible stuff-seems to lift the whole affair out of the supernatural miasma in which some of us have been tempted to plunge it. One-hundredth of the moons has been found.

"The rest will also be!"

Edmund had turned his back on the window. Frieda and Theodor had switched off their projectors.

"Meanwhile, Earthlings are going about their business with a minimum of commotion, meeting with considerable calm the strange threat to the fabric of their Solar System. Many, of course, are assembled in churches and humanist temples. Kometevskyites have staged helicopter processions at Washington, Peking, Pretoria, and Christiana, demanding that instant preparations be made for-and I quote —'Earth's coming leap through space.' They have also formally challenged all astronomers to produce an explanation other than the one contained in that strange book so recently conjured from oblivion, *The Dance of the Planets*.

"That about winds up the story for the present. There are no new reports from Interplanetary Radar, Astronomy, or the other rocket ships searching in the extended Mars volume. Nor have any statements been issued by the various groups working on the problem in Astrophysics, Cosmic Ecology, the Congress for the Discovery of New Purposes, and so forth. Meanwhile, however, we can take courage from the words of a poem written even before Dr. Kometevsky's book:

> "This Earth is not the steadfast place
> We landsmen build upon;
> From deep to deep she varies pace,
> And while she comes is gone.
> Beneath my feet I feel
> Her smooth bulk heave and dip;
> With velvet plunge and soft upreel
> She swings and steadies to her keel
> Like a gallant, gallant ship."

While the TV voice intoned the poem, growing richer as emotion caught it up, Celeste looked around her at the others. Frieda, with her touch of feminine helplessness showing more than ever through her business-like poise. Theodor leaning forward from his scarlet cloak thrown back, smiling the half-smile with which he seemed to face even the unknown. Black Edmund, masking a deep uncertainty with a strong show of decisiveness.

In short, her family. She knew their every quirk and foible. And yet now they seemed to her a million miles away, figures seen through the wrong end of a telescope.

Were they really a family? Strong sources of mutual strength and security to each other? Or had they merely been playing family, experimenting with their notions of complex marriage like a bunch of silly adolescents? Butterflies taking advantage of good weather to wing together in a glamorous, artificial dance-until outraged Nature decided to wipe them out?

As the poem was ending, Celeste saw the door open and Rosalind come slowly in. The Golden Woman's face was white as the paths she had been treading.

Just then the TV voice quickened with shock. "News! Lunar Observatory One reports that, although Jupiter is just about to pass behind the Sun, a good coronagraph of the planet has been obtained. Checked and rechecked, it admits of only one interpretation, which Lunar One feels duty-bound to release. *Jupiter's fourteen moons are no longer visible!*"

The chorus of remarks with which the Wolvers would otherwise have received this was checked by one thing: the fact that Rosalind seemed not to hear it. Whatever was on her mind prevented even that incredible statement from penetrating.

310

She walked shakily to the table and put down a briefcase, one end of which was smudged with dirt.

Without looking at them, she said, "Ivan left the Deep Space Bar twenty minutes ago, said he was coming straight here. On my way back I searched the path. Midway I found this half-buried in the dirt. I had to tug to get it out-almost as if it had been cemented into the ground. Do you feel how the dirt seems to be *in* the leather, as if it had lain for years in the grave?"

By now the others were fingering the small case of microfilms they had seen so many times in Ivan's competent hands. What Rosalind said was true. It had a gritty, unwholesome feel to it. Also, it felt strangely heavy.

"And see what's written on it," she added.

They turned it over. Scrawled with white pencil in big, hasty, frantic letters were two words: "Going down!"

The other gods, Dotty dreamt, *are combing the whole Universe for us. We have escaped them many times, but now our tricks are almost used up. There are no doors going out of the Universe and our boats are silver beacons to the hunters. So we decide to disguise them in the only way they can be disguised. It is our last chance.*

Edmund rapped the table to gain the family's attention. "I'd say we've done everything we can for the moment to find Ivan. We've made a thorough local search. A wider one, which we can't conduct personally, is in progress. All helpful agencies have been alerted and descriptions are being broadcast. I suggest we get on with the business of the evening-which may very well be connected with Ivan's disappearance."

One by one the others nodded and took their places at the round table. Celeste made a great effort to throw off the feeling of unreality that had engulfed her and focus attention on her microfilms.

"I'll take over Ivan's notes," she heard Edmund say. "They're mainly about the Deep Shaft."

"How far have they got with that?" Frieda asked idly. "Twenty-five miles?"

"Nearer thirty, I believe," Edmund answered, "and still going down."

At those last two words they all looked up quickly. Then their eyes went toward Ivan's briefcase.

Our trick has succeeded, Dotty dreamt. *The other gods have passed our hiding place a dozen times without noticing. They search the Universe for us many times in vain. They finally decide that we have found a door going out of the Universe. Yet they fear us all the more. They think of us as devils who will some day return through the door to destroy them. So they watch everywhere. We lie quietly smiling in our camouflaged boats, yet hardly daring to move or think, for fear that the faintest echoes of our doings will give them a clue. Hundreds of millions of years pass by. They seem to us no more than drugged hours in a prison.*

Theodor rubbed his eyes and pushed his chair back from the table. "We need a break."

Frieda agreed wearily. "We've gone through everything."

"Good idea," Edmund said briskly. "I think we've hit on several crucial points along the way and half disentangled them from the great mass of inconsequential material. I'll finish up that part of the job right now and present my case when we're all a bit fresher. Say half an hour?"

Theodor nodded heavily, pushing up from his chair and hitching his cloak over a shoulder.

"I'm going out for a drink," he informed them.

After several hesitant seconds, Rosalind quietly followed him. Frieda stretched out on a couch and closed her eyes. Edmund scanned microfilms tirelessly, every now and then setting one aside.

Celeste watched him for a minute, then sprang up and started toward the room where Dotty was asleep. But midway she stopped.

Not my child, she thought bitterly. *Frieda's her mother, Rosalind her nurse. I'm nothing at all. Just one of the husband's girl friends. A lady of uneasy virtue in a dissolving world.*

But then she straightened her shoulders and went on.

Rosalind didn't catch up with Theodor. Her footsteps were silent and he never looked back along the path whose feeble white glow rose only knee-high, lighting a low strip of shrub and mossy tree trunk to either side, no more.

It was a little chilly. She drew on her gloves, but she didn't hurry. In fact, she fell farther and farther behind the dipping tail of his scarlet cloak and his plodding red shoes, which seemed to move disembodied, like those in the fairy tale.

When she reached the point where she had found Ivan's briefcase, she stopped altogether.

A breeze rustled the leaves, and, moistly brushing her cheek, brought forest scents of rot and mold. After a bit she began to hear the furtive scurryings and scuttlings of forest creatures.

She looked around her half-heartedly, suddenly realizing the futility of her quest. What clues could she hope to find in this knee-high twilight? And they'd thoroughly combed the place earlier in the night.

Without warning, an eerie tingling went through her and she was seized by a horror of the cold, grainy Earth underfoot-an ancestral terror from the days when men shivered at ghost stories about graves and tombs.

A tiny detail persisted in bulking larger and larger in her mind-the unnaturalness of the way the Earth had impregnated the corner of Ivan's briefcase, almost as if dirt and leather co-existed in the same space. She remembered the queer way the partly buried briefcase had resisted her first tug, like a rooted plant.

She felt cowed by the mysterious night about her, and literally dwarfed, as if she had grown several inches shorter. She roused herself and started forward.

Something held her feet.

They were ankle-deep in the path. While she looked in fright and horror, they began to sink still lower into the ground.

She plunged frantically, trying to jerk loose. She couldn't. She had the panicky feeling that the Earth had not only trapped but invaded her; that its molecules were creeping up between the molecules of her flesh; that the two were becoming one.

And she was sinking faster. Now knee-deep, thigh-deep, hip-deep, waist-deep. She beat at the powdery path with her hands and threw her body from side to side in agonized frenzy like some sinner frozen in the ice of the innermost circle of the ancients' hell. And always the sense of the dark, grainy tide rose inside as well as around her.

She thought, *he'd just have had time to scribble that note on his briefcase and toss it away.* She jerked off a glove, leaned out as far as she could, and made a frantic effort to drive its fingers into the powdery path. Then the Earth mounted to her chin, her nose, and covered her eyes.

She expected blackness, but it was as if the light of the path stayed with her, making a little glow all around. She saw roots, pebbles, black rot, worn tunnels, worms. Tier on tier of them, her vision penetrating the solid ground. And at the same time, the knowledge that these same sorts of things were coursing up through her.

And still she continued to sink at a speed that increased, as if the law of gravitation applied to her in a diminished way. She dropped from black soil through gray clay and into pale limestone.

Her tortured, rock-permeated lungs sucked at rock and drew in air. She wondered madly if a volume of air were falling with her through the stone.

A glitter of quartz. The momentary openness of a foot-high cavern with a trickle of water. And then she was sliding down a black basalt column, half inside it, half inside gold-flecked ore. Then just black basalt. And always faster.

It grew hot, then hotter, as if she were approaching the mythical eternal fires.

At first glance Theodor thought the Deep Space Bar was empty. Then he saw a figure hunched monkeylike on the last stool, almost lost in the blue shadows, while behind the bar, her crystal dress blending with the tiers of sparkling glasses, stood a grave-eyed young girl who could hardly have been fifteen.

The TV was saying, "... in addition, a number of mysterious disappearances of high-rating individuals have been reported. These are thought to be cases of misunderstanding, illusory apprehension, and impulse traveling —a result of the unusual stresses of the time. Finally, a few suggestible individuals in various parts of the globe, especially the Indian Peninsula, have declared themselves to be 'gods' and in some way responsible for current events.

"It is thought —"

The girl switched off the TV and took Theodor's order, explaining casually, "Joe wanted to go to a Kometevskyite meeting, so I took over for him." When she had prepared Theodor's highball, she announced, "I'll have a drink with you gentlemen," and squeezed herself a glass of pomegranate juice.

The monkeylike figure muttered, "Scotch-and-soda," then turned toward Edmund and asked, "And what is your reaction to all this, sir?"

Theodor recognized the shrunken wrinkle-seamed face. It was Colonel Fortescue, a military antique long retired from the Peace Patrol and reputed to have seen actual fighting in the Last Age of Madness. Now, for some reason, the face sported a knowing smile.

Theodor shrugged. Just then the TV "big news" light blinked blue and the girl switched on audio. The Colonel winked at Theodor.

"... confirming the disappearance of Jupiter's moons. But two other utterly fantastic reports have just been received. First, Lunar Observatory One says that it is visually tracking fourteen small bodies which it believes may be the lost moons of Jupiter. They are moving outward from the Solar System at an incredible velocity and are already beyond the orbit of Saturn!"

The Colonel said, "Ah!"

"Second, Palomar reports a large number of dark bodies approaching the Solar System at an equally incredible velocity. They are at about twice the distance of Pluto, but closing in fast! We will be on the air with further details as soon as possible."

The Colonel said, "Ah-ha!"

Theodor stared at him. The old man's self-satisfied poise was almost amusing.

"Are you a Kometevskyite?" Theodor asked him.

The Colonel laughed. "Of course not, my boy. Those poor people are fumbling in the dark. Don't you see what's happened?"

"Frankly, no."

The Colonel leaned toward Theodor and whispered gruffly, "The Divine Plan. God is a military strategist, naturally."

Then he lifted the scotch-and-soda in his clawlike hand and took a satisfying swallow.

"I knew it all along, of course," he went on musingly, "but this last news makes it as plain as a rocket blast, at least to anyone who knows military strategy. Look here, my boy, suppose you were commanding a fleet and got wind of the enemy's approach-what would you do? Why, you'd send your scouts and destroyers fanning out toward them. Behind that screen you'd mass your heavy ships. Then —"

"You don't mean to imply —" Theodor interrupted.

The girl behind the bar looked at them both cryptically.

"Of course I do!" the Colonel cut in sharply. "It's a war between the forces of good and evil. The bright suns and planets are on one side, the dark on the other. The moons are the destroyers, Jupiter and Saturn are the big battleships, while we're on a heavy cruiser, I'm proud to say. We'll probably go into action soon. Be a corking fight, what? And all by divine strategy!"

He chuckled and took another big drink. Theodor looked at him sourly. The girl behind the bar polished a glass and said nothing.

Dotty suddenly began to turn and toss, and a look of terror came over her sleeping face. Celeste leaned forward apprehensively.

The child's lips worked and Celeste made out the sleepy-fuzzy words: "They've found out where we're hiding. They're coming to get us. No! Please, no!"

Celeste's reactions were mixed. She felt worried about Dotty and at the same time almost in terror of her, as if the little girl were an agent of supernatural forces. She told herself that this fear was an expression of her own hostility, yet she didn't really believe it. She touched the child's hand.

Dotty's eyes opened without making Celeste feel she had quite come awake. After a bit she looked at Celeste and her little lips parted in a smile.

"Hello," she said sleepily. "I've been having such funny dreams." Then, after a pause, frowning, "I really am a god, you know. It feels very queer."

"Yes, dear?" Celeste prompted uneasily. "Shall I call Frieda?"

The smile left Dotty's lips. "Why do you act so nervous around me?" she asked. "Don't you love me, Mummy?"

Celeste started at the word. Her throat closed. Then, very slowly, her face broke into a radiant smile. "Of course I do, darling. I love you very much."

Dotty nodded happily, her eyes already closed again.

There was a sudden flurry of excited voices beyond the door. Celeste heard her name called. She stood up.

"I'm going to have to go out and talk with the others," she said. "If you want me, dear, just call."

"Yes, Mummy."

Edmund rapped for attention. Celeste, Frieda, and Theodor glanced around at him. He looked more frightfully strained, they realized, than even they felt. His expression was a study in suppressed excitement, but there were also signs of a knowledge that was almost too overpowering for a human being to bear.

His voice was clipped, rapid. "I think it's about time we stopped worrying about our own affairs and thought of those of the Solar System, partly because I think they have a direct bearing on the disappearances of Ivan end Rosalind. As I told you, I've been sorting out the crucial items from the material we've been presenting. There are roughly four of those items, as I see it. It's rather like a mystery story. I wonder if, hearing those four clues, you will come to the same conclusion I have."

The others nodded.

"First, there are the latest reports from Deep Shaft, which, as you know, has been sunk to investigate deep-Earth conditions. At approximately twenty-nine miles below the surface, the delvers have encountered a metallic obstruction which they have tentatively named the durasphere. It resists their hardest drills, their strongest corrosives. They have extended a side-tunnel at that level for a quarter of a mile. Delicate measurements, made possible by the mirror-smooth metal surface, show that the durasphere has a slight curvature that is almost exactly equal to the curvature of the Earth itself. The suggestion is that deep borings made anywhere in the world would encounter the durasphere at the same depth.

"Second, the movements of the moons of Mars and Jupiter, and particularly the debris left behind by the moons of Mars. Granting Phobos and Deimos had duraspheres proportional in size to that of Earth, then the debris would roughly equal in amount the material in those two duraspheres' rocky envelopes. The suggestion is that the two duraspheres suddenly burst from their envelopes with such titanic velocity as to leave those disrupted envelopes behind."

It was deadly quiet in the committee room.

"Thirdly, the disappearances of Ivan and Rosalind, and especially the baffling hint-from Ivan's message in one case and Rosalind's downward-pointing glove in the other-that they were both somehow drawn into the depths of the Earth.

"Finally, the dreams of the ESPs, which agree overwhelmingly in the following points: A group of beings separate themselves from a godlike and telepathic race because they insist on maintaining a degree of mental privacy. They flee in great boats or ships of some sort. They are pursued on such a scale that there is no hiding place for them anywhere in the universe. In some manner they successfully camouflage their ships. Eons pass and their still-fanatical pursuers do not penetrate their secret. Then, suddenly, they are detected."

Edmund waited. "Do you see what I'm driving at?" he asked hoarsely.

He could tell from their looks that the others did, but couldn't bring themselves to put it into words.

"I suppose it's the time-scale and the value-scale that are so hard for us to accept," he said softly. "Much more, even, than the size-scale. The thought that there are creatures in the Universe to whom the whole career of Man-in fact, the whole career of life-is no more than a few thousand or hundred thousand years. And to whom Man is no more than a minor stage property—a trifling part of a clever job of camouflage."

This time he went on, "Fantasy writers have at times hinted all sorts of odd things about the Earth-that it might even be a kind of single living creature, or honeycombed with inhabited caverns, and so on. But I don't know that any of them have ever suggested that the Earth, together with all the planets and moons of the Solar System, might be...."

In a whisper, Frieda finished for him, "...a camouflaged fleet of gigantic spherical spaceships."

"Your guess happens to be the precise truth."

At that familiar, yet dreadly unfamiliar voice, all four of them swung toward the inner door. Dotty was standing there, a sleep-stupefied little girl with a blanket caught up around her and dragging behind. Their own daughter. But in her eyes was a look from which they cringed.

She said, "I am a creature somewhat older than what your geologists call the Archeozoic Era. I am speaking to you through a number of telepathically sensitive individuals among your kind. In each case my thoughts suit themselves to your level of comprehension. I inhabit the disguised and jetless spaceship which is your Earth."

Celeste swayed a step forward. "Baby...." she implored.

Dotty went on, without giving her a glance, "It is true that we planted the seeds of life on some of these planets simply as part of our camouflage, just as we gave them a suitable environment for each. And it is true that now we must let most of that life be destroyed. Our hiding place has been discovered, our pursuers are upon us, and we must make one last effort to escape or do battle, since we firmly believe that the principle of mental privacy to which we have devoted our existence is perhaps the greatest good in the whole Universe.

"But it is not true that we look with contempt upon you. Our whole race is deeply devoted to life, wherever it may come into being, and it is our rule never to interfere with its development. That was one of the reasons we made life a part of our camouflage-it would make our pursuers reluctant to examine these planets too closely.

"Yes, we have always cherished you and watched your evolution with interest from our hidden lairs. We may even unconsciously have shaped your development in certain ways, trying constantly to educate you away from war and finally succeeding-which may have given the betraying clue to our pursuers.

"Your planets must be burst asunder-this particular planet in the area of the Pacific-so that we may have our last chance to escape. Even if we did not move, our pursuers would destroy you with us. We cannot invite you inside our ships-not for lack of space, but because you could never survive the vast accelerations to which you would be subjected. You would, you see, need very special accommodations, of which we have enough only for a few.

"Those few we will take with us, as the seed from which a new human race may-if we ourselves somehow survive-be born."

Rosalind and Ivan stared dumbly at each other across the egg-shaped silver room, without apparent entrance or exit, in which they were sprawled. But their thoughts were no longer of thirty-odd mile journeys down through solid earth, or of how cool it was after the heat of the passage, or of how grotesque it was to be trapped here, the fragment of a marriage. They were both listening to the voice that spoke inside their minds.

"In a few minutes your bodies will be separated into layers one atom thick, capable of being shelved or stored in such a way as to endure almost infinite accelerations. Single cells will cover acres of space. But do not be alarmed. The process will be painless and each particle will be catalogued for future assembly. Your consciousness will endure throughout the process."

Rosalind looked at her gold-shod toes. She was wondering, *will they go first, or my head? Or will I be peeled like an apple?*

She looked at Ivan and knew he was thinking the same thing.

Up in the committee room, the other Wolvers slumped around the table. Only little Dotty sat straight and staring, speechless and unanswering, quite beyond their reach, like a telephone off the hook and with the connection open, but no voice from the other end.

They had just switched off the TV after listening to a confused medley of denials, prayers, Kometevskyite chatterings, and a few astonishingly realistic comments on the possibility of survival.

These last pointed out that, on the side of the Earth opposite the Pacific, the convulsions would come slowly when the entombed spaceship burst forth-provided, as seemed the case, that it moved without jets or reaction.

It would be as if the Earth's vast core simply vanished. Gravity would diminish abruptly to a fraction of its former value. The empty envelope of rock and water and air would slowly fall together, though at the same time the air would begin to escape from the debris because there would no longer be the mass required to hold it.

However, there might be definite chances of temporary and even prolonged survival for individuals in strong, hermetically sealed structures, such as submarines and spaceships. The few spaceships on Earth were reported to have blasted off, or be preparing to leave, with as many passengers as could be carried.

But most persons, apparently, could not contemplate action of any sort. They could only sit and think, like the Wolvers.

A faint smile relaxed Celeste's face. She was thinking, *how beautiful! It means the death of the Solar System, which is a horrifying subjective concept. Objectively, though, it would be a more awesome sight than any human being has ever seen or ever could see. It's an absurd and even brutal thing to wish—but I wish I could see the whole cataclysm from beginning to end. It would make death seem very small, a tiny personal event.*

Dotty's face was losing its blank expression, becoming intent and alarmed.

"We are in contact with our pursuers," she said in the familiar-unfamiliar voice. "Negotiations are now going on. There seems to be-there *is* a change in them. Where they were harsh and vindictive before, they now are gentle and conciliatory." She paused, the alarm on her childish features pinching into anxious uncertainty. "Our pursuers have always been shrewd. The change in them may be false, intended merely to lull us into allowing them to come close enough to destroy us. We must not fall into the trap by growing hopeful...."

They leaned forward, clutching hands, watching the little face as though it were a television screen. Celeste had the wild feeling that she was listening to a communique from a war so unthinkably vast and violent, between opponents so astronomically huge and nearly immortal, that she felt like no more than a reasoning ameba ... and then realized with an explosive urge to laugh that that was exactly the situation.

"No!" said Dotty. Her eyes began to glow. "They *have* changed! During the eons in which we lay sealed away and hidden from them, knowing nothing of them, they have rebelled against the tyranny of a communal mind to which no thoughts are private ... the tyranny that we ourselves fled to escape. They come not to destroy us, but to welcome us back to a society that we and they can make truly great!"

Frieda collapsed to a chair, trembling between laughter and hysterical weeping. Theodor looked as blank as Dotty had while waiting for words to speak. Edmund sprang to the picture window, Celeste toward the TV set.

Climbing shakily out of the chair, Frieda stumbled to the picture window and peered out beside Edmund. She saw lights bobbing along the paths with a wild excitement.

On the TV screen, Celeste watched two brightly lit ships spinning in the sky-whether human spaceships or Phobos and Deimos come to help Earth rejoice, she couldn't tell.

Dotty spoke again, the joy in her strange voice forcing them to turn. "And you, dear children, creatures of our camouflage, we welcome you-whatever your future career on these planets or like ones-into the society of enlightened worlds! You need not feel small and alone and helpless ever again, for we shall always be with you!"

The outer door opened. Ivan and Rosalind reeled in, drunkenly smiling, arm in arm.

"Like rockets," Rosalind blurted happily. "We came through the durasphere and solid rock ... shot up right to the surface."

"They didn't have to take us along," Ivan added with a bleary grin. "But you know that already, don't you? They're too good to let you live in fear, so they must have told you by now."

"Yes, we know," said Theodor. "They must be almost godlike in their goodness. I feel ... calm."

Edmund nodded soberly. "Calmer than I ever felt before. It's knowing, I suppose, that-well, we're not alone."

Dotty blinked and looked around and smiled at them all with a wholly little-girl smile.

"Oh, Mummy," she said, and it was impossible to tell whether she spoke to Frieda or Rosalind or Celeste, "I've just had the funniest dream."

"No, darling," said Rosalind gently, "it's we who had the dream. We've just awakened."

The Last Letter

*Who or what was the scoundrel that kept
these couriers from the swift completion
of their handsomely appointed rondos?*

On Tenthmonth 1, 2457 A.D., at exactly 9 A.M. Planetary Federation Time-but with a permissible error of a millionth of a second either way-in the fifth sublevel of NewNew York Robot Postal Station 68, Black Sorter gulped down ten thousand pieces of first-class mail.

This breakfast tidbit did not agree with the mail-sorting machine. It was as if a robust dog had been fed a large chunk of good red meat with a strychnine pill in it. Black Sorter's innards went *whirr-klunk*, a blue electric glow enveloped him, and he began to shake as if he might break loose from the concrete.

He desperately spat back over his shoulder a single envelope, gave a great *huff* and blew out toward the sorting tubes a medium-size snowstorm consisting of the other nine thousand, nine hundred and ninety-nine pieces of first-class mail chewed to confetti. Then, still convulsed, he snapped up a fresh ten thousand and proceeded to chomp and grind on them. Black Sorter was rugged.

The rejected envelope was tongued up by Red Subsorter, who growled deep in his throat, said a very bad word, and passed it to Yellow Rerouter, who passed it to Green Rerouter, who passed it to Brown Study, who passed it to Pink Wastebasket.

Unlike Black Sorter, Pink Wastebasket was very delicate, though highly intuitive-the machine equivalent of a White Russian countess. She was designed to scan in 3,137 codes, route special-delivery spacemail to interplanetary liners by messenger rocket, and distinguish 9s from upside-down 6s.

Pink Wastebasket haughtily inhaled the offending envelope and almost instantly turned a bright crimson and began to tremble. After a few minutes, small atomic flames started to flicker from her mid-section.

White Nursemaid Seven and Greasy Joe both received Pink Wastebasket's distress signal and got there as fast as their wheels would roll them, but the high-born machine's malady was beyond their simple skills of oilcan and electroshock.

They summoned other machine-tending-and-repairing machines, ones far more expert than themselves, but all were baffled. It was clear that Pink Wastebasket, who continued to tremble and flicker uncontrollably, was suffering from the equivalent of a major psychosis with severe psychosomatic symptoms. She spat a stream of filthy ions at Gray Psychiatrist, not recognizing her old friend.

Meanwhile, the paper blizzard from Black Sorter was piling up in great drifts between the dark pillars of the sublevel, and flurries had reached Pink Wastebasket's aristocratic area. An expedition of sturdy machines, headed by two hastily summoned snowplows, was dispatched to immobilize Black Sorter at all costs.

Pink Wastebasket, quivering like a demented hula dancer, was clearly approaching a crisis. Finally Gray Psychiatrist-after consulting with Green Surgeon, and even then with an irritated reluctance, as if he were calling in a witch-doctor —summoned a human being.

The human being walked respectfully around Pink Wastebasket several times and then gave her a nervous little poke with a rubber-handled probe.

Pink Wastebasket gently regurgitated her last snack, turned dead white, gave a last flicker and shake, and expired. Black Coroner recorded the immediate cause of death as tinkering by a human being.

The human being, a bald and scrawny one named Potshelter, picked up the envelope responsible for all the trouble, stared at it incredulously, opened it with trembling fingers, scanned the contents briefly, gave a great shriek and ran off at top speed, forgetting to hop on his perambulator, which followed him making anxious clucking noises.

The nearest human representative of the Solar Bureau of Investigation, a rather wooden-looking man named Krumbine, also bald, recognized Potshelter as soon as the latter burst gasping into his office, squeezing through the door while it was still dilating. The human beings whose work took them among the Top Brass, as the upper-echelon machines were sometimes referred to, formed a kind of human elite, just one big nervous family.

"Sit down, Potshelter," the SBI Man said. "Hold still a second so the chair can grab you. Hitch onto the hookah and choose a tranquilizer from the tray at your elbow. Whatever deviation you've uncovered can't be that much of a danger to the planets. I imagine that when you leave this office, the Solar Battle Fleet will still be orbiting peacefully around Luna."

"I seriously doubt that."

Potshelter gulped a large lavender pill and took a deep breath. "Krumbine, a letter turned up in the first-class mail this morning."

"Great Scott!"

"It is a letter from one person to another person."

"Good Lord!"

"The flow of advertising has been seriously interfered with. At a modest estimate, three hundred million pieces of expensive first-class advertising have already been chewed to rags and I'm not sure the Steel Helms-God bless 'em! —have the trouble in hand yet."

"Judas Priest!"

"Naturally the poor machines weren't able to cope with the letter. It was utterly outside their experience, beyond the furthest reach of their programming. It threw them into a terrible spasm. Pink Wastebasket is dead and at this very instant, if we're lucky, three police machines of the toughest blued steel are holding down Black Sorter and putting a muzzle on him."

"Great Scott! It's incredible, Potshelter. And Pink Wastebasket dead? Take another tranquilizer, Potshelter, and hand over the tray."

Krumbine received it with trembling fingers, started to pick up a big pink pill but drew back his hand from it in sudden revulsion at its color and swallowed two blue oval ones instead. The man was obviously fighting to control himself.

He said unsteadily, "I almost never take doubles, but this news you bring-Good Lord! I seem to recall a case where someone tried to send a sound-tape through the mails, but that was before my time. Incidentally, is there any possibility that this is a letter sent by one *group* of persons to another group? A hive or a therapy group or a social club? That would be bad enough, of course, but —"

"No, just one single person sending to another." Potshelter's expression set in grimly solicitous lines. "I can see you don't quite understand, Krumbine. This is not a sound-tape, but a letter written in letters. You know, letters, characters-like books."

"Don't mention books in this office!" Krumbine drew himself up angrily and then slumped back. "Excuse me, Potshelter, but I find this very difficult to face squarely. Do I understand you to say that one person has tried to use the mails to send a printed sheet of some sort to another?"

"Worse than that. A written letter."

"Written? I don't recognize the word."

"It's a way of making characters, of forming visual equivalents of sound, without using electricity. The writer, as he's called, employs a black liquid and a pointed stick called a pen. I know about this because one hobby of mine is ancient means of communication."

Krumbine frowned and shook his head. "Communication is a dangerous business, Potshelter, especially at the personal level. With you and me, it's all right, because we know what we're doing."

He picked up a third blue tranquilizer. "But with most of the hive-folk, person-to-person communication is only a morbid form of advertising, a dangerous travesty of normal newscasting-catharsis without the analyst, recitation without the teacher —a perversion of promotion employed in betraying and subverting."

The frown deepened as he put the blue pill in his mouth and chewed it. "But about this pen-do you mean the fellow glues the pointed stick to his tongue and then speaks, and the black liquid traces the vibrations on the paper? A primitive non-electrical oscilloscope? Sloppy but conceivable, and producing a record of sorts of the spoken word."

"No, no, Krumbine." Potshelter nervously popped a square orange tablet into his mouth. "It's a hand-written letter."

Krumbine watched him. "I never mix tranquilizers," he boasted absently. "Hand-written, eh? You mean that the message was imprinted on a hand? And the skin or the entire hand afterward detached and sent through the mails in the fashion of a Martian reproach? A grisly find indeed, Potshelter."

"You still don't quite grasp it, Krumbine. The fingers of the hand move the stick that applies the ink, producing a crude imitation of the printed word."

"Diabolical!" Krumbine smashed his fist down on the desk so that the four phones and two-score microphones rattled. "I tell you, Potshelter, the SBI is ready to cope with the subtlest modern deceptions, but when fiends search out and revive tricks from the pre-Atomic Cave Era, it's almost too much. But, Great Scott, I dally while the planets are in danger. What's the sender's code on this hellish letter?"

"No code," Potshelter said darkly, proferring the envelope. "The return address is-hand-written."

Krumbine blanched as his eyes slowly traced the uneven lines in the upper left-hand corner:

> *from* Richard Rowe
> 215 West 10th St. (horizontal)
> 2837 Rocket Court (vertical)
> Hive 37, NewNew York 319, N. Y.
> Columbia, Terra

"Ugh!" Krumbine said, shivering. "Those crawling characters, those letters, as you call them, those *things* barely enough like print to be readable-they seem to be on the verge of awakening all sorts of horrid racial memories. I find myself thinking of fur-clad witch-doctors dipping long pointed sticks in bubbling black cauldrons. No wonder Pink Wastebasket couldn't take it, brave girl."

Firming himself behind his desk, he pushed a number of buttons and spoke long numbers and meaningful alphabetical syllables into several microphones. Banks of colored lights around the desk began to blink like a theatre marquee sending Morse Code, while phosphorescent arrows crawled purposefully across maps and space-charts and through three-dimensional street diagrams.

"There!" he said at last. "The sender of the letter is being apprehended and will be brought directly here. We'll see what sort of man this Richard Rowe is-if we can assume he's human. Seven precautionary cordons are being drawn around his population station: three composed of machines, two of SBI agents, and two consisting of human and mechanical medical-combat teams. Same goes for the intended recipient of the letter. Meanwhile, a destroyer squadron of the Solar Fleet has been detached to orbit over NewNew York."

"In case it becomes necessary to Z-Bomb?" Potshelter asked grimly.

Krumbine nodded. "With all those villains lurking just outside the Solar System in their invisible black ships, with planeticide in their hearts, we can't be too careful. One word transmitted from one spy to another and anything may happen. And we must bomb before they do, so as to contain our losses. Better one city destroyed than a traitor on the loose who may destroy many cities. One hundred years ago, three person-to-person postcards went through the mails-just three postcards, Potshelter! —and *pft* went Schenectady, Hoboken, Cicero, and Walla Walla. Here, as long as you're mixing them, try one of these oval blues —I find them best for steady swallowing."

Bells jangled. Krumbine grabbed up two phones, holding one to each ear. Potshelter automatically picked up a third. The ringing continued. Krumbine started to wedge one of his phones under his chin, nodded sharply at Potshelter and then toward a cluster of microphones at the end of the table. Potshelter picked up a fourth phone from behind them. The ringing stopped.

The two men listened, looking doped, Krumbine with an eye fixed on the sweep second hand of the large wall clock. When it had made one revolution, he cradled his phones. Potshelter followed suit.

"I do like the simplicity of the new on-the-hour Puffyloaf phono-commercial," the latter remarked thoughtfully. "The Bread That's Lighter Than Air. Nice."

Krumbine nodded. "I hear they've had to add mass to the leadfoil wrapping to keep the loaves from floating off the shelves. Fact."

He cleared his throat. "Too bad we can't listen to more phono-commercials, but even when there isn't a crisis on the agenda, I find I have to budget my listening time. One minute per hour strikes a reasonable balance between duty and self-indulgence."

The nearest wall began to sing:

Mister J. Augustus Krumbine,
We all think you're fine, fine, fine, fine.
Now out of the skyey blue
Come some telegrams for you.

The wall opened to a small heart shape toward the center and a sheaf of pale yellow envelopes arced out and plopped on the middle of the desk. Krumbine started to leaf through them, scanning the little transparent windows.

"Hm, Electronic Soap ...Better Homes and Landing Platforms ...Psycho-Blinkers ...Your Girl Next Door ...Poppy-Woppies ...Poopsy-Woopsies...."

He started to open an envelope, then, after a quick look around and an apologetic smile at Potshelter, dumped them all on the disposal hopper, which gargled briefly.

"After all, there *is* a crisis this morning," he said in a defensive voice.

Potshelter nodded absently. "I can remember back before personalized delivery and rhyming robots," he observed. "But how I'd miss them now-so much more distingué than the hives with their non-personalized radio, TV and stereo advertising. For that matter, I believe there are some backward areas on Terra where the great advertising potential of telephones and telegrams hasn't been fully realized and they are still used in part for personal communication. Now me, I've never in my life sent or received a message except on my walky-talky." He patted his breast pocket.

Krumbine nodded, but he was a trifle shocked and inclined to revise his estimate of Potshelter's social status. Krumbine conducted his own social correspondence solely by telepathy. He shared with three other SBI officials a private telepath —a charming albino girl named Agnes.

"Yes, and it's a very handsome walky-talky," he assured Potshelter a little falsely. "Suits you. I like the upswept antenna." He drummed on the desk and swallowed another blue tranquilizer. "Dammit, what's happened to those machines? They ought to have the two spies here by now. Did you notice that the second-the intended recipient of the letter, I mean-seems to be female? Another good Terran name, too, Jane Dough. Hive in Upper Manhattan." He began to tap the envelope sharply against the desk. "Dammit, where *are* they?"

"Excuse me," Potshelter said hesitantly, "but I'm wondering why you haven't read the message inside the envelope."

Krumbine looked at him blankly. "Great Scott, I assumed that at least *it* was in some secret code, of course. Normally I'd have asked you to have Pink Wastebasket try her skill on it, but...." His eyes widened and his voice sank. "You don't mean to tell me that it's —"

Potshelter nodded grimly. "Hand-written, too. Yes."

Krumbine winced. "I keep trying to forget that aspect of the case." He dug out the message with shaking fingers, fumbled it open and read:

Dear Jane,

It must surprise you that I know your name, for our hives are widely separated. Do you recall day before yesterday when your guided tour of Grand Central Spaceport got stalled because the guide blew a fuse? I was the young man with hair in the tour behind yours. You were a little frightened and a groupmistress was reassuring you. The machine spoke your name.

Since then I have been unable to forget you. When I go to sleep, I dream of your face looking up sadly at the mistress's kindly photocells. I don't know how to get in touch with you, but my grandfather has told me stories his grandfather told him that his grandfather told him about young men writing what he calls love-letters to young ladies. So I am writing you a love-letter.

I work in a first-class advertising house and I will slip this love-letter into an outgoing ten-thousand-pack and hope.

Do not be frightened of me, Jane. I am no caveman except for my hair. I am not insane. I am emotionally disturbed, but in a way that no machine has ever described to me. I want only your happiness.

Sincerely,

Richard Rowe

Krumbine slumped back in his chair, which braced itself manfully against him, and looked long and thoughtfully at Potshelter. "Well, if that's a code, it's certainly a fiendishly subtle one. You'd think he was talking to his Girl Next Door."

Potshelter nodded wonderingly. "I only read as far as where they were planning to blow up Grand Central Spaceport and all the guides in it."

"Judas Priest, I think I have it!" Krumbine shot up. "It's a pilot advertisement-Boy Next Door or-that kind of thing-printed to look like hand-writtening, which would make all the difference. And the pilot copy got mailed by accident-which would mean there is no real Richard Rowe."

At that instant, the door dilated and two blue detective engines hustled a struggling young man into the office. He was slim, rather handsome, had a bushy head of hair that had somehow survived evolution and radioactive fallout, and across the chest and back of his paper singlet was neatly stamped: "RICHARD ROWE."

When he saw the two men, he stopped struggling and straightened up. "Excuse me, gentlemen," he said, "but these police machines must have made a mistake. I've committed no crime."

Then his gaze fell on the hand-addressed envelope on Krumbine's desk and he turned pale.

Krumbine laughed harshly. "No crime! No, not at all. Merely using the mails to communicate. Ha!"

The young man shrank back. "I'm sorry, sir."

"Sorry, he says! Do you realize that your insane prank has resulted in the destruction of perhaps a half-billion pieces of first-class advertising? —in the strangulation of a postal station and the paralysis of Lower Manhattan? —in the mobilization of SBI reserves, the de-mothballing of two divisions of G. I. machines and the redeployment of the Solar Battle Fleet? Good Lord, boy, why did you do it?"

Richard Rowe continued to shrink but he squared his shoulders. "I'm sorry, sir, but I just had to. I just had to get in touch with Jane Dough."

"A girl from another hive? A girl you'd merely gazed at because a guide happened to blow a fuse?" Krumbine stood up, shaking an angry finger. "Great Scott, boy, where was Your Girl Next Door?"

Richard Rowe stared bravely at the finger, which made him look a trifle cross-eyed. "She died, sir, both of them."

"But there should be at least six."

"I know, sir, but of the other four, two have been shipped to the Adirondacks on vacation and two recently got married and haven't been replaced."

Potshelter, a faraway look in his eyes, said softly, "I think I'm beginning to understand —"

But Krumbine thundered on at Richard Rowe with, "Good Lord, I can see you've had your troubles, boy. It isn't often we have these shortages of Girls Next Door, so that temporarily a boy can't marry the Girl Next Door, as he always should. But, Judas Priest, why didn't you take your troubles to your psychiatrist, your groupmaster, your socializer, your Queen Mother?"

"My psychiatrist is being overhauled, sir, and his replacement short-circuits every time he hears the word 'trouble.' My groupmaster and socializer are on vacation duty in the Adirondacks. My Queen Mother is busy replacing Girls Next Door."

"Yes, it all fits," Potshelter proclaimed excitedly. "Don't you see, Krumbine? Except for a set of mischances that would only occur once in a billion billion times, the letter would never have been conceived or sent."

"You may have something there," Krumbine concurred. "But in any case, boy, why did you-er-written this letter to this particular girl? What is there about Jane Dough that made you do it?"

"Well, you see, sir, she's —"

Just then, the door re-dilated and a blue matron machine conducted a young woman into the office. She was slim and she had a head of hair that would have graced a museum beauty, while across the back and-well, "chest" is an inadequate word-of her paper chemise, "JANE DOUGH" was silk-screened in the palest pink.

Krumbine did not repeat his last question. He had to admit to himself that it had been answered fully. Potshelter whistled respectfully. The blue detective engines gave hard-boiled grunts. Even the blue matron machine seemed awed by the girl's beauty.

But she had eyes only for Richard Rowe. "My Grand Central man," she breathed in amazement. "The man I've dreamed of ever since. My man with hair." She noticed the way he was looking at her and she breathed harder. "Oh, darling, what have you done?"

"I tried to send you a letter."

"A letter? For me? Oh, darling!"

Krumbine cleared his throat. "Potshelter, I'm going to wind this up fast. Miss Dough, could you transfer to this young man's hive?"

"Oh, yes, sir! Mine has an over-plus of Girls Next Door."

"Good. Mr. Rowe, there's a sky-pilot two levels up-look for the usual white collar just below the photocells. Marry this girl and take her home to your hive. If your Queen Mother objects refer her to-er-Potshelter here."

He cut short the young people's thanks. "Just one thing," he said, wagging a finger at Rowe. "Don't written any more letters."

"Why ever would I?" Richard answered. "Already my action is beginning to seem like a mad dream."

"Not to me, dear," Jane corrected him. "Oh, sir, could I have the letter he sent me? Not to do anything with. Not to show anyone. Just to keep."

"Well, I don't know —" Krumbine began.

"Oh, *please*, sir!"

"Well, I don't know why not, I was going to say. Here you are, miss. Just see that this husband of yours never writtens another."

He turned back as the contracting door shut the young couple from view.

"You were right, Potshelter," he said briskly. "It was one of those combinations of mischances that come up only once in a billion billion times. But we're going to have to issue recommendations for new procedures and safeguards that will reduce the possibilities to one in a trillion trillion. It will undoubtedly up the Terran income tax a healthy percentage, but we can't have something like this happening again. Every boy must marry the Girl Next Door! And the first-class mails must not be interfered with! The advertising must go through!"

"I'd almost like to see it happen again," Potshelter murmured dreamily, "if there were another Jane Dough in it."

Outside, Richard and Jane had halted to allow a small cortege of machines to pass. First came a squad of police machines with Black Sorter in their midst, unmuzzled and docile enough, though still gnashing his teeth softly. Then-stretched out horizontally and borne on the shoulders of Gray Psychiatrist, Black Coroner, White Nursemaid Seven and Greasy Joe-there passed the slim form of Pink Wastebasket, snow-white in death. The machines were keening softly, mournfully.

Round about the black pillars, little mecho-mops were scurrying like mice, cleaning up the last of the first-class-mail bits of confetti.

Richard winced at this evidence of his aberration, but Jane squeezed his hand comfortingly, which produced in him a truly amazing sensation that changed his whole appearance.

"I know how you feel, darling," she told him. "But don't worry about it. Just think, dear, I'll always be able to tell your friends' wives something no other woman in the world can boast of: that my husband once wrote me a letter!"

Yesterday House

Meeting someone who's been dead for twenty years is shocking enough for anyone with a belief in ghosts-worse for one with none!

I

The narrow cove was quiet as the face of an expectant child, yet so near the ruffled Atlantic that the last push of wind carried the *Annie O.* its full length. The man in gray flannels and sweatshirt let the sail come crumpling down and hurried past its white folds at a gait made comically awkward by his cramped muscles. Slowly the rocky ledge came nearer. Slowly the blue V inscribed on the cove's surface by the sloop's prow died. Sloop and ledge kissed so gently that he hardly had to reach out his hand.

He scrambled ashore, dipping a sneaker in the icy water, and threw the line around a boulder. Unkinking himself, he looked back through the cove's high and rocky mouth at the gray-green scattering of islands and the faint dark line that was the coast of Maine. He almost laughed in satisfaction at having disregarded vague warnings and done the thing every man yearns to do once in his lifetime-gone to the farthest island out.

He must have looked longer than he realized, because by the time he dropped his gaze the cove was again as glassy as if the *Annie O.* had always been there. And the splotches made by his sneaker on the rock had faded in the hot sun. There was something very unusual about the quietness of this place. As if time, elsewhere hurrying frantically, paused here to rest. As if all changes were erased on this one bit of Earth.

The man's lean, melancholy face crinkled into a grin at the banal fancy. He turned his back on his new friend, the little green sloop, without one thought for his nets and specimen bottles, and set out to explore. The ground rose steeply at first and the oaks were close, but after a little way things went downhill and the leaves thinned and he came out on more rocks-and realized that he hadn't quite gone to the farthest one out.

Joined to this island by a rocky spine, which at the present low tide would have been dry but for the spray, was another green, high island that the first had masked from him all the while he had been sailing. He felt a thrill of discovery, just as he'd wondered back in the woods whether his might not be the first human feet to kick through the underbrush. After all, there were thousands of these islands.

Then he was dropping down the rocks, his lanky limbs now moving smoothly enough.

To the landward side of the spine, the water was fairly still. It even began with another deep cove, in which he glimpsed the spiny spheres of sea urchins. But from seaward the waves chopped in, sprinkling his trousers to the knees and making him wince pleasurably at the thought of what vast wings of spray and towers of solid water must crash up from here in a storm.

He crossed the rocks at a trot, ran up a short grassy slope, raced through a fringe of trees-and came straight up against an eight-foot fence of heavy mesh topped with barbed wire and backed at a short distance with high, heavy shrubbery.

Without pausing for surprise-in fact, in his holiday mood, using surprise as a goad-he jumped for the branch of an oak whose trunk touched the fence, scorning the easier lower branch on the other side of the tree. Then he drew himself up, worked his way to some higher branches that crossed the fence, and dropped down inside.

Suddenly cautious, he gently parted the shrubbery and, before the first surprise could really sink in, had another.

A closely mown lawn dotted with more shrubbery ran up to a snug white Cape Cod cottage. The single strand of a radio aerial stretched the length of the roof. Parked on a neat gravel driveway that crossed just in front of the cottage was a short, square-lined touring car that he recognized from remembered pictures as an ancient Essex. The whole scene had about it the same odd quietness as the cove.

Then, with the air of a clock-work toy coming to life, the white door opened and an elderly woman came out, dressed in a long, lace-edged dress and wide, lacy hat. She climbed into the driver's seat of the Essex, sitting there very stiff and tall. The motor began to chug bravely, gravel skittered, and the car rolled off between the trees.

The door of the house opened again and a slim girl emerged. She wore a white silk dress that fell straight from square neck-line to hip-height waistline, making the skirt seem very short. Her dark hair was bound with a white bandeau so that it curved close to her cheeks. A dark necklace dangled against the white of the dress. A newspaper was tucked under her arm.

She crossed the driveway and tossed the paper down on a rattan table between three rattan chairs and stood watching a squirrel zigzag across the lawn.

The man stepped through the wall of shrubbery, called, "hello!" and walked toward her.

She whirled around and stared at him as still as if her heart had stopped beating. Then she darted behind the table and waited for him there. Granting the surprise of his appearance, her alarm seemed not so much excessive as eerie. As if, the man thought, he were not an ordinary stranger, but a visitor from another planet.

Approaching closer, he saw that she was trembling and that her breath was coming in rapid, irregular gasps. Yet the slim, sweet, patrician face that stared into his had an underlying expression of expectancy that reminded him of the cove. She couldn't have been more than eighteen.

He stopped short of the table. Before he could speak, she stammered out, "Are you he?"

"What do you mean?" he asked, smiling puzzledly.

"The one who sends me the little boxes."

"I was out sailing and I happened to land in the far cove. I didn't dream that anyone lived on this island, or even came here."

"No one ever does come here," she replied. Her manner had changed, becoming at once more wary and less agitated, though still eerily curious.

"It startled me tremendously to find this place," he blundered on. "Especially the road and the car. Why, this island can't be more than a quarter of a mile wide."

"The road goes down to the wharf," she explained, "and up to the top of the island, where my aunts have a tree-house."

He tore his mind away from the picture of a woman dressed like Queen Mary clambering up a tree. "Was that your aunt I saw driving off?"

"One of them. The other's taken the motorboat in for supplies." She looked at him doubtfully. "I'm not sure they'll like it if they find someone here."

"There are just the three of you?" he cut in quickly, looking down the empty road that vanished among the oaks.

She nodded.

"I suppose you go in to the mainland with your aunts quite often?"

She shook her head.

"It must get pretty dull for you."

"Not very," she said, smiling. "My aunts bring me the papers and other things. Even movies. We've got a projector. My favorite stars are Antonio Morino and Alice Terry. I like her better even than Clara Bow."

He looked at her hard for a moment. "I suppose you read a lot?"

She nodded. "Fitzgerald's my favorite author." She started around the table, hesitated, suddenly grew shy. "Would you like some lemonade?"

He'd noticed the dewed silver pitcher, but only now realized his thirst. Yet when she handed him a glass, he held it untasted and said awkwardly, "I haven't introduced myself. I'm Jack Barry."

330

She stared at his outstretched right hand, slowly extended her own toward it, shook it up and down exactly once, then quickly dropped it.

He chuckled and gulped some lemonade. "I'm a biology student. Been working at Wood's Hole the first part of the summer. But now I'm here to do research in marine ecology-that's sort of sea-life patterns-of the in-shore islands. Under the direction of Professor Kesserich. You know about him, of course?"

She shook her head.

"Probably the greatest living biologist," he was proud to inform her. "Human physiology as well. Tremendous geneticist. In a class with Carlson and Jacques Loeb. Martin Kesserich-he lives over there at town. I'm staying with him. You ought to have heard of him." He grinned. "Matter of fact, I'd never have met you if it hadn't been for Mrs. Kesserich."

The girl looked puzzled.

Jack explained, "The old boy's been off to Europe on some conferences, won't be back for a couple days more. But I was to get started anyhow. When I went out this morning Mrs. Kesserich-she's a drab sort of person-said to me, 'Don't try to sail to the farther islands.' So, of course, I had to. By the way, you still haven't told me your name."

"Mary Alice Pope," she said, speaking slowly and with an odd wonder, as if she were saying it for the first time.

"You're pretty shy, aren't you?"

"How would I know?"

The question stopped Jack. He couldn't think of anything to say to this strangely attractive girl dressed almost like a "flapper."

"Will you sit down?" she asked him gravely.

The rattan chair sighed under his weight. He made another effort to talk. "I'll bet you'll be glad when summer's over."

"Why?"

"So you'll be able to go back to the mainland."

"But I never go to the mainland."

"You mean you stay out here all winter?" he asked incredulously, his mind filled with a vision of snow and frozen spray and great gray waves.

"Oh, yes. We get all our supplies on hand before winter. My aunts are very capable. They don't always wear long lace dresses. And now I help them."

"But that's impossible!" he said with sudden sympathetic anger. "You can't be shut off this way from people your own age!"

"You're the first one I ever met." She hesitated. "I never saw a boy or a man before, except in movies."

"You're joking!"

"No, it's true."

"But why are they doing it to you?" he demanded, leaning forward. "Why are they inflicting this loneliness on you, Mary?"

She seemed to have gained poise from his loss of it. "I don't know why. I'm to find out soon. But actually I'm not lonely. May I tell you a secret?" She touched his hand, this time with only the faintest trembling. "Every night the loneliness gathers in around me-you're right about that. But then every morning new life comes to me in a little box."

"What's that?" he said sharply.

"Sometimes there's a poem in the box, sometimes a book, or pictures, or flowers, or a ring, but always a note. Next to the notes I like the poems best. My favorite is the one by Matthew Arnold that ends,

'Ah, love, let us be true
To one another! for the world, which seems
To lie before us like a land of dreams,
So various, so beautiful, so new,
Hath really neither joy, nor love, nor light,
Nor certitude —'"

"Wait a minute," he interrupted. "Who sends you these boxes?"

"I don't know."

"But how are the notes signed?"

"They're wonderful notes," she said. "So wise, so gay, so tender, you'd imagine them being written by John Barrymore or Lindbergh."

"Yes, but how are they signed?"

She hesitated. "Never anything but 'Your Lover.'"

"And so when you first saw me, you thought —" He began, then stopped because she was blushing.

"How long have you been getting them?"

"Ever since I can remember. I have two closets of the boxes. The new ones are either by my bed when I wake or at my place at breakfast."

"But how does this-person get these boxes to you out here? Does he give them to your aunts and do they put them there?"

"I'm not sure."

"But how can they get them in winter?"

"I don't know."

"Look here," he said, pouring himself more lemonade, "how long is it since you've been to the mainland?"

"Almost eighteen years. My aunts tell me I was born there in the middle of the war."

"What war?" he asked startledly, spilling some lemonade.

"The World War, of course. What's the matter?"

Jack Barr was staring down at the spilled lemonade and feeling a kind of terror he'd never experienced in his waking life. Nothing around him had changed. He could still feel the same hot sun on his shoulders, the same icy glass in his hand, scent the same lemon-acid odor in his nostrils. He could still hear the faint *chop-chop* of the waves.

And yet everything had changed, gone dark and dizzy as a landscape glimpsed just before a faint. All the little false notes had come to a sudden focus. For the lemonade had spilled on the headline of the newspaper the girl had tossed down, and the headline read:

HITLER IN NEW DEFIANCE

Under the big black banner of that head swam smaller ones:

Foes of Machado Riot in Havana
Big NRA Parade Planned
Balbo Speaks in New York

Suddenly he felt a surge of relief. He had noticed that the paper was yellow and brittle-edged.

"Why are you so interested in old newspapers?" he asked.

"I wouldn't call day-before-yesterday's paper old," the girl objected, pointing at the dateline: July 20, 1933.

"You're trying to joke," Jack told her.

"No, I'm not."

"But it's 1953."

"Now it's you who are joking."

"But the paper's yellow."

"The paper's always yellow."

He laughed uneasily. "Well, if you actually think it's 1933, perhaps you're to be envied," he said, with a sardonic humor he didn't quite feel. "Then you can't know anything about the Second World War, or television, or the V-2s, or Bikini bathing suits, or the atomic bomb, or —"

"Stop!" She had sprung up and retreated around her chair, white-faced. "I don't like what you're saying."

"But —"

"No, please! Jokes that may be quite harmless on the mainland sound different here."

"I'm really not joking," he said after a moment.

She grew quite frantic at that. "I can show you all last week's papers! I can show you magazines and other things. I can prove it!"

She started toward the house. He followed. He felt his heart begin to pound.

At the white door she paused, looking worriedly down the road. Jack thought he could hear the faint *chug* of a motorboat. She pushed open the door and he followed her inside. The small-windowed room was dark after the sunlight. Jack got an impression of solid old furniture, a fireplace with brass andirons.

"Flash!" croaked a gritty voice. "After their disastrous break day before yesterday, stocks are recovering. Leading issues...."

Jack realized that he had started and had involuntarily put his arm around the girl's shoulders. At the same time he noticed that the voice was coming from the curved brown trumpet of an old-fashioned radio loudspeaker.

The girl didn't pull away from him. He turned toward her. Although her gray eyes were on him, her attention had gone elsewhere.

"I can hear the car. They're coming back. They won't like it that you're here."

"All right they won't like it."

Her agitation grew. "No, you must go."

"I'll come back tomorrow," he heard himself saying.

"Flash! It looks as if the World Economic Conference may soon adjourn, mouthing jeers at old Uncle Sam who is generally referred to as Uncle Shylock."

Jack felt a numbness on his neck. The room seemed to be darkening, the girl growing stranger still.

"You must go before they see you."

"Flash! Wiley Post has just completed his solo circuit of the Globe, after a record-breaking flight of 7 days, 18 hours and 45 minutes. Asked how he felt after the energy-draining feat, Post quipped...."

He was halfway across the lawn before he realized the terror into which the grating radio voice had thrown him.

He leaped for the branch over-hanging the fence, vaulted up with the risky help of a foot on the barbed top. A surprised squirrel, lacking time to make its escape up the trunk, sprang to the ground ahead of him. With terrible suddenness, two steel-jawed semicircles clanked together just over the squirrel's head. Jack landed with one foot to either side of the sprung trap, while the squirrel darted off with a squeak.

Jack plunged down the slope to the rocky spine and ran across it, spray from the rising waves spattering him to the waist. Panting now, he stumbled up into the oaks and undergrowth of the first island, fought his way through it, finally reached the silent cove. He loosed the line of the *Annie O.*, dragged it as near to the cove's mouth as he could, plunged knee-deep in freezing water to give it a final shove, scrambled aboard, snatched up the boathook and punched at the rocks.

As soon as the *Annie O.* was nosing out of the cove into the cross waves, he yanked up the sail. The freshening wind filled it and sent the sloop heeling over, with inches of white water over the lee rail, and plunging ahead.

For a long while, Jack was satisfied to think of nothing but the wind and the waves and the sail and speed and danger, to have all his attention taken up balancing one against the other, so that he wouldn't have to ask himself what year it was and whether time was an illusion, and wonder about flappers and hidden traps.

When he finally looked back at the island, he was amazed to see how tiny it had grown, as distant as the mainland.

Then he saw a gray motorboat astern. He watched it as it slowly overtook him. It was built like a lifeboat, with a sturdy low cabin in the bow and wheel amidship. Whoever was at the wheel had long gray hair that whipped in the wind. The longer he looked, the surer he was that it was a woman wearing a lace dress. Something that stuck up inches over the cabin flashed darkly beside her. Only when she lifted it to the roof of the cabin did it occur to him that it might be a rifle.

But just then the motorboat swung around in a turn that sent waves drenching over it, and headed back toward the island. He watched it for a minute in wonder, then his attention was jolted by an angry hail.

Three fishing smacks, also headed toward town, were about to cross his bow. He came around into the wind and waited with shaking sail, watching a man in a lumpy sweater shake a fist at him. Then he turned and gratefully followed the dark, wide, fanlike sterns and age-yellowed sails.

The exterior of Martin Kesserich's home —a weathered white cube with narrow, sharp-paned windows, topped by a cupola-was nothing like its lavish interior.

In much the same way, Mrs. Kesserich clashed with the darkly gleaming furniture, persian rugs and bronze vases around her. Her shapeless black form, poised awkwardly on the edge of a huge sofa, made Jack think of a cow that had strayed into the drawing room. He wondered again how a man like Kesserich had come to marry such a creature.

Yet when she lifted up her little eyes from the shadows, he had the uneasy feeling that she knew a great deal about him. The eyes were still those of a domestic animal, but of a wise one that has been watching the house a long, long while from the barnyard.

He asked abruptly, "Do you know anything of a girl around here named Mary Alice Pope?"

The silence lasted so long that he began to think she'd gone into some bovine trance. Then, without a word, she got up and went over to a tall cabinet. Feeling on a ledge behind it for a key, she opened a panel, opened a cardboard box inside it, took something from the box and handed him a photograph. He held it up to the failing light and sucked in his breath with surprise.

It was a picture of the girl he'd met that afternoon. Same flat-bosomed dress-flowered rather than white-no bandeau, same beads. Same proud, demure expression, perhaps a bit happier.

"That is Mary Alice Pope," Mrs. Kesserich said in a strangely flat voice. "She was Martin's fiancee. She was killed in a railway accident in 1933."

The small sound of the cabinet door closing brought Jack back to reality. He realized that he no longer had the photograph. Against the gloom by the cabinet, Mrs. Kesserich's white face looked at him with what seemed a malicious eagerness.

"Sit down," she said, "and I'll tell you about it."

Without a thought as to why she hadn't asked him a single question-he was much too dazed for that-he obeyed. Mrs. Kesserich resumed her position on the edge of the sofa.

"You must understand, Mr. Barr, that Mary Alice Pope was the one love of Martin's life. He is a man of very deep and strong feelings, yet as you probably know, anything but kindly or demonstrative. Even when he first came here from Hungary with his older sisters Hani and Hilda, there was a cloak of loneliness about him-or rather about the three of them.

"Hani and Hilda were athletic outdoor women, yet fiercely proud —I don't imagine they ever spoke to anyone in America except as to a servant-and with a seething distaste for all men except Martin. They showered all their devotion on him. So of course, though Martin didn't realize it, they were consumed with jealousy when he fell in love with Mary Alice Pope. They'd thought that since he'd reached forty without marrying, he was safe.

"Mary Alice came from a pure-bred, or as a biologist would say, inbred British stock. She was very young, but very sweet, and up to a point very wise. She sensed Hani and Hilda's feelings right away and did everything she could to win them over. For instance, though she was afraid of horses, she took up horseback riding, because that was Hani and Hilda's favorite pastime. Naturally, Martin knew nothing of her fear, and naturally his sisters knew about it from the first. But-and here is where Mary's wisdom fell short-her brave gesture did not pacify them: it only increased their hatred.

"Except for his research, Martin was blind to everything but his love. It was a beautiful and yet frightening passion, an insane cherishing as narrow and intense as his sisters hatred."

With a start, Jack remembered that it was Mrs. Kesserich telling him all this.

She went on, "Martin's love directed his every move. He was building a home for himself and Mary, and in his mind he was building a wonderful future for them as well-not vaguely, if you know Martin, but year by year, month by month. This winter, he'd plan, they would visit Buenos Aires, next summer they would sail down the inland passage and he would teach Mary Hungarian for their trip to Buda-Pesth the year after, where he would occupy a chair at the university for a few months ...and so on. Finally the time for their marriage drew near. Martin had been away. His research was keeping him very busy—"

Jack broke in with, "Wasn't that about the time he did his definitive work on growth and fertilization?"

Mrs. Kesserich nodded with solemn appreciation in the gathering darkness. "But now he was coming home, his work done. It was early evening, very chilly, but Hani and Hilda felt they had to ride down to the station to meet their brother. And although she dreaded it, Mary rode with them, for she knew how delighted he would be at her cantering to the puffing train and his running up to lift her down from the saddle to welcome him home.

"Of course there was Martin's luggage to be considered, so the station wagon had to be sent down for that." She looked defiantly at Jack. "I drove the station wagon. I was Martin's laboratory assistant."

She paused. "It was almost dark, but there was still a white cold line of sky to the west. Hani and Hilda, with Mary between them, were waiting on their horses at the top of the hill that led down to the station. The train had whistled and its headlight was graying the gravel of the crossing.

"Suddenly Mary's horse squealed and plunged down the hill. Hani and Hilda followed-to try to catch her, they said, but they didn't manage that, only kept her horse from veering off. Mary never screamed, but as her horse reared on the tracks, I saw her face in the headlight's glare.

"Martin must have guessed, or at least feared what had happened, for he was out of the train and running along the track before it stopped. In fact, he was the first to kneel down beside Mary —I mean, what had been Mary-and was holding her all bloody and shattered in his arms."

A door slammed. There were steps in the hall. Mrs. Kesserich stiffened and was silent. Jack turned.

The blur of a face hung in the doorway to the hall —a seemingly young, sensitive, suavely handsome face with aristocratic jaw. Then there was a click and the lights flared up and Jack saw the close-cropped gray hair and the lines around the eyes and nostrils, while the sensitive mouth grew sardonic. Yet the handsomeness stayed, and somehow the youth, too, or at least a tremendous inner vibrancy.

"Hello, Barr," Martin Kesserich said, ignoring his wife.

The great biologist had come home.

"Oh, yes, and Jamieson had a feeble paper on what he called individualization in marine worms. Barr, have you ever thought much about the larger aspects of the problem of individuality?"

Jack jumped slightly. He had let his thoughts wander very far.

"Not especially, sir," he mumbled.

The house was still. A few minutes after the professor's arrival, Mrs. Kesserich had gone off with an anxious glance at Jack. He knew why and wished he could reassure her that he would not mention their conversation to the professor.

Kesserich had spent perhaps a half hour briefing him on the more important papers delivered at the conferences. Then, almost as if it were a teacher's trick to show up a pupil's inattention, he had suddenly posed this question about individuality.

"You know what I mean, of course," Kesserich pressed. "The factors that make you you, and me me."

"Heredity and environment," Jack parroted like a freshman.

Kesserich nodded. "Suppose-this is just speculation-that we could control heredity and environment. Then we could re-create the same individual at will."

Jack felt a shiver go through him. "To get exactly the same pattern of hereditary traits. That'd be far beyond us."

"What about identical twins?" Kesserich pointed out. "And then there's parthenogenesis to be considered. One might produce a duplicate of the mother without the intervention of the male." Although his voice had grown more idly speculative, Kesserich seemed to Jack to be smiling secretly. "There are many examples in the lower animal forms, to say nothing of the technique by which Loeb caused a sea urchin to reproduce with no more stimulus than a salt solution."

Jack felt the hair rising on his neck. "Even then you wouldn't get exactly the same pattern of hereditary traits."

"Not if the parent were of very pure stock? Not if there were some special technique for selecting ova that would reproduce all the mother's traits?"

"But environment would change things," Jack objected. "The duplicate would be bound to develop differently."

"Is environment so important? Newman tells about a pair of identical twins separated from birth, unaware of each other's existence. They met by accident when they were twenty-one. Each was a telephone repairman. Each had a wife the same age. Each had a baby son. And each had a fox terrier called 'Trixie.' That's without trying to make environments similar. But suppose you did try. Suppose you saw to it that each of them had exactly the same experiences at the same times...."

For a moment it seemed to Jack that the room was dimming and wavering, becoming a dark pool in which the only motionless thing was Kesserich's sphinx-like face.

"Well, we've escaped quite far enough from Jamieson's marine worms," the biologist said, all brisk again. He said it as if Jack were the one who had led the conversation down wild and unprofitable channels. "Let's get on to your project. I want to talk it over now, because I won't have any time for it tomorrow."

Jack looked at him blankly.

"Tomorrow I must attend to a very important matter," the biologist explained.

Morning sunlight brightened the colors of the wax flowers under glass on the high bureau that always seemed to emit the faint odor of old hair combings. Jack pulled back the diamond-patterned quilt and blinked the sleep from his eyes. He expected his mind to be busy wondering about Kesserich and his wife-things said and half said last night-but found instead that his thoughts swung instantly to Mary Alice Pope, as if to a farthest island in a world of people.

Downstairs, the house was empty. After a long look at the cabinet-he felt behind it, but the key was gone-he hurried down to the waterfront. He stopped only for a bowl of chowder and, as an afterthought, to buy half a dozen newspapers.

The sea was bright, the brisk wind just right for the *Annie O.* There was eagerness in the way it smacked the sail and in the creak of the mast. And when he reached the cove, it was no longer still, but nervous with faint ripples, as if time had finally begun to stir.

After the same struggle with the underbrush, he came out on the rocky spine and passed the cove of the sea urchins. The spiny creatures struck an uncomfortable chord in his memory.

This time he climbed the second island cautiously, scraping the innocent-seeming ground ahead of him intently with a boathook he'd brought along for the purpose. He was only a few yards from the fence when he saw Mary Alice Pope standing behind it.

He hadn't realized that his heart would begin to pound or that, at the same time, a shiver of almost supernatural dread would go through him.

The girl eyed him with an uneasy hostility and immediately began to speak in a hushed, hurried voice. "You must go away at once and never come back. You're a wicked man, but I don't want you to be hurt. I've been watching for you all morning."

He tossed the newspapers over the fence. "You don't have to read them now," he told her. "Just look at the datelines and a few of the headlines."

When she finally lifted her eyes to his again, she was trembling. She tried unsuccessfully to speak.

"Listen to me," he said. "You've been the victim of a scheme to make you believe you were born around 1916 instead of 1933, and that it's 1933 now instead of 1951. I'm not sure why it's been done, though I think I know who you really are."

"But," the girl faltered, "my aunts tell me it's 1933."

"They would."

"And there are the papers ... the magazines ... the radio."

"The papers are old ones. The radio's faked-some sort of recording. I could show you if I could get at it."

"*These* papers might be faked," she said, pointing to where she'd let them drop on the ground.

"They're new," he said. "Only old papers get yellow."

"But why would they do it to me? *Why?*"

"Come with me to the mainland, Mary. That'll set you straight quicker than anything."

"I couldn't," she said, drawing back. "He's coming tonight."

"He?"

"The man who sends me the boxes ... and my life."

Jack shivered. When he spoke, his voice was rough and quick. "A life that's completely a lie, that's cut you off from the world. Come with me, Mary."

She looked up at him wonderingly. For perhaps ten seconds the silence held and the spell of her eerie sweetness deepened.

"I love you, Mary," Jack said softly.

She took a step back.

"Really, Mary, I do."

She shook her head. "I don't know what's true. Go away."

"Mary," he pleaded, "read the papers I've given you. Think things through. I'll wait for you here."

"You can't. My aunts would find you."

"Then I'll go away and come back. About sunset. Will you give me an answer?"

She looked at him. Suddenly she whirled around. He, too, heard the *chuff* of the Essex. "They'll find us," she said. "And if they find you, I don't know what they'll do. Quick, run!" And she darted off herself, only to turn back to scramble for the papers.

"But will you give me an answer?" he pressed.

She looked frantically up from the papers. "I don't know. You mustn't risk coming back."

"I will, no matter what you say."

"I can't promise. Please go."

"Just one question," he begged. "What are your aunts' names?"

"Hani and Hilda," she told him, and then she was gone. The hedge shook where she'd darted through.

Jack hesitated, then started for the cove. He thought for a moment of staying on the island, but decided against it. He could probably conceal himself successfully, but whoever found his boat would have him at a disadvantage. Besides, there were things he must try to find out on the mainland.

As he entered the oaks, his spine tightened for a moment, as if someone were watching him. He hurried to the rippling cove, wasted no time getting the *Annie O.* underway. With the wind still in the west, he knew it would be a hard sail. He'd need half a dozen tacks to reach the mainland.

When he was about a quarter of a mile out from the cove, there was a sharp *smack* beside him. He jerked around, heard a distant *crack* and saw a foot-long splinter of fresh wood dangling from the edge of the sloop's cockpit, about a foot from his head.

He felt his skin tighten. He was the bull's-eye of a great watery target. All the air between him and the island was tainted with menace.

Water splashed a yard from the side. There was another distant *crack*. He lay on his back in the cockpit, steering by the sail, taking advantage of what little cover there was.

There were several more *cracks*. After the second, there was a hole in the sail.

Finally Jack looked back. The island was more than a mile astern. He anxiously scanned the sea ahead for craft. There were none. Then he settled down to nurse more speed from the sloop and wait for the motorboat.

But it didn't come out to follow him.

V

Same as yesterday, Mrs. Kesserich was sitting on the edge of the couch in the living room, yet from the first Jack was aware of a great change. Something had filled the domestic animal with grief and fury.

"Where's Dr. Kesserich?" he asked.

"Not here!"

"Mrs. Kesserich," he said, dropping down beside her, "you were telling me something yesterday when we were interrupted."

She looked at him. "You *have* found the girl?" she almost shouted.

"Yes," Jack was surprised into answering.

A look of slyness came into Mrs. Kesserich's bovine face. "Then I'll tell you everything. I can now.

"When Martin found Mary dying, he didn't go to pieces. You know how controlled he can be when he chooses. He lifted Mary's body as if the crowd and the railway men weren't there, and carried it to the station wagon. Hani and Hilda were sitting on their horses nearby. He gave them one look. It was as if he had said, 'Murderers!'

"He told me to drive home as fast as I dared, but when I got there, he stayed sitting by Mary in the back. I knew he must have given up what hope he had for her life, or else she was dead already. I looked at him. In the domelight, his face had the most deadly and proud expression I've ever seen on a man. I worshiped him, you know, though he had never shown me one ounce of feeling. So I was completely unprepared for the naked appeal in his voice.

"Yet all he said at first was, 'Will you do something for me?' I told him, 'Surely,' and as we carried Mary in, he told me the rest. He wanted me to be the mother of Mary's child."

Jack stared at her blankly.

Mrs. Kesserich nodded. "He wanted to remove an ovum from Mary's body and nurture it in mine, so that Mary, in a way, could live on."

"But that's impossible!" Jack objected. "The technique is being tried now on cattle, I know, so that a prize heifer can have several calves a year, all nurtured in 'scrub heifers,' as they're called. But no one's ever dreamed of trying it on human beings!"

Mrs. Kesserich looked at him contemptuously. "Martin had mastered the technique twenty years ago. He was willing to take the chance. And so was I —partly because he fired my scientific imagination and reverence, but mostly because he said he would marry me. He barred the doors. We worked swiftly. As far as anyone was concerned, Martin, in a wild fit of grief, had locked himself up for several hours to mourn over the body of his fiancee.

"Within a month we were married, and I finally gave birth to the child."

Jack shook his head. "You gave birth to your own child."

She smiled bitterly. "No, it was Mary's. Martin did not keep his whole bargain with me —I was nothing more than his 'scrub wife' in every way."

"You *think* you gave birth to Mary's child."

Mrs. Kesserich turned on Jack in anger. "I've been wounded by him, day in and day out, for years, but I've never failed to recognize his genius. Besides, you've seen the girl, haven't you?"

Jack had to nod. What confounded him most was that, granting the near-impossible physiological feat Mrs. Kesserich had described, the girl should look so much like the mother. Mothers and daughters don't look that much alike; only identical twins did. With a thrill of fear, he remembered Kesserich's casual words: "... parthenogenesis ... pure stock ... special techniques...."

"Very well," he forced himself to say, "granting that the child was Mary's and Martin's —"

"No! Mary's alone!"

Jack suppressed a shudder. He continued quickly, "What became of the child?"

Mrs. Kesserich lowered her head. "The day it was born, it was taken away from me. After that, I never saw Hilda and Hani, either."

"You mean," Jack asked, "that Martin sent them away to bring up the child?"

Mrs. Kesserich turned away. "Yes."

Jack asked incredulously, "He trusted the child with the two people he suspected of having caused the mother's death?"

"Once when I was his assistant," Mrs. Kesserich said softly, "I carelessly broke some laboratory glassware. He kept me up all night building a new setup, though I'm rather poor at working with glass and usually get burned. Bringing up the child was his sisters' punishment."

"And they went to that house on the farthest island? I suppose it was the house he'd been building for Mary and himself."

"Yes."

"And they were to bring up the child as his daughter?"

Mrs. Kesserich started up, but when she spoke it was as if she had to force out each word. "As his wife-as soon as she was grown."

"How can you know that?" Jack asked shakily.

The rising wind rattled the windowpane.

"Because today-eighteen years after-Martin broke all of his promise to me. He told me he was leaving me."

White waves shooting up like dancing ghosts in the Moon-sketched, spray-swept dark were Jack's first beacon of the island and brought a sense of physical danger, breaking the trancelike yet frantic mood he had felt ever since he had spoken with Mrs. Kesserich.

Coming around farther into the wind, he scudded past the end of the island into the choppy sea on the landward side. A little later he let down the reefed sail in the cove of the sea urchins, where the water was barely moving, although the air was shaken by the pounding of the surf on the spine between the two islands.

After making fast, he paused a moment for a scrap of cloud to pass the moon. The thought of the spiny creatures in the black fathoms under the *Annie O.* sent an odd quiver of terror through him.

The Moon came out and he started across the glistening rocks of the spine. But he had forgotten the rising tide. Midway, a wave clamped around his ankles, tried to carry him off, almost made him drop the heavy object he was carrying. Sprawling and drenched, he clung to the rough rock until the surge was past.

Making it finally up to the fence, he snipped a wide gate with the wire-cutters.

The windows of the house were alight. Hardly aware of his shivering, he crossed the lawn, slipping from one clump of shrubbery to another, until he reached one just across the drive from the doorway. At that moment he heard the approaching *chuff* of the Essex, the door of the cottage opened, and Mary Alice Pope stepped out, closely followed by Hani or Hilda.

Jack shrank close to the shrubbery. Mary looked pale and blank-faced, as if she had retreated within herself. He was acutely conscious of the inadequacy of his screen as the ghostly headlights of the Essex began to probe through the leaves.

But then he sensed that something more was about to happen than just the car arriving. It was a change in the expression of the face behind Mary that gave him the cue —a widening and side-wise flickering of the cold eyes, the puckered lips thinning into a cruel smile.

The Essex shifted into second and, without any warning, accelerated. Simultaneously, the woman behind Mary gave her a violent shove. But at almost exactly the same instant, Jack ran. He caught Mary as she sprawled toward the gravel, and lunged ahead without checking. The Essex bore down upon them, a square-snouted, roaring monster. It swerved viciously, missed them by inches, threw up gravel in a skid, and rocked to a stop, stalled.

The first, incredulous voice that broke the pulsing silence, Jack recognized as Martin Kesserich's. It came from the car, which was slewed around so that it almost faced Jack and Mary.

"Hani, you tried to kill her! You and Hilda tried to kill her again!"

The woman slumped over the wheel slowly lifted her head. In the indistinct light, she looked the twin of the woman behind Jack and Mary.

"Did you really think we wouldn't?" she asked in a voice that spat with passion. "Did you actually believe that Hilda and I would serve this eighteen years' penance just to watch you go off with her?" She began to laugh wildly. "You've never understood your sisters at all!"

Suddenly she broke off, stiffly stepped down from the car. Lifting her skirts a little, she strode past Jack and Mary.

Martin Kesserich followed her. In passing, he said, "Thanks, Barr." It occurred to Jack that Kesserich made no more question of his appearance on the island than of his presence in the laboratory. Like Mrs. Kesserich, the great biologist took him for granted.

Kesserich stopped a few feet short of Hani and Hilda. Without shrinking from him, the sisters drew closer together. They looked like two gaunt hawks.

"But you waited eighteen years," he said. "You could have killed her at any time, yet you chose to throw away so much of your lives just to have this moment."

"How do you know we didn't like waiting eighteen years?" Hani answered him. "Why shouldn't we want to make as strong an impression on you as anyone? And as for throwing our lives away, that was your doing. Oh, Martin, you'll never know anything about how your sisters feel!"

He raised his hands baffledly. "Even assuming that you hate me —" at the word "hate" both Hani and Hilda laughed softly —"and that you were prepared to strike at both my love and my work, still, that you should have waited...."

Hani and Hilda said nothing.

Kesserich shrugged. "Very well," he said in a voice that had lost all its tension. "You've wasted a third of a lifetime looking forward to an irrational revenge. And you've failed. That should be sufficient punishment."

Very slowly, he turned around and for the first time looked at Mary. His face was clearly revealed by the twin beams from the stalled car.

Jack grew cold. He fought against accepting the feelings of wonder, of poignant triumph, of love, of renewed youth he saw entering the face in the headlights. But most of all he fought against the sense that Martin Kesserich was successfully drawing them all back into the past, to 1933 and another accident. There was a distant hoot and Jack shook. For a moment he had thought it a railway whistle and not a ship's horn.

The biologist said tenderly, "Come, Mary."

Jack's trembling arm tightened a trifle on Mary's waist. He could feel *her* trembling.

"Come, Mary," Kesserich repeated.

Still she didn't reply.

Jack wet his lips. "Mary isn't going with you, Professor," he said.

"Quiet, Barr," Kesserich ordered absently. "Mary, it is necessary that you and I leave the island at once. Please come."

"But Mary isn't coming," Jack repeated.

Kesserich looked at him for the first time. "I'm grateful to you for the unusual sense of loyalty-or whatever motive it may have been-that led you to follow me out here tonight. And of course I'm profoundly grateful to you for saving Mary's life. But I must ask you not to interfere further in a matter which you can't possibly understand."

He turned to Mary. "I know how shocked and frightened you must feel. Living two lives and then having to face two deaths-it must be more terrible than anyone can realize. I expected this meeting to take place under very different circumstances. I wanted to explain everything to you very naturally and gently, like the messages I've sent you every day of your second life. Unfortunately, that can't be.

"You and I must leave the island right now."

Mary stared at him, then turned wonderingly toward Jack, who felt his heart begin to pound warmly.

"You still don't understand what I'm trying to tell you, Professor," he said, boldly now. "Mary is not going with you. You've deceived her all her life. You've taken a fantastic amount of pains to bring her up under the delusion that she is Mary Alice Pope, who died in —"

"She *is* Mary Alice Pope," Kesserich thundered at him. He advanced toward them swiftly. "Mary darling, you're confused, but you must realize who you are and who I am and the relationship between us."

"Keep away," Jack warned, swinging Mary half behind him. "Mary doesn't love you. She can't marry you, at any rate. How could she, when you're her father?"

"Barr!"

"Keep off!" Jack shot out the flat of his hand and Kesserich went staggering backward. "I've talked with your wife-your wife on the mainland. She told me the whole thing."

Kesserich seemed about to rush forward again, then controlled himself. "You've got everything wrong. You hardly deserve to be told, but under the circumstances I have no choice. Mary is not my daughter. To be precise, she has no father at all. Do you remember the work that Jacques Loeb did with sea urchins?"

Jack frowned angrily. "You mean what we were talking about last night?"

"Exactly. Loeb was able to cause the egg of a sea urchin to develop normally without union with a male germ cell. I have done the same tiding with a human being. This girl is Mary Alice Pope. She has exactly the same heredity. She has had exactly the same life, so far as it could be reconstructed. She's heard and read the same things at exactly the same times. There have been the old newspapers, the books, even the old recorded radio programs. Hani and Hilda have had their daily instructions, to the letter. She's retraced the same time-trail."

"Rot!" Jack interrupted. "I don't for a moment believe what you say about her birth. She's Mary's daughter-or the daughter of your wife on the mainland. And as for retracing the same time-trail, that's senile self-delusion. Mary Alice Pope had a normal life. This girl has been brought up in cruel imprisonment by two insane, vindictive old women. In your own frustrated desire, you've pretended to yourself that you've recreated the girl you lost. You haven't. You couldn't. Nobody could-the great Martin Kesserich or anyone else!"

Kesserich, his features working, shifted his point of attack. "Who are you, Mary?"

"Don't answer him," Jack said. "He's trying to confuse you."

"Who are you?" Kesserich insisted.

"Mary Alice Pope," she said rapidly in a breathy whisper before Jack could speak again.

"And when were you born?" Kesserich pressed on.

"You've been tricked all your life about that," Jack warned.

But already the girl was saying, "In 1916."

"And who am I then?" Kesserich demanded eagerly. "Who am I?"

The girl swayed. She brushed her head with her hand.

"It's so strange," she said, with a dreamy, almost laughing throb in her voice that turned Jack's heart cold. "I'm sure I've never seen you before in my life, and yet it's as if I'd known you forever. As if you were closer to me than —"

"Stop it!" Jack shouted at Kesserich. "Mary loves me. She loves me because I've shown her the lie her life has been, and because she's coming away with me now. Aren't you, Mary?"

He swung her around so that her blank face was inches from his own. "It's me you love, isn't it, Mary?"

She blinked doubtfully.

At that moment Kesserich charged at them, went sprawling as Jack's fist shot out. Jack swept up Mary and ran with her across the lawn. Behind him he heard an agonized cry-Kesserich's — and cruel, mounting laughter from Hani and Hilda.

Once through the ragged doorway in the fence, he made his way more slowly, gasping. Out of the shelter of the trees, the wind tore at them and the ocean roared. Moonlight glistened, now on the spine of black wet rocks, now on the foaming surf.

Jack realized that the girl in his arms was speaking rapidly, disjointedly, but he couldn't quite make out the sense of the words and then they were lost in the crash of the surf. She struggled, but he told himself that it was only because she was afraid of the menacing waters.

He pushed recklessly into the breaking surf, raced gasping across the middle of the spine as the rocks uncovered, sprang to the higher ones as the next wave crashed behind, showering them with spray. His chest burning with exertion, he carried the girl the few remaining yards to where the *Annie O.* was tossing. A sudden great gust of wind almost did what the waves had failed to do, but he kept his footing and lowered the girl into the boat, then jumped in after.

She stared at him wildly. "What's that?"

He, too, had caught the faint shout. Looking back along the spine just as the Moon came clear again, he saw white spray rise and fall-and then the figure of Kesserich stumbling through it.

"Mary, wait for me!"

The figure was halfway across when it lurched, started forward again, then was jerked back as if something had caught its ankle. Out of the darkness, the next wave sent a line of white at it neck-high, crashed.

Jack hesitated, but another great gust of wind tore at the half-raised sail, and it was all he could do to keep the sloop from capsizing and head her into the wind again.

Mary was tugging at his shoulder. "You must help him," she was saying. "He's caught in the rocks."

He heard a voice crying, screaming crazily above the surf:

> "Ah, love, let us be true
> To one another! for the world —"

The sloop rocked. Jack had it finally headed into the wind. He looked around for Mary.

She had jumped out and was hurrying back, scrambling across the rocks toward the dark, struggling figure that even as he watched was once more engulfed in the surf.

Letting go the lines, Jack sprang toward the stern of the sloop.

But just then another giant blow came, struck the sail like a great fist of air, and sent the boom slashing at the back of his head.

His last recollection was being toppled out onto the rocks and wondering how he could cling to them while unconscious.

VII

The little cove was once again as quiet as time's heart. Once again the *Annie O.* was a sloop embedded in a mirror. Once again the rocks were warm underfoot.

Jack Barr lifted his fiercely aching head and looked at the distant line of the mainland, as tiny and yet as clear as something viewed through the wrong end of a telescope. He was very tired. Searching the island, in his present shaky condition, had taken all the strength out of him.

He looked at the peacefully rippling sea outside the cove and thought of what a churning pot it had been during the storm. He thought wonderingly of his rescue —a man wedged unconscious between two rock teeth; kept somehow from being washed away by the merest chance.

He thought of Mrs. Kesserich sitting alone in her house, scanning the newspapers that had nothing to tell.

He thought of the empty island behind him and the vanished motorboat.

He wondered if the sea had pulled down Martin Kesserich and Mary Alice Pope. He wondered if only Hani and Hilda had sailed away.

He winced, remembering what he had done to Martin and Mary by his blundering infatuation. In his way, he told himself, he had been as bad as the two old women.

He thought of death, and of time, and of love that defies them.

He stepped limpingly into the *Annie O.* to set sail-and realized that philosophy is only for the unhappy.

Mary was asleep in the stern.

What's He Doing in There

He went where no Martian ever went before-but would he come out-or had he gone for good?

The Professor was congratulating Earth's first visitor from another planet on his wisdom in getting in touch with a cultural anthropologist before contacting any other scientists (or governments, God forbid!), and in learning English from radio and TV before landing from his orbit-parked rocket, when the Martian stood up and said hesitantly, "Excuse me, please, but where is it?"

That baffled the Professor and the Martian seemed to grow anxious-at least his long mouth curved upward, and he had earlier explained that it curling downward was his smile-and he repeated, "Please, where is it?"

He was surprisingly humanoid in most respects, but his complexion was textured so like the rich dark armchair he'd just been occupying that the Professor's pin-striped gray suit, which he had eagerly consented to wear, seemed an arbitrary interruption between him and the chair —a sort of Mother Hubbard dress on a phantom conjured from its leather.

The Professor's Wife, always a perceptive hostess, came to her husband's rescue by saying with equal rapidity, "Top of the stairs, end of the hall, last door."

The Martian's mouth curled happily downward and he said, "Thank you very much," and was off.

Comprehension burst on the Professor. He caught up with his guest at the foot of the stairs. "Here, I'll show you the way," he said.

"No, I can find it myself, thank you," the Martian assured him.

Something rather final in the Martian's tone made the Professor desist, and after watching his visitor sway up the stairs with an almost hypnotic softly jogging movement, he rejoined his wife in the study, saying wonderingly, "Who'd have thought it, by George! Function taboos as strict as our own!"

"I'm glad some of your professional visitors maintain 'em," his wife said darkly.

"But this one's from Mars, darling, and to find out he's —well, similar in an aspect of his life is as thrilling as the discovery that water is burned hydrogen. When I think of the day not far distant when I'll put his entries in the cross-cultural index..."

He was still rhapsodizing when the Professor's Little Son raced in.

"Pop, the Martian's gone to the bathroom!"

"Hush, dear. Manners."

"Now it's perfectly natural, darling, that the boy should notice and be excited. Yes, Son, the Martian's not so very different from us."

"Oh, certainly," the Professor's Wife said with a trace of bitterness. "I don't imagine his turquoise complexion will cause any comment at all when you bring him to a faculty reception. They'll just figure he's had a hard night-and that he got that baby-elephant nose sniffing around for assistant professorships."

"Really, darling! He probably thinks of our noses as disagreeably amputated and paralyzed."

"Well, anyway, Pop, he's in the bathroom. I followed him when he squiggled upstairs."

"Now, Son, you shouldn't have done that. He's on a strange planet and it might make him nervous if he thought he was being spied on. We must show him every courtesy. By George, I can't wait to discuss these things with Ackerly-Ramsbottom! When I think of how much more this encounter has to give the anthropologist than even the physicist or astronomer..."

He was still going strong on his second rhapsody when he was interrupted by another high-speed entrance. It was the Professor's Coltish Daughter.

"Mom, Pop, the Martian's —"

"Hush, dear. We know."

The Professor's Coltish Daughter regained her adolescent poise, which was considerable. "Well, he's still in there," she said. "I just tried the door and it was locked."

"I'm glad it was!" the Professor said while his wife added, "Yes, you can't be sure what —" and caught herself. "Really, dear, that was very bad manners."

"I thought he'd come downstairs long ago," her daughter explained. "He's been in there an awfully long time. It must have been a half hour ago that I saw him gyre and gimbal upstairs in that real gone way he has, with Nosy here following him." The Professor's Coltish Daughter was currently soaking up both jive and *Alice*.

When the Professor checked his wristwatch, his expression grew troubled. "By George, he is taking his time! Though, of course, we don't know how much time Martians ... I wonder."

"I listened for a while, Pop," his son volunteered. "He was running the water a lot."

"Running the water, eh? We know Mars is a water-starved planet. I suppose that in the presence of unlimited water, he might be seized by a kind of madness and ... But he seemed so well adjusted."

Then his wife spoke, voicing all their thoughts. Her outlook on life gave her a naturally sepulchral voice.

"What's he doing in there?"

Twenty minutes and at least as many fantastic suggestions later, the Professor glanced again at his watch and nerved himself for action. Motioning his family aside, he mounted the stairs and tiptoed down the hall.

He paused only once to shake his head and mutter under his breath, "By George, I wish I had Fenchurch or von Gottschalk here. They're a shade better than I am on intercultural contracts, especially taboo-breakings and affronts..."

His family followed him at a short distance.

The Professor stopped in front of the bathroom door. Everything was quiet as death.

He listened for a minute and then rapped measuredly, steadying his hand by clutching its wrist with the other. There was a faint splashing, but no other sound.

Another minute passed. The Professor rapped again. Now there was no response at all. He very gingerly tried the knob. The door was still locked.

When they had retreated to the stairs, it was the Professor's Wife who once more voiced their thoughts. This time her voice carried overtones of supernatural horror.

"What's he doing in there?"

"He may be dead or dying," the Professor's Coltish Daughter suggested briskly. "Maybe we ought to call the Fire Department, like they did for old Mrs. Frisbee."

The Professor winced. "I'm afraid you haven't visualized the complications, dear," he said gently. "No one but ourselves knows that the Martian is on Earth, or has even the slightest inkling that interplanetary travel has been achieved. Whatever we do, it will have to be on our own. But to break in on a creature engaged in-well, we don't know what primal private activity-is against all anthropological practice. Still —"

"Dying's a primal activity," his daughter said crisply.

"So's ritual bathing before mass murder," his wife added.

"Please! Still, as I was about to say, we do have the moral duty to succor him if, as you all too reasonably suggest, he has been incapacitated by a germ or virus or, more likely, by some simple environmental factor such as Earth's greater gravity."

"Tell you what, Pop —I can look in the bathroom window and see what he's doing. All I have to do is crawl out my bedroom window and along the gutter a little ways. It's safe as houses."

The Professor's question beginning with, "Son, how do you know —" died unuttered and he refused to notice the words his daughter was voicing silently at her brother. He glanced at his wife's sardonically composed face, thought once more of the Fire Department and of other and larger and even more jealous-or would it be skeptical? —government agencies, and clutched at the straw offered him.

Ten minutes later, he was quite unnecessarily assisting his son back through the bedroom window.

"Gee, Pop, I couldn't see a sign of him. That's why I took so long. Hey, Pop, don't look so scared. He's in there, sure enough. It's just that the bathtub's under the window and you have to get real close up to see into it."

"The Martian's taking a bath?"

"Yep. Got it full up and just the end of his little old schnozzle sticking out. Your suit, Pop, was hanging on the door."

The one word the Professor's Wife spoke was like a death knell.

"Drowned!"

"No, Ma, I don't think so. His schnozzle was opening and closing regular like."

"Maybe he's a shape-changer," the Professor's Coltish Daughter said in a burst of evil fantasy. "Maybe he softens in water and thins out after a while until he's like an eel and then he'll go exploring through the sewer pipes. Wouldn't it be funny if he went under the street and knocked on the stopper from underneath and crawled into the bathtub with President Rexford, or Mrs. President Rexford, or maybe right into the middle of one of Janey Rexford's Oh-I'm-so-sexy bubble baths?"

"Please!" The Professor put his hand to his eyebrows and kept it there, cuddling the elbow in his other hand.

"Well, have you thought of something?" the Professor's Wife asked him after a bit. "What are you going to do?"

The Professor dropped his hand and blinked his eyes hard and took a deep breath.

"Telegraph Fenchurch and Ackerly-Ramsbottom and then break in," he said in a resigned voice, into which, nevertheless, a note of hope seemed also to have come. "First, however, I'm going to wait until morning."

And he sat down cross-legged in the hall a few yards from the bathroom door and folded his arms.

So the long vigil commenced.

The Professor's family shared it and he offered no objection. Other and sterner men, he told himself, might claim to be able successfully to order their children to go to bed when there was a Martian locked in the bathroom, but he would like to see them faced with the situation.

Finally dawn began to seep from the bedrooms. When the bulb in the hall had grown quite dim, the Professor unfolded his arms.

Just then, there was a loud splashing in the bathroom. The Professor's family looked toward the door. The splashing stopped and they heard the Martian moving around. Then the door opened and the Martian appeared in the Professor's gray pin-stripe suit. His mouth curled sharply downward in a broad alien smile as he saw the Professor.

"Good morning!" the Martian said happily. "I never slept better in my life, even in my own little wet bed back on Mars."

He looked around more closely and his mouth straightened. "But where did you all sleep?" he asked. "Don't tell me you stayed dry all night! You *didn't* give up your only bed to me?"

His mouth curled upward in misery. "Oh, dear," he said, "I'm afraid I've made a mistake somehow. Yet I don't understand how. Before I studied you, I didn't know what your sleeping habits would be, but that question was answered for me-in fact, it looked so reassuringly homelike-when I saw those brief TV scenes of your females ready for sleep in their little tubs. Of course, on Mars, only the fortunate can always be sure of sleeping wet, but here, with your abundance of water, I thought there would be wet beds for all."

He paused. "It's true I had some doubts last night, wondering if I'd used the right words and all, but then when you rapped 'Good night' to me, I splashed the sentiment back at you and went to sleep in a wink. But I'm afraid that somewhere I've blundered and —"

"No, no, dear chap," the Professor managed to say. He had been waving his hand in a gentle circle for some time in token that he wanted to interrupt. "Everything is quite all right. It's true we stayed up all night, but please consider that as a watch-an honor guard, by George! —which we kept to indicate our esteem."